MW00579354

A QUEEN OF RUIN

Also by K.F. Breene

DELICIOUSLY DARK FAIRYTALES
A Ruin of Roses
A Throne of Ruin
A Kingdom of Ruin
A Queen of Ruin

DEMIGODS OF SAN FRANCISCO
Sin & Chocolate
Sin & Magic
Sin & Salvation
Sin & Spirit
Sin & Lightning
Sin & Surrender

LEVELING UP
Magical Midlife Madness
Magical Midlife Dating
Magical Midlife Invasion
Magical Midlife Love
Magical Midlife Meeting

DEMON DAYS VAMPIRE NIGHTS WORLD
Born in Fire
Raised in Fire
Fused in Fire
Natural Witch
Natural Mage
Natural Dual-Mage
Warrior Fae Trapped
Warrior Fae Princess
Revealed in Fire
Mentored in Fire
Battle with Fire

A QUEEN OF RUIN

BY K.F. BREENE

Copyright © 2022 by K.F. Breene

All rights reserved. The people, places, situations and craziness contained in this book are figments of the author's imagination and in no way reflect real or true events.

Contact info:
www.kfbreene.com
books@kfbreene.com

PART ONE

CHAPTER 1

HADRIEL

*W*HAT IN THE *absolute fuck?* I thought as silence descended on the after-battle crowd. The prince stood at the top of the steps in jeans and no shirt, in front of the castle, staring down at his mother, the queen.

The fucking queen!

How the hell was she alive?

Well, obviously I knew *how*—she'd somehow escaped before the curse and hidden in the collection of dragon villages in the Flamma Kingdom, safely tucked away.

I didn't know her story, and already I wasn't sure I could forgive her. She hadn't aged. In all this time, she looked exactly the same as the last time I'd seen her in the castle. So did her chief lady-in-waiting. The magic affecting us had obviously impacted them, too, but they'd gotten the fun antiaging side effect without having to pay the price. She'd hung out in that cute little village while her people were slowly dying or being indoctrinated into some pretty fucking weird sexual kinks.

3

Like…what the fuck?

Had the king known? Probably not. He'd never been much of an actor, and he'd convinced Nyfain his mother was dead.

It took Leala's wide-eyed glance for me to realize I'd said that last bit out loud.

Almost like he'd been slapped, the prince jerked. Soon after, his body bristled and he unleashed a thick wave of stinging power. It washed over me and threatened to pull me under its tide. My wolf curled up inside of me and did the equivalent of a whimper. The queen flinched, along with almost everyone else in the room. Not Finley, though. Her eyes blazed as she stood beside the ferocious dragon prince. She was the only person in the whole fucking world who liked to bathe in his dominating power, the nutcase.

As if in response, a different sort of power suffused me. A calming magic full of steadfast strength, utterly unbreakable. It was a message of unity. Of pack. Of protection. Power in numbers.

Weston, the alpha wolf, was responding to the dragon's fury. This was why strong wolf shifters and dragon shifters never really got along. Dragons liked to swing their dicks or tits around, and wolves linked arms and said, "Come at me, fucker!" Too much ego all around.

And now I was stuck right in the fucking middle of it, because my goddess-cursed wolf had connected with that alpha wolf and did not plan to let go. He wanted to join Weston's pack. To belong. To bask in that sense of unity and try to muscle our strength to its full potential rather than remain a lone wolf curled up at the feet of dragons.

And while I got where the fuzzy bastard was coming from, I needed him to understand that Finley created unity just like that alpha wolf did, only she didn't have to use wolfsong to do it. My loyalty to her had been earned by her actions alone, no magic involved. She would protect us just the same or better. She'd let us flower within her care.

He was not listening, the horrible cumgoblin.

Within Weston's magic, my wolf slowly uncoiled. Adrenaline seeped through my blood and my back straightened. For the first time ever, I didn't have idle thoughts of shitting myself within the prince's hostile golden stare.

At least that was a nice change.

"Please," the queen said, a small quiver in her voice. "Give me a chance to speak with you." She must have felt all the eyes on her, and a lesser woman would've looked around at the spectators. But she'd learned mastery of her emotions after living with the late king. She'd had to. She'd had to be the people's rock within the storm.

Right up until she left us.

She lifted her chin. "Let me explain, and then I will respect your decision about my fate," she continued in a strong, even voice.

The prince clenched and unclenched his fists, his expression stony and his body straight and tall. Finley, though, let unease crease her expression. Her eyes darted between the prince and the queen, full of concern for one, anger for the other. The prince might not be showing his emotions, but she'd feel them through their bond. He probably didn't want to hear his mother's explanation for fear it would damn her, destroying his opinion of the woman who'd been everything to him. The woman he'd put above all the other people in his life.

I took a deep breath, my heart breaking for him. For all of us. The king had been a horrible bastard. I didn't know if I could handle it if it turned out the queen had been just as bad. It would tarnish all my good memories of this place. Because she was the one who'd made it livable.

Fuck. I couldn't believe this was happening!

The prince's nod was minimal before he looked away, not sparing her any more of his attention. It was a slight to her position, both as the crowned queen and as his mother. It must've killed him to do it.

"I will send for you," he said indifferently. He panned his gaze over the crowd gathered before him. "You've all fought and won a hard battle. Those of you joining us from outside my kingdom, welcome. I apologize that we don't have more to offer you, but we will at least organize warm beds and offer you what food we have. Those of you who have returned after imprisonment in the demon kingdom, I will hear your stories, one and all. You will be avenged, that I promise. And lastly, those of you who rose up against the demons, congratulations! It was a battle well fought. You clinched our victory today. Be proud of yourselves. We've taken our kingdom back!"

A cheer went up from the periphery of those gathered, those mediocre fuckers feeling the glow of our win.

"Hadriel," the prince said, wiping the smile off my face immediately. I hated when he zeroed in on me. "Get everyone settled. We'll all take a rest to get our bearings, and then we have much to do. We're still weak as a kingdom, but I mean to rectify that issue as quickly as possible. After you get everyone settled, see me for a list of those I need to meet with and when."

Power rode the prince's rapid-fire commands. My wolf thrashed within me, not wanting me to bend to the dragon. My wolf only wanted to recognize commands that came from his alpha.

I grimaced, hesitating, not able to stop from glancing back at Weston. If this were a normal situation, he'd take grave offense to an outsider telling his pack wolf what to do. It would be seen as a challenge. Then again, the prince probably wouldn't take kindly to Weston snagging the loyalty of his people. What a clusterfuck.

I opened my mouth to speak, still not really sure what I planned to say, when understanding dawned in the prince's eyes. His gaze turned hard as it flicked to Weston.

"I can sever the connection at any time," Weston said, his tone as hard as the look the prince was giving him. "His wolf doesn't wish it. None of them do."

A wave of power washed over us again, the prince not liking what he'd just heard. My wolf clearly wasn't the only one who'd responded to Weston. Other villagers had been drawn to him too. After such turbulent times, the feeling of safety and unity offered by a pack led by a powerful, balanced wolf alpha was beyond enticing.

The prince and Weston stared at each other for a

long beat, the dragon power pounding around us and the wolf power throbbing in our middles. Weston held steady. It felt like the two alphas were gearing up for an explosion, and we'd all be slammed in the process.

That wasn't what was tearing me apart, though.

Finley was looking at me with sudden understanding. Sorrow lined her features.

"Your wolf wants to join his pack, is that it?" she asked me quietly. Each word was like a nail hammered into my heart. I'd wanted to do this differently. I'd wanted to explain.

Everyone waited quietly for me to answer.

I nodded mutely. "I tried to resist, but I saw the queen fly overhead, freaked out a little, and accidentally let down my defenses. My wolf…took over."

A breath left her parted lips. She reached out and hooked her hand around Nyfain's scarred forearm, seeking support.

He shifted his attention to her.

"We'll talk about this later," she told him, her gaze still on me. When she finally ripped it away, it came to rest on Weston. "We'll need to talk this through. I want to better understand how wolf shifters work. But this isn't the time. We have a lot of tired people that are due a rest. We need to get everything organized, as Nyfain said, and to do that, we need our people. All of them. Can you…release them or whatever you do for long enough for that to happen? It'll help all of us in the long run. After that…we'll figure out what happens next. Is that a good enough compromise?"

Nyfain wrapped his arm around her waist possessively, hooking it on her hip. He didn't comment, just watched Weston quietly. Despite being his mate, she wasn't technically the princess yet, and in this kingdom the queen had never shared the full weight of the throne's power. That was the way it had always been. It was clear the prince didn't care, though. He clearly intended to treat her as his equal in all things, including leading his kingdom. He had always made way for Finley, respected her, even when he wanted to throttle her.

If he wasn't so fucking terrifying, I'd pat him on the back for being better than the king before him, even now, on the doorstep of hell. I'd praise him for putting his faith in Finley.

You're going to make me miss her rising to her mantle and being a kickass fucking queen, you gibbering fuck puppet, I thought-yelled at my animal, my heart still breaking. *I don't want to leave her. I don't want to go with that alpha.*

Being with our own kind is what is best for us, and you know it, he replied. *Our father was a beta. Our mother was just as powerful. There is more to you than a mediocre butler or a stable boy. We should be in a pack so we can pull out our true potential.*

I gritted my teeth, my eyes prickling with heat. I hated being torn in the middle—because he was both right and wrong. If we left, we'd be missing the opportunities *she* could give us. She'd always tested my mettle, and in the demon dungeons she'd trusted Leala and me to help in the best way we knew how. She'd worked with us to create a solid team that had gone on to save the fucking day. *She* had led, not Weston.

"Yes, of course," Weston said, cutting through my thoughts, and the tangling power of the two alphas subsided. "They want to stay connected to the pack, but I will step aside as alpha—as their commander—so you can see to your affairs. Please let me know how I can help."

Finley breathed out a smile. "Thanks. Get some rest. We'll chat soon."

Weston visibly relaxed, as did the wolves around him.

"We need to grab the faeries and the demons before any of the villagers find them," Finley murmured to the prince, running her hand down his stomach.

"The demons?" he growled.

"Yes. A small group of demons helped us get out of the dungeon. They want to overthrow their ruling party and are offering us inside information so we can help them do it. I'll explain everything, but first we need to secure them before someone gets the wrong idea and kills them."

He nodded, looking out at the members of his court she'd returned from the dungeon. "Take a team of dragons," he told her. "I'll work on getting everyone settled here. See me when you get back. We haven't finished imprinting."

She shivered, her eyes going starry for a moment.

"Okay," she said in a breathy whisper before she seemed to get a hold of herself. "But also…" She turned and pointed at Weston. "Wolves are better on the ground. Can you spare me an escort, Weston?"

The prince stiffened momentarily. Finley didn't know how things were done here. All official business was typically handled by the court, and positions of power had always been held by dragons.

Finley was breaking protocol by asking for Weston's help, even for something as simple as guard duty. She was essentially asking a wolf to do a dragon's job, or at least that was how it would be perceived.

But the prince didn't correct her. He didn't call her down, like the mad king certainly would've. He was allowing her to make the faux pas without comment to ensure she saved face in front of their subjects. And honestly...he probably realized Finley was right. Wolves *were* better on the ground. It made sense to bring them to help, especially since any problems would come from the villagers who were ground-bound shifters.

Weston glanced at the prince, obviously wondering if the dragon alpha would have a problem, before stepping forward. "Of course."

"Great," Finley said. "Tamara, grab a couple of people, and let's go."

Tamara didn't move. She looked at the queen, technically her commander, waiting for the go-ahead.

Fear gripped me. How would this go for Finley? Would anyone support a commoner when they had the real thing back in the flesh?

I should've known the prince wouldn't stand for that.

"Until we know how she escaped the curse," he barked, looking over his mother's head, "my mother will not retain any power. And as most of you are aware,

11

queens are not afforded the capacity to independently rule. With my father gone, the crown and its duties have passed to me. I am its steward until the coronation. Finley, as my mate, is acting princess, soon to be crowned queen. At such a time, I will amend the laws to give her equal power and authority, and to grant any female offspring the same rights to the crown as their male counterparts. You will treat any command given by Finley with the same weight as you would if it came from me. You *will not* obey any commands by the former queen until I say otherwise."

His words blasted through the day, and if the queen felt their power, she gave no sign. She stood up straight, her expression stoic, seemingly undaunted by his sentiments. I'd never seen her so cool to him in my life. Her chief lady-in-waiting, however, standing behind her, scowled like a motherfucker. I did not forget that she'd also escaped the curse. The two of them had gotten out in the nick of time. And then, because of the queen's supposed death, the prince had been trapped in the kingdom.

I noticed a slight tremor in the prince's hand as he reached for Finley's cheek and ran a thumb along her jaw.

"Hurry back," he told her softly before giving her a lingering kiss. "We have many things to discuss, and we will do so…after we've exhausted our efforts with the imprinting."

Her gaze turned eager as he glanced at me and then turned away, heading back into the castle. Finley gasped, reaching for him, and I saw what she was responding to.

The prince's back, scarred and covered in tattoos,

had two strips of gleaming golden scales carved down each side. Hours ago, they'd been nothing but scars. Neither strip was complete, however—there were patches that showed only old scar tissue. It was like someone had scratched away sections. He hadn't completely healed with the release of the curse. The other scarring on his body hadn't gone away at all.

He shivered as she traced parts of the mended scales.

He turned back to her, his eyes intense. "I thought they felt different but…other matters stole my focus."

"They aren't complete. But…they're gold," she said softly.

He didn't speak, continuing to look at her for a long moment before his eyes flicked beyond her. He had an audience. He wouldn't want to shift in front of everyone in case his scales hadn't returned to their original color. Not to mention his wings might be all jacked up, since the scales were. I'd seen dragons with damaged wings, and it usually showed in the scales on their backs. After spending so much tortured time with the guy, I could now read the prince really well. He wouldn't want everyone seeing this new facet of himself before he understood what it meant.

"Hurry back to me," he murmured, and then finished his walk into the castle.

I jogged after him. He probably needed someone to yell at. It always seemed to make him feel better. And after that little powwow, he had some real bad shit to sort through. He'd need someone to take his mind off things, and until Finley could do it, he'd have to settle for his trusty butler.

Mediocrity for the win.

CHAPTER 2
FINLEY

"**H**OLY SHIT, RIGHT?" Tamara said as we jogged away from the people gathered around the castle steps. "I never, ever would've thought she was still alive. That collection of villages had *no idea* she was the queen of Wyvern until the curse was lifted. Lucille, did you see how confused they all were at first? Then all the blinking as their brains tried to make sense of everything?"

"She taught me to fly," I said, still unable to believe it. "She heard my story. She smelled *her son* on me, saw her sword, and never said anything. It explains why she didn't want anyone else from Wyvern hanging around, though. Why do you think that is?"

"Yeah, good question," Lucille said softly as Jade and Xavier, two of the dragons from the old court, joined us. We stopped just inside the tree line, waiting for Weston's wolves.

"The king was incredibly broken up about her death," Xavier murmured, stripping in preparation to shift. "Do you think he knew?"

"He must have known," Jade replied, her green eyes flashing.

"But it was a closed casket funeral," Tamara said.

"He would've wanted to see her," Jade replied. "It was probably a closed casket because she wasn't in it."

"So then why lie to us?" Tamara frowned, anger sparkling in her eyes. "Why lie to her guard? Do you think he was just trying to get the prince home?"

"It worked, didn't it?" Xavier said.

"The king was crazy, though," Lucille said. "He wouldn't have allowed her to leave. If he'd known she was alive, he would've followed her and dragged her back.

Xavier shrugged. "Maybe she made a deal—I'll leave, and it'll bring back the prince. Him for me."

"She wouldn't sacrifice him like that," Tamara hissed.

"She would if she thought he could leave," Xavier said. "I doubt anyone would've thought the mad king would make a deal with the demon king. She probably figured she could save herself without causing any harm to her son."

"But why didn't she age?" I asked, replaying all that had happened, going over all of my dealings with the woman I'd known as Ami. "She and Claudile were affected by that curse even if they weren't here."

"First of all, her name isn't Claudile." Xavier smirked. "It's Delaney."

I grimaced. "And the queen's name is…"

Tamara and Lucille's eyes widened. Xavier's gleamed.

"You don't know the queen's name?" Lucille asked.

"I was young when she supposedly died, and I was in one of the smaller and more detached villages," I replied. "I didn't know any of their names. I'm sure I would've if life had been normal, but they were all supposedly dead by the time I was old enough to retain that kind of information, the court with them, and we were fighting for our lives. It didn't seem important to know."

Xavier grinned. "Nor do you know any of the customs. You've already fucked up in a major way, and it's only day one."

My stomach twisted, and Tamara scowled.

"Remember who you're talking to," she told Xavier. "Show some respect."

"I'm talking to a commoner who stands in the shadow of the most beloved queen in history," he replied. "Finley might be the prince's mate, but she hasn't been sworn in. She's not official."

"Didn't you hear the prince?" Lucille shoved him. "He made her official in word, if not yet in deed. Not to mention that as soon as he's king, he's going to change things. She won't be just a figurehead. It's about damn time."

"We'll see," Xavier said in a low tone.

"Power or not, being sworn in or not," I said in an even tone, "keep talking to me like that and we're going to have a problem."

He smirked. "Except the queen took her sword back."

"Do you think I need a sword to slit your throat?" I ground out. "I'll find a fucking piece of glass if I get desperate enough, and I doubt I will, because a dagger or pocketknife will do just fine."

His eyes narrowed, but his mouth shut. He correctly realized I didn't give idle threats.

My stomach didn't stop churning, though, something I wouldn't allow to show on my face. I hadn't been ready for his sudden swagger. It was like he didn't remember all we'd been through. It was like he somehow thought the old hierarchy was alive, and his place in it was assured. Well, he'd be slapped with the dick of reality soon enough. The kingdom he'd returned to wasn't the golden one of times past. It was broken, and swagger had no place here.

Still, his sentiments would be shared by others. I'd probably have more dissenters than supporters.

Maybe you should make an example of him. You wouldn't need a blade to put him in his place, my dragon thought. *You just need me. I'll take his dragon any day. I'm bigger, more alpha, and most importantly, I am so much meaner.*

Five men and women walked up, the men tall and broad, with clearly defined muscles and hard eyes. The women were a bit shorter, with not as much girth, but their curves spoke of hard muscle.

"The alpha sent us," said the man at the front, brown-haired and with a chiseled face and deep-set, velvety brown eyes. "I'm Ehno. I'll be heading up this subsection of pack. I'll be following your lead."

Tamara's eyes widened, and Xavier frowned and shot me a look. This was significant in some way, but I had no idea why. My lack of knowledge about shifters and court in general was already hindering me. I needed to get some lessons, ASAP. I wondered if Tamara would give them to me.

"Do you know where we're going?" I asked Ehno.

"Yes. Back to where we came in, right?"

"Right. Hopefully they didn't get any dumb ideas about wandering into Wyvern after the magical wall lifted. I doubt the villagers would be happy to see those demons." I nodded at him. "We'll be flying overhead. We'll keep pace with you."

Ehno nodded, stepping away to shift.

I did the same, leaving the trees for a moment so my dragon could take over. We shifted, and she rose into the sky, beating her wings lazily as she took us over the trees. The other dragons joined me, and we soared over the Forbidden Wood—or the Royal Wood, I guessed, now that it wasn't forbidden anymore.

A thrill arrested me. Was this for real? Was I a fucking princess?

A *princess*?

I still remembered the wonder I felt watching Nyfain soar through the blue sky in dragon form, his gold scales glittering. Back then I was a young girl, separated from him in every way that mattered, but he was mine now. My mate. Maybe one day the father of my children, if I was blessed enough to have any. My forever. I couldn't believe we were finally back together, the curse lifted.

There is still a lot of work to be done, my dragon warned me. *Forever won't mean much if that demon horde comes back and cuts the legs out from under you. Or that queen rips the throne out from under your ass.*

Can you just let me have one damn second to marvel at my good fortune?

Marvel when he's fucking you. Start thinking about his wing issue now.

She had a point. Demon magic had ripped the wings from his back. Stripping it away had returned some but not all of the scales. Why? Could some of their magic have gotten tied up within him when he forced the shift?

If so, Calia, the powerful faerie who'd helped us break out of the dungeons and into our kingdom, should be able to sense the magic. Hopefully, she would also be able to unravel it or strip it away.

Patrols of village shifters roamed the trees below us as we made our way, cut through with Weston's wolves. I made sure not to outstrip them, flying slowly as they loped beneath us. I wanted to show that we were a unit, all of us. That our success against the demon king hadn't been a fluke and we'd be stronger if we stuck together.

My heart started to hammer as we approached the edge of the kingdom without a glimpse of the demons and faeries.

Land, I told my dragon.

She angled down quickly, the ground rushing up to meet us, and shifted, and my human body tumbled along the ground.

I know you know how to fucking land, you asshole, I told her, dragging myself to my feet and shaking it off. *You're making me look like a fool in front of the others.*

I only kinda know how to land. This made it look like we were in a hurry.

The list of things we needed to work on was growing

rapidly.

The other dragons landed behind me, joining me just outside of the previously erected magical wall. The wolves jogged up in their animal forms.

In this spot, it was easy to see the effect of the demon magic on our land—one side of the invisible line was lush and green, the other side twisted and blackened and robbed of life.

"Where'd they go?" Tamara asked, pointing out heavy treads from what must've been demon boots.

While I caught whiffs of their scents, it wasn't distinct enough for me to follow them, and the treads disappeared after a few steps. It was almost like they'd tried to keep their path hidden.

"No bodies," Jade said, circling out to scan the area. "No blood. Those are good signs."

Ehno, now a large gray wolf, growled softly before making a show of putting his nose to the ground. He jogged forward like that, then turned back, asking me to follow.

I needed to learn to read *wolf* better so he didn't have to mime his intent.

"Their noses are clearly better than ours," I said, motioning for him to continue and then jogging after him. "They're better at tracking. Follow on two feet so that we can communicate if we have to. I don't think I have the energy for rapid-fire shifting."

"Me neither," Tamara murmured. "I'm exhausted. Thank the goddess the prince has a heart and will let us rest before we start to rebuild. I don't think I can keep going much longer."

I didn't bother asking what the mad king would've demanded. It was pretty clear.

In a moment, it was evident where we were going—right back to the boats. Once there, we saw the rowboats we used to get to shore had been taken in and tied up, keeping anyone from heading out to them.

"Smart," I said, readying to shift. "They probably worried one of our people would come out this far, searching for demons, and didn't want to risk a confrontation."

"Or maybe they were just tired and wanted a bed." Jade rubbed her eyes.

"Or that, yeah." I smirked and shifted, wondering how the hell I was going to get onto the demons' boat without crashing into it. My dragon shifted in the air, and I dropped like a stone onto the deck, landing hard on my butt and then falling back and clunking my head.

Problem solved, she thought.

There weren't enough swear words in the world to properly get my feelings across, so I just pushed myself to standing and thought about how to get revenge without killing us both.

As the rest of the dragons circled overhead, the captain emerged. He quickly alerted the others to our presence.

"It worked," Govam said when he met me on the deck. His dusky gray eyes twinkled. "Is your kingdom in one piece?"

"It hasn't been in one piece for years, Govam, you know that. But we did do it, yes. We chased them out."

I heaved a shuddering sigh and let myself smile, still

struggling to process everything. Nyfain and I had freed our kingdom from the demons' clutches.

I was banging the golden prince!

Would you calm the fuck down? my dragon thought in annoyance. *Don't make me keep reminding you that—*

Yes, yes, I know.

I tried to wipe what I knew was a stupid grin from my face, except desire was pooling within Nyfain now, curling and growing and heating up. I felt his longing for me and my equally strong need to get back to him. To feel his body under my fingers. To get lost in his touch. It wasn't just a sexual need for him—it was a strange sort of throbbing. A pull that gripped my middle and kept yanking to get me moving toward him. He felt like a part of me, like half of me, actually, and everything in me was desperate to merge those halves. It had to be a side effect of the imprinting. There was so much to do, and now so much to sort out—the queen, the wolves, establishing trade again, getting supplies—but all I wanted was to revel in Nyfain's body. To feel his soft lips glide down my scorching flesh.

"We need to get you guys safely back to the castle," I said as Calia drifted to the side of the railing on the deck of her sleek ship, anchored not far away. She waved. I raised my voice. "I have a favor to ask you. I want to see if you can help my mate shrug off the rest of the demons' magic."

"Your golden prince will undoubtedly want to establish a connection with her people," Govam said, watching as her sister and the other faeries joined her. "He will want to secure an invitation to speak with the king and queen, I have no doubt. She is high up in their hierarchy. I've heard it mentioned throughout the years."

Add it to the list.

Then, unbidden, a thought drifted up. Was she from the same kingdom as Nyfain's ex-fiancée? Would that woman think she had some sort of claim to him, even after all this time? To his plant-growing magic that was so rare and powerful?

My dragon growled low, but I pushed the thought away. I had enough to do—I didn't need more dread heaped on my pile. I'd worry about it when the time came.

CHAPTER 3
FINLEY

FLANKED BY THE wolves, the faeries made a circle around the demons, and my dragon escorted them back through the wood and to the castle with the rest of the dragons in the air. Those who caught sight of us stared, their faces screwing up in anger at the sight of the demons.

At the castle, the stairs were cleared except for a couple of people hurrying this way or that. Vemar came walking out and did a double take upon seeing me.

"There you are, Strange Lady." He stopped in front of us, hands on his hips.

I shifted back into my human form. The wolves followed suit, and the dragons landed and did the same.

"What's up?" I asked Vemar, feeling the constant pull of Nyfain as though a string were attached to my ribs. I could actually feel his location now, like a beacon calling me home.

"Just looking for a way to be of use. I've spent much too long being idle in a dungeon. I'd rather not be idle here."

"I'm sure they could use help dusting rooms or putting sheets on beds or whatever needs to happen."

"Yes, they could, but they don't seem to want that from me. They shooed me away. They didn't think it was any place for a dragon. My question, of course, was 'Well then, where is the place for a dragon?' To that, they said, '*In the court*.'" Vemar stretched his arms wide and looked around. "So where is this magical court where the dragons belong? It looks to me like there is not much of anything around here except random streaks of glitter and abandoned costumes. I found a bear costume in the corner. I would've looked closer, but it had some worrying stains on it. I decided it was best not to touch it anymore. And there are candles in all the light sockets. That has to be dangerous, doesn't it?"

I couldn't help but chuckle. "Don't touch the costumes, no. Back in the day, the dragons—and only the dragons, I think—were the nobility. They made up the court. Nobility don't do menial tasks. That's probably what they meant."

"Only dragons?" Ehno asked.

"Only dragons," Tamara replied, a growl in her voice. "This is a dragon kingdom, or did you miss that? Just like the Flamma Kingdom only has wolves in the court."

"Hey, hey, whoa, whoa." I quirked an eyebrow at Tamara. "Remember that there wouldn't *be* a dragon kingdom without Ehno and the rest of Weston's pack. Anyway, he's right to ask the question. Neither hierarchy makes sense when you have other shifter types in the kingdom," I said, rubbing my eyes. "There should be fair representation. I mean, in the Flamma Kingdom, they have all those strong dragons hanging out in the mountains. Think of how much more powerful that kingdom would be if they incorporated the dragons into the court. They'd be unstoppable."

"Dragons and wolves don't really get along," Lucille said.

"Well, if everyone stopped being such cunts, maybe they could." I refocused on Vemar. "Just go force the issue. I doubt they'll pick a fight with a mad dragon. Or get some sleep. You have to be exhausted."

"I am exhausted, yes, but it feels good to be busy." He leaned in a little closer. "By the way, you have a very ruthless mate. I'm glad I knew better than to mess with him. I don't think Micah realized what he was getting into."

Micah being the dragon who'd attempted to tear me from Nyfain. He'd challenged him and suffered badly for it.

I swallowed. "How is Micah?"

Vemar straightened up with a smirk. "He cheated death, and he knows it." He laughed and turned. "I don't think he'll trouble you again. He has learned his lesson." He disappeared into the castle.

I glanced back at Tamara. "You guys can go and get some rest. I think we'll be fine in the castle."

Tamara glanced at Ehno before giving me a curt nod and walking around us and into the castle. The other dragons followed her in, probably headed to check out their old lodgings and see what state they were in. They'd all been in the demons' clutches with me, and many of them had been away from home for years.

"I didn't mean to cause trouble," Ehno said quietly as we started forward, heading inside at a slower pace.

"You all need to stop being at odds with each other," I replied, feeling a flutter as I neared Nyfain. "Because I will tell you this—when we were all charging in here, I realized how effective it was to have the dragons in the air and the wolves on the ground. What we couldn't do from above, you finished from below. Just think if there were faeries throwing magic into the mix, too." I glanced back at Calia. "Now *that* would be a good time, wouldn't it?"

A small smile blossomed on Calia's face. "Dragons," she murmured, shaking her head slightly. "Battle is a treat to you."

"A strong unit crushing one's adversaries...yeah. It excites me." I shrugged with a laugh. "Still, we'd be unstoppable."

"It is my hope that we will put that to the test before long," she replied as we climbed the stairs. "We will need to work together to rip Dolion down from his perch."

My stomach flipped when I saw Nyfain. He was on the second floor, checking rooms with Hadriel in tow. Nyfain had donned a rumpled shirt and some shoes, one of the laces still undone. His tousled hair tumbled down over his forehead, and his muscles rippled beneath the threadbare fabric.

"Oh my," Calia said softly, a note of alarm in her voice. "That's..."

Nyfain glanced my way as we neared, frustration in

his expression, and held up a single finger for me. He couldn't walk away just yet. Hadriel gave me a long-suffering look from behind him.

"I recognize him," Calia whispered. "It's hard not to remember a man who is so very beautiful but in a terrifying way. He was betrothed to someone in our court a long time ago. I very clearly remember his intensity. He scared half the court, even when he was on his best behavior."

A sudden flash of rage stole my breath. I pressed a palm to my chest, trying to still the feeling that threatened to drag me under.

I hadn't been ready for the intensity of my reaction. When Nyfain's ex-fiancée crossed my mind before, it hadn't torn through me like that.

What'd you expect? my dragon thought. *He's ours. We've claimed him. Obviously we're going to kill anything that touches him. Logic.*

That was going to take some getting used to.

"Sixteen years ago," I said through gritted teeth, "and please don't mention her again. I'm not exactly…rational when it comes to him just now."

"Sorry, yes, of course," Calia said. "He's a Syflora, isn't he? Am I remembering correctly?"

"What's a Syflora?" asked Denski, Govam's second-in-command, who stood right behind him, at the head of the demon group.

"They have magic in their song," Calia replied, studying him. "They can help natural things grow and flourish. It is a very rare gift, helpful for the healing arts and creating natural remedies. I remember the royal family thinking it would be a great blessing to introduce that magic into their bloodline."

The rage blistered this time, tinging my vision and making me wobble where I stood.

"Stop talking about that," Govam barked at her, stepping forward quickly and putting himself between me and her. "Can't you see it is affecting her?"

"It's fine." I wiped my suddenly slick forehead. "It's fine. Just a little rage among friends. But yes, Calia, please stop mentioning…"

The thought of him having babies with another—

I bent over and braced my hands on my knees.

"Just…stop mentioning that whole thing," I said.

"Are dragons really so possessive?" one of the faeries whispered.

One of the female wolves answered her. "The imprint is still fresh, probably not even fully settled. I remember wanting to rip the face off anyone who so much as looked at my Raymond. I don't think I would've had the control to stop from braining someone who talked about my mate… Well, what she just talked about."

I squeezed my eyes shut. "That's the gist of it, yes. And dragons are very possessive, yes. They will fight to the death if someone touches their mate."

"Not just dragons," Ehno murmured.

"See? We're not so different, are we?" I straightened up with effort as Nyfain walked toward us. His gaze stuck to me all the way down the hall until he was right in front of me, his heat bathing my flesh, his proximity loosening the tight coils of anger within me.

"Hey," he said softly. It was like he neither knew nor cared that guests stood at my back. He ran his knuckles down my cheek before leaning in to kiss me softly. "You good?"

"Calia…" I half turned and motioned to her. He didn't follow my movements with his eyes, still giving me his undivided attention. "Knows you. From…before."

Realization flowered through the bond. He'd put two and two together.

He shook his head slowly. "There is no before you. There is no after. There is only you. Always."

I let out a slow breath and stepped closer, running a hand up his chest. The heat of his body seeped through my palm and invigorated me. I closed my eyes for a moment, letting the last traces of anxiety and anger drain away. When I was back to myself, I fluttered my eyes open and stepped to his side.

He dropped his big arm around me and hooked his hand around my hip. He finally tore his eyes away.

I pointed at Govam. "This demon is the leader of the group that helped us get out of the dungeons. Dolion doesn't treat his guards well. They want to overthrow him."

Nyfain stepped forward and put out his hand. Govam shook.

"Thank you for helping her get out," Nyfain said in a menacing growl. "I look forward to hearing more about your role and why I shouldn't kill you."

The faeries shifted and looked at each other with wide eyes as the wolves rolled back their shoulders and puffed out their chests in approval. I felt my eyebrows drift up and my mouth go slack. Before I could decide if I needed to do damage control, Govam replied, "Then I will make sure I am very convincing."

He stepped back as Nyfain saw Sonassa in the very back of the group of demons.

"If you use your magic in this castle," Nyfain told her, his teeth bared, "I will make an example of you. My mate has brought you here, and so I will honor her wishes and keep you safe…until you use your magic on one of my people. Then I will kill you gruesomely. Do you understand me?"

"Yes, sire," she said in a tight voice before dropping into a low bow.

"Govam is very good at staying alive," I told Nyfain. "He can read dragons really well."

"If he steps out of line, his ability to read my rage won't save him from me," Nyfain responded.

"I have no doubt," Govam replied in a matter-of-fact tone.

Well, this was going swimmingly.

I held out my hand to indicate Calia, still standing with her crew of faeries. They'd drifted backward a few steps, no doubt alarmed by Nyfain's handling of the demons.

"As I said before, she knows you—"

"Forgive me, I know *of* you." Calia blushed. "I know of your magic. We've never met."

"Speaking of," I said before she could go on, "she has a special magic that allows her to essentially pick apart the magic of others. She's the one who got us past the

31

magical wall surrounding the kingdom. She also dis-
pelled the suppression magic used on the other
prisoners. I wondered…" I met her indigo eyes. "Can
you see if he still has any demon magic within him? His
scales haven't fully healed, and I wondered if maybe that
is why…"

Her eyes flicked from me to him. "Yes, of course,
but…I might have to touch him."

"It's fine. I'm good. It was just with—" A flash of
rage kept me from mentioning that other woman, or her
court, or their plans.

Nyfain ran his comforting touch along my back, easing my anger.

"And that is Ehno," I said, wiping my face of the
sudden perspiration again. "He's one of Weston's pack
members. I didn't get the others' names."

"I'm Weston's beta," Ehno said, nodding at Nyfain.
"The alpha was detained, looking after his wolves. I
assisted Finley, giving her the lead of the hunt."

Nyfain tensed, gripping my hip a little more tightly.
Shock bled through the bond, but he didn't show it on
his face. He offered Ehno a curt nod. "She doesn't
understand what that means. Because of the curse, she
didn't grow up as a shifter. This is all new to her. But I
know."

"Of course." Ehno returned the curt nod with a little
crease forming between his dark brows, giving me a
glance. He clearly didn't know my backstory. Or any of
our backstories, maybe.

"Thanks for your help," I told him, and then nodded
to the others. "You can head out now, I think."

The shifters peeled away, moving back the way they'd come. They were probably going to find Weston and get their accommodations.

"Hadriel," Nyfain barked without turning, expecting Hadriel to come running, no doubt. While he waited, he said to Calia, "And how do you feel about working alongside demons?"

She spared them a long look. "It sounds like it is a means to an end, but I will not lie—I do not like the idea of being their keeper."

"Have no fear. I am more than happy to take on that task," Nyfain said in a rough tone. The demons drifted backward, except for Govam, who held his ground. He clearly knew Nyfain wouldn't kill him just yet. Not without cause.

"Yes, sire?" Hadriel hurried toward us. "Oh, Finley, love, you're still here. Good." He stopped at my side. "Very naked, though, my darling. Is that going to be the new normal? Because I thought we could get away from the nakedness for a while. I am desperately tired of seeing tits and dick within the castle walls…"

"Hadriel, find our new guests lodgings," Nyfain commanded, power twisting through his words. "We'll need eyes on the demons at all times. Put them on the third floor so they cannot get out through a window, and make sure their rooms are watched at all times. Ask some of the dragons to do it, the members of court and the guests. And offer a rotation to the alpha wolf."

"The…alpha wolf, sire?" Hadriel said haltingly, traces of delight coloring his words.

"Yes. Finley set the precedent by including them earlier. The alpha replied in kind. I will honor my mate's decision. If they wish to help us, we'll be glad for it."

"Yes, sir—Fuck. Sire, I meant. Yes, *sire*."

"And Hadriel?"

"Yes, sir? Sire?"

"Get the seamstress and seamster ready to receive work. The alphas will need to be seen and dressed, and then we will meet over dinner to discuss particulars. It will all have to be arranged."

"Yes, sire."

I could hear the fatigue in Hadriel's voice. I laid my hand gently against the dip in Nyfain's back. He turned a little and bent to me, giving me his full attention again.

"He's tired too, baby," I said quietly, not wanting to make a big deal of it or publicly disagree with him in any way. "Maybe let…the *fully dressed* housemaid, hopefully without her big purple dildo, handle some of it?"

Nyfain kissed the top of my head. "Of course. Hadri-el, make sure to delegate and get some rest. I'll need a butler who is not so mediocre before long. I am hoping you can rise to the challenge."

"Yes, sir—sire! Yes, sire." Hadriel winked at me before turning and muttering, "Thank the goddess and her dirty secrets, I thought I'd never get away from him."

Nyfain pretended not to hear as a smile bloomed on the faces of a few of the faeries. The demons clearly knew better than to show any mirth at Hadriel's craziness.

"Please, rest," Nyfain told the faeries. "Everyone has earned it. Let us know if you need anything. We don't have much, but we'll try to accommodate you in any way we can. Thank you for helping take back our kingdom. I owe you a debt."

"No." Calia shook her head before stepping closer. "I owe Finley a debt. Two, in fact, because she also saved my sister. We have not done much to help, but we will. I will discuss that with you when we have all had a chance to refresh." She held her hands out, close to him but not touching, then shut her eyes before slowly nodding. "Yes, there is something within you. Something lingering." Her hands drifted closer. "It feels like the suppression magic, but it is...festering, almost. Like...there is a fissure within you where the demon magic has taken root. It is entwined in there. It grips tightly."

Nyfain's fingers dug into my skin, but he didn't comment.

Calia opened her eyes and took a step back, shaking her head. "It isn't something I can help you with, although maybe the healers of my people can."

"Can Dolion fix it?" I asked Govam.

His eyes narrowed a little. "His people surely could. Similar to the way they tried to find your bond and sever—"

He abruptly stopped talking and took a large step back, jostling his people out of the way. His gray eyes were focused on Nyfain, who hadn't so much as twitched.

"You're right, sweetheart," Nyfain growled to me, his fury burning within the bond. "He is very good at reading the room. I wouldn't mention that again, demon."

"Didn't need to be said, sire," Govam responded easily. "His people likely *could*, but they could also do more damage while they were at it. Even if it would mean their death, I doubt they would miss the opportunity to cripple a dragon."

"I wouldn't let them try," Nyfain replied.

He had a point. I'd just been grasping at straws. Trying to find an easy way. But when in my experience had anything concerning healing ever been easy?

Nyfain slid his hand up the back of my neck possessively, and I could feel his desire swell through the bond. I swayed toward him, my knees going weak. He hoisted me up into his arms and started walking, backtracking to call one of his dragons to him. I couldn't focus on what he was saying, though, lost as I was in his heat. His balmy smell cocooned me, pine and lilac with a hint of honeysuckle, like a warm summer evening in a high mountain meadow. Like coming home.

His lips seared fire along my jaw and his passion throbbed, his dragon right near the surface, needing to finish the imprint with his cock deep inside me.

CHAPTER 4
FINLEY

W E WALKED DOWN the hall to his rooms. I dragged my lips along his neck before nipping at his jaw.

He shivered, angling his head so that I could run my teeth down the side of his throat and suck in my mark at the base of his neck.

"No tower?" I asked, my lips now against the shell of his ear.

"No," he rasped. He slowed and turned his head to claim my lips, thrusting his tongue into my mouth. His taste drove me wild, chasing away my worries and the long, long to-do list I was creating. "No tower. And no separate rooms. Traditionally the king and queen sleep in separate chambers. Not us. I want to go to sleep with you in my arms, and wake you up with my cock deep in your pussy."

I melted around him, liking when he talked dirty. I feathered my tongue across the edge of his earlobe, my core pounding with arousal.

"We're not going to waste time on the 'proper' way

K . F . B R E E N E

of doing things," he went on. "Not after all we've been through." He pulled back a little and looked down into my eyes. "We have an opportunity to start over. We have an opportunity to build something here, in this kingdom. You've already shaken things up, and I want to keep heading in that direction."

His eyes dipped to my exposed chest.

A little grin pulled at his lips. "I do think clothes should be a requirement within the castle, however. Hadriel did have a point."

I chuckled. "Fair point. I just didn't have any at hand."

"Yes, Leala is helping settle people in." His eyes turned serious. "We'll discuss the changes as soon as we can cobble together some sort of council. A council that is interested in the wellbeing of people—all of them, not just the rich. I want Hannon to be on that council."

I widened my eyes, pulling back a little. "H-Hannon? But he's...common. Who will listen to him?"

"The same people who will listen to you. We'll make sure of it. But as I said, all of that can come later. I will not rush our imprinting, not even with the...shocking revelations of earlier and all that is going on. It's time we lost ourselves in each other, regardless of what waits for us outside of these walls."

He carried me into his rooms, and I got a glimpse of high ceilings, artful paintings, and the deep blue-green décor before he slammed the door shut behind us and lowered me down his body. My bare skin slid against the rough seam of his pants; his bulge was hard and ready for me.

"The good thing about clothes not being worn is that I can get at you so much faster," he murmured, bending to take my hard nipple in his hot mouth.

He ran a finger through my wetness, moaning as he felt my heat. I spread my legs wider, and he ran his digits up across my clit before threading two fingers into me. They curved just right, pumping in and out, and his thumb pressed and circled my clit.

I fisted his hair, my hips gyrating in time with his ministrations.

He fell to his knees before grabbing one of my knees and guiding it up and over his wide shoulder. He dragged his tongue through my wet folds, teasing it around my opening before thrusting inside.

I shivered, letting my head fall back against the wood with a *thunk*. He feathered his tongue up toward my clit before sucking it in hard. I gasped as he plunged his fingers into me again, working me hard and fast.

"Oh fuck," I said, my eyes fluttering. "Oh goddess, oh fuck—"

With the other hand, he reached up and tweaked a nipple, sending shooting sparks of pure bliss straight to my needy cunt. I wanted to hold out, wanted to savor these fucking amazing sensations, but without warning, a wave of pleasure engulfed me, and then I was falling down into my orgasm, moaning, shuddering against his hot mouth.

"Goddess help me, you taste so sweet," he murmured, his lips against my pussy, the vibration of his words tickling me pleasantly. "Better than anything I've ever tasted. I hadn't heard this was a side effect of imprinting. Maybe it's because we're true mates."

"Let's see, shall we?" I shoved his head away to put some space between us, quickly pulled in my foot, and shoved him backward, using my will to help the cause. He toppled back onto the ground, splayed for a moment before he rolled over slowly to his hands and knees.

Sudden anger turned to blistering excitement as he rose to his knees, his golden eyes pinning me to the spot.

"Are you trying to dominate me, princess?" His voice was rough and wild, raw and full of danger.

A thrill of warning zinged up my spine.

"I'm going to suck that cock until you are hopelessly writhing on the floor and begging to come down my throat," I said, full of bravado I wasn't sure I felt.

Fire lit in his eyes and burned through the bond. Power coiled around him; he'd heard my challenge and needed to answer. Needed to do what was in his nature—force me to submit.

Suddenly I couldn't get enough air. I felt like running. Whimpering. Rolling over and spreading my legs.

Fight that fucker until we come, my dragon growled.

Sounded good to me.

I crashed my will down on him, flattening him to the ground. He grunted as I pounced, using all my strength to rip him over onto his stomach and tear the shirt across his back. His golden scales, broken down his back, glittered in the low light in the room, so fucking beautiful.

I straddled his hips, tightening my body to keep him put in case he tried to buck me off. I leaned forward to shove his hands over his head, holding them there for a moment while my brain tried to catch up to my body. I probably needed a plan or something. He was much stronger than me. More ruthless. Pinning him to the ground probably wasn't the best idea.

He clearly thought the same thing.

I heard his low, dark chuckle. The sound caressed my skin with little shocks of pleasure. I shivered with the feel of it, the *promise* of it.

"Ten…" he said in a low voice, not fighting me. Not moving, his hands above his head, the muscles on his big arms flared. "Nine…eight…"

A shock of adrenaline coursed through me.

Oh shit, my dragon thought with the equivalent of a squeal of excitement. *Get his clothes off and get the fuck to the other side of the room. We can't fight him on the ground. We need to charge into him with a running start.*

Not a great game plan, but it was better than nothing. She was right about one thing—I needed to fight on my feet. I wouldn't do much on the ground, not against this huge slab of lethal muscle.

Wasting no time, I scrabbled off him and rolled him over. He complied easily, his eyes hooded and a lazy grin drifting up his face. Fire bled through the bond, the thrill of a challenge about to be met.

"Seven…six…"

I grabbed two fistfuls of his ripped shirt and yanked. More fabric tore across that muscled, scarred, and tattooed chest. Goddess help me, I loved the play of violence on his flesh. I loved to see the evidence of his hard-earned prowess, and his utter confidence in it. He wasn't hiding what he was—he couldn't. I didn't want him to.

My core tightened and my wetness leaked down my thighs as I slowed down a little, savoring the look of him. Running my hands down his chest and delighting in the feeling.

"Fi—" He stopped counting for a moment, watching me as I bent to kiss between his pecs, then run my lips down his chest.

"You're so beautiful," I whispered, licking across one of his nipples and then kissing over his heart. I stayed there for a moment, my lips against his skin, his heart gently pulsing back against me. "Calia was right when she said you were beautiful in a terrifying way."

I drifted down his chest again, unbuttoning his threadbare jeans, a remnant from a different time. It didn't need to be anymore. We could trade for more of them, or send people into the human lands to buy or steal them, depending on whether we could work out how to get at that last bit of gold in the reserves—the gold Dolion hadn't been able to steal. Now that the curse had been broken, the world and all its spoils were once again open to us.

"The parts that make you terrifying," I murmured, unzipping and kissing downward, "are incredibly sexy."

I worked around to his hips, my fingers in his belt-line, and pulled his jeans lower. He lifted, allowing me to tug them down to his ankles before finally getting off his shoes. I climbed back up his body slowly, licking and kissing my way, savoring the salty taste of his skin. The warmth on my lips and tongue.

"Your scars…" I ran my tongue across a jagged scar

that must've hurt something awful when he got it. "Your ink…" I sucked in his flesh over an intricate design, wondering who'd applied them for him. Wondering how. I'd never thought to ask. And honestly…I wasn't in a rush to learn everything about him all at once. I wanted to savor some of the secrets so that I could unravel him little by little over the years to come. We had all our lives. "Your passion…"

I reached his cock and sucked it in without warning or finesse, taking it deep. He pulled in a breath, his body tensing, all his muscles popping. His groan was pure carnal sin, and he flared his big thighs.

I backed off, coating his cock with my saliva, rolling my tongue across the head. I pumped his shaft once and then flicked my tongue down the underside and tracing a vein to the base before sucking at the seam of his ball sack. His release of breath was heady, and he snaked his fingers into my hair.

"Now you're at my mercy, little dragon," he growled, pulling me up by the hair until his cock head rested against my lips. "My dragon wants to take over and make you scream with pleasure." He let me lick the tip, his eyelids growing heavy. "But I think I'll be selfish."

He thrust up suddenly, his ass lifting off the ground, his fist in my hair yanking. His cock pushed in deep, way to the back of my throat.

"Swallow it down, princess," he said as he backed off and did it again. "Take it all."

My gag reflex went active, but I pushed past it, doing as he said, feeling the excitement in the loss of control. There was a time to fight, and a time to revel in my big golden dragon taking what was his.

My dragon purred in delight, and an incredible wave of desire overcame me. Suddenly I couldn't suck hard enough. Fast enough. I devoured his cock with my need.

"Oh fuck, Finley—"

Soon I wasn't the only one lacking control.

His movements turned harried. Wild.

He yanked me down harder, grinding into my mouth. I bobbed furiously, and tears ran down my cheeks from the effort. I ran my fingers against the seam of his balls, massaging one testicle and then the other while I worked my other hand around his base, squeezing down as I sucked.

"Hmm," he said, two hands in my hair now, fucking my face in coarse strokes. "That's right. Take it all. You wanted to taste? I'm about to give you a big fucking taste. Look at me."

Power ripped through my body. I moaned from the delicious feel of it, from the pleasure he was pumping through the bond, echoing the sensations I was causing.

I lifted my eyes, feasting on his body as it worked, curling in a fantastic show of cut arms, abs, and pecs. Above me were those golden eyes, on fire with passion. He strove harder, breathing rapidly, cutting off my air. He clutched my hair, and my chin hit off his balls as he yanked me down while thrusting up, swinging his ass off the floor.

"Swallow this down, princess," he grunted, filling my mouth.

The taste exploded across my senses, sweet as salted caramel, a treat I hadn't had in a long time, only better.

Addictive. De-fucking-*licious.*

I groaned, massaging his balls to get every last drop. He slowed, breathing hard, watching me. I finished swallowing as his fingers loosened in my hair.

"Fuck, Finley, that is so sexy." His words rode a tortured sigh.

"Definitely a different flavor," I murmured, licking down his softening shaft before placing a light kiss on his hip and then kissing down to his inner thigh.

My dragon surged, then, out of the blue. She bit into his flesh, *hard*, piercing the skin and drawing blood.

He grunted, spreading his thighs and bracing his palms on the ground beside him. I struggled to get control back while she flitted our tongue over the bite mark before moving to the other side. She kissed his other inner thigh, lifting our eyes to his, locking gazes.

His lush lips stretched up into a lazy smile right before she bit down again, marking him ruthlessly a second time.

He chuckled darkly. "Come back, princess. Tell your dragon that I am not nearly close to being done. She needn't worry."

A naughty smile played on my lips, her reaction, before she did as he said, receding so that I could wrestle back control.

Mark him some more. I want everyone to know he's ours, she said with a swirl of possession.

He must've felt it through the bond because his smile stretched and his eyes glittered. He hooked his fingers under my chin and used pressure to make me sit up and then climb closer, not at all worrying about the blood

45

welling from the bite marks.

"She just wanted to enact a little violence, apparently," I said as he grabbed one of my knees and guided it to the side of his hip.

"Understandable. I never got to finish my count." My adrenaline must have swirled through the bond because he shook his head a little. "That's a game for another time. I found a book in the library, and I want to act it out. I want to fuck you the dragon way."

My belly fluttered. "What's the dragon way?"

His smile was wicked. He didn't answer. Instead, he pulled my other knee into position so that I was straddling his semi-hard cock.

"Mmm," he said, pulling my hair to tilt my head back. He ran his teeth down my neck before licking his mark. "You're so fucking wet."

He ran his mouth back up to my chin before crossing over to the other side.

"I want to hear how wet you are," he rasped. "Reach down and finger-fuck your pussy."

I groaned with his dirty words as he continued his slow, teasing torment. I reached between us and slid my fingers over my clit, feeling a jolt of pleasure before I tilted up my hips a little so I could slip a finger, and then two, into my cunt. My juices flowed around the digits and leaked down, coating his hardening cock.

"Fuck that's hot," he whispered as the slick sounds filled the air.

He sucked in the fevered skin on my neck as he sat up and rearranged my legs again, now totally wrapping them around him. He pushed me back a little, holding me in place so that he could bend and lick across one pebbled nipple.

"Keep fucking yourself, Finley," he said before he sucked it in and rolled it around his mouth. "I want you to come on top of my cock before I put it back inside of you."

I gyrated my hips up, using the heel of my hand to press into my clit while I curved my fingers into my pussy like he wanted. Eyes closed, I soaked up the sensations as his arms encircled me, keeping me steady, a band of immovable strength that made me feel as though I weighed nothing.

His cock was rock hard under me, its length pushing against the crack of my ass. He leaned over and sucked in the other nipple, dragging it through his teeth and sending a sudden jolt of pain turned pleasure racing through my body.

I groaned. The sensations heightened, on the point of blistering pleasure.

"Come for me," he commanded, power ripping through me.

I cried out, shaking in his arms as he hauled me up against his chest. He fused his mouth with mine, angling to deepen the kiss, sucking in my groans of climax.

"Good girl," he murmured against my lips, grabbing an ass cheek in each hand and lifting me.

The head of his cock dragged against my opening, stalling one moment before he yanked me down over him. It slammed home with satisfying roughness. He did it again, lifting me easily before crashing me back onto him, so deep and consuming. So thick.

He took a hand from my hip and wrapped it around the back of my neck, holding me to him. He pressed his other large hand to the back of my shoulder, passion mixed with power, his and mine. Our dragons were right near the surface, soaking it all in, the love, the lust, the ache for each other, the *need*. This was what they'd always craved. It was what they'd always worked to fulfill.

As if keeping them in mind, he broke the kiss so that he could rake his teeth down the flesh of my neck and settle his lips over his claiming mark, one hand still on my neck, keeping me put. The pads of his first two fingers on the other hand glided over my scales as his teeth skimmed against my mark.

A surge of pure carnal bliss shot through me, making me gasp. I jerked my hips against him wildly, arching as he finished running his hand over my scales.

"Oh goddess, that's good," I groaned, bobbing on him now, feeling the delicious friction inside of me.

He braced both hands beneath my columns of scales this time and rubbed a finger along the edge of each side. The pleasure was minimal, more of a hint of what was to come. A promise. Something to liven up a boring meeting, perhaps, or a dinner.

"Interesting," he said softly, and I knew he'd file that away for just such a boring meeting or dinner.

He ran his fingers back down, this time with a hint of his nails. He thrust up as he did so, our coupling now wet and messy and loud and so fucking hot because of it. He sucked over my mark as his nails traveled my scales, and I lost all semblance of control.

I might've screamed. Or yelled something. The pleasure doubled and throbbed, pulsing within my body, across my back, along my fevered flesh. I couldn't think through it, felt like I was pleasantly drowning within it.

I bobbed and jerked on top of him, no finesse, no sense of rhythm or composure. I couldn't seem to control my body.

"That's right, princess," he growled, jerking his hips under me, thrusting up as I was coming down. "Let go for me." Power laced his words, stripping away any defenses I might've possessed. "Let go."

He kept stroking my scales, sometimes with nails, sometimes with just pressure, fanning his breath on the mark, scraping his teeth over it. It was like toying with a clit, but *so much better.* The pleasure continued to build, compounded, until it was too much. Pleasantly, gloriously *too much.*

He bit down on my mark, and I shattered, screaming out wordlessly, coming apart at the seams. I felt like I was convulsing, shaking against him while clinging tightly. The orgasm lasted and lasted, Nyfain shuddering with me while still stroking my scales softly, lightly kissing his renewed mark.

My head lolled on his shoulder as we came down slowly. His heart beat frantically against my chest.

"Unlike that horse-riding scenario, I think we can repeat that one," he said with laughter in his voice.

"That was a scene in a book?"

"Actually, more of a how-to. It was a chapter on using the scales and mark together during sex. Good?"

"Yes. Very."

He pushed to standing, holding me in his arms the whole time, his cock still buried within me.

"Very good," I murmured, my lids getting heavy.

"I guess I'll need to scour that book for more tips and tricks."

I laughed. "Yes, please."

His legs wobbled as he walked into the other room to his large bed before pulling back the covers. He slipped out, and I knew a moment of disappointment and loss before he slid into the covers and gathered me up beside him. I fit my head into the hollow between his chest and shoulder and felt my eyes droop, relishing in his strong arm around me and his heat and power thrumming within.

We stayed like that for a moment, lying together quietly, his thumb lightly tracing a path over and back across my shoulder.

"I don't want to believe it," he finally whispered. "All this time I've blamed myself for her death. For not being here to save her. For sixteen years I've been living with her ghost. I've been living with soul-crushing guilt. And the whole time she's been alive?"

He stroked down the center of my back.

"My brain just doesn't want to believe it," he murmured. "While at the same time…"

"At the same time, you're desperate to have her back," I finished.

"Yes. Except…I saw the guilt in her eyes." He shook his head. "And then there's the *way* she came back. She hid herself. Hadriel told me she didn't want any Wyverners going to her house in the village. She was keeping her situation a secret until she couldn't anymore. Why? And, most importantly, what am I going to do if she was responsible for that curse? For my father's last descent into madness?"

I grazed my fingertips across his chest. "We'll find out soon enough. Whatever has to be done, I'll stand by you. I'll help."

"If her aim is to position herself on the throne, you won't be able to."

CHAPTER 5
FINLEY

THE NEXT THREE days were a haze as I checked in with the kingdom and helped bring some order after the battle and the demon occupation. The living conditions in some of the villages were still atrocious. The village leaders had worked to help their poorer people through the sickness, like I'd insisted, but hadn't done anything to improve their living conditions.

Nyfain insisted I stay by his side, dressed in my fine clothes and with my hair intricately done. He wanted to make sure the people knew my position, and also for me to see for myself the work that had to be done. We wanted our kingdom to be strong and prosperous, and he agreed with me that there was only one way to accomplish that: to focus on ensuring the wellbeing of its people. *All* its people. The wealth, such that it was, would need to be distributed more evenly.

That sentiment did not go over well with some of the village leaders, of course, who then quickly lost their roles. Nyfain would tolerate no animosity toward me. If people hated my common roots and sneered at my ideas because of it, they were thrown across the room in a fit of rage. It wasn't altogether kingly but...well, learning curve.

Speaking of learning curves, I didn't have one clue how I was supposed to act or what I was supposed to say. I included the wolves on what was typically dragon business, accidentally forgot to dress nicely or at all after flying, and told several pompous village leaders where they could stick their traditional views. Nyfain bore all of it with great patience, quietly letting me know when I'd made a faux pas and helping me determine whether to correct course or create a "new normal."

Nyfain was creating just as many new normals. When visiting a village, he might pick up a broom and help an ailing woman sweep out her front room, something his father's servants wouldn't have dreamt of doing, let alone his father. Or he would lend his strength to someone trying to erect a stall in their little market. He'd been so far removed from these people for so long, doggedly going about his duty, that he enjoyed connecting with them now. It seemed like he wanted to be a bigger part of the people's lives.

Today, though, he was being fitted for some princely clothes or robes or whatever he needed, allowing me a much-needed reprieve. Of course, I didn't intend to spend it resting.

I crossed the brittle grass at the back of the castle with two books under my arm and Hannon at my side. Govam and Denski followed behind us, flanked by Tamara and two of Weston's pack. Between the demons and the few books on demon magic that Hannon had recommended from his few months of studying their kind, I was going to figure out how to cure Nyfain.

He still hadn't shifted. He hadn't brought it up, but I could tell he was afraid to see what his wings looked like. I didn't rush him, but his hesitation certainly made me rush myself. I *would* find a cure for that magic that still tainted him. There had to be one.

He also hadn't spoken to his mother. I got the impression he was putting it off, scared of what he'd hear. I didn't rush him on that, either.

"The prince asked for my assessment of who should be on the advisory circle from each of the villages," Hannon said as we made our way to the working shed near the everlass field. "I think he's giving me too much responsibility, for one, and two, I'm too young for that sort of post. Too inexperienced with how a kingdom—or village—should be run."

"Everyone who is left is inexperienced in those things," Tamara said. "Except for one person…"

We fell silent for a beat, knowing she meant the queen.

"You are calm and steadfast," Govam told Hannon. "You are levelheaded and courageous. You watch more than you speak, and think before you do. Those are good qualities in an advisor. I think your sister will benefit from your advice."

"I'd be offended, Govam, if you weren't right." I chuckled. "I've always needed it, in fact."

"Your upbringing has made you wise beyond your years, Hannon," Tamara said. "Just like it has made

Finley tough. I think you'll both do great. Certainly a lot better than those jokers in the villages. What a bunch of wankers. Most of the 'leaders' aren't fit for that role—they got it by default."

"They are what's left after sixteen years of harsh treatment by demons," I said. "Though you're not wrong."

I stalled when we reached the doorway of the work shed, my stomach dropping and my heart speeding up.

Ami and Claudile—the *queen* and her lady-in-waiting, whose real name I'd already forgotten—stood within it, one crushing some dried everlass and the other eyeing one of the cedar trays I'd brought from home. They looked up when they noticed my shadow darkening the floor, and each immediately stiffened. Irritation flickered across Claudile's face, but the queen's expression showed none of her thoughts.

"Finley," she said, putting down her pestle and mortar and clasping her hands together.

"Ami," I replied, trying to ease my tight muscles as I crossed the threshold.

"It's Queen Arleth," Claudile barked.

"I used the name Ami because no one in the villages could seem to remember the name Arleth," Ami—Arleth—explained in a patient tone. "Because of the curse, I imagine. They have no trouble now."

I wanted to say, "Ah yes, the curse that didn't affect you except to pause your aging," but I held back. I didn't want to spark additional animosity with her and create a larger chasm for Nyfain to cross.

"And you are?" I asked Claudile.

"Delaney," she replied stiffly.

"Fantastic." I couldn't help the dry tone. "What are you doing, Arleth and Delaney?"

"It's *Queen* Arleth, girl," Delaney said.

Arleth held up her hand. "It's fine, Dee. I doubt very much that Finley will respect my position. Isn't that right, Finley? You never called my son Prince Nyfain, correct? Or addressed the demon king as such."

Right. She knew a lot about me. After all, I'd shared my history with her in the village, thinking she was a fellow healer. She'd been studying up on the woman who wore her son's mark. Was she now going to attempt to use that information to bring me down?

She can try, my dragon thought with a growl.

"Correct," I replied, stepping over to the corner of the large worktable. "I'm sure you remember, I was raised common in a ruined kingdom. How to act around royalty wasn't important at the time. I was more interested in keeping my family and neighbors alive."

Not to mention I never imagined I'd meet a royal in my lifetime.

I set my books on the table and realized none of the others, not even Hannon, had followed me in.

I sighed, suddenly supremely annoyed.

"Listen," I said, the need to get to work overriding this sticky situation we were in. "I know you used to work here, and maybe you think it's still yours. I don't really care. I assume you still have some love for your son, and he's the one I mean to help. Why don't we just agree to ignore each other until you and Nyfain sort everything out? You can work over there, and I can work over here, and we don't have to bother each other."

I unstacked the books, laying one next to the other before opening the first one to the section about suppression magic.

After a quiet beat, Arleth said, "How do you mean to help my son?"

I blew a breath out slowly. "I'm not sure yet. That's what I'm doing here."

"Maybe I should've asked—what's wrong with him? His scarring?"

I flicked a glance her way and saw genuine concern. A mother's concern. So I explained what Calia had said as I pulled Govam and Denski inside and sat them on chairs near the corner I would take over.

"Okay," I told Govam when I'd finished, not bothering to weigh Arleth's reaction. "Explain Dolion's magic to me. When it's strongest, how it works, if you know of any healing that seems to work on it…"

"I thought you had a cure for their demon magic?" Delaney asked, crossing her arms.

"Crowded everlass handles the sickness brought on by demon magic, yes, but that's not what's plaguing Nyfain. The magic that's caught inside him is blocking his magic, but it's not a poison. I don't want to give him the crowded plant. It's too dangerous. His life is more important than wings."

"Do you really mean that?" Arleth asked with a blank face and even tone.

"Dragons put a lot of weight on their ability to fight in the air," Delaney explained brusquely. "A king wouldn't be able to lead his army without wings. I've known dragons who would prefer death to a life without wings."

"Dragons need to straighten out their priorities. Now please *shh*." I waved them away. "Let me work."

Thankfully, they returned to what they were doing, making salves and ointments. I listened to Govam's explanations, checked the books, and thought about the various elixirs and concoctions I'd made to counteract demon magic. Minutes tugged hours behind them. The sun started lowering toward the horizon. My guards had likely swapped out with replacements at some point, but no one had come in to alert me.

Through it all, Govam and Denski sat in their chairs, answering my questions when I had them and sitting quietly when I didn't. No one prodded me when I leaned against the table for long periods of time, staring out at the dimming light, thinking. Wondering where to start. Wondering *how*.

Finally, when a course of action started to take shape, I straightened up with a pop in my back and grabbed the cedar tray.

"Here." Turning from the simmering pot she'd been tending, Delaney grabbed one of the pine trays.

"No, thanks. I want really strong everlass for this one. Hannon…" I called.

Vemar poked his head in through the door. "He left a while ago. Said he wasn't needed."

"Can someone see if Nyfain has the time to help me? I need him to sing to the plants. And maybe track my sister down, too. She harmonizes well with him. She's in a room on the second floor of the castle—"

"Yeah, yeah. Fiery little thing, right?" He put out his hand like he was measuring the top of her head. "Takes no shit? I'll go get her. You got this?" He pointed to the demons.

"Yeah, I'm good. Or you can let them go back, if you want. I have all I need for the moment. Now it's time for some trial and error."

"We'll stay, if you don't mind," Govam said.

"It's calming, sitting in here, watching you ladies work," Denski added.

I shrugged, hefting the cedar tray. "Suit yourself. I'm heading out to the field to harvest. Try to run, and I'm sure a bunch of dragons would be happy to hunt you."

"Didn't need to be said," Govam murmured.

"If you want stronger leaves, you'll want the pine trays," Arleth said, setting down the collection of herbs she'd pulled off the drying racks in the corner. They'd been there since I'd last used this place, probably not in the best shape but serviceable enough.

I turned enough to look at her and Delaney, who'd taken her concoction off the fire. It looked like they were readying to leave.

"That's a common misconception," I replied. "I had this talk with Nyfain once. Long story short, cedar works better. Try it and see." I headed out the door as the demons stood.

A few wolves lounged outside in their furry forms, their noses twitching from the scents filtering out. They lifted their heads at my exit and then stood, waiting for the demons to emerge. I ignored them, glancing toward the castle. Vemar was already out of sight, but a collection of dragons soared overhead—two large dragons, one of them Lucille, with five smaller dragons fanned out in obvious disarray behind them, their wings rolling and tilting and occasionally flapping erratically. The new dragons were learning to fly.

My heart beat faster with the sudden urge to shift and join them. I hadn't flown in the last couple of days, and I could feel my dragon's eagerness. Her desire to master her craft so we could fight Dolion from the sky.

Not yet, I thought, my feet crunching in the brittle ground as I made my way to the everlass field. *We'll get to it, I promise. First we need to figure out how to get our mate up there with us.*

Did I say anything?

Clearly she was feeling a little salty.

Arleth and Delaney followed me, neither of them carrying trays.

I stopped in confusion, half turning back.

"Your plants are safe. You don't have to monitor me," I said.

They kept walking, passing me and threading their way into the everlass field. I placed my tray on one of the sawhorses resting just outside of the field. One of them had probably set it up.

"You wish to harvest, yes?" Arleth ran her fingers along the plants and started humming softly. "We'll help sing to them. They like when there are multiple people giving them attention and love. You'll get the strongest working leaves with our help."

I must've had a dumbfounded look on my face because Delaney said, "We don't have to like each other, or even get along, but when you work the everlass, you do it on the plants' terms. You do it with respect."

It was something I might've said. So I walked in with them and started touching the plants as they were doing. I let my mind wander as the air moved across my skin, a slight chill hinting of the night to come. I watched the dragons soar through the sky, awash with pinks and oranges with pockets of deepening purple. And I scanned the various plants as I thought through the problem at hand.

I would heal Nyfain first, easing his pain and loosening him up, and once that happened, I would scrape out the magic trapped within him.

His remedy would have to be administered in stages, I thought. A softer sort of elixir at first, working through all the tired muscle and residual scar tissue. Then I could get a little more aggressive, and more aggressive still, until I yanked that foreign magic out of him by the roots. This was all guesswork, of course. Maybe I could do it with one elixir. That would be ideal.

Regardless, I knew in my bones that I'd need to eradicate the magic within him before we went up against Dolion. I knew, without knowing how, that Dolion would be able to use that magic to hinder Nyfain.

Pleasure curled across my flesh and fluttered in my stomach a moment before shock and longing exploded through the bond. I glanced up, catching Nyfain coming our way with Sable half jogging at his side. Vemar and a few of the Wyvern dragons trailed them, all eyes on us.

I straightened up, pulling my fingers from the plants, wondering if I should have fought Delaney more and made them leave. Maybe I was crossing a line again without realizing it.

But in the next moment, Nyfain was threading his way into the plants with us, his eyes darting between all of us and settling on me.

"Hey, baby," he said softly as he met me, leaning over one of the plants to kiss me. "I heard you needed some help singing to the plants."

The desire to touch him, to stay near him, to drape myself around him, clawed at me.

His smile was sanguine as he reached out and took my hand.

"That's the imprinting," he whispered, his gaze rooted to mine. Clearly my expressions and body language showed what I was feeling. "I've heard that it fades, but for us I suspect it will never totally go away."

"I'm okay with that." I laid my other hand on his chest and then hooked it around his neck, pulling him closer and brushing my lips across his. "And yes, I do. I want…"

I pulled back again and turned away, needing to think.

"I want melancholy." I looked back at him to make sure he understood that I needed his special magic, the Syflora, and that I understood my request was weird. "I want…gloomy. Think of shadows and pain, and of dank, dark places. I want you to…" I thought about dropping his hand but couldn't bear the thought, so I tugged him along instead. I stopped at a weakened plant, not crowded but not vibrant. "I want you to sing to the ailing ones especially. The ones that are struggling."

A crease formed between his brows, but he nodded without questioning me.

I shrugged. "Maybe I'm on the wrong track, but…" I shook my head. It felt right. We'd always used the healthiest, most vibrant leaves, figuring those were the strongest. Of course we'd think that. But the crowded plants were the strongest. Maybe the plants in between packed a bigger punch without verging on poisonous?

As far as singing a melancholy tune… Well, sometimes my feelings and hunches didn't make sense.

His fingers entwined with mine, he started singing, walking through the field and stopping at the struggling plants. Without being told to help, my sister Sable roamed with us, creating a beautiful harmony with Nyfain, taking what was already lovely and enhancing it into a melody so rich and complex it brought tears to my eyes.

By the time we were done, long shadows reached across the grounds. A collection of people had gathered around the edges of the field, sitting or standing, gazing at us with dreamy looks or fondness on their faces.

"You have quite the gift, girl," Delaney told Sable, patting her shoulder as she passed. "Quite the gift."

"And she is your sister?" Arleth asked me, in a different row of plants about five feet away. Her gaze kept flicking to Nyfain, roaming his face, picking out his scars.

He was staring off into the woods, waiting for me, still holding my hand. Pain and unease radiated through the bond, but he held his pose, refusing to break in front of his people.

"Yes. She doesn't seem to be able to help plants grow like Nyfain, but she does have a beautiful voice."

"Yes, well…" Arleth picked her way to the edge of the field before pausing. The Wyverners who were present bowed, one and all. She inclined her head, and they shuffled to the sides, clearing a path for her back to the work shed. It seemed they had forgotten the *former* part of her title.

"What more do you have to do?" Nyfain eyed the empty tray. "Do you need to harvest?"

I shook my head as Sable met Hannon and Dash in the crowd of onlookers. I'd been so caught up in the music that I hadn't even noticed them drifting closer.

"I was going to, but I want to see how the plants respond to your singing. I might pick tomorrow or in a couple days, depending."

He straddled the plants and then scooped me up, squeezing me tightly to his chest before leaving the field.

"I've been thinking about setting the date for our coronation," he said, and a wave of nervous tingles flowed over me. "Before we do that, though, there are a couple of matters we need to address."

My voice quivered. "Such as?"

The crowds only haltingly bowed for him, not entirely used to it after sixteen years of lax protocol. They did, however, quickly get out of his way, scattering to the sides as he carried me forward.

"I can walk, you know," I murmured, draping my arms across his shoulders. I kissed his warm neck, running my lips up to his ear and sucking in an earlobe.

"Why would I let you walk when this is much more

pleasant?" He squeezed around me, obviously craving the closeness like I did. "The first order of business concerns Weston."

Tingles rolled over my skin. "I need to speak with Hadriel before you tell Weston he's no longer needed. I want to see how attached he is to the alpha."

"That is certainly part of the problem, yes—the wolves attaching themselves to him. I've met very powerful alpha wolves in the past, but none of them have called wolves the way Weston does. It's almost like he's a siren. I spoke with a few of our wolf shifters today, and they told me he gives them a sense of pack unity they've never experienced before. Ever. Our kingdom hasn't been nurturing the other shifters."

"And Weston makes them feel like they belong."

"Yes. To do that takes more than just magic and power. It takes a certain type of leader. A natural-born alpha."

"What's the difference between a natural-born alpha and a regular alpha?"

"Common alphas achieve their status through sheer power and prowess. If they're not royalty, they challenge for their placement. They learn to be leaders, and the better ones help their packs or townships thrive. Micah is an example of a common alpha. A natural-born alpha is someone who...just has something extra. They don't demand loyalty—they inspire it. Weston, I'm very sure, is a natural-born alpha, with power and prowess in plenty, but also a knack for cultivating the unity and balance wolves clearly crave."

"I think everyone craves that."

"Maybe so, but dragons aren't connected in the same way. It's odd, though…"

"What's odd?" I asked, stroking my thumb across the dark, red-tinged stubble lining his chin.

"Someone of his caliber would usually be snatched up by a wolf king. I'm surprised Weston had an average sort of pack. Large—much larger than most non-royal packs—but tucked away in a rural area, away from court. A wolf of his stature would usually seek to elevate himself."

"Not everyone's main goal in life is to suck up to royalty."

"It wasn't yours?" he asked darkly, heat soaking into his tone and then through my blood.

"It wasn't the royalty aspect that I wanted to suck up to, it was a certain dragon that I wanted to suck on. And look, dreams do come true."

"Dreams or nightmares—I guess it's all in the eye of the beholder."

"Obviously." I kissed the corner of his lips as he entered the castle. "Which type of alpha are you?"

"The third kind. The one who inherits it and wonders if the role shouldn't have gone to someone more deserving."

"So the defeatist kind."

He laughed, slowing so that he could give me a deep, consuming kiss. "That kind, yes."

"What about the cat shifters, or bears, or…"

He shook his head. "I'm still trying to understand the situation, but it's a weakness, that much I know. We simply *cannot* have a kingdom this diverse entirely ruled by one type of creature."

"Well, yeah. Logic, right? I've brought that up a time or two."

"It is logic to you, looking at it with fresh eyes. But for us…" He walked through the halls slowly, peering through doors and scanning the ceiling and floor. His eyes caught a few times on a smattering of glitter or a streak of dirt. "We've only known one way of doing things. This is a dragon kingdom, so of course it is ruled by dragons. In a wolf kingdom, they are ruled by wolves. Anyone with power, like Weston, usually seeks out a ruler who shares their animal. There, they can elevate themselves within the court. Those not of note, or without power…file in."

"They get shuffled into the cracks and forgotten about, you mean?"

His sigh ruffled my hair. He didn't respond. He didn't need to. We both knew my whole village had essentially been forgotten.

"Except the dragons in the Flamma Kingdom didn't seek out the dragon kingdom," I said.

"Yes. Before the curse, I heard a lot of stories as to why, but I doubt any of them were accurate. My mom, the one person who knew the other dragons, never said a word to me about it. I suspect that meant my father or this kingdom was probably part of the problem."

"And yet no one overthrew him."

"This kingdom was wealthy, and my father had a strong army—outside kingdoms wouldn't wish to upset the status quo, and the people… Well, what could they do? I'd hoped to change things, but…my life took a few strange turns."

"But you ended up in the right place. You have the chance to change things."

He squeezed me as we walked.

"I've been to the dragon villages in Flamma—they are small and quaint and peaceful. They're ruled by a council of elders, I guess, and there's no widespread poverty like in many of the villages here. No obvious class system or stuffy court with lofty ideals." I was still annoyed about Xavier's personality shift, something that had gotten a bit bolder over the last couple of days. It had been mirrored, to some degree, in the other Wyverner dragons.

Dragons had always been placed on a perch in this kingdom, and they knew it.

"But they are essentially ignored by their kingdom," I continued. "And then there are the dragons from other kingdoms. That surprised a few people in the dungeons."

"The dungeons, yes," Nyfain growled, meeting his valet, Urien, just inside the door to his rooms. *Our* rooms, now. "One of the things on my list is to listen to you and the other dragons recount your experiences in the demon kingdom. But not yet. It will overwhelm me with rage, I'm sure, and I can't have that distraction until I can act on it."

"Sire, milady." Urien gave us a stiff bow.

"Finley needs to see the seamster," Nyfain told him. "Find her lady's maid and Hadriel and tell them she is ready. They will escort her. I've told Leala what Finley may need. Cecil should remember the particulars. He was a great favorite of my mother before—"

He clenched his jaw. He had been about to say *before she died.* Except…those words no longer applied. In reality, they never had.

"Sire." Urien bowed again before excusing himself, closing the door behind him.

Nyfain let me slide down his body, his eyes hooded as I did so. He pushed in close, crowding me with his heat and his scent.

"You allowed my mother to work with you today," he murmured, his voice deep and rich and intoxicating.

"She was helping me with the everlass. She and her friend don't seem to like me much—or at least Delaney doesn't—but they respect the plants and work together really well. So I figured…if they could help, I would accept their help. And then you joined us…"

He ran his fingertips down the side of my throat before bending to follow them with his scorching mouth. He stopped to nibble my collarbone but continued to glide his hand down my body, flowing over my budded nipple and then the side of my stomach. He pushed his palm firmly against my lower abdomen, his fingers pointed downward, and kept sliding. His fingers slid over my clit, the sensation dulled by my pants, and continued, curving under and cupping my mound.

I sucked in a breath as I melted against the wall, pounding for him.

"We need to meet with her," he murmured against my skin. "I'm having the formal dining room and cutlery polished up. I need to know if she is a threat. If she had a hand in the curse."

Pain bled through our bond, and he pulled me

against him, breathing me in.

"I don't want to have that meeting," he admitted. "I'm dreading it. At the same time…being in the everlass field with you two, with Sable singing with me… It was like a dream. It reminded me of tending to the fields with my mother and her ladies when I was a boy, only it was better, and we had half of the help. I want that for us. I want it for all of us. I want her back."

I ran my hands up his broad back and looped them around his neck, holding him tightly.

"I know. If you want her back badly enough, maybe…well, if she admits the worst, it might just be a matter of forgiveness."

"There are some things that cannot be forgiven."

CHAPTER 6
NYFAIN

I LOOKED STRAIGHT ahead as I crossed the brittle grass toward the Royal Wood. Urien had told me moments before that there was a disturbance outside of the gold reserve that I had to see to immediately. I'd been loath to part with Finley, a feeling that I doubted would ever go away, but I'd been more nervous about the shift I knew I must make.

I'd been avoiding this. My scales weren't completely healed. I dared not hope my wings had been returned to me, but what of the color of my scales?

"Are you sure that was wise, sire?" Urien asked, speaking about my instructing Finley to take the dragons in hand and scrub away any pompousness the old court might be attempting to resurrect. I'd done it right before heading out.

Urien followed me at a respectable distance. He had always kept with the old customs, even when the world was falling down around us.

Perhaps I should do the same. The returning drag-

ons were certainly trying to scrape together the reality—
and hierarchy—they remembered. They wanted to
pretend the curse hadn't ruined us.

The curse *had* ruined us, though. It had put us
through a grinder, scrambled the result, and then tried to
burn the remains. Going back to what life had been like
before didn't seem possible. Hell, to be honest, it didn't
seem smart.

This kingdom had been struggling before the curse.
No, it had been decaying from within. Touring the
villages this last year had opened my eyes in a way
nothing else could have. Now, learning how dissatisfied
the wolves and other shifters had been with the old
hierarchy?

We had to do better. I was done letting my people
down. In my youth, I'd locked myself in a prison of
indifference, trying to ignore the despicable things my
father did in the name of solidarity. When I couldn't
contain my disgust any longer, I'd left. I'd abandoned my
people to my father's tyranny. I'd saved myself and, in
the process, damned the kingdom.

My mother's sudden reappearance had made me
realize I'd been living with the wrong ghost. I'd been
plagued with guilt about walking out on *one* person, my
mother, instead of everyone else I'd abandoned.

Now I could *see*.

And one of the things I saw was my mate. Finley was
a natural alpha like Weston. At a young age, she'd forced
her village to band together to fight the sickness unleashed by the demon magic. Given their social standing
in the kingdom going into the curse, they should have

fared the worst, and instead they'd been impacted the least.

Then there was the way she'd spread her cure for the demon sickness, insisting that the poor and rich had equal access. And the role she'd played in breaking the curse and freeing us from Dolion.

If she saw fault in the royal court, then I'd damn well let her fix it. I had faith in her.

To Urien, I said, "It's time for the people to learn a queen isn't just a pretty figurehead. A queen is a leader. She's someone to shoulder the weight of the royal duty alongside the king. We'll rule together, or we'll all crumble."

"Yes, sire," he said crisply. He wasn't the sort to argue, so that tone was the only pushback I would get.

I needed to surround myself with people who weren't afraid to tell me their thoughts. People who weren't stuck in the past.

"How is Hadriel doing with his extra responsibilities as butler?" I asked, breaking through the tree line into a clearing big enough for me to shift.

"He shows promise, but his heart isn't in it. He wasn't bred for a life of service, and it shows. Which is just as well, because I've heard his wolf is refusing to give up Weston's pack bond. The man and the wolf are at odds, and the wolf is flexing his strength to hold on to that bond."

I shook my head and stared out at nothing for a moment. Finley would be heartbroken if Hadriel left. To be honest, I'd hate to see him leave as well.

"Find someone in the villages who can stand in for

him," I said, poring over how I could fix this. There was a way—I just had to find it. "When you do, shift him to the role of the princess's personal advisor."

"You would have a stable hand turned butler advise the future queen on her role and duty?"

I took it back—Urien *did* give his thoughts on my decisions, he just did so passively, parroting my orders back to me as questions of confirmation.

I chuckled. "Not advise her so much, no. More…rein her in as much as possible. He has a *way* about him. He'll keep her out of trouble if anyone will. Mostly because he'll be too scared to tag along, and it'll give her pause."

"Yes, sire."

I stripped my clothes and handed them over. Urien stripped as well and tucked our clothes into a small satchel he'd carry around his neck in animal form. As an owl, he would follow me from the air. Usually we'd have someone trail us on horseback with clothes, but it was getting too dark. I didn't want to risk a horse's broken leg.

Moment of truth.

I held my breath and let my dragon surge up, his anxiety matching mine. It was vain, this worry. The color of our scales didn't matter in the grand scheme of things. It wasn't life or death. Even so…I wanted my golden scales, which would so match the gold dusting on Finley's red ones. I wanted to look like I belonged with her. Like she belonged with me.

Our head rose into the foliage above us, our body filling the clearing and shoving branches out of the way. My dragon squeezed his eyes shut.

A QUEEN OF RUIN

I'm afraid to look, he admitted.

Aren't you always telling me that you own the balls and I own the brain? Where's your courage now?

I don't want people talking about that beautiful little dragon next to that great, dulled beast. At least if we were gold...

We're needed. We've taken too long already. Look.

He peeled open one eye, and then the other, before stretching his lips across his teeth in the dragon equivalent of a grimace. He looked down, letting me see our body. My heart sank, and he took a deep breath.

It's not as bad as it was, he thought, eyeing the gold peeking out of the darkened scales. It was like someone had taken a flame to large sections of his body. *At least we'll partially match her gold dust.*

No wings adorned his back, though he could feel their nubs sticking out from the rest of his hide. Whatever plagued his color also plagued his wings. We still weren't a complete dragon. Poor Finley. What a mate she'd been strapped to.

If we can't wow people with our appearance, we'll have to do it with our ferocity, I thought.

I'd hoped for both.

He took off through the trees, the brittle branches harmlessly sliding along our sides. I'd need to spend time in this wood, working on my Syflora magic and trying to sing some life into it. Finley probably knew more about my power than I did, what with all her reading and research. She could help me harness its gifts. When we had time.

The reserve, which was a pompous name for the

mines, resided on the far end of the kingdom, not terribly far from Finley's village. We made it there in no time, slowing as we approached, and a great growl rumbled from deep within my dragon's chest as he smelled the other alpha dragon. Micah, the one who had challenged me for my mate.

My dragon had wanted to kill him, as was his right, but I pulled him back. That man had helped save this kingdom, and he could be a great asset. I'd sacrificed glory for practicality.

I hadn't stopped monitoring his whereabouts, however. He wouldn't get a second chance. Another lapse in judgment with my mate, and I'd finish the job.

. Thankfully, he'd kept out of my way. He hadn't volunteered to watch the demons or patrol the grounds. He'd stepped back, letting everyone know who ranked as alpha in this kingdom.

My dragon pushed through the last of the trees before the clearing, finding the other alpha standing off to the side with some people from his village, all nude. In another cluster, closer to the opening of the mine, stood Xavier, Lucille, and Jade, their bearings uncomfortable, their clothes loose-fitting, like the ones I'd brought.

My dragon shifted as Urien landed on a tree branch near me, his owl head swiveling. When I was in human form, Urien fluttered down beside me before setting down the bag and shifting as well. He handed over my clothes.

"What's all this?" I walked forward, stopping equidistant from the two parties. "I heard there was a disturbance."

"Sire." My people bowed. The foreign dragons turned toward me, not even offering a nod. That sort of thing would've driven my father crazy, but I'd long since stopped caring if people paid homage to my station.

Xavier stepped forward. "It seems the foreign dragons have been monitoring the actions of our...former queen."

I noticed the pause before *former*, as though he didn't accept my decision on that front. I also noticed the tone around *foreign*, signifying the visiting dragons were lesser than the court dragons, regardless of their respective power levels. His impertinence aggravated me, but Finley could sort out the latter and I'd handle the former soon enough.

"And?" I asked, keeping my facial expressions neutral. They couldn't know how much the issue with my mother pained me.

Micah stepped forward. "Alpha," he said, driving home the status quo. I offered a curt nod. "The way Ami—Arleth—handled the situation in Flamma doesn't sit right with me. There were many opportunities for her to meet with your people after they came to our village. They would've recognized her, yet she only met with the princess and her brother. She chose to gain information and insight about this place from the only two people who would not know her on sight."

"And?" I prompted.

"She hid her involvement in the battle for Wyvern," he continued. "Rather than alert anyone to her presence, she instead snuck in through the back door, so to speak. She joined the forces of one of the villages and further concealed herself."

"I am aware," I said. "What does it have to do with these reserves?"

"My room faces the everlass field. I watched her and Finley...and you in the fields. She stayed in that little dwelling beside the field until everyone had left, and then she skulked away with Claudile."

"The queen does not skulk," Lucille snapped. "And her name is Delaney, chief of the...former ladies-in-waiting. Show some respect."

"We met her as Claudile, Angry Lady," Vemar said, spreading his hands.

"Well, now you know better," she replied through her teeth. "You're a visitor here. You should know the names of the royal circle."

"Enough," I barked, power riding my command. "Micah, make your point."

"I left the castle to follow her, and I met Vemar and the others along the way. They shared my concern. The women shooed away the guard who was here and went down into the mines. I confronted them, knowing what is down there, and they tried to fight their way out. We thought it might be best to detain them. If they had no guilt, they wouldn't have panicked and tried to flee. They have offered no explanations for their behavior."

"Sire," Xavier said, his tone angry and his words clipped. "With due respect, the queen and Delaney don't have any tools. They don't even have a rock hammer or shovel. What harm could they possibly do? These foreigners need to mind their own affairs. This is a court issue, not—"

"If you say 'these foreigners' one more time, Xavier," I said, my patience fleeing, my stomach twisting at the implications of the story, "I will rip your tongue out. You shared a dungeon with some of them for years, did you not?"

"Yes, sire," he said hesitantly.

"Then act like it," I roared, accidentally releasing a peal of thunderous power. "They are your brothers and sisters in arms. The court ideal you're trying to prop up like a stick man died long ago, and I never much cared for it, anyway. Without this collection of dragons, you wouldn't have a court to bolster your overinflated ego. Consider that."

Xavier visibly quailed. All the Wyverners did, and all of the visiting dragons, save Micah and Vemar, flinched and backed away.

I should've let Finley handle it, I told my dragon.

Probably. You always sing about decorum and then lose your temper and scare all the village-folk.

Or court, in this case.

"Where is she?" I asked, power still pumping through me, anger and unease coloring my words.

"Th-there, sire. She's in there." Lucille pushed Xavier to the side and turned, putting out her arm to indicate the gaping black hole. The other Wyverners stepped out of the way quickly and silently.

I didn't let my agitation show as I stepped into the mouth of the mine and caught sight of my mother's stoic face and raised chin. It was the same look she'd always given my father after doing something she knew he wouldn't like.

A little behind her stood Dee, a woman who had been like a second mother to me. A woman who had beamed at my accomplishments and nurtured me throughout my youth. Her face was screwed up in a ball of anger, the look she would've given my father right before my mother was violently punished.

The strength nearly went out of me.

"You don't need to fear me as you did him," I told my mother, my heart breaking because they were words I'd never wished to utter. "I won't hurt you."

"On the contrary," my mother said quietly. "I fear you so much more. You have the power to do the most damage."

Fabulous.

"Why are you here?" I asked, refusing to run my hand down my face because it would show my sudden exhaustion.

"I was given matewealth by the late king. A dowry, essentially—"

"A bribe to marry that mad fool, that's what you were given," Dee mumbled.

"We agreed on a large sum of gold. It was supposed to be transferred to me on the day we mated. Instead, he sectioned off part of the reserve for me. He never allowed me the workers to have it dug out, though, nor the tools to do it myself. Before I left, I secured it with a spell purchased from the faeries. I didn't want him to have access to it any more than he wanted me to."

That spell was clearly what had kept Dolion from taking it. He'd thought it was an ancient form of magic. And maybe it was. Faeries could be wily. My mother obviously knew that.

My heart sank a little more, if that were possible.

"You came back for the gold," I said evenly.

Her eyes flicked over my shoulder. She knew we had an audience and didn't want to voice a truth I might not like. She'd done that a lot when speaking to my father in front of their subjects or guards.

In defeat, I turned away. I couldn't take being treated as though I were my father's son, some sort of tyrant to be feared and pacified.

Though maybe I was. Hadn't people always told me I had a terrible temper? My rage made people quail. A moment ago, I had threatened to rip someone's tongue out. Surely that spoke of an unhinged individual, made worse by sixteen years of struggling to survive. Sixteen years spent constantly fighting.

Those sixteen years had made me harder, I knew. Less able to bend. Less reasonable. My mother was obviously responding to what I had become. A nightmare in the flesh.

A beast.

"Take whatever is yours," I said, and I couldn't hide the misery I felt. "I'll supply you with the crew and tools to get it. When you have what you need, you may go."

"I would still like my audience with you," she replied as I stepped out of the mine. "You owe me an audience."

I laughed sardonically and then felt my gut churn.

If she thought I owed her something, she believed I'd wronged her. Although she was the one who urged me to leave the kingdom all those years ago, maybe she'd expected me to take her with me.

Pain vibrated through me. Anguish.

I didn't have the strength for more of this.

"You'll get your audience." It came out a growl. "Tomorrow. Then we can be done with it."

I shredded my clothes as I shifted, letting my dragon take over and run us out of there. I didn't want to look at the others. I feared I'd see pity in their eyes, or loyalty to my mother, even though she'd essentially told me she'd take the last of the kingdom's wealth and leave. We were on our knees, and she was taking her money and walking.

Our mate is there to distract us from the pain, my dragon thought as he ran through the trees. *Let her calm you before you do something foolish, like scare the whole castle with your temper. If you don't impress the people with your leadership, they will gravitate toward your mother. You can't let that happen, not when she has the remainder of the wealth of the kingdom.*

My father had scared people with his punishments, not his temper. He hadn't had the power to really make people quail. He'd relied on his commanders and whips for that. But my dragon had a point. People surely remembered the atrocities my father used to dole out at the smallest slight. They might think my temper would easily devolve into that sort of behavior.

If I raged, they might turn to her, as they used to. It would feel comfortable to them.

Damn her for forcing me into this position, I thought. *Damn her for making it even harder for Finley to gain traction.*

Finley is a hero. She's the warrior queen we need to

defeat Dolion for good. They will remember that if all goes well. We just need to make sure your mother doesn't win them to her side before Finley can claim their hearts.

Go to her, I thought.

But in the next moment, my dragon caught a whiff that pulled out a growl from deep within our throat.

Demons.

CHAPTER 7
NYFAIN

M Y DRAGON CHANGED course in a moment, putting on a burst of speed.

We crashed through the trees, breaking off branches. We caught sight of a wolf, loping off to the side. One of Weston's. The wolf alpha had said he would help keep us secure until I had things in hand, and he was keeping his word. My dragon huffed out a burst of fire. *Come to me.*

The wolf caught on quickly, dashing through the trunks and brush and falling in just behind me. Another wolf cut in from the other side, joining us, and my dragon slackened his pace so we could stay together.

The demon scent was stronger by the old portals, the magic torn down but the ground still heavily trodden and marred from so much use after the portals had stopped moving. A lone demon was running about, obviously not powerful enough to teleport. Where there was one, there were usually more.

My dragon roared as he launched forward, stomping across any vegetation in our way. Careful not to swing his tail and take out a wolf coming up behind, he chomped into the demon and slowed.

Don't kill it, I thought quickly. *You can damage it, but don't kill it. I want to take it back to the castle and see what it knows.*

A growl rumbled through my dragon's chest, but he did as I said, controlling his bite so that he could rip the demon off the ground. The creature was now screaming and twisting, trapped within his teeth. He looked down at the wolves, whose numbers had grown. Through a series of huffs and postures, he relayed that they should keep patrolling. Then we took off running again, taking the demon back to the castle. Hopefully Weston wouldn't think I was stepping on his toes, commanding his wolves. He'd given that trust and privilege to Finley, after all, not to me. But without him here, someone had to take point. Besides, they were showing their prowess in guarding our borders while the dragons squabbled.

Finley and I both would have to take the dragons in hand. The wolves were making a mockery of us.

IT HADN'T TAKEN long to deposit the demon in the dungeon and get Finley's demon, Govam, down there with him. I wanted to see how the one would react to the other.

Govam walked into the dungeon with a cool demeanor, flanked by Tamara and one of Weston's wolves. The demon watched me as he cautiously approached. Ready to react. He clearly knew I was particularly dangerous just now.

"We found this demon lurking on the edge of the

kingdom," I told Govam, my hands at my sides. Still, his gaze lingered for a moment before he turned his attention to the demon in the cell.

"The king uses his kind as spies or scouts," Govam said, returning his focus to me. "There should be others. They usually travel in packs of a half-dozen. They get their tongues cut out young and are taught to speak with their hands in a language only certain factions of demons know. This is to prevent them from being tortured for information, obviously."

"Let me guess: you don't know the language."

"I do, actually. I made sure to learn it. But you don't need to torture him to get information. These demons are usually a precursor to an attack. If you can find them all and kill them, that's your best bet. They'll have to send in more, which will grant you time. Dolion wants to know what he's facing. If any of these creatures get back to him, you'll have anywhere from a few days to a month before Dolion attacks in force. I'd suggest getting a plan together to defend your kingdom, and to defend yourself, personally. He'll be looking to kill you. He does not like fear, and he fears you."

The demon in the cell hissed, spittle flying at Govam. He gestured in front of his chest, which was accented by little movements of his body.

"I have only chosen the wrong side if Dolion wins," Govam told him, looking away. "And given what I have seen so far, I don't believe he will."

"Who else in your crew knows the language?" I asked.

"All except Sonassa, the succubus."

I looked at the wolf. "Make sure Weston knows of this conversation. Have him look for the other demons. I agree that there are likely more." I shifted my gaze to Tamara. "Get the dragons in the air so you can help the search. Round the demons up and bring them here." I swung my attention back to Govam, speaking to the others. "Keep him separate from the rest of his party. Call me when we're ready to pry information out of those we capture. I want to see if our resident demon is telling the truth."

"Yes, sire," Tamara said, grabbing Govam's arm.

"Find me when you have something."

"Yes, sire," they both said, escorting Govam out of the dungeon.

The captured demon hissed again, but I ignored it as I made my way out.

I would be the one to torture whatever demons were captured. It was a job I'd detest doing, but I didn't want to force it on someone else, not so soon into my tenure. I wanted the people I governed to know that I wouldn't ask them to do something I wouldn't do myself.

It would also give me the opportunity to fact-check Govam and his resident demons. Finley had a hard-earned trust with them, I knew, but I wanted to test them for myself.

I let myself into our collection of rooms, utterly drained from dealing with my mother. It felt like my heart had been torn out of my chest and all that remained was a ragged hole.

Finley glanced up from a circular table in the corner where she was organizing a stack of books.

"Hey, baby," she said, wearing the shapeless slip I'd helped her into earlier. "I stopped by the library for us. I was thinking an action-adventure for you and a mystery with romance in it for me, and then we can switch and talk about them. If you hate that idea, though, I got a couple other options—"

She paused when she looked at my face and then down my nude body. I wasn't adhering to the rule of always wearing clothes within the castle. I didn't give a fuck.

She put the books down without another word and turned to me.

"It'll be okay," she said softly, and I knew she was reading me perfectly. She knew what I was going through and why. "There will be an explanation, I know there will."

She reached for me as I came close, cradling my cheeks in her hands, her eyes supportive but fierce. Soft but full of fire.

I didn't tell her about the gold. I didn't tell her about the demons. I didn't want to talk at all. I just wanted to feel her body envelop mine. I wanted to lose myself in her.

I ran my hands up her sides, lifting the fabric as I did so.

"I spoke to Hadriel," she said, and now I felt her pain. She was worried she'd lose him.

I was determined not to let that happen.

So I shook my head and captured her lips. We'd worry about this shitstorm of a kingdom later. This was a time to express love.

I opened her lips with mine, swiping my tongue through, and then lifted the slip over her head. I tossed it to the ground and walked her backward. She looped her arms around my neck as I ran my hands down her supple skin. Her nipples budded under my fingers, and she sucked in a breath as I gently rolled the pads of my thumbs over each of them.

Once in the bedchamber, I walked her up the couple of steps leading to the bed until the back of her legs bumped the mattress. I bent to run my tongue over the peak of her breast before sucking it in. My hands drifted lower, moving across her fevered flesh and settling between her strong thighs. I ran my fingers over her wet pussy before dipping them inside her, teasing out a little feminine mew. I curled my fingers, rubbing as I circled her clit with my thumb. For a moment I pulled my fingers out again, running them up and along her clit before pushing them back inside her, getting everything slippery.

"You are a blessing in my life, Finley," I mumbled, my heart full to bursting in a way that eclipsed my pain and anxiety.

I cupped her cheek and took the weight of her head as I ran my lips down her neck and over my mark. I kissed and flicked my tongue across it, feeling the ache to mark her again. Again and again, I doubted I'd ever get enough of doing it.

I sucked in her flesh as my fingers worked, rougher now, feeling the fire of her in my blood. And then, when I couldn't help myself anymore, I bit down into her flesh and cut the skin. She sucked in a breath and then moaned, jerking her hips in time with my fingers.

Her dragon fed us power in a gush, wanting it harder. Wanting me to dominate. She seemed to love the force it took me to make them submit. To crave the evidence of my strength and power.

I fisted her hair and yanked, pulling her head back and kissing up her exposed jugular while I finger-fucked her harder, keeping pressure on her clit. The sounds of her moans and wetness filled the room. I sucked in a nipple, hard, and she jolted. Her groan was long and rich, and her cunt clenched around my fingers in her first release. It was so easy with her. So gratifying.

After straightening up, I slowed my fingers, still within her, now dwarfing her with my height and size. Angling her head with my hold on her hair, I forced her to look up at me.

"I didn't say you could come," I told her with extra gravel in my voice.

Her eyes flashed fire and a challenge. Anticipation curled through the bond.

"I do what I want," she replied, and a shock of pain lanced through my middle. I gasped and stepped back, loosening my hand in her hair so I didn't jerk her neck and hurt her.

A sly smile curled her lips, and she scampered across the bed, putting distance between us.

"Do you think you can run, little dragon?" I asked, prowling around the other side of the bed.

Her eyes widened as she took in my popping muscles and slow advance. Her power thrummed, but my dragon was already ripping power from our bond and hoarding it, ready to unleash.

She shook her head a little, clearly realizing we had the upper hand. Realizing I would not stop until she was forced to submit.

"Don't I get a countdown?" she said with nervous excitement.

My laugh was low and rough. "No."

I reached the corner of the bed and darted forward a moment before she sprang onto the mattress and attempted to scamper over it and to the door. Her magic shot out, trying to spear me and block my advance.

My dragon released his great well of power and cut through it, leaving her at the mercy of my physical strength and speed. I was on her in a moment. I curled my left hand around her ankle and managed to grab her wrist with my right. I hauled her back as she struggled, kicking out at me, her desire raging through the bond. I trapped her against my body, pinning her arms to her sides with one arm and cinching the other around her stomach. I bit her shoulder as she thrashed within my hold, and then dragged my teeth across to her neck. Magic and power thrummed through me as though we were preparing to place our mark on her for the first time.

She panted as my teeth hovered over her left shoulder, on the opposite side of my mark. Still my power pulsed, pounding higher, gathering.

I thought marking didn't work in more than one place, I told my dragon, pushing against her, my cock trapped between our bodies. *I've never seen it done.*

I need to, my dragon thought, desperate, wanting to

be in the air with her dragon and leave the human skin behind. He was driving me hard, not settling for less than what his baser needs urged of us.

Still she struggled against me, but there was no true fight in it. She gripped my thighs, and her head was thrown to the side, offering her flesh to me. She wanted what my dragon was desperately trying to give her.

I squeezed her a little tighter with a small shake.

"Submit," I ground out.

Her words were barely audible through her pants. "Make me."

I bent her over the bed, fisting her hair roughly again, and pressed my palm against her back to keep her there. Her body practically melted onto the soft surface, head angled back, fists grabbing the bedclothes. I grabbed the base of my cock and directed the head over her puckered asshole and then down, gliding through her glistening wetness. My knees almost gave out when I felt that wet heat, the desperation to be inside of her blotting out everything else. I resisted, though, teasing her pussy before running my cock up over her asshole again, taking the wetness with it. I'd meant it as a tease, but I didn't get a chance to glide it back down through her folds. She pushed into me hard, her cheeks enveloping my cock.

My breath hitched and my hands fell away from her immediately, braced beside her on the bed as I watched my cock slip into her ass like an out-of-body experience. My knees wobbled, my desire pumping up exponentially.

"Fuck," I managed, unable to help a small thrust.

She groaned, pulling a little forward and then pushing back, working me in. I watched as my shaft sank in deeper, nearly there. It was so fucking hot I couldn't handle it, mostly because it was so unexpected.

You've lost control of her, my dragon thought. *Her dragon wanted—*

Shut up. Both of you. I'm busy.

Finley was proving there was more than one way to dominate a dragon, and I'd absolutely go quietly if this was how she chose to handle me.

Her back arched and she stalled, letting out a breath. She pulled back and pushed, not seating herself entirely.

"I need..." Her breath hitched, and I reached around her and sank two fingers into her pussy, curling them and rubbing before pulling them back out. Her groan was soft, and then she yelped as I slapped my other hand against her firm, round ass.

I pulled out a little and thrust, my pelvis meeting her flesh, working her clit while feeding her pleasure through the bond to minimize her pain.

"Oh!" she said, the sound melting into a long moan as I stroked her scales and then hooked my hands over her shoulders and pumped into her. My balls slapped against her clit, my cock gripped nice and tight.

"Fuck me, Nyfain," she said breathily, pushing back into me.

I raked my hands back down her scales again before pulling her up off the bed, her back to my front, thrusting up into her. I kissed her neck and felt down to her breasts, rolling her nipples between my fingers.

"Who do you belong to?" I asked in a rough growl, my dragon feeding me power, wanting to take over again.

"You," she said on a sigh. "My golden prince."

"I'll make you worship this cock." I slipped a finger into her pussy, groaning at how wet she was. I used my other hand to assault her clit, getting her on all levels. "I'll ruin you for anyone else."

"You already have."

Her admission, followed by her mew of pleasure, sent white-hot desire ripping through me.

"Then use me. Take your pleasure from me."

I dropped my lips to her neck, kissing and licking. I stroked within her, and she rocked more solidly on my cock, doing as I asked, taking what she wanted. She reached back and grabbed my ass cheeks, her fingers digging in, yanking me to her faster. Making me fuck her harder.

Our little dragon has detoured. Let her play, my dragon growled. *Do not come until you mark, and do not mark while between her cheeks. I doubt that's a story she'll want to repeat.*

He was asking the impossible.

Still I gritted down, stroking her, kissing, letting her ass-fuck my cock.

That thought made my balls tighten with the need to explode, to let loose into that tight hole. I worked my fingers faster, rubbed against her clit, and then just needed her to come already because I was desperate.

I pushed her head forward a little and sucked across one of her scales.

"Holy—!" Her cunt pulsed against my fingers as she climaxed, shuddering against me, wordlessly yelling her glory. "Fuck," she finished, sagging.

You're weak, my dragon thought. *You're less than a man should be. You should be able to hold out without resorting to a quick trick to make her come.*

Seriously, shut the fuck up.

I cleaned things up quickly and then flipped her onto her back. I settled between her spread thighs, loving her soft pink flush and heavily lidded eyes. She looked up at me dreamily and offered me a soft, satisfied smile.

"You aren't done yet, princess." My chest glowed with warmth, but my voice was harsh. I kissed her, hard and demanding.

"Yes, sire," she cooed, and a shock of need pierced me.

I growled as I drove into her, seating myself fully. Her surprised "oh!" turned into a decadent groan of pleasure.

"Claim me, Nyfain," she murmured, her fingernails digging into my back. "Claim me again. Mark me as yours."

Her legs encircled my hips. I started a hard rhythm, pounding into her on each thrust. Her jaw went slack and her eyes fluttered closed as she grunted with each firm slide of my cock.

"Look at me," I commanded, power pumping between us once again. Her dragon wasn't keeping any of it, though. Instead, she was offering it up to us, gleefully submitting.

Finley's eyes peeled open slowly, finding mine. I strove harder, falling into her beautiful gaze, open all the way down to her soul. Within us, I could feel the bond

K.F. BREENE

pulsing and throbbing until I was sucked into that place where only she and I existed. Where the world fell away.

"Nyfain," she said, raking her hands across my scales and scars. "Nyfain," she said again, and I couldn't tell if she was begging or praising me.

I worked within her, keeping my body flush with hers, feeling her hard nipples on my chest and her skin against mine. I kissed her sweet lips and thrust my tongue into her mouth to match my movements, faster now, wilder. She gyrated up to catch the swing of my hips, crashing into me. I ground against her, my control gone, leaving behind a desperation to claim her for good.

My dragon throbbed power, and then I bit her neck on the opposite side of her first mark, sinking my teeth into her flesh again and releasing the magical serum that would brand her. She cried out, shaking around me, her pussy walls gripping my cock. Pleasure overwhelmed me, and then I groaned against her, erupting inside of her. Two more pumps, and I was spent, melting down around her.

We lay still for a moment, locked in each other's arms, panting.

"I've never seen someone with two marks," I told her softly, pulling out and then moving her into the sheets. I probably wouldn't be able to stay long, but I wanted a few minutes with her in my arms before I had to deal with the demons.

She curled up against my side, resting her head on my chest. "Now you have."

I breathed in her scent, resting my cheek on her head. "Getting back to the earlier conversation, I would love to swap books and discuss. I've read that action-adventure one you picked out, though. Twice. We'll need to pick another."

"Hmm," she said, stroking my chest. "What was the blast of alarm you felt earlier, after your mom?"

I debated not telling her, but she was not the type of woman who would allow me to save her from the less savory parts of ruling a kingdom. Hell, she'd probably offer to torture them herself to save me the unpleasantness.

"Demon scouts. Govam says they travel in packs. We've only found one so far, but they're looking for more."

She jerked up to sitting. "Are you serious? We should be out there searching with them."

I grabbed her shoulders and pulled her back down, forcing her to nestle against me again. "Part of being a prince and future king is delegating. I can't handle everything myself. I need to be able to trust my people to handle some of these tasks."

"Right, well, delegate to me, then. I want to help secure the kingdom."

"You *are* helping secure the kingdom. You are working on making an heir."

She moved her fingers over my chest and then flattened them against my heart. "I'm going to assume you're too smart to reduce me to nothing more than your broodmare. I can do both, one after the other, or even at the same time. Or don't you know how 'sperm meets egg' works?"

I smiled and stroked her hair off her shoulder.

"Honestly, I needed you here. With me. I'll be interrogating the demons and assessing the trustworthiness of your demon friends."

"They aren't my friends, and that's probably wise."

A soft rap at the door announced Urien. I sighed, dreading getting up and going back to my life.

"I can do it," Finley said, making me smile again. I'd known she'd offer. "I can make the demons talk. Actually, anyone from the dungeons will be glad to. You can delegate this. I can feel your hesitancy to do it."

The rap sounded again. I called out for Urien to enter. He wasn't accustomed to knocking, but we'd needed to make adjustments for Finley's comfort. She still wasn't too keen on having people walk in on our lovemaking, and there really was no telling when and where we'd go for it.

"No, I need to do it." I explained why as Urien popped his head in.

"Good evening, your highnesses." Urien offered a slight bow. "Sire, they have tracked down four more demons and put them into the dungeons. They are looking for more, but don't think it is likely they'll find them. They've mostly combed the kingdom."

I kissed Finley's head and rolled out of bed. "Thank you, Urien, I'll be right there."

Finley moved to get up, and I put out my hand to stop her. "Rest. Read. Relax. I'll be back as soon as I can, and then you can try to mark me again."

She paused, her eyes darting to the open door, and then threw back the covers.

"While you're doing that, I'll work the everlass," she

said. "I want to harvest some at night for the elixir I'm making. How were your scales? Back to normal or still affected?"

"It doesn't matter."

She paused, giving me a stern look. "It does matter. I want to know the extent of what I'm trying to fix."

I almost told her not to bother, that I doubted this was something that could be fixed. Hope could be a dangerous thing. I didn't want to dream of wings and scales if it would never come to pass. I didn't want to insult her, though. She would try regardless, and if anyone could figure it out, it was her.

I described my color and the state of my wings while she listened avidly. Then she nodded, finished dressing, and went out the door. When there was a job to do, the woman didn't know the meaning of *rest* or *relax*.

"Did you still want to meet…your mother over dinner, your highness?" Urien asked as I stepped into some leather pants.

"Yes. Tomorrow. Have Cook make her favorite. She might as well go out with a bang."

"Of course, sire. And shall we have our crew excavate the gold?"

"I'll see if she wants to be there for it or not. When I know, I'll send word to organize it. We'll only use those who are not also competent fighters. It seems we'll have another battle soon. We need to prepare for it."

CHAPTER 8

FINLEY

THE NEXT DAY, I returned to the everlass field while Nyfain slept. He'd spent most of the night "interviewing" the trespassing demons and comparing notes with the friendly demons, who had translated out of earshot from each other so that their stories could be checked. When he'd finally trudged through the door, he had dark circles under his eyes and mussed hair. He'd washed off all remnants of his activities, but I could see the disgust in his eyes. He hadn't liked the job.

I didn't ask him about it. For all my bravado, I wouldn't have liked it either. Killing demons as a means of survival or in the heat of the moment was one thing— it was a rough world and we all knew the stakes—but slowly and methodically inflicting pain to get information? It wasn't ideal, and if the whole kingdom wasn't on the line, I doubted he would've attempted it. But as Tamara was quick to tell me when she met me in the everlass field (she was *not* pleased I'd gone off by myself the night before when there were demons on the loose), the kingdom *was* on the line. Those scouts meant Dolion was readying for an attack.

I couldn't wait to meet him on the battlefield.

"That seamster is certainly...something," Hannon said, leaning over a sawhorse and cutting into a piece of wood. In addition to his advisory duties, he'd been helping people rebuild their homes. He often made his workstation here, where I came and went, so we'd have a chance to chat despite my busy schedule.

I straightened up from my workstation next to the shed and drew my forearm over my slick forehead. The afternoon sun beat down on us at our respective stations. He had a woodworking station set up, and I was drying and cold-seeping everlass leaves in the bright sunlight. The first step to a cure you'd never made before was trial and error. I used to have to do that one idea at a time, but now, with all the castle resources, I was humming along. It would cut my time in half. More, hopefully.

Assuming I could actually find a cure.

"He's colorful, yeah," I said absently, remembering my trip to the seamster yesterday when he'd measured me with a lot of tsking and head shaking, grumbling about all the weight I'd lost. Which set off Hadriel's defensive streak; he made the very logical comment that, when starved, a person tended to lose weight. The conversation devolved into bickering.

I looked down at the large pot filled with shimmering water. Everlass leaves floated within the brew, swaying gently.

"You'll do it," Hannon said softly. "You'll cure him if anyone can." He put down his tools and sighed, looking off into the field, then turned and leaned on the saw-horse. "Would it really be so bad if you couldn't, though? I didn't think it bothered you. His condition, I mean."

"It bothers *him*." I took a few steps to join him, looking out at nothing, and then put my hands on my hips. "After the curse was lifted, he wouldn't shift in front of me. He was scared of what he'd see. When he did eventually shift, he didn't want to admit to me that his scales hadn't returned to normal. I already knew his wings hadn't been restored. It bothers him, and *that* bothers me."

He nodded. "He's been through so much. It would be nice to see him live in peace."

"I don't think he'd know what to do with peace. Would any of us?"

"Self-peace," he said softly. "He tries to hide his turmoil, but…he's not just scarred on the outside."

I looked at him for a long moment. My brother had always been perceptive, and he knew a lot about Nyfain's struggles through me, but his tone was filled with a deeper kind of knowledge.

"And the dinner with his mom is tonight?" he asked, not meeting my gaze.

I narrowed my eyes at him. "What are you hiding, Hannon Mosgrove?"

"Nothing. I'm just worried about you guys, is all. Despite your hero's journey, most of the kingdom is rooting for the former queen. When I'm in the villages, helping, I hear what they say. They loved her before the curse. And while they respect and put their faith in Nyfain, he doesn't shine as brightly as he once did. Now he's...broken. Like their kingdom. Like *them*. The queen symbolizes a time of glory in their minds."

Fire burned through my blood.

"It wasn't a time of glory. The kingdom still had money, sure, but it was faltering. Nyfain himself told me so—" Cutting myself off, I narrowed my eyes at Hannon. "You're trying to get a rise out of me."

"Yes, while also informing you about the current state of affairs. The villagers must not remember it faltering. Or, if they do, it can't possibly seem as bad as the last miserable sixteen years. Besides, you do your best work when you're riled up. I figured I'd...give you a nudge."

"One day, Hannon, that nudge is going to have me pushing back."

A smile stretched across his face. "I doubt it. You think I am breakable. You wouldn't harm me any more than you'd let someone else harm me."

"I wouldn't be so sure," I grumbled, stalking into the shed.

It was infuriating that he was right. And while I'd seen firsthand that he was anything but breakable, he'd always be the soft touch between the two of us. The sensitive one. The caretaker. I couldn't beat on a guy like that.

And he knew it, that dickface.

"I can hear you," he called with laughter in his voice.

Apparently I was mumbling to myself, something I tended to do when working the plants.

"Good," I called back.

I looked around the messy shed before deciding it

was time to restore some order to it in case Arleth and her grumpy sidekick wanted to come work together before the big dinner. They might need to get their heads straight, and this was a good place to do it. That could only help Nyfain. Hopefully.

"Well, hello," I heard a while later.

I glanced up to find Gunduin filling the doorway, an easy smile on his face. He lounged against the door with his arms crossed. I'd met him in the dragon villages when I knew Arleth as Ami. He was her cousin and a delight to have around.

"How goes it?" he asked. "I haven't seen much of you since we got here."

I wiped the hair out of my face. "Yes, I've been helping Nyfain with the kingdom."

"I know. I've been part of your brother's crew, helping with the woodwork. But you've probably heard that."

I had heard, yes. Gunduin had been rolling up his sleeves and getting his hands dirty. He wasn't the only one. Many of the visiting dragons from the villages had also been helping, along with Weston's wolves and a few of the faeries. That kind of cooperation was what we needed.

"Not just woodworking, I hear." I moved a trial elixir off the fire. "You've been helping flight-train the dragons."

"Yes, though I don't know how much my presence is appreciated. I get the feeling the local dragons would rather train their own."

"The local dragons don't seem to realize that we need all the help we can get. They need a little…guidance."

He laughed, coming into the shed and looking around the tables. "I think your guidance will be very…compelling. And probably violent."

"I hear that's the best way to reach dragons."

"As if you know another way." His expression shifted, turning more severe. "I know you have a duty to your mate. If you can cure what ails him, it'll be to the betterment of the kingdom, not least of all because it'll help him as a dragon. But you also have a duty to your dragon, Finley. She needs to learn to fly properly. To land. The fast shifting you've mastered is impressive, but it won't save you from breaking your neck in a bad landing. You can't expend all your efforts on everyone else and neglect yourself and your animal."

I have always liked him, my dragon thought.

I rolled my eyes, and he clearly thought I was reacting to him.

He leaned over the table a little, power curling around him. His demeanor darkened, and an uncharacteristic viciousness rang through his tone.

"In doing your duty to yourself and your dragon, you will also spark wonder and pride in your people's hearts. There is no dragon prince with his glimmering golden scales to fly through the sky right now. So it has to be you. Your dragon is a vision, larger than most and so exquisitely colored. You yourself are entrancing. I know you don't care, but people are drawn to beauty. I've heard that the prince used to be a great looker. He stopped people in the lanes as he rode by on his dashing horse or flew overhead. Now he is terrifying—a mess of scars, his scales tarnished. He is nightmarish."

I curled my fist. "Be careful what you say about my mate."

"Your true mate." He pointed at my fresh mark, one on each side of my neck now. "Only a true mate can apply more than one mark. That shows you belong together, but you still have to hold up his mantle. Do you understand? Part of your job in curing this kingdom is upholding the ideal of the throne. You need to capture the hearts and minds of those you would lead. If you don't, your kingdom will be divided."

He stared at me for a solid beat, willing me to understand.

Your kingdom will be divided.

What Hannon had said echoed through my mind: most of the kingdom was rooting for the queen. Nyfain and I might've helped get them out of the blackness, but the queen symbolized better days.

Damn her.

"Why would you tell me this?" I asked him, not hiding my confusion. "You're her cousin. Her family."

His demeanor softened again, but I didn't miss the edge in his voice.

"I'll let you in on a little secret, Finley. It doesn't sit well to be a dragon in a wolf's kingdom, ignored. No, not ignored...pushed aside. The elders might like to think the wolf king and queen will push back on the demon king for us, but they won't get involved. We have no voice in the Flamma Kingdom."

"Then why stay there?"

"Where else would we go? It's said the rulership here

has been less than savory for generations—Arleth herself implored us not to come to Wyvern after she took the throne. And then the curse wiped it from our minds until recently. When she was young, Arleth had grand ideals about crowns and thrones and change, and instead... Well, I'll let her tell her story. Suffice it to say she didn't make those changes. *Any* changes. I love my cousin, but I am a practical man. I want to live in a place that respects *all* of its people. Here there is a real chance at a fresh start with two leaders who have sacrificed everything for their kingdom and want to see their people thrive. I see such potential in the golden prince...and in you, Finley." He paused for a long moment. "Except you are in grave trouble. The laws, as they stand, forbid a queen from ruling. But in a broken kingdom, laws can be remade. If there's a royal rift, it'll leave the kingdom wide open for the demon king to come back and deliver the deathblow. I would rather not see that happen. You must bridge that gap."

Why the fuck are we always stuck between a rock and another rock right before a fucking rockslide barrels down the hill toward us? my dragon thought. *This has gotten ridiculous.*

I couldn't agree more, but Gunduin spoke a lot of truth. We couldn't afford to have the kingdom split, so apparently I had to go to war with a queen. Super.

CHAPTER 9
HADRIEL

S HOWTIME.

I gave Leala a nervous nod, and she opened the tower door. Finley had been bathed and dressed and her hair done perfectly, ready for dinner with the queen. We'd attended to her in the tower so that she could have a grand entrance and descend the stairs to the waiting prince.

Everything rode on her performance right now. People would be able to directly compare her with past royalty, and she not only had to prove she had the merit, but could also outshine the former, beloved queen. No pressure.

She stood at the window, looking out. I could tell she was nervous as fuck, thanks to that assclown Gunduin. It was a nervousness she didn't know how to hide. She wasn't trained to hide her feelings behind passive-aggressive words. She didn't even know the proper etiquette for a formal dinner. When something bothered her, she handled it like a dragon did—with rage and fire.

Yes, Finley was definitely out of her league, and she knew it. Poor thing. Part of me wanted to steal her away and run. Run from the queen, this broken kingdom, the alpha wolf, the fucking demon king and all his minions—just run.

She never would, though. And I'd stay and fight right beside her, for whatever that was worth.

You hear that, you dick-faced shitbasket? I told my wolf. *I will not go with that alpha.*

Your language is as colorful as your outfit.

Cecil did this, you know he did, I replied. *I asked for* professional *and* chic, *something that befit a queen's advisor, and he gave me this flowery fucking dongshow.*

Literally. The fabric was covered in dongs barely hidden within the floral pattern.

Fucking Cecil.

A wave of power washed over us, and then Finley rolled her shoulders as if preparing for battle. "Okay," she said, turning from the window.

My heart caught in my throat, and my eyes suddenly misted. Leala gasped and dusted her chest with her fingertips.

I was standing before the goddess reborn, I knew it.

Finley's eyes shone with a strange golden tint, like they were literally flickering with fire. Her head was held high, face composed but determined. Her body, tall and lean muscled, stood in a way that bespoke blood-soaked battlefields on a cold winter's morning.

That wasn't what stole my breath, though, or made Leala gasp.

The air shimmered around Finley as she let her power uncoil within her. Tiny flames licked up her arms and curled from her back. Actual fucking flames!

"Apparently this is my lot in life," she said in a strong, clear voice, stalking forward like a predator. "This kingdom is now my duty, and I will own it. Hopefully Nyfain doesn't cast me out."

"He would *never*," I said, aghast. "Leala, love, go make sure everyone is ready."

"Is that a…" Finley looked closer at my jacket with the burgundy velvet lapels. It was the only part of the look Cecil had gotten right. "Is that a golden penis?" She pointed at my right breast area.

I huffed and covered it with my palm. "Don't ask. Seriously."

"Okay, okay!" Leala reappeared in the doorway and gestured us on wildly. "The prince is there." She put both her hands out. "But don't hurry. Princesses don't hurry. Saunter. This is a big entrance. Use it."

"Yes, love, that is good advice." I motioned Finley in front of me. "Go now. Big moment. Keep up the fire, that's a helluva trick."

"I don't know how I'm doing it. I just have so much power raging through me right now, what with Nyfain's nervousness and my own and our dragons trying to compensate…"

"I've heard some of the most powerful dragons can do that," Leala said as she got out of the way. "And you guys are definitely in that league, especially together. Just go with it. It looks great!" She gave a thumbs-up.

"Why isn't it burning my dress?" Finley murmured as she took the stairs.

"I have no fucking idea, love. Let's just count our blessings." I followed behind her, Leala waiting a beat before joining us, not part of the procession (unlike me, as Finley's royal advisor), but definitely eager to watch.

Butterflies swarmed my belly as we reached the third-floor landing. The first of the staff was there, pretending to clean or examine light fixtures or count their fingers. They looked up as Finley approached, and their eyes widened…and then lit up…and then burned brightly.

"Milady." The first staff member bowed, though I was looking straight ahead with my chin up in measured importance and didn't see who it was. "Milady," another said, bending lower.

"Yes!" I recognized Cook's voice on that one. I was sure he was shaking his fist in appreciation, as well. Why he was way up here and not in the kitchens preparing for dinner was anyone's guess. Mediocre bastard.

At the next set of stairs, Finley paused for a moment, and I inched a little closer in case she was losing her nerve. But then she started moving in a measured pace again, not using the handrail for guidance like all the ladies before her had done. I wasn't sure it was wise, but I didn't want to undermine her by telling her so. I had to trust she wouldn't take a tumble, and if she did, that she'd end it in a fabulous swan dive or something.

More bows and "miladys" came as the staff pushed to the sides of the stairs to let her down the middle, another first. When we reached the second-floor landing, she paused again, a little intake of breath giving her away.

I chanced a look.

She wasn't noticing the staff gathered all around, some on the landing and some down below, gazing at her with stars in their eyes. She didn't so much as glance at the collection of visiting dragons on the first floor, Micah a step in front and Vemar a little to the side, grins sliding up their faces. Nor did she notice Weston and a few of the wolves who'd gathered around him. The alpha had a stoic expression, but through our pack bond, I could feel the call of the hunt thrumming through him— and us. The need to rise up and defend. To protect. To battle and to win. The wolves around him grinned in excitement.

The faeries, one and all, stood on the second-floor landing, watching her closely. Her sister, at her side, pushed forward a little with a small smile.

But Finley noticed none of them. Her focus was entirely on Nyfain. He waited at the bottom of the stairs, right in the middle, staring up at her with such supreme devotion in his expression that another tear leaked from my eye.

He was as much of a sight as Finley. He wore a perfectly fitted black suit with a slight shine, like satin, molding to his powerfully built body. He wore a black waistcoat embroidered with gold under the jacket, along with a bow tie with the same design. His dark brown hair was stylishly tousled, absent of the crown long ago stolen by the demon king, giving a slight wildness to his overall appearance. His golden eyes sparkled with menace and power, and fire licked at his shoulders and up his arms despite the suit. His striking face, cut through with scars, tipped his image from alpha dragon into a *nightmare*, ruthless and vicious. If Finley was concerned she'd appear too hard for polite company, she needn't have worried. Compared to him, she was every bit as soft and demure as her old village had tried to make her.

Together they looked like they would burn the world down and laugh in the ashes.

The prince didn't start up toward her or put out a hand to hurry her along like his father would've. He just waited patiently for his mate, allowing her to keep the spotlight.

I hurried a little bit because I was still mediocre and didn't really care that I was supposed to stay behind her. I forced my way to the side of the stairs and then hurried down so I could watch her final descent.

I was glad I did. Finley's expression melted into the same expression as Nyfain's, rife with longing and devotion. All of the tension drained out of her bearing as she continued down the stairs, her eyes on only him.

Soft murmurs filled the crowd, but nothing pulled the couple's focus away from each other. When Finley was close, the prince climbed up a step, meeting her at last.

The prince leaned toward her, his lips nearing hers. Her mouth fell open slightly, ready for a kiss; their eyes were hooded as they breathed the same air, not even an inch apart.

He hesitated, though, his hands coming up. The fingers of his right hand brushed against the side of her jaw and the fingers of the other skimmed down the side of her neck. Her eyes fluttered closed as he bent forward, angling to place a kiss on the edge of her lips and then her jaw before skimming his lips down the side of her neck, following his fingertips. When he got to her mark, he gave it a lingering kiss, and she shivered beneath his touch.

He was greeting her not as a royal or a member of the court, but as a mate greeted his other half after an absence. Their absence had been less than a day, but clearly they'd both felt it. Obviously this was what it meant to be true mates and desperately in love.

They were going to be the best royal couple in history, I just knew it.

Taking his time, not worried about the attention directed toward them, Nyfain skimmed his lips up before placing another kiss to the other side of her mouth, and then followed the same trail on this side until his second lingering kiss was on the other mark.

Her hands drifted up his chest and around his shoulders as his lips returned to hers. His eyes feasted on her face, their bodies humming with power and fire. Finally, slowly, methodically, he pressed a soft, sweet kiss to her lips.

When he pulled back this time, he said softly, "You look stunning, sweetheart. You're an absolute vision."

She smiled at him, love-struck, her eyes a little misty.

His gaze flicked back and forth between her eyes, a little crease forming between his brows.

"Your eyes...have changed color. There's some gold in them now."

"There is?" she asked, reaching up to wipe away the color that had transferred to his lips.

His smile stretched as he wrapped an arm around her waist. "Yes. Come on. Let's let the servants get to gossiping."

Her little giggle was sweet and very unlike her. It was amazing what love could do to a person. She waited until he turned, hooking his arm onto her hip, before stepping down next to him. They took the last step onto the ground floor together, and she threaded her fingers between his where they rested on her hip.

It was only then Finley looked around. She paused, not letting the prince start forward yet, and nodded to Micah, off to the side. Then Tamara, dressed in battle gear and probably just off duty from watching the demon prisoners. Weston also got a nod, which he returned, and the faeries leaning over the banister earned a smile.

As they finally walked forward, Finley nodded and said hello to several staff members in passing. The prince walked beside her, following her gaze but saying nothing. The crowd watched her depart, many with smiles, some blotting tears, and a few with tense postures that suggested they were thinking about battle. About what she stood for.

Leala and I were fucking geniuses.

It wasn't until that moment of congratulating myself that I noticed the former queen. She stood ahead of them, having just entered from a wide doorway. Her expression mirrored her son's stoicism. The lady-in-waiting was slightly behind her, as was the tradition for the royals and aristocracy of the past. A fine dress hugged her curves and jewelry twinkled along her neck, on her wrists, and circled a few of her fingers. Her posture was stately and reserved. She hadn't aged a day. And while she was still in her prime, her magnificence paled in comparison to the couple that had just passed and gone before her. She spoke of the past, of an ideal that had fallen by the wayside. Of a full staff, impeccably trained, and a castle with actual fucking light bulbs so we wouldn't have to eat by candlelight.

She didn't fit in today's harsh climate, and it showed.

I hurried down the stairs so I could get in front of her. I wanted to see if I could sneak into the dining room and continue to watch. I was no longer worried about my girl. Now I just wanted to see the fireworks.

CHAPTER 10
FINLEY

"I'M SORRY FOR having you dress in separate quarters," Nyfain said in a low voice as we made our way to the dining room. "I wanted that entrance for you. Hadriel assured me that you would enrapture everyone, but..." He took a deep breath. "I will remember the image of you walking toward me just now for the rest of my life. It stole my breath."

My heart heated. "I'm not going to be as eloquent when I say that you are incredibly handsome."

He squeezed my fingers where our hands were still joined at my hip. "Eloquence often gets in the way of truth. Hearing you say that, knowing how I look, and feeling that you actually believe it..." He leaned over and kissed my temple. "It is everything."

The doors stood open with two black-suited staff members standing at attention on either side, one with pants too long and the other swimming in his pressed shirt. Inside, the candles glimmered, sparkling across the beautiful glassware and against the laid-out silver. Three places were set at the right end of the table, two on one side and the other across from them.

"Since I'm not officially king and we are in limbo before the coronation, my mother technically has higher status." He took his arm from my waist and pulled out my chair. "She would therefore sit at the head of the table. Given the current...situation, I thought this was the better option."

"And we can't do the coronation until we're ready to go to the council meeting?"

"Correct. Once we are king and queen, we'll have very little time before we need to officially establish ourselves on the council. If we were to do that now, we'd go in as a poor, broken kingdom. The other kingdoms would view us in low esteem, and it would give Dolion a lot of power over us. They'd side with him, essentially, no matter what we said. We need power and might and financial security if we're going to have a chance to stand against him." He took a deep breath. "But the council also won't wait forever. Time is ticking, and this thing with my mother is slowing everything down. It's muddling my plans to lift this kingdom onto its feet. Plans that already have a slim chance of success."

He didn't say it, but I could read him easily. *Why is she doing this to the kingdom??* he was wondering. He must be. I certainly would be.

My dragon rolled within me, and I knew what she was thinking as well: we had precious little time to cure him if he was to show up at that council meeting in all his golden glory.

I sat and waited for him to sit beside me, but he remained standing, reaching down to lay his hand on my shoulder.

"You aren't going to sit?" I asked softly, not wanting to be overheard in case the guest of horror was nearby.

"I was taught that a gentleman stands until all ladies are seated."

My heart swelled at his chivalry. Even though he and his mother were at odds, and she posed a threat to both of us, he would keep himself to his high standards.

A swish of fabric had me glancing toward the door. The sparkling necklace she wore caught my eye first.

I turned a little more as Nyfain's mother walked in wearing a shimmering dress that had probably been made from silk or some equally as expensive and currently unattainable fabric. More jewels sparkled on her earlobes and shimmered around her wrists and on her fingers. She was covered in the things, more gems than I'd ever seen, let alone on one person. Her face had that firm expression Nyfain had worn, and her bearing and poise screamed *regal* and *important*. Her hair was done up on her head, and although her face had been heavily made up, her refined beauty shone through. Even without a crown, so did her position.

There was nothing former about this queen.

Oh my god, I was about to have dinner with the queen. Me, a commoner, meeting the *queen*!

Young me was squealing. A thousand childhood memories crowded me: my make-believe tea parties with the queen, palling around with her son, getting ready for a formal dinner in the castle...

Watch, folks, as the queen sits down to tea with the

fine and esteemed Princess Finley.

Fucking hell, my dragon thought. *Not that again.*

If this wasn't the perfect time for it, then when was?

Too bad this time the queen wasn't happy to see me.

My heart sped up, and soon it was racing. Perspiration formed on my brow.

I struggled to call up images of "Ami" in her quaint house or in her backyard in plain clothes, working the plants like anyone else. Now, in this formal dining room with her, watching her glide to her chair, I once again felt completely and utterly out of my depth.

Nyfain ran his palm up my shoulder to rest on his mark. He squeezed, probably to comfort me...or himself. I could feel his anxiety rise like mine. I could feel his uncertainty.

If only Claudile—Delaney—were here to scowl at me so my anger could drown out this annoyingly debilitating, star-struck horror...

A staff member met Arleth at her chair. If she was annoyed not to be at the head of the table, she gave no sign. She sat down gracefully and was helped closer to the table, where she folded her hands into her lap and lifted her gaze slowly to Nyfain.

He ran his thumb across my mark, cutting through my anxiety with a jolt of pleasure, before pulling his hand away and taking his seat. Another staff member made a show of helping him push the chair closer to the table before crossing to the other side of me. The staff member on the queen's side leaned forward, and then, in a little dance that was almost choreographed but not quite, they took our folded napkins off the porcelain plates in front of us and snapped them out before dropping them into our laps. Nyfain was next, and once his napkin had been dropped into place, the staff members moved away toward a silver tray-stand holding two carafes of a reddish-brown liquid at the other end of the dining room.

"Mother," Nyfain said by way of greeting before stretching his arm across the back of my chair, just barely low enough not to be awkward for him. "I'm surprised to see you here, in this kingdom. I was told you'd died."

The staff was back, filling our crystal goblets with what looked like some sort of brandy-wine.

She waited until they'd gone again, her hands still resting gently in her lap.

"Yes, I know," she told him, and the flash of guilt in her eyes sent a spear of pain and anger and frustration through the bond. "I know what a shock it must be to see me here. I wanted an opportunity to explain. After I am through, I will accept any course of action you deem fit."

Nyfain stared at her, saying nothing. In a moment, her gaze shifted to me, and she inclined her head.

"Finley. It's nice to see you again."

"You too…" I said, trying to stay composed.

The first course, a creamy soup dish, was brought out. Nyfain and the queen waited for the staff to move away before politely reaching for their soup spoons, Nyfain taking his arm from around my chair to do it.

Not really hungry, my stomach turning, I took up my spoon as well.

The queen took a dainty spoonful, and Nyfain followed suit. I dipped my spoon in and then just let it stay there for now. There were only so many things I could pretend at one time.

Nyfain finished his mouthful, but instead of going for another, he laid his spoon down beside the bowl and left his forearm propped against the table.

I remembered the way he'd followed my lead the first time we had dinner. He was doing it again, letting me call the shots so that I felt more comfortable, even in a formal dinner with his mother.

With a surge of emotion, I reached over and placed my hand on his thigh. He really was too good to be true.

The queen dabbed her mouth for some reason (not a drop on it), set down the spoon, and took a sip of her wine.

"Truth be told," she said, setting down her glass, "I'm not exactly sure where to start."

"Did Father think you were dead?" Nyfain asked.

She reached for her spoon again but hesitated and let out a small breath. "So much of this is complicated."

"Then uncomplicate it," he said, and she tensed, as though stopping herself from flinching.

She let her hand fall to her lap. "At first, yes, he thought I was dead. He thought he'd killed me."

I felt the scowl drop from my face. Nyfain froze.

"He blamed me for you leaving, of course," she continued. "I'm sure you could guess that. He was a man who blamed everyone else for things that happened, never himself. You remember that, I'm sure."

He didn't nod, but emotions stirred through the bond. He clearly did.

"Our relationship was bad after you left, but he kept the bruises in covered areas. He was good at hiding those, as I'm sure you also remember. I had a plan, though. Before you even found someone to marry—"

Rage rushed through me, and I sucked in a breath, leaning back to try to control it. Nyfain glanced over before placing a hand on my shoulder. His touch helped calm the rage, the thrashing of my dragon.

"I apologize," she said to me, and it sounded sincere. "After you left, Nyfain, I got all my affairs in order. When all the arrangements had been made, I told him I was leaving. That I was going home. You were safe, and there was no one else I needed to—or had the ability to— protect. While I should've felt a keener duty to the kingdom, he'd stripped away all my power by then. He'd torn away all my duties but the things concerning the plants—the things specifically concerning trade. So I told him I was leaving."

"And he tried to stop you," Nyfain said in a measured voice. Pain seeped through the bond.

"Yes. I knew I'd get beaten for it, but I was prepared. My plan accounted for the likelihood that I would not be able to walk or fly. And so I summoned my courage and stood my ground."

She lifted her chin a little, with her hands in her lap and her back straight, and even so, she'd never looked more fragile. If she weren't so composed, I knew she'd be shaking. I barely dared to breathe.

"And he nearly killed you," Nyfain said softly, his trembling hand moving to take mine on his thigh. This was what he'd always been afraid of. The guilt he'd lived with for years.

"Yes," she said, her tone even. "When I refused to back down, he just kept going and going. His commander at the time, a sniveling wretch of a man, did nothing. He stood by and watched. It was Dee who finally tore him away from me, taking damage herself. She broke through the door of his quarters, took down that commander, and put herself between me and the king. It was her words that finally broke through his wrath. She told him he'd already killed me, so what was the point in beating a dead body? She said I'd have to have a closed casket, and the whole kingdom would blame him for my death."

Arleth took a sip of her wine, her hand steady. Nyfain's arm now shook.

"If not for her, I would have died," she said. "Even after she stopped the beating, I still would have died if not for the everlass draught she dribbled into my mouth."

"So they carried you out?" I asked.

"Not that night. I couldn't be moved. They put me in the casket and summoned the king to look at me. My face and body were a mess. Extensive bleeding, broken...everything. When he looked, he didn't notice the slight rising and falling of my chest. He just saw his handiwork. He believed that he'd killed me, giving me a perfect way out." She huffed. "He had the gall to cry, that disgusting pig." She paused for a moment, as though to gather herself. "They lied to him the next night, saying they were going to prepare my body for burial, and moved the entire coffin with me in it. My ladies-in-waiting scurried me away to the ship we prayed was still waiting just offshore. I still needed constant tending. I was healing, but very slowly. Someone needed to go with me, and it was Dee who volunteered to leave her life of luxury for a simpler existence. A village life." Her gaze slid to me. "As you saw. There were fewer people at the time. Dragons have found us over the years, looking for a place to belong. We're really not as solitary as everyone tries to believe."

She took another sip of her drink, quiet descending on the table until she continued.

"How did he find out you weren't dead?" I guessed.

"I don't know. Maybe he wanted to cry over my dead body again, or maybe he doubted their word. He was paranoid at the best of times. He always thought people were lying to him. Soon after we set sail, though, three members of the court came after us. I was on the deck, drinking an everlass draught and getting air, barely able to sit up. Dee had just gone to get me a shawl, so no one was with me. I couldn't move on my own. I couldn't get to cover. It was Durrel who landed, insisting I stop the ship immediately. That I go back with them." She took a shuddering breath, and for the first time, fear glimmered in her tight eyes. "I did not understand why anyone would want to stay in a broken kingdom with a mad-man, but the court had it good in those days. They were the lords of the land, as you remember, Nyfain. The king saw to it that they had everything they could want. They weren't trapped in his shadow, subject to his bad moods and fast fists.

"Amazingly, it was one of the crew, a lion shifter,

who came to my aid. I hadn't spoken to him once. But he came out of nowhere and stepped between Durrel and me. He kept Durrel from snatching me, and then the rest of the crew came and threw him overboard."

"What about the other dragons?" Nyfain asked, a growl riding his words.

She gave a slight smile. "I'd planned for that. It is a well-kept secret within the court that a certain type of magical pulse made by the faeries can keep dragons at bay. It rattles our dragons' senses for a time, and they lose control of their body mechanics. I procured the pulse before you left, Nyfain. I had it, waiting for the right moment. Dee activated it on the ship, and it kept the dragons at bay as the boat moved farther and farther from shore. Eventually, thankfully before the magic ran out, the dragons couldn't follow anymore. We were too far out. So they returned to shore, and I eventually made it to safety."

"Durrel…that was the one who couldn't swim, wasn't it?" Nyfain asked.

Arleth's grin said it all.

"But then why did the curse affect you?" Nyfain asked. "Why didn't you find a way to get word to me?"

Guilt creased her eyes before she smoothed it away.

"I failed you," she said softly. "I should've gotten word to you right away. I know that now." She paused for a moment, guilt soaking into her features. "But I wanted to be safe and settled before I sent you a message. I wanted to be in better condition before you saw me. Unfortunately, that took longer than I expected. By the time I did send a message…" She shook her head. "They didn't know who you were. Had never heard of Wyvern. At first I thought there had to be some mistake, so I traveled to the faerie kingdom." She shook her head again. "I didn't know about the curse, of course, but I knew something had gone gravely wrong."

"They didn't know me."

"No, but they were in the process of cleaning out your bedchamber. They couldn't explain the various mementos you'd left behind."

Nyfain's fingers entwined tightly with mine as rage simmered within me at the mention of his other life.

"I'd wondered if they'd...done something. Killed you, maybe, but they didn't seem to recognize me, either," she said. "It was like the whole history of the kingdom had been wiped from their minds. I know much about faerie magic, and I could tell they hadn't been bamboozled by their own magic. The only other creatures with magic powerful enough to wreak such a change were the demons. It was then that the reality of the situation started to dawn on me. I knew there must have been a dark trade of some kind. A curse."

"You did not suspect that Father would call me home?" Nyfain asked guardedly.

She took a deep, steadying breath and locked eyes with him. It looked as though it took a lot of effort. "Yes, I did suspect the mad king would come up with a lie to cover my disappearance. He did it often with his subjects, staff, court, and army. Saying I'd actually died was of course the easiest excuse for my absence, and he must have known my funeral would be the easiest way to bring you home."

Heavy silence crowded the air, and I held Nyfain's hand tightly. We all knew the words that were coming next—it just took her a few moments to summon the courage to speak them.

"When I realized how long it had taken me to heal, I figured you'd probably gotten—and answered—his summons by then. I suspected you were in Wyvern. At that point... At that point, I should've followed you to Wyvern. I should've joined you there to spare you the pain of my death. That would've been the courageous thing. But I couldn't bear to return to him." Her body shook with sobs. "So I told myself that I would visit you once you returned home, because I knew you wouldn't stay in Wyvern. I decided I'd go to you and beg forgiveness for the grief I'd caused you. I figured you could work yourself around to accepting that. But then the faeries didn't know you, and so I went to find out why. I could never have imagined the fate I'd forced upon you with my cowardice."

I barely stifled the deep breath I needed to let out. Turbulent emotions rolled through the bond.

"Did my father have dealings with the demons in the past?" Nyfain asked. "Is that really why you made the connection to demon magic?"

She looked like a cornered rabbit cowering at the feet of a wolf. But she answered. "He'd dealt with them in the past, yes. Not to such a large extent, but..." She held up her palms. "He threatened to harm *you* if I told you of those dealings. I only knew because I'd stumbled into a meeting. He'd meant to keep those secrets from me, from everyone."

Nyfain looked away from her, his jaw set, his eyes landing on our entwined fingers. So many emotions rolled through the bond that I couldn't pick any out.

"The curse affecting you..." He didn't look back up at her. Gravel lined each syllable. "Did you have some hand in its creation? Is that why it froze your aging?"

She swallowed and shook her head, her eyes filling with tears. "No. I swear to you. I couldn't come home, either. After my trip to the faerie kingdom, I hired a shipmaster, who thought I was crazy, and forced him to follow the old maps. The demons can erase memories, but they can't erase the lines on a map. But magic blocked me out. I was locked outside. I have no idea why the magic in the court impacted Delaney and me. I didn't even realize I'd stopped aging for many years, and until I met Finley, I didn't fully understand why. I didn't know the details of the curse, or even if it was specifically a curse, only that the magic was affecting me."

She swallowed and dabbed at her cheeks.

"I failed you. I damned you to...to *this*. But I did not have an active hand in that curse. Please believe that. My only goal was to break free. And then, after I healed, to get to you. My motives were simple, please..." A sob ripped free. "Please believe that."

Nyfain was squeezing my hand so hard it hurt. He let out a breath, bending forward.

"It's as much my fault as yours," he said softly. "I left you here. I left the kingdom. I knew what I was leaving you to—them to—and I still walked away. You weren't strong enough to dominate him, but I was."

"His army would've killed you," she replied, her

struggle to straighten up plain. Her eyes were rimmed red. "He would've had them kill you."

"He wouldn't have killed his heir."

"You are only his heir in name. You aren't his heir by blood."

The air seemed to flash-freeze over the table. Nyfain's lifted his gaze to hers slowly, his profound confusion evident.

"I beg your pardon?" he finally said.

She took a deep breath. "The king's animosity toward you probably stemmed from many things, but one thing in particular. The king knew he was not your father."

CHAPTER 11
FINLEY

"**G**ET OUT." THE staff at the other end of the room, standing by the drink station, flinched. "That'll be all, thank you. Close the doors behind you. Do not come back in until we summon you." Then, realizing how hasty and panicked I probably sounded, I added, "The soup is delicious. We need time to eat it."

No fucking way did the staff need to hear that Nyfain might not be the heir to the throne. It wouldn't do much for our cause. Not to mention this was clearly the first time Nyfain was hearing this information. If the king wasn't actually his father, Nyfain had a lot more to digest from this conversation than some iffy decision-making by his mom. He might not be so keen to have strangers listening in.

The door clicked behind the last staff member, who peered through the crack for as long as he could before it latched. They'd heard the first bit of that, and they'd talk.

Fuck.

"Are you telling me that the man I called Dad," Nyfain said, each word clipped, "was not actually my biological father?"

His mother took a couple of deep breaths, trying to get her emotions under control. This new topic was clearly easier for her to discuss. She didn't seem to feel guilty about siring Nyfain with someone other than the king, or having lied to Nyfain all his life.

Nyfain must've realized that as well, because he leaned forward, bristling, his anger starting to rise. He pushed back his soup and leaned on the table, staring at his quickly sobering mother.

"If my father wasn't the king, who was he?" he asked in a growl.

"You never knew him. You were too young—"

"Who?" Nyfain shouted.

She flinched, her whole body tense. I placed a hand on his shoulder to help him keep his head. I could feel his dragon roiling within him, feeding him fire and power. My dragon started to gently siphon it off and stash it away, making sure they didn't destroy the whole room in a rage.

"It was the king's commander. Not the commanders you knew over the years—his first, from what I understand. Please, allow me to explain."

I rubbed Nyfain's back, sensing he needed the contact. In all honesty, though, I couldn't fault the queen for seeking comfort away from the mad king. Then again, I hadn't been lied to my whole life. I doubted Nyfain would be so quick to see reason after a betrayal of that magnitude. It was a helluva thing to learn after all he'd been through, and right before he was supposed to assume the throne.

He didn't comment, which she must've known was his acceptance, because she quickly jumped into the story.

"I was only eighteen when I permanently moved here, only seventeen when the king first started courting me. He'd wanted a wife with power and prestige, and I ticked all his boxes and had a pretty face. He dazzled me with riches and splendor, luxury and doting servants. He talked about the two of us sitting on the throne of his great kingdom. About my child being his heir, a future king…"

She took a sip of her drink, her soup long forgotten.

"I was warned by many in my village to talk to the elders about this kingdom. They said the king's honeyed words would not be my reality. In my foolishness, I thought I could handle the situation, and when he offered me a handsome mateprice, an assurance that I would be well provided for if it didn't work out, I agreed to marry him.

"I came to this kingdom with stars in my eyes, but it took barely a year for me to realize I'd made a grave mistake. A year after that, and I wanted to get out. He'd talked about the power I would have, the duties I would do—lies. Even if I had wanted to change things—and I did—I had no way to actually do it. I asked for my mateprice so that I might leave."

"The gold reserve," Nyfain said, his tone flat.

"Part of it, yes. Back then, there was plenty more. He said that I could have it, but I'd have to dig it out myself. I said that was fine."

"But he wouldn't give you the resources or the tools," Nyfain said.

"Correct," she said, inclining her head. "He had many excuses, and I believed them for a time, but finally I pushed the issue. That was the first time he struck me. Just the once, but it was enough."

I wrinkled my brow. "Enough for what?"

She assessed me for a moment, and a little smile played across her lips.

"I was not as hard as you, young Finley. I was not forged in fire as you were. I knew he could dominate me, and I didn't push the issue. I didn't learn how to manifest my will to rise higher, fight harder. Instead, for many years, I cowered."

"Not all women will randomly stab someone with a pocketknife, sweetheart," Nyfain told me, and through his rolling emotions I could pick out his brief flare of humor.

"That wasn't random," I mumbled. "Or did you forget you had me by the throat?"

"Yes, well." Arleth quirked her eyebrow at us, and I wondered if I'd forgotten to mention the stabbing bit when I was recounting my history to "Ami" in the everlass fields of her village. "The mad king would not have tolerated someone pushing back. I tried to make the best of my situation, but his ill treatment of me went beyond physical abuse. He took all his frustrations out on me. Belittled me. He spent his idle time tormenting me for his own amusement. Often it was unbearable.

"His commander at the time tried to help as much as he could. He tried to intercept, even if he was punished for it. When the physical abuse did happen, and the king wouldn't let my ladies-in-waiting see me, the commander often nursed me himself, tending my wounds and trying to make me laugh. To say I fell hard for him would be an understatement. He was my light in a very dark place, a joy amidst so much anguish."

She wiped away another tear.

"We fought the attraction at first. I knew the king would lose his mind if he knew, especially since he hadn't been able to get me with child. Given our circumstances, we'd never imprint, the king and I, and because of that I'd never go into heat to help things along. So even though the king was notoriously unfaithful, something I didn't mind because it kept him away from me, I needed to stay true. Except inevitably..."

Nyfain didn't speak, tense beside me. I leaned against him and wrapped my arm around him, hugging him while watching Arleth. He dropped his hand from the table, reaching over to place it on my thigh.

"It was about a year after I'd first given in to temptation with the commander," she said, "that I learned I was with child."

"So it wasn't just the one time," I surmised.

"No. Not remotely. Once it started..."

"Were you in love?" I asked.

"Madly. Desperately." She wiped away another tear. "His dragon wanted to lay his claim over the king's mark. The commander had more than enough power to do so. He was a great alpha dragon, the most powerful dragon in the kingdom. It was how he'd challenged his way up to commander from humble roots. My dragon also had a fierce need to mark him. But we knew it would mean his death. Maybe mine too." She took a deep breath. "I knew the baby was his. There could be no doubt. I hadn't been with the king in many months. He was busy with the new servants, and at any rate, he knew I hated his touch. He often lost his…"

"Hard-on," I added.

Her lips tightened fractionally, and she gave a slight nod. She hadn't been schooled in the sexually outspoken ways of Hadriel.

"He *serviced* me, as he called it, when he was drunk with brandy or power. There was no love there. So when I fell pregnant, and the only man and dragon I'd been with for months was the commander…"

"The only man…and *dragon* you'd been with?" I asked with a crinkled nose. "Your dragons banged, too?"

Her look was more than enough answer.

Get our big-dicked dragon up into the sky, and I'll show you how dragons fuck, my dragon thought, and I wanted to scrub out my brain. It was weird enough to fuck in human form while the dragons were in control.

"Why won't you say his name?" Nyfain asked, tensing again.

She lifted her chin a little. "Because you will have heard his name. I'd like you to know the real story so you won't let lies tarnish his name."

Ugh, that didn't sound good.

"Did the king suspect?" I asked.

She took a deep breath. "It didn't seem like it at the time, but looking back on it, I think he probably did. He wasn't a dumb man. Not to mention…he'd apparently known his chances of producing offspring were limited. That was something I found out later. He'd kept it from me—from most everyone—not wanting word to get out that he was all but sterile. He thought it would...defeat his manhood, or some such nonsense. Still, he probably thought there was some chance, however miniscule. We all hope for the impossible, every now and then."

I leaned back, knowing this was in the past, but scared for her all the same. I could only imagine what a guy like the king would do if he found out that another man had done what he could not.

"And did the commander know?" I asked.

She shook her head. "No. I breathed not a word of it to anyone. His mark was not on me, so he didn't display the possessiveness many dragons would, but if he'd known I carried his offspring..."

A blast of power pumped from Nyfain, and he pulled his hand from my thigh to settle it around my shoulders. It didn't have to be said that he'd bring possessiveness to a new level if I got pregnant.

She nodded. "So I kept it to myself and enjoyed the months that followed. The king, warned by the midwives that I was in delicate condition, kept away from me lest he lose his temper and hurt me. Lest he lose the baby, basically. Because even if he knew it probably wasn't his, the child would still be born with his name. He was hoping for the powerful heir he'd dreamt of. It was the reason he'd sought me out, after all. He'd put his hope in my bloodline."

"Did you continue to see the commander?" I asked, caught up in the story despite myself.

"Yes, when I could. He delighted in watching my belly grow and feeling the baby move inside of it, and continuing to…"

"Bang?" I supplied, forgetting to mind myself.

She ignored me entirely this time. "We were very careful, of course, helped by my most trusted ladies-in-waiting. Dee in particular. She watched over me like a mother hen. And when the baby was born, it was a dream come true. I loved my son immediately, of course." Her eyes shone as she looked at Nyfain. "He was perfection, from his tiny fingers and toes to his cute little scrunched-up face when he wailed for that first time, strong and angry, even then."

I rubbed Nyfain's thigh.

"And the king…well, he got his heir. He gave me the space to raise you, to nurture you. He couldn't be bothered with children, so he allowed you to spend your days with us, working the plants, and run free in the wood and play. It wasn't until you were entering your teens, when you got your first growth spurt, that it became clear you had great potential. That's when he started to…take you in hand, as he called it. As you advanced in age and power and stature, he took more of an interest. I don't have to fill you in on the rest."

I remembered from Nyfain that "the rest" wasn't pretty. Beatings, harsh treatment, unkind words and actions, days locked in the tower… It hadn't been an easy childhood for him once his father—or the king, I guessed—stepped in.

His emotions boiled within him, now seasoned with more anger. Maybe he was wondering if he would've been spared the ill treatment had he been declared someone else's. Or maybe if his real father had stepped in and saved him.

I put my hand to his side in comfort and asked the queen a question to help move things along.

"And all that time, his real father had no clue?" I asked.

Her countenance fell. "He wasn't alive to see Nyfain reach his teens. Even when Nyfain was a baby, he was the spitting image of his father. No one noticed at first. They'd look between me and the king and squint and say, 'Who is he like, then?' I'd say the king, of course, which pleased the king, but my unease grew. By the time Nyfain was five…it was painfully clear. People were starting to notice the similarities. The *commander* was starting to notice. He didn't say anything—he was more the strong and silent type—but I could see him studying Nyfain. His possessiveness was starting to grow as well. His need to be near me, near his son, was increasing.

"When Nyfain was six, just after his birthday, the king summoned his caregiver for an examination. Afterward, the king confronted me. Cornered me. Whatever he heard must've made him realize Nyfain wasn't his. I was intent on denying it, but Ta—the commander burst into the room and tossed the king away like he was a doll. The commander took his place in front of me, shielding me, and told the king that if he touched me or *his* son again, he'd kill the king, repercussions be damned."

"He must've overheard the king and put two and two together," I said.

Tears again trailed down Arleth's cheeks. "It would seem so, yes. He was the king's right-hand-man, so to speak. The wolves would have called him a beta. He was with the king often."

"What did the king do?"

"He killed him," Nyfain said. "Taerhael, that's who you're speaking of, isn't it? I barely remember him, but I know he was killed for treason."

Arleth wiped her cheek with the back of her hand. "Yes. His treasonous deeds were all related to me. As the king would say in later years, *I* was the reason Taerhael had to be killed. My wicked ways beguiled the most powerful and loyal dragon in the kingdom. I was his ruin—the kingdom's ruin. He said it again and again until I started to believe it. The king could be incredibly manipulative. He'd tell you something in such a way that you questioned your own mind. I still believe it, mostly. It is true, after all. Taerhael was killed because of his deeds with me."

Before I could push back on that assessment, because she obviously wasn't the one to blame, Nyfain cut in.

"Whenever he punished me for some misdoing or imagined slight, he'd say I would never amount to anything. That I'd turn out just like that traitor Taerhael. The name meant little to me then, but his tune changed in later years. He started saying I'd never amount to Taerhael. I was constantly compared to him and found wanting. In my mind, that meant I wasn't even as good as a traitor. I was worthless. I grew to loathe that name."

"No." The queen shook her head and leaned forward, resting her hand on the table between them. "That didn't have anything to do with you. That had to do with the past. Taerhael would've been so *proud* of you, Nyfain. He was so good with you when you were little, playing with you outside, teaching you to ride a horse, letting you crawl all over him and pull his hair. He had infinite patience with you, even when he didn't know you were his son. He would've protected you to the last, had he known. He tried, in the end. He killed a lot of people before they were able to take him down. But he was no match for a king and his army."

"Why didn't you tell me?" Nyfain's voice was ragged, his composure cracking. "Why did you let me believe, all this time, that I was the spawn of *that man*? That...miserable man. He showed me no love. No...compassion. *Ever.* Even when he tried, it often resulted in a cuff to the ear, or a bark to get out of his sight. Then the beatings, the punishments, being locked in the tower..."

Arleth shook her head. "I couldn't tell anyone. I was told by the king, in no uncertain terms, that if the truth got out, even a rumor, he'd kill you. He maintained that there was no point to you if people didn't believe you were his son. Your only value to him was in the perception that you were his heir. Still, he came to see you as a mockery of his manhood because he couldn't get me with a child of his own. I told you to leave to protect you. You were never safe here, not while he was alive. *I* was never safe here. I told you to leave, and as soon as you were safely away, I left too. I had damned this kingdom with my indiscretions. I didn't want you to suffer in the fallout."

The strength went out of Nyfain, and he leaned back,

gripping the top of my chair.

"When I asked where my size and strength came from, since I was so much larger than D—" Nyfain gritted his teeth. "Than the king, you told me it was from your family line."

"You would've been a hair taller than Taerhael now, with wider shoulders. It might've been from my line..." Her voice trailed away.

He stared at her, obviously reeling. I didn't know how to make it better. I didn't know how to comfort him through this other than to keep my hands on him and offer my soft support through the bond.

I certainly didn't want to point out that the only way she'd fucked up was by not writing to Nyfain sooner. By not warning him as soon as she could. She'd known enough about the king to guess he'd do something crazy. Then again, she'd barely gotten out of her nightmare life alive. She had been clawing her way back from the dead. She was a survivor. Her story wasn't pretty, but surviving never was.

Still, I wasn't the one who had been lied to all my life. Nyfain would need to come to grips with that fact before logic could rule.

Besides, sad story aside, there were still questions on the table.

When the truth broke—which was inevitable, since two staff members had heard her claim the king wasn't Nyfain's father—what would happen?

What would happen when only one official royal was left in the kingdom—the favorite royal—and she had ownership of the gold?

CHAPTER 12

FINLEY

TIME TO DO my part and get this dinner back on track.

"Right." I clasped my hands together and rested them in front of me on the table. Leaning over them, I speared Arleth with my hard look. "As I understand it, you are technically the queen, and Nyfain is technically a nobody. You just told the staff that he is not the heir. If we can't hush it up, and they believe you, he no longer has any standing as a royal. I, as we know, am common. I technically have less than zero standing here. Regardless of how things went in the dungeon, most of the court dragons would be happy enough for things to go back to normal, and for me to resume my place at the bottom of the proverbial heap. Technically speaking, you hold all the power."

I paused to monitor her face. She gave nothing away, her eyes dry now despite the tear stains streaking her cheeks. She studied me silently.

"I'm sure you know by now that *technicalities* don't

143

amount to dick," I said, and she flinched. Sometimes a little crudeness went a long way. "The curse changed things. The old rules are broken. You could use that to your advantage right now, but we could do the same. And while you have more money, we have something more important: might. The dragons from your village seem intent to follow Micah or me, and I have it on good authority that Micah stands with Nyfain. Weston's wolves will also follow us. We have the power to stand against the demon king. The hope of this kingdom rests on Nyfain's and my shoulders, money be damned."

She clasped her hands in her lap, her eyebrows lifted. "And what of the people? I am their favorite, not you."

I huffed out a laugh. "You are their comfort blanket. I'll make them realize they don't need one. They'll follow me because I'm more than a figurehead. I'm the hero of this tale, and I'll promise them the glow of victory."

She swayed back just a little. "My goodness. You burn as brightly as the sun, young Finley. No wonder my son is enamored with you." She leaned forward just a bit. "It seems Gunduin's advice registered after all. I had wondered, when you didn't leave the everlass house."

"He told you about that, did he? When I'm in one of those moods, it's best to steer clear."

"It was I who sent him in there. What would he know about the politics of the crown?"

"*You* sent Gunduin?" I pointed at her.

She sighed before reaching into her top to pull something out of her cleavage. "Sometimes undergarments are useful, Finley, remember that."

She placed a little vial wrapped in paper on the

stretch of table separating her and Nyfain.

"This is the spell breaker for the magic that secures the remainder of the gold," she said. "I placed that spell right before I left, as you probably guessed. The gold was mine, and though I hoped to never come back, I didn't want the kingdom to gobble it up. The king was spending frivolously, more going out than coming in. This was always a wealthy kingdom, with much to trade, but even a wealthy kingdom, mismanaged, can fall into desolation. I feared that was the way it would go. So I protected what was mine."

"If you never thought to return," Nyfain said, not looking at the vial, "why did you secure it? Spite?"

"For you." She tapped the table next to the vial. "That spell breaker needs three to five drops of blood. Your blood, freely given. It then needs to be poured into the crevice indicated on that slip of paper. I had intended to give it to you in person after we both left the kingdom. After all this time, though, the original drawing has faded. It is barely legible. I went into the reserve last night to remind myself where the specific crevice is so that I might re-trace the lines."

Nyfain's shock mirrored my own.

"Wait…" I said, trying to wrap my brain around all of this.

"Why didn't you say?" Nyfain asked, pulling the paper from the vial and examining it. "Why didn't you tell me what you were doing?"

The queen smiled sadly. "Would you have believed me? I knew you mistrusted me. I wanted this audience to thoroughly explain myself. I knew you would at least give me the chance to explain. You are your father's son, and I don't mean the king."

"Probably too soon," I murmured.

"Why did you keep yourself hidden from the court?" Nyfain asked. "Why didn't you tell Finley who you were in the village?"

She sighed softly again and ran her hand across her forehead. "I have so much to answer for, I know that. And I know you need to hear all to see if you will allow yourself to forgive me, even in part. But I am also famished and tired and in need of getting drunk. Might we move our conversation to a more comfortable location, maybe in front of a fire, and eat like normal people? Like simpler people? I have been away from this style of dining for sixteen years. Happily, I might add. I never much liked it. And if Finley were any more uncomfortable here, we would be in danger of an extreme reaction, like her overturning the table or throwing a wine glass."

My eyebrows pinched together and my eyes narrowed at the dig, but I had to admit that the alternative she'd suggested sounded great.

Our mate is the explosively destructive one of our pair, my dragon grumbled. *Talk about putting one's son on a pedestal.*

I ignored her and looked to see Nyfain's reaction, or maybe beg him to say yes. He felt my gaze and met it, his eyes going from hard to pillow soft in a moment. My middle warmed despite the situation.

"Of course," he rumbled.

NYFAIN HAD THE hallways cleared, and then we moved to a little den at the back of the castle that seemed familiar to both him and his mother. Based on the emotions rolling through the bond, I suspected they'd shared many other meals like this, sitting quietly in front of the fire. Nyfain had mentioned as much.

Our dinner had been kept warm, and the servants turned it into a little buffet for us to pick at. We sat around it on the floor with forks in our hands, stabbing in turns. I sat between Nyfain's legs, leaning against his chest as he draped an arm around me, wanting the closeness the imprinting seemed to demand. It was such a welcome change from the formal dinner that I couldn't help relaxing.

"You were a shock, Finley," Arleth said after we were settled. "In the village, I mean. An absolute shock. I reeled from it."

"You could've fooled me," I retuned.

Her smile was slight. "I was taught to conceal my reactions. Dee saw my—the sword first, of course." She finished chewing and sipped her wine, which sat on the ground in front of her. "She assumed it had been taken by the demons or someone and sold. That it was mere coincidence that you had it. But then I smelled you."

She shook her head and speared another piece of meat.

"Did you recognize my scent?" Nyfain asked.

"Of course I did. You're my son. I'd recognize your scent anywhere. But I did not recognize the woman who wore it. At that time, I didn't know that only some of our people had aged."

"I basically told her my life's story," I murmured to him.

"Yes, she did, giving us a much better picture of what had happened in the kingdom after the demons came."

"Why didn't you tell me who you were?" I asked, resting my hand on Nyfain's knee, stopping myself from rubbing his thigh. Not appropriate. But damn it, the urge was there.

She sighed and leaned back onto her hand. "A few reasons. The first was that I'd walked away from that life. I didn't identify as the queen anymore, and it felt wrong to present myself as such. The second was Dee's prodding. She thought it was an outrage that you should be so ignorant of your own queen. She didn't trust you were being truthful."

"She doubted Hannon?"

Arleth paused and then chuckled softly. "She didn't even think of Hannon. I suppose he's not doubted often, is he? He has a certain…way about him. His honesty is kind and genuine. He'd be a terrible royal. At least in the old days."

"We're no longer in the old days," Nyfain growled.

She didn't comment on that. "The third was because…I'm a mother. I wanted to see what kind of woman my son had supposedly chosen."

Nyfain tensed, and power curled through the bond.

Arleth bowed her head slightly. "I apologize. But you can't blame a mother for wanting to know if a suitor is good enough for her child. You'll see one day, hopefully."

"And?" Nyfain asked.

"My old judgments made me look down on her background, it's true," she said. "A member of the court—a prince—mating a common girl from one of the poorest villages?" She blew out her breath and shook her head. "Ridiculous. But then I worked the plants with her. I've never seen such skill. Even now, watching her strive to make an unheard-of cure for you..." She shook her head again. "I thought I knew everything about the herbs, but I'm learning from her. Why are you keeping some of the everlass in cold water, Finley? After you left, I went to check on your operations."

"You can discuss that another time," Nyfain said.

Still, I felt his pride seeping through the bond, matching my own. I couldn't help but preen a little. The *queen* had just complimented me on one of the things that mattered most to me. If not for all this drama, I'd feel a little euphoric at that.

Arleth continued. "Her power is exceptional. She is a true match for you, son. It's clear the goddess crafted her—crafted you both—to save this faltering kingdom. But what won me was the fight I saw in her—her dragon's fearlessness in the face of a challenge. After that first day of flying, I knew that she would do you proud. She'd do this whole kingdom proud. I knew she was strong enough to stand up to the might of the crown and force her own way, something I'd set out to do but couldn't."

"And yet...you were always so frosty to me," I said, mystified. "Delaney has always acted like she downright hated me."

"Dee takes a while to come around. She's very protective of Nyfain. But I...didn't know what the future held. I didn't want to influence any of your future decisions."

"And what decisions are those?" Nyfain asked.

"First..." She held up a hand. "You should know two things. Micah's suspicion of me is not unfounded. I moved into his village on purpose because he was such a powerful alpha. I kept my eye on him to ensure he didn't abuse that power. My history in this kingdom should tell you why. I'm sure he always felt my eyes on his back. His attachment to Finley—"

Nyfain squeezed me and ran his teeth along my neck, scraping across his mark. His power pulsed. It rolled through me, deliciously wild, and I shuddered and leaned harder into him.

"Sorry," Arleth murmured. "I forget that the imprint bond is so new. I avoided the court dragons in the village for the same reason I sent Gunduin into the everlass house earlier today, Finley. I know how the people respond to me. I knew Tamara would've resumed her old post with barely a word from me, and the others with her. She knew the abuse I endured, and she would not fault me for leaving. They all knew. If I had showed myself in the villages, I would've stolen focus from you, Finley, and no matter what I said, I would've divided your army as I am starting to divide the kingdom now.

"I am so tired of being the one who ruins. I'd like a chance to restore this kingdom instead. I know you suspected I coveted the crown for myself, but honestly, it couldn't be farther from the truth. I gave it up. I do not want it."

Silence fell again, and I didn't know where to go from there. I believed her, every last word, and didn't think she deserved the guilt she'd heaped on her own shoulders. The king had seduced her with riches and a luxurious life…and then trapped her in an impossible situation. What choices had she had? Her lies and deceit had made the difference between life and death for her child. I imagined any mother would do the same.

On the other hand, given she didn't want to continue to divide the kingdom, my job here was done. This was no longer any of my business. It was now officially a matter between mother and son. I could do nothing but quietly support Nyfain and lend an ear and an opinion when asked.

I did have one question, though.

"You have a huge library. Why didn't you poison the bastard?" I furrowed my brow. "Crowded everlass would be too risky, given your vocation, but I can think of three poisons right off the top of my head that I'd use. And I only had one book about trees with information about poison in the notations! I'm sure there were a dozen poisonous solutions to your problem. Feed him a muffin, stop his heart. Ta-da! Then, after he died, your son would be king, governed by you, protected by his actual father and now commander, and Bob's your uncle. It sounds like no one would've missed that mad bastard if you'd kept the status quo and made changes slowly." My mind started turning. "Actually, I should learn more about poisons. What if we go to a dinner with Dolion or some other idiot who tries to poison our meals? I'll need to know what might work its way into our food and have ingredients ready for antidotes, just in case."

As I thought of the section of the library I'd need to hit, I realized silence hung around us. Arleth was staring at me with widened eyes.

"What? Am I being insensitive?" I grimaced. "Or do you think I'm nuts? Because someone poisoning our meals is a very real concern. It's a great way to off someone, and if they're good at it, no one will be able to pin it on them."

Nyfain started to laugh, hugging me closer. "It is safe to say, Mother, that I will never live to see the day when madness overcomes me. Finley will kill me long before that."

"I..." Arleth continued to stare. "I'm at a loss for words." She started to laugh. "What a very different upbringing we've had, Finley. I think the other kingdoms won't know what to do with you. So beautiful. So fierce. Mildly terrifying..."

"She'll be hard to kill," Nyfain said.

"Yes, she will. Once she learns her way around a court, that is. She will need to know the protocol of formal dining, for a start."

"Add it to the list," I murmured. It was becoming a long list.

Nyfain turned solemn. "Where does this leave us, Mom? You indirectly told servants that I am not the rightful heir. Why would you do that in front of them if not to force my hand somehow?"

"I wasn't thinking, but it doesn't matter. On the one hand, I think they'll be glad the madness won't spread to you. Maybe they won't even believe it. On the other hand, without me to get in your way, who else would step up for the throne? The king has no remaining family. His cousins are not here anymore—"

"They were killed by demons. Most of the dragons were."

"Yes. So there is no one to pass the throne to. It is essentially up for grabs. For someone to take it, they would need to challenge you."

"I'm not worried about a challenger," he growled.

"Or they might challenge Finley's right to become queen…"

"A challenge to her is a challenge to me. They would raise that issue only once."

She nodded. "The mad king kept his court in luxury and privilege because he wanted them to covet the life they had. He wanted them to protect it and, in so doing, protect him. As long as they were happy, no one would challenge his right to rule. No one would challenge *him*."

"And that's why he filled his court with dragons," I said with sudden clarity. "Any wolves strong enough to stand up to them would've left for the wolf courts. He didn't care about the ones who stayed behind because they couldn't pull him from his mantle. He didn't need to have equal representation because he wanted only his strongest defenders to have power."

"And those in the villages who could yield the best commodities for trade," she said, and that was clearly the origin of the disparity we were now fighting.

Nyfain ran his fingers down my neck, making me shiver. "With you to balance my temper, little dragon, we won't make the same mistakes. We'll make something great out of this kingdom. Something prosperous."

"Was never a question in my mind." I leaned against him before angling my head, nuzzling my face into the warmth of his neck.

"It's time that I adjourn with my mate," Nyfain told his mother, pushing away our dishes and glasses before gathering me up into his arms. "I need to think on the things you've said. I need to...replay memories of my past. I need some time."

"Of course."

I could hear the hope in her voice. The desperation that what she'd said would be enough. That he could forgive her.

I held my breath, waiting for what he would say next.

"But I would be honored if you would stay in the castle and help my mate and me navigate this new kingdom. Help us build something powerful that we can pass on with pride. Help us raise our children, if we should be so blessed. They will need a retreat when their father gets into a temper, or their mother gets into a mood."

He stood, and I looped my arms around his neck, secure in his strong hold. Normally, I'd be incredibly uncomfortable to be held like this in front of his mother, but I just didn't have it in me to care. I craved his power and strength wrapped around me. I was delighted he'd given her a fair shake.

"Yes, of course," she said, tears immediately coming to her eyes and her lips trembling. "Of course. I will have a room prepared for me immediately so that Finley can take her place in the queen's chambers."

Nyfain shook his head. "Stay there. Enjoy it. I know it was your sanctuary. Finley will be with me in the king's chambers. As soon as I am sworn in—" He paused for a moment. "I need to figure out who will take over the role of royal documentation. But as soon as I am king, I will give her equal power. We will share the rule."

She nodded mutely, her eyes overflowing. Nyfain turned to leave, but she stopped us before we reached the doorway.

"I heard it was you, Finley, who revitalized the garden."

Nyfain turned slightly so I could see her. "I mostly just organized it. A few of the others did the hard labor."

"I let her pick a garden to regrow," Nyfain added. "Any garden. She chose that one."

"Thank you. It is beautiful."

Nyfain closed the door softly behind us. When we were only a few steps away, a ragged sob broke free from behind it. Arleth was letting herself give into her emotion.

"It is good of you to start on the road to forgiveness," I whispered, leaning my head on his shoulder.

"There is nothing to forgive. I just..." He stopped talking as he made his way down the hallway, moving past staff who bowed or curtsied as we passed. A few of them smiled and tilted their heads, reacting to the sight of him carrying me. If nothing else, no one could question how we felt for each other. How ardently we loved. That, in itself, was a change from the past.

He made it to our rooms, finding Urien and Leala

working quietly to put away clothes and set everything to rights.

"That'll be all," Nyfain said, turning toward the bed-chamber.

When they'd gone, he set me down softly before looking deeply into my eyes. He traced my jaw with his fingertips before putting pressure beneath it, tilting my head up a bit so he could lean down and slide his lips across mine.

"Thank you for being there tonight," he said. "Thank you for standing by me. For never refusing to back down to my rage. I need it. The kingdom needs it. I like knowing that you'd poison my breakfast if I ever get out of hand." His lips curled up into a smile, but I could hear the seriousness in his tone. "I like knowing you'd never allow me to turn into the man who raised me. If I should ever turn into the thing I loathe, I know you'll never allow me to treat you the way my—what I thought of as my father treated my mother. You'll ensure I don't continue the cycle, and that gives me comfort. I will never hurt you, little dragon, and if I try, I expect death."

"That is oddly romantic," I whispered. His lips merged with mine and swallowed my chuckle, his slow and languid kiss sending shivers racing across my flesh. "I would never poison your breakfast, though," I murmured against his lips as he pulled the straps of my dress off my shoulders. The fabric cascaded down my body.

He leaned back just enough for his gaze to take me in. He glided his hands down my sides, his fingertips barely skimming my flesh. Goosebumps erupted across my skin as he reached the band of lace around my hips, tracing it.

"No?" he asked softly.

"No. I'd poison your late afternoon tea, or your dinner, depending on how quickly the poison worked. That way you'd die in your sleep of what the doctors would hopefully assume were natural causes."

His fingers skimmed my outer thighs now, his mouth next to mine, breathing the same air.

"I love that about you—you're so smart and vicious."

He moved his fingers back up, gliding them over the tops of my thighs and then my pelvic bones, avoiding all the places that were suddenly aching for his hard and fervent touch. They danced across my stomach and along my ribs, curving to sweep up the sides of my breasts, annoyingly avoiding my nipples.

"I've been nervous to take my place as king," he admitted, which surprised me, because I hadn't read that through the bond. "Nervous that I'll end up like the king before me, and the king before him. That I will only be there because of titles and bloodlines."

I wanted to scoff but didn't, instead closing my eyes as his fingertips lingered over his claiming marks before moving upward.

"How about now?" It came out a breathy whisper.

"Now?" His lips glanced off mine. He pulled away before I could deepen the kiss.

His light touch moved over my shoulders and down my back, avoiding my scales.

"Now I am excited. The throne is not technically mine for the taking anymore. It is not a duty to bear. Instead…"

His fingers flowed over my butt cheeks, heading to the backs of my thighs.

"It is a position to fight for. It is a challenge to rise to. I will welcome challenges from anyone who feels they can strip me of the throne. And I will crush them all."

Power rang through his words. It slithered across my skin and hardened my nipples. I groaned from the delicious feeling of it.

"I liked fucking your ass last night," he said darkly, his lips on my neck, his palms spreading across my ribs. "What would you have me fuck tonight?"

His filthy mouth made me shiver. "I want you to fuck me with your tongue."

He growled softly, his hands disappearing from me for a moment so he could quickly strip out of his jacket and what lay beneath it.

"Look at me," he commanded. "Look at the monster who occupies your bed."

Soft candlelight glinted off his robust frame, ink and scars and muscle winding together in perfect, battle-worn harmony. His golden eyes glinted in his beautiful face, his scars not detracting from his appearance. Adding to it, if anything, showing the dangerous edge he wielded like a sword.

Gazes locked, I slowly reached for him. His pec flinched when my palm touched it. My other hand went for his pants.

"You are only a monster to my enemies," I said quietly as his pants dropped to the ground. "You are a guardian to me."

I pushed down his underwear, salivating when his

cock sprang free. I gripped it in my hand as I moved closer, sliding my other palm up his rippled stomach and back to his pec.

"Or did you mean this monster?" I gave his cock a tug.

He slid his hands up, running his thumbs over my nipples, then bent and took one in his mouth in a move that sent sparks of pleasure through me.

Pulling back, he said, "Bend over the bed so I can tongue-fuck that pussy."

He hadn't taken off my garter or the knife stitched in there. I turned toward the bed, and he pushed me down, one hand pressing to the center of my back while the other traced that knife before running up over a cheek. He kicked my ankles with his feet, spreading me wide, before pinning my arms with the hand on my back. The digits of his other hand traced down my crack to my soaking pussy.

"I love how wet you get for me, baby," he groaned, pushing two fingers into me and pumping for a moment, curving toward my front just right, on the pleasurable side of rough. I whimpered from the sudden onslaught, clenching around him and jerking my hips, my body already wound up from the teasing. A sudden jolt of pleasure had me panting and moaning, trying to push back against his fingers. My body neared the edge, ready to break apart, but he stopped, pulling free.

"No," I begged, moving my ass, tilting up my cunt for him.

"You said tongue, not fingers, princess," he said. "My dragon insists on me worshiping you." He fell to his knees. "I'm happy to comply."

He freed my hands so he could grip the sides of my thighs and push them farther apart. His deliciously hot, wet tongue flicked across my clit before moving through my slippery folds, so wet they were dripping. His groan of pleasure preceded his tongue delving in deep, as deeply as it could go, before he backed off and sucked down to my clit and then back. He started doing as I'd asked him, moving his tongue in and out of my pussy while running his knuckles along the outsides of my clit, teasing me again.

"Fuck, I love the taste of you," he growled.

I shoved back into his face, but he pushed with the hand that still held me, forcing me to endure this torture. He continued until I was so turned on, so frustrated, so desperate, that I just kept saying his name, over and over.

With a dark chuckle that licked down my body, he straightened and crawled onto the bed beside me.

I looked at him wild-eyed as he lay down, smirking.

He reached out for my hand before dragging me closer, throwing my knee over his stomach and making me scramble over to straddle him, not at all where I needed everything placed.

"Do you want to fuck the face of your golden prince, little dragon?" He applied pressure to the backs of my thighs. "Put that pretty little pussy over my lips and take what pleasure is yours."

I was over him in an instant, knees on either side of his head. His tongue attacked me, swirling across my clit as his fingers delved into my cunt. He covered my clit with his mouth, sucking twice, bringing me to the edge again, only to steer me down with his hand.

"Come all over my tongue before I make you come around my cock," he said.

I tilted my head back in ecstasy at his words, on fire, desperate to hit the peak again and again.

I sat on his mouth, feeling his tongue delve in deep before he pushed one of his hands in behind it. He moaned, pushing me away so that he could dip those fingers into my cunt before spreading the slickness back. He returned to my pussy with his hot mouth, devouring it, as his other hand did lazy circles around the outer ring between my cheeks. I waited a moment, gyrating, building, and then grabbed his other hand and directed it to my clit. As he got into position, I slid my hands up over my breasts and grabbed my nipples, rolling them between my fingers. I wanted to see what it was like when absolutely all my points of interest were covered.

The finger at the back shallowly thrust in, his tongue delved, and he grabbed my clit between his knuckles, *hard.* Sensation was everywhere, hitting me all at once.

I screamed with the release, blasting apart at the seams, shaking and shuddering over him, wringing out every last ounce of pleasure before sagging to the side. I didn't want to suffocate the guy.

He rolled me easily, pushing aside the covers and pausing to finally remove my blade and garter belt. He straightened me on the bed and slipped between my spread thighs, guiding his cock into me.

"The first thrust always feels like coming home," he said against my lips softly, seating himself fully.

He opened my lips with his, stroking his tongue

through and letting me taste myself on his lips. I wrapped my arms around his neck and legs around his hips, holding him tightly.

"I didn't mention it before," he murmured, the movement of his hips measured and powerful. I groaned from the wonderful friction. "When I was talking about you killing me."

"Hmm?" I said with a smile.

"I love you." His pace picked up, and he kissed me again, tilting his head to bring the kiss deeper, fucking my mouth with his tongue. His pace matched that of his cock.

"In a life created of nightmares," he murmured, "you have become my paradise."

I held on to him tightly as our bodies moved together, as he drove into me, his cock filling me, his tongue wrestling with mine. I swung up into him, ground against him, panted into his kiss. Lights danced behind my closed eyes as I relished his body. His touch. Our intimacy.

"Come with me," he commanded, and my orgasm exploded through me. I cried out, calling his name. He shuddered, filling me with his release, clutching tightly.

He breathed heavily, stilling, and then kissed me languidly while my legs were still wrapped around him.

"Take a small break, princess," he said, kissing along my cheek to my ear. "I'm not going to give you much reprieve tonight. I have a need for your body, and I'm going to take my fill."

PART TWO

CHAPTER 13
ARLETH

T HE NEXT DAY, my heart in my throat, I walked
through a castle I'd hoped never to set foot in again.
It was larger than I remembered. Grander. Many things
were scratched or needed replacing, and there was a
worrying amount of glitter, but overall it was much the
same as I remembered it. It felt different, though. People
were laxer now. *Much* laxer. They were looser with their
smiles and shallower in their bows, not quite sure how to
do their jobs but trying their best all the same.

The most important change, however, was that no
one lived in fear. Not of the king or his court. Sure, they
quailed when Nyfain was in a temper, but they didn't
think he'd randomly hurt them. Or kill them. They
trusted in him. Were willing to put their lives on the line
for him.

They respected him.

My heart swelled as I walked down the hall toward
one of the rear doors.

I'd always known he'd make a magnificent king if

given the opportunity to do things his way. The late king never would've given that to him. He would've tried to corrupt Nyfain into his way of thinking. Now, without that obstacle, my son could spread his wings.

A pang hit my heart at the thought of wings, and I teared up before I could blink away the moisture.

When I first saw his dragon, I'd had to choke back a sob. Then, seeing his human body, covered in scars that attested to years of pain and turmoil, had sliced off a piece of my heart. I'd done that to him. My negligence in not getting word to him quickly had allowed that insane king to trap him here. The demon king had obviously tried to kill him, and any lesser dragon would've succumbed long ago.

Anger kindled in my belly. I had to own that I was not born a fighter. Unlike other dragons, I'd never reveled in rage. But seeing the torment that had been visited upon my son made my blood burn until all I could think about was the destruction of the demon king.

We'd get our vengeance. I might not be an asset in the actual battle, but I had a talent for finding the weaknesses in a royal court. I'd had to develop that skill to shield Nyfain from harm. Finley wasn't the only survivor in this family—she'd just had to deal with a different kind of hardship.

With my help, she would learn to hide her dagger behind her beautiful smile. To dazzle and delight while exploiting the weaknesses of our enemies. She'd become the best queen this kingdom had ever known.

"Hello, my darling."

I slowed upon hearing that voice as the strange man who used to be the butler and was now apparently Finley's advisor stepped out from a room and fell in at my side.

He smiled at me with straight white teeth below an odd little mustache. His coat, a vibrant spectacle, was closed in front with two buttons embedded in the bright pink...velvet? His...what could only be described as slippers, nearly matched his lapels, the pink a shade darker with faux-gold buttons.

I vaguely recognized him from my tenure as queen, but I couldn't place him. I was sure the servants would know, but I'd been keeping a low profile around the castle so as not to make my presence any harder for my son and his mate.

"Hello," I said cordially, if a bit frostily. My old training on the "proper" way to address those of lesser status was hard to unravel.

"I hear you're joining the team. Fantastic!" He motioned me forward. "I have to say, I was a little worried. We all were, weren't we? But this is great. Finley is absolute crap at a formal dinner. Like...literally the shits. I tried to help, but I only know the basics. You're going to be a lifesaver when she has to meet other royals. She'll need to show well to get their support..." He put a hand on my arm as we neared the rear door, slowing me. "Assuming the demon king doesn't blow through sooner than expected and kill us all, right?"

He laughed as though he'd made a grand joke, and I suddenly didn't know what to say. Or how to act. Or...where to look. He was at once disarming, confusing, and completely unexpected. I barely managed a closed-mouth smile, probably blinking too heavily within his easy profanity.

"I just wanted to introduce myself," he went on, his gaze drifting down my front. "I'm Hadriel, the princess's advisor and confidant, and you are wearing the wrong outfit, love. We can't have you wearing that if she is to steal everyone's focus. You look too...ordinary."

My eyebrows drifted upward. I'd never been spoken to this informally in this castle. Ever.

"You know who I am, right?" I asked, suddenly unsure and even more confused because of it.

He laughed again. "Obviously I do. Who are you kidding? I am practically shitting myself with giddiness right now. But..." He tilted his head down a little. "In my job, I have to put my *best moments ever* aside so that Finley is taken care of. And you do not have the right look, lamb. We can't have the former queen running around in pants and ordinary clothes. It'll make you seem like you're trying to be *one of the people* instead of royal, and that'll make her look a little out of place, since she is somewhere in between. The woman is an odd duck. It's why I love her, but it is a little challenging to create an image for her because she fits in no standard boxes. Not a single one. We're calling her unique instead of weird, but...she is weird. Always has been. Now"—he held up a finger—"you *can* wear pants, but they have to be a finer version of pants, get me? You can fit with Finley, or you can be stuffier and fancier than Finley, but you can't just..."

He quirked an eyebrow and ran his finger through

the air in front of me. Then he smiled, slowly reached out, and lightly touched my shoulder. Before I knew it, I was being ushered back to my room, into my dressing quarters, and Finley's lady's maid was providing me with something "a little more suitable" that had been recently created for me without my knowledge. It didn't even occur to me to tell them no. What they dressed me in was not even remotely my style, but I allowed it all the same and eventually found myself outside, blinking at the door Hadriel had just closed behind me with a smile and a wink.

When I walked into the everlass house, I realized I had a dazed smile on my face.

Dee looked up from a collection of assorted herbs and frowned, taking in my outfit.

"Did you lose a bet?" she asked.

"I think so," I responded, my smile growing as I looked back the way I'd come. "Finley's advisor is…"

"Odd."

"Yes."

"Crass."

"Definitely yes."

"Strangely likable."

I laughed. "Yes! His strangeness is…"

"Disarming."

I shook my head and walked in farther. "Yes, it is."

"He used to be the stable hand. All the dragons used to pick on him, but they'd protect him against other shifter bullies."

The memories came rushing back, helping me place him—he hadn't had that silly mustache back then, and smears of dirt had usually marred his complexion.

"I thought he looked familiar." I looked over the various items within the work area. Finley must've been here this morning. Everything was moved from where it had been yesterday afternoon when Dee and I snuck back to see what she was up to. We hadn't dared confront her again. She could be as wild as Nyfain when she was in a mood. "I never understood that—they bullied him, but forbade anyone else from bullying him."

"They didn't bully so much as…retaliate, I think. From what I gather, he had a smart mouth that always got him into trouble."

"I can see that. Yet they clearly liked him enough to keep him in their bubble of protection."

She pointed at a mixture floating in murky water. "Look at this. She's cold-seeping the everlass. It is starting to release its components. She's added other herbs to the mixture, all raw except for sprinkles of…coriander, I think, which seems to have been…roasted—there's a stray bit here—and then ground. She sprinkled it on top. It doesn't seem like she has stirred it in."

"Cold-seeping everlass." I shook my head, meeting Dee there and then looking over the various ingredients she had gathered. "Have you ever heard of such a thing?"

"No. I've also never heard anyone else claim it matters *when* everlass is harvested, or that cedar is better, or that the type of water used with it alters the potency but only with certain elixirs… The list goes on."

Dee shook her head, continuing to look over the various elixirs that had been started and a couple that had been moved off to the side, clearly abandoned.

"We're not helping as we ought," she finally said. "A *child* is showing us up, Arleth. We've been too complacent. We need to start using our brains and show her that we are just as competent as she is."

I laughed as I gathered the materials we'd need. We were creating a stock of the elixirs and draughts for Nyfain and the kingdom. These had always fetched the highest prices in trade. When he opened communication and commerce with the other kingdoms and traveling merchants, he'd have something to sell.

"And we need to teach her to fly," Dee said as she braced her hands on her hips and looked at the books still splayed open under a protective sheet at the back of the worktable. Finley seemed to value books very highly. I wondered if Nyfain had showed her the secret section of the library. I hadn't noticed anything out of place in there, though order had never ruled in there. "Do you see how she lands? She is utterly reckless. She'll kill herself, and then where will this kingdom be? Your son will go mad with grief."

"He would," I murmured. Nyfain had found true love. His true mate. It was clear to all who saw them together that they were made for each other. It was as sweet as it was inspiring. It almost made me want to start looking again. Maybe find someone who suited me so I could fully experience love again without the fear that a jealous king would kill us both if he found out.

I took a deep breath. "And she needs to teach us how she works with will. We can all do it to some degree, but I should have enough power to use it the way she does.

She's weaponized it…"

"If you'd had that ability, the king might not have been so liberal with his fists," Dee muttered.

We got to work. Dee sang softly, and I occasionally harmonized as we went through the familiar steps.

It took me a while to gather myself, but finally I said, "He came to check on me this morning." My eyes filled with moisture that I blinked away. Dee looked up. "Like he always used to, remember? He passed a moment with me in the garden."

A warm smile pulled at her lips. "He has forgiven you."

A tear overflowed. I couldn't help it. "Yes, I think so."

"And Finley? I couldn't quite understand you through your slurring last night."

Dee had helped me get back to my room through the secret passages so no one would see their former queen blind drunk. It was a path we'd traveled many times in the past. My old life had been full of stress and ugly emotions. Sometimes I'd needed a night of overindulgence. Other times, it had been fun to drink a few glasses and have a singsong.

Last night, though, I'd cried so hard I threw up. Despite what I'd gone through with the king, the last sixteen years had been the hardest of my life. I'd been separated from my son. Unaware of whether he was alive or dead, of whether he was suffering…

A chasm had opened up in my chest, a hollow that was a constant presence while I waited for…something, *anything* to change.

And then, when he was freed, and he doubted me—

I wiped away another tear as more welled up.

I'd lived in agony these past few days, compounded by the sixteen years I'd spent wondering and worrying. When he'd been gracious enough to allow me to stay, to resume my life with him...

It was still hard to get around the emotion. I'd missed him more than a person would miss air. He was my son, my little boy—to lose him was to lose a large piece of myself, and knowing I was the one who'd caused it...

"You need to find a way out of the darkness, Arly," Dee said softly, coming over to wrap her arms around me. "He's safe, as much as he can be. He's free. You're free. The mad king can't hurt him now, and the demon king should not try if he knows what's good for him. It's time to find peace."

I nodded, using the back of my hand to cover my nose and mouth as I tried to master my emotions. She was right. That time had passed. I needed to learn to live with my guilt so I didn't miss any more of my son's life. So I could enjoy seeing him mated and happy.

Swallowing, I answered Dee's question. "Finley doesn't seem to care whether I like her. Or whether you do. She was quick to forgive, it seemed like. I've never met anyone like her."

"How do you know she was quick to forgive?"

"She advertises her every thought on her face and body. We have to work on that. She should only show her rage, and that should seem to come out of nowhere. That will have the greatest impact on the other royals."

I'd been keeping a close eye on the movements of the other kingdoms and their courts, hoping to hear news of my son. I had informants everywhere, people I paid a small amount to write me news. They weren't people Nyfain could really make use of, mostly servants or groundspeople, but they'd relayed plenty of news and gossip. Now, I could help Finley learn intimate details about their courts before she even met them.

"We've always known she doesn't care what people think of her," Dee said.

"Yes, but I'm the mother of her mate. The former queen. I would've thought…"

Dee laughed. "You should've known better." She paused for a moment. "You shouldn't have spoken about his real father in front of servants."

"I know. You said that last night."

"I wasn't sure you'd remember. It might've gravely undermined him."

"Well, he has my support now, and no one is powerful enough to challenge him. Not at present."

"Unless they band together…"

"Under whose leadership?"

Dee was quiet for a moment. "Make peace with Micah. He might not like that you've suddenly aligned yourself with Nyfain. He might worry Nyfain isn't the dragon he seems. Explain yourself to him. Put yourself at his mercy if you have to."

I huffed. I would never allow myself to be at the mercy of any man ever again.

"Manipulate him, I mean," Dee said. "Make him *think* you're at his mercy. Appeal to his ego."

"I knew what you meant."

"He is Nyfain's greatest threat, I think. He is strong enough to lead a revolt, and everyone knows he wants Finley."

I gave a small smirk. "Finley has the true mate mark. One mark and another can lay a claim over it, but two? She'll be Nyfain's forever. Besides, he wouldn't be able to handle Finley. She'd turn him inside out. You should've heard what she said about poisoning the late king."

"I did. You told me three times last night."

I grimaced. I didn't remember that.

"Anyway," she said, "you know better than anyone that alpha males don't always have sense. He might not want to back down. Finley's a beautiful and fierce alpha. Any male of standing would kill to have her, for her offspring if nothing else. You need to douse those coals so that they don't ignite."

There was truth in what she said. I wanted to clear the way for my son as much as possible, and Micah would be an easy obstacle to push to the side.

"I heard you're here to stay," my cousin Gunduin said with a smile as he stopped in the open door and leaned against the frame.

"You're late to the gossip," Dee said, not looking up.

"No, I just spent my morning helping Hannon fix a villager's wall before it collapsed." He pushed off and wandered in a little farther, looking over everything. "Listen…" He slipped his hands into his pockets. "I was thinking about going back…"

Dee and I slowed in our work, both of us looking at him for a long beat.

"I need to get my things," he continued. "And try to convince more people from the villages to come back here with me. A couple of us are going."

My heart quickened as excitement rolled through me. I shared a quick look with Dee.

"You meant to give us a scare," she said, narrowing her eyes at him.

He laughed again. "Yes, I did. I'm glad you two are staying. It makes my decision simple. There is nothing for me back home. Here we'll get to actually be part of a kingdom. A kingdom where we're appreciated. I really like Hannon, too. I think you should join him on the advisory circle he's forming, Arleth. He's aiming to make it a fair representation of all who live here, and I think your knowledge of the kingdom could greatly help."

I shook my head. "He is welcome to speak with me, but I will not take an authoritative position in this kingdom. I had my chance to affect change, and I failed."

"But—"

I held up my hand. "No. My word will carry more weight, I know it will, and that is not fair or helpful. I will aid Finley in her role, advise my son if he needs it, and help with the management of goods and gold. That is it."

"That is plenty," Dee told me, picking up the larger dried everlass leaves.

"Well…should you change your mind…" Gunduin let it linger.

"No," I said.

He lifted his eyebrows. "Well, anyway, almost all of the dragons who came with us plan to stay. Most of them plan to go home at some point to make arrangements for the move. When they do, I have every belief they'll try to convince others to join us. It's inevitable that some will, and I think they'll like what they find."

"It might be hard for them to get used to people telling them what to do," I said. "The dragons from the villages are used to holding their own council."

"He's a great natural alpha, Arly." He leaned in a little to try to catch my eye. "That's what they'll respond to, and word got around about Finley before we left. People saw the way she flew, courageous and crazy, and then she handed Micah his hat in that final meeting with the elders. They'll want to visit to see how she leads, and when they get there, they'll fall under the couple's spell. I think many will come, and most will stay."

"We shall see," I said.

"We shall hope," Dee said. "We need the bodies. We're sparse on people here, and even sparser on warriors."

CHAPTER 14
FINLEY

"**D**O WE HAVE to have a formal dinner, though?" I asked quietly as my spirited mare pranced beside Nyfain's grumpy stallion.

I ducked to avoid a low branch scraping across my mostly coiffed hair that Leala had done up earlier. We'd been visiting villages for the last few hours, showing our faces, greeting people, and answering their questions.

"Weston is a powerful alpha," Nyfain responded, humor coloring the bond. The sinking sun painted his handsome face in a soft glow, easing the severity of his sharp cheekbones and smoothing out his scars. "We've asked him to dinner to discuss his role in this kingdom and the length of time he plans to stay. He'll expect that dinner to be formal. I've heard a suit was made for him. We all have to play our parts."

He was playing his. He wore his golden livery collar over his shoulders, something he hadn't worn to dinner last night because he hadn't wanted people to notice that I didn't have one. That was before word got out that he wasn't the true heir. Hadriel had reported a great many people talking about it. Nyfain wore it now to remind people he'd be taking that title regardless of his bloodline.

I did not envy the idiot who chose to fuck with him, not when his dragon was eager for the challenge. Or the fool who decided to mess with me, for that matter. I wouldn't get a chance to defend myself. Nyfain's dragon had made it abundantly clear that he would rip the face off anyone who threatened his mate. My dragon purred every time it even partially came up.

Still, neither she nor I were purring now as we crossed the threshold into the last village on our list. Mine.

Hannon, who now had the very official-sounding title of head advisor, followed behind us. Although he hadn't asked for his role any more than I had asked for mine, he was giving it everything he had, checking out each applicant for the advisory circle thoroughly and nominating a few of his own applicants based on those he met.

Hadriel kept pace beside him, and Tamara and a few others from my guard followed, along with a couple of other dragons from the old court, like Xavier. They were supposed to be our formal procession.

We were a parade of dragons through mostly non-dragon villages. Something I'd pointed out softly to Nyfain before we left.

He'd nodded, squinting a little as he watched them mounting their horses.

"We'll fix it," he'd replied. It sounded like he had

some kind of plan, or maybe that was wishful thinking.

Eyes turned our way as we rode the horses at a walk down the lane, faces I'd known forever going a little slack upon seeing the prince and all his (modest) finery. When they shifted their gaze to me, it was as though they'd never met me. Their eyes sparkled with excitement. That was, until I saw a couple of Jedrek's close friends loitering outside of the village pub.

"Why are they glowering at you?" Nyfain asked.

"They were Jedrek's friends," I replied, looking away, only to lay eyes on my ex-boyfriend, standing with his wife, looking at me with wide eyes. Smugness weaseled into me before I quickly looked somewhere else. I wasn't sure how Nyfain would take a past romantic interest. I hadn't been great at hearing about his, and I was nowhere near as possessive as he.

Kinda.

Nyfain still hadn't heard the full account of my stay in the dungeon—we both knew he wouldn't take it well, and he wanted to wait until he could do something about it—but he'd correctly surmised that Jedrek hadn't made it out.

He slowed his horse's walk a little, his anger curling through the bond.

"It's fine," I said, wanting to reach out and put my hand on his shoulder. I didn't dare, though. I was liable to lean too far and fall off. "I can't really blame them."

"They will not show disrespect to my mate and their princess," he said as a wolf's song drifted out of the wood behind us. Another rose up, a warning weaving through the melody.

"We've got trouble," Hadriel said, pulling his leg from over his horse and jumping off. "We're being attacked. I feel it through the bond."

"So soon?" Hannon asked, jumping down from his horse as well. He might've done better to stay on, since he still couldn't shift, but he didn't have much experience on horseback, let alone while fighting.

Nyfain's boots hit the ground, and Urien trotted his horse up quickly before meeting him there, taking his clothes and jewelry as he quickly shed them.

"He must know striking soon and hard would be to his advantage," Nyfain said as my feet hit the ground. "He can't afford to let us get our feet under us, or for me to officially assume the crown and have to report to the council too soon. It's a good play."

"It's a fucking attack," I said as Leala hastened up with her whip held snugly in its holster at her side. She reached for my clothes.

"Get to the other villages," Nyfain told me as I stripped out of my pants. "Get everyone to defend their homes. Once you're done, find me." He gripped my shoulders for a moment, staring into my eyes. "Stay safe. Protect yourself. Do not take any risks. You hold my heart. Keep it safe."

"Yes, yes, I got it."

He kissed me hard. "I love you. Find me."

With that, he was running, yelling commands at the other dragons as he went. All but two of my guard ran after him, shedding clothes. When Nyfain had the space, he shifted into his large, magnificent dragon. Gold peeked out around the tarnished scales, glittering in the late-evening sun the way it had in the past.

"Let's go," I said to Tamara and Jade, who would be accompanying me.

"If I shift, I'll join the wolves," Hadriel yelled at me, out of his clothes and looking for the go-ahead.

I gave him a nod, knowing what that meant. His wolf would suck him into Weston's pack, and he would no longer take commands from me. In this situation, it would be the best place for him. I couldn't get hung up on it when we needed the hands. Or paws, in this case.

"I'll help defend our village," Hannon told me. "I need to get some weapons from the house anyway."

"You need to start carrying those," I told him before I started running.

Tamara and Jade fell in with me as dragons up ahead took to the sky, keeping pace with my ground-bound golden prince. Villagers, catching on to what was happening, ran every which way, securing things in their homes, closing doors, or shifting into their animals. Hannon walked through them calmly as if he hadn't a care in the world. As though danger didn't faze him and walking into a battle was an everyday occurrence.

When we had some space, I took a running leap and shifted.

You...dickhead, my dragon thought with a grunt, surging up and taking over. Her feet scraped against the ground, pitching her forward as she snapped out her wings and took to the air.

Payback, asshole.

You'll look just as stupid if I fall on my face.

It never seemed to stop you.

I didn't wait for the others, who fully stopped to shift. There would be no demons in the sky to bother me. Tamara and Jade could catch up.

My village was already active, so we hurried to the next. Through the trees, I could just make out the shapes of demons running through the darkening wood. They were all headed in one direction: toward Nyfain.

My insides ran cold.

Somehow they knew where to find him. The demon king was making a play to take down his biggest threat. If he brought down Nyfain, he'd bring down the kingdom.

Hurry, I thought. *We have to get to him.*

I know. But we have to warn everyone, too. We need more help.

My dragon circled the next village, roaring out her warning. Like she had when we first came back, she threaded in a call to rise up in defense of our homes. The people below slowed, looked up, and watched us for a moment as though transfixed. My dragon roared again, shocking them into action.

The villagers scrambled, some stripping down and shifting into their animals immediately, others running for their houses.

On the second circle, Tamara and Jade caught up, fanning out behind me. I didn't stand on ceremony—which I didn't actually know anyway—and took off for the next village, quickly outstripping them. My dragon was faster by far, probably owing to the larger wingspan.

Fear riding us hard, we roared out our warning as we approached the next village. And the next, flying by the castle as people ran out of the doors. I saw Micah hurriedly strip and shift before taking to the sky, Vemar joining him. They joined me as I flew.

Wherever I looked there were more demons, all running in the same direction.

How do they even know where he is? I asked as Vemar's dragon dipped. Fire belched from his mouth and scoured the ground, washing over the demons and burning across two struggling trees. Flame stuck to the trees, crawling up the trunks, quickly burning out, since there was no fuel in dead things. The demons kept running, unaffected.

Shit, I thought. *They must have some sort of magic spell protecting them from fire.*

It looks like they're coming from all angles. They seem to have a homing beacon on Nyfain.

My dragon swooped down. Her belly scraped across the tops of trees until a clearing gave her space. She landed too fast, snapped in her wings, and slid across four demons who quickly painted her underside red. She barreled into a tree, unfortunately took it out with her sliding body, and sprang to her feet as she turned. Her tail whipped around, smashing into three demons and sending two wolves scattering.

Watch, folks, I thought, *as the big, dumb dragon takes out the wrong people.*

Fuck's sake, not that stupid invisible audience again. I thought we'd gotten over that.

Desperate times, as they say.

She launched back into the sky as the other dragons circled overhead, probably all wondering, *What the fuck?*

In the next clearing, she landed behind another

group of demons and trampled them with her feet. Then she was up again, flying over the next village in a race to get to Nyfain. Young dragons were already popping into the sky. The wolves of the villages must've felt Weston's warning through their pack bond and spread the word. That was handy.

One of the young dragons veered out of control and crashed. Like us, they needed training. They needed direction. We'd have to put that on the never-ending list of things to do.

Now to Nyfain, I thought, having a hard time not being in control when his safety was on the line.

I felt his rage burning hot but also a shock of pain. She soared over the wood, this time a little slower to make sure all the other dragons could keep up. More demons streamed through the trees, all of them intent on getting to Nyfain.

My own rage pumped higher with each pump of my wings. This would not happen again. Dolion's reign on this kingdom was done; I would make sure of it. We'd been plagued with him and his kind for long enough.

Adrenaline and power filling us, she spotted Nyfain ahead. He was in a clearing of his own making, having knocked down smaller trees and trampled bushes and brambles to open up the area around him. His dragons flew low, dipping and snatching demons off the ground before chomping them and throwing their lifeless bodies. Their fire didn't work on the demons, though, even with multiple streams from many dragons that had the trees burning down below. Without it, they were at a disadvantage in the air. Dolion had prepared for this.

That was when I saw the wolves.

Weston stood at Nyfain's side, ducking and dodging around Nyfain's swinging tail or swiping claws to maul anyone who dashed close enough. His wolves fanned out around him, taking down five demons to every swooping dragon's one kill. This was a ground battle, and in order to beat this horde, wings were ineffectual.

Get down there, I thought-shouted, but my dragon was already on it, not even slowing as she dove to the ground. She hit the earth and slid, crushing a crowd of demons under her scales.

I should've brought weapons, I thought, used to fighting with my body when on the ground.

I got plenty.

She swung her tail, taking out three demons while bending to snatch up another in her jaws. Wolves quickly came to our sides, ducking in and around us as we clawed one group and stomped through another, their claws raking our sides but doing little damage.

A slash made her flinch, though, searing pain cutting into her leg.

She turned, catching a demon with a sword held high, ready for another slash. Dark red blood leaked down her leg, just above the ankle.

A mighty roar from Nyfain's dragon trembled the earth, infused with blistering rage and incredible power. He tromped the short distance to get to us.

Just kick the thing, I told her as the demon swung.

A wolf lunged from behind, chomping into its neck and then ripping its great head to the side. Blood splattered, but I didn't have any time to congratulate him on the kill. There was a cluster of demons right behind the first, sacrificing the sword wielder so they could go for the wolf.

Nyfain's dragon stepped in and swung, his tail taking out four demons and barely missing the wolf and us. His aim and control were absolutely incredible after so many years spent fighting on the ground.

I can't let that big sonuvabitch show me up, my dragon thought.

Same team!

It might be the same team, but I want to be the most valuable player.

Watch, folks, I thought miserably, *as the big, dumb dragon goes beyond her abilities and gets us killed.*

I got this, she thought back, and it really seemed like she believed it. Dipshit.

She raced beyond Nyfain to where several demons were closing in on Weston. There were too many, and Weston's wolves were too few to protect him. My dragon roared even as she bore down on the enemy, summoning our people to help. To land and fight with teeth, claws, and tails rather than take missing shots from the air.

She went after the demons like a wild thing, not nearly as graceful or controlled as Nyfain but making up for her deficits with a viciousness that made demons and wolves alike pause for a moment, staring in shock or horror. She took the hesitation to her advantage, ripping into them savagely and huffing and snorting for the wolves to fall in.

Tamara and Jade landed not far away, with Lucille and a couple of others following suit. They echoed our roars before awkwardly fighting anything in their path. Their size—all of our sizes—worked against us, only Nyfain able to turn and stomp and bite seemingly all at the same time to catch the much smaller bodies darting in and scratching and cleaving. But the wolves quickly fell into a rhythm with us, letting the dragons scatter the enemy and kill what we could and seamlessly taking out the rest.

A mighty roar beat down on us from above, and then another, before Micah and his dragons touched down. Trees cracked; branches fell like rain. Fire coated the ground, not burning the demons but blinding them, suffocating them. Our teeth and claws ended them. Wolves from the villages came in next, not as practiced as Weston's wolves but following his unspoken commands all the same. They stayed to the outside by Micah's dragons, finishing off what the dragons started. And then other creatures came, big cats and one honey badger so insane it had three demons give up the fight and start running blindly.

Creatures wailed, and I couldn't tell if the cries were coming from our side or the enemy's but didn't stop to check. I could cure our people when this was done. When the demons were gone.

Nyfain let out a frustrated roar, and I belatedly saw what the problem was.

No, not what. *Who.*

There he is, my dragon thought, taking a shallow sword strike to the chest as she followed Nyfain's dragon through the melee. *Dolion!*

Not letting the pain register, she knocked aside two

demons as she burst between a couple of burning trees. The fire didn't bother our scales, but Weston hung back and tried to work his way around it. A wall of demons blocked him, trying to crowd us in, and he darted back toward us. My dragon, realizing what he meant to do, slowed and veered, scraping first one tree with her side and then the other, snuffing out the fire around us. She widened her legs and slowed more, allowing him to dart under her and run out the other side. Four more wolves did the same maneuver before she followed them, watching them span out around Nyfain again.

Nyfain crashed through the demons with the wolves at his side, their attacks perfectly synchronized, Weston allowing him to take the lead. Emotion grabbed hold of me. It was a fucking beautiful sight.

This is no time to get sappy, my dragon said as she again rushed into the fray.

I can do what I want. I don't have fuck all to do but sit here and watch you flailing around like a gobshite.

How about you get mad, Miss Useless? I'm getting tired. I don't have as much stamina as that big fucker. I need power.

There was going to be one helluva battle for dominance between true mates when this was all over. I doubted either dragon liked to be shown up, even by the other. Idiots.

I can hear your thoughts, asshole, my dragon thought as she came up behind the others. Weston pushed to the side to make room, the wolves reconfiguring to put Nyfain and me at the front.

Well, maybe try to work with *him instead of outdoing*

him.

I can't. He keeps trying to protect me and cut me out of the action.

Yeah, I should've expected that. He wouldn't want us getting hurt. How annoying.

See? my dragon thought as she caught sight of Dolion again, back behind the line of his demons, staring at Nyfain with frustration and hate etched into his features. *But guess what? I'm not ground-bound.*

She fell back and then snapped out her wings, quickly taking to the sky.

I hate that motherfucking demon, she thought as power pumped through her, her sights locked on Dolion.

Nyfain roared his frustration behind us. He couldn't keep my dragon from taking this risk. I wasn't about to help him.

If you can't get him in this form, shift, I thought, searching those around him for a weapon I'd be comfortable using. *I can handle him on two feet.*

She thought-grunted her acknowledgement as she dove, going for the old *smoosh* approach. I braced for the impact, right near the surface, wanting to see him smeared across the ground. But right before she reached him, he looked up in surprise and popped out of sight.

Fuck, she thought as she twisted her head back and snapped at the place he'd just been. Her teeth raked across something before she slammed into the ground and rolled over a few bodies that couldn't get out of the way in time.

He teleported. Get him! I hollered.

I got a piece of him, she said, quickly righting herself.

It's not teleporting—it's some sort of invisible transferring of his body.

Yes. Teleporting.

Ignoring me, she climbed to her feet and did a quick spin, wiping her tail in a circle to give us a little room. The more powerful demons we hadn't killed teleported immediately, avoiding her strike, but the expendable grunts swarmed in with no wolves to help us and no other dragons to give us aid.

She stomped and bit, trying to clear enough space so she could snap out her wings and take to the sky. There were too many, though, some with swords at the ready. If she exposed the fragile membranes of her wings, they could easily slash through them.

Run out of here, I thought, feeling our heart quicken. *Hurry! Crush them beneath your feet.*

A sword slashed her hind leg. Then another, as Dolion appeared about twenty feet away. His right thigh glistened with blood, his pants ripped away to reveal a bloody tear. My dragon had just barely gotten him.

Found you. With grit and determination, she ignored the sword strikes coming at us faster now, and pushed through them. Swinging her tail and stomping, she tried to get out, to get enough room to stretch her wings.

Micah and Vemar soared above us. Micah dove to Dolion, spitting fire, but Vemar circled back toward me, stopping just above us.

Why doesn't he land and help? my dragon thought, taking more blows, one cutting deep. *Fuck, this is dire. Suggestions?*

I was a master at getting myself out of terrible situations, since I found myself in them so often, but it was hard to get my brain working in another body.

Spin in a tight, fast circle three times. Keep your tail low. Get everyone. As you finish the last spin, snap out your wings and jump. You might be dizzy, but pump your wings anyway. If we can just get above them, we can fly in circles for all I care.

You're a fucking genius.

I lost sight of Micah dipping toward Dolion, moving much too slowly—he'd never get the demon king like that—as my dragon started to spin. Her tail whipped out, crushing through demons. On the end of the third spin, she snapped out her wings and pumped them quickly. Our gaze didn't settle. The world spun around us. But up we went, our feet leaving the ground.

Before we could get far, though, white-hot agony seared across our lower side as something stabbed into her belly.

She roared and thrashed, veering to the side because of the dizziness and now the muscles in the right side of her belly screaming in pain and going lax. She crashed down.

A bloody long sword lay not far away—the object that had been stuck in our side. It must've been thrown. That was the only explanation for why it hadn't gone in deeper.

Unfortunately, it had gone in deeply enough.

The pain throbbed deeply. Blood gushed out of the wound, and her mind went woozy.

He got me in a soft spot, she thought, pushing back at the pain. It wasn't easy, though, and given how experienced we were with being tortured, that meant very bad things.

Vemar roared, a call for aid, and Micah rose higher into the sky to look back.

No! I wanted to yell out. *Don't let him get away! Ignore us.*

Except I knew he wouldn't be able to get Dolion, not with slow swoops and bites. Not when Dolion could blink in and out like that.

Vemar landed next to us, and Tamara was there a moment later, taking my other side.

About fucking time, my dragon thought sourly.

Most valuable player, huh? I replied, knowing we couldn't shift back to human form, that she had to get us out of this mess or we'd be killed for sure.

Pain slashed across our ankle and more stuck us in the rear haunch area, a dragon's version of a butt cheek.

You have to get up, I told her, pulling power from Nyfain. He needed it, I knew, but we needed it more. *You have to get out of here! We need Hannon to patch us up.*

Vemar and Tamara fought by my side, keeping the largest force of demons off us. Lucille and Jade landed a moment later, one in front and one in back, surrounding us.

This is embarrassing, my dragon thought, forcing herself to struggle up. Blood pooled on the ground below us.

A great, thunderous roar quaked the earth, full of rage and fire and power.

Damn it—

She cut off as Nyfain reached us, the wolves quickly filling in the gaps between the other dragons and forcing space around us. He stood over us, Dolion clearly forgotten, the demon grunts of no consequence to him.

His size and intensity bore down on top of us. He growled, the sound rumbling deep in his chest.

What does he want? I asked as his power rose through us, diminishing some of the pain.

He wants us to shift. He wants to take us out of here.

She straightened herself, and I knew she was willing our body to stitch itself back together more quickly.

Nyfain growled again. He cuffed our neck with his teeth, a direct command. *Shift.* The pull of his power washed over us. Weakened by blood loss, we weren't powerful enough to resist.

She yanked me up to take over as she got out of the way.

Our body reduced quickly until I wobbled where I stood, my bare feet sinking into the blood-soaked dirt.

Don't you fall, she said.

My knees shook and my vision swam. Pain throbbed through me, and I looked down at a large gash in my side, streaming blood.

"Fuck, you idiot, that's bad," I said.

It's not like you didn't feel it that whole time. How is this my fault?

I'd find a way to blame her.

Nyfain's dragon bent with his mouth open, his teeth coming around us, gently pinching my skin, before he lifted back up. His tongue pushed against our back, trying to make us more comfortable on his teeth. He did a few grunts and a soft growl, the vibration slithering pleasantly across my flesh. The other dragons and wolves cleared the way, and then he was running back toward the castle.

"It's her fault," I said, because I knew his fear that something had happened to me would turn to anger that I'd put myself in harm's way.

Ass, my dragon thought, but didn't push back. She liked when his dragon raged.

Tamara and Lucille kept pace with us in the air, probably ready to swoop down at a moment's notice. But what few demons had remained outside of the main fight were running now, sprinting and yelling with wolves hot on their heels. They were lower in power, the kind that wouldn't fight without their master forcing the issue.

Nyfain made it to the castle steps, and then I was falling.

CHAPTER 15
FINLEY

H E CAUGHT ME, as I knew he would, but I wasn't prepared for the shock of pain as I landed in his arms.

"How bad?" he asked, stalling on the steps. "Goddess help me, Finley, you're bleeding too heavily. *Fuck*."

I pressed my hand to my side as he started jogging, holding me tightly against him.

"I'm okay," I said, and it was almost certainly true. I was sure I'd been worse than this a time or two. "Get me to the everlass house or shed or whatever your mom calls it and send someone for Hannon. He can patch this up. It'll be fine. You need to go back to the battle."

He cut through the castle quickly instead of going around. "There's no need for me to go back to the battle."

"Make sure the demons don't scatter and plague the villages. The villages aren't equipped to handle them."

A woman's voice came from the side of us. "Sire, is the princess hurt?"

I didn't bother opening my eyes to see who'd said it. If she couldn't answer her own question by noticing the blood dribbling over his arm and onto the ground, then I didn't have high hopes for her brainpower.

"Find the head advisor, quickly!" he barked. "Find Hannon. Tell him to get to the everlass house. The princess needs him urgently."

"What about Dolion?" I let my head rest against his large shoulder. "My dragon nipped him as he was teleporting. Maybe Micah was able to follow him and eventually grab him."

"Dolion was running like a coward by the time I got to you. A dragon nip is no small thing. He couldn't put weight on that leg. Even still, Micah was too slow to get him. Dolion's demons were leaving, though. You ended the battle, sweetheart." His tone was probably meant to be soft because I was hurt, but he missed the mark. I heard the anger coloring his words.

I grimaced because he was sure to fly into a spectacular rage once I made it through this.

Nyfain reached the back door of the castle and paused, kicking out. The door busted from the hinges and fell away to the side. He continued on as though that hadn't been a bit extreme.

"He came here with one purpose," Nyfain said, jogging again. "To kill me. He didn't expect to nearly get killed by my mate, his former prisoner."

This time, the pride in his tone was clear.

Spectacular rage followed by incredible sex was definitely in my future.

"It helped greatly that you pushed the dragons to

fight on the ground." His voice was a soft rumble now.

A wave of dizziness swept over me. That would be the blood loss. I needed to patch that thing up, and quick.

"The question is," I said, a tiny bit slurred, "why didn't *you* push them to do that? Their efforts from the air were mostly ineffectual."

He didn't answer for a moment; we were nearly to the shed.

"Because dragons aren't used to fighting on the ground," he finally replied. "They aren't trained for it. I didn't want to force them to abandon their flight."

I pulled away somewhat so I could look into his golden eyes. What he wasn't saying was louder than what he was.

"You have to stop that shit," I told him firmly.

His brow furrowed.

"You have to stop feeling sorry for yourself and assuming you are bringing everyone down," I continued. "Flight can have a great many advantages, like moving from point A to point B quickly to reach your target—"

"We'll talk about what you did later," he growled.

I swallowed as he reached the everlass shed but ignored his comment.

"But Dolion somehow protected his people from fire, which is the other main strength a dragon has going for it in the air. And then there were the trees and the number of enemies surrounding you and the wolves…"

He set me down gently on the workstation, looking around with wide eyes.

"It's fine—this place is controlled chaos. I know

where everything is." I grimaced as I struggled to get down. He set me on my feet but kept his hand firmly pressed against my wound. "Yeah, good call. Keep pressure on that. I don't think I have any bandages in here."

"Here." Nyfain took down bandages from a high shelf in the corner.

I braced my hands on the tabletop to keep from falling as I made my way around, knowing Arleth and Delaney had been working on healing elixirs and draughts to trade. It would get my healing started while I mixed up something stronger, and then a salve for Hannon's patchwork. I just had to stay ahead of the damage and give my body time to heal.

"You should've seen yourself, Nyfain," I mumbled as I found one of their draughts. I unscrewed the top and drank it down. It was supposed to be diluted with water, but the stronger the better.

"Ugh," I said as I breathed out what felt like fumes. "That tastes rough. They need to fix that."

I took some dried everlass, the kind I knew would work, dumped it into a stone bowl, and motioned Nyfain toward the pot in the corner. "Water. Heated. I need a rolling boil. Half a bucket is enough. I don't need much, and less water means faster heating."

"What about the bandages?" he asked.

"Bandages are a patch. This elixir is a cure. I need that water going."

"Sure, yeah." Nyfain dashed over to the pot and was quickly out the door, doing my bidding. His mother had trained him well.

I chose the herbs I needed, shaking now, this remedy one I'd used for years. It was fast, efficient, and didn't require much work. Perfect for when I came home half-dead, something I'd done a few times before.

"You were amazing," I said as he jogged back in, set the pot in place, and got working on the fire. The coals were still hot, never really cooling down with us always in and out, so it would be a quick job to get it going. "You worked—"

Dizziness overcame me and my knees gave out, pitching me against the table and down. I clutched on lest I fell and couldn't get back up—force of habit. I sucked in breath, willing that first draught to start working quickly, willing myself to hang on until this next one was done.

"Goddess help me, Finley—" Nyfain was there in an instant, hoisting me back up.

"It's fine. This is nothing. Work on that fire!" I said, sucking in air. Just needed a little oxygen and I'd be ready to go.

"What have we got?" Hannon jogged in, assessing me quickly. I was thankful he didn't grimace, because that would've set Nyfain off, but I could tell he wanted to. This was definitely an occasion for his grimace.

"I nearly got Dolion, and then his demons nearly got me," I replied.

I finished putting in the herbs as Hannon pulled a chair from the corner and set it behind me.

"Here, you don't need to stand for that," he said as he pushed my elbow out of the way and had a look. "What do you need me to do if you lose consciousness?"

He peeled off his shirt, dirty and sweaty but not bloody, before turning it inside out and readying to pull it around me.

"Here." Nyfain grabbed the bandages that Hannon had obviously overlooked in the state of chaos and handed them over. "She said she wanted water first—I'm not used to having healing...draughts at my disposal. I didn't know which was best to do first."

"Not a problem. This is perfect," Hannon replied, taking the bandages so Nyfain could go back to the fire. "Thank you."

"I won't pass out, I'm good. Don't scare Nyfain." I took a seat. "Sorry about my bare butt on the wood."

"Of all the things you worry about," Nyfain mumbled, straightening from the fire. "How bad is she?"

"She'll pull through," Hannon said, and while that was almost certainly going to be the case, I was glad he didn't elaborate.

"How'd it go with you?" I asked, my vision swimming again, my body cold. I had lost a lot of blood, but at least the pain had dulled. The everlass was starting to work.

I went back to grinding the herbs. Or had I even started?

"Here, let me—"

"No, no." Hannon put out his hand to stop Nyfain. "She needs something to do. Let her work those plants. It'll keep her conscious longer."

Fear and anxiety seeped through the bond even though Nyfain's face was now flat and emotionless. With Hannon in the room, he didn't want to show his emotions.

I rolled my eyes and then swayed. I grabbed myself before I could go too far, feeling Nyfain's hand on me, holding me steady.

"I love you," I said, because I was about to tell him off, "but you need to go check on the battle. Even if Dolion took off, you need to make sure everyone is okay. You have a broader responsibility than just me. You're the prince and future king. You need to put them before me."

He flicked my hair out of the way and put his soft, comforting touch against my upper back.

I fluttered my eyes closed but continued to grind, knowing the movement really would help keep me awake. Sleep, in these situations, was the enemy. If you slept, you had a chance of never waking up.

"There are two incredibly powerful and competent alphas on that battlefield," he said. "I left Weston in charge of the ground, and Micah will handle anyone in the air. As I said, the battle was disbanding, thanks to you diving headfirst into Dolion and managing to somehow bite him, so the rest will just be cleanup. I am sure they can handle it without me. If anything, they'll want to know you're taken care of. They all saw what happened. They will have recognized that my princess has more courage than any battle-hardened warrior."

"I mean...not to brag, but I kind of am a battled-hardened warrior. You don't hunt wild boar and stay naïve."

"She's not lying," Hannon said, wrapping me up. "She got a couple bad scrapes like this from them, actually."

"I got those kills, though."

"Victory at a cost," he replied, something he'd often said when patching me up in the past.

I repeated the words I always answered with: "The cost is worth it for our loved ones."

"Yes, it is," he replied.

Nyfain stepped over to the water, looking down into the pot, probably willing it to go faster. His muscles flared, and his whole body looked tense with worry.

"Shouldn't she be lying down?" he asked Hannon.

Hannon glanced at me, moving quickly but not hurrying. He stepped around Nyfain, taking something from the shelves and carrying it over to the table. He was making a poultice, no doubt.

"No, I don't think so. She typically does better when she's sitting through it. If she lies down, she'll surely pass out, and then I won't be able to get the elixir into her fast enough. She knows how to get through a near-fatal wound."

I probably should've told him not to elaborate.

"It's fine," I said. Searing agony rolled through me. "It'll be fine."

"I can feel that you are lying," Nyfain replied.

"She's not lying to you, she's lying to herself," Hannon said, very unhelpfully. "I suggest you let her. It seems to help."

"Very chatty all of a sudden, aren't you, Hannon?" I said. "Very chatty."

Nyfain's worry increased. His power pumped through me, helping.

His dragon is freaking the fuck out, my dragon thought. *We must look bad.*

If only he'd seen me after a torture session. He has no idea what we can handle. Don't worry about it.

"It was mostly quiet where I was," Hannon told me conversationally as he peeled away the already bloody bandages before applying his poultice that would hopefully close the wound a little quicker. "Demons were either trying to run around the village or through it. With help from some of the villagers, we were able to quickly disband them."

"You got here fast." I leaned an elbow on the table and propped my face onto my fist, angling to look at him. "Nyfain didn't even tell them where to find you."

"I was already on my way." He stepped closer and peered at my work. "Is that how you want it?"

He was just trying to distract me, I knew. I glanced into the mortar anyway, but the image swam before my eyes. I closed them as Hannon continued.

"The villages weren't under threat, it seemed like. I came here to see if anyone needed help. A couple of the house staff found me as I came out of the wood."

"Lucky, lucky." I took a deep breath and then went back to the pestle, grinding it against stone. This recipe was hardy. It could take me grinding it a little too much. Or too little. "The villages were quiet because Dolion was making a play for Nyfain. There was an entire horde there, trying to surround him and box him in."

I fluttered my eyes open to see Hannon peering across me at Nyfain. He was looking to see if Nyfain had taken any damage, not like it would matter. With me hurt, no way would Nyfain let Hannon spare his attention for anyone else.

"And it apparently didn't work, I see." Hannon went back to his workstation as I slowly turned to look at the water. A wave of dizziness swept across me, and the next thing I knew, I was pressed against Nyfain's chest, cradled in his arms.

He kicked the chair a little with his foot, turning it, and sat down with me on his lap. He turned me sideways before leaning me more thoroughly against him.

"Stay like that," he commanded, his power rolling over me and his deep voice rumbling through his chest. Shivers coated my flesh. "Stay upright. Keep your eyes open. Hannon, go outside and tell Tamara to find my mother. Tell her I need help in here."

"It's fine, seriously—"

"If you tell me it is fine one more time," he ground out, his tone savage, "I will make you regret it. Now sit there quietly while I finish grinding this. Or talk if you need to, but stop saying ridiculous things."

Apparently I didn't look fine.

"It's—" I just barely stopped myself from saying it was fine.

In a moment, Hannon came back in.

"If that water is at a rolling boil, go ahead and take out a large cup's worth," I told him.

"A large cup?" Hannon peered in the pot. "How much time?"

That had to mean it wasn't ready yet. He was asking how much time until I passed out.

I blew out a breath. It wouldn't be long now. My

whole world was starting to float. Next would be spinning. Then passing out. This wasn't the first time I'd lost
a lot of blood. The problem was, we usually had hot
water on standby. We'd had to with Father on the verge
of death.

"We should always have water going here the way we
did at home, Hannon, remember?" My eyelids were
heavy. I fluttered them against the encroaching darkness.

"Okay," I said, and jerked, my whole body suddenly
tensing. Had I fallen asleep? Nyfain's hand spread across
my back. "Okay, Nyfain, grind that until it is almost a
powder. The second the water is ready, get that cup and
pour in the contents. Let it sit for—"

"I know how long," Hannon cut in. "Fight it. Stay
awake. You've lost a lot of blood. You'll need to fight the
desire to sleep."

"Yeah, yeah, I know."

"What annoys you?" he asked, resorting to our old
standby: making me mildly angry to keep me awake.

The wheels in my head started to turn. There were
always so many things that annoyed me. Not as many
now, though. But still...

"Why doesn't Tamara get called a great alpha?" I
said, clawing to consciousness, holding on to Nyfain to
stay upright. Or maybe he was holding me. I couldn't
feel my body at this point. The everlass draught had
effectively numbed me, which was great for dulling the
pain, but I was at a point that I needed pain to keep me
going. I needed to feel something. "Why didn't she get to
stay behind and lead a group of people? She's experienced in it."

"She didn't stay behind because she is supposed to guard you," Nyfain replied. "*Supposed to* being the operative words. You were left wide open."

"I'm not an easy one to anticipate. That's not her fault."

"It is her *duty* to anticipate you. It is her entire job—to anticipate and protect. You are inexperienced in battle, your dragon is inexperienced in all things, and you have no fear. You are a fucking nightmare on a battlefield, Finley. For me. I need to keep alive a woman who does not seem to want to stay alive herself."

Rage was pulsing through the bond, seeping into his words. I fell into it, letting the power consume me, wondering how much longer until that water started boiling.

"You have that wrong, sire," Hannon said as he crossed behind us to the pot. "She absolutely wants to stay alive. Train her how and then stand back. That's all you need to do."

"That's all I need to do, is it, Hannon?"

I grabbed Nyfain's shoulder, trying to struggle up. "Don't take that tone with—"

"It's fine, Finley," Hannon said as he lifted the pot off the fire and set it aside. "It's his fear talking. He can let out his rage. My animal is not afraid of it. He says it is a natural part of life."

Arleth strode in, dirty, nude and with blood spattered through her wild hair. She had a shallow gash already healing across her stomach. Shock and fear rolled over her expression before she turned entirely stoic.

"I heard she was stabbed," Arleth said. She walked straight to her store of draughts and elixirs. "What happened?"

"She went after Dolion," Nyfain said, his tone flat. "His demons had a great sword, and they knew where to use it."

"I know those details. I meant why were they able to get a sword that close to her in the first place?"

"I was too far away to help. I couldn't get to her to stop it."

"Where was her guard?" She pulled free a little canister and unscrewed the top before shooting a blazing look at Nyfain. "Why was she in the heat of battle? Her dragon might as well be an infant with what little she knows. She can barely get up off the ground. She definitely doesn't know how to get out of the air properly. I heard she tried to dive straight into him. She could've killed herself!"

"She was crash-landing at him to squish him," I said, my voice wispy, leaning my cheek against Nyfain's neck. "Mmm, your skin feels good. Cool. If you land just right, it works."

"She's burning up," Nyfain said.

"It's nearly ready," Hannon, the only one not riled up, replied. "It just needs to cool a little, and I'll mix in her ingredients."

"I'm—" I gritted my teeth to keep from saying I was fine. "Just get me that elixir and I'll be fine, seriously." I wilted over Nyfain's shoulder now, very little strength left. My mouth felt like I had a cloth in it. "I've been this bad before."

"Once, yes," Hannon said, "and that was without her animal to help. I just need this water ready and...well, what's a little throat burn, eh, Finley?"

"My throat will heal," I slurred, draped around Nyfain, so, *so* sleepy. "Probably don't have much longer."

"Here. Have her breathe in this," Arleth said, bending behind Nyfain to put a canister close to my face.

"Whoops." Hannon put a hand to her arm and moved her to the side. "Sorry, ma'am, but I don't know what that is, and she is getting close to unconsciousness. I'm surprised it hasn't happened already. It must be her mate riling her up. Let's just stick with what works, shall we?"

Thunderclouds crossed her face. "Did you just push the former queen of Wyvern, young man?"

Hannon ignored her, pulling the mortar close, removing the pestle, and dumping the contents into the mug.

"There is some debate as to your position, ma'am," Hannon said, mixing the ingredients with his finger. "I beg your pardon, but I'd do it regardless. The prince cares more about his mate than your outrage. I figure I'm safe enough."

He bent to me, his hand on my forehead.

"Here we go, Finley. This is going to hurt. It's only a burn, though. The elixir will help heal it as it heals you. I know you remember the last time. Get it in you, and then you can go to sleep. I'll stitch you up."

I knew better than to try to grab the mug. I knew better than to worry about the pain it would cause going down. When his eyes looked like that, we were in a dire situation.

"Crashing into him would've been so much more effective than the current outcome," I grumbled.

"You wounded him, sweetheart," Nyfain said softly. "That's more than I'm sure he expected. We'll get him in the end. He's just going to force us to do it politically. He probably thinks I'm all brawn and no brain. Won't he have a shock when we show up at the council?"

"When *you* show up," I said, babbling now. "I will crash-land into that just the same as I did on the battlefield."

"Not at all, dear," Arleth told me in a kind voice, so different than when she was speaking to Nyfain earlier. "We'll start training as soon as you are well. Nyfain will have his warrior queen, but she won't have to crash into anything."

"Hold her head, Nyfain," Hannon instructed, forgetting to use his title.

Nyfain didn't hesitate, angling me so Hannon could nurse me more efficiently.

"I'd rather be the one under his care," Nyfain murmured. "It means you would be spared this pain, baby."

Arleth picked up the pestle and smelled it. She scanned the ingredients I'd used, her brow pinching. She had no idea what this elixir was.

It was going to blow her mind, I knew it.

Hopefully after it saved me.

CHAPTER 16
FINLEY

S LEEP RECEDED SLOWLY, pulled back from my mind like a blanket. Softness enveloped me, supporting my body and my head, lying heavily over me. I breathed in slowly, savoring the sweet, floral scent of the air.

Blinking my eyes open, I saw an arrangement of roses on the little table beside my bed, the crimson petals glistening with beads of water. At the base was a note, my name written in a familiar, eloquent scrawl.

I smiled but knew better than to reach for Nyfain's letter with a greedy snatch. Something would undoubtedly hurt if I did that. Instead, I slowly pushed back the covers and fingered the soft cloth draping over my body. Someone had cleaned me up and dressed me.

"Good morning, my darling."

Hadriel sat in a chair across the room, his pink-clad ankle resting on a black-clad knee. A simple black jacket covered his torso, the lapels velvet but matching the rest.

"No penis jacket this time?" I asked, feeling down my wounded side and finding bandages under my slip.

"No, thankfully. I coaxed the seamstress into making something decent for me. I told her it would be our little secret, and I wouldn't tell one joke or speak hardly at all. I think she did a fabulous job. The problem is, all the fucking dragons have decided they should pick on me whenever I wear normal clothes. It's like we've stepped back in time. Except it's not even the same dragons! It's new dragons—the visiting ones. The whole situation is utterly ridiculous. Why me, you know? What did I do?"

"Talk a bunch of shit to the wrong people?"

"Okay, yes, I did do that. But honestly, Finley, darling, you have to believe me. It's like they purposely say stupid shit so I can't help but poke fun at them. You should hear what they come out with. One actually asked another if his new pants made his dick look bigger!"

I couldn't help grinning. "And what did you say?"

"I told him the truth—the pants made it look big enough to distract from what came out of his mouth."

My smile widened, and I started to chuckle. "Was that it?"

He smoothed one side of his mustache. "Well, I *may* have also pointed out there was such a thing as *too* big, and he was never gonna get any offers for blow jobs or anal wearing those pants."

I laughed harder.

"The problem is," he went on in a huff, "I say these things to people who don't have the ability to trade witty responses, and then I end up in a compost pile or some other unsavory place."

I laughed harder, doubling over, not feeling the slightest tinge of ache. "You do keep life interesting."

"Apparently," he said, picking up a book from the table at his side and opening to the bookmark.

"How long have I been out?" I looked out the sunny window, seeing blue sky peek out from a few puffy white clouds.

"Just the rest of last night and this morning. How do you feel?" He lowered his book again.

I pushed the bedcovers back more and pulled up my slip and then the bandage. The wound was stitched together with black string, with Hannon's telltale straight lines and even threading. The puffy pink skin spoke of healing, and the gash was much smaller than it had been yesterday.

"Great. Record fast healing time."

You're welcome, my dragon said.

Your crashing got us in trouble. I wouldn't say you're welcome *just yet.*

I'm blaming that on you.

I leaned over and captured the note at last, running my finger across a burgundy seal pressed with what had to be the royal crest.

"He's getting fancy." I slipped my finger under it and broke the wax.

"He hunted around until he found that color. It's close to your scales."

My ~~impossibly stubborn mate~~ dearest Finley,

I realize a letter isn't strictly necessary, since I am close at hand—I'm in the castle or on the grounds looking after things—but I worried that if you didn't hear this from me, you'd ignore it. I am hoping you don't ignore it anyway.

Please don't ignore it anyway.

You lost a lot of blood yesterday after doing something incredibly ~~courageous~~ stupid, and while you might feel good or *fine*, you need some rest. You can heal faster than most, but you do still need time to recuperate.

There is nothing pressing that you need to see to today. All of your appointments have been pushed back. In fact, after you wake up and feel up to it, I will push back mine as well. You gave me a scare yesterday, and I would like to take some time to revel in your touch and your scent.

To add weight to my request, Hannon has advised that you don't do any physical exertion. I'm reasonably confident he meant flying or learning the sword, both things my mother is now hellbent on teaching you. I am decently sure he didn't mean sex, but just in case, I'll do all the work, I promise.

Leala will supply you with a leisure dress, what women used to wear around the castle. It's casual wear. ~~Undergarments not required.~~ <— that should've been an underline and not a strikethrough...

Stay to the rooms and rest, if you'd like. Hadriel should be on hand to fetch you a book if you need it. Or I can meet you in the library, or the study. Wherever you wish to go <u>within the castle</u>, I will meet you there. They'll get word to me so I know where to find you.

I love you, my courageous little dragon.

Best,
Your ~~once~~ handsome mate

P.S. That last strikethrough was a joke. Kinda.

P.P.S. Don't mind the random bouts of rage you'll undoubtedly feel through the bond. I will not direct it at you. Yet. My dragon will instead wait until he can have at your dragon. He has some issues to work out, he says. I'm sure you can anticipate his reaction to ~~the close call~~ your normal state of affairs in a dangerous setting.

I shivered with desire before reading the note again, laughing through it a second time.

"Find his note funny, do you?" Hadriel asked before turning a page. "He must not be expressing himself to you as he has been expressing himself to the castle all morning."

"He's mad at me." I tucked his note under my pillow so Leala would know I wanted to save it. I needed to find a place to put them.

I swung my legs over the edge of the bed and checked in with my body again. Nothing. No aches. No pain. A slight pulling with the stitches, but that was normal.

"He's mad at the whole fucking castle, love. He is not impressed that the princess of this kingdom, his *mate*, was badly injured. You should've been fighting with people. Instead, you attacked on your own and, as I understand it, were buried in demons. My giddy goddess, *Vemar* was the one who roared for aid! It should've been someone from your guard. Or from the kingdom, at least. We need some serious training in this kingdom, that much is painfully obvious. And dragons need to learn to fight on the ground. If not for Weston and your chomping on the demon king's leg, we would've been fucked. And then *you* got fucked, and here we are. The prince has lost his mind, and we're all afraid to breathe."

I ran my fingers through my hair. "I'll talk him down. I'm just not used to fighting alongside people. I've always been on my own. When I see a chance, I take it. Since it was Dolion, I went for it. And yes, this did happen in a battle, where the stakes *seem* to be higher, but honestly, this sort of thing has happened throughout my life. I mean, talk to me about wild boar!"

"Why?" He cocked his head at me. "What the fuck do wild boar have to do with the princess being in mortal danger?"

"Because I've been in mortal danger from wild boar a few times in my life, and one of those assholes almost killed me once. But guess what?"

"Well, I hope you learned to stop messing with those asshole wild boar—"

"No, I got better. Wiser. And the next time, I took one down. And the next time after that, I didn't get hurt when I took one down. I do stupid shit, yes, and that battle was admittedly on a larger scale than normal, but I've learned from it. Or I will…when I can process it."

Hadriel ran his hand down his face, mussing his mustache. "Slap my ass and call me Winky, what is my life right now?"

"It's exciting, Hadriel. Welcome to an exciting life. Now, where's this leisure dress I'm supposed to wear?"

Before I could even see it, Leala bustled in with some breakfast. After I ate, she insisted we wash and re-dress my wounds before she took over dressing me. Hadriel stuck around, getting yelled at for nibbling off my plate and reading his book while Leala got me ready. Once done, she set to changing the bedsheets as though I had the plague and she didn't want anyone else catching it.

"She was worried about you," Hadriel said, patting my forearm as we walked down the stairs.

The *anything but leisure* dress, a slinky, silky affair that draped down my neckline and swooped down my back, dragged on the floor with a small train behind me as we made our way down the hall.

"You looked like absolute death, love. You were incredibly pale, and your lips were kinda blue, and by the time I saw you again, you were unconscious in the master's arms. I must say, even I had a fright. I would prefer not to see you like that again. I have a formal request in to see the wolf alpha. I'm going to ask him to reject me today so I can be done with his pack. It'll mean I can't shift until he's gone, but I have a lockdown on this shaggy bastard." He pointed at his chest. "I'll be good, I promise. I'll learn to fight on two legs if I have to. I'm capable of it, just like you."

My heart swelled, and I put my hand on his shoulder, stopping for a moment and facing him. "I don't want to jeopardize your future, Hadriel. I know what a pack would mean to you. There must be some other way this can work."

"I fit in here, with you. I mean, yes, we both stick out like sore thumbs, but at least we're doing it together. Besides, I'll be a queen's advisor. That is *something*! I'll have clothes and go to nice parties and participate in all the things I watched from a distance all those years ago. Sign me up!"

I chuckled softly and kept walking. Although I had a destination in mind, I didn't mention it to him, knowing he wouldn't approve.

"Whatever you decide," I said, "aim for happiness over *stuff*. Dresses and parties aren't fun when you're lonely."

"Don't leave me, and I won't be lonely."

"Hello, Strange Lady." Vemar pushed off the wall down the way, and I couldn't help but stagger to a stop. A smile stretched across his face, showing off newly whitened teeth that stood out against his dark brown skin. His deep-set brown eyes glittered, and he tucked one of his large hands in the pocket of his...extremely colorful jacket.

"What..." It was all I could get out.

His smile growing, if that were possible, he ran a hand down the yellow velvet of his lapel, setting off some of the yellow in the jacket's busy design. Fitted black pants draped from his trim hips, though they couldn't completely mask his powerfully robust thighs. Yellow velvet—or something like it—dress shoes and a blue pocket square "completed" the ensemble.

"What..." I said again.

"Surprise," Hadriel said drolly, grabbing my arm to get me walking again. "The prince placed him as your temporary bodyguard until you are elevated to queen. By then, it is the hope that your normal guard will be properly trained. They seem to forget who they should be protecting as soon as the prince is in their midst. So, since he correctly realizes you'll stop at nothing to get into danger, he's going to work with them. You'll all learn together eventually, but until you know how to properly fly, Arleth and Dee will be handling you."

"And in the meantime"—Vemar spread his arms—"I am dressing the part. Look…" He drew closer and pointed to a little yellow dick within the pattern. "There are thirty-seven of them on my person, and I am asking all the pretty little wolves I meet to try to find them all. For each hint I have to give, we must both lose a piece of clothing."

"Let me guess…" Hadriel said, his tone flat. "Thirty-six in the jacket and one that isn't so hidden after the hints are handed out?"

Vemar braced his hands on his hips and winked. "Very smart, Mr. Butler. How did you know?"

Hadriel huffed. "You think you're the first guy to trick people into looking for your junk? Trust me, 'find the sausage' is a well-known game around these parts. If you want more takers, ask the house staff. They will be more than grateful for something new to stick in their mouths. And it is now Mr. *Advisor*."

Vemar threw back his head and guffawed, shaking with laughter.

"You know that working with me doesn't require ridiculous clothing, right?" I asked as we continued on, me leading and them not paying attention.

"This isn't ridiculous." Vemar smoothed down his

jacket.

"It is absolutely ridiculous, yes. I tend to wear that clothing *because* it is ridiculous," Hadriel replied. "It disarms people. You aren't going to disarm anyone. They'll probably be *more* worried seeing you walking around looking like that. It basically screams *unhinged.* What's next? Are you going to grow a mustache and try to pass yourself off as my twin?"

"If you like."

"Please don't." Hadriel groaned. "I get picked on enough."

Vemar looked over, power pulsing around him, suddenly incredibly intense. My small hairs rose.

"Who is picking on you?" he growled.

Hadriel shivered before waving it away. "Don't you worry about it. I don't need you swinging your dick around, making me look like a fool. I'm fine."

We reached the back door, and suddenly both guys stopped dead.

"Where are we going, lamb?" Hadriel asked as I pushed open the door.

Vemar quickly ran around me, hands out, blocking my way. "I'm sorry, Strange Lady, but you aren't supposed to be outside. Prince's orders. Turn back, now."

"I'm just walking. There is absolutely no exertion involved." I hit him with my will, knocking him out of the way.

"You have a lot to learn," Hadriel muttered to him. "My love, listen to me. The prince wants you resting and relaxing. Not for you as much as for him, do you understand? You scared the life out of the poor guy. Give him a break. Just stay in today, let him coddle you, and then tomorrow, when he forgets to command you to stay indoors, you can do whatever you please. Then it won't be my fault."

"He won't even know," I replied. "Just a quick stop and back in I'll go. I have to do a quick thing with the everlass or it'll be ruined. Seriously, it'll take no time at all."

"Strange Lady, please." Vemar caught up to me, now on my other side. "This is my first day. I don't want to disappoint the prince on my first day. I'm going to live here now. I need a job."

"Oh, that's great!" I said as we walked across the grass.

"Yes. I see a great future here. We're going to try to convince more dragons to join us. But in order for me to succeed, I need to be on the prince's good side."

"You will, Vemar, I promise. He won't even know."

I neared the everlass shed and gazed out at the plants, seeing Delaney within the rows, roaming and stroking her hands against the leaves. She was likely pruning.

Inside, Arleth sat at the back corner of the worktable, clearly making sure not to disturb my setup. Except there was one new collection of leaves drying with the rest.

"What is this?" I asked, stopping next to it.

She looked up at me with hard eyes before her gaze zipped to the corner, where my brother sat with a notebook. Hannon set it down and came over to me.

"Leisure dresses are meant to stay in the castle," Arleth said, going back to her work.

I pointed at the leaves as Hannon frowned at my dress.

"Leisure dresses aren't great for checking wounds," he said, reaching down to grab the hem.

"Oh—whoa. Wait!" I grimaced at him. "I didn't realize you'd be here. I...didn't exactly wear underwear."

He dropped the fabric like he'd been burned.

"You saw her without clothes yesterday," Arleth said. "Every time she shifts and gets in a tiff in the castle, she wanders around without clothes. What's the difference?"

There was the woman I'd known as Ami, free of any royal pretenses. I was happy for her return.

"Seeing her after shifting is less jolting," Hannon said. "Lifting up her dress to find out she's not wearing any underwear would be a mindfuck."

Arleth popped out a hip and stared at him for a moment. "My goodness, Hannon. Blushing at your age?" She motioned at Hadriel and Vemar, who'd stalled at the door. "One of you help Hannon. She should be examined"—I got a severe look—"before she goes back into the castle."

"All due respect, but I'm not about to lift the dress of the alpha's mate, for whatever reason. I value my life. I think I'll be the lookout." Vemar backed away, pushing past Hadriel to get out the door.

Hadriel straightened himself up. "Well. If I must get yelled at, then these are good pants to do it in. They'll hide the stains..."

"Oh, for heaven's sake." Arleth dropped the herb she was trimming and came around the corner of the table. "Hadriel, get out," she barked. "Make some use of yourself and that dragon and fill the pots near the waterspout. Bring them inside to boil when you're done, and then ask Dee if she needs help. If you are going to be hanging around, you *will* make some use of yourself."

"Yes, ma'am," Hadriel said with wide eyes, and quickly scooted away. Now there were probably two people who would make him soil himself.

Arleth reached me and unceremoniously grabbed the straps on my shoulders.

"Get ready to cover your nipples," she murmured, dragging the fabric down to my waist.

I did as instructed, feeling incredibly awkward. Thankfully, that seemed to be enough for Hannon. When he saw the bandages, he immediately relaxed and pushed my elbow out of the way.

"How's the throat?" he asked, peeling away the side of the bandage.

I flinched as it pulled at my skin. "Fine. No aches or pains. Healing is so much quicker now that I have access to my dragon."

He nodded and replaced the bandage. "Did you look after this already?"

"Leala did."

He nodded again, stepping back. "It'll be fine. Take it easy today and mind yourself tomorrow. You know what you can handle, but the prince does not. Keep him in mind as you recover. I have some time before I meet with the next applicant for the advisory circle, so I'll help the others...make myself useful."

"Your calming presence is always useful, Hannon, if you'd like to sit." Arleth motioned to the chair in the corner.

Hannon studied her for a moment. "If you'd like."

CHAPTER 17
HANNON

I KNEW EXACTLY what the queen wanted—for me to monitor Finley until Nyfain showed up to claim her. The queen's worry curled through the air, sinking deep, where my animal gathered it up. The queen thought Finley was wild, rash. She just didn't know my sister.

Finley took great risks, it was true, but that was always for a cause bigger than herself. She would battle a wild boar because her family was starving and needed the meat. She'd trade herself to the demon king because it was the only way to save the people she loved. And she would take the opportunity to crush Dolion on the battlefield because it would end his threat to her people.

And yet Finley had an ironclad will to survive and the instincts to see her through danger. She also knew when to lean on the people she trusted. Before Nyfain, I'd always been there to patch her up and share the duties of caregiver to our family. Now, she had me *and* a big, strong alpha dragon who would set the world on fire to ensure she stayed safe.

I turned my back on my sister as they fit her elegant dress back in place and then took my seat in the corner. It was a place I was trying to grow accustomed to, just as Finley was trying to grow accustomed to her new role. We weren't facing the same dangers as before, or the same demands. With Dad healthy enough to reassume his role as father and caretaker, living in the castle and protected, he didn't need us to take on those roles for him anymore.

My sister and I had both lost the life we'd been forced to adopt, and in so doing, lost our purpose.

She'd found a new one, though. I hadn't. Not completely. I was trying to put my time and effort into this new advisory circle, but I wasn't taking to it as much as Nyfain had hoped. My animal wasn't embracing the challenge the way he'd savored the task of looking after my family and old village.

I sat down again and picked up my notebook. The time had almost come to make my final selections for the advisory circle. I wasn't sure what happened after that. Hopefully something that took more of my time.

"What is this?" my sister asked again, pointing at a batch of everlass leaves.

"That is an addition to your experiment," Arleth replied, heading back to her herbs. "I've been reading some of the books you brought in, and found a few more in the library that might be of use. I was thinking…" She paused for a moment, unreadable to me. She was as good at hiding her emotions as the prince. Clearly it was a learned skill. "The everlass has always seemed to have a mind of its own. Have you noticed that?"

Finley's "thinking expression" covered her face. Her eyebrows pinched, her eyes got faraway, and her lips pulled to the side a tiny bit. It was essentially a warning expression. Don't bother her when she wore it, or something awful would happen to you. Her temper wasn't much better than the prince's.

"If you give it a task, it sets out to do that task to the best of its ability," Arleth went on. "When it comes to dragons, that goes double. Everlass elixirs and draughts seem to work best on us. Our elixirs need to be tweaked for other creatures—faeries do best with formulas that are basic. Shifters need them to be a little more acidic. Demons…" She shrugged. "What do demons need? I've never heard. Dragons haven't been in the habit of making things for demons."

"I didn't know that about the other creatures. Is that why your painkilling draught was so rancid tasting?"

Arleth slowed in her ministrations, her brow lowering.

No, then. Finley wasn't great at breaking things to people gently. Hopefully the queen could teach her how.

Finley didn't seem to notice. "So if we find out what sort of draught would work best for a demon, we could possibly use the opposite to counteract the effects of their magic?" She squinted. "Or maybe not the opposite. I'll have to try both." She looked up at me suddenly. "I didn't even ask about the demons and faeries after the battle. Are they okay? Are all the demons still with us?"

"Yes," I responded, crossing an ankle over my knee. "The dragons were on guard duty, and they remained, just in case. The faeries stuck to their rooms. I get the feeling Calia is eager to speak to the prince, though. She's probably feeling the call of home."

"I know," she replied, already pulling ingredients to her. She mixed her herbs with the ease of someone that had been doing it all her life. In her case, it was mostly true. Since she was old enough to garden, at least.

As she got to work, she said, "Nyfain seems to think the different groups of visitors each need some elaborate dinner. Which, fine, as a prince with official business, he's probably right. But it seems like a waste of time."

"Have you told him that?" I asked.

"No," she replied.

"And you shouldn't," Arleth said. "He's doing official dinners so they will be prompted to invite him to their courts. Or at least that's true of Calia. It's how things are done. He might appear rough and tumble now, ruthless even, but he was schooled in the finer workings of a court, and he's using that knowledge to make allies. Trust him. He knows what he's about."

Finley didn't respond, looking at me through her lashes. A new emotion wafted my way—anxiety. I knew what she was thinking: *He might know what he's about, but I have no clue how to exist in that world.*

I gave her a small smile and an encouraging nod, letting her know she wasn't alone. And she wasn't, truly—I'd need to make sure I learned how to sit at a proper dinner table.

I reached down to grab my notepad to jot that on my to-do list.

"I picked some everlass that the demons fought in," Arleth said, going back to a more comfortable topic for

Finley. "The field is struggling with all the damage, but it will rally. I've seen fields look worse and come back strong. But I thought you might try using some of the plants that were trampled by the disgusting creatures. Maybe they'll work harder to eradicate the enemy from my son."

Finley glanced at me in that way of hers, and I immediately set down my notebook and stood, grabbing a cup and going to the water. She took the cup from me and poured in the ingredients before handing it back.

"There should be a ladle—"

"I got it," I told her, taking it from the shelf.

"That elixir you made yesterday..." Arleth started, regarding her with a shrewd look. "It heals very quickly."

"It has to," I said, pouring in the water and setting it beside Finley to cool. "With all the times she limped into our house, she needed something quick and effective."

"And easy to make," Finley added.

"You need to meet and understand other creatures, Finley, so that you can alter your recipes to suit their needs, but then I think you will make this kingdom money with your skills. A *lot* of money."

"Do we need it? You've given Nyfain your gold, haven't you?" she replied, working on something else now, picking from various pots and steaming things from around the room.

"Nope, not that one. It'll be too watery. Over there." Arleth pointed at a pot that sat on a patch of dirt, cooling. The two were like dancing partners switching off who led and who followed. "What I've given him is a mere fraction of what the kingdom once had. We need it, trust me. To see greatness, we'll need a lot of it."

"We don't need greatness all at once," Finley replied. "We just need to cut the throats of our enemies so we have time to do this right."

A puff of Finley's rage had me smiling. Give her an enemy and stand back. She was like Nyfain in that way.

The queen's eyebrows rose to her hairline, but she didn't comment.

Finley froze, looking down at the everlass the queen had picked. Her hands came out slowly to grip the edge of the worktable.

"Yes," she said softly, her gaze going far off.

I got butterflies in my stomach and my heart quickened, something that always happened when Finley slipped into one of these moods. My animal rolled within me in a flurry of excitement, something I didn't much understand but liked the feeling of.

Arleth opened her mouth to ask what was happening, but I held up a hand to silence her. Finley was having an epiphany. It was something that happened to her from time to time when she was working on a complex cure. An idea would strike her, seemingly out of the blue, that would lead to exponential gains in whatever she was working on.

Some might attribute these leaps to intelligence and an enhanced analytical ability, and my sister *was* intelligent. But this was more than that. This was magic. Just as Nyfain could sing plants into growing, Finley could sense new ways to cure ailing people. It was a gift from the goddess, I knew it. She was goddess-touched.

"The gold," Finley whispered, turning to look out the

window. "Blood."

Arleth furrowed her brow and shook her head in apparent confusion.

I kept my hand in the air to keep her from speaking. If Finley's concentration was broken now, she'd lose the thread of whatever had struck her, and she might never grab hold of it again.

She turned back around and stared at Arleth. "The spell in the reserve. You used blood to counter it. Nyfain's blood. It needed to be freely given."

"Yes…" Arleth replied slowly. "But that was a magical spell."

Finley turned away again.

"A curse is a magical spell, too, it's just more sinister. Nyfain altered the curse when he forced a shift. He punched a hole through it, in essence, and fragments were left behind, burrowing into his internal scars. He left fragments that burrowed into his internal scarring—" She pointed at me while continuing to look out at the bright sunlight. "You said he has scars on the inside, Hannon, and you were right. Scars on the inside, festering with those fragments. The curse's magic was stripped away, but the altered portion was not. It needs a different counter-spell."

Finley turned back, eyes sparkling. Radiance filled the air. She was on the right path now, I could feel it. *She* could feel it. She'd cure Nyfain, just like she'd cured the demon sickness. Just like she'd cured hundreds of other ailments over the years.

A proud smile graced my lips, and I basked in her moment of glory, passing the emotions down to my animal.

Finley sprang into action, tossing what she'd already created and starting anew. She pushed ingredients away and pulled new ones toward her.

"Demon blood," she murmured. "The everlass works differently on different species. If you give it a job, it will try to do that job. But it needs direction, and the fragments of the spell festering inside of Nyfain have to be coaxed out."

Her hands stilled on a pot of cold-seeping everlass, and she closed her eyes, very still. My animal roiled within me. A wave of goosebumps spread along my skin.

"The demon-trashed field, yes," she whispered, gold-speckled eyes opening and narrowing on me. "The one by our village, Hannon, where you protected Sable from the demons, remember? I noticed the damage at one point when passing through the Royal Wood, though I haven't had time to stop in. I'll pick some of those and cold-steep them. That and…"

She knows what we are, my animal said as Finley started touching all the herbs one by one and looking around the room, her eyebrows low over her eyes.

"That and…" she said again, wandering among the pots.

She can't know what we are, I replied. We *don't know what we are.*

She feels it, though. She senses it, just as that big dragon senses it. Why else did he put you in charge of the advisory circle? He's trying to forge a connection between us and his kingdom so we'll guard it as we guard our kin and our community. So that we'll die for it as we'd die for them, without thought, without emotion.

I shook my head minutely so that no one else would notice. I didn't like sharing the things my animal said. Some of it unnerved me. Some of it would damn me.

"I'm not following," Arleth told Finley, moving closer.

"Blood, freely given, has a certain kind of a magic," Finley mumbled. A bookworm tended to have a lot of information stored in her head, just waiting to become useful. Finley loved when a random factoid could be pulled out and put into action, especially in her remedies. "It's a wholesome magic. It is based on someone's desire to help with their very essence—their life's blood. Demon blood freely given, put into a healing mixture, *might* coax those shards of magic out of Nyfain's scars. Ingredients that work well with demons will further entice them. And then the everlass mixture must attack the demon magic and burn it away, healing in its wake. The struggling plant *should* have the right potency. I think a crowded plant will be too much. This is what will free him, though. I *feel* it. I just need all the right ingredients."

"*Koo-kooo,*" filtered in through the door. Then again.

"Freely given demon blood," Finley murmured, ignoring the fake bird call. "I bet Govam will give it to me. He owes me, the bastard."

Hadriel poked his head in. "In case you were wondering, that wasn't a bird. The prince is coming. He's coming, and he's pissed. Again."

"Damn it…" Finley glanced at the door, then looked

around the room. "Is there a way to sneak out of here? I need to get to that field. I want to—"

An imposing presence filled the doorframe, his massive shoulders nearly spanning the width and his robust body projecting the sort of power and grace only a predator could possess. Finley froze as his golden eyes scanned the interior of the work shed, lingering on his mother for a moment, taking in his mate, and then slamming into me.

My animal moved within me as power curled from the large dragon, scraping against our spirit in barely contained menace. Liking the feel and wanting more of it, I squared my shoulders and stood. The dragon was issuing his challenge without consciously realizing it. I was pretty sure he couldn't help himself. It was natural for one of his kind to force submission.

I lifted my chin just a little and hardened my gaze, prodding him to use more power.

His eyes sparked, the alpha in him internalizing my posture and bearing as a returned challenge. His rage intensified. His muscles flexed one by one. His dragon moved behind those golden eyes, a terrifying sight.

The prince would act on my challenge soon. The only reason he hadn't yet was because of my relationship to Finley. Brutality to me would hurt her. He didn't want that for her. Neither did I.

But my animal craved what we were getting from the alpha dragon right now, and he reveled in the power it manifested within us.

Nyfain's rage billowed into the room, drawing the queen's notice and visibly melting my sister with desire—an uncomfortable sight.

While they were distracted, I breathed it in, sucked it down. The rage was intoxicating. Equally as intoxicating as joy, pleasure…as an enemy's fear. Equally as useful as pain. As suffering.

I had a dirty secret, one I hadn't told a soul. One I hoped Nyfain, very good at reading people, hadn't guessed.

Ever since my animal was drawn out, I'd had the ability to internalize strong emotions. I could suck them in, like air, and feed them to my animal. There they brewed, churning, until they flowered out in the heat of battle and expanded, filling me with strength and power. Speed and agility.

I'd told my animal we had qualities similar to the demons in the demon king's castle.

They have qualities similar to us, not the other way around, my animal had replied. *Demons specialize in one type of emotion, or none at all. Sex demons seek pleasure. The creatures in the dungeon sought misery. But what demons seek joy? Love? What demons feed off rage or the effulgence of spirit?*

Maybe we just don't know about them.

Fine. Then I'll ask you this—what demons seek to care for and guard those they love? We use emotion as a source of power, and we apply that power to improve the lives of those we love. That is not a demonic characteristic. We are not reprehensible, Hannon. We are certainly not a demon.

I'd had my misgivings. Still did. Even when he added, *Besides, have you seen any demons with wings?*

He'd stretched within me then, trapped in the confines of my body but desperate to take to the sky.

I hadn't seen any demons with wings, no, and therefore desperately hoped he had them. I worried about the alternative.

The dragon's rage continued to pump into the small cabin, feeding my animal. I held his gaze, knowing it was dangerous, that I'd send that big dragon over the edge and feel his wrath. He was reaching the edge of his tolerance, and my goading him on only fanned the flames.

But his rage was so sweet, so powerful. It intoxicated my animal. It felt as though it expanded through my body. It was hard to resist.

In a moment, though, I realized with horror that I'd waited too long.

Suddenly he sprang into action.

CHAPTER 18
FINLEY

M Y BREATH CAUGHT in my throat as Nyfain surged toward my brother. I barely managed to get myself in front of him. He stopped short, reaching out to grip my arm so he didn't knock me over, his hard eyes directed over my shoulder.

"Hey, hey, whoa." I ran my hands lightly up his chest and then hooked them delicately around his neck.

The sweetness of the gesture counteracted the rage billowing from my mate. His muscles loosened just a bit, and he swung his gaze down to me almost as if he couldn't help himself. His anger dimmed somewhat as he locked eyes with me, anchoring himself.

"What's going on?" I asked, not daring to look away from him and release his focus. I had no idea what Hannon had done to set Nyfain off, but I didn't want to give Nyfain a chance to "fix" it. "You okay?"

Nyfain took me in and softened further, his thumb stroking my arm. I was still tense, though, and I could tell he was preventing himself from looking up again, not wanting to make eye contact with my brother.

"Your brother is walking a very dangerous line, princess. I'll give you a chance to talk him down. Next time I'll handle it myself. Meet me outside."

He abruptly turned and walked out the door.

I took a deep breath and sent a questioning look at Hannon, who had his face tilted downward.

"Sorry, Finley," he said immediately, looking up through his lashes to see if Nyfain had gone. He lifted his face to look at me bashfully. "I apologize. My animal is getting to me. He likes to set off the dragon's rage."

I studied my brother, noticing the tension in his shoulders and the slight tilt of his head. Hannon was a terrible liar. I saw the pleading in his eyes. There was something he wasn't telling me, but he wanted me to drop it.

I flicked a glance to Arleth, who was watching acutely, and thought better of trying to pry it out of him. This was now family business, and she wasn't the sort of family I wanted to share it with. Not yet, anyway.

I said, "I can get away with inciting his rage, Hannon. You cannot."

"I know. My mistake."

"You heard what'll happen if you make that mistake again."

"Yes."

I glanced over the ingredients I'd collected and felt the unmistakable urge to get to work. My brain was exploding with ideas. I felt the rightness of this approach. Of working the struggling everlass. It had been ignored all this time, poor thing. It deserved a chance to shine.

Nyfain was waiting for me, though, worried about my wellbeing. I'd given him a scare. He needed to take care of me for a while to reassure himself that I was okay. I knew this because I'd felt the same way after he nearly died.

I inhaled deeply, let it out slowly, and tried to temper the fire and excitement raging through my blood.

"Okay." I turned toward Arleth. "Here's what you do." I crossed to her stockpile of elixirs, draughts, and salves. Although I'd only tried the one, I knew what they all did. "You take this one…this one…and this one…"

I pulled out the ones I was certain could use a little more oomph.

"Make a new batch of each using the cold-seeped everlass over there." I pointed to the basin that didn't have any added herbs in it. "Same recipe, different type of plant."

"Dosage?" she asked.

I probably should've been surprised by her ready cooperation, but I was too wrapped up in my head.

I started to answer and then stopped, thinking it through, listening to my intuition. Hannon rubbed at his arms like he was cold, but I turned so it didn't distract me.

"Three-quarters the usual amount," I said softly, letting it hang in the air for a moment, not quite sure. Would that be too strong? Something told me the cold-seeped struggling plant would pack a punch. "I really wish I could be the one experimenting."

"We must balance the duty that hangs around our shoulders and use others to do the things we cannot,"

Arleth said, as though reciting something she'd heard often.

"True. Fine. I'd say…try a half—No. Two-thirds. Try two-thirds. Let's see how that stacks up."

She nodded and quickly began packing away the things she was working on so she could do as I said. I watched in misery for a moment but forced myself to take a step back. And then another.

"You'll be able to start on it first thing tomorrow," Hannon said softly, reading my mood. "You can get up early and head in before…whatever thing you have to do."

"We'll be flying first thing," Arleth said. "First thing in the court means right after a light breakfast."

"There, see?" Hannon moved to me and braced a hand on my shoulder. "Get up early and come out here. I'm sure the prince would gladly go with you. You can breakfast here and then the queen can meet you for flight."

"Sensible, as always, Hannon," Arleth said, rehanging the herbs she'd no longer be needing and taking down those she did.

"Fine," I said, my mood blackening.

"Yes." Hannon nodded. "Anger and annoyance are much better than sadness."

I frowned and gave him a light shove. "You're getting a little too good at reading me, Hannon," I said darkly. "Violation of privacy, maybe?"

"It's my job," he replied quickly.

"It's not, actually. Go pick an advisory circle."

With a last look at my chaotic station, I exited the

everlass shed and found Nyfain waiting not far away, his hands clasped behind him, looking out over the grounds. Hadriel and Vemar stood to the side, shoulder to shoulder, their backs straight, probably afraid to move and draw Nyfain's attention.

"Hey," I said, trying to even out my tone. "Ready."

He didn't look at me when I stopped beside him but turned his head farther away, letting out a little sigh.

"He's sorry—" I started, but Nyfain cut me off.

"What's a compromise you will accept?"

"What?" I asked.

He did look down at me then, a smile working at his lips. "What is a compromise you will accept? I know you want to work your plants. And yes, I will do it with you early tomorrow. But I don't want you overextending yourself today."

"I know." I put out my hands. "I'm here. Let's go to the library."

He shook his head a little. "I can feel how keyed up you are, sweetheart. You're in a piss-poor mood because I am tearing you away, and you'll be incredibly distracted. I know you're only doing it for me. So. What is a compromise you can live with?" A dangerous glint entered his eyes. "A very tranquil compromise without much effort."

I beamed at him, I couldn't help it, and slipped my arm around his waist so I could lean into him. He enclosed me in his arms.

"I'd be satisfied with harvesting some leaves. Just that, and I'm all yours."

He glanced out at the field.

"No," I said. "Not from there. From the one near my village. The one I helped create."

His expression fell.

Before he could say no, I said, "We can take the horses. Those aren't strenuous. Or...your dragon can carry me in his mouth." His eyebrows pinched together. "Piggyback?"

He huffed and looked away. "Damn you, Finley. Why can't you ever make my job easy? I'm supposed to be protecting you, but I can't seem to protect you from yourself."

"I know. What a shit job. But seriously, baby, it'll be worth it. You'll see. I know how to fix your scales and get your wings back. I know I do!"

He claimed my lips in a rush, running his teeth over my bottom lip before sucking it in.

"I should say no," he said. "I'm not worth your discomfort."

I pulled back and gave him a skeptical look. "Who are you kidding right now?"

"Never mind—"

"Walking to an everlass field in the middle of the day, when I hardly feel my wound, is not worth my discomfort when—"

"I said never mind—"

"—I've been tortured—who the fuck are you kidding right now?"

He captured my lips again, and I could feel his smile as he moved his lips against mine. I tried very hard to keep from turning to liquid against him—and failed. He groaned softly as he chased my tongue, devouring my mouth, spreading his hands across my back and holding me tightly. His hard length pressed against my belly, begging to be taken out and sucked. Or sat on.

"Okay," he said, pulling back just enough so he could speak. "You win. Let's go get your leaves. But promise me that we can go somewhere we can be alone after that."

"Our nook in the library," I whispered, eyes closed, not wanting to move away. I ran my hands up over his impossibly broad shoulders and then lightly traced the mark I'd given him. He shivered. "I feel like reading a dirty book."

"How about I read the dirty book to you?"

My smile curled my lips. "Sounds like a dream."

I forced myself to break away from him, my body humming as much as my mind. Wanting him but also wanting to find a cure. I wanted both equally. *Thank you, goddess, for giving me a man who would let me do both.*

"I just need to get—"

"Here we go." Arleth exited the everlass shed with Hannon in tow, my brother carrying two cedar trays. She motioned off toward the grounds. "Maybe you can have...one of your trusted advisors alert the castle that we'll need horses and a cart to go to the field? Delaney and I can fly there with the large dragon in the colorful jacket. That'll save some horses—I confess, I haven't checked what the stables look like." She put a finger to her lip. "Do we have a cart for the everlass leaves?"

I blinked dumbly at her and blurted the first thing that came to mind. "You're coming?"

She gave me a condescending look. "Of course I am coming. You mean to harvest. We will help."

Delaney stood in the everlass field, arms at her sides, watching us. She clearly wondered what was going on but didn't want to walk all the way over to find out.

"Maybe your sister would like to come?" Arleth asked pleasantly before giving Hadriel a stern look.

"Finley, darling, I'm getting nasty looks." Hadriel slouched where he stood, and a large grin worked up Vemar's face. "Should I heed her passive-aggressive orders? It might save us all a lot of trouble."

Arleth waited patiently for me. I could feel Nyfain's humor weaving through the bond.

"Yeah, sure, why not. Vemar, go grab my sister, will you? She's probably in the castle somewhere. She's intent on learning every inch of it. Ask the staff. They can't keep track of Dash, but they always seem to know where she is."

"Sure thing, Strange Lady." He took off at a jog.

"Hadriel, do as the queen has passively commanded and see to the horses and a cart," I said, somehow managing to keep a straight face.

"Thank the goddess for the ability to sin," Hadriel muttered as he sprinted away.

"He never would've lasted under the last king," Arleth said, watching him go.

I held up my finger for Nyfain. "I'm not allowed to fly, right?"

"No," he said, scooping me up into his arms. "Nor walk. You should rest."

I looped my arm around his neck and snuggled in

close. "I should be embarrassed about this."

"Why?"

"Your inability to see the problem is worrying. It means you'll never stop."

"Do you want me to?"

I tucked my lips together to keep from answering because I wouldn't be able to help myself from being honest, and I really shouldn't let my mate carry me everywhere like I was a child. It wasn't a good look regardless of how it felt.

Instead, as Nyfain started to walk me across the ground wrapped up in his arms, and Hannon and Arleth waited for Delaney, I asked quietly, "What happened with my brother back there?"

He sobered a little. "He has a lot of power he's keeping under wraps. When his animal finally decides to show itself, I think he'll widen a lot of eyes."

"Why does that worry you?"

"I've never been afraid of a challenge in my life. I've also never met someone I thought could overpower me. I'm not sure about him. I think it would be a battle, and for your sake, I hope it never comes to that."

"Because you wouldn't back down?"

"Not from a challenge, no. It isn't in me. Nor is losing."

Shivers rolled across my skin, and I snuggled into him a bit more. "It won't come to that. I'll make sure it doesn't."

"He might not always let you call the shots."

"You need to pay more attention. I don't call anything. I do me, and he does him. Together we kept our family alive. I only tell him what to do when it pertains to the *me* side of things. He's not in charge of anything at the moment, so he doesn't need my help. When he has the advisory circle, though, just you wait. He can get bossy when he needs to be."

Nyfain grunted, and I hoped that satisfied him.

I hoped the advisory circle satisfied Hannon. He was definitely keeping something under wraps, and while I really wanted to press him, I didn't sense it was danger-ous. Not to him or to anyone else. I did sense, though, that he was uncomfortable with whatever was going on with his animal. Maybe that was why he hadn't shifted yet. Goddess knew I'd had a rocky start with my animal. He probably just needed time.

SABLE AND DASH both came, Dash tagging along because Father had asked Vemar to keep him out of trouble. My little brother rode with Hannon while my sister rode behind Hadriel. The cart had a squeaky wheel, and Hadriel grumbled about it the whole way out to the field.

I swung my foot over the saddle but was given a command to wait. The power caressed me like a lover, however, so I allowed Nyfain to come around and lift me down so I didn't "hurt myself." I was pretty sure he was using my wound as an excuse to baby me without my pushing back, but given he'd let me come all the way out here after he'd expressly told me not to leave the castle, I let him.

"Over there, Hadriel, hurry now." Arleth pointed toward the large birch tree at one end of the field.

"What happened to the kind queen from back in the

day?" he murmured, walking his horse before throwing the reins over a tree limb to keep the horse from wandering. "This one is pushy."

"Sawhorse…just there." Arleth pointed. "Nyfain?"

"Of course." Nyfain gave me a kiss on the temple and walked to the cart to retrieve it.

"And there." She pointed to another. "Hannon?"

Hannon followed Nyfain without a word.

"Vemar, clothes, if you please," she said without turning to look. Vemar stood at the edge of the field, watching everyone. "There's a reason we dressed quickly. There are children present."

"My apologies, Miss Queen. Let me just go don my dick jacket."

She shook her head lightly. Dee's attempts at a scowl were undermined by the telltale tilt at the corners of her lips. I hoped the kids weren't listening, but then again, they were in the castle now. Although it was much less likely they'd walk in on an orgy now than it had been a few months ago, language was harder to tone down.

While Arleth barked out orders, I followed Nyfain over to the birch out of curiosity. When I got close, it burst into life, shaking and shimmering, its branches waving.

"Holy shitstains, Finley, watch out!" Hadriel jumped away from the horse and ran a few steps, turning to shield his face with his arm while he looked up at the shaking tree.

Everyone but Nyfain stopped and stared, wide-eyed, as I worked around the tree to the little bush where Nyfain had always stored his notes and things for me.

"Nyfain put your sword right here, Arleth," I told her, pointing. "When I needed weapons. We weren't...seeing each other at the time, but we communicated through letters. He didn't tell me that the sword was yours."

"You wouldn't have accepted it if you'd known," he replied, fondness in his voice as he set up the sawhorse.

I pulled my lips to the side, not quite sure that was accurate...

"I have not seen you wear that sword since the battle, young Finley," the queen said, motioning for Hadriel to grab a cedar tray for collecting leaves.

The sword had been waiting in our room after our dinner with Arleth. There had been no note. Obviously she'd meant to give it back to me, but no way would I wear something I could not use and that did not belong to me. I'd told Leala to return it.

Later that day, it had shown up again, this time with a note.

It's pretty if nothing else. Use it in the ceremony
when you don the crown. It'll secure your place –
A

"Tamara keeps threatening to teach me how to use it," I told Arleth, wandering out into the field. "I decided that I won't wear it until it serves a purpose. And that purpose won't just be ceremonial, unless the ceremony includes cutting off Dolion's head. No one follow me in here yet. Stay out." I paused. "Dash, what did I just say?"

I didn't have to turn around to know he'd frozen and started backtracking. He might be incredibly sneaky and hard to catch, but that didn't mean he was unpredictable. He'd always loved following me.

I closed my eyes as I walked one of the rows, running my hands along the plants, remembering all the time I'd spent in this field. I'd always been trespassing. I'd always been afraid of getting caught. Dark had covered me in its embrace as I stealthily moved through the plants, pruning as I went, harvesting into my little sack.

Now look at me. Here in the light of day, with the queen and the golden prince. What an amazing turn my life had taken. It was worth the agony I'd endured in the demon lands, no question. I'd do it again in a heartbeat.

I took deep breaths as I reacquainted myself with the plants. The demons had damaged them, many of the plants wilting as if poisoned. And yet…

I found a patch amongst the sickliest plants that had sprung back totally. Not just that, but there was a strange sheen to the leaves. They almost looked coated in light.

I braced my hands on my hips. I'd never seen anything like that before. I'd certainly never read about it.

Something made me turn…and I caught the guarded gaze of Hannon.

"That's where Hannon played hero," Sable said, hanging on to him. "I helped, though, didn't I, Hannon? I played decoy so you could get closer."

"You did. I couldn't have saved you if you hadn't played along," Hannon replied, watching me.

I shook my head and turned back around. What the fuck kind of animal was he hiding?

I did another tour in the field just because I could, shouting halfway through, "Dash, I said *get out!*"

"You're such a pest," Sable called to him.

"Be nice, Sable," I muttered, heading back to the demon-distressed area. "Nyfain, please bring the tray."

I got to work harvesting from the plants as everyone else filtered into the field. Vemar hadn't worked much with everlass, but he took to it easily, knowing the importance of the plants. All dragons did. Not to mention they'd saved us from the dungeons. Hadriel's new love of gardening made him an apt student. Hannon mostly just wandered, trailing his fingers along the plants. He'd never been one for gardening and clearly didn't want to learn, but he was happy to go with the flow.

"You taught your little brother well, Finley," Arleth said as she pruned and nurtured the healthy plants, leaving me to choose what to harvest.

"It's not that hard," replied Dash, who was just as nimble with the plants as he was at sneaking into dangerous situations.

"Can we sing now?" Sable asked.

"Not yet," I replied, finished with the demon area and approaching the plants with the sheen.

"I've never seen that before," Nyfain said as he returned to me with a fresh tray, looking at them.

Arleth made her way over and glanced over my shoulder. She touched one of the leaves as she stepped a little closer. Then Delaney joined us, both of them bending to get a closer look.

"What is it?" Delaney asked Arleth quietly.

Arleth shook her head. "Maybe the effect of enemy bloodshed?" She raised her voice. "Hannon, you said you killed those demons here?"

Hannon looked over. "Fought them, yes. Not sure where they actually died."

"This is gruesome talk in front of children," Arleth murmured.

"These kids have seen a lot more horrors than that bad guy dying, I assure you," I replied. "Okay, scatter. I want to harvest some of these. Nyfain and Sable, go ahead and sing, if you'd like."

"Why didn't you want us singing with the collection of the other leaves?" Nyfain asked, waiting patiently as I circled the plants and looked at all their leaves. None had wilted. None needed pruning.

"Because the singing will cure the wilting plants, and I wanted to collect some leaves from them first. These are already in great health."

I shook my head, not really understanding. Not even wanting to pick them, they were so beautiful. What if the leaves didn't come back the same?

"I'd love a private garden with plants like these," I said, touching one of the leaves with a finger. "These are more beautiful than any rosebush could ever be. More majestic."

"You'll have to figure out how they came to be and duplicate it," Nyfain said as I pulled a leaf free and then studied it to see if the strange light would fade from the natural waxy surface.

"I'd rather not drag a demon into a private garden to kill it."

"Maybe we could take it from here and plant it there. It wouldn't like it, but I might be able to keep it alive with song."

"Thanks, babe, but that's okay. They're happy here. Probably. I don't know. It's like a super everlass plant or something. Maybe it'd be happy anywhere. We shall see."

I watched the leaf a while longer and then put it into the tray before bending to pick another. Nyfain started to sing, and the others joined in as I worked my way around the plants, feeling in my bones that this was the plant to do it. This was the one that would make one helluva difference.

I just wished I knew how it came to be.

CHAPTER 19
FINLEY

"CONTENT?" NYFAIN ASKED after we'd reached the castle grounds again and stabled the horses.

"Yes, thank you," I said as I watched Vemar pull the cart toward the everlass shed so he could unload the contents. Arleth had had the foresight to bring covers for the trays. Dash got to sit in the cart and hold on to them, something he found incredibly fun.

"Finley, darling…" Hadriel called from behind us, holding the reins of his horse with Sable still in the saddle. "Sable wants lessons. Do you mind?"

"Me too!" Dash yelled, running out of the stable. I hadn't even seen him duck in.

"Don't let them get hurt," I said.

Hadriel put his hand to his chest. "What do you take me for?" he responded indignantly.

I rolled my eyes and let Nyfain take my hand and walk me back to the castle.

Before we'd left the field, I'd pulled Hannon aside quietly and asked if he knew anything about those glowing leaves. I'd watched him closely, very good at reading him after all this time. When he'd answered *no*, I pushed him until he admitted his animal thought they might've been transformed by a burst of power he'd given off when preparing to rescue Sable. He'd felt it happen but didn't understand it.

"Can you do it again?" I'd asked.

A little crease had formed between his brow as he studied me. "I don't know," he'd said. "I think someone I care about has to be in grave danger. I don't seem to be able to turn it on and off. But I can try."

"Try," I'd said, "but not for me. You need to learn to work with your animal, whether you shift or not. Trust me, it'll help down the road."

He'd studied me for a moment, then said, "My animal says we'll try so that you can have the everlass in your garden."

Great, my dragon had grumbled. *I can handle him being the better sibling, since you're a nutcase, but his animal is more gracious than me, too? Bullshit. Disown him.*

I wasn't in complete disagreement.

"Where to?" Nyfain asked, releasing my hand and wrapping his arm around my hip.

I wrapped my arm around his waist. "Library. Dirty book. Remember?"

"Just making sure you didn't change your mind." He was quiet for a moment before he said, "You and my mom work exceptionally well together. I thought you'd take offense to her barking orders at everyone when we got to the field."

"She knew what she was doing. Might as well let her do it."

"And when you told everyone to stay out…she did."

"I knew what I was doing. She was letting me do it."

He leaned over and kissed the top of my head. "I feel like I've died and am living in the goddess's paradise. Harvesting like that, with my mate, Mom, your family—"

"Don't forget the dick jacket. No harvesting is complete without a man wearing a bunch of dicks hidden in the design of his jacket."

"My fa—the mad king is probably turning over in his grave."

"As long as he is rotting in hell, I don't much care." I slowed him so I could look up into his golden eyes. "You deserve this happiness, Nyfain. You refused to let the dark path you were forced to walk consume you, and you finally found the dawn. We've worked for this, you and me. We've fought for it. So let's enjoy it to its fullest and not let a single day pass where we don't love hard, laugh hard, play hard, and fuck hard."

"Fuck, I love you." He swooped me up into his arms.

I laughed. "I wondered how long it would take you to pick me up again."

We crossed the threshold into the castle. "I was trying to give you your space."

"That was your version of space?"

"It wasn't yours?"

I laughed again as he carried me to the library, making everyone scatter as he walked through the halls. After all his blustering earlier in the day, the staff apparently preferred not to be in his company. I was not complaining.

"Dirty book?" I asked as he lowered me onto our lounger in the back corner, mostly obscured from view of the rest of the library by a huge tapestry that hung in front of it. A large bust sat on the small table behind it, and the plant next to it was large enough to block from sight anyone sitting on the lounger in the nook. Still, there were enough gaps to allow that person to peek through it and spy on others in the library. "Should I pick one?"

"No. Let that joy be mine. I know just the one."

When he came back from the secret room in the corner, a room that no longer needed to remain secret now that the mad king was gone, he sat behind me, putting his legs to either side of me so I could curl up onto his chest.

"Should I read from the beginning, or just skip to the first steamy scene?" he asked, reaching the book around me and opening it so he could hold me and read at the same time.

"Maybe read a bit until I get impatient to touch you, and then we'll skip ahead."

"Right." With that, he turned the first page and got to work.

His reading voice was rich and expressive, his cadence ebbing and flowing as he read, changing his voice just slightly for each character. I sat in rapture, utterly sucked in, not wanting him to skip ahead at all—not even wanting him to get to the steamy parts where I knew I would feel compelled to take off his pants, distracting him and interrupting this magical moment.

K.F. BREENE

I was just about to suggest we change books when he bristled, pausing in the middle of a sentence. One of his hands came away from the book and drifted toward my arm, grabbing it as though anchoring me to the spot. He looked to the side, bending up a little to see through or around the plant.

"Weston has entered," he said softly, and I turned to see the alpha wolf stop in the opening to the library. He walked forward, eyeing the couches and looking around the corner. When he didn't see anyone, he tilted his head downward a bit, pausing. Even from here I could tell he was sniffing, and then he turned in our direction.

"Wolves' sense of smell is better than ours," I whispered, wondering about their hearing as well. "Or at least that's so for wolves of his caliber."

"Highnesses, I wished to have a word," Weston called out, not taking a step closer. "I heard you were in here. I can see that you're secluded. Should I come back another time?"

Nyfain pulled in a breath, lowering the book slightly, his hand sliding down my arm. "I'm sorry, princess," he mumbled. "We'll have to pause here for a moment." He raised his voice. "Back here. Bring a chair."

I lost sight of Weston for a moment, and then I heard footsteps coming our way. He appeared in our secluded little area with one of the chairs from the round table in the far side of the library. Once near us, he placed it just off the foot of our lounger and walked around to sit.

I pushed off Nyfain to sit on my own, since we weren't exactly in an official-looking pose, but Weston put up his hand.

"Don't worry, highness—"

"Please, call me Finley," I told him.

"Finley, then." He held my gaze for a beat, and it seemed poignant in some way. "Please don't move on my account. I'm a wolf. I've seen my fair share of imprinted mates. Some of them never unglue themselves from their partners."

I gave him a sheepish smile and leaned back, not cuddling like before but still using Nyfain for a chair. He snaked his arm around my waist, holding me tightly to him.

"What can we do for you, alpha?" Nyfain asked.

"Call me Weston."

Nyfain inclined his head.

"There are a few things I'd like to discuss," Weston began, "and I thought you'd be amenable to a casual setting instead of a formal dinner."

I knew he'd heard about my loathing of those dinners.

"Of course," Nyfain said.

"First, let me be frank. I have more than half of your kingdom's wolves patched into my pack."

He paused, his eyes boring into Nyfain's.

"Please don't tell me you came here to interrupt our reading time with a challenge." I groaned. "Because that is unforgivable, and I'll have to kill you myself. I like you, Weston. I don't want to have to kill you."

His gaze darted to me, his eyes widening. A flash of humor stole over his expression before he threw his head back, exposing his throat, and laughed in a deep, rich tone.

"That's not what he was doing, sweetheart," Nyfain murmured into my ear, laughter riding his words. "But at least now he knows where he stands when it comes to you and your reading."

I wasn't even embarrassed. He was better off knowing.

"No, Finley, I wasn't issuing a challenge. I'm not suicidal." Weston wiped his eyes with the back of his hand. "The alpha is more than aware of his people's craving for a pack. I was simply helping him assess the situation."

"Ah." I pressed my lips together.

"There are too many people," he went on, wiping his left eye again, a smile playing across his lips, "and they are too spread out for me to be effective. I had to let many of them flounder in the last battle so I could focus on the most important action. Thankfully, the demons didn't seem overly concerned with the villages. It was a stroke of luck. However, for safety and practical reasons, the pack should be broken down into a functioning hierarchy so I can maneuver the few, who can in turn help me control the whole." He paused. "Are you following me?"

He was looking at Nyfain, but the change in his tone suggested he was talking to me.

"Yep," I confirmed.

He nodded slightly. "Since the last battle, however, I have received a large number of requests from shifters to be rejected from the pack. That means these people wish for me to sever their connection. To free them. Your... I'll just say his name, because honestly, his entire situation in this court confuses me. One of those requests came from Hadriel."

"Did you grant it?" I knew my voice relayed what I was feeling, equal parts anxiety and hope, but I couldn't help it. His call mattered to me, and I couldn't pretend otherwise. I wanted Hadriel to be happy, and regardless of what he'd said, I knew a pack could do that for him. I saw the confidence the connection gave him, the strength. He needed Weston, more than I needed him. I couldn't let my selfishness stand in his way. Still...I wanted to.

"I wanted to speak with the alpha before granting any of their requests."

"Just..." I held up my finger. "For clarity, what would happen if they wanted out and an alpha wouldn't allow it? Would they be forced to stay in against their will?"

"Most alphas aren't capable of holding a wolf to the pack so tightly they can't escape with enough distance and willpower," he said. "I am rare in this instance."

"So, then...an alpha like you. What happens if you don't let go?"

"That alpha would need to be challenged and defeated—"

"In this case, killed," Nyfain murmured.

"If that wasn't possible, the pack could work together to defeat the alpha. If *that* didn't work, they would need to escape the pack on two legs and try to find someone who *could* win the challenge. It's a very real concern with an alpha of my power level and magical ability. Being alpha is a great honor but also a great responsibility.

Someone like me would be a real problem if corrupted by power."

"Yikes." I grimaced. "Well, in that case, I'll say it again. Please don't make me kill you."

Weston's smile stretched, and his slate-gray eyes glittered. "I'll try my best. In seriousness, we all know what happens when power corrupts. I am very conscious of my role and very receptive to feedback from my pack. Should a time come when I am not, I hope I am taken down brutally."

His gaze bored into Nyfain, and I could feel Nyfain nod slightly. A promise asked, and a promise made. It was basically like Nyfain asking me to kill him if he stepped out of line. These guys were at the top of the power scale, and they worried what would happen if they morally lost their way. They were such good men they were seeking the protection of their people, pack or mate, against themselves.

I leaned my head back against Nyfain for a moment, rubbing his thigh to express my sudden gush of feeling. He gave me a little squeeze, warmth coming through the bond.

"Some of those requests," Weston said, not at all bothered by our display of affection, "were from the pack mates I brought here."

Surprise flitted though the bond.

"It seems they find it thrilling to battle amongst dragons," Weston said. "As far as I know, it has never been done before. Maybe it has here…?"

"No," Nyfain responded. "Dragons don't typically fight on the ground. I have to, obviously, and have sixteen years of practice. The others wouldn't have if not for Finley calling them down. Her will is incredibly strong, and she's figured out how to use it to force her commands."

I pulled away and frowned at him. "My dragon issued the command, but we didn't force them."

"Your dragon should be using her will as a weapon, as well, like you do. That's why Vemar didn't land right away when you were in trouble. He worried you'd lash out with your will, and he'd be caught in the crossfire. It wasn't until he realized your dragon wasn't using it that he lowered to your aid, nearly too late. But she does snake will around her commands and *helps* people do what she thinks they must."

Did you know that? I asked my dragon.

I knew I wanted them to do what I said, but no, I didn't know I did it with will.

Well, you better fucking learn or else it'll be us they kill for misuse of power.

Dramatic.

"She is such a dickface," I muttered. Weston grinned, the sentiment leaking into his previously somber eyes.

"It's no different than when I infuse my commands with power," Nyfain said, pulling me back to him. "Or when Weston commands his wolves through their bond. They won't resent you for it, if that's what you're thinking."

"First Hannon, and now you. Is everyone a mind reader all of a sudden?" I grumbled.

To Weston, Nyfain said, "As you know, she's new to

shifting because of the curse. She hasn't been conditioned in how dragons normally go about things. The first time she shifted was after leaving the dungeons."

Weston squinted a little. "I heard that you now intend to train your dragons to fight on the ground?"

"Yes," Nyfain replied. "It was thought *by some*"—he squeezed me—"that in certain instances, we might be more useful on the ground. Obviously, even though they might not like it, no one could argue the point. The dragons were mostly useless in the air yesterday."

"They did seem a little out of their element on the ground," Weston said. "But even though your dragon isn't patched into my pack, we worked with you seamlessly. Finley too. It was like...a wolf pack of epic proportions. Safer for us all. Much more effective. Even when the dragons kept to the air when we first came in, there was a thrilling element to the battle. Being covered from the sky is a decided advantage for a wolf pack."

"Having you on the ground was a decided advantage for us," I responded. "We may be large and strong, but we're not as good at working together. We're not *patched in*, as you said. We can also be too big and cumbersome, or too high and far away, to deal with certain threats. Your wolf pack filled in the gaps. It made us a solid force."

Weston's eyes were bright as he stared at me. "I knew you were different from the first time I met you. You don't have the usual arrogance of a dragon, if you'll pardon my frankness, alpha. And while you, sire, own your position, I see the differences in you as well. You didn't balk at using us in the battle. You led with presence of mind, even if it meant relying on the wolves more than your dragons—"

"I meant to win," Nyfain said. "I have no pride when it comes to fighting. Not anymore. You win, or you die. It's that simple. It's a lesson I've learned over and over since the curse, sometimes barely hanging on until the next day. There is no room for vanity in battle."

Weston inclined his head. "Agreed, though I learned that lesson in the dungeons. Even then, it didn't hit home until a strange sort-of dragon with no scales, an equally strange wolf, and a whip-cracking...monkey thing fused us all together and forged a path out of hell." He crossed an ankle over his knee. "I will, of course, let the wolves out of the pack. Especially those from this kingdom. But I wanted to make sure there was a safe place for them here. They weren't appreciated in the past."

"The past went up in flames," Nyfain growled. "I know what you offer the wolves, and that the other creatures need to feel included as well. I'm looking into how to make that happen. Finley's brother Hannon is creating an advisory circle that will speak to the court regarding the needs of the villages, and he will have voices from all animals within it. He himself is not a dragon. He will be impartial. We will create a better kingdom for all, where *all* will be represented. Unfortunately, though, we don't have anyone strong enough to create that overall pack unity like you have done. We'll have to make do."

The guys' eyes locked on each other, and I wondered if I'd have to get out a ruler for the dick-measuring contest that was surely in progress.

CHAPTER 20
FINLEY

"Let me tell you something about me," Weston said, leaning back and relaxing a little, but with power still coiling around him. "My parents grew up in court. Which one doesn't matter. They were both mighty in their own right. They had three boys, me being the middle. My brothers were great additions to the court, but I had a rare blend of power and pack magic, and the court treated me like gold. Usually a wolf has to fight his way up, learning as he or she goes, but I was fast-tracked through the beginning stages, something rarely done. The challenges for placement I did issue were easily won. I was in line for beta very young. The youngest in history, in fact. My parents couldn't have been prouder. The court was their life. Their parents had been in it, and their parents before them. It was like air to them—something they couldn't do without. They tried to train my brothers and I the same.

"Unfortunately, because of my gifts, my younger brother was soon largely ignored by them. My older

264

brother too, but by then he was old enough to have his own life. My younger brother started to pull away. And my parents let him. He was the weakest of us, after all. Below their notice.

"As he was slipping, I was being showered with attention. I soon learned what my duties would entail. When the royals traveled, I would accompany them as their beta. They told me I was to seek out wolves that would be assets to our kingdom and…steal them, essentially, capturing them with a pack bond."

Nyfain stayed very still, but turbulent emotions rolled through the bond. If his father had possessed that ability, he would've jumped on it.

"At first this wasn't a grave concern for me. I was young, and my parents saw no fault in it. It would make our court mighty, they said. Everyone tried to steal members from other courts, they said. It was easy. And after I'd taken someone, the royals would snatch up their families to *ensure they stayed together*."

"To ensure the royals had first pick of future generations," Nyfain growled.

"Yes. And I might've continued to go along with it. After all, I seemed to naturally understand how to make a pack thrive, and the royals allowed me to make changes for the betterment of the pack. They didn't ask much more of me than I was willing to give. That is, until my brother tried to leave the court."

He paused and looked at me.

"You see, Finley, my brother might not have been a bright star, but he was from a very strong bloodline. A bloodline that had churned out me. The royals didn't want to lose that. So they ordered me to make him stay."

Weston ran his fingers through his hair and looked away for a moment, expressing more emotion than I'd seen from him before.

"I did, I'm ashamed to say. To keep my life of luxury and my standing in the court. With the blessing of my parents, I did as they asked." He sucked his lower lip through his teeth. "My brother became wild, after that. Self-destructive. Violent. He became more animal than human. That was when my older brother came to me and told me I was failing in my duty to protect those who were weaker. To protect my family." He shook his head. "Such simple words that struck me to my core. He was right. What kind of alpha harmed his people rather than protected them?"

He paused for a moment, staring out at nothing.

"I didn't release my younger brother," he went on. "I held my bond to him tightly...and released everyone else. I took what little was actually mine and left the court with him, keeping him close until I could nurse him back to health, forcing him into two legs as often as needed, fighting or running or hunting with his wolf until the poison in his thoughts finally bled away. Only when his mind was right did I release him. At that point, he wanted to stay of his own free will. So we moved to the nearest town, spent some time learning the pack there, and I finally challenged, took over, and watched as he worked his way up to my beta."

I blinked through misty eyes. "That's a really sweet story."

"The royals allowed you to leave?" Nyfain asked, his

tone unusually somber. I couldn't read the emotions rolling through the bond, which was unusual for us.

Weston locked eyes with him for a moment. "Let's just say they got tired of losing valuable wolves trying to keep me."

"When you returned from the demon lands…" Nyfain let the sentence linger.

"My brother had assumed the role of alpha. He'd found a new beta. The rest of the pack structure was still in place. The wolves in his care were happy and healthy and prosperous. He was leading the life he always should have. While he was not quite cut out for the court, he is more than capable for a large, remote pack. Moreover, once I was presumed dead, the seemingly random attacks on the pack stopped. They had found a level of peace I wasn't able to give them."

"That sweet story took kind of a shitty turn," I mumbled.

Weston shook his head. "Not shitty. My brother is finally out from under his siblings' shadows. He got his happily ever after."

"He couldn't have been happy to see you return," Nyfain said.

"Salt in wound," I whispered to him.

"He was happy I was alive. But worried I'd take over, yes. Thankfully, I had a prior obligation." Weston looked at me. "I did him the courtesy of staying on two legs, took what money and belongings were solely mine, and left again. Those closest to me from the past insisted on leaving with me. It will hinder the pack somewhat, because they are strong wolves all, but my brother has a large, healthy group of young to bolster the numbers. He'll be fine. Even still, I would've tried to deter them if we hadn't needed numbers. As it was…"

"Will word of your return get back to the royal family?" Nyfain asked, and I crinkled my nose because I wasn't sure why it mattered if Weston had left both the pack and the kingdom.

"It will, yes."

Nyfain released a breath, ruffling my hair. Weston looked at him steadily, placidly, and I sensed a decision being made. I also sensed the issue had to be more complicated than it seemed, because if Weston was looking for a new job and a place to stay, the obvious answer was *fuck yes, when can you start?*

"Hang on a minute," I said, holding up my hand. "What am I missing?"

Nyfain's hand came to rest on my upper arm. "I apologize, princess. I didn't think to explain."

"A talent like me has a very hard time walking away from a court," Weston told me. "At least in my kingdom."

"Usually no one *wants* to walk away from a court," Nyfain said. "As you heard from my mother, my—the mad king used to shower his court in luxury and hold them on a pedestal. It wasn't just so they would defend him. It was so they wouldn't be able to find a better life elsewhere. It was so they didn't want to leave."

"And when they tried, like your mother, he got violent?" I asked.

"Not quite the same as that, but close," he replied. "He made it very difficult for people to walk away. Many courts do, I believe."

I bristled. "We won't. Because that's bullshit."

A smile played on Weston's lips. "I believe, if you were in that position, you would've made it a point to walk away, yelling curse words all the while, and taking half the court with you."

"Very likely," Nyfain said. "There are advantages to approaching a situation with a fresh pair of eyes."

I didn't miss the implication. There were disadvantages too, and I was very glad that Arleth was in the picture to help me through them.

"So the random attacks were the old court trying to haul you back in, obviously," I said.

"Yes," Weston replied. "Sometimes they came in force, and sometimes they tried to sneak in. But there was a reason they gave me so much power—I excel at my position. I can take mediocrity and make it shine. A strong army requires unity. It is the result of standing and fighting together, of learning to work together for the common good. It's about instilling trust and pride."

"You clearly know this is a kingdom of mediocrity, then." I lifted my eyebrows at him.

He huffed and bent forward, shaking his head. "This is unlike any professional meeting I've ever had in my entire life, even between my brother and I."

"We'll get to why in a moment," Nyfain said. "Finley, to spell out the problem, the queen and king from the Red Lupine Kingdom will not take kindly to his being in our court. If we were equal in power, they wouldn't have much sway. But they're prestigious and powerful, and we're...us. They might accuse us of stealing him from them. They could lobby to the council to demand his return, and if we don't oblige, we'll have to pay a fee. A very large fee, I imagine, given his magical talents and power level."

"What?" I sat forward. "His whole job was to steal people from other kingdoms!"

"Because those courts couldn't lobby against someone mightier than they," Weston said. "We can certainly explain the history of the situation, but that would take arbitration. They could drag it out for long enough to bleed you dry. In the eyes of many, a kingdom is only as good as its gold coffers."

"Moreover," Nyfain said, "they would feel inclined to set their allies against us, weakening our overall voice on the council. Given Dolion will be out to destroy me, the Red Lupine monarchs' accusations might cripple us. We might never recover."

"Do they have to know he's here?" I asked. "We can just say he left."

"No." Nyfain's power surged. "I will not hide anything. If I choose to take him on, I will do so openly."

"If…who decides to take him on?" I scooted away a little and turned, hitting Nyfain with a scowl. My dragon blasted a wave of power up through me, right near the surface. "I must be silly. I thought you implied this was solely *your* decision, as if I'm to be nothing more than a pretty queen to bounce on your knee. I must've misheard."

His dragon is ashamed of the man, my dragon growled, and I very nearly spat out laughter.

Rage boiled through the bond.

"I misspoke, princess," Nyfain said. "Let me explain. If I decide against it, we will pass the decision along to our advisory circle and ask for their feedback. This is possibly the most crucial decision for the kingdom thus far. We can't make a hasty call."

I'm pleased with that answer, my dragon said before slinking back down.

Oh sure, hang me out to dry.

Nyfain was right, though—this did require more thought.

I pushed away from him, freezing his arms with my will so he couldn't grab me and haul me back. I walked into the open space where his proximity wouldn't muddle my brain.

"Okay, here's what we know." I rubbed the back of my neck. "We are currently on our knees, yes, and we have a shocking lack of people in this once mighty kingdom. That said, Dolion just marched through with a full force of expendable soldiers, and we sent him sprinting away. So while we are financially vulnerable, we *do* have physical might. Most of the dragons will be staying. More dragons will undoubtedly come—Micah himself told me he'd be gathering them. If Weston can create a powerful wolf force, then that's us stronger still. So our greatest issues are financial, and probably also how we are perceived in the political sphere."

Nyfain looked at me for a very long moment, and he didn't have to say what he was thinking.

I lifted my hands. "I know I am the biggest hindrance with the political piece. I *know.* But I will fix that, I promise. Arleth said she can teach me if I'm willing to learn, and Nyfain, I promise, I will do you proud. Some-fucking-how, I will act like I'm supposed to. I'll be ready when it's time. Push off the coronation if you have to, but when the time comes, I'll be ready. I won't even complain about it." Under my breath, I added, "To you, at least."

A grin worked at Weston's lips.

"The financial piece is probably the biggest issue, and the Red Lupine Kingdom has its fair share of money," Nyfain countered.

I put out my hand. "Well, we have that bit of gold…"

He sat forward before swinging his legs over the edge of the lounge chair and bracing his elbows on his knees.

"We have the armory," he said. "Dolion wasn't over-ly interested in it since he had the gold reserve, and when he tried to show an interest, I…made him think again. Dragons like shiny things, and those swords have gems and gold in plenty. We always wore them to formal events."

"I never did understand a shifter wearing a weapon on two feet, no matter how pretty," Weston said, re-crossing his ankle over his knee.

It occurred to me that we were discussing his future right in front of him. Also that I'd essentially called Nyfain down, and he'd returned fire. We felt so comfort-able with him that we weren't worried about our positions or saving face. That had to mean something.

"I think it makes a bigger statement if we don't wear them," I said. "Our dragons are our weapons, and they are a helluva lot more terrifying than a bunch of spar-kling, pretty swords. Not having the option of the sword will make people think of the weapons we *do* have. And that'll lead them to remembering there is a very unhinged dragon in the room."

After a moment, Nyfain said, "Agreed. So we can melt the weapons in the armory, and we have the gold reserves. That'll get us the interest of tradesmen, at the very least. My mother also mentioned your improvements on common medical remedies will increase our profits from them, possibly exponentially. If we can get enough merchants coming through, we can start commerce. The only problem is that the kingdom needs so much that the money coming into the coffers will go right back out again."

"We've lived with very little for sixteen years," I replied. "Very little."

"My pack never had any riches," Weston said. "Your kingdom isn't as lacking as you imagine. Not to the people currently living in it." He paused. "But I do have some remaining questions."

"After all that?" Nyfain asked in faux anger before settling back and putting out his hand for me.

I took it and let him reel me back in.

"You were always going to say yes, weren't you?" I whispered as I settled into his arms.

"You should probably teach her the art of bartering," Weston said.

Nyfain chuckled, squeezing me close. "Weston hasn't been patrolling so diligently, asking nothing in return, out of goodwill. He's been taking measure, seeing if he could settle here. When he decided he could, he started gathering up reasons why we wouldn't be able to let him go."

"I'm not quite that ruthless," Weston cut in. "I *would've* done those things out of goodwill. Finley did me a great service. Actually, she did all of us in that dungeon a great service. If you've heard the stories, you know what I mean."

Nyfain tensed. "I haven't heard the stories yet, no. On purpose. I will hear them when I have an outlet for my rage."

"Wise," Weston said softly. "Well, believe me when I say that I would have done everything possible to help secure her and this kingdom. My honor dictated at least that much. But if I'd had a pack to go back to, I would've given you a definite departure date."

"Be that as it may, Weston understood that the might of our army is no small thing, Finley. We all know what he brings to the table there."

"And the number of village wolves who are now in his pack," I said, now seeing all the nuances of this conversation. "You guys have been circling each other this whole time."

"You really don't know *anything* about shifter life, do you?" Weston asked me with awe in his voice. "I know you've said it, but…"

"A lot of the shifters in this kingdom don't," Nyfain said with no ounce of humor. "For years, no one could shift or even feel their animals. After a while, they stopped talking about it, I gather. Instead of teaching their children the meaning of being a shifter, they struggled through sickness and famine, change and fear. This kingdom is not a clean slate, it is a broken one, and we must mend it and create anew all at the same time. But forgive me. You had some questions?"

Weston was watching Nyfain intently again. "They might not know the ways of shifters, but you seem very well versed in shifter ways as well as those of a court and crown."

"Very well versed. My fa—the late king gave me a solid education on such things. Sometimes it was trial by fire. But I am well armed for the political circuit, my mother even more so. We just need to get our financials up to speed."

Weston leaned forward, and I got the impression this was another battle between the two men.

"You'll follow through with giving Finley equal power? I saw it just now, but then, she wasn't really pushing back, since you were angling for that decision anyway."

"I will." A smile played on Nyfain's lips. "I have to. If I ever fuck up, I'm counting on her to set me straight. She has an extensive knowledge of poison, I recently learned. It isn't something I want to test."

Weston jerked back as though slapped. "You certainly don't speak like any king I have met. Nor any alpha."

The mirth drained out of Nyfain. "At one time in my life, I was the prince you'd likely expect, pompous and arrogant. The crush of the curse changed my perspective on a lot of things. But Finley's the one who will bring balance to the kingdom. I'm giving her the power now without formality. It'll be concrete as soon as I take the throne."

"Where will I fit in here? I've heard this kingdom typically has a dragon commander, similar to a beta. I must press upon you, though, that I will not answer to Micah. There is a reason alpha wolves and alpha dragons do not typically get along, and while we are doing well to play nice right now, if I have a permanent position, I doubt things will be so smooth."

"Yes, I've noticed the space you give each other." Nyfain let out a breath as he toyed with my hair. "I made a quick assessment in the last battle. I think it was a wise one, though it'll bear more thinking about. You rule the ground, Micah rules the sky, and I rule you both."

"What about me?" I asked. "And Tamara?"

"You'll do whatever you damn well please regardless of what I say"—he flicked my hair—"and Tamara will do everything in her power to lead the guard and try to keep you alive until I can come to your rescue."

I huffed. "Just wait. As soon as I have even an inkling of what I'm doing out there, juuust wait. It'll be me who has to rescue *you*."

"You did that already. You rescued the whole damn kingdom. It's getting old." He snaked his arms even tighter around me and brushed his smiling lips against my neck and up to my jaw.

My eyes fluttered shut, and I sank into the delicious feel of his muscular body. I tilted my head, moaning softly as his lips slid back down my neck and skimmed across one of his marks before I remembered myself and jolted, snapping my eyes open.

Weston had stood and grabbed the back of his chair. He paused before leaving. "Enjoy yourself, Finley. Don't worry so much about displaying your affection for each other. It's good for the kingdom to see that their king and queen are truly in love. It'll inspire a sense of trust and give them hope."

He lifted the chair, about to carry it out, but paused and set it down.

"I'm sure you'll learn this from the former queen's teachings, but meetings like this usually go down differently. Most of the time they're about people on the top wanting to show their underlings the height of their pedestal."

"I don't care about maintaining an image," Nyfain said, his knees to either side of me, his hard length pressing against my back. He ran his palms across my stomach. "How could I? By now, the whole kingdom knows I'm a bastard."

I frowned at him. "What a horrible thing to say—"

"Fine." He laughed as he buried his face against my neck. "That I'm not the rightful heir. Regardless, I don't care about seeming lax. I know I'll get challenges before long. I welcome them. I also know Weston won't be stupid enough to be one of those challengers."

Weston huffed, lifting the chair again. "You, seeming lax? Only here, with Finley. The second she steps away, your whole kingdom goes running."

Cowards, my dragon thought as Weston slipped away. I couldn't help rolling my eyes at her.

CHAPTER 21
FINLEY

N YFAIN CHUCKLED SOFTLY as he gave my mark an open-mouthed kiss and sucked in my suddenly fevered skin.

"Wait until he leaves the library," I said, my eyes fluttering closed again as he teasingly flicked his tongue across my skin.

"He'll be gone in a minute." He tilted his head, feathering his lips up my neck. "I need to get into that tight little pussy. I should've come inside you twice by now."

Heat enveloped me as he slid his hands up over my breasts, kneading and caressing them.

"Did you wear underwear?" he whispered, lightly pinching my nipples between his fingers and sending pleasure shooting straight down to my cunt. "I see that your beautiful breasts are free."

He pushed one of his palms down my stomach, over a hip and to the top of my thigh. He fisted the material before dragging it up, exposing my bare pussy.

"But what about—"

The click of the library door signified we were alone—not that Nyfain cared in the least.

"When they see me fucking you, they'll know you're mine," he growled, slipping a finger through my folds.

I lost my argument as his digit traveled through my heat and then circled my clit, getting everything slick.

"I want to lick this wet pussy, but I don't think I can wait." He dipped two fingers into me, hitting me just right and making me arch against him. His fingers sloshed through my wetness, the sound incredibly erotic.

"Maybe I'll lick you clean after I fill you up."

I moaned loudly at the filthiness of the statement, spreading my legs, pushing his wider. He hooked his feet on the insides of my knees and dragged them wider still.

"Do you like that, baby?" he said in a rough voice. "Do you want me to keep fingering you until you come so pretty for me?"

"Yes, Nyfain," I said, rolling my hips in time with those thrusting fingers. He pinched my nipple gently, giving it a soft tug as his fingers thrust.

"Tell me what you want, baby. Let me hear you say it."

"Fuck me with your fingers, Nyfain. Please. Make me come."

He worked harder then, rougher, the heel of his hand hitting my clit and his digits rubbing against that perfect spot within me.

The library door clicked open, and murmuring voices suggested we weren't alone anymore.

I sucked in a gulp and jolted, trying to peer around the tapestry. My dress was pooled around my waist, my knees spread wide, showing my bare, glistening pussy with his hand smacking against me as he finger-fucked me.

"Didn't we say we were going to try fucking at one of the sex parties?" He took his hand from my breast and grabbed a fistful of my hair. "Now we have an audience. They won't see you, Finley, but let them hear you. Let them hear how much you like getting fucked by your alpha."

Oh, goddess help me, his dirty words turned me on so fucking much.

I couldn't deny I wanted that. I'd seen a lot by now, even masturbated to a threesome, but I'd never been the one on display. I was still too shy to actually *do* any of that stuff.

This was my chance to safely explore my boundaries.

The tension left me and I melted back into him, releasing a little mew of pleasure as his hand smacked against me, the heel banging against my clit.

"That's my girl. Pull down your top. I want to look down at those pink nipples."

Desire flooding me, I pulled off my straps and helped my top fall down to add to the puddle at my waist. The air caressed my budded nipples.

"Suck this like it was my cock."

He pushed a digit into my mouth, and I sucked greedily.

"Hmm, that's right. Fuck, Finley, you're a goddess." He swapped the finger with this thumb before he moved down to roll the wetness across a nipple. He angled my body, leaning me to one side so he could bend over my torso and softly blow across the newly wet nipple.

"Holy—"

I exploded in an orgasm, the fingers he still had inside of me heightening the pleasure as they smacked against my clit.

He turned me enough to claim my mouth, sucking in my lingering moans as shivers coursed through my body. He pulled out his fingers and lifted his hand, breaking away from me long enough to suck in the digits as he held my gaze. His eyes blazed, and his cheeks hollowed.

He made a sound of enjoyment before moving me again and pushing me forward. He took a moment to pull off his shirt before snaking an arm under my breasts and lifting me enough so that he could undo his pants and push them down his strong thighs, that big cock breaking free and springing up.

"I realize I am being a hypocrite right now, pulling and pushing at you when you should be relaxing without strenuous activity, but... Well, I need to fuck you, so I guess this is me saying you were right and didn't need to be on bedrest."

I chuckled softly as he settled me down a little. He pushed my knees closed, looking down my body as his cock settled between my folds. A little bead of precum glistened on the tip.

Back leaning against his front, I reached down and ran my fingers under his cock while sliding forward a little. When I slid back, I left his shaft glistening with my juices.

His growl of pleasure competed with a soft moan

somewhere else in the library. Our efforts had inspired the others.

"Fuck," he said softly. "This place was always off-limits."

"Let it pass this time. You can make a royal decree or something tomorrow that we're the only ones allowed to have sex in here."

"Wait until tomorrow? Why is that?" he asked devilishly. "Is my little voyeur wanting to get off on someone else fucking in tandem?"

I ran my thumb over the head of his cock, making him suck in a breath. I wiped off the moisture and slowly lifted it to my lips as I turned my head. He angled me a little so he could watch as I took my finger in my mouth and sucked on it.

"Yes," I answered, rubbing the underside of his shaft again. Another moan filtered through the library, louder this time, as though someone were testing the waters.

I smiled as I ever so slowly ground my hips forward and then back, holding his cock tightly to me with my hand, rubbing it with my cum. More precum beaded, and I rolled it around the head before sliding his cock back down, moving forward again. He breathed softly against my neck as he slid his hands up to cup my breasts, sliding his thumbs over my nipples.

I put my head back, my urgency rising.

"Hmm, yes," I heard—a woman. Rhythmic grunts preceded the slapping of skin.

"We better hurry in case he has no staying power," I whispered, tilting up a little more and pushing with my hand so that his tip caught against my opening. He reached down to either side of my butt, lifting slightly for a better angle. The tip popped inside, and then I pushed back slowly, groaning loudly as he filled me.

"Hmm, harder, baby," I heard.

The slick smack of fucking rang through the library. I pulled my hips forward, his cock rubbing against all the right places, before jerking back, his cock slamming home.

"Oh fuck," Nyfain growled, reaching for my clit.

I gyrated, going faster now, listening to someone else fucking in our vicinity and moaning loudly enough to be sure they heard me. Naughtiness overcame embarrassment. As I boldly moaned, taking my pleasure from my mate with reckless abandon, I listened to them. My hips swung faster, and faster still, control fleeing.

"Yes, baby," Nyfain said. "Use me. Use your alpha's cock."

With a sudden frenzy, I leaned forward and braced my hands on his hips, bouncing hard, slamming down onto him over and over, getting louder and louder. The other couple joined us, sex filling the room. Nyfain's and my juices trickled down over his balls.

I spread my legs, looking down at where his cock disappeared into my glistening pussy. I reached down to cup and knead his balls. He was thrusting up, hard and fast, but not completely out of control yet. On the verge.

I wanted him to be lost with me.

Appealing to his dragon, knowing its weakness, I found the seam of his sack with my thumb and pressed as I said, "Fill me up, Nyfain. Fill me with your cum. *Breed me.*"

A strangled sound issued from his throat. My dragon pushed up close to the surface in a needy rush, and I felt his dragon do the same. They felt breed lust, just like I knew they would.

Nyfain's arms constricted around me.

"Finley," he said. And then his control utterly fled. I could feel it.

In a shock of motion, he grabbed my hair and pushed me forward, rolling me toward the other side of the lounger. I couldn't get my legs up in time, so they flattened, pitching me onto my stomach. He crawled up behind me, his cock having come free, and roughly pulled my hips higher before ramming forward. His cock seared into me, driving down deep.

I cried out, barely getting my knees to the edge of the lounger for purchase. He railed into me, rutting blindly, crashing home over and over, no rhythm. No sense.

A deep swell of fire raged through me, burning me inside and out. All thoughts fled within it. It felt like my motor ability had been taken over by someone else. My dragon purred, thrashing to get out, thrashing to get at Nyfain's dragon. I felt the same urge from his beast, the two of them feeling each other through the bond but wanting to experience this connection in their own physical bodies. Wanting to take to the sky and dive, rolling together as one.

Someday was my only thought as I shoved back against his thrusts, mindless, desperate. No way should I have been in rhythm with his erratic movements, but as his body took mine, pleasure continued to tear through me. I came, then built, then came, then built, then cried out with the sheer blissful agony of our blind lust. Deep love. Incredible desire.

We went at each other like mad things. We came repeatedly but kept going, over and over, his cock never losing hardness. The lounger broke under us, and we tumbled to the ground, Nyfain landing on top and wasting no time before getting back inside me. His lips fused with mine and his dragon started swapping out, pumping into me and then giving way to him. My dragon and I mirrored the change, naturally, seamlessly, until finally I couldn't handle coming anymore. I couldn't handle the pleasure, which was unlike anything I'd ever experienced. He wasn't even trying to help me by paying attention to my clit or mark or scales, and still I couldn't stop.

"Nyfain," I gritted out when it was my turn to take control. We were going at it in equal turns now, sometimes him on top, sometimes me, rolling around the floor in a frenzy. "Nyfain, please."

"Yes. One more," he said, and then bit on his mark a final time, his cock deep within me, our bodies slick with sweat and our flesh sensitive to the touch. One more thrust, and then the seams of my body unraveled and I blasted apart, shaking beneath him, clutching him desperately, holding on for dear life.

"I love you, my little dragon," he said before he hit his final peak and roared so loudly it shook the walls.

Light and color drifted behind my eyelids as I came down, breathing hard, his body a comforting weight over me. I had no idea how long we'd been at it, but I was sore in all the best of ways and half eager to try again.

He pulled up slightly, his chest heaving. Wonder lit his face. His gaze locked with mine for a very long moment, and I felt something move within my chest, such a profound love that tears sprang to my eyes. It wasn't enough to say the words. This feeling couldn't be properly expressed.

"I will get someone to fuck in the same room as us every day for the rest of our lives if that's the kind of sex it leads to," he said, a smile tickling his lips. "Although, as soft as you are, I think I rubbed my dick raw."

"I think you rubbed *me* raw."

He kissed me in a rush that turned languid in a moment.

"That's the breeding frenzy, then?" I guessed when he pulled out and sat, lifting me into his lap. I leaked all down around him and didn't feel self-conscious because if I had to deal with pooling, so should he. He'd made most of this mess.

"Yes. That's you in heat, sweetheart. So soon after imprinting. That's true love." I could hear the devotion and excitement in his voice. He cupped the back of my head and kissed me again before hugging me to him. "I'll feel it whenever you need me. Don't resist it. If you do, it'll cause you pain, I've heard."

"But..." I traced my fingertips down his cheek. "What about the dragons? They want to fly."

A glimmer of sorrow dulled his eyes for a moment, but he shrugged it off. "Maybe next time, if your cure works. Or they can attempt a very awkward and likely very gross ground-bound situation."

Fix their wings, my dragon thought. *I'd rather em-*

barrass myself in the sky than on the ground.

Nyfain stood and picked me up, cradling me in his arms. "Let's go to our rooms. I'm not in the mood to share you anymore."

"What about the mess?" I looked over his shoulder. "You're...productive."

Totally naked, not at all fit to be seen, he strutted toward the library doors. Once we left our little nook, I realized we did indeed have an audience. A big one. Whoever had been banging had either dressed or gone, and everywhere I looked, there were staff and wolves and dragons, all clothed. They all beamed as Nyfain carried me through the library. Some of them even clapped.

"This should be very embarrassing," I murmured, strangely not feeling the need to hide my face. "What in the world is going on?"

"They were sharing in the alpha pair's heat-mating. It's a ceremony in some packs of wolves, it almost always means greatly coveted offspring for dragons, so they probably liked the idea of a ceremony, and...well, some of the staff are kinky as fuck. They were probably just reminiscing." He opened the door and walked through it. "Don't worry about cleanup. After all the things I've seen in this castle, it's my turn to leave a little filth for them."

I giggled, looking forward to the days ahead, but it didn't happen again. I couldn't spark another frenzy. I could incense Nyfain's dragon, and that sort of banging was very fun and enjoyable, but it wasn't the same. It didn't kindle the heat and fire that had brought on our sex marathon.

Arleth said this generally happened when the dragon wasn't quite ready. It was the dragon who sparked the heat, not the human.

I knew, of course, that my dragon was more than ready to get with child, so I wondered if she was trying to suppress it so that I could cure them. She'd want to partake, I knew, and she wanted Nyfain's dragon flying with her to do it. She was waiting for me to cure them, apparently confident in my ability to do so, and quickly.

That bitch was hard to please.

CHAPTER 22
VEMAR

I STROLLED DOWN the large and clean hallway with a hand in my pocket, wearing a wild jacket that made me laugh every time I looked down at it. Hadriel sure had some crazy taste. He'd made an art out of absurdity.

Before being kept in a demon dungeon and forced into all kinds of heinous acts, I would *never* have been caught in clothing like this. I'd always been much too worried about my image. About my perceived strength and power and status among dragons.

But fuck, being a prisoner had bent my brain. I'd learned a thing or two about perceptions and how useless they were. I'd also learned that there was power in the abnormal. There was power in throwing people off-kilter, and these colorful clothes certainly did that. I didn't have Hadriel's flair, but a manic smile went a long way when wearing a jacket with a bunch of golden dicks hidden in the pattern.

"Well hello, Ms. Lovely," I told Charlette as I passed by.

She straightened up and turned to me with a sweet smile and fluttering eyelashes before her gaze roamed down my body and stuck to my cock. She was probably a few years older than me (or looked a few years older, at any rate) and was way, *way* more sexually evolved. I thought I'd seen some things with the demons, but this lady proved me a novice. I'd heard stories about this castle during the curse, but clearly the extent of the debauchery had been lost in translation.

"Hmm," she said as she stuck out a curvy hip. "Do you want to play 'find the dick' again?"

She'd seen this jacket before but hadn't played by the rules. The second I'd asked her to find the dicks, she was pulling at my pants.

"Can't right now, I'm afraid. Have you seen my little buddy?"

She pouted before gesturing down the hall. "He went that way not long ago. He was muttering something about the faeries and dinner plans. Check in with me later?"

"Maybe so. Maybe not."

I kept walking. There was no point in making plans with the cursed staff, as I called them—the staff members that had survived the curse within the castle. They might make plans with you, and then plans with another, and then plans with five more, and all of a sudden there was an orgy in one of their cramped quarters and that fucking guy named Liron randomly tried to stick his dick in your ass.

Speaking of dicks in asses...

"Hello, Miss Smith. Lovely evening."

I smiled at the head housemaid, all prim and proper with her ironed clothes, stiff back, and squared shoulders. She was great at her job by day and visited the impromptu orgies with a big purple dildo strapped to her person by night.

I'd wanted to know what pegging was, and she'd shown me. Boy had she shown me. I wasn't sure I'd ever be the same. I definitely-mostly didn't like it. Almost-mostly hated it a little. Kind of liked it some, but only with a reach-around. The whole experience had been quite confusing.

The cursed staff were careful to keep the kinky fuckery under wraps and behind closed doors, but if you knew where to go or whom to talk to, there was always fun to be had or weird experiences to endure and mostly quite like.

Fuck, this place was turning me. What had I gotten myself into, hanging out with Leala and Hadriel?

"Dragon," Miss Smith said by way of greeting as she passed by.

None of the cursed staff called me sir. It was a sign of respect amongst them, apparently. I had no idea why or what that meant, but also didn't care so didn't ask. I just watched out for that big purple dildo and that dipshit Liron.

The clock chimed down the hall. The faeries were supposed to be dining with the royals in half an hour. They needed to be ready for their walk down the stairs to show off their...sparkle or clothes or whatever it was that people wanted to see. That was why Hadriel had hastened to check on them, I'd wager, but Leala needed him to put the finishing touches on Finley. It wasn't like him to run late.

"No, please!" I heard from down the way, a woman's voice. She sounded like she was in anguish.

My heart skipped a beat and then I was running, shedding the silly slipper-shoes and staying as silent as possible. If some assfuck was forcing himself on a lady, I didn't want him knowing his death was coming until I was looking him right in the fucking face. I liked surprising people with extreme violence.

"Please don't," the lady cried, unshed tears in her voice.

Two rooms up, the one with the door slightly ajar.

I forced myself to slow a little so that my footsteps were nothing but a whisper. My ears tuned in, my hearing having always been good but now fucking excellent since the demon dungeon. When the darkness cut out your eyesight, you learned to rely on your other senses. I was an apt pupil at surviving.

"You can't tell, Hadriel, *please*," I heard, and I stopped up short, two paces from the door.

My heart still thundered in my ears. Confusion raced through me.

"Listen…"

That was Calia. I knew her voice. The other must've been her sister, Dessia. The lady hardly spoke, so I hadn't recognized it.

I looked around, getting my bearings. Yes, that was their room.

"All she wants is to stay hidden," Calia went on in a calm, even tone, presumably speaking to Hadriel. "You wouldn't even know any of this if you hadn't barged in here. In this, Hadriel, ignorance really is bliss, I promise. We've just told you why. We've told you her history. Please, have a heart. Keep this to yourself. She deserves peace and safety, doesn't she, after all she's been through?"

"Of course she does, lamb," Hadriel replied, and his voice reduced to a faint whisper. I doubted anyone but me would have the eavesdropping capabilities to pick up his next words. "But she puts everyone at risk, and I will not let any harm come to Finley. It's my duty to watch her back, and you must see the threat Dessia poses."

"She's no threat," Calia said earnestly. "Not to anyone. Not at all. Please, Hadriel, we explained why."

I leaned in a little closer, trying to catch every word as she went on.

And then I wished I hadn't.

CHAPTER 23

FINLEY

Three months later

T HIS WAS IT.

This was the elixir that would give Nyfain his wings back...unless it didn't.

I took a deep breath and, with shaking hands, poured the powder into the mug with the other ingredients.

"Hey," Hannon said softly as he entered the shed. "Sorry I'm late. Arleth asked that I create another one of the illuminated plants."

Although we still didn't understand why Hannon had the ability to create the illuminated plants, he'd figured out how to make more by "sprinkling" his power. His animal would only do it sparingly, though. He'd sprinkled my garden, and he'd sprinkled a few of the plants in the main everlass field, but that was it. He hoarded the rest of his power for when it was needed to defend his kin and community.

I wasn't complaining. Sprinkling a few plants was

plenty. The leaves kept growing, and in my tests so far, they seemed to work wonders. I hoped they did for this concoction as well.

He stopped beside me and looked down at the mug with the mixture in it.

"This is it?" he asked.

I took a shuddering breath, bracing my hands on the table's edge. "This is it. It has blood from Govam, the most powerful of the demons, the healing mixture the demons love, and the illuminated everlass. I think the illuminated everlass will essentially bridge the gap between Govam's power and that of the demon king. If I didn't have the everlass, I think I'd need Dolion's blood, freely given. Which...would not happen. You might've saved the day, Hannon. Hopefully. We'll see if it's enough."

Tears filled my eyes, and I backed away.

"What if it doesn't work?" I asked softly. "What if I wasted all this time and effort and it doesn't work?"

"Hey, hey." Hannon rubbed my back, careful to avoid the strips of my scales. "So what if it doesn't work? You'll keep trying until it does. You'll find the solution, Finley. You always do."

I shook my head, utterly exhausted. I'd been waking up early and going to bed late, always busy with this and the kingdom, always challenged, for months now. The only breaks I'd allowed myself were to sleep and bang Nyfain. I knew I needed to slow down, but I'd wanted to get this done. I'd wanted to solve this problem and finally put the stigma of the demons behind us.

Dolion had left us alone since that last battle. He was

likely preparing to meet us in the political sphere. We'd be heading into that fray soon, and I wanted Nyfain to be free of any demon taint when we did.

"I don't have any other ideas," I said as a tear overflowed. I wiped it away with the back of my hand. "This isn't like the other times. I have literally zero other ideas. I have nowhere to go from here."

Hannon put his arm around me. "You've said that before. You might not remember, but I do. You said it about the nulling elixir a million times. And look, you kept trying new things until you finally found the answer. You'll do the same thing here."

"Nyfain has been so patient with me. He keeps taking my trial elixirs, gets his hopes up, and nothing comes of it."

"What do you mean nothing comes of it? He sparkles now. He matches your gold dusting on most of his body. He's really proud of that, Finley. He's happy every time his dragon walks beside yours. You've given that back to him."

"But his flight—"

Hannon squeezed me. "He doesn't care about that anymore—you told me so yourself. After winning all those challenges, and with all the other dragons fighting on the ground with the wolves, he's happy and confident the way he is."

"People hate fighting on the ground with the wolves," I grumbled, knowing he was right.

Weston had taken on the alpha role, and he was excelling at it. All of the kingdom's wolves were now a part of the pack, something that pleased Hadriel to no end, since he could stay with me *and* be part of the pack. The dragons were less pleased, which had led to many challengers taking on Nyfain over the past few months. They'd lost, all of them, from the ambitious young village dragons to the power-thirsty outsiders, thinking they could best him because he was ground-bound. In the end, Micah, who'd taken on the position of commander of the dragons, encouraged Nyfain to deal a killing blow to the next challenger. He'd done it, reluctantly, brutally, and there'd been no more challengers since.

The spectacle had also scared a little humility into some of the court dragons, most notably Xavier.

Our people, dragons and wolves and other shifters, had been learning to fight together on the ground and in the sky, and they were excelling at it. We, as a kingdom, were excelling.

"They don't hate working together," Hannon said. "They might whine, but most of them actually like it because of how effective it is. I can feel a change coming, Finley. Weston is an incredible alpha, and he is amazing at directing his troops. Most of the dragons haven't worked with anyone like him. Even Micah is taking notice, and those two don't really get along. If it were any other wolf, they'd probably still have a problem, but not him. They're even mirroring his wolves' strategies in the air. Nyfain would rather you take a break than kill yourself trying to grow back his wings. He's told you that. I know he has."

I took a deep, shuddering breath, and said what I hadn't admitted to even myself before now.

"This is all that I am, Hannon." Sobs bubbled up. "My ability to cure is the one thing that sets me apart from everyone else. I've cured friends, neighbors, strangers. It has always been my *thing*. It's my identity, almost." I paused to wipe my tears away. "What if I can't cure the one person who means the most to me?"

Emotion dragged me down as Hannon hugged me, squeezing me tightly. He didn't speak, just waited for me to purge. We'd each had our fair share of breakdowns over the years, and we knew how to navigate each other's rock bottoms.

"I want to give that gift to Nyfain. I want to personally show him my worth, you know? Not to sell, or to help his subjects, but to benefit him directly." I shrugged. "I just want to prove that I'm special in some way. That I have a right to be at his side. Giving him back his shimmer and wings felt like the key to that." Another sob broke out of me. "What if I have nothing to offer but a bad attitude and the true mate bond that *nature* chose, not him? I'm common, and he's a prince. I'm not meant for this role. Nothing is coming naturally to me. I'm trying my best, but I don't fit here, Hannon."

I clutched at his shirt and cried into his chest, the real reason this meant so much thickening the air around us. My many failures crowded my memory, things like flight issues, fucking up the names of the key players in the other courts, which fork to use at dinner, and all manner of other things that just didn't seem to make sense. They were required all the same, though. For everything I did properly, there seemed to be eight things I got wrong.

"*Shh, shh, shh,*" he said softly, rocking me. He petted my hair, something he hadn't done since my freak-out when Father was deteriorating in health. "You are trying to learn a lifetime of mannerisms and education in a few short months. You need to be easier on yourself. You've come so far in such a short time. Arleth is incredibly pleased with your drive and determination. She thinks you are doing great."

I let out a ragged breath before more sobs racked me, all the fear, worry, and anxiety bubbling up and spewing over. I'd tried to be strong and keep it down, but it had grown to be too much. It was too consuming.

"You've already shown Nyfain your worth ten times over," Hannon said. "You saved his kingdom. You saved *him*. You chased the demon king away, nearly dying to do it, and you cured his people. Now, your elixirs and draughts are helping fill our coffers. You're creating unreal expectations for yourself, Finley. You're not seeing things clearly."

I wiped my eyes and took deep breaths, trying to calm down.

"Nyfain isn't a prince," he said, pulling back so that he could look me in the eyes. "He doesn't have the blood of kings. He has the blood of a villager from another kingdom and a strong and determined commoner, like us. He is blazing his own path, and he wants you beside him. He wants the woman who doesn't care whether he has wings. Who doesn't care that he looks like some sort of handsome nightmare. You've never judged him. You've always supported him, even when he didn't think he was worthy of it. You've always loved him unconditionally. *That* is what makes you perfect for him. Don't sell yourself short because you might not have created a cure that no one has ever heard of. You're more than that."

The tears flowed freely. "That stuff doesn't take any effort, though. I need something else to bring to the table."

His smile was sweet. "No you don't, you idiot. Not to him. And as for the rest of the kingdom, what more could you do for us than produce cures that fetch the highest price in the kingdom's history? I hear they are more sought after than the faerie remedies, especially with my special plant in the mix. You need to sleep, Finley. Fatigue is muddling your brain."

I frowned at him. "It's time for hard truths, is it?"

"You know the drill. This isn't the first time you've been like this. I could basically write up a script for it."

"Oh yeah, Mr. Perfect?" I pulled away and wiped my face. "You never freak out?"

"You know that's not true. I just haven't been the focus for a while. I'm waiting in the rafters, hoping for the time when I can be useful."

Which wasn't entirely true. He'd been leading the advisory circle these last months, and he'd come up with ideas that had helped bring our people together, including bringing in a traveling circus and merchants. It had also helped word get out about my cures. While he was kicking ass there, he was also sticking his nose into the budget, using his years of handling our family's accounts in hard times to save the kingdom money hand over fist. He was the only one that could scold me for wasting supplies and have me actually listen. I knew not to push back when he had the *tone*, something that had surprised a great many people. Still, I could tell he was unsatisfied. That he felt incomplete.

"You need to get out from under my shadow." I pulled a cloth from the workstation and blew my nose before tossing the soiled cloth into the corner of the floor. I took a deep breath.

"I'm okay here for the moment," Hannon said. "When you stop needing me, I'll find someone else to baby. Maybe Sable will be getting into trouble by then."

"Not her. It'll be Dash we have to worry about."

"That's probably true. He has found all the secret passages in the castle and gotten caught in countless rooms he shouldn't've have been in."

"Getting caught is his problem."

Hannon rolled his eyes. "Not the lesson he needs to learn, Finley." He paused for a moment. "Maybe you shouldn't give Nyfain the elixir just yet? Why don't we wait until you get some rest and shake off your expectations? You don't need to go into heat to fall pregnant. It just helps. It's not the end-all and be-all. Dragons do get pregnant without it."

I stared at him for a second. "How did you know my dragon was holding out on the heat until Nyfain's dragon could fly?"

A crease formed on his brow. "Didn't you tell me that?"

I frowned. Maybe I had, but I couldn't remember doing it. Still, there was no other way he'd know.

"It's probably a bad time, anyway," I admitted, feeling my cheeks flush. "But the feeling of it is…indescribable."

"Ah." He cleared his throat. "Still, there will be plenty of opportunities for you to try again down the road. And if you never find a miracle cure, well…even stubborn dragons have to face reality eventually."

One day his animal is going to show himself, my dragon thought, *and that is the day I'm going to ring his motherfucking bell.*

"Let's get this over with." I grabbed the ladle and took the mug to the fire. I scooped in water before letting it rest for a moment and then giving it a stir. The fragrance curled around my face and seeped into my senses—sparkling and vibrant with a hint of darkness. The smell had changed just a bit from the trial elixirs, owing to the different everlass I'd used, and my stomach somersaulted with the feeling it gave me. It felt right. It felt like a key I'd found to a lock that had always remained engaged.

I set it aside for Hannon and began cleaning up the workstation. He had always been the one to administer my concoctions. He was the one with the good bedside manner. I'd called him here specifically for this reason.

"Tell him to drink it immediately," I said as Hannon took the mug. "Tell him to get some sleep. I'll sleep in the tower tonight. I need to sort myself out."

Hannon picked up the mug. "I'll just remind you that, unlike with the cure for the demon sickness, this elixir isn't in danger of killing anyone. The worst that will happen is nothing at all. It's hard when we get our hopes up and we don't get the outcome we were going for, but at least no lives will be lost."

I sucked in air to settle my head and nodded. I knew that. Of course I did. This really wasn't the big deal I was making it out to be. But I couldn't help it. For some reason, this moment felt monumental. Not just because of Nyfain's wings, but because of the possibilities presented by the illuminated everlass and the mystery surrounding my brother's animal.

I was worried it wouldn't work, but I was just as worried it would.

"Just go," I said, my head a mess. I grabbed a couple of the dried, bundled herbs to return them to their rack.

"Okay," he said, walking out. Before he crossed the threshold, he said, "Take it easy on yourself, Finley. If you need me, or Dad, or the kids, just send word. We'll always be there for you. That hasn't changed."

I nodded and wiped away another tear, my heart ragged.

The shed felt empty when he left, and I sagged against the table. I really did need to get some sleep. My dramatics right now were way overboard.

As I was finishing cleaning up, the sky outside turning dark and a flickering candle my main source of light, Arleth entered with Delaney right behind her.

"Sorry, I know I'm late for dinner—" I started.

Each night was a new formal dinner, a new exercise in all the ways I could embarrass myself by not knowing which fucking fork to use.

"Dinner has been canceled tonight," Arleth said, stopping for a moment and gazing at my virtually clean workspace. She arched an eyebrow before continuing on to the corner to grab a few things. "I thought maybe you'd like to help me improve the taste on a few of these draughts."

Delaney was looking at me closely, her eyes narrowed. "No. I don't think that's a good idea, Arly. Let's go read by the fire—what do you say, Finley? How about a cheese plate, some fruit, too much wine, and a good book followed by dirty jokes?"

I frowned at her. "Dirty jokes?"

Arleth stopped what she was doing and started to put her things away. Then she came around to slip her arm through mine. "Yes, dirty jokes. When you drink as much wine as we are about to, the lines in the book start to run together. That's about the time we'll stop reading and start telling the dirtiest jokes we can think of. Come on. Let's get your lady's maid, too. I bet she has a whole store of dirty jokes."

"And if not dirty jokes, she should have a great many interesting stories," Delaney said, taking my other arm.

"And we'll get the funny little wolf butler."

"The butler can't come. This is a girls' evening," Delaney said as she bent to blow out the candle, and I let them lead me out of the shed. "We need to finally get electricity out to this shed. Now that the castle has it again, there's no reason for us to do without."

"The wolf butler will do fine as one of the girls," Arleth said. "I bet he'll have the dirtiest jokes of all."

"What's going on?" I asked as they marshaled me across the grass and to the back entrance of the castle.

"What's going on is that you are in need of a distraction, Finley," Arleth said, patting my arm. "We are going to provide it. The mass quantities of alcohol will be good for your stress and will also force you to sleep. Tomorrow, you'll be too hungover to worry about whatever your elixir did or didn't do to my son. You see? Sometimes alcohol is the answer."

"Alcohol is always the answer," Delaney said, and they both laughed.

I didn't have the energy to resist.

We ended up in the back study doing exactly as they'd said—eating, drinking, and eventually cackling at various dirty stories and jokes. I didn't have many, though I did tell them about Mr. Pee-body, the demon who'd paid for me to pee on him when I was imprisoned in Dolion's castle. Hadriel and Leala did not disappoint, though, and Hadriel was even dressed in the little maid outfit he'd had Cecil make for him for shits and giggles. He'd worn briefs to hide his junk, which would've otherwise been on display because Cecil apparently found that hilarious. We couldn't tell whether he'd noticed the red target sewn into the ass of the dress and decided against mentioning it.

Nyfain came to the door at about the time we usually went to bed, asking to take me out of there. He could obviously feel my worry and impatience and wanted to settle me, or sex it away, or both. I didn't want to see his scales, though. The elixirs usually took the whole night to work, and I didn't want to spend all night repeatedly checking them. So I resisted the incredible urge to go to him and instead downed my glass of wine and asked for another.

"Let me in, Mom," he growled from just outside the

doorway.

Hadriel shrank into his chair with a deep grimace, and Leala did the same.

Not Arleth, though. She stood her ground, with Delaney right behind her, both of them propping their hands on their hips and swaying a little.

"You're not welcome," his mother told him. "This is ladies' night."

"Since when do you have ladies' night?"

"Since we aren't ruled by a paranoid, small man who is threatened by women getting together for drinks and fun. Or are you, in fact, just such a man?"

Nyfain huffed, and Hadriel's eyes widened.

"Finley is unsettled, Mother. Let me in to see her."

"No," Arleth replied. Delaney crossed her arms over her chest. "She is happy as she is. Sometimes a woman needs her mate, and sometimes a woman needs her mate to fuck off. This is the latter. Go, Nyfain. She's just fine."

"I love that woman," Hadriel mouthed to Leala. She nodded adamantly.

There was a long pause. I felt Nyfain's anger swirling through the bond, but he didn't push.

"Tell her to come to me when she's done," he said.

"I will tell her no such thing. She'll make up her own mind, and you'll figure out which decision she made based on whether she comes to bed."

"Mom, you're drunk. You don't need to protect her from me. I'm not Da—I'm not the mad king."

"I *am* drunk, yes. I plan to get drunker. And she clearly does need my protection. She's way overtired, she's incredibly stressed, and she's been pushing herself too hard. Part of protecting your mate, son, is knowing when she needs to be forced to relax. I am doing that for you. You're welcome. If you knew what was good for you, you'd let me. Now go. The night is wasting, and I haven't had my fill of raunchy jokes."

"Goddess above," he said in exasperation. Laughter bubbled up, and then I was shaking with it, Leala and Hadriel with me. "Have it your way, Mother. Send for me if she needs to be carried out of there."

Arleth closed the door, probably in his face, and turned around indignantly.

"Carried out of here..." she mumbled. She and Delaney walked back over, poured more wine, and said, "Now, where were we?"

CHAPTER 24
NYFAIN

I LAY WITH an arm under Finley's head and my other secured around her waist, holding her tightly to my body. Soft morning light streamed in through the windows of the tower.

I'd gone to bed in the tower, knowing Finley would attempt to put distance between us by coming here. Hannon had warned me of that. She got nervous after administering a new medical treatment, afraid she'd be a failure, and I knew the elixir she'd given me last night was especially important to her. My mother had clearly intuited that too. She was very good at knowing when people were on the edge and needed to be pulled back. She'd had that job when she was queen and the king was terrorizing people.

Sure enough, Finley had arrived in the small hours of the morning, escorted by an equally drunk Leala and Hadriel, who quickly staggered away when they saw me.

Finley hadn't protested when I gently stripped her and then lifted her into bed. She hadn't rebuffed me when I slid in beside her and gathered her up in my arms. And she hadn't pushed me away a few minutes later when I held her hair as she threw up into the washbasin.

I lightly ran my thumb back and forth across her belly, appreciating the warmth of her against my skin while I listened to her soft, even breaths. I was content with her in a way I'd never been content before. At peace by her side, my dragon purring softly and her dragon sounding just as blissful. It was amazing how well we fit together. In all things, we were like two pieces of a perfect whole. I couldn't fathom not having her in my life. I couldn't even remember how I'd gotten by without her before the curse.

She stirred and moaned lightly, her hand coming up to rest on her forehead. She said, "Ugh," before turning and snuggling up against my chest.

"How do you feel?" I asked quietly.

"My head is pounding, and it feels like I have sweaters on my teeth," she murmured, eyes closed.

"Maybe you should take it easy today?"

"I can't. I have a million things to do. I have a hangover cure. It was in great demand in my old village."

"Of course you have a hangover cure." I laughed softly and was about to jokingly ask if there was anything she *didn't* have a cure for when I remembered the elixir for my wings. Given that I didn't feel much different than after any other one she'd given me, there was one thing, yes, and today I'd stop her from continuing her pursuit. The strain was too much on her. I knew she wanted to help me, and her dragon wanted to fly with mine, but enough was enough. I didn't need it—I needed her healthy, and her fatigue and anxiety were draining her too much. She'd end up distracted when flying and make a bad judgment call that would get her hurt or worse.

The fight we would have about it would likely be epic.

"I'm not in the mood for sex," she said, and then kissed my pec, followed by my neck.

"Don't mind my cock. It's always like that when I'm with you. I wasn't planning on—"

I sucked in a breath when she wrapped her hand around my shaft.

"I'm not in the mood, but I need it." She sucked the skin on my neck to the point of pain before releasing it, marking me. She pushed up to sitting, grabbed her head, and then swung a leg over my hips.

I couldn't help laugh. "I can be on top if you want? Or I can fuck you while you're on your side? Being on top is probably the worst possible idea when your head is pounding from a hangover."

"My dragon is insisting I bob on your cock," she grumbled, sliding her deliciously wet pussy along my shaft, leaving a glistening trail.

"Well, who am I to argue with your dragon?" I said, gripping her thighs as she pushed her hips forward and then grabbed the base of my cock, running the head through her folds before bracing it at her opening.

"I should be arguing with her, but..." She sat down hard.

My cock drove up into her, and we both groaned

loud and long. Her wet depths hugged me tightly, and then she started to move, hard and fast, no frills or nonsense, just fucking. She arched back, the ends of her hair dusting my thighs. She cupped my balls and then kneaded them in the way I loved, increasing my pleasure.

I squeezed her clit between two of my knuckles, making her jolt and then groan. She ran a hand up her belly and over her breast, kneading and then pinching the nipple. I watched, transfixed, and then looked down to my cock disappearing into her tight little body.

"Come inside me," she said softly as I worked her clit and she rubbed my balls. "I need you to come inside me."

My dragon pushed up to the surface, filling me with power. Her dragon took it and then gave it back with more, feeling the moment. Feeling our connection.

Finley had been doing this off and on since the mate-heat. She would get into these moods where she needed my cock and my seed. It was like she was a woman possessed, her thirst hard to quench, but it wasn't with the frenzy of that heated mating in the library. It didn't overwhelm my dragon.

I'd asked my mother about it, since I didn't know who else to ask, and she said she suspected Finley's dragon was suppressing the heat. That her dragon was hoping she could cure me so our dragons could experience the heat while flying. These moments of need were likely the heat trying to resurface.

"Nyfain," Finley said, her voice husky. She jerked her hips over me, working my cock in a way that made my eyes roll back in my head. "Fill me up, Nyfain."

I bucked up into her without meaning to, my hands slapping down onto her hips. I did it again and again, my dragon half stealing control, desperate to fulfill our end of the bargain.

Fuck she felt good.

I pushed up to sitting, ramming my cock up as she slammed down. Her breasts bobbed, and I captured a nipple with my mouth, making her groan and her head loll. She worked her clit as I pushed into her, chasing my orgasm, knowing she was getting close. Power pulsed between us.

"Nyfain," she begged, over and over, needing me to come. Needing me to explode inside her.

Out of control, loving it, I rolled her over and settled between her legs, still inside her and now pounding into her tight cunt. The sounds of wet slapping filled the room. She groaned and writhed, and I was right there with her, on the edge.

"Command me," she said, her eyes fluttering. "Command me to come."

She raked her fingers down my scales, and I barely managed to do as she said, the command almost incoherent as I hit my peak and shuddered over her. Her eyes snapped open, wide, and her fingers stilled. Sweat made her beautiful face shiny, and then she moaned, her insides squeezing me tightly as she hit her climax.

"*Yes.*"

She said it like she always did when she hit these moods, long and low. It was like she was giving me a pat on the back for fulfilling her wishes.

This time, though, her eyes went wide again after her

final shudder. She looked almost scared, like a cornered rabbit.

I frowned and pushed up a bit. "What is it?"

"N-nothing. Get off. My head hurts."

Turbulent emotions raged within her. I suddenly understood. She'd run her hands down my scales and felt the brokenness. She'd felt the failure. This wasn't the first time her hopes had been dashed.

"Listen, sweetheart, it doesn't—"

"Off!" Her will gave me a mighty shove, toppling me backward.

Something is amiss, my dragon said, confused. *Her dragon is delighted.*

Her dragon is always delighted after we service her when she's in these moods.

He couldn't argue the point, so he fell silent, still close to the surface but watching. He'd never admit it, but when Finley got unpredictable, he got a little nervous. There weren't many who could rattle him, but our mate was high on that short list.

I slowly stood as Finley climbed off the bed, holding her head. In silence, she dressed in the clothes I'd brought up for her last night. I pulled mine on as well, intending to shadow her until she'd had her cure and I could talk to her somewhat rationally.

She brushed her hair and teeth in a rush, not waiting for her maid's help, and then ran into Leala on the stairs.

"Good morning, milady." Leala offered her a curtsy and a smile. "How do you feel this morning?"

"How do *you* feel this morning? You don't look affected at all by last night."

"No, milady. I've had a lot of practice with parties and heavy drinking. May I bring you some breakfast?"

Finley pushed past her, her mood dark.

"She'll breakfast in the everlass house, as usual," I told Leala.

Finley continued down the stairs, and I followed. She didn't spare me a backward glance, but she didn't tell me to fuck off, either. I considered that a win.

When we reached the everlass house, Mom and Dee were already inside working on their elixirs and draughts, earlier than normal. Usually they waited until after flight training. Then again, given how much wine they'd plied Finley with last night, maybe they didn't expect to do flight training at all. Finley grunted in acknowledgment and went about gathering up herbs and dried everlass, presumably for her hangover cure.

"How's the head?" Delaney asked Finley, barely looking up from her work.

"Not ideal," Finley mumbled.

Mom glanced at her with a little smirk. "Do you have a remedy that will help you? Dee and I have one if you don't."

"I do." Finley ground the herbs and everlass and then mixed it with water before drinking it down. After she was done, she went and stood in the doorframe, staring out at nothing.

"And how are you, son?" My mom glanced up at me before doing a double take. Her eyes narrowed. "Is it just me, or are your scars less defined?"

I shrugged. I hadn't noticed. It had been a long time since I'd cared about my reflection.

"Take off your shirt," Finley said, rubbing her temples.

"Me?" I asked, taken aback.

"I am certainly not talking to your mother," she replied tersely.

A high-wattage smile lit up Dee's face. She clearly liked when Finley was in a dark mood.

"Finley, listen, about the elixir—"

"Take off your shirt," Finley barked, power riding the command.

My dragon roiled within me, not liking being told what to do. Still, I did as she said.

Mom gasped.

"What is—" Dee stopped mid-sentence, her eyes widening. They were all looking at my back.

My mom moved quickly, slapping her hand on my shoulder, turning me a little so Dee could see better.

"Did it work?" Mom asked breathlessly. "Finley—"

"I don't know," Finley replied curtly. "I'm too afraid to ask him to shift."

The words I might've said dried on my lips. I spun to face my mother.

Her eyes had filled with tears. "Go shift, son," she said quietly. "Go see if your mate is a genius."

"Don't be ridiculous. Of course she's a genius," Dee said, moving around to keep inspecting my back. "Do you feel any different, Nyfain?"

I shook my head, but then assessed again. Before I'd been too focused on Finley, maybe. Too worried about her mood and her possible disappointment.

Finley turned to survey me as I looked inward, immediately noticing a new lightness in the center of my being. An easiness that I didn't quite remember. I didn't feel that dark weight that I'd grown used to, tugging on me, dragging me down.

A frown crept onto my face. I looked into the gold-speckled, guarded eyes of my mate. Staring back was hope and fear. Anxiousness.

Couldn't be.

"Shift," my mother urged me.

"I'll stay here." Finley turned toward the back corner as Hannon jogged into the everlass house, out of breath. His red hair stood up all over his head, like he'd just rolled out of bed. His eyebrows lifted when he noticed my shirt was off, and I turned, showing him my back.

"He hasn't shifted yet," Finley told him, sitting on a chair and entwining her fingers as she settled in to wait.

Hannon gestured me out. "She never watches the patients, remember?"

For the other elixirs, she'd had me shift first thing in the morning, standing by while I did so. She'd observed the results closely, made notes, and then gotten to work. But this one was clearly different. This one was the culmination of months of work, and if it hadn't done what she hoped, she was at a dead end.

"It won't matter if it didn't work, sweetheart," I told her softly. "I'm fine the way I am. I've overcome my disappointment. Wings don't define me. I don't need them to lead our army or win challenges. Your health and wellbeing are much more important."

She lifted her chin and turned her head away, like she didn't want to hear it.

I didn't understand her reaction. I'd never seen her like this, so full of nerves. So unwilling to face the results of an elixir she'd made.

"Come on," Hannon said, motioning me out again.

At a loss, trusting him to know what was best for Finley, I did as he said. Once we were outside and out of earshot, Mom and Dee following behind, he explained.

"Hope and failure are funny things. In the past, she knew people would literally die if she failed. She knows you won't, of course, but old habits die hard. Her dragon wants this very badly, too. I think Finley's nervous about disappointing her. So there are a few things going on, and she's withdrawing to try to protect herself. It happens sometimes."

"You two are very close," my mother commented. "You know her very well."

"She's my sister, and we've spent the past several years taking care of our siblings and our father in a very small house. We've learned how to be a good team, because we had to work together to stay alive. That included learning when to avoid each other and when to interfere. Annoying her when she's in a dark mood is…not fun."

I took several steps away from them, buying myself some room. Trying to pretend my stomach wasn't flipping and sending nervous tingles through my body.

She couldn't have managed it, my dragon said, hope eating through him. *There's no way.*

I undressed and put my clothes in a pile, then walked farther away. Here it was. The moment of truth.

It doesn't matter if she did or not, I thought, trying to

317

maintain a level head. *Either way, we'll make a name for ourselves and this kingdom. Either way, we will own our place as king. We are still a dragon without wings. A mostly golden one. We can feel confident by her side.*

Shut up and get out of the way. I'm shifting, he said with a burst of urgency.

I did as he asked, allowing him to surge up and take over. We grew into his large dragon body, and I felt them immediately. I felt them growing up from our back and then out to the sides, large and glittering and *complete.*

We had wings.

She'd done the impossible and healed us. She'd given us back our flight.

CHAPTER 25

FINLEY

THE ROAR OF triumph blasted through the air and rumbled the ground, even from the distance. The emotions coursing through the bond were jubilant, excited, and awestruck. In a moment, the sound of wings beating at the air drifted toward us.

"Fuck," I said, emotion rising through me and clogging my throat.

It really worked? my dragon asked, imploring me to go outside.

My heart hammered. I could barely breathe. The butterflies in my belly had turned ravenous, eating their way through my middle. Still I sat there, desperate with hope. Terrified of failure.

A shape filled the doorway. The morning sunlight shone through my brother's red hair.

A *whoosh* sounded above the shed. Air wafted into the cabin, something large overhead messing with the air currents.

"You're wanted," Hannon said with a small smile.

"You did it. You cured him of the demons, once and for all."

I let out a ragged sob, bending over to put my face in my hands. If I messed up everything else in this new role, at least I'd done this. I'd completely reclaimed my mate from the demon king.

"Was he happy?" I asked through my tears. I felt his happiness, but I needed someone else to confirm it.

"Of course he's happy. I'm sure you heard the roar. C'mon. Go fly with your mate. He's waiting for you."

I felt the disturbance of the air, Nyfain still doing circles around the shed.

"What about his scales?" I asked, stalling.

I hope I don't embarrass us, my dragon thought.

I hoped so too. We could definitely hold our own in the air now, and we were incredibly fast, faster than even Micah, but I remembered seeing Nyfain in the air years and years ago. He'd been so graceful, so regal.

Maybe he's rusty, I thought. *Besides, we're still learning. We have a pass.*

That's exactly what I'm worried about. If he babies us...

I stood, knowing I needed to face this. Scared and excited and nervous to do so.

"Go and look, Finley," Hannon said softly.

Taking a deep breath, I straightened my posture, steeled my will, and walked to the door. Hannon stepped out of the way, and I passed through, feeling another whoosh of air. I swallowed the lump in my throat and looked upward, using my hand to shield my eyes from the sun.

The sight took my breath away.

He was just as I remembered. His golden scales glimmered against the deep blue of the sky. His great body moved through the air with incredible grace, turning with a beautiful fluidity of movement that I'd never seen in any other dragon. Not now, and not before. His scales gleamed without a single dull spot, and his wings spread out to his sides, large and whole. He was like a dancer, born to the sky, so incredibly comfortable up there.

For how exceptional he was on the ground, it was nothing compared to him in the air, even after all this time.

"You did it," Hannon said again, watching Nyfain circle above us.

I let out a breath slowly as Nyfain's dragon roared, the command tearing at me, telling me to get into the sky. He was tired of waiting. Arleth and Delaney had shifted and lifted into the sky too, I noticed, but they were a distance away, clearly giving us our space.

Let's go, my dragon thought. *Hopefully I don't look stupid next to him.*

Oh, how the tables had turned. Now we were the ones worried about looking bad next to him.

I stepped away and quickly stripped before taking a running leap into the sky. She exploded into her form, wings pumping immediately, lifting us before any of her feet touched the ground. She rose quickly, and if I'd had a stomach, it would've dropped out. The wind rushed at us as the ground fell away.

Nyfain lazily cut toward us. Two pumps of his

mighty wings, and he was next to us. His dragon rose over us, so fucking beautiful with his glittering scales, and did a quick swoop over our back, lightly dragging his tail up the middle.

My dragon shivered violently and purred, the warmth in our middle seeping through us and desire pooling hot. I felt Nyfain's mirth and love through the bond, and then he put on a burst of speed, stretching his returned wings.

Oh, he wants to play? my dragon thought, and put on her own burst of speed. She wasn't great at detailed maneuvering, but speed we had in plenty. No one could keep up with us once we got going.

She came up behind him and went to pass, but he veered into our path, blocking us. She tried to go over, and he rose, cutting us off. Around the other way, and he was there, anticipating us. Not letting us pass.

What's he doing? I asked.

He's toying with us, the fuckface.

Her frustration and anger rose just as fast as her excitement. Adrenaline coursed through our body. I yanked power from Nyfain and felt his amusement, his utter joy.

Give him hell, I told her, pulling more power.

No problem.

She flew higher, waited until he moved to block her, and then swooped down at a breakneck pace, something Arleth had advised us not to do, saying it was too dangerous. We could hit a current wrong and dump the wind from our wings. My dragon didn't care. She was an aggressive flier, never happy unless she was pushing the limits.

She did so now, curving to the side as she dove past Nyfain, scraping along the underside of his stomach with the claws at the ends of her wings. And then she was pumping her wings for all that she was worth, gaining speed quickly, closing the translucent parts of her eyelids, which allowed her to see through the rushing wind.

A huge roar rose behind us, and then the chase was on. We could hear Nyfain's great wings beat at the sky, pushing for speed. Pushing to catch us.

Get crazy, I thought, inwardly grinning, wishing I could look back and see him.

My dragon couldn't waste any time, though. She felt his proximity. She felt his swell of strength and power as he bore down on her.

Fuck, he's intimating, she thought with glee as she slanted her wings and tore down in a loop, another thing Arleth absolutely hated. *I've never felt anything like it. It's terrifying even though he's on our side.*

Not when he's trying to dominate, he's not.

He always wants to dominate.

She pulled up fast, gaining altitude, catching him just as he turned in the air. Since he was so much bigger than us, he needed more space and time to react. Speed was our advantage.

Go, go, go! I urged her.

She didn't need to be told. She was already putting on a burst of speed and power, flying toward the Royal Wood at a breakneck pace. It wasn't long before he was on us again, too damn big and fast and powerful.

Let's see him do this, my dragon thought.

No, no! I thought desperately, knowing what she intended to do. Arleth hadn't just expressed her disapproval of this maneuver—she'd forbidden it.

My dragon never listened.

She pulled up and fluttered her wings in the air, stalling, losing the wind. Gravity grabbed us, sucking us down to the ground. A shock of fear went through Nyfain, and he moved to intercept, intending to catch us as we fell. I had every belief he'd be able to. My dragon knew he'd try. He was too gallant for his own good. *She* only cared about winning.

She fell, slowly at first and then faster. Nearing him, she suddenly tilted, angled, and then put on a burst of strength to pull out of the fall. She zoomed past him, roaring, looking back at him and slapping down her tail. The spikes at the end raked across his back, not at all the sweet caress he'd given her earlier.

Manic glee stole over me as shock and surprise drifted through the bond—followed by pumping excitement and rage. She'd just issued a challenge to the alpha dragon.

Oh shit, oh fuck, oh no, I thought, giddy, wishing I could be the one in charge of her body. I'd been in charge plenty, though. It was her turn to frolic with our big golden dragon.

She was racing again, not really knowing how to fight in the air. We were still learning the basics.

His roar froze our heart for one moment, and then adrenaline pumped through our veins.

Come at me, fucker! she thought-hollered, banking in

the air and catching him hard on our tail.

She moved up and out, slapping him with her tail again before angling into a quick downward spiral and then lying low over the trees. She was using all her tricks for this one. Hopefully Arleth wasn't watching. And since she probably was, hopefully the lecture wouldn't be too bad.

Ready to shift? my dragon thought as she waited for Nyfain to turn and come back for us. It was only a matter of time before he caught us, but the fun was in the chase. The tops of the trees tickled our belly. Dragons rose from the villages in the distance, hearing the roars and probably wanting to check it out. Some of them would get to see their future king in the air for the first time, having been too young to remember before the curse. What an amazing sight. It would stick with them forever, like it had stuck with me.

His wings thundered through the air. Sharp pain lanced our tail. His teeth.

Fuck, he's on us already. Now! She yanked her tail away, found the first break in the trees, and dipped in, tilting her wings just right to dramatically slow us.

I took over, shifting when her body was a safe distance from the ground. My legs buckled and I rolled, catching myself and then popping back up. Soon I was running in the safety of the tree cover, looking up at that golden belly as it passed over.

Now what? I asked, out of breath. *If we rise now, he'll have us in a moment.*

Now we see what he does.

I jogged through the wood just to keep moving, feeling the power pumping through me, searing through my blood. Flames danced along my skin.

Several wolves ran from the trees and flanked me, keeping pace easily.

"Hey, guys," I said as I saw the big dragon pass over the wood again. "Let's get to thicker trees and force him to make a decision."

The wolves ran with me, joined by Weston, who stayed just behind me, protecting me while I played my games with Nyfain.

Breathing heavily, smiling too big, I ducked deeper into tree cover, which was slowly starting to come back thanks to Nyfain's Syflora gift. When he passed overhead this time, his shadow blended in with the ones cast by the trees. The sun dimmed, and I lurked, the wolves all around me, none of us sure of my plan.

"Don't let him see you," I told the wolves, hearing the disturbance of wings above us. My stomach fluttered with this game of cat and mouse, especially since I had no illusions about which of us was the cat. Nyfain was biding his time, deciding how much rope he wanted to allow me before he reeled me back in.

NYFAIN

FLUSH HER OUT, I told my dragon as I watched this all play out, so fucking excited and aroused that I could barely contain myself. We'd have that little dragon in the sky today. I didn't care who saw, and I'd make sure she didn't either. I knew her dragon wouldn't bat an eye. After she was forced to submit, obviously.

I can't shift that fast, said my dragon, who had a deep and profound respect for the aerodynamics of Finley's dragon.

She was sensational. The things she did were incredibly dangerous, and it had always been frowned upon in the court to take such risks, but the more advanced dragons, the ones with more courage than sense, practiced their trick maneuvers away from the castle. They would twist and turn just like that, so hard to catch. So effective in battle. My dragon couldn't bank that fast. He was too large for quick moves and fast spirals. He had to outwit her.

Land farther away and stalk her, I told him.

Excitement pumped through him. The glory of the hunt sang in his blood.

He chose a clearing far removed from her hiding spot, watching the air in case she again took to the sky. With the stealth born of sixteen years of hunting and fighting in this wood, he closed the distance separating us from her in no time. He slithered through trees and took the softer, spongier ground so she didn't hear us coming.

We caught sight of the wolves before we saw her. They caught our movement a moment later, freezing and then quickly racing out of sight. She was going to be pissed they'd given her away.

I heard Finley's whisper within a group of trees just up ahead.

"Does anyone see or smell or hear him?" After a beat

she said, "I know that body position, Weston. What are you hiding?"

Go now—

My dragon didn't wait for me to finish the thought. He charged forward, bursting through the trees and tearing off any branches that stood in his way. Finley screamed as she turned, her eyes fully rounded and terror lining her face.

A pang hit my heart. This might be a game, but I still didn't like seeing her that way. My dragon clearly had the same thought, because he slowed a little, giving her a moment to get her bearings.

We were fools, the both of us.

In a shift faster than I had ever seen in my life, she was a dragon again, forcing her body into the press of trees and breaking branches to fit. She charged us with such ferocity that we could do nothing but stand there and blink for one full second.

It was a second too long.

She reached us with teeth and claws and somehow also her tail, spinning and running while still managing to hit us. As her rump disappeared, the wolves scattered, and we were left standing there, dumbstruck, our side throbbing from where her tail had pierced our thick hide.

What in the fuck was that? my dragon said, launching forward to run after her.

But she'd already taken to the sky with a burst of speed. We'd have to push ourselves to catch her.

Finley has always thought very quickly on her feet. Clearly her dragon has the same merits.

I was not prepared.

I felt like laughing as he found a break in the canopy and pumped his mighty wings.

I can't believe she cured us, I thought as he rose and caught sight of her gorgeous burgundy scales dusted in gold. She was heading toward the sea. *I cannot believe she figured out how to cure us.*

Of course she did. I cannot believe you doubted her.

As if he hadn't also been surprised.

I never thought we'd fly again, I thought.

You need to have more faith in our mate.

Power pumped through us as we gained on her, faster than her when moving in a straight line. Through the bond we could feel that Finley and her dragon both felt the adrenaline—they were hoping we'd catch them, and pissed by the inevitability that we would. They hated being outdone but loved that final moment when they submitted and let pleasure carry them away. They didn't seem to realize this, but *I* submitted each time too, giving myself to Finley totally. Losing myself in her. Letting control flee, holding on to her as my lifeline to tether me to this place.

My dragon was about to prove the same.

They were just ahead of us now, losing their head start, unable to keep us from closing the distance.

I belatedly noticed other dragons in the air, lazily soaring, watching us play with our little mate. They were giving us plenty of space, either knowing or instinctively feeling that my dragon would give up the game the instant another dragon encroached on his space. He could fight in the air now, which made him exponentially deadlier than he'd been on the ground. He'd always excelled in the air above all things, and he was not shy in proving it.

Finley's dragon banked right, glancing back, her tail slicing through the air just above.

I'm going to take her here, my dragon thought, a swell of heat and desire pounding through him. *In the air. I want her to claim us for the second time, here, on our first flight together.*

Does she know how?

If not, she'll learn.

Instead of following her, he cut the other way and curved backward, swooping up and over his body to twist in the air. He angled and pumped his wings, quickly on her again. She cut down and then swooped to the left, so fucking quick it was unbelievable, but he adjusted—more powerful and experienced—and was on her again, just overhead. He pushed forward a little, but instead of overtaking her, he reached down with his tail and felt just at the base of hers, stroking firmly.

A wave of pleasure rolled through the bond. He'd never fucked another dragon in the air, but we'd heard plenty of stories. *Plenty* of stories. He might not get things perfect on the first time, but instinct was driving him, giving him ideas of what to try.

Finley's dragon fluttered her wings, losing a bit of speed, trying to fight the raging desire to get at her alpha dragon. She still wanted to play the game, and I hadn't missed the nervousness trickling through the bond, but she was desperate for her mate. Always had been. She wanted this with everything that she was. My dragon felt the same way. These two had always wanted each other. Always. Even back when Finley and I were mucking everything up.

Still, keeping up appearances, she pushed ahead again. The sea glimmered in the distance, a beautiful backdrop. Finley's emotions pumped through our connection, desire tinged with disgust. I would've laughed if I could. She didn't know shifter life, so this would seem very unsavory to her.

She'll get used to it, my dragon growled.

Finley's dragon cut right and then tried to twist over her body, copying the maneuver we'd just used. She got halfway, but her wings didn't flare properly and her body was positioned wrong. A shock of fear coursed through the bond, and she was falling, struggling to right herself. My dragon was there immediately, swooping beneath them and flipping, grabbing her with his teeth and front feet. Twisting over again, he pumped his wings hard, aiming upward, needing altitude.

Her dragon struggled, but just barely. She wasn't a fool. She didn't want to be let go and figure out how to stop plummeting to her death.

A strange sort of fervor rose through our middle, echoed in the bond.

Is that the heat? I asked, not recognizing this feeling from the other night.

He didn't answer me, and soon I felt Finley's dragon go still within his hold. Finley's confusion matched mine as the strange feeling flared, throbbing within us like a drumbeat. Fire curled out of my dragon's nostrils and rolled over Finley's skin. Still we climbed. Still that throb

K . F .   B R E E N E

pounded through us, harder and harder, seeping
through them too.

When we were very high, almost unable to breathe
in the thin air, my dragon twisted again and let go,
falling away. Finley's dragon caught herself quickly and
swooped down to meet us as we righted and pushed back
up high.

The pounding feeling reverberated all around us,
scraping along our bones, thrumming in our chest. He
let out a roar unlike I'd ever heard, sensual and erotic,
calling her to him.

As if in a trance, zero fight in her now, the little
dragon flew close, clearly enraptured by the feeling
thrumming between and within us.

A dragon's mating call. He was going all out.

She fluttered her wings and curled through the air
around him, quick and darting, barely sliding against the
tip of his tail before fluttering her wings against his
underside. He purred loudly, liking his little mate's
attentions, staying stoic in the sky as he pumped his
erotic mixture of sound and feeling through the air,
spurring her on.

I felt Finley through the bond, and I sank into that
special place where we seemed to share one soul. She
gripped me as tightly as I gripped her, feeling each other
as our dragons did their dance.

The magic entwined through us all, the four-way
bond pulling all of us together. I heard Finley's purr now,
and it matched my dragon's. I felt their love and excitement, their desire. And then it was happening, the
dragons locking together and hurtling through the air,

wings and teeth and claws all scrabbling for purchase as they tried to figure things out. When they did, I felt my dragon's eyes flutter closed as he sank into his mate for the first time, seated exactly as he'd always wanted. Exactly as he'd envisioned it.

The dragons clung together, the wind rushing by them, their pleasure pumping through us all. I would've groaned if I could've, and I could sense Finley's answering pleasure. The feeling was indescribable. The danger, the height, the *falling*, all while entwined with a lover. All while giving and taking from each other, sharing everything we were and holding nothing back.

The trees swam into view. The ground spun up to meet us.

My dragon pushed away before pumping his wings, getting his bearing and watching to make sure his mate did the same. When she steadied herself, they soared upward again, swirling around each other, reaching high and then crashing together again, nimbler and more confident this time. He fit into her like a last puzzle piece: perfection. Their pleasure rose—all of our pleasure rose—as we fell. He plunged in deep, and she held on, receiving him in ecstasy. Their purrs were a cacophony, their bodies merged as one. And then Finley's dragon growled before she bit into him, claiming us again, only this time in dragon form.

My dragon let out a loud roar of victory as he released into her for the first time. I felt her climax through the bond, the dragon shuddering against us. She held his flesh in her teeth as we continued to tumble, all of us coming down from the pleasure, Finley and I holding each other tightly through the bond.

Soon, though, the dragons had to shove back from each other and get their bearings. They weren't ready to go back to the castle, though. They weren't ready to let the "two legs" take over. Instead, they made lazy tours around the kingdom, inviting other dragons up to join them, soaring and dipping, playing by each other's side. Those who couldn't fly filled the villages and crowded the open spaces, watching us pass overhead. Many pointed; some shifted and ran on the ground under us. It seemed like the whole kingdom had turned out to see the royal pair glide through the sky in all their glory.

Finley had given this to me.

There weren't words for what I felt.

It wasn't until the coming of the afternoon, when the burn of flight was settling into my dragon's bones, and Finley had started to lag, that we finally headed back to the castle. We touched down, Finley having mastered her landing, and shifted. I was barely back in my body again before I had her in my arms, hugging her tightly and walking her back to the castle. We wouldn't be doing anything today but basking in each other's touch.

"We're moving the coronation closer," I told her as I walked her in through the back of the castle. "We're ready. I want you as my official queen, and then I want to take on the world."

CHAPTER 26
FINLEY

"**Y**OU LOOK GORGEOUS, dove," Hadriel said, looking over Leala's handiwork as she put the finishing touches on my *look* for the coronation. "You're going to steal the show."

"I can't believe this is real," I said as I stared at my reflection in the mirror.

The likeness of me looked back, softer than I remembered, with gold-flecked eyes underneath a large, stately crown. Jewels adorned the band, climbing up in four sections to meet at the top in a spire topped with a large ruby, twinkling for all to see. The velvet covering my head was supposed to match the scales of the king's dragon, but Nyfain had altered the practice. My velvet was burgundy to match the scales of my dragon, and his would be gold.

He was getting ready in the king's suite. According to him, he wanted to see the full effect rather than witness my transformation in stages, and I suspected he wanted the same for me.

"Here we go, let's get you up." Leala reached for my arm, and Hadriel stepped closer on the other side, helping me out of the chair with the crown still in place. Usually, they apparently put the crown on when the walk was about to start, but Leala had been worried about the curl she'd done *just so.*

"I cannot believe this is real," I whispered, admiring the beautiful, glimmering gown inlaid with specks of ruby, hugging my bust and then flowing down my legs and into a long train behind me, currently held by a couple of chairs. "This has to be some mistake."

"Just remember," Hadriel said, pressed into my side, smiling at me in the mirror. "The master is not the true prince either. He doesn't have the blood of Wyvern's kings. He fought for his place, just as you did."

"I didn't fight for anything."

"What's that?" He pulled away a little and put a finger to his temple. "Am I an idiot, or didn't we take a tour around the demon king's dungeons and then battle him *twice*? Leala, is it me who's the idiot?"

"Yes," Leala said as she held out a pair of burgundy gloves for me to slip into. "But you did certainly fight for your place, milady. No one in this entire kingdom questions that. There are some very large stories going around about you."

"You're welcome," Hadriel said. "I had *no idea* the villagers were such gossips. Worse than the castle by far."

"They just aren't used to your theatrics," Leala replied.

Hadriel squinted one eye. "Yes, good call. I better be a little more discreet. I don't want to blow my load too quickly."

"For once," Leala murmured with a little smile.

Hadriel sucked in a breath and put his palm to his chest dramatically. "How *dare* you! You know I'm no one-pump chump. I've worked very hard on stamina."

She laughed as she stepped back to survey me. Her smile grew wider. "You make a very beautiful queen, milady."

"Yes, you do, I must say," Hadriel said. "You'll easily shine among all the simp queens from the other kingdoms, and when it's time to swing your tits around, you'll shock or scare or intrigue them all. I am *so* excited for going on our tour once we're official with the council. How many kingdoms have written in and expressed interest in having us visit?"

"Five," Leala supplied, turning me toward the outer room, something made more difficult by the train. "Calia asked that we visit her kingdom before the council. So four have requested to meet us some time after."

We'd piqued the curiosity of the other kingdoms. Arleth had said their requests for meetings were basically the equivalent of them circling us. One of those kingdoms was Red Lupine, and Nyfain wondered at their decision to send a note before the council. They had to know we had Weston. I could feel his unease whenever we spoke of it.

Still, none of that mattered right now. Not because of the coronation, but because of where it would lead: the council meeting. It would give us a chance to size up the other kingdoms. After that, we'd have a better idea of which of them to seek out for possible alliances, hopefully with the help of the faeries.

"Other than the demon kingdom, which was a pretty shitty vacation, I've never left the kingdom, and I am so fucking excited I can't even believe it." Hadriel clapped. "I can't believe this is real either, love. But it is, so let's make it official."

Sucking in a deep breath, I walked toward the outer room where Arleth, my family, and Vemar were waiting. Even though my guard, led by the incredibly competent Tamara, was now set, Vemar hadn't taken the hint that he was no longer needed. He'd basically taken up the role of hanging around and scaring away anyone who didn't expressly belong. He was big and powerful and crazy, and no one wanted to mess with those traits in a dragon.

Impatience swirled through the bond, followed by urgency. "Nyfain's nervous," I told the others as I crossed the threshold.

"Don't worry about that, dear," Arleth said. She came forward as she scanned me with glimmering eyes. "He wants to hurry and make it official. Ever since you gave him back his wings, he's been looking forward to this moment. My goodness, Finley. The goddess herself wouldn't look as perfect as you do. You are a dragon queen, through and through. Your dangerous edge cuts through all that sparkle and glamour. Your power and the fire curling across your skin—you are an absolute vision."

Father came forward then, tears brimming in his eyes, the wisps of hair across his balding head artfully combed over. His suit was tailored and fine and better than anything he'd probably worn in his whole life.

"I knew you'd live among the stars one day," he said with a tremor in his voice. "I wish your mother could've been here to see this. She would've been so proud." A tear overflowed, and he grabbed my hands. "So proud!"

Heat prickled my eyes, and my chest felt heavy. "Thanks, Dad," I said, hugging him.

"I gotcha—here we are." Leala grabbed the crown so that it didn't topple off my head. It had been made with my exact measurements in mind, but it was heavy and cumbersome, made with jewels we'd taken from the ceremonial weaponry in the armory. Despite the booming demand for our cures and elixirs, we didn't have a lot of funds to spare. With Nyfain's and my approval, Hannon had poured most of the kingdom's profits back into the people, continuing to fix houses, lanes, and get them set up with supplies to make sellable goods. There was an incredible expense involved, but Nyfain was confident it would be better for the kingdom in the long run.

Sable and Dash stepped up, Sable in a satin dress with a smudge of dirt around the hem, with really cute curls bobbing around her head. Dash had his hair combed with a little splash of unruliness around his cowlick, and he wore a beige suit that had one more dirt smear than Sable's. They'd clearly not done their best to keep things clean, but given their normal state of attire, I counted myself lucky.

"Wow, Finley." Sable's eyes sparkled as she looked me over. "You look really pretty."

"I thought you didn't like looking pretty," Dash objected. "What's the point of it?"

"To make people envious." Sable elbowed him. "To make them desire you."

"Ew. Finley, that's not right, is it?"

I laughed and ran my thumb across his cheek. "No, that's not right. I'm playing a part. People like to look at pretty faces, and so I am distracting them with mine while plotting a way to get my knife in their ribs." I winked at him.

"Finley, now, that's not the kind of thing a queen should say to children," Father admonished.

"Ever the dragon queen," Arleth said, motioning me toward the door. "Go make my son the proudest king this world has ever known."

Vemar stood with the door handle gripped in his large hand. "You sure do clean up well, Strange Lady," he said with a crooked smile. "But look at this." He smoothed down the burgundy satin lapels of his suit coat. The rest of his ensemble was black except for the burgundy loafers adorning his huge feet. "Pretty slick, huh? I was so excited to represent, I barely noticed that weird ol' seamster talking about getting his eye poked out while fitting me. He's obsessed with eye safety for some reason."

"Yes, yes, we know your cock is huge," Hadriel cut in dryly. "Let's move along."

"As you wish, Sir Butler." Vemar opened the door with a flourish and then bowed as I passed.

Tamara waited just outside the door in a loose slip of burgundy, ready to shift at a moment's notice if any threats should arise. The rest of my guard waited beyond her, along the sides of the hall—a collection of dragons and wolves, returning and new, women all. Nyfain would have a collection of men in his guard, and our burgeoning army would be a free-for-all, spots going to those best suited for them.

"I think I am getting a little tired of the color burgundy," I murmured as I reached her.

Speak for yourself, my dragon thought.

Tamara gave me a tight smile. "The mad king was obsessed with seeing the color of his scales everywhere," she said as we walked down the line of the guard. The guards toward the end started walking, keeping to my sides to box me into their protection (or not let me get in trouble). "The whole castle was essentially a dull green. Right this way, your majesty."

She gestured me toward the grand staircase.

"You're going to use my title all the time now, aren't you?"

"Only when it's necessary, I promise."

She increased her speed to walk directly in front of me with Jade and Lucille at my sides.

I'd wondered if there was a throne room in this castle back in the day, and had since realized that yes, there had been, and the demons stole it piece by piece so it could be rearranged in Dolion's castle. Dolion had obviously changed the colors, however, wanting to fit the stolen riches to his tastes.

"Was there ever a contract drawn up regarding the mad king's dealings with Dolion?" I wondered aloud. "I can't imagine it was expressly noted that Dolion couldn't steal anything, or that he could, but surely there were some ground rules. Besides, it seems like the council must have some rules of warfare they ascribe to, and stealing would be frowned upon."

"What does that matter?" Tamara asked. Her near-whisper reminding me I wasn't supposed to be talking. I never did things the way I was supposed to. Ceremonies made me impatient. Nyfain too. They just seemed like a colossal waste of time.

"It matters for when we see him at the council," I said. "We might not be able to get the kingdom's stuff back, but we can surely make him look even more despicable. That goes a long way in polite society, or so the queen always says."

"You will need to call her the queen mother, or by her name," Jade whispered. "You're going to be the queen now."

"Right, right." I didn't tell them that this all felt far-fetched. They weren't wrong, but I didn't feel like a queen at all.

People gathered around the stairs and the first floor, smiling and cheering as I made my way down. As a procession, we turned toward the rear main ballroom, which had been modified into a new throne room. Grander than the last, it was furnished in high style and with large oil paintings of past kings and queens and scenery on the walls. It was here the villagers would come every month to pay respects or make petitions, asking us to sort out their grievances. It would also be a place where we'd hold court, which was basically like giving the nobles a turn to bitch.

As I approached, I kept my gaze down for a moment, the nervousness so extreme it felt like it would choke me. But then I looked up slowly, finding Nyfain at the rear of the room, facing front. Steps had been built leading up to a dais, and two golden-sprayed wooden chairs waited for us, fairly plain because we'd run out of armory to melt, with burgundy-cushioned high backs and seats. The sprayed woodwork was intricate and exquisite, made by a really fine master craftsman from one of the villages who liked banging demons and had thus escaped their culling of talented people.

Eventually we'd up our game, but they would do for now.

A long, flowing velvet cape spread across the floor behind Nyfain, arranged in such a way that I couldn't see any other pieces of his outfit, just his somewhat tamed brown hair peeking out from a similar crown to mine. Heart thumping, palms sweaty, I started forward, only then seeing Hannon at the top of the stairs, looking down at me.

Nyfain and I had agreed that, in place of anyone more suitable, our former head advisor (a role that had been given to Arleth) and current treasurer would draw up the official documents. Hannon had asked for the privilege and responsibility to go to someone else, and at first I agreed with him, but Nyfain was adamant. I'd relented and so had Hannon, mostly because it wouldn't be prudent for the former queen to do it (for some reason) and we were short on time. Nyfain wanted this done and done now. He was tired of waiting for his queen.

How could a girl let her brother refuse that? She couldn't. Poor Hannon was locked in.

He wore a strange rectangular hat that was likely reserved for religious people (they'd long since succumbed to the demons), and a long cream robe with gold and burgundy lines down the front. A little smile played across his lips, and a strange sheen, like the full light spectrum, filtered into the air around him.

I took a deep breath and walked at a measured pace toward Nyfain, following the red velvet rug without glancing at the various people gathered in the room. I almost wanted to turn around; my feelings of unworthiness were beating into me.

Then Nyfain turned just a little, looking back at me. I met his golden gaze, now with a light speckle of my burgundy from the double claiming, and locked on to it. He reached me through the bond and brought me closer to him. We were intimately connected in a way most people couldn't be. True mates in all things. We were in this together.

So I stepped up next to him, still looking at him, and even though we were supposed to give Hannon our undivided attention as he said the official sermon, I couldn't bear to tear my eyes away from my golden dragon prince, asking me to take his hand and remain by his side forever.

"Are you ready?" he asked me in a subdued voice when Hannon had finished. Light drifted from Hannon, glowing down around us, making the air wavy with pastel light and power. Little sparks danced around Nyfain's face and against his crown, playful and beautiful, a perfect accent to this amazing moment.

Nyfain reached out, and I took his hand. After a

beat, during which the staff grabbed our long trains and lifted, he circled me, turning me as he did. For one solid beat, he looked into my eyes, hand in hand, and then we walked forward as king and queen of Wyvern.

AFTER A SLOW walk down the halls and up a flight of stairs, Nyfain led me to the king's chambers, moving from the prince's chambers we'd been sharing since I came back. It was a grand set of rooms I'd never entered before, at least twice as big as the queen's, with a large washroom, a large bedchamber with a bed much too big for just two people, a study, a personal library…and that was about when I stopped looking around. I rushed to the library immediately, nearly knocking off my crown and sending Leala lunging after me.

"We still have work to do, sweetheart," Nyfain said.

Leala unstrapped the train from around my neck as Urien saw to Nyfain. The livery collar—I had one too, now!—weighed heavily on my shoulders, and Nyfain took my hand again before leading me toward a balcony at the far end of the room. Two staff I didn't know opened the glass doors, and Nyfain paused.

He took a deep breath. "When I was young, I used to dread this day. I knew it was my task to lead this kingdom to greatness, and I didn't see how it could possibly be done. Then, years later, I walked away without the intention of looking back. Through a sick twist of fate, I was forced to return, to bleed for this kingdom. To learn the true meaning of duty." He looked at me. "And I thank the goddess from the bottom of my soul it happened this way. Now I *can* see a way forward. I can see a future. And when I wake up next to you, smelling your scent and feeling your hair brush across my chest, I can see my forever. Every trial I've been through was worth it to find myself here, with the woman I love by my side and a great kingdom at my feet. The nightmare king with his warrior queen. You've given me a chance to rise to my full potential, and I cherish you for that. I will love you always."

Tears crowded my eyes. "I am literally living my dream right now, Nyfain. The dream I had since I was young. I've found my golden prince, and I'll love my golden king until the day I die."

You are absolute shit at making speeches, my dragon murmured.

Nyfain smiled, though, and asked me again, "Ready?"

I gave a slight nod, and we walked forward, hand in hand, stepping out onto the balcony overlooking the grounds. The area below us was crowded with people who wanted to see their king and queen. They cheered and waved in the bright sunshine, yelling things like "all hail" and "long live" and "yee haw." We waved demurely, as was customary, and then I felt adrenaline rise through the bond.

"I would like it to be known by all four of us," I said through mostly shut lips so no one below would know that I was talking, "that we are not going to bang in the air tonight. Got it? No dragon sex on the day of the coronation. I will stage a hostile takeover and send us careening to the ground if you fuckers even try."

I could feel my dragon grumbling and a surge of

frustrated power from Nyfain's dragon. Nyfain just laughed. He was never embarrassed when the dragons went at it, something they'd done at least once a day since Nyfain's recovery a little over a week ago. My stupid dragon had learned how to hoard the heat for just herself, something Arleth had never heard of, and so she saved it all for herself, the selfish dipshit. I was no longer opposed to dragon fucking, even though it had been very awkward that one time they tried it on the ground (the tail was a problem), because it was a pleasurable thrill, but I was opposed to it becoming a spectator sport.

I took a step away from Nyfain and held my hands a little to the side. He did the same. We were about to attempt something that had never been done before. Something that not many shifters could do. Riled up by competition, though, hating to be outdone by my dragon, Nyfain's dragon had risen to the occasion.

That was what Nyfain said, anyway. I had a feeling he had worked just as hard to make this happen.

Leala took my livery collar, and two more staff peeled off my long gown.

"Just so we are absolutely clear, Strange Lady," Vemar murmured from beside the curtains behind us, "you *have* practiced this, right?"

"You should call her Dangerous Lady, not Strange Lady," Leala whispered, coming back for my undergarments.

"Answer, please, *Crazy* Lady," Vemar said.

"You've seen me do it, Vemar. You know it's no big deal," I responded.

"I think he was talking about that prickly king beside

you, love," Hadriel mumbled.

I glanced at Nyfain. He met my gaze but didn't comment.

"That look means *mind your own fucking business, or I'll rip your spine out through your dick*," Hadriel told Vemar.

"Noted," Vemar responded.

"Was this one of your dreams, as well?" Nyfain asked me, humor quickly filtering into the bond as his jacket and shirt were stripped away. "Stripping down in front of a kingdom?"

"No. I'm trying to ignore it, actually. *Shh.*"

My crown was the last item to be taken, at the same time as Nyfain's, and then we stood there naked in front of all of our subjects. Whose dumb fucking idea was this?

Mine. And it's a damn good one.

"Ready?" I asked.

"As planned." Nyfain waited patiently.

He *had* practiced, yes. He'd jumped off cliffs, lower and lower until he jumped off the mast of the faerie ship, and finally a tree about as high as our balcony. He was ready.

I hoped he was fucking ready. Otherwise he might go splat.

He helped me up onto the edge of the balcony, and a loud *whoa* drifted out below us. Cheering and shouts died down until they were soft murmurs of excitement, everyone staring up at us with wide eyes.

And then I jumped, smiling, feeling the rush as the wind streamed past me. I'd always loved this part, the free fall when I was still in my own body. My smile turned to a laugh, and then I tucked in so the dragon could take over.

She exploded into being and then whooshed down toward them, sailing just over their heads before climbing and turning, issuing a loud roar to her mate.

Nyfain stepped up to the railing, tall and broad and bronzed by the midday sun. Scars crisscrossed his body, caught by the rays, some hidden by the intricate lines of ink that had been drawn over and around them, some a fierce reminder of what life had been like in this kingdom. His powerful frame was corded with muscle, showcasing his hard-won strength. The breeze worried his unruly hair, and his golden gaze, too far away for most in the crowd to make out, speared down into them. He looked ruthless and menacing, utterly terrifying. He was the defender of this kingdom, and now he finally had the title to go with it.

The crowd had gone deathly silent. A little tremor of fear rolled through them, more than a few people shivering. And then he was jumping, a swan dive toward them, not waiting until the last moment like I had—he was not able to shift fast enough to wait at all. The moments ticked by, and down he fell, nearly too low now.

My dragon tensed, ready to rush forward, but then the big golden dragon emerged. Sun glimmered on his scales as his wings snapped out and started pumping. Dragon-made wind slapped down on the people below, making them duck, ruining their hairstyles, and then Nyfain was sailing past them. His roar rumbled the ground and sent some people scattering to the sides.

Others stayed low, turning to watch him take to the sky.

He joined us, and then, wing to wing, we went back for another swoop before we flew out over the kingdom.

No banging, seriously, I told my dragon.

If you say so.

I was suddenly a little worried about what she planned to do in retaliation.

CHAPTER 27
FINLEY

THE BANQUET HALL was crowded for the coronation dinner. The large dining table that sat in the middle of the room had been in storage for years, taken away during the demon residency to make room for sex parties.

At least Dolion hadn't stolen it.

I shared the place of honor with Nyfain, both of us back in fine clothes, our plates heaped with food. Arleth sat by Nyfain's side as head advisor—she hadn't wanted the post in the beginning, but she was so good at it that the other advisors pushed her into it—and Hadriel sat by my side for no reason other than that he'd basically forced his way past whoever was supposed to be there. Calia and her sister sat across from Nyfain and me, in a position that declared them our special guests, with Hannon next to them. Govam sat just beyond them, with Denski by his side, not so far down that they couldn't be a part of our conversation. The rest of the faeries and demons, as well as the rest of my family, sat closer to the other end, not important to matters of the kingdom. Arleth's words.

She'd been the one to plan this out. In times past, that duty would have gone to a team of people, who'd decide who warranted a seat near the king and queen. Given that that team had all likely died tragically, and no one left really knew what they were doing in terms of official business, Arleth had gracefully accepted the role.

"How do you feel?" Hadriel asked me, beaming, constantly looking around to see who was noticing him at the right-hand side of the queen.

I looked out over the people seated at the table and those waiting on the sides in attendance. Laughter rang up, and wine was being poured freely.

"Fine. Impatient." I reached for my glass.

Nyfain glanced at me, his eyes sparkling. He dropped his hand to my thigh before turning back to his mom.

"Impatient for what?" Hadriel replied.

"Working. Doing my job. I don't know. This seems like it's gone on too long."

Calia's sister, Dessia, whom I'd never spoken to directly, leaned toward me. She was in her early twenties, with white-blonde hair that framed a very pretty face that bore a close resemblance to her sister's. She seemed incredibly shy. She always let Calia, a few years her senior, do the talking. Always.

Until now, apparently.

"Congratulations," she said in a voice like a soft breeze. Her startlingly blue eyes held mine. "I have never seen a queen quite like you."

"It's only day one. I'll grow into it." I gave her a thumbs-up.

She shook her head. "You mistake me. I hope that you don't. Most royals live for fancy parties and dinners such as these. They look down on their kingdoms from their great towers, so they don't see the people anymore. They just see taxpayers. Land owners. Bloodlines that will continue to build their kingdom in power and those that will not."

"Ah. Well, again, it's only day one. Who knows what the crush of time and power will do to me." I gave her a thumbs-down this time.

Dessia laughed, covering her mouth. "No, you will not let anything crush you, I don't think. And if they try, your great love will surely prevent it." Her gaze flicked to Nyfain.

I wrapped my fingers around his where they rested on my thigh.

"I would like to have a great love like that someday," she murmured, her face going red and her back bowing. She took up her fork and pushed some peas around her plate.

"Honey, we would *all* like to have a love like that someday, with the orgasms to show for it." Hadriel leaned over the table to catch her eye, his smile disarming. "Have you tried one of the dragons on for size? They specialize in defending their mates. If you can stand their possessiveness, arrogance, growling, and rage issues, and—"

"Hadriel, I am getting the idea that you don't like me," said Vemar, on Hadriel's other side for the same reason Hadriel had earned a spot in the seats of honor. He was enjoying himself immensely. "That hurts my feelings."

"You don't have feelings," Hadriel responded. "You just have a sick sense of humor about where you randomly stick your dick."

"C'mon," Vemar said, leaning back. "Pretending my dick was the meat in that sandwich was funny. The bread was shaped for it and everything. A few of those condiments and *ta da*. Dick dog."

"Leala should've actually bitten into it instead of just pretending," Hadriel replied.

"She is the one who likes pain, not me. I told her I'd slap her bottom with these big hands she seems to like so much." Vemar held up his large, scarred hands.

"You're about to walk down a dark path, buddy." Hadriel shook his head. "A very dark path. She will coax out kinks you didn't even know you had. Despite all that time you spent in the demon castle, I'm not sure you're ready for it. She *liked* all that crazy shit in that castle, remember?"

"I am just fine with having her as a guide, Sir Butler. She said she doesn't mind sharing, and I don't mind being shared. All at the same time, occasionally. It is a dream come true. Everyone is happy."

"Don't listen to them," I told Dessia as Calia turned her attention our way. "They have long since forgotten what polite conversation is supposed to sound like."

"Oh, don't worry about my sister, highness—"

I put out my hand. "Call me Finley unless you absolutely have to call me highness, and then do it sarcastically so it won't be so weird."

Dessia laughed softly. When Calia heard it, a smile crossed her face. She inclined her head and lowered her voice. "I think *now* is the time it is absolutely necessary, but I will work on the sarcasm, if it pleases you." She laughed. "Dessia has seen things most people can't imagine. It is why she is so quiet. Sometimes, to escape one's horrors, one must lock one's mind inside of flesh and bone." She spread her hands to indicate Hadriel and Vemar. "Over these many months, they have drawn her out again. And you, warrior queen, with your golden king, have intrigued her. Please, tell me you will hurry to visit us. I am pressing the king to hasten."

I'd opened my mouth to answer when a strange feeling swept through me. My vision swam for a moment and my head spun before tingles crept up my spine.

"Are you okay, highness?" Calia asked, her smile slipping.

"Yes, I'm fine." I cleared my throat and sat up a little straighter as goosebumps pebbled my skin. My face flushed, and then my body. My nipples hardened under my clothes.

I reached for my wine as Nyfain turned toward me slowly, looking confused, his nostrils flaring.

"What's happening?" Hadriel asked, drawing eyes to us.

"No, no, it's fine, really." I finished reaching for my wine while pressing the back of my hand to my cheek, needing to be grounded by the coolness of my fingers.

The tingles intensified and spread, coursing through me like my blood had been aerated, and then they sank low. My chest tightened as an aching need stole over me. It rose through me like its own entity, searching.

A gush of wetness flooded my panties. My breath came out in pants, my breasts pushing against their confinement, wanting to be released. Wanting to be touched and sucked.

I bit back a moan as my vision swam again. I tried to push the feeling away. It would've helped if I could leave, but I wasn't sure I could get myself out of here and to a washroom without staggering.

Should've let me fuck the dragon in the air, my dragon said smugly.

Oh no. Not here.

The heat.

In horror, I looked up at all the people crowding the room, eating, laughing, enjoying their dinners. At the people serving and those lingering around the perimeter, excited to be a part of it all. I remembered what happened when I'd gone into heat before, how long it took, how crazy and loud we were. If we left to do that now, we wouldn't come back before the dinner was over.

We couldn't leave our own coronation dinner!

Breathing deeply, I tried to regain my sense of composure. I took a sip of wine and smiled at a swimming Calia and Dessia across the way, their expressions serious. Hannon seemed uncomfortable.

"My love, what is happening?" Hadriel asked in a low voice.

Nyfain tensed beside me, and a shock of power flowed over us. I groaned within the feeling, fluttering my eyes closed and swaying toward him.

Hadriel grabbed my shoulder and yanked me back. "Oh fuck, is this what I think it is? Vemar, look. I wasn't in the library for the heat-fucking that other time."

"It's fine," I said, waving them away, fighting back the urge to melt against Nyfain's side. "It's good."

Vemar studied me from behind Hadriel. After a beat, his eyes widened.

"Fuck," Vemar said, all signs of joking gone. "Tamara!"

Nyfain ran his hand up the back of my chair and curled his arm around me. He pressed toward me possessively, and I couldn't help another groan. Only Hadriel was keeping me from leaning into him.

"Don't give in to it, Nyfain," I said through my teeth. "I can hold off until the dinner is done. We can—"

Another huge swell of power rolled from Nyfain, slowing and then stopping conversation in the large room. Weston and Micah popped up from their chairs farther down the table, and Tamara appeared by my side.

She took one look at me, and then she was all action.

"C'mon, highness. Let's get you up. Here we go. Micah, Vemar, Weston," she barked, "secure the king until I can get his mate out of here."

Delaney pulled Hadriel's chair away—with him in it—before reaching for my arm.

"Son, listen to me," Arleth said from behind me. I belatedly realized her hands were on Nyfain's arm along the back of the chair. "You need to let go. Let her get to another location, and then you can join her."

"This is ridiculous," I said. "I can hang on until after dinner. I've ignored my arousal before."

"It's not you that's the problem, highness," Delaney said as Arleth tried to pry Nyfain's arm off the chair. "It's him. He is a very powerful alpha, which means he is very possessive, and if you go into heat around all these males and you smell like *any* of them, his dragon will assume control and try to kill them to defend his right to you. I've heard being true mates makes it that much more intense. We need to get you away from all these males— from *everyone*—and get you cleaned up. He can have you then."

Ready to see him in a possessive rage? my dragon thought gleefully.

"This is nuts," I said, pushing to stand and then staggering into Delaney. "We did this in the library, and it was fine."

"Everyone stayed well away from you in the library," Tamara said. "And it sounded like you were already making love when it came upon you, right? That's the start of it. This is…"

"Her dragon has been suppressing it," Arleth said. "She was defying nature, and now it'll cost them. Let's just make sure it doesn't cost us all."

"What do you meant *it'll cost them*?" I asked, pulled farther away by Delaney.

"You know how you like rage fucking, Finley?" Hadriel asked as he crawled over the table toward Dessia to get away. "Well, given how worked up he already is, you're about to get a hard ride."

This is your doing, you know. You didn't want us to fuck earlier, so here we are. I'm looking forward to it, though. If things get too crazy, the dragon and I can always take over.

What about all the times Nyfain and I had sex as humans? I thought as a menacing growl ripped out of Nyfain's throat. *Everything's been perfectly normal. Why is he like this now?*

Because the golden dragon and I were taking the edge off. It comes in waves, and when we feel it rising, we take to the sky, fuck until he fills me with his seed, and safely return so that you and the human can do it at your leisure. But hey, it's fine. He'll work you in hard now, and then we can share the heat while it lasts, huh? Won't that be fun?

Nyfain's arm finally came away from the back of the chair. He grabbed the edge of my seat and then ripped it backward. The chair went flying, barely missing Tamara and Arleth and hitting two people near the wall.

Look at him, he's like some sort of wild thing, I thought.

Yes, he is. And when that wild thing captures you, he's going to rip off that dress and fuck you senseless. If you don't want that to happen in this room, you better get the fuck out of here. I'm good with whatever. As long as his dick is in us and everyone else clears out, he shouldn't need to kill anyone.

What the holy fuck had I gotten myself into?

Nyfain rose slowly, like he was uncoiling, and my knees went weak at the sight. Saliva pooled in my mouth, and wetness dribbled down my inner thigh.

Unable to help it, my body on fire, so aroused I could barely think, I took a step toward him. Hands grabbed me, ripping me around and pushing me away.

"Is she okay?" Calia cried.

"She'll be good," Hadriel replied. "She loves rage fucking; this shouldn't be too much different. The mighty vagina can take some real pounding. Well, I don't have to tell you that. Don't worry, she'll be fine."

Weston, Micah, and Vemar rushed by me, giving me a wide berth, hurrying to stand in front of Nyfain.

"Arleth, stay behind to stall him," Tamara said as more of my guard joined her. They pushed me ahead of them, jogging now. "Delaney, you too. He won't want to go through you two."

Those two broke off as we tried to push past people who didn't have the sense to get away.

"Clear a path, you idiots!" Tamara yelled. "An alpha in heat is about to come through."

A roar followed us out the door, thick and heady, a sound that shouldn't be able to come from a human throat.

"Why isn't he chasing us?" Jade asked, looking over her shoulder as we turned the corner.

The rising tide within the bond was answer enough. I could feel his adrenaline. The desire he didn't want to control. The touch of mischief.

"He's counting down," I said, shoving them away but still jogging with them. A surge of matching adrenaline tore through me. I couldn't help a giddy laugh.

"Counting down to what?" Tamara asked as they ushered me toward the stairs.

"He's giving me a head start," I said. "Then the chase is on."

"Are you insane or something?" someone asked

from the back. "This doesn't seem like something to be excited about. You'd best go somewhere quiet and try to calm him down when he gets to you. He didn't look like a guy I would want after me in that state."

"She's a dragon, and he's her mate," someone else said. "She knows what she's getting, and crazy or not, clearly she likes it."

"I do not understand dragons," the other, obviously a wolf, replied.

I let them run me up the stairs as Tamara yelled at all the staff to scatter before the incensed alpha came through. She needn't have bothered. He didn't want anyone else. He only wanted me, and he wanted me with a fire I could barely understand. A fire I felt deep down in my very core, burning, pulsing.

When we reached the king's suite, I stopped them from stripping me, from trying to wash me. I forced them to leave, saying I'd be okay, that I'd ensure no one came to harm after he found me.

Uneasy but unable to deny me, both because of my station and my weaponized will, they left, and I got to work.

I'd given Dash a few lectures about going into rooms he wasn't supposed to, and confiscated one of the maps he'd made of the castle. Specifically, the hidden tunnels. I grabbed that now and went to the corner of the bathroom indicated on the map, searching the little crevices and nooks. Nothing I found looked like it would trigger a hidden door.

A shock of power sang through me. A burst of adrenaline.

K . F .   B R E E N E

Time was up.

Breathing heavily, desperate and excited and loving the thrill of running, I turned the map over and went to the other corner. There I found it easily, a little knob tucked behind a cabinet. Dash really needed a compass rose or a better sense of direction.

I pushed it, pulled the door wide, ducked in, and closed it behind me. Following the map, I took the turns that would bring me to a small back stairway and up to the third floor. Except when I got there, it was a dead end.

"Damn him and his map making," I said, looking back the way I'd come.

A slight tremor shook the ground. I cocked my head. Was that a roar of frustration? He must've gotten to the king's room and found me gone.

With a thrill and an excited laugh, I raced back the way I'd come for a bit until I reached another junction. I wound through the corridors, finding one that wasn't on the map, and then looked for one that should've been there but wasn't. Turned around, confused, I jogged toward the last location that had seemed legit. Around the next corner, I checked my whereabouts, thought about turning the map, and looked up to see if anything matched.

A huge frame filled the small corridor. His golden eyes flecked with burgundy glowed softly in the dim light. My heart stopped for a moment.

"Did you think you could run from me, my queen?" he asked in a gravelly voice. "Did you think you could hide?"

362

Is that the dragon? I thought.

No. But in his current state, with as many phero-mones as you're secreting, you probably won't be able to tell the difference.

Fear rode my adrenaline. My survival reflex went active. Usually it urged me to fight, but this time it urged me to run like fucking hell.

"Shit," I let out before I turned and sprinted.

I could hear his shoes hitting the floor as he launched after me. The map fluttered to the ground, and I rounded a turn too fast, going wide and bouncing off the wall. My slippered feet nearly lost traction, but I kept going, around another turn, hoping to hell I'd find the damn staircase.

Dead end.

"No. Fuck." I slammed up against the wall and then pushed off and spun around to find another way.

Nyfain filled the corridor up ahead, coming fast.

Heart beating like a rabbit, I ran right at him before ducking into a corridor on the left. He skidded as he reached it, grabbing the corner. He swung himself around and in.

Up ahead, jiggling in my vision, the stairs climbed out of sight.

"Oh thank fuck," I said with a ragged breath.

His feet pounded the ground not far away, his long legs carrying him much faster than I could go.

I reached the stairs and jumped up the first two.

A large hand grabbed the back of my dress and ripped backward. Fabric tore, and I screamed. My back hit Nyfain's front, and his arm wrapped around me.

"You are *mine*," he growled, putting me down onto the ground before shoving me forward with one hand and ripping at my dress with the other. I caught myself with my hands on the steps, bent over. Nyfain ripped again, tearing my dress completely off me.

He growled again when he saw I wasn't wearing underwear. He held me in place with one hand and pushed in close, using the other to thread two fingers into my molten pussy. He sucked in a breath through his teeth. "Goddess help me, Finley, you're so fucking wet. You're so ready for me."

He worked faster, curving his fingers just right as they glided in and out of my cunt, making wet sounds. Without warning, he flipped me over and shoved me down against the cold, hard stairs. The corners bit into my back as he slapped my knees wide and slipped his middle two fingers into my pussy, bending over me in his fine suit. He restarted his fast, hard pace. His thumb pressed into my clit and his fingers rubbed my upper wall, his hand slamming into me, the sensations jarring and brutal and—

Holy fuck, it was so good.

I braced my elbows against the stairs, no longer even conscious of the bite of pain from the wood. He kept at me, leaning down a little more to place a bruising kiss on my lips. I opened my mouth to him, but he backed off, working my pussy, wiggling his thumb over my slick clit. His palm against me made a wet cupping sound. Each thump of his hand, each rub of his fingers, sent me higher, over the edge but still climbing. He was rubbing too much but not enough. Thrusting too hard, but I needed more.

"C'mon baby," he urged, power flowing around us. "Come around my fingers before I load you up. Squirt for me."

A naughty little thrill arrested me as I remembered the threesome I'd witnessed. The woman squirted, something I hadn't known was possible until that moment.

"I don't know how," I said as I gyrated against his fingers, the fire of the moment burning me alive gloriously.

"Yes, you do. Keep building. Hold the feeling until you can't possibly do it anymore. Don't come until I say you can."

I whimpered as he kept at it, his other hand now pressed against my mound, creating more pressure, creating a need I couldn't quite extinguish. His thumb worked me, his fingers pumped, and suddenly the need to come clawed at me.

"Not yet," he commanded, sensing it, his power stopping me short.

I didn't fight him. I didn't push back, wanting the bigger climax he was promising me.

"Yes," I said through my clenched teeth as his hand slammed against me harder, his fingers working furiously. "Wait, too much—"

"A little more, sweetheart," he said, leaning far over me.

I cried out with the pent-up need to let go.

"Come, baby. Come for me," he commanded.

He tore his hands away right before I exploded,

pleasure pulsing through me as I gushed all over the bottom of the steps. My mouth dropped open even as I panted, shuddering from my release.

"Hmm, that's right." He fell to his knees between my legs and sucked in my clit before licking down my slit, tasting me. Back to my clit, he worked me again, slower this time, draining all my pleasure until I lay in an uncomfortable heap against the steps.

The waves of heat still tore through me, though, an orgasm not enough. The craving still ached.

"Nyfain," I begged miserably.

"I know, sweetheart." He stripped out of his clothes quickly, tossing them to the side. His large cock stood out proudly from his deliciously cut body, the tip glistening. "I'll make it better."

I licked my lips and sat up, wanting to get at it. He chuckled darkly, changing his position so he was on his knees on the steps, his cock jutting out. I reached for it, wrapping my fingers around it, and then sucked it in deep, loving his growl of approval. My cheeks hollowed as he hit the back of my throat. I backed off and then took him in again, swallowing him down, choking on his cock. I reached down to work my clit as he pumped into my mouth, but it wasn't doing enough to release the consuming desire that pounded within me. I put two fingers in my pussy, rubbing, trying to calm my desperate need.

Nyfain pulled himself from my mouth, slid onto his back on the steps, and guided me on top of him. He claimed my lips as I fitted my knees onto the steps, reaching between us to roughly grab his cock. He groaned from the treatment as I lined him up and rolled my hips, kissing my opening with his tip.

"Fuck, I want you so badly," I murmured against his lips, sitting down on top of him.

He swallowed my moan, gripping my hips tightly.

I meant to go slow, to savor this, but as soon as I lifted, I had to crash back down again, eager to be closer to him. Needing more of him. All of him.

I whimpered, riding him hard. I sat down with all my weight, crushing him against the steps before squeezing my pussy around him as I lifted up and then repeated the process. I worked my clit, rolling my hips, not getting the friction I so desperately needed. "Nyfain, please, *more*."

He sat up in a rush, pushing me off him and getting us to our feet. He swung me around, bent me over, and slammed himself home. I groaned and fell forward, against the steps again, knees bent, ass in the air. With his hands on my hips, he pulled me back as he pumped forward, pounding into me savagely. He took to me like a wild thing, raw and vicious. His cock branded me with pleasure. His balls slapped off my clit. I dropped my head and squeezed my eyes shut, wanting this. Needing it.

Power curled around us. Our dragons threw it back and forth, feeling each other through the bond. As the power and pleasure built, I bucked against him wildly. He crashed into me, his hipbones bruising, our skin slapping.

I screamed in carnal pleasure as I broke apart at the seams, the heat within me releasing in a huge torrent.

Nyfain roared so loudly it shook the foundation as he emptied himself into me. There was so much of it that it ran down my legs—a sensation so sensual, so dirty, it made me come again, and then again somehow. I quaked so badly my teeth chattered!

When the waves of pleasure subsided, my knees gave out totally, and I dropped to the steps. Nyfain grabbed me just in time, hauling me up and draping me over his wide shoulder.

"Not as comfortable as you carrying me in your arms," I wheezed, feeling like my bones had turned to liquid.

"I want everyone to see my prize. I want them all to see our combined cum leaking down your legs as I carry you back to our rooms. And when we get there, I'm going to fuck you again, and again, until you are hoarse from screaming my name. And then, one last time, I'll make you call me alpha as you sob with pleasure."

It was a wicked display of dominance, and it had me so turned on that I didn't care when he did exactly as promised. I liked it, in fact, especially when we reached the second-floor landing and he decided he'd rather go to our sanctuary, the tower. He pulled me back into his arms then, and I basked in his fierce gaze, daring anyone to come close. Daring anyone to step forward and challenge the claim he had on his mate. I knew he'd meet the challenge ruthlessly. Just as ruthlessly as he'd protect me—or his child—from danger. He was every bit the nightmare alpha he'd said he was, and I couldn't get enough of it.

The heat was already rising at that point, and I needed him again. Wanted him inside me so badly that I could barely form words.

Now that the coronation was over, though, it was time for this ruthless alpha to show his cunning.

It was also time to go to the faerie lands, and a thought I'd been ignoring and repressing was finally weaseling its way to the forefront of my mind.

His ex-fiancée was a member of the faerie court. I'd be seeing her.

Would I be able to stop myself from giving my own show of dominance and protecting my claim?

PART THREE

CHAPTER 28
HADRIEL

"**U**GH," I SAID for the millionth time in the last three days, hanging over the railing of the sleek and fast and still-horrible faerie ship after another bout of seasickness.

One of Govam's demons stood a few paces away, looking out at the sea, searching for the vessels that Govam was positive would come. He believed we'd be attacked by Dolion somewhere along this journey, our deaths made to look like an accident. After all, his biggest threats were all in this fleet. The new and former royals of Wyvern, the powerful wolf alpha, and the prized faerie sisters. Not to mention the dragons who could severely damage Dolion's forces. The rebel demons had been vigilant in their watch.

It had been suggested that we go a longer route to try to avoid a possible confrontation, but Dolion had ships in plenty and knew our final destination—he could have his people waiting anywhere. Probably did, in fact.

The royal couple had been keeping watch

too...when they weren't fucking like rabbits. Or like dragons in heat.

My stomach heaved. The demon beside me gave me side-eye and moved another step away.

Finley and the king had taken three weeks to get their affairs in order before finally taking a very patient Calia up on her offer to visit her kingdom. The royal pair had left Weston's beta in charge of the wolves and ground shifters, and a dragon from Micah's village had been put in charge of the air. Most of the guards and army had stayed behind as well, to protect the kingdom.

"How you doin', bud?" Vemar walked up and roughly patted me on the back.

"Ugh," I said again, hanging a little lower. "Stop. Not funny."

Vemar crossed his arms over his chest and turned, leaning his butt up against the railing. "Sailing is boring, huh?"

"Yeah, super fucking boring. Hanging my head over the side of the ship, trying to purge an empty stomach, is very humdrum. What a snooze."

He nodded as though he agreed, clearly missing my very on-point sarcasm.

"One more day," he said, turning again and bracing his hands against the railing, looking out at the sea. "No sign of any demons yet."

The demon a few steps away ignored Vemar's comment.

Three more ships accompanied us, carrying guards and staff and goods for gifts and trade. I was pretty sure the ships had been rented from somewhere, but I hadn't asked for any of the boring details. I'd been too busy throwing up over the side of the very lovely but not any smoother-riding faerie ship.

"I'll probably have lost another five pounds in that time." I wiped my mouth with the back of my hand and straightened up a little, keeping my eyes on the horizon. That was what Dessia had said. Keep my eyes on the horizon to steady my stomach.

She was a filthy fucking liar, and I did not appreciate her laughing at me when I told her that.

"Let's go for a walk." Vemar grabbed my shoulders. "Come on, it'll make you feel better."

"Don't you have any dragon friends to bother?"

He manhandled me until I was facing the bow and then lightly shoved me to get me walking. "None of them need cheering up."

"*I* don't need cheering up. I need to be left alone."

"Being left alone to your misery is no way to go through life, Hadriel. We talked about this."

"First of all—" I held up a finger, paused, and thought about attempting to throw up. I burped instead and then groaned to finish it off. "Jacking off into an open window is not an act of misery. I'm telling you, you should try it. There's something very liberating about it. Second, I am not throwing up after a demon sex party. I don't need someone to watch my asshole so that a demon, or that fucking idiot Liron, doesn't try to stick something in it. I am seasick. I just need to grin and bear it until we reach dry land, and then I can get back to life as usual."

Vemar patted my shoulder as we made our way past

a faerie cleaning the decks with a weirdly clean mop. How was that possible? Was the ship so well looked after that even the mops remained clean? There was something not right about the whole scenario.

"You got me now, little buddy," Vemar said, patting me again. He was a handsy guy. Usually I didn't mind, but on most days I didn't spend the majority of my time being sick over the banister of a ship. "I'll make sure no one tries to stick anything in your asshole unless you want them to."

"That's…" I gave him side-eye. "I mean, thank you, but that was not my point."

He turned to me with a furrowed brow. "Then what was your point?"

"Leave me alone, that was my point! I was explaining why it is okay for you to leave me the fuck alone!"

He laughed like that was a grand joke. We rarely communicated properly. Very rarely.

Calia stood with Dessia at the bow, their hair billowing out behind them and their pastel dresses whipping around their feet. Govam and Denski stood down a ways, scanning the horizon, and Hannon was just beyond them.

Dessia glanced in their direction, and I knew she was checking out Hannon. She always seemed to know his location when they were in the same room, but she'd never actually spoken to him. Unfortunately, he seemed oblivious to women finding him attractive, so at this rate they'd never bang. And given what I knew of both of them—everyone in the castle loved gossiping about attractive single people—they weren't getting laid by anyone else. What a waste.

"Ladies, wonderful day, isn't it?" Vemar stopped beside them and braced his hands against the railing.

Dessia started, curling into herself just a little, before realizing who it was. She glanced beyond him, saw me, and offered me a light smile. I narrowed my eyes at her in return. I was still mad about the crap seasickness advice she'd given me.

"It is very clear and mild, yes," Calia responded, straight and tall and confident. "Summer is nearly here. The gardens will be in full bloom when we arrive."

Vemar nodded, falling into silence. I took that as my cue to slink to the side and hope I didn't have to wilt over the railing and further embarrass myself in front of the faeries. I should've just stayed in the stables all those many years ago.

"What brings you to the upper deck?" Vemar asked.

Dessia leaned her forearms against the railing, and I could just barely see her cheeks turn red. It was Calia who answered.

"The royal couple have found their heat again, and it seems incredibly violent. We thought we might take a turn around the deck while they...exhausted themselves."

"Ah, yeah." Vemar chuckled. "Dragons really get into that heat cycle. I hope I'm lucky enough to experience one someday. I hear they are incredibly fun. Lots of dominance games, but the female doesn't put up nearly as much of a fight. That's a good way to make a man feel powerful, eh?" He puffed up his chest. "You get to breed your mate with power and fire and gusto, and she never takes the wind out of your sails by slapping you around."

"You force dominance to breed?" Dessia asked, aghast.

"No, no." I snaked myself in between Vemar and Dessia then held up my finger to get my bearings while focusing on that damn horizon. She apparently thought that was hilarious. "Your giggle is very annoying, my darling, I don't mind telling you. Anyway, shifter males like to dominate the females. It's their *thing*. Alpha females usually like to fight back, challenging the male. And then they both rage until finally the male gets his way or the female lets him have his way, and then they bang. Dragons are more violent than wolves. Much more violent."

"Dragons live for challenges," Calia said.

"Where's the fun if there's no challenge?" Vemar spread his hands. "Except for breeding. When you're trying to get your mate with child, you don't want any obstacles. It's hard enough as it is."

"He means that dragons have a harder time getting with child. I'm not sure why—"

"Because we're stronger, faster, and bigger. We fly, and we blow fire," Vemar growled. "If we could breed as easily as wolves, we'd dominate the world. The whole place would be out of balance. The goddess knows this."

"That is their reasoning as to why." I turned just enough to make a face at Dessia, and this time her laugh was okay. "Anyway, Finley used to fight back a lot harder. The two of them would rage at each other, I'm telling you, and he'd barely get past her will. Things changed not too long after she stopped the tea, especially

A QUEEN OF RUIN

once her heat started. She seems to put up enough of a fuss to excite them both and then relishes in his dominance. I've seen a few glimpses—she's having a good time."

"It's what females crave," Tamara said, wandering over to stand beside Vemar.

"Hello, eavesdropper," I said dryly. "Where'd you skulk from?"

"I noticed no one was watching your asshole, so I was thinking of a way to get at it," she replied. "I don't have the right equipment, sadly."

"Or any sort of imagination," I said. "I've dodged my fair share of broom handles."

"I'll take that under advisement," she said with an arched eyebrow. To the others, she said, "Female dragons thinking about offspring crave shows of dominance by their mates. They want continual proof that their mate will be able to protect them and their offspring."

"But surely Finley is well able to protect herself?" Calia asked. "I've seen her fight."

"It's a vulnerable thing to grow and birth a child," Tamara responded. "During that time, she must be protected."

"And the heat…" Calia started.

"Makes it easier to beget a child," Vemar said.

"How…" Calia cleared her throat. "How long does it last, exactly? The cycle duration, I mean. At this point in the journey, given their room is next to ours, we're pretty well aware of how long each episode lasts."

Vemar tipped back his head and laughed.

"It shouldn't be much longer," Tamara said with a smile that devolved into chuckles.

"But Calia, sweetie," I said, "don't think they're suddenly going to chill out once the heats ends. If anything, they'll probably be louder and more violent. They've always been...spirited. Remember what I said about Finley fighting back? Well, when she's in the mood, she really goes for it."

Calia grinned and shook her head. "It is amazing that dragons have a harder time procreating when they spend so much time trying."

"Not everyone, trust me," Tamara said, glancing across the deck. "Their desperation for each other is a rarity, not the norm."

Her gaze snagged on Govam. He was leaning over the railing, his hand up to block the failing sun. Her reaction prompted Vemar to push away from the railing to see what had interested her. Then he looked out over the horizon.

I followed suit, needing to look there anyway. I didn't see what they were noticing at first. And then there it was, a black spot directly in our path. There shouldn't be any landmasses out there. It had to be a ship or a trick of the eyes, and I doubted we'd all fall victim to the same trick.

"Get the royal couple," Govam barked to no one in particular.

"It could be anyone," I said as Calia squinted at the horizon. "There are a lot of ships on this sea. It could be tradesmen—"

"Or pirates," Dessia said softly. Calia put a hand on her sister's shoulder.

"Get the royal couple," Govam said.

Denski pointed at something off the starboard side. "They are covering their bases," he told Govam. "You were right. The most credible witnesses against Dolion are all here. If he kills them in one fell swoop, he won't have nearly as much opposition."

"Wait, wait, hold on," I said, holding up a hand. "First, yes, what you just said is obviously true. But we can't be sure those ships belong to the demons. They are tiny specks on the horizon! Let's wait until we can at least make them out before we interrupt the *very busy* royal pair. The king will not like to be interrupted, trust me. He'll get violent. Where are the telescopes?"

Govam turned to me, his face blank. "We don't need them. Those ships are exactly where we expected them to be. If you are too much of a coward to interrupt dragons in heat, then I will do it. There is no time to waste." He turned and started walking.

"He just called you out there, little buddy." Vemar's hands were on my shoulders, pushing me behind the demon. "We need that demon, though, and if he goes in there before they're done, the alpha dragon will see it as a breach of territory and kill him. He won't kill you. You need to be the one to sound the alarm."

"He *will* kill me!"

I felt myself pushed along. "Nah. Finley will stop it. Probably. You should be fine."

"You don't sound all that sure."

"Well…life isn't fun without taking risks, right? Here, I'll go with you."

"Why are dragons so fucking crazy?" I hollered, pushed forward.

CHAPTER 29
FINLEY

M Y CLIMAX TORE through me, harder and higher and more intense than the last, and the one before that, and the ones before that. I shook with it, clutching Nyfain as he emptied into me. The strange euphoria I'd come to expect quickly settled over me as our dragons purred their contentment. It was as though my body realized I'd gotten what I needed and could relax again.

I let my arms slip from around his shoulders and flop down onto the bed. His chest heaved against me, his arms still wrapped around me possessively, his softening cock lodged inside. His eyes roamed my face, so full of love and devotion it made my breath catch. He kissed me gently before nibbling my bottom lip.

"I wish we didn't have official business so we could just stay in bed for the whole heat," he murmured, kissing along my jaw and sucking little patches of skin along my neck and down to his mark. "I want to lie here with you until it comes on again."

It's our turn next, my dragon said, just fine with public displays of fucking. She had zero shame. She and Nyfain's dragon barely removed themselves from the ships to have at it.

"I'm actually starting to get sore at this point." I angled my head so he could kiss across my throat to the other mark. "Which is pretty good, I think, since we've been at it for a few weeks now."

"Will you deny me?" he growled, and the hint of command sent a delicious thrill down to my core.

I moaned softly, my eyes fluttering closed. I drifted my fingertips down his back and over his scales.

"Maybe," I purred, feeling his shudder. I continued to let my hands drift lower until they were resting on his perfect, muscular ass. I kneaded firmly, pushing my knees a little farther out and pulling his hips in tighter. I clenched my pussy around him. "Would that stop you from fucking your cum into me nice and hard?"

He sucked in a breath, his cock hardening again, and this time it had nothing to do with the heat.

I scraped back up his scales, grinding my hips against him.

"Do you want me to fuck you again, little dragon?" he asked in a deep voice, his hand coming to rest on my right knee. His other hand grabbed my left as he leaned back a little, forcing me to open wider for him. "Have I been taking it too easy on you? Clearly you aren't sore enough."

He pulled back before slamming forward, the sound wet and sticky from so many combined releases.

"Is this what you need?" He pulled back horribly

slowly, and juices ran down my slit and over my asshole. The euphoria still throbbed. My body ached. His thrust ended in a wet slap. "You need it rougher? You want more pain with your pleasure?"

His hips banged against my bruised thighs. His cock drove in deep. My desperation for him surged, spiraling higher. The soreness throbbed in time with the pleasure.

Yes, I fucking did. I'd been craving his dominance for weeks. I'd been mewing like a little kitten while he took me over and over.

It was time to act like a dragon while the heat was at bay.

Just as long as you get that good cock, my dragon said, *you do you. I'm here for it.*

I surged up, grabbing his hair and yanking to the side. My will slammed into him, forcing him to roll over. The bed wasn't that big, though. Not like in the castle. He hit the edge with blazing eyes and tried to grab on. His hands slipped and he went crashing over the side.

I rolled off the other way as he slowly pushed to standing. He turned sideways so that his arms could flare as he stood between the bed and the wall. His eyes swept down my body, catching between my thighs and sticking for a moment. When they returned to me, excitement glittered in them. A spark. He recognized my challenge and savored it.

"Come and get it," I said. "If you can."

He chuckled darkly and stepped forward, closing the distance. I didn't move, waiting. We didn't have much room to maneuver.

His hand shot out, faster than a blink, his fingers

wrapping around my throat and squeezing.

Oh, so that's how we're going to play, is it? my dragon thought as fire flooded my blood. *Right for the throat?* She paused. *Kick his fucking ass.*

I slammed him with my will, the blow so hard he grunted as he flew backward. His legs hit the back of the bed and his body kept going. He windmilled to try to keep upright, but I jumped up and kicked, my foot hitting him center mass.

His grunt was even more pronounced this time, but he was rolling as soon as his back hit the bed.

I was there when his feet hit the ground, my fist already sailing through the air. It hit him in his face and snapped his head back. He grabbed my wrist as he fell, yanking me down with him. I tried to pull free, but his grip was too hard. I couldn't escape.

"You should've stayed on your feet," Nyfain said in a rough, menacing tone. "Now you're at the mercy of the big, bad dragon."

"I'm at no one's mercy." I punched his throat and then reached around his erection to hit him in the balls.

He groaned, and not from pleasure, jerking away and creasing in the middle. He almost looked like he was headed for the fetal position.

"Is that how we're going to play it?" he asked as I finally pulled my hand away and quickly shoved off the bed.

"That's what my dragon said after you grabbed my throat," I replied as he pushed to standing like he was slowly uncoiling. A thrill arrested me, but I hid it. "So yeah, that's exactly how we're going to play it."

He lunged at me again, not grabbing this time but barreling into me. He slammed me into a small desk against the wall, forcing my ass up and onto it. He pushed in between my legs, hand at my throat again. His other hand grabbed the back of my knee and shoved it up, giving him plenty of room.

Power pulsed within me. Desire ramped up.

The tip of his cock kissed my opening, and my eyes fluttered. I wasn't done yet, though. *I'd* be fucking *him* this time.

I twisted as I brought my arm around, slapping his hand off my throat. My leg pulled down too forcefully for him to stop me. He bent in the direction I was twisting, and I hit him with will to keep him going so I could roll out from under him.

Wood snapped under me. The legs of the desk gave out, and the whole thing dropped to the ground.

I squealed as I went down, surprised. Nyfain caught me, the game forgotten for the moment while he kept me from hitting the ground.

This was definitely going to be a *cheat to win* situation.

I took advantage of his protective instincts and shoved him back with my hands *and* my will, hitting him high so as to knock him off balance. He staggered backward, surprise lighting his face. Then humor. His feet couldn't get purchase in time, and he fell, his ass hitting the ground hard enough to shake the room and his back hitting the side of the bed.

I was on him a moment later, tamping down his hands with will and wrapping my fingers around his throat, squeezing. I ran my slippery pussy along his hard shaft before angling and sitting down onto him.

"Oh fuck," he groaned, fighting against my will's hold, struggling to breathe. "*Yes. Fuck, I love when you use me.*"

Does it need to be mentioned that you shouldn't kill him? my dragon asked patiently.

He can breathe. This is just a little asphyxiation kink, that's all. Leala told that story about it, remember? He'll get off. It'll be fine.

I bounced on top of him, letting my head fall back as I continued to squeeze. The euphoria from the heat was still there, adding a glorious double layer to the sensations. It was unlike anything I'd yet felt, complex and violent and so fucking right.

His dragon seems delighted, at any rate, my dragon thought, purring deeply. *He likes when you get feisty.*

I gyrated my hips, rubbing his cock against all the right places.

"Fuck up into me," I commanded as he continued to struggle against my hold, his eyes closed in ecstasy.

He did as I said, even though I doubted I had the resources of will to really make him. All my efforts were going toward keeping his hands down. I could barely contain him, even with all my power.

His hips swung off the ground, his cock punching into me. I moaned, my head thrown back, soaking up the violence. Struggling to take him deeper. Loving that continued euphoria.

"Fuck me, little dragon," he wheezed, his eyes fluttering now.

The sound of the door handle caught my lust-soaked awareness. Someone was coming in.

Nyfain's eyes snapped open. "Fucking bad timing," he said, his throat tight from my hold. "Almost there. Keep going. They can wait."

Do not stop, my dragon thought desperately.

"I realize this is a bad time," Hadriel said.

I released Nyfain's arms so that I could throw my will back. It hit the door and slammed it shut, knocking Hadriel away.

A proud smile lit Nyfain's face, and he closed his eyes again, raking his hands down my scales and thrusting his hips up into me. I worked him harder, knowing our time was running out, because we wouldn't be interrupted if it wasn't important. I was thankful this wasn't part of the heat so that Nyfain wouldn't lose his mind and throw someone overboard. So that I wouldn't urge him on in doing it.

"Squeeze...harder," he whispered, his throat bobbing.

I adjusted my hands, squeezing with one hand and my will while I dropped the other hand between my spread thighs. I worked my clit as I fucked Nyfain, lifting and sitting down onto him wildly, relishing in the power of this strong dragon under me, of this powerful alpha at my mercy, even if he was letting me keep him pinned.

He lifted my hips and pulled down as he thrust. The sounds of sloppy sex were interrupted by the door opening again.

"Is she choking him?" someone asked.

I felt a strange thrill at being witnessed doing something a little kinky. So maybe my dragon wasn't the only one who enjoyed public displays of fucking. So what?

Nyfain didn't let up. He thrust wildly, and I jerked my hips in his hold to get more friction. Almost there. I rubbed my clit and squeezed his throat.

"Come with me, Nyfain," I commanded.

He groaned and shuddered as I hit my peak, that naughty feeling giving me a glorious boost. I exploded, crying out and falling against him. I released my hold on his throat, and he shuddered again, thrusting a few more times as he emptied himself inside me. Our release seeped down, over his balls, visible from our spectators' vantage point. A territorial part of me liked them seeing me fuck my big dragon, knowing he was my alpha to use as I pleased.

As if hearing me say it, or maybe feeling it through the bond, Nyfain put his arms around me and held me close. He kissed me languidly, not at all hurried by the unwanted visitors.

"I really do hate to interrupt your...kill fucking, or whatever it is you're doing," Hadriel said nervously, "but we have an issue. Govam is certain we do, at any rate."

Nyfain met my eyes for one solid beat, allowing me all his focus. "Time for duty," he said softly. Louder he said, "Leave us so that we can get cleaned up. We'll be out momentarily."

"Yes, sire."

The door closed with a loud bang, Hadriel not able to get away fast enough.

I leaned against Nyfain for a moment, resting my head on his shoulder and enjoying the warmth and comfort of him before I disentangled myself and pushed to standing.

"Govam's instincts are on point," I said. "He hasn't been wrong yet."

"I don't expect him to be wrong about this, either. Dolion's going to throw everything he has at us, and he's not stupid. It'll all be from the shadows." Nyfain pulled on a loose shirt. "I suspect there will be assassination attempts at every turn from now on. Fun time is over. We're heading into war."

"Fun time is over?" I pulled on my clothes as fire roared through my veins. "Are you saying there'll be no more time for fucking?"

He chuckled as he paused next to me, sparing a glance for the ruined desk. He pulled me in close and kissed the top of my head. "There will always be time for fucking, sweetheart. I want to try that choking thing again while you hold me down. That felt dangerous. I liked it. Kill fucking, Hadriel called it."

"He's right. Dragons are crazy."

"It was your idea."

I laughed as he grabbed the door and pulled it open.

Hadriel waited beside Govam with Vemar, Calia, and Tamara standing behind them. Calia peered around Hadriel, spying the desk.

"We'll obviously pay for that," I said quickly, vaguely gesturing.

She looked bewildered.

"Please, your highnesses." Govam held out his hand, indicating we should walk to the front of the ship.

At the bow, one of the faeries held out a golden telescope. His face was blank, his eyes tight. This obviously wasn't good news.

Nyfain gestured for Govam to take the telescope. He peered through it. A ship was on the horizon, large and black and familiar. Then he swung the telescope toward another ship approaching from the right.

"Well, fuck," I said, putting my hands on the railing.

"Those vessels aren't used for piracy," Govam said, handing the telescope to Nyfain. "They are used for battle."

"Would Dolion be on one of them?" Calia asked.

"Definitely not," Govam replied. "He wouldn't jeopardize himself on the water like this."

Nyfain's lips tightened as he studied each of the ships in turn. He then turned the other way, scanning. Finally he pulled the telescope away and handed it to Micah, who'd walked up with Weston. Someone had clearly gotten word to them.

"Check the back," Nyfain said. "Make sure they aren't closing in from all sides."

"Yes, sire." Micah took the telescope and got to work.

Another faerie, holding an additional telescope, took off the other way without a word. She'd scan the other side and also hopefully double-check the back. There couldn't be too many lookouts right now.

"Those ships will have cannons," Govam said.

"Range?" Nyfain asked.

"They're twenty-pound balls. At max, we're talking five thousand yards. Over two and a half miles. But for targeting and effectiveness, they'd need to be about a half a mile out. Half a mile, and they'd be guaranteed to get a hit. There might be reason to suspect they'll have magical weapons. Demons are very rarely on good terms with faeries, but there are many places to get faerie magic."

"I can handle the faerie magic," Calia said. "Any spells that are sellable are within my power to null. It would only be a problem if they had actual mages on hand, and mages would never work for demons."

"Agreed," Govam said. "Still, there is a type of spell that will prevent a dragon from flying."

"Arleth said that was a well-kept secret," I murmured.

"Nothing is a well-kept secret from Dolion," Govam said.

"I know of it, of course," Calia replied. "Get me close enough, and I can null it."

"We have harnesses," Vemar said. "We can fly her in, no problem."

"That leads me to the next issue." Govam glanced at the dragon shifters stalking closer, wanting to hear what was going on. "As long as the bottom deck of a ship is protected, the boat or ship will never sink by fire. Going up against dragons, I would assume Dolion will have thought of this. Therefore, if you rain down fire on him and his crew, you might kill them all, but you will not destroy the vessel. It's almost certainly protected by spells or even a thin layer of water in the lowest level."

Nyfain studied him for a moment. "And then he will have proof that dragons attacked one of his vessels. He won't be able to prove which ones, but given the route we took, the timeline, and whatever holes our ships suffer from their guns…"

"But if we have holes, we can prove he started it," I said.

"Lots of holes to worry about today," Hadriel murmured.

"We can't prove he started it, no," Nyfain replied, looking out over the waters. "We won't even be able to prove he shot at us. His guns will likely fall off the burning ship and sink to the bottom. Twenty-pound cannons are the most common in the world. Or at least they were…"

"They still are," Govam supplied. "That's why he uses them on vessels like this—for missions like this. They are cheap and common. Even poor pirate ships have one or two. He has the crews keep them in pristine condition so they can deny they were ever used. He doesn't even load them unless he plans to use them. My guess is they'll dispose of them after they shoot at us. He can claim someone else was responsible. Or he might say you killed all his people to keep them from speaking for him at the council meeting."

"Meanwhile," Nyfain said, "we'll be bringing a different grievance against him before the council. A grievance that most people would assume we'd want vengeance for. There would be motive for us to have started an altercation."

"But there's motive for him to start an altercation as well," Hadriel said.

"Yes," Nyfain replied, "and then it would become a battle of he said/he said, taking focus away from the actual issue: his dungeons and what he did to those imprisoned there. It's best if we avoid the whole thing."

"Fine." I shrugged. "Then let's board their ship and kill them the old-fashioned way, with swords and knives. I'm great in close quarters. Give me a dagger, and I'll wreak havoc. Even a sword. I know how to use one of those now." Tamara and the guard's teachings had been on my daily duty list. I much preferred the sword instruction to that of the formal dinner lessons. "Then we can tie their precious cannonballs to their ankles and send them down to Davy Jones's Locker. We can help the boat drift way off route, and there will be no way for them to pin anything on us. Problem solved."

"I like the way you think, Your Royal Strange Lady." Vemar grinned.

"No," Nyfain growled, and everyone near him took an involuntary step back. His hard eyes found mine, and fire rolled across his shoulders. "You could be carrying our child. You will not put yourself into harm's way. You may command *from a distance*, but until we are sure you are not putting another life in danger, our child's life, you will not take an active part in the battle."

I flinched within his intensely possessive stare. My hand involuntarily went to my belly. It was silly, really, given I knew what the heat was for, but I hadn't given that possibility much thought. There had been so much going on that I hadn't paid attention to the calendar.

My mind raced, trying to place when I'd bled last. It seemed like such a long time ago. Had it been a month? More? Would I still have the heat if I were already pregnant?

Nyfain, clearly feeling my turbulent emotions, grabbed the back of my neck and pulled me closer, looking hard into my eyes. I stared back at him and then glanced away, still thinking. The heat had started in the library—which hadn't yielded new life—but then resurged after Nyfain's first flight. That was a week before the coronation. Then it had taken three weeks, give or take, to get ready to leave. It might've been a week before that that I'd had my period? Less? More?

Fuck.

This was terrible timing.

"You're not going anywhere near that battle," Nyfain said in a low, gruff voice.

Leala spoke from behind the gathered crowd—too short to be seen among so many tall dragons and robust wolves. "How about you burn the ships, with them in it, and then blow holes in the bottom deck with cannons. It'll sink them. No proof, no hassle."

"And this is why she is the genius among us," Hadriel said, although the compliment lacked the usual pride he used when speaking of her. His gaze was rooted to me.

In fact, everyone's gaze was rooted to me.

I twitched up a shoulder, still held in Nyfain's grasp, suddenly feeling like I was standing at the edge of a very high cliff and he was the only thing keeping me from falling off.

"I probably have a week or so before I know for sure," I said without confidence.

More fire rolled across his shoulders. He closed his eyes and blew out a steadying breath as joy and excitement burst through the bond.

"I don't know yet, Nyfain," I said softly, because it was true, and I didn't want him to get his hopes up again. Not like he had that one time at the beginning of our relationship.

His eyes opened slowly, and though we had things to plan and demons to hopefully kill, he held my gaze for a tender moment. His grip was firm on my neck, holding me close. His other hand drifted to my arm, further rooting me to the spot. His smile was soft.

"Okay," he murmured. Then his gaze hardened. "But you aren't going anywhere near this battle."

CHAPTER 30
FINLEY

"IT'S FOR THE best, your highness," Tamara said as she kept pace with me, headed to the stern of the ship. Harnesses were being laid out all over the deck as Weston chose who would be going in them. *He* would not be left out of this fight. I had not been given a choice.

"I don't even know if I'm pregnant, though," I whined, watching the demon ship as our ship turned. We'd be going left, putting some distance between the oncoming demon ships. There were only two coming. No one could spot any others on the horizon. For now.

When we reached a clear bit of deck, Tamara put a hand on my arm and signaled for Hadriel, Vemar, and Leala, who'd been following us, to hang back. Lowering her voice, she asked, "Have you hit the stage of euphoria in the heat? Where, at the end of the heat wave, you feel a certain extra…high?"

I stiffened and couldn't keep my eyes from widening. I'd used that exact word to describe how it felt lately at the end of our frenzied rush of lovemaking, when a floating sort of bliss swept through me. It was more than the intense pleasure of the heat, more than the best orgasms I'd ever had—it was almost like my world exploded into color and my entire body was alive for the first time.

I didn't answer Tamara, afraid to.

Her eyes softened, and a little smile crossed her face.

"Why?" I whispered. "What does that stage mean?"

"How long have you been in that stage?" she asked.

I shook my head, thinking back. "I don't know, a few days? Nearly a week? First my dragon felt it with his dragon, and then I felt it with Nyfain. I just thought it signaled we were nearing the end of the heat."

She nodded, and her smile grew. "When you hit the stage of euphoria, it almost always means your heat has been successful."

"But…why does it still go on?"

She shrugged. "I don't know. Maybe just to ensure it's definitely taken hold? It always does, though. A heat never stops before the euphoria unless it wasn't successful."

It was hard to breathe. My thoughts turned internal, sinking into my belly where new life had possibly been started. Where Nyfain's child might have taken root. Where the fate of the kingdom's future generations might reside.

I might have just sired an heir.

Holy fuck.

My world exploded in colors, so many emotions rolling through me that I could barely feel them all before new ones usurped them. Joy, fear, wonder, anxiety, excitement—

"This is terrible timing," I whispered.

"Are we doing girl talk?" Vemar shuffled closer. "I love girl talk. Can I do the girl talk, too?"

"No, you cannot." Hadriel shoved him out of the way. "Were you invited by the former queen to drink with the girls? No, you were not. I was, though." He hurried closer. "Darling, what is going on? Why do you look so terrified? What did Tamara say? I was doing my best to eavesdrop, but there is so much yelling going on around us that I couldn't hear. Do you have solid news you should be sharing with your dearest friend and trusted advisor?"

Leala drifted in right behind him, a smile curling her lips. Vemar peered over their shoulders.

"Does she have the euphoria?" Vemar asked. "Is that what we're talking about?"

"What's the euphoria?" Hadriel asked.

Tamara stared hard at me, silently asking me if I wanted to share.

I shook my head minutely. Not until I was sure. Not until I had my bearings. We had demons chasing us, and our people were preparing to attack. It wasn't the time for...huge life events.

"Come on." I turned and continued down the deck. "We need to get ready to go."

"You heard the king, your highness," Tamara said, keeping close. "You aren't going."

"I *am* going. I'll just stay at a distance. Which is fine. I can't blow fire anyway." I paused. "Can I shift if I'm..."

"Yes," Tamara answered. "Dragons are actually incredibly hardy with their young. You can shift all the way up until about eight months, and then no because there is about a five percent chance of triggering preterm labor. Male dragons tend to get very dramatic if their offspring is in danger. Especially alpha dragons." She paused for a moment. "*Especially* an alpha of the king's caliber."

"I get it, I get it," I said.

"What's the euphoria?" Hadriel asked again, practically jogging to keep up with my fast walk. "Is this a sure thing? Goddess spank me, I suddenly got so fucking excited. Oh shit, I better practice not swearing. Can't swear around babies. Well, maybe around babies. They can't understand anything. How many years do I have to practice not swearing? I'm going to push it to the very last minute. Do you know for sure if you are, love?"

"Focus, Hadriel," I barked, noticing my dragon was very quiet within me. Very still.

"You just blew your invitation to the next girl talk, I'll tell you that much," Vemar told him.

What's going on? I asked my dragon, reaching the stern of the boat and checking on the activity there.

The dragons that would be in the first wave of the attack, all heavy fire breathers and experienced fliers, waited back here.

I'm processing, she answered.

That made one of us.

The ships behind us would have the same sort of setup. The plan was that Calia would go first, needing to take down any magical defenses, with the dragons right behind her. They would clear away the top deck of enemies so that the wolves could head below decks to clean up the remainder of the enemy there.

Nyfain was on the second ship now, explaining how this would go. Micah had flown to the third.

"We ready?" I asked the dragons here, touching shoulders and forearms, meeting eyes. I received excited nods and grins in return.

"We're going with the first wave, right, highness?" Jade asked me when I reached her. Her gaze dipped to my stomach so quickly that I nearly missed it.

I took a deep breath and kept a stern face. "You and most of the guard are going with the first wave, yes. I will fly behind you this time. The overly cautious alpha has demanded it. I am choosing my battles. Literally. I'd love to fight the demons, but I'd rather not fight him. He's damn hard to keep pinned down."

Lucille pushed into Jade with a laugh. "Especially now that he might have successfully bred his mate. Oh gracious, he's going to be a handful, highness. I definitely recommend picking your battles. Don't worry, we got this."

"Did you reach the euphoria?" Jade asked, her eyes flashing with excitement.

Suddenly all the chatter around the back deck died down. Eyes turned my way.

"Everyone knows about that, huh?" I murmured. Butterflies filled my stomach. "You could've filled me in, you know."

Before they could press me for a proper answer, I saw a distinct azure dragon rise from the second ship and fly our way.

"Damn it," I said through my teeth. "He sicced his mother on me."

A moment later, Delaney followed.

"Oh great, and the enforcer, too," I grumbled.

"And it begins," Tamara said with a huge smile.

"How long?" Jade whispered to Tamara, and I guessed she was asking how long I'd been in the euphoria stage.

"So euphoria means it is a done deal?" Hadriel said.

"Yes," Vemar answered. "What a blessing on their rulership. This is good luck, so soon after taking the throne. The goddess shines on us all."

"Focus, people," I barked, my will whipping the command through them. "Remember, you need to stay behind Calia. Wait until she gives you the all-clear and then unleash hell. Those of you who need to return to pick up the wolves can peel away as soon as the first deck is cleared. The rest of you, remember to wait until the wolves have gone below before you drop in and start destroying things. Nyfain and…"

I paused as I watched Arleth and Delaney circle once, looking for a landing place close to me. Oh yeah, she was coming to make sure I didn't put myself in harm's way. Thankfully, there were too many dragons just here. They'd need to go to the front of the ship to find enough space to land.

I ignored Tamara, Jade, and Lucille's smirks at my predicament with my formidable mate-parent and her sidekick.

"Nyfain and Micah will direct you on where to blow fire when the wolves are on the ship. We don't want to be overzealous and trap our people in the flames. They'll clear a section, and then you will burn the hell out of that section. Those who brought the wolves in will take them back out again. *Remember your harnesses.* Do not burn them. Wolves can swim better than dragons, apparently, but the water is cold, and they will have a long wait before the ship can pick them up. Look after them so that they can look after you, got it?"

The group erupted in excited barks of "yes, highness," or "yes, queen" as I felt a presence drawing close behind me. Lucille's grin widened and Jade bit her lip.

"The demons have wronged us," I went on, feeling the pulse of adrenaline running through the bond. Nyfain was gearing up, probably delivering a speech to the second ship. "They've imprisoned us, tortured us, subjected us to unspeakable horrors, killed our families, and hurt our loved ones. It ends now! *We* will end it. We will fight back! We will not allow them to do this anymore!"

Roars and cheers went up. Fists rose into the sky.

"Wait for my signal and then rise," I told them. "Take to the sky and follow me into battle. I will take you as far as I can and then cut away—king's orders."

I gritted my teeth, because when had I let Nyfain keep me out of a battle before? I wanted to tell these people why I was listening to him and leaving them to go without me. But I didn't want to admit conclusively that I'd hit the euphoria stage without having told Nyfain first. The daddy deserved to know.

Holy fuck.

I tried to calm my suddenly rampaging heart and the

gush of joy that ran through me.

Then I couldn't help myself.

"But I will only sit out as long as you are all safe. So make sure you take them down so that I don't have to save your asses and get in trouble with the king. If I get in trouble, I will absolutely blame it all on you fuckers!"

Laughter rose, and then I turned and walked toward the front of the ship, feeling Nyfain's adrenaline and power pulsing now. Feeling the call of battle.

Fuck, I wanted to join in. I wanted to go with them. Not just to the edge of battle, but right into the heart of it. That was always where I found myself. I didn't want this time to be any different.

"Finley." Arleth jogged up from behind me in a slip, having clearly jogged down the other side and swung around the stern to find me. "Finley!"

"Yes, Arleth." I didn't slow. Nor had I meant for my reception to be so frosty.

"How long have you been in euphoria?" She kept pace a little behind me, as was proper for someone walking with the queen. She did everything properly outside of private quarters.

"Nearly a week, I think," I told her, pausing by a wolf who was picking at a harness. "Do you need help?" I asked him.

He looked up with a frown. His eyes widened and he offered a bow.

"I'm fine, your highness. It's just that…" He looked down.

I bent to show him how he should wear it in wolf form. They'd been altered before the trip to better accommodate our ground troops.

"Thank you, your highness." He smiled at me.

"Be safe out there, okay?" I touched his arm. "Wouldn't want to lose you."

He bowed again. "Yes, highness. I won't let you down."

"I didn't know what the feeling was," I told Arleth as I continued on, picking up where we'd left off. "I didn't know what it meant. There's been so much going on that I wasn't counting the weeks or realizing that…"

"You're late," she surmised.

"I think so. I'm pretty sure."

"You're probably about a week late. That's why you have the euphoria." I could hear the excitement in her voice. "You didn't tell Nyfain you had it?"

"No. I mean, I mentioned that the sensations felt really amazing, and it was getting more and more intense, and—"

"No need to elaborate," she replied.

"Like I said, I didn't know it meant something. I just thought that's what happened toward the end."

"Well…it is."

"Oh goddess, someone pinch me," Hadriel said. "I didn't realize I'd get this excited. Leala, aren't you excited? I told you. I told you all that fucking would definitely lead to a little dragon. Didn't I tell you? There is no way two people could fuck that much without it leading to—"

"Hadriel," Arleth barked.

"Yes, ma'am. Sorry, ma'am," he muttered. "Question, though: baby dragons aren't as scary as their parents, right? It takes a while before the crazy sets in?"

"You are very strong-willed, Finley, we all know that," Arleth said, ignoring Hadriel. "You are a woman who likes to take care of herself. You are very competent. But now is a time to rely more heavily on your mate."

"Please don't tell me we are doing this now," I muttered, finding Weston at the bow of the ship with two of his beta stand-ins.

"Protecting you and your young is one of his major purposes as a mate and a dragon," she continued. "Nyfain is a very strong alpha, and he will take that duty so seriously he might seem overbearing at times. Overly possessive. But it is in his nature." I stopped a couple feet from Weston, waiting for him to finish so I could interrupt Arleth. She must've realized it, because she started talking faster. "You will feel the natural urge to let him protect you. Give in to that urge. Allow him to do his duty as your mate. Practice patience if you must, and know that you won't be held back from the battle forever. Just until your young are safely out of harm's way."

Weston turned to me with raised eyebrows.

I gave him a flat stare, relaying my annoyance.

His eyes sparkled, but he didn't let the sentiment curve his lips.

"Do you have all you need?" I asked him.

"Yes, thank you, highness. We'll check on the harness setups as soon as the dragons take to the sky. The wind from their wings might disrupt their layout, and I don't want to have to do the job twice."

"Great. As you know, I'll be leading the first wave.

I'll cut out near the ship to the north. With me will go Tamara and Vemar—"

"And me," Arleth said. "And Dee."

"I really don't think you need to babysit me, head advisor," I said through clenched teeth.

"A member of the advisory circle doesn't engage in battles, or who would lead the kingdom if its leaders were to perish?" She chuckled softly. "No, no, we'll be happy to monitor the queen and heir."

She had probably just made that rule up. No doubt, by the time we got back, it would be law.

I stared at Weston with all the frustration I wanted to unleash on her. His lips started to wobble as he lost the battle to hold back that smile. He had no end of fun with my trying to learn my new position.

"The rest of my guard will help with the ship. I'll be on hand if you need me."

"No, you will not," Arleth cut in. "You will do your duty as figurehead *only*. You will let them handle the rest. Your duty is to protect the future of the kingdom, which is almost assuredly in your womb. This is exactly what I was talking about."

I didn't take my flat stare away from Weston.

"Anyway, moving on," I said dryly. "What of Hadriel? Are you leaving him behind?"

"Yes. We don't need him for this. Plus, he's clearly flustered by the...possible news. I'll leave him here in case you need to come back early."

"Thanks, alpha," Hadriel murmured behind me. He was being genuine.

I nodded and turned from him. No one had ever

been this intense when someone in the village was with child. While I realized it was different now that I was queen of the realm, I wasn't even sure I actually was pregnant. I hadn't used the herb concoction the mid-wives had taught me back when I was starting to treat people with my remedies. I had no proof.

As if sensing my bewilderment, Weston said, "Highness…"

I paused and looked back.

He bowed low and straightened, his eyes intense. "You are possibly carrying the future of our pack. It is an incredibly important duty. I will protect you and your young with my life."

"There, see?" Arleth said, stepping closer and sweeping her hand toward Weston. "He has expressed the situation perfectly."

He winked at me. "Stay out of that battle. We won't need you, promise. That and…I don't want to see the alpha lose his ever-loving mind."

"I don't even know if I am actually with child," I grumbled, finishing my turn and doing a sweep of the deck. I checked on Nyfain through the bond. His power was pumping, his adrenaline up, but he wasn't quite ready to fly into battle yet.

"It would be extremely rare for you to feel the euphoria if you weren't with child," Arleth said, shadowing me with everyone else trailing behind her.

"Except my body could reject the pregnancy." I reached one of the only open spaces on the deck large enough for us to shift. Originally I had planned to just jump over the side and shift before I hit the water, but I had a feeling that wouldn't go over well just now. "I could miscarry. The first three months are a precarious time."

Arleth waited just behind me. "Dragons are a lot hardier than other creatures once they are with child. It takes us time and patience to conceive, if we ever do, but once that happens, the chance of miscarriage is very low."

I wanted to ask why they were making such a big fuss about my fighting, if that were the case, but decided against it. It wouldn't take a genius to guess the answer.

"Okay, let's just focus on the situation at hand, shall we?" I pushed the hair out of my face. "We're about to go into battle."

"A battle you will take no part in, your highness," she replied in a firm tone. "A battle you will stay very far away from. Your task now—"

I stepped away and pulled my dragon to the surface. I couldn't take it anymore. I needed quiet to think. I needed to know if I was actually with child. I needed...Nyfain. I wanted to figure this out with him, especially if there were going to be all these strings attached.

My dragon surged up and took off, wasting no time. She was still quiet, her mood still subdued, but she'd always been quick to help when I really needed her.

I really needed her.

CHAPTER 31
FINLEY

S HE FLEW AROUND to the stern, scanning the horizon as she did so. The demon ships were in pursuit; they clearly thought we were trying to run. They were still separated by a lot of sea. They were too far away from each other to join forces in any way. They were definitely too far from us to use their cannons successfully, and our ships were faster.

We didn't check on Calia and her sister, I thought.

My dragon angled, flying over the deck, where Calia and her sister stood within their harnesses, waiting for someone to connect them up to their dragon carriers. Both beasts were from the dragon villages, steady fliers with patient and calm dispositions. For dragons, anyway.

Calia looks determined, my dragon thought as she dipped, swooping low. *Dessia looks resolute.*

Calia looked up and caught sight of us. She smiled and lifted her hand in salute, then gave us a thumbs-up. Dessia gave a small wave, her smile slight and barely visible. She was a trooper. I got the impression she'd prefer to be safe and comfortable, far away from trouble, yet she'd been Calia's companion through all of this, and she wasn't turning back now.

I didn't see Hannon on the decks and wondered if he'd hitched a ride to the ship the rest of our family was on to make sure they were safe. He knew I was protected and would want to make sure the same was true of them. I was glad for it.

How is Calia going to do this if she can't see in the dark? my dragon thought as she puffed out air and flicked her tail in greeting as we flew by. *The sun is nearly down.*

The moon is bright, and for her it is about feeling the magic. The dragon will keep her out of harm's way. She just has to do her magic.

Nyfain's dragon exploded in power, and then he shot up into the air, gorgeous and golden in the dimming sunset. The darkness would pump up the demons' power. We'd had unlucky timing.

Then again, the full moon wasn't far off. We'd benefit from the strength of the moon.

I did a circle as my limited guard and overbearing mate-parent and Dee rose into the sky, one by one, Tamara and Vemar thankfully following me first. Nyfain stayed above the other ship, but I felt his longing clearly through the bond. He wanted us closer. Wanted us together. It nearly undid me to deny the call.

Finally, Micah rose from the third ship. We were ready.

Nyfain's roar ripped through us, a command for everyone to join him. My dragon issued her own roar, uniting our people behind us.

I pushed away the pang of frustration that I couldn't participate in the battle more directly and felt Nyfain's supportive answering emotions through the bond. He pulled us closer again, yanking us, almost, not liking the distance. Wanting us by his side.

Dragons from all three ships rose into the sky as my dragon finally gave in to temptation. She sped off toward him, gushing delight and need when he banked right and cut the distance between us in half. He soared over us, dipping his tail so it would skim across our back. My dragon shuddered in pleasure, turning to meet him in the air.

Like a dance, the two dragons fit into their personal formation, practiced over the last month by nothing more than their desire to fly together, to be in each other's company as they soared over their kingdom.

They looked a picture, I knew, elegant and sleek, their sizes and colors complementary. They provided a united front for our people, calmly cutting through the darkening sky as the rest of the dragons rose to meet them. This was the figurehead job. The show we were obligated to put on. In a moment, it would turn into a battle.

Adrenaline started to throb in me as more dragons took flight. I saw Hannon standing on the deck of the second ship, and I knew he had his new double-edged axe and dagger tucked into a sheath and harness on his person. He'd been training, and those weapons had proven his most effective. But he wouldn't be joining the wolves. I'd made Nyfain promise to make Hannon stay behind. It was Hannon who had insisted our family come, anyway. He could stay in safety and make sure they didn't get up to mischief.

You're treating Hannon like Nyfain and Arleth are treating you, my dragon thought as Nyfain roared. He pumped his wings and rose a bit so the other dragons could assemble into their formations, doing large laps around the ships. They needed to wait for the last of the first wave dragons.

And it is fine for me to forcefully protect my family and not fine for them. I am a very firm believer in certain double standards. Hannon can't come to any harm. He is the glue of our family. He needs to stay safe.

And we are the glue of the kingdom, especially if we're with child. I think Nyfain and Arleth have a very good point about what our duty is now.

No one asked you.

My dragon huffed as the last dragons found their formation. With another roared command from Nyfain's dragon, it was time to unleash our secret weapon.

Calia and her sister slowly rose into the sky, gripping their harnesses tightly even though they were thoroughly strapped in. Their hair blew in the wind from their dragons' wings.

I was excited on their behalf, for the thrill and the flight and the impending battle. It probably made one of us.

I hoped we wouldn't need them, though. I hoped this was just a precaution and they could return to the ship quickly. They didn't seem to savor violence.

What if the demons have that magic where fire won't

413

work? I don't think Calia can help with that, especially from a distance, I said to my dragon, a question I hadn't thought to raise earlier. My mind had been on other matters. Like the euphoria.

Then the dragons land and physically destroy their whole world. They are all great at fighting on the ground now. They'll figure out how to fight on a ship. We got this. With Calia to make flying safe, we got this.

She was right. I knew she was right. But I worried ten times as much when I had to watch the action unfold without being able to negate the threat myself.

Nyfain pushed forward, and my dragon was right there with him, following Calia and her sister. Calia would dictate the speed of their initial approach by pulling on cords attached to the dragon above her.

Here we go, I thought, my heart speeding up.

We could clearly see the demons as they scurried across the top deck of the targeted ship. Flaps in the sides of the ships opened and barrels surged forward, the cannons being readied. Oh yeah, they were gunning for us.

Calia's escort slowed and then angled a bit, no longer heading straight for the ship. As I watched, I saw Calia yank the cord on her right, prompting the dragon to angle a bit more. She was guiding him in an arc around the ship, which suggested she felt magic that would affect him and didn't want to go for a swim.

Dessia's dragon got closer to the other, as close as she could. Calia and her sister's magic worked better in close proximity to each other.

The other ship continued to close the distance, demons racing across the deck. Cannons popped out, still out of range but not far now. They could hit us from there with blind luck, but pretty soon they'd be in range for better targeting.

Come on, come on, I thought. *Get that magic down.*

The dragon carrying Calia flapped his wings wildly for a moment, tilting and dropping in the air.

I surged up near the surface of my dragon, desperate to go to their aid but trying to stay out of it.

As if knowing my struggle, Nyfain's dragon cut in front of us, blocking the way. Micah pushed forward, intent on helping, but Calia's hands dropped and the dragon regained flight. He rose into the sky, the signal that all was clear.

She'd broken the spell.

Nyfain's dragon stalled a moment, his tail swinging around and lightly bumping against my dragon's neck. It slid up delicately, an intimate touch, before he surged forward. His roar vibrated through us. *Attack!*

Heart hammering, my dragon pulled up, clearing away. The dragons behind us followed Nyfain in perfect formation, descending on the ship like falling stars. The dragons dove and spouted flame before soaring away, making room for the next wave. Hair and skin and clothes caught fire. Wood began to burn. Sails went up.

The demons had put all their faith in the magic to keep the dragons at bay. They hadn't made a backup plan.

The first blast made my dragon flutter her wings and angle away. Cannons.

Scratch that—they hadn't made a *good* backup plan.

Another explosion of fire and gunpowder. I saw the glint of the ball as it whizzed toward us, much too low. Those cannons were made to hit ships, not objects in flight.

Tamara flew on my right and Vemar on my left, staying close. Delaney moved in over me as Arleth went below. They were boxing me in. No. As Tamara pushed in close, Vemar giving me space, and Delaney crowded me from up top, I realized they were herding me.

It's one thing to stay out of the fight, but it is entirely another to be herded away from my mate, my dragon grumbled.

They clearly think you're going to do something reckless.

I said I wouldn't? My dragon huffed.

Like that has ever stopped you.

She didn't comment, but I could feel her unease at being separated from him. She allowed them to lead her but still repeatedly looked over her shoulder, watching Nyfain.

He dipped along the side of the black demon ship, roaring as he swung his tail into the side. He tore open a large gash in the wood and caught cannons in the process, shoving them back or dragging them forward. Two of them pitched over the side, a terrified demon clinging to one of them as it splashed down into the water.

Another dragon—Xavier, I thought—followed behind him, narrowly dodging a cannonball exploding from the ship. He smashed his tail into the gaping hole, knocking cannons farther back and crushing whoever was in the way.

A third dragon puffed fire before following Xavier. The others in the vicinity pumped their wings and gave the dragon some space. In a moment, I saw why.

He dove past the ship and breathed fire into the gaping hole that Nyfain and Xavier had rent into the side. Bursts of flame exploded back out, large plumes coughing from all the openings. He was hitting the highly flammable black powder used to launch the cannonballs. Any loaded cannons went off, but the barrels had been turned askew. Balls burst through the back of the ship or the other side. The cannons jumped back with the force, some too near the opening. Their bases went over the edge, and then they fell into the waiting waters below.

The pull of Nyfain clawed at our middle. My dragon's anxiety rose, and she slowed. She didn't want to be herded. She didn't want to leave her mate. Something in her said we needed to stay close to him. That we had to stay by his side.

I felt Nyfain pull me in through the bond, holding me tightly. He was trying to ease my worry. Or was he trying to ease his own concerns? Whatever he was doing, it wasn't enough. We didn't want to let him out of our sight.

This had to be one of those natural urges Arleth had spoken of. She asked that we gave in, but that was impossible right now. I wasn't supposed to go to him. The feeling of resisting, though, was like being split in half. As though this feeling, this all-consuming need, was something we could simply ignore.

This might take some getting used to, I thought. *Keep* ·

to our duty. He's not in danger. He'll be fine, but Calia might need us. She's more vulnerable. She's also our first line of defense against that other ship.

Watch, friends, my dragon said, *as the dragon's entire middle is ripped out through her side because of this fucking feeling. Watch as she bleeds out before falling out of the sky.*

Well, well, well, I thought with utter delight. *Look who has decided to adopt talking to an invisible audience in times of great stress.*

It seems more logical than whatever the fuck is going on with me.

She gritted her teeth against the urge to get back to Nyfain. She doggedly continued along, right behind Calia, boxed in by guards. The rest of the dragons had probably fanned out behind—who was to say? We could barely focus, desperate as we were to turn around.

A ragged roar boomed behind us. Pain pierced our middle. And then he was coming. He was flying toward us, easing the ache caused by our separation.

Oh thank fuck, my dragon thought, breathing deeply, slowing.

Clearly he felt it too, I replied. *Turn around so I can see.*

No. He felt it too, but he broke first. We have a stronger will. We're going to own that.

Or he loves us more and you're a horrible bitch.

It is impossible to love us more than we love him. He is just weaker.

There really was no use arguing with her.

The guard around me fell away, giving me space.

The ache at our separation diminished, easing little by little, until it relaxed. My dragon took another deep breath.

Nyfain's tail grazed the middle of our back as he flew overhead, and then he fell in beside us, the early moonlight catching his golden scales. His dragon looked over, giving a huff of fire. The sentiment, whatever it meant, flipped my dragon's belly. Our chest glowed warm, filled with his proximity. His presence. All our fears and worries eased.

This will definitely take some getting used to, I thought.

Yes, she said, though she didn't seem too beaten up about it.

The second ship had clearly watched their brethren's fate in horror and decided they weren't heroes. The large black vessel was in the process of turning, a slow affair. They wanted to get the fuck out of there.

Too late.

Calia and her sister circled the second ship from a distance again, staying just outside of the magic while Calia pulled it down. This time she worked even faster, and before I knew it, she was lowering her arms, signaling the second ship was open for destruction.

Nyfain led the charge, roaring as he descended on the ship and blasted it with fire. The others went after him. Micah wasn't with them, which suggested he'd stayed behind to oversee the ruination of the first ship.

Our dragons ran their tails through the sides and filled the space with fire. Flame billowed out and up in no time. Demons dove into the water to get away, only to be scooped up into the jaws of dragons and crunched.

I'm glad I'm a dragon and not someone prone to getting attacked by them, I thought as I watched the fast and brutal destruction of the ship. The wolves wouldn't even get a chance to play their part. There would be nothing left for them to attack.

Nyfain returned to us before the destruction was complete, flying in front of us and flicking his tail against our neck as he passed. My dragon followed him, finding her place at his side. He checked on the other ship, finding it engulfed in flames and half sunk. Either the explosions or the cannons' misfires had punched enough holes in the lower deck to send it down to a watery grave. Dragons circled it like carrion birds, some of them swooping down to pluck an escaping demon out of the waters and end its struggles.

Matters were clearly well in hand, and after a glance at the other ship, also in flames, he turned back to our ship.

Calia and her sister are definitely secret weapons, my dragon mused as she soared lazily at Nyfain's side, a victor without having done anything. *And they should remain secret. We don't want to reveal our hand. You need to make sure Nyfain the human knows that.*

I will. I would just like it to be known, though, that I've always known it would be beneficial to have faeries on our side.

Any idiot would know that. She paused. *Also, I did plenty. I held my position as a figurehead and led the charge.*

Sure, yeah. Great job...leading the charge.

420

She huffed at me, and I smiled to myself. It relieved me to know that we honestly hadn't been needed. Not even the wolves had been needed. Without a proper deterrent, the demons hadn't stood a chance on a couple of wooden ships in the open water.

Nyfain beat his wings over the faerie ship, waiting for me to land and shift. I did so very delicately so as not to incite his rage. After being the reason he'd left one battle for the other, I didn't want to exacerbate matters. Or get a lecture from anyone else, like his mom, who was watching my every move.

He landed next, shifting and walking toward me as Urien and Leala met us with clothes to change into. The azure dragon touched down before he reached me.

"Damn it," I said between my teeth as Leala helped me get a slip on. His mother wasn't done with me yet.

She's probably going to push you to take a test so we can know for certain we're carrying Nyfain's child, my dragon thought.

A shiver swept over my flesh as Nyfain stepped close to me, slinging his arm around my waist. My dragon was probably right. I needed to take the "probably" out of things, for Nyfain and for me.

I turned toward him and ran my palms up his hard chest. He pulled me in close, dipping his head to run his lips against mine.

"Are you ready, Nyfain?" I met his eyes as I hooked my arms around his neck. "Do you want to find out if you're going to be a daddy?"

CHAPTER 32

NYFAIN

MY MOM AND Finley worked in the galley of the ship, done arguing for the moment. The resolution to their (long) argument about whose concoction for verifying if a woman was with child was better was that they'd each make their own. Finley would use them both.

I shuddered as I tried to take a deep breath and wiped the perspiration from my forehead as I sank deeper into my chair at the dining table just outside the galley. Finley and my mother were within view, because I needed to see them right now.

I hadn't thought to ask Finley about the euphoria. The heat had been getting more pleasurable for me, more intense, so I hadn't thought much of it when she said the same was true for her. I'd forgotten she knew so little about shifters and even less about dragons.

It had been going on for nearly a week.

"How are we doing?" Hadriel slunk in, somewhat bent over and with his fingers entwined. He glanced at the women silently making their brews, then grimaced at me. "Are they getting along any better?" he whispered.

My mother was being a little overbearing. She had good reason for it, though. If Finley was with child…

My child…

My dragon moved within me, impatient. Hopeful. Incredibly protective, not wanting Finley or her dragon out of his sight. He'd nearly lost his mind in the battle earlier. He couldn't stand to see her moving away from him, potentially putting herself in danger. His need to wrap his wings around her, shield her from anything that might hurt or upset her, tore at us every second. Every moment. Even now, I wanted to pull her over here and wrap her in the protection of my arms. I wanted to head back home and lock her in that tower. I'd stay there too, guarding the door.

The emotions were crazy. Illogical. So fucking intense I could barely think straight. And yet I wanted them. I wanted the power they brought, the crystal-clear focus when she was near. I wanted the enhanced intimacy of her touch and the glorious tranquility I felt when I was at her side, ensuring nothing could harm her.

I tightened my fingers where they lay entwined on the dining table.

"They are ignoring each other at the moment," I murmured.

"Oh good. That's better than yelling at each other like earlier. Though…" Hadriel leaned his elbow on the table, propping his face in his hand, and leaned toward me. "Not allowing Finley near a stove is a bit overboard. Can we agree on that? Not allowing her to battle, yes.

That makes sense. Not allowing her plants and elixirs, the one thing that calms her? Hmm."

"My mother is worried Finley doesn't understand the gravity of the situation. She's worried she'll do too much and hurt herself and the...possible baby." My heart started to hammer and butterflies exploded through my stomach. "Finley was raised among wolves and other shifters that have an easier time getting pregnant. She doesn't realize how lucky we are and how quick it was. Possibly was. Dragons are hardy, but they aren't invincible."

"Ah ha." Hadriel put up a finger. "Not to worry. I have asked Vemar to go get Hannon. Her brother is probably the only one that can talk sense into her. Remember the fight they had about bringing the whole family instead of leaving them in the castle?" He paused and narrowed one eye at me. "Hannon won. He said they'd be safer here, protected by our best people, and everyone in the family came. Before that, they were yelling at each other and everything. But Hannon won. He's your best bet, I think. Don't worry, I took care of it."

He turned away and clasped his fingers to mimic my pose. I couldn't tell if he annoyed the shit out of me or was a good type of distraction. The question would probably always remain.

Finley sprinkled herbs into a pot.

"I thought you'd want to know, sire," Hadriel went on. "The demon ships sank. Both of them. The wolves weren't needed, as you know, but neither were the cannons from our ships. Which you also probably know, since you haven't heard any cannon fire. The only problem is, there are bodies and debris floating all over the place. Body parts, too. The dragons are trying to burn any floating wood, but the wood is wet now, so…that's not going well."

I nodded. There wasn't much they could do about that. This situation would never have disappeared without a trace. But Dolion had no proof who'd done it.

"The wolves are annoyed, of course," Hadriel said, back to looking at the women finishing their brews. "They wanted to help. They felt left out. I took care of it."

"And how did you do that?" I asked, raising my brows.

"I told them the truth. If they'd been brought to the barbecue, they'd have ended up roasting on a spit or drowning. When there were still some grumbles, I mentioned that dragons are so crazy, they'd piss on the flames to put them out. So charred and pissed on, or a watery grave. Neither of those options were very appealing to them."

I blinked. Hadriel had a habit of tumbling off the deep end of absurdity, to the point where you had to wonder if something was fundamentally wrong with him.

I slowly swung my gaze to him, hoping he was kidding. As if we were a comic duo, he swung his gaze toward me at exactly the same speed. When our eyes met, he waggled his eyebrows. He very clearly was not kidding.

"And how are you, sire?" he said, his posture still perfectly mimicking mine.

I found myself answering without meaning to. "Scared."

A shock of adrenaline coursed through me. I hadn't meant to use that word. I didn't even know where it came from.

Feeling the emotion, Finley glanced back. When our eyes connected, something tight in my middle loosened. My muscles relaxed. She gave me a nervous smile but then went back to what she was doing.

More words tumbled out, unbidden. "I'm scared she won't be with child. That she has built her hopes up again, that *I* have built her hopes up, and she'll be disappointed. I don't think I can see that vulnerable, sorrowful look on her face."

I leaned back, pulling my hands to the edge of the table.

"I'm scared that I'll never be able to give her children. That we'll have to go through this again and again. She wants to be a mother, and she'd be such a great one. I hope I can give that to her. On the other hand, I'm also scared that she is with child. I'm scared that I won't be able to protect her. I'm scared, above all else"—my voice caught—"that I will lose her. I can't lose her. If I lose her, I will lose myself. Without her, there will be a hole in my center that I'll never be able to fill."

I blinked away moisture in my eyes, trying not to focus on the uncertainty of this moment. On the terror of waiting for my future to be laid bare.

"And what do you hope for?" Hadriel asked me, and I noticed his hands were on the edge of the table like mine. I had no idea why he was mimicking me like that.

Was it on purpose? Or was he just incredibly odd and off-putting?

Once again, because I was so off-kilter with him right now, I opened my mouth and the words came tumbling out.

"I hope she will soon find out she is the mother of my child. That'll make me the happiest man this world has ever known."

Hadriel put his palms up and nodded. "Then let's just focus on that, shall we, sire? Fear helps us pass the time, sure as shit, but it doesn't actually get us anywhere. Unless you're being chased, obviously. When I'm being chased, I run like a motherfucker. You might remember that from my years of being picked on by dragons. Ol' Hadriel is very quick."

As with before, he dragged my focus to him, kicking and screaming. He also mimicked the head turn from earlier, moving with the same deliberate slowness as I had.

"Hello," he said when our eyes met, and suddenly I wanted to strangle him.

"Okay. It's ready." Finley stared down into the pot as a small knock came at the door.

"Oh. Fantastic. Just in time." Hadriel hopped up. "Hang on there, Finley, my love. We have a visitor."

"I don't want any visitors, Hadriel," Finley said.

"Don't I know it. That's why I have Leala guarding the door."

A rush of chilled air blew through the space. A moment later, Hannon walked in with his usual calm, measured pace. He stopped between the galley and the table, facing Finley.

"Oh, it's you," she said, holding out a shallow bowl. "Good timing."

"What's going on?" Hannon looked her over as he took the bowl. Not seeing any wounds, he assessed my mother before turning to look at me. His eyebrows knotted. "What's going on?" he asked again.

I'd only told my mother about Finley, who had of course told Delaney, but that was as far as it had gone. At the time, I hadn't known about the euphoria. I'd just mentioned she might be late and it would be good for her to have someone knowledgeable around. Given Hannon had been left on the other ship, he clearly hadn't heard the gossip from this one.

"I might have an affliction," Finley said. "I have a very pushy mate-parent."

Hannon took the bowl, glancing at my mother. "I don't understand."

"I might be pregnant, Hannon. This is the test that will tell me." She moved toward the table. Toward me.

Hannon stared after her for one beat, and then color shed from him in waves, shimmering in the air around him. It was his magic. His power. Family connections brought it out in him. His drive for protecting his loved ones was even stronger than a dragon's.

"So soon?" he asked. "I thought it took a while for a dragon."

"The heat cycle often brings on babies," I said, "but yes, it was very soon after imprinting for a heat cycle. We were blessed."

I pushed my chair back and stood, then held out a

hand to Finley. She took it, and I reeled her around the edge of the table and into my lap, sitting with her. She looped her arms around my shoulders and waited until I tipped my head back so she could kiss me softly.

"I heard what you said," she whispered. "Don't be afraid, baby. Whatever comes, we'll face it together. We will hope together, and we'll be scared together, and we'll be disappointed together. You won't fail in protecting me, we both know that. You won't fail in providing for me. I won't let you." Her laughter lifted my heart. "As long as we're together, we have everything we need."

"Preferably without your mate-parent looking over your shoulder with that disapproving look, am I right?" Hadriel grinned and lifted his eyebrows.

Mom turned back to give him a look of death.

Hadriel virtually sank into himself. "Yes, that should've been much quieter. I realize my error. Whoopsie." He put his hand beside his mouth and said to Finley and me, "Tough crowd."

"It's a bit weird, helping my sister with this," Hannon said as he ladled a bit of liquid into the bowl.

"Well, maybe one day I'll make the concoction for your mate. We'll be even, how's that?" she replied.

"If I'm ever that blessed," he said.

"How does it work?" Hadriel asked, watching Hannon.

"I'll take both bowls into the bathroom and pee in them," she said, then murmured, "I had some practice with Mr. Pee-body." She shook her head. "If they turn bright green, I'm pregnant."

"What if one turns bright green and the other

doesn't?" Hadriel asked.

"It depends which one turns," Finley said dryly. She earned a *look* from Mom. She ignored it, of course, and leaned into me, running her lips along my cheek and nibbling my earlobe. "I know I said all that stuff about togetherness, but I'm a little scared, too. This is such a big deal, and there's so much danger ahead of us. What am I going to do if I can't fight?"

I cupped her cheek. "You're going to stay by my side. No one will touch you if you're next to me."

She gave me a nervous smile that sank down to my heart and then excused herself to the washroom.

Hadriel tapped his fingers rhythmically against the table as Hannon and my mom cleaned up the galley. Nervousness traveled back and forth through the bond.

"And you're sure it's yours, right?" Hadriel asked conversationally.

I had his throat in my hand and his body shoved against the wall before I could register moving. The table lay on its side and chairs were strewn around the floor, one still spinning.

"Whoa, whoa, whoa." Hannon grabbed my arm with one hand and put his other hand on my chest. "Let's not hurt him. Finley loves him."

"If you *ever* say that to me again," I growled, ignoring Hannon, "I will finish you. Do you understand me? You get to stay alive because of Finley. That is the only reason."

I leaned in close, making sure my message was delivered. When I saw the fear deep in his eyes, I released my hold and pulled my hand away.

Hadriel coughed, sliding to the ground. He grabbed his throat and curled up into a ball.

"Good reaction time, sire," he wheezed, coughing again. "I was expecting violence, but I did not expect it so fast." He groaned, getting to hands and knees and dropping his head. "Wow. That was fucking terrifying. I thought I was going to die. I think I sharted. Did anyone hear it? That was good, though. That was good. You had zero doubt in those crazed peepers of yours, sire. I was worried, what with the situation with your real father, you know? Sometimes our past can cloud our judgment. Not you, though. No clouds in that psycho stare. None whatsoever. You have perfect trust in our girl. Phew. I think that gave me heartburn."

"Here, let me help you up." Hannon reached down for him.

"Wait, wait." Hadriel held up his hand. "Is he still looking at me?"

Hannon looked my way, a wrinkle in his brow. "Yes."

"Then I'll just stay down here, nice and small. I don't think he'll kick me when I'm down."

Mom threaded between Hannon and me, looking down on Hadriel. "You flirted with an alpha dragon's rage to see if he had any doubts about his mate?"

"Flirted? That wasn't flirting." He pushed back to his knees. "I punched his rage right in the fucking nuts. I needed to know, though. Even a little doubt can grow into the kind of parasite that eats you alive. I needed to know if Leala and I would have to protect Finley from the king's misguided rage down the road. I'm sure I don't have to explain that to you, ma'am. This kingdom isn't known for its sanity."

My mother turned and looked at me incredulously, her eyes shining with tears.

"Keep him with her, always," she told me, her voice wavering. "Always. He'll protect her in ways you probably won't even think of." She turned and headed back into the galley.

"Pick him up," I told Hannon, bending down to grab one of the overturned chairs.

"There would have been other, less rash ways to accomplish the same thing," Hannon murmured to Hadriel, setting him on his feet.

"I don't have that mood-consuming thing like you do," Hadriel said, straightening his plain gray sweatshirt.

"What?" Hannon asked, his eyes rounding and face going slack.

Hadriel heard the change in his tone and abruptly stopped smoothing out his sweatshirt. "What?"

"What did you say?" Hannon asked.

A look of terror bled through Hadriel's eyes. "Oh fuck, I don't know. What did I say? Was it bad? What did I do, black out? I haven't even been drinking on this trip!"

"The mood-consuming thing he does?" I asked.

Hadriel's eyebrows climbed and his eyes got cagey. "What am I missing? Why was that the wrong thing to say?"

Something moved behind Hannon's eyes. Uncertainty, maybe. Fear?

"Isn't that what you do?" Hadriel whispered, leaning

toward him a little. "Hey, look, to each their own. As long as you're not a dragon, I don't care what you're up to. No offense, sire. And ma'am."

"How did you—" Hannon cut off, and though he didn't glance at me, I knew he wanted to.

Mood consumption.

Pieces started aligning.

Before they could converge, there was a light knock at the door.

Leala stuck her head in. "I think you should stop fighting or whatever you were doing and clean everything up. She's coming."

CHAPTER 33
FINLEY

I SET THE bowls onto the crooked table and stood back, looking for Nyfain's reaction. His eyes darted down, first to one bowl, then to the other. Then back to the first. An explosion of emotion ripped through the bond, and I could feel his dragon reach through our connection and grab mine.

Nyfain's eyes hooded, and his mouth slowly tipped into a smile. When he met my eyes, their golden depths shimmered with emotion.

"Love." He grabbed me and pulled me close, wrapping his arms around me and rocking me softly.

"Let me see." Arleth shoved Hadriel out of the way. He rammed into Hannon, and they both crashed into the wall, nearly tripping over a waylaid chair. She looked at the green in each bowl before clapping her hands together. "You are!" She faced me, tears clouding her eyes. "You are!"

She started jumping up and down, laughing.

"She is?" Hadriel tried to climb over Hannon to see.

"Oh my—Finley, lamb, what wonderful news. Sire, what a treat to share this with you. We will always have that time when you tried to kill me and I narrowly escaped so we could share in the news of your first child."

"Wha—?" I furrowed my brow at Hadriel, who had wrapped his arms around half of Hannon's thick chest.

"Oh, honey." Arleth hugged Nyfain from behind, her arms making it to my shoulders. "What a blessing. I am so happy. I so hoped for grand-babies. Dee will be thrilled." She laughed, squeezing me tightly, before excusing herself and running off to tell Delaney.

"Congratulations, Finley," Hannon said, standing nearby. Power shed from him in beautiful waves.

I unwrapped myself from Nyfain so that I could hug him, and then hug an increasingly loud Hadriel.

"It's still early," I said. "Many things could go wrong. I've helped many women who didn't make it through the first trimester—"

"Yeah, Finley!" Vemar walked in with an enormous smile. "I just heard. Sire, you got some warrior swimmers, eh?" He slapped Nyfain on the back. "Finley. Congratulations, hon!" He waved at me from a few feet away.

I stepped toward him in confusion, my arms out for a hug.

He held up his hand and took a step back. "No, thank you. Let's wait until we all know how reactive the king will be now that you're with child."

"Very wise," Hadriel said to Vemar. "Very, very wise. You wouldn't be as lucky as me if he went after you. You're not as likable."

"What happened?" I asked as Nyfain slipped his arm around my shoulders.

"Congratulations, sire," Tamara said as she filled with the doorway with a big smile. She inclined her head to me. "Highness. Congratulations!"

Someone else stepped in behind her, shouting congratulations at me too. Then another. My anxiety started to rise, and then dread took its place. What if something happened? I didn't want to have to tell all these people. I didn't want to have to explain my heartache over and over.

"Hey." Nyfain lifted me up into his arms, already walking toward the door. People cleared away instantly. "Leala, keep them back."

"Yes, sire. No problem." Leala led the way toward our room as I dug my face into Nyfain's neck so I wouldn't have to see how quickly the news was spreading.

A whip crack rang out. Leala always carried her whip in the holster at her hip, opposite clothes pins, scissors, and other things she might need in tending me.

"Holy fuck," someone said.

Another crack. "Back off, we're walking here!" Leala yelled.

"You probably have the coolest lady's maid in the history of the job," Nyfain murmured, such sublime happiness in his tone that I couldn't help tightening my hold around his neck.

"Congratulati—" someone started.

Crack.

"Ow!" they shouted. "Fuck! What the fuck? What

was that for? Why the fuck do you have a whip?"

Once we were at our room, Leala rubbed my arm consolingly before shutting the door behind us. Her whip cracked again, and someone shouted before all fell quiet around us but for the murmuring of water along the side of the ship.

"Hey," Nyfain said softly, sitting on the edge of the bed and nestling me into his lap. "What's the matter? Aren't you happy?"

I told him about my fears. About what we'd have to face if things didn't work out.

"I can't…I can't imagine having to tell a kingdom full of people if I lose the pregnancy."

"Hey, hey. *Shh.*" He stroked my hair back from my face, his touch infinitely gentle. "Dragons are hardy, didn't my mother tell you? Once the child attaches, there are usually very few preterm issues. The odd exceptions usually have to do with physical exertion, and by that I mean fighting or excessive combat training. That's why my mom was being so overbearing. You're a risk taker, Finley—it's one of the things I love about you. You'll have new limits now, though, and you shouldn't learn what those are by nearly dying. I don't want you to lose our baby."

His eyes were so deep. So full of love.

"I'll be good," I whispered. "I promise."

He smiled, his severe features softening into utter perfection. He was so handsome it took my breath away. He wrapped his arms around me again, tucking my head underneath his chin and rocking me slowly.

"I don't have words for how happy I am," he said, his

voice rumbling from deep within his chest. "I don't have words for how full my heart is. I can't…"

His voice broke and he hugged me tighter.

"I can't believe my good fortune," he said in a ragged whisper. "Thank you for believing in me when I'd lost all hope. Thank you for forcing me to find my way out of the darkness so that I might once again enjoy the light. I love you, Finley. Please guard my heart. It is yours forever."

A tear slipped down my cheek. "I love you too." I sniffed. "But you did actually help, you know. I didn't just do this on my own."

"Hadriel asked me if I was sure it was mine," he said.

I pulled back so he could see my frown. "Was he trying to die or something?"

Nyfain chuckled. "He was apparently testing me. He wanted to see if I had any doubts because of what I learned about my real father."

I lifted my eyebrows. "Ah. I guess I can see that. And you rushed him. That's what he meant when he said he'd almost died."

"He was exaggerating."

"Yeah, I'll bet he was." I quirked an eyebrow at him. "And? What was the result of the test?"

"He apparently sharted, but my reaction pleased him. Especially the part where I didn't kill him."

"That was sweet of him, I guess. There were probably better ways he could've gone about it, though."

Something flashed in Nyfain's eyes, so fast I almost doubted I'd seen it at all. The next moment, his eyes had cleared and he was standing me up.

"We should arrive at Narvos Kingdom tomorrow evening," he said, his eyes liquid gold. He unfastened the three buttons at my neck. "News will have spread among the ships about your...condition." I arched my eyebrow at him again, and he smiled, trailing his fingers along the sides of my neck. I closed my eyes, savoring his touch. "They won't begrudge us some alone time before we have to go to work."

He bent down and grabbed the hem of my slip before lifting. He peeled it away gently before tossing it to the side, pausing when he noticed the desk we'd ruined.

It looked like it had been patched up by a child. Random pieces of wood had been stuck to splintered sections with nails that were too big or nailed halfway in and then bent sideways. The top slanted right at a downward angle, no two corners at the same height. A folded-up sock propped up the back right leg, and the other three legs were broken and taped.

"I didn't think we'd broken it that badly," I said.

"Forget us breaking it, what sort of a fix is this? I would've thought the faeries had more skill in wood-working, even deck hands."

I laughed softly and stripped Nyfain's shirt the same way he had removed my slip: slowly, delicately.

I kissed his hard, inked chest, right above his heart. "I think it was Hadriel. Weston let him stay behind—even though I guess they all technically stayed behind—so he could prepare for my return. It was after everyone heard about the euphoria."

I dragged my lips along his fevered flesh, licking and tasting as I did so. I flicked his nipple with my tongue before scraping my teeth across it.

"With all the weirdness in that body," Nyfain murmured, sliding his hands down my upper arms, "how does he have room for a heart of that size?"

I laughed as I pushed down his sweats, finding him bare underneath. I ran my hands along his smooth shaft, my mouth watering for him. I fell to my knees in front of him, pushing his cock up so I could suck and lick his balls before running my tongue up the underside to his cock head. He sucked in a breath as I flitted my tongue over his winking slit, licking up the precum I found there. The imprinting really had made it taste like candy, and I couldn't get enough.

He groaned as I sucked him in. I ran my hands up the insides of his thighs and cupped his balls. As I took him deeper into my mouth, I massaged his balls with one hand and used the other to stroke his shaft in rhythm with my mouth.

"Hmm," he said as he threaded his fingers into my hair.

I ran my hands over his muscular thighs and up to his mouth-watering ass, feeling his firm cheeks. He pulled back before thrusting, taking over, his fingers tightening in my hair. I sucked and angled so that he would be pumping down into my mouth. Throat elongated, I moaned as I took him, knowing the vibration would run up his shaft and spear through his body.

I wasn't disappointed. His groan of pleasure soaked down into me as he sped up, pulling my head forward and ramming his cock in, fucking my face. His ass clenched under my gripping fingers. His hips swung. I sucked him in deep, my eyes starting to water. That was when I looked up at him, meeting his eyes as he looked down.

"Fuck, Finley," he groaned, going faster now, chasing his orgasm.

I left one hand on his butt but returned the other to his balls, kneading and massaging, feeling when they tightened up into his body.

"Swallow it down," he commanded as drool ran down the side of my lips. "Swallow what I give you."

I groaned at his filthy talk. At his power pumping through me.

"That's right, baby, choke on this thick cock," he said, knowing what I liked. "Play with your clit. I want to see you get off as you suck me down."

He yanked my head back with one hand, still holding my gaze, and reached down to grab my throat with his other. He moved my head up and down his cock, squeezing my throat gently, taking complete control.

My body heated up. The ache for him rose, slowly at first but building to a fever pitch. My heat was coming on again. I already carried his child, and apparently the euphoria was my reward. I intended to make the most of it.

But first I'd please my man until he was goo in my hands.

I pulled my hand away from his butt and ran it over my breasts, pinching a nipple. Then let it trail down to my clit and through my slick folds. I pulled the moisture up and around my clit before heading back down again, slipping two fingers into my pussy.

"That's right, baby, fuck your tight little cunt with your fingers."

Nyfain took a harder grip on my hair and tilted my head to the side a little so he could more easily hold on to my throat. He thrust his dick into my willing mouth. I groaned around him, back at my clit now, stroking myself.

"Play with your nipple with your other hand," he said, power still pumping through me.

My body throbbed for him. My blood burned.

I wanted to tell him to fuck my face harder. To own me. To use me. But I didn't want to stop sucking his dick down deep. I worked myself harder, toying with my nipple and rubbing my clit, liking the roughness. Needing it.

"That's right," he said, his movements jerky. Wild. Getting closer. "You're so gorgeous."

He stroked in deeper, slapping his balls against my chin. His hold on me tight. Waves of pleasure ran through me, from the bond, from myself. They swirled within my body until I was as tight as a bowstring, humming with the need to release. With the need to suck down his climax. I was really going to miss this heat when it left. It enhanced sex in the best way possible, making even choking on a cock the most amazing thing to have ever happened in the world.

He grunted as he fucked my face in long strokes. He tilted my head back farther, just this side of pain. Dominating. Taking his pleasure.

I whimpered, right on the edge. Sucking for all I was worth.

"Swallow it all," he said before he growled his release.

His delicious taste flooded my mouth and slid down my throat. I gulped, savoring the sweet and exotic taste. My own climax ripped through me, and I groaned in chorus with him, shuddering in delight.

Still the heat pounded through my veins. Pleasuring him was nice, but it wasn't enough. It wasn't what would satisfy me.

I backed off and then licked him clean before straightening up to standing. Holding his eyes, I fed him my glistening fingers, letting him suck off my climax. I followed that with a kiss to his lips, letting him open my mouth with his and mix the flavors. The thought of it spiraled, and then I was running my fingers into his hair and taking hold, assaulting his mouth with mine. Wrestling with his tongue. The kiss deepened as we lost ourselves to it.

"Fuck me, dragon," I told him, pulling him backward toward the bed. "Worship me."

His growl of pleasure slithered across my flesh.

"As you command," he replied, and he fell across me onto the bed. His hip and elbow touched down beside me, though, so his weight wasn't directly pressing on my front. He was already trying to protect the baby.

Suddenly I couldn't wait. I couldn't get enough. I needed him inside me. I needed his seed, regardless of whether it mattered at this point.

I pulled up my knees to either side of him. I reached between us and grabbed his already stiffening cock. I angled my hips and placed him at my opening before reaching both hands around and raking them across his scales.

He sucked in a gasp and then rammed forward, driving down to his base.

"I've never heard of a dragon losing a baby from sex," he said as he ground against me, moaning when I clenched my cunt around his hard cock. "But if you feel like I'm being too rough, tell me and I'll back off. I won't ever forget that you're carrying my child, but that doesn't mean I know what is best for your body. Do you understand me? You are in control here. Always."

"Yes," I breathed, jerking my hips to get a little friction. "Come inside me, Nyfain. I need you to come inside me."

He kissed me hard as he pulled his hips back. His tongue swiped through my mouth as he thrust back into me. Then he started a fast rhythm, perched on the edge of the bed, filling me up. I ran my fingers along his scales, back and forth, liking the feel of it. Wanting to get to our climax faster. Pleasure pulsed through me, through our bond, and then a rush of sweet oblivion hit me, pulling me under and setting off sparklers behind my eyelids. I cried out with the climax. He groaned my name and then shuddered over me a moment later, filling me up and running over.

The euphoria settled over me immediately, and this time I rode it, drifting within the bliss of it.

In a moment he pulled out and situated me so that I was in bed, snuggled and warm, the euphoria pulsing softly within me. He climbed in beside me, facing me with his head propped up on his elbow. We'd have a few minutes of bliss before the heat would start pounding again, requiring more servicing.

He traced his fingers along the edge of my bottom lip before running it over and along my chin. His eyes tracked the movement, sliding down my neck and lingering on his mark. Then lower, over my collarbone and down between my breasts. Only when he got to my stomach did his fingers slow and flatten until his palm was flush with my belly.

"Last time...when we thought you might be with child," he murmured, turning his palm so he cupped the base of my stomach as though holding what lay inside of it. "And you were late?"

"Yes," I whispered.

"I meant all the things I told you. It was incredibly dangerous for you to have my child at that time. I didn't have my full power. I didn't have my wings or my kingdom. I didn't have an army or my freedom."

"I know."

He slid down the bed until his face was even with my belly and hooked his hand around my hip, hugging me. "I would've forced you to get out somehow. To go find safety for yourself and the child. I needed you two, above all else, to *live.*"

I didn't respond this time. Leaving him for any reason didn't bear contemplation.

He kissed my navel softly, then a little more firmly, leaving his lips pressed to my skin. I felt the glow of his heart pumping through the bond. I felt the solid contentment of his dragon.

He moved up the bed, propping himself on his elbow and looking down at me. His eyes glowed softly, fire burning within them.

"Well, now I have my full power," he said, a growl riding his words. "I have my wings and my freedom, both thanks to you. Most importantly, I have an up-and-coming kingdom and a vicious army at my back. I misspoke earlier about being afraid that I wouldn't be able to protect you. That's bullshit. I'm not afraid. I'm fucking exhilarated. This is the role I was born for. This is what I was made for, as an alpha. As your mate. No one will ever hurt you. I will protect you until my last breath. Absolutely no one will get through me to get to you."

Everyone had always said, *Give a dragon a challenge and then stand back.* Given he was one of the most powerful alphas the kingdom had ever seen, I'd known fear wouldn't ride him for long.

He put his hand on my stomach again. "And this I promise you," he continued. "Our child will want for nothing. He or she will be cherished, and for the first time in generations, the royal heir will have parents who ardently love and respect each other. Don't bother reading fairytales to our child." He tucked a lock of hair behind my ear. "The love in those stories will pale in comparison to ours. The heroine will never compare to my warrior dragon queen. And only the villain could be as ruthless and vicious as I will be when faced with my enemies. We're going to write our own story, in blood if need be. No one who goes up against me will live. Dolion made a grave mistake the day he imprisoned my kingdom. It is that mistake that will cost him his whole world."

I sucked in a deep breath as my body sparked with adrenaline and desire. My dragon moved within me, incensed, ready to go to war.

"That's all well and good, but this warrior queen can't join in the fun."

Humor sparkled in his eyes. "Has my mother taught you nothing? You don't have to use your fists to fight, Finley. You can just as easily use your brain. You'll have entire courts to manipulate, and I'm sure before the end we'll find *someone* who needs poisoning."

I laughed delightedly. Yes, dragons were crazy. "Then there will be two villains in this story."

"You cannot appreciate the light if you don't spend any time in the darkness."

His humor died away.

"We won't rest all day tomorrow," he said. "We'll have our whole lives to rest. No, tomorrow I will finally hear everyone's stories of the dungeons. It is time I let my rage sharpen me into a knife. The moment we land, the games of living and dying will begin. Dolion will have spies. He might have his people working there in the shadows. We'd best get ready."

CHAPTER 34
HADRIEL

I'D NEVER BEEN so happy to see dry land in my life. Finley had promised to find a cure for my seasickness, but she couldn't very well do that on a boat.

I climbed from the rowboat and clutched Leala for a moment, steadying myself. The faerie ship gently swayed in the harbor behind us, the evening sun glinting off its surfaces. The anchor kept it in place, just in front of the other ships our people had sailed in.

"You good, little buddy?" Vemar asked, putting a heavy hand on my shoulder.

I shrugged him off. "Stop calling me that. It's insulting."

"Which part?"

I rolled my eyes as Leala grabbed my arm to steady me. "Why did you guys decide to wear the same clothes?" she asked, turning to look at the few rowboats coming in behind us. They carried Finley's trunks, containing clothes, plants, and a case full of quick cures in the event someone got poisoned. She might look really elegant with her fancy clothes and hair done just right, but she was always prepared for extreme violence.

Urien stepped out of the rowboat like he'd been holding court in it. Absolutely nothing ruffled that fucking guy. It was really annoying.

"I have no idea, Leala. Ask the fucking dragon," I said, holding my stomach.

"I thought we should present a united front." Vemar smoothed the lime-green blazer down his broad chest and dusted off his canary-yellow slacks, not displacing the water that had sprinkled them on the boat ride over. His pink shoes, matching the random pink lines threaded throughout the whole ensemble, were entirely overkill on him.

"You look ridiculous," I told him, waiting for Leala and Urien to give orders to the staff about what should go where and with whom.

"I look just as ridiculous as you do," he replied. "It's the same outfit."

"First, it is an *ensemble,* not an outfit. Second, I look eccentric. I act a certain way, I look a certain way, and I disarm people so that they are easier to manage—"

"Or get information from," Leala murmured, joining us again. "Remember, we have a job to do here. We are in charge of circulating among their staff. We'll need to get or spread gossip, depending on how things are going. It might not be so dire here, since Calia will hopefully pave the way toward an alliance, but kingdoms down the line might be dangerous. We'll need to practice networking."

"Yes, exactly," I said as we joined Urien and headed

to meet up with Finley and everyone else. They were assembling on the docks, Finley getting constant congratulations and the king staring straight ahead like he wanted to burn the world to the ground.

He'd spent all day hearing various people's accounts of the dungeons. When it was time for me to give mine, I realized I didn't feel so seasick when I was afraid for my life. And while I wasn't in danger from him directly, the vicious rage that radiated from him made my balls tighten up.

Finley had gone last. I wasn't sure whether she got to finish, because the next thing I knew the king ripped the door off its hinges, threw it, and made short work of getting into the sky. His dragon roared with such rage that my heart jiggled in my chest and the poor sod next to me, a faerie deck hand, pissed himself. The king painted the sky in fire and flew for a long time after that.

It did not seem to help.

That motherfucker was still fuming. He stood stoically, straight and tall and broad and fucking terrifying. Only Finley and Hannon would stand close to him. Not even Weston or Micah kept their usual proximity.

"I can pull off eccentric," Vemar said, tugging on his oversized lapels.

"You're too big and mean to pull off eccentric," I replied. "You're a dragon. When you fuckers try to be eccentric, it just comes off as dangerous. What do you even do anymore, anyway? The queen has her guard now. She doesn't need a bodyguard."

"I look after you so that you can look after her," he replied. "I'm the guardian of the asshole."

"Aw. That's sweet," Leala said, giving him a smile.

"What in the fuck?" I honestly couldn't tell if he was serious. Then I decided I didn't really care. He did actually keep people from picking on me. One look from him and people found somewhere else to be. "Well, just don't scare people who I need to get information from."

"Unless scaring them will help," Leala murmured as we drew closer.

"When would it help?" I whispered.

Vemar chuckled. "You have so much to learn, little buddy."

Once everyone was assembled and the trunks and supplies and goods were being unloaded from the various ships, Calia and Dessia met the royal couple on the docks. It was only then that I looked around, following the progression to the banks, where several large carriages drawn by four or six horses each had rolled to a stop.

"Is it just me," I murmured to Leala as Finley and the master stepped off the docks and onto a cobblestone lane, walking beside Calia and Dessia at a measured pace, "or are these docks incredibly clean and...I don't know, organized?"

Flowers bloomed all around us as we reached a small market, where vendors in stalls and booths were selling fish and other goods. They were all in orderly rows, each evenly spaced from the next, and separated by patches of grass. No one yelled out prices or called to their friends. Not one piece of garbage or stray fish part marred the ground. No whiffs of rot or unsavory smells mingled with the lovely floral bouquet passing my nose. It was like this place wasn't real. It was just too…nice.

"They must be hiding something." I narrowed my eyes at the stall owners, all impeccably dressed. Only one had a stain on his shiny blue shirt. "This loveliness probably covers up some sort of devious horror."

"Everyone says the faerie kingdom is lovely," Leala whispered as we entered a more densely populated area of the town. "They obviously go to great lengths to make sure it stays that way."

Finley and the king stopped with Calia near the biggest and grandest of the carriages. Six well-bred draft horses waited in front, one stamping its hoof impatiently. A golden insignia was etched into the body of the carriage, and the windows and door were outlined in gold to match.

All of the faeries in the area slowed, their eyes riveted to either Finley or the king. When the two were helped into the carriage, Dessia and Calia following, the crowd's attention swept over the rest of the gathered party. They gaped at Micah or Tamara as they stripped off their clothes and took to the sky. More dragons handed their clothes off to staff and followed. Weston did the same before shifting, organizing his wolves to lope around the procession of carriages as the dragons flew in perfect formation overhead. They were all making a statement. The king might still be pulling himself up by his bootstraps, but he had a well-organized and well-disciplined defense.

I didn't follow with the wolves. My place was in a carriage, monitoring Finley's plants and elixirs. It was essential that those weren't meddled with or lost. They might eventually be the difference between someone living and dying.

Arleth and Delaney had the same idea. They watched the most important of the trunks get loaded before gracefully slipping into an open carriage at the back, able to see who was coming or going. They clearly had very little trust in this kingdom. That would probably serve us well.

NYFAIN

I HELD FINLEY'S hand as the carriage took us along a familiar lane to the large castle sitting on a rolling green hill. Flowers bloomed along the road, magically altered to be there all year long. Perfect bushes dotted the countryside, and not one speck of grime marred the perfection that was the royal grounds.

"Do you recognize any of this from the last time you were here?" Calia asked with an excited smile.

My mate tensed beside me, and unease rolled through the bond.

I pulled my focus from the beautiful scenery gliding by the window and pushed away the burning, throbbing rage that had been pressing down on me ever since I heard the first account of the demon dungeon.

"There is only you," I reminded Finley, meeting her eyes. I ran my thumb across hers. "There was no before you, and there is no after. Just you."

Her smile was sweet and grateful, but her dragon

thrashed at the thought of my ex-fiancée. She was an alpha female—she wouldn't like another female having any sort of claim to me, even if it was nothing but history. Hopefully Hadriel and my mother could run interference between Finley and Eris. While I would never disrespect my mate and keep her from protecting her territory—me—there was a lot at stake. We needed everything in this kingdom to go perfectly. Our future depended on it.

"I know," she whispered.

To Calia, I said, "I do, yes. It's exactly the same."

She looked between Finley and me uncertainly for a moment before smiling joyfully and looking out the window. She had pride in her kingdom, and well she should. They treated their people well and gave them many opportunities for success. They looked after the aging and sick and didn't ask for more than was fair in taxes. Their kingdom, at least when I left, had been happy and healthy and, because of that, strong.

I didn't mention that the faeries' focus on beauty was a little overkill. In my opinion, using magic to keep flowers in eternal bloom took away the natural beauty of the seasons. The fresh growth and bloom of spring after a chilly and barren winter had always moved me. If nothing ever died, there could be no rebirth. Perfection got old.

I kept my expression free of emotion, but Dessia was watching me in a way that suggested she knew my thoughts.

"I'll want to move Govam and his demons into the castle as soon as possible," I reminded Calia, something we'd discussed after she gave me her account of the dungeons. I didn't want her to slip into her life here and forget her promises. "Someone will need to keep a close eye on them to make sure they mind their manners."

"Yes, of course," Calia said. "I just have to clear it with the king and queen, and then we can establish which rooms they're given. With a guard, of course."

"Of course. I'll have one of my people watching them at all times, but I'm sure the king will also want someone of his choosing to do the same."

"Yes. You obviously remember his paranoia."

"Thoroughness," I corrected her. "He's kept this kingdom safe for a long time."

"Wow," Finley breathed as we neared the castle.

The castle sprawled across the gentle hills covered in green grass and fragrant flowers. Shimmering blue spires topped gray-white stone towers decorated with arched windows and a multitude of flower boxes. Again, the whole place was impeccable, not one visible blemish upon it. The faeries spent an obscene amount of time, money, and magic on keeping up appearances. It was another thing I'd never been that into, though I could certainly see the appeal for visitors. The look of wonder on my mate's face was enough to make me rethink my entire plan for our castle.

"I knew you'd like it." Calia beamed. "Wait until you see the gardens. I'll take you to meet the healers tomorrow."

Dessia continued to study me. She never said much, preferring to use her sister as a shield and watch from the shadows, but I got the feeling she wasn't as shy and

timid as she acted. I had nothing on which to base that
suspicion other than that she clearly had layers, ones that
went deeper than if she were simply a faerie whose magic
had not manifested but, even still, could somehow boost
her sister's magic. Beneath those layers, I sensed a
curling darkness within her, kept hidden. She hadn't
been as rattled by the demon dungeons as the others. She
hadn't been as scarred. I got the feeling that her scars had
already been present; I just didn't know how or why.
Something neither of them had offered up.

"Ready?" Finley asked me as the carriage stopped in
front of the castle.

"Always."

"I will be monitoring your environment closely,"
Calia said, and Dessia nodded.

"Our environment?" Finley shook her head a little.

"Who comes and goes around you," Calia replied.
"The mood of those around you, their motives for being
in your company. You are our guests, and I will ensure
you have a pleasant stay. You are in no danger here, I
will make sure of it."

"Thank you for that," I told her, pleased that she
should take such an interest. Still, it wasn't an offer she
could make. She had the king's ear and a decent amount
of power in the court, but she didn't have the authority
to organize the king's guard or give them commands.
Only the king could do that. If any servants or guards
were compromised, we'd be in plenty of danger.

I had every suspicion servants *and* guards had been
compromised by Dolion. The attack on the water had
made it clear he knew exactly where we were headed.

"Shall we?" Calia smiled and climbed from the carriage.

Dessia stalled for a moment, her gaze shifting back and forth between Finley and me. She studied me for another moment before climbing out of the carriage.

"Here we go," Finley said softly.

She moved to get up, but I held her back so that I could climb from the carriage first and help her down. The evening sun glinted off my livery collar, and I assumed my crown. My black suit was cut through with a golden sheen, shining in the failing light. I had dressed the part even though I'd felt a lot more like putting on battle gear and going off to find Dolion right now.

Servants lined the walkway into the castle, all dressed exactly the same in their white jackets over dark waistcoats with gold buttons on either side. Their tight white pants ended in stockings the same dark blue as the waistcoats and loafers with golden buttons. It was something Hadriel might have worn, a thought that nearly cracked my stoic and self-important facade.

Finley took my hand, her other hand touching her belly, where our child was safe and snug.

And just like that, my heart surged and I couldn't breathe. I pulled her to me, lifting her out of the carriage and then holding her tightly.

We all had certain parts to play on this visit, and mine was the role of the ruthless, scarred dragon king. I needed to play up the typical dragon stereotype. I needed to cultivate a stoic and aloof image.

I couldn't help it, though. I had to touch her. I had to hold her and put my hand on her belly, so fucking honored that she was going to be the mother of my child. So fucking excited that I would get the chance to be a dad—a *good* dad.

"I love you," I murmured, kissing her.

Her lips curved upward under mine, and she looped her arms around my neck. "Aren't you supposed to be the grumpy one who hates everyone?" She sucked in a gasp as I ran my fingers down the scales on her back, displayed by her slinky dress.

"I'm still the grumpy one. They'll just think I hate everyone but you. It'll be fine."

She laughed and went to pull away a little, but then surprised me by tightening her grip on me, her cheek against my chest.

"Are you okay?" I asked.

"Yes. Probably. I don't know. I've had these incredible urges since that battle. At the moment I'm desperate for closeness, and it's a little tricky to ignore. It feels like my heart is trying to rip out of my chest and burrow into you."

She peeled herself away from me, tears in her eyes.

"Yeah," she said. "I'm fucking crying. Why am I fucking crying? I have no idea. I think I've gone insane. Is that part of a dragon being pregnant? It should be much too early for crazy hormones."

Without thinking, I scooped her up into my arms and walked toward a patiently waiting Calia.

"No, no." Finley patted me even as she clung to my shoulders. "This isn't what our plan was. This isn't a proper image of royalty. Put me down. I can get my emotions sorted."

Take care of your mate, my dragon said. *That's more important than a cultivated first impression. Your plan was stupid, anyway.*

He could always be counted on to choose our mate over literally anything else. He wasn't exactly the brains of this outfit. Still, I couldn't help myself. The knowledge of her pregnancy had changed things for both of us. We'd need to work that into the plans, somehow. Hopefully my mother would have some ideas.

Ahead of us, Calia and Dessia entered the great arched doors of the castle. Finley gasped as we crossed the threshold after them. Crystal lights and chandeliers caught the light from the windows and splashed it around. Plush furniture kept in immaculate condition spotted the floor, and oil paintings done by masters throughout the years hung on the walls.

Nothing had changed from when I was here last. Not that I could tell, anyway. Even the scent seemed the same, pleasant and eternal. Too nice. The whole place was too nice, in my opinion, like you didn't want to sit down for fear of messing up the carefully arranged pillows.

Had I thought that when I was here last? Or had sixteen years of ruin left a larger mark than I'd realized?

The throne room was huge and extravagant, done in the same style as everything else. A kaleidoscope of color speckled the walls, and the large windows showed the sunset blazing across the sky. Attendants working in perfect synchronicity closed the doors behind us. Various members from their court sat on tasseled stools along the red carpet leading to the royal dais. There the king and queen sat in their golden thrones, older than I remembered them. Wrinkles pulled at their expressions and clustered around their eyes. Their hands were a bit more gnarled and their postures not quite as straight. Time hadn't stopped for them. They wouldn't have much longer on the throne before it was time to pass it along.

Many of the court showed expressions of delight and joy upon seeing Calia and Dessia, lighting up as though the sun had made an appearance after a long, hard winter. Very few were able to smooth their expressions into a polite welcome. A great many saw me and startled, looking at my scarred face and hands. Men noticed Finley, and their eyes sparked with pleasure or lust, churning my guts. Some looked at us in confusion, probably wondering why I was carrying my mate.

And then I saw her.

Eris. My ex-fiancée.

CHAPTER 35
NYFAIN

S HE SAT IN the second row, indicating she still had
mid-tier status in their court. If she'd mated me—
married, in their culture—she would've upped her status.
She would've brought in the bloodline of a powerful
dragon and a Syflora, a connection to a throne. In return,
I would've gotten out of my duty to Wyvern and, in so
doing, reduced my status. In my desperation to be away
from the king, I'd never realized how stacked in her
favor the mating would've been.

She was older now, of course, time not having
stopped for her. She had deep lines near her eyes and on
her forehead. Her oval face and soft brown eyes still
looked kind, though her skin had lost some of its flawless
radiance. She wore a vibrant blue and yellow dress with
frills and dizzying lines, a style she'd adopted in her
youth to hide what she thought was a plain appearance.

I'd never been in love with her, and I was almost
positive she hadn't been in love with me. She'd been my
ticket out. Marrying her would have allowed me to keep

the luxurious life to which I was accustomed without having to face the mad king's rage, since I would have had protection from the powerful faerie king. It would've been a marriage of convenience, and at the time, I was fine with that. I hadn't wanted anything more. I'd thought our affection for each other and a decent enough time in the bedroom would be plenty fulfilling.

How incredibly wrong I'd been. I now thanked the goddess every day for how my life had turned out. If I hadn't been forced onto the path I now walked, one day I would've woken up and looked around and wondered how I'd ended up in such a miserable existence.

Or maybe I just felt that way now because I'd realized how amazing life could really be. How transformative love could be.

Eris's eyes widened when she saw me. Her gaze roamed my face and disgust crossed her countenance. She was none too thrilled with how my appearance had turned out.

I nearly laughed.

Her gaze then found Finley. Her eyes widened for the second time, but this time it wasn't because of disgust. Red bloomed in her cheeks, and her face closed down in what I could only imagine was jealousy. She looked over Finley's body, her dress, but always she went back to her face. Taking in every inch, every line. It was almost like she was mesmerized by Finley's beauty. Beauty that Finley herself couldn't give a shit about.

I kissed Finley on her temple and wiped my memory clean of the past. I hadn't lied to Finley—there was nothing of substance before her. There would be nothing after. There was just her. If I'd needed any proof, I'd just gotten it.

"Your highness." Calia dropped into a perfect and deep curtsy in front of the faerie king.

Dessia mumbled the same thing, her curtsy not nearly as deep.

King Starvos looked down at the pair with a stoic expression not unlike the one I'd meant to affect.

"Calia, Dessia, good to have you home," he said as though intensely bored. "We've missed you these many long months. If not for your correspondence, we would've worried you'd been caught again."

"Now, now," Queen Ayre said, patting the arm of her throne. "You know that Calia never stays caught for long. She is in and out—no one can keep her." She laughed.

Finley tensed, confusion and unease coming through the bond, and the faerie sisters also seemed discomfited.

Years ago, there had been rumors about the queen's memory starting to slip. No one had been allowed to talk about it. I wondered if that had progressed.

The king's brow furrowed. He glanced at the queen in annoyance but didn't comment.

"I've organized a dinner on your behalf, of course," the king went on, looking at Calia. "We'll have all your favorites." His smile just barely reached his eyes. Although the man kept a beautiful kingdom, he had a ruthless streak. All good kings did. He wasn't in the habit of gaily carrying on like much of his kingdom, even though he clearly had a soft spot for Calia.

His steely blue gaze came to me. If he noticed the

difference in me, he gave no sign.

"Prince Nyfain—excuse me. *King* Nyfain now, I hear." He paused for a beat, and I waited for him to continue. "You have had your coronation after a little hiccup. Is that all settled now?"

So Calia had passed on the information that my father wasn't the mad king. I should've guessed as much. And now the king was using it to hammer home his royal dominance between the two of us. He had the prestige, the larger and richer kingdom, and an ancestral right granted him by a bloodline that went back centuries. He hadn't needed to fight for anything.

I barely stopped myself from grinning.

Before I could answer, verbally waving the slight away, a surge of anger rocked through the bond. Finley pulled her arms from around me, and a slap of will had me letting her go.

When she got to her feet, her body was a little in front of mine. Protecting me, I realized. Ready to go to war if he should further demoralize her mate.

My dragon surged up, fire and power swirling around us, liking when our mate showed her grit.

"It is settled, yes," I answered, bending an arm around her and hooking it on her hip. Unable to help myself, I curled my other arm around her, resting my touch on her stomach. "I will be presenting in front of the council when it is next in session. Along with my queen. May I introduce Queen Finley of Wyvern. She is my true mate and was instrumental in breaking the curse the demons had on my kingdom. I'm sure you've heard of it by now."

He was already looking at her, his face blank, his eyes calculating.

"Finley is the one I told you about, your majesty," Calia said. "She is the reason we were able to make it out of the dungeons." She smiled back at us. "She just recently found out she's expecting."

"Oh my goodness!" Queen Ayre clapped, her eyes lighting up. "Oh, congratulations, my dear. That is wonderful! No wonder the big, brooding dragon was carrying you—"

"My dear," the king said between his teeth, clearly trying to subdue her.

"They are so protective, are they not?" she said. "I've always heard they were. And look, he stands with his hand on your belly. Yes, so protective! So romantic, isn't it, Starvos? Remember when we first heard—"

"Ayre, my dear," the king barked, and magic curled into the air, stinging. "This isn't the time."

Ayre jolted, gripping against the arms of the throne. Her jaw tightened and her eyebrows dipped. He was magically silencing her. He was calling his queen to heel. If Finley had had any doubt about the power structure in this kingdom, it had just been settled.

"I have heard a lot about you, Queen Finley." Starvos bent his head. "Calia is taken with you. You rendered this kingdom an incredible service in those dungeons. It's something I would like to speak to you more about."

"Of course, sire. I'm at your disposal," Finley said, and then bent down into a flawless curtsy. "Thank you for hosting us. What I've seen of your kingdom so far is absolutely stunning."

He studied her for another moment. "I must say, my dear, King Nyfain has found himself a queen just as splendid."

"Please, call me Finley," she interrupted delicately, inclining her head. "And I thank you."

"Finley, then."

I could just see her serene, demure smile.

Starvos's eyes fluttered just a little. He was clearly taken in. Entranced by her display of that natural beauty he clearly coveted. She was essentially a human equivalent of his grounds, always in bloom. Always pleasing to look at.

Goddess help me, the woman could be taught. She was executing my mother's teachings beautifully. Wild but well mannered. Protective, territorial, but domesticated. She was perfection.

Pride warred with the overwhelming urge to swoop her up into my arms again. I refrained, just barely.

"Yes, well," Starvos said, studying her a little longer, a slight wrinkle in his brow. He'd probably heard she'd been brought up common and couldn't quite believe it.

"She is also a great healer, highness," Calia said. "She has a natural gift. I believe she has a touch of the goddess about her."

"Yes, you mentioned as much in your letters." He rested his elbow on the arm of the chair and touched his finger to his lips in thought. "You should introduce her to the royal healers. Show her some of our plants. She might be surprised to discover we kept some everlass alive from when Nyfain was here last. I'm sure they'd like a tutorial from a master worker."

Calia's eyes widened a little and her smile stretched. "I will, highness. I'm sure they would have a lot to talk about."

"Yes, well," he said again, a phrase I remembered him using often when I was here. "Hmm," he said, his gaze lingering on Finley again.

Annoyance rolled through the bond, but it did not show on her face or in her bearing.

"I'm sure you are tired," he said to me, finally prying his gaze from my mate. "There are rooms prepared, of course. I'm sure your people are settling you in as we speak. Don't hesitate to let someone know should you need anything. Not much has changed since you were here last. Other than your appearance, of course. I'd like to hear more about that, too. There is a very dark underbelly in a kingdom we both know. I will need more information so that I don't fall into its snare."

"I know far more about that kingdom than anyone else," I replied. "Even its allies. I'll tell you more when we have some privacy."

"Of course. While Finley visits the healers, you should come for a boat ride with me. We have revamped the lakes. I remember those were always a favorite of yours."

They weren't, but I nodded anyway. "Fantastic. I look forward to it."

His gaze flicked to Finley, to my hand resting on her stomach, before he met my eyes again.

"I know something of dragons, so with respect to your mate, I will be vague," he said. "I am sad that your journey took you away from here. Selfishly, I had hoped you would stay."

Finley bristled, and her power ballooned. She kept herself in check, though.

"Still, I think it was for the best," he continued. "Despite what I have lost, I am now hopeful for what I might gain. Calia is impressed with your operations. With the speed at which you are building your kingdom. She has been all over the world, I'm sure you've heard. Learning things, occasionally getting caught and needing to escape."

Spying was what he was really saying. "I'm sure you've heard" actually meant "you've surely figured out."

I hadn't known Calia when I was here, but I wasn't green like Finley was. It hadn't taken me long to figure out her situation. She was a little too diligent in her offers to help. A little too smooth in her questions. A little too analytical. I wasn't quite sure how her sister fit in, but it hadn't taken me long to figure out why they were hanging around. Given everything was going well and I could sense her growing regard for us, her task actually helped my kingdom. It was why I'd let it continue, something I was sure she knew.

Emotions swirled through the bond. Confusion and then hurt and then anger. Finley had probably thought Calia was staying out of the goodness of her heart. And while she probably wasn't far off—Calia could've left before we did—it would likely tarnish her feelings toward the other woman. It would weaken any budding friendship.

This was exactly why I hadn't told her. Why my mother hadn't. She needed this lesson. She needed to realize that we all had a duty, and those who played with crowns dealt in secrets and half-smiles. We could have friends, but we always had to be conscious of our duty. Finley was a queen now, and our world was never black and white. It was never as glamorous as this kingdom looked.

"She is an excellent judge of a kingdom's value," Starvos said. "I expect great things."

"Thank you, that means a lot," I replied, moving my hand from Finley's stomach down her arm until I found her hand and entwined our fingers. "I'd be lying if I said I wasn't making some decisions with the memory of this kingdom in mind."

Now his smile did reach his eyes. He breathed in a little, his chest rising.

"I wondered, based on some of the things I'd heard. It's good to know we have the esteem of the golden dragon king." He chuckled. "Yes, well. You must be tired. I'll have my people show you to your rooms. Hopefully I'll see you and your beautiful queen at dinner tomorrow. And a…" He put up his finger, searching his memory for something. "And um…Haddle, isn't it?"

"Hadriel, sire," Calia helped. "Hadriel the butler."

"He's the advisor now," Dessia said softly.

"Oh yes, that's right." Calia laughed. "He's the queen's advisor now. In addition to the former queen, of course."

Starvos's eyes sparkled. "Former Queen Arleth, yes. Yes, I remember her. Lovely woman. I always had a great time chatting with her. Anyway, Had…"

"Hadriel and Leala, the lady's maid," Calia supplied

patiently. "They were both key players in getting us all communicating so Finley could get us out of the dungeon."

The king waved it all away. "Yes, yes. Fine. Nyfain, I hope you don't mind, but we'd like to extend the invitation to the servants Calia mentioned. The ones who were integral to her escape. Then there are the other prisoners from the dungeons..." He let his sentence linger.

"I'll make sure one and all are at your disposal," I replied, stepping around Finley so that I could bow. "I waited until recently to hear all of their stories. I wanted to have the information fresh in my mind. It is not easy to hear. Not even for a man who was trapped in hell for sixteen years while his kingdom died around him. You might want to take it in doses. And you'll want to do it in privacy."

His eyes were clear as they took my measure. He'd know what I meant. If he planned to do anything with the information, he'd want to guard it. Every court as old as his had leaks. When one was found and plugged, another invariably popped open. If he planned to take on the demons, he'd want to safeguard every scrap of information.

He stood, and after a moment, so did the queen. She followed him off the dais with a stiff back and jaw, her eyes tight. Calia turned back to us with a smile.

"I'll take you to your rooms."

Finley was quiet as we walked, taking in the various paintings and décor, her hand held tightly in mine. Once in our room, we found Leala and Urien putting away our things and Hadriel yelling into the room from the balcony. After Calia said her goodbyes and promised she'd see us tomorrow, she closed the door behind us.

"You okay?" I asked Finley, running my fingertips down the middle of her back, grazing her warm skin.

She stared off at nothing for a moment, drawing Leala's attention. "You knew," she said, leaning against me.

"About Calia?"

She nodded.

"Yes. I had a feeling she was intentionally being obvious about her position to tip us off."

"Obvious to whom?" Finley shot me a scowl. "I had no idea." She braced her hands on her hips and turned to Leala. "Did you know Calia was a spy?"

Leala's expression was guarded. "I heard a rumor, but I didn't realize you were in the dark."

"What—Oh, Finley, you're back." Hadriel's eyes narrowed. "Uh-oh, what did I miss? What happened?"

"Finley just learned that Calia is a spy," Leala murmured.

"Did everyone know?" Finley asked in a surge of anger. "Was I the only idiot?"

"Goddess goose me, no." Hadriel put up his hands and walked forward before giving me a wary look and halting.

I took that as my cue to cross the room and check out the various amenities. This kingdom had always loved their luxuries, and after going so long without such small comforts, I could do with all they had to offer.

"The staff had no idea, trust me." He patted her

shoulder and then led her to the dressing table, where Leala stepped in behind her and started undoing her hair. "They should've known, too, because they've been in other courts before. They're clearly rusty. She visited Cecil and learned a great deal, mostly about stuff that probably made her blush, but didn't give him much in return. That's a real tip-off. Cecil is a master at knifing information out of people. He says these absurd things with only a *kernel* of truth in them just to get a rise out of you. He likes to tell all sorts of stories about me in particular, and I swear—"

"Get to the point, Hadriel," Leala admonished.

"Right, right. Yes, sorry. Anyway, I clued in and told Leala, and *she* clued in, but not many other people knew."

"Then why didn't you tell me?" Finley asked.

"Because of me," I said. "You needed to learn this lesson, sweetheart. As we continue to socialize with other courts, you're going to meet people you like and want to be friends with. You need to remember, though, that you have a duty and, more importantly, *they* have a duty. You can be friends with Calia, but if you do, you'll need to remember that anything you say will work its way back to this kingdom. There are no secrets between you two. None. Not unless you hold one of her secrets to assure her silence. Royalty deals in secrets and lies, always. You need to be very slow to trust, and even then, always keep your eyes open."

Finley blew out a breath and shook her head. "I had no idea what I was getting into. Being queen is nothing like I thought it would be, and I've barely begun."

I crossed to her again, unconsciously shooing Hadriel and Leala away with my proximity. I massaged her shoulders.

"It'll get easier, I promise. Eventually this will be second nature. You won't even notice it. Friendships will be easier to cultivate."

She leaned back into me. "I'm mad at you."

I laughed. "You certainly seem like it."

"These fucking emotions that make me crave your touch won't let me be as mad as I want to be. I might have to start resisting. It's getting ridiculous."

"I know. I haven't heard of emotions like this, but it's bound to end soon. Maybe when the last of the heat ends? It should be any day. It's usually a week after the start of the euphoria stage."

"It must've looked absolutely ridiculous when you *carried* me into the throne room. Like...what were we thinking? How embarrassing! But it felt perfect at the time. And now, when I'm trying to be mad, or thinking I want my much smaller emotional range back, I recoil from the idea. Part of me likes going crazy for you. It's really fucking annoying. I logically can't stand that I'm being this dependent and sappy, but then, I love being this dependent and sappy and *needy*. Goddess help me, I am so incredibly needy. Hadriel, aren't I needy?"

"Will you cry if I answer that?" he asked.

"Yeah, probably. Fuck, I don't know. I need to look all this up. This has to be in a book somewhere."

"You know what?" I leaned over and gave her a sneaky smile in the mirror. "They just so happen to have an incredible library here."

Her eyes lit up, as I'd known they would.

I worked her shoulders for a moment longer before getting out of the way so Leala could tend to her. "Get yourself dressed down, and then we'll go for a fly," I told her. "We'll come back, have some dinner in and a good night's rest, and then tomorrow we'll see *all the things*, okay? I know my way around. They won't begrudge me showing you. They delight in people enjoying their kingdom. The parts they spend so much effort to keep up, at any rate."

"You saw her, didn't you?" she asked in a low voice. "She was the one in the dizzy dress."

Cold dripped down my back. I knew she was talking about Eris.

"Yes," I replied.

She didn't speak for a moment. Very little emotion came through the bond.

"You never would've been happy with her," she finally said. "And she wouldn't have been happy with you. The first time you thoroughly lost your temper, you would've scared the pee out of her. Holding back is no way to go through life."

I'd assumed she hadn't noticed my glance at Eris, since I hadn't felt any rage. Instead, she'd clearly waved the thought away because she felt how wrong the match was. How incompatible. There was no danger to her claim on me, and so she'd ignored it.

"I love you," I told her, laughing.

"Well, with choices like that, no wonder."

I just hoped Eris felt the same as Finley and I did. She'd been seated in between couples, indicating she was still single. I hoped her obvious disgust for my appearance would help her forget any attachment she might've had. I hoped it would deter her from taking out her jealousy on Finley.

CHAPTER 36
FINLEY

"**F**INLEY!" CALIA BEAMED from the doorway to our rooms the next morning. "How did you sleep?"

She'd be taking me and my entourage to the healing tents while Nyfain met with the king.

I kept my face neutral. It still stung that she'd spent months in our kingdom doing her job—a.k.a. spying on us—and not because she believed in us. I knew it had worked to our benefit, but still...I was annoyed, to put it lightly. I felt a little betrayed even though she'd probably thought I knew the score. All the other intelligent people seemed to have figured it out.

"Great, thank you."

I turned as Nyfain approached me. He wrapped his arm around my waist before kissing my temple, then my lips, then bending to kiss my stomach.

"Be good," he told me as he straightened. "Keep our baby safe. I love you both."

I smiled because I couldn't help it, then melted against him because he was irresistible.

476

"*You* be good," I replied, wrapping my arms around his middle. "*You* be safe. Don't take any chances or get in a fight, because if you do, I'm going to have to pull hero. Some things can't be helped. I love you both."

He pulled back, his brow furrowing.

I laughed and pointed at his chest...and then moved my finger down to indicate his cock.

His lips stretched into one of his irresistible smiles, softening his features, and he shook his head as he pulled away from me.

"I'll make you love both of us even more later tonight, don't worry."

He fitted a small knife into a holster at his ankle, covered by his tailored slacks. His black shoes had been polished to a mirror shine, and a ribbed dress shirt hugged his fantastic torso. The sleeves were rolled up to expose his scarred and inked forearms, and the top two buttons had been undone, showing a few scars along the side of his neck, disappearing below the fabric. He was putting his suffering on display, and given his infallible confidence, the effect was like a steel mace to the face. Holy fuck, I was suddenly sopping wet between my thighs.

He tensed, probably feeling my rush of desire through the bond, before shaking his head again. "Maybe this afternoon."

I grinned wickedly as he slipped by Calia, nodding in response to her greeting.

When she looked at me again, her face was flushed.

"You must be used to sexual innuendo at this point, having survived the demons' castle." I grabbed a wrap in

case it got cold and fitted my dagger into the sheath at
my hip. While I now knew how to use a sword, I was still
much better with a dagger. It was more comfortable and
worked much better as a surprise howdy-do.

"I am, but you guys are…different."

She pushed to the side of the hall so that I could
leave the room. Weston and a few of his wolves waited
on one side with Arleth and Delaney, and Tamara and a
few of her guard waited on the other. Nyfain would get
Micah and some of his dragons, plus a few of the lesser-
powered wolves. There wasn't much trust regarding our
safety at present.

"Leala, you coming?" I called behind me.

"Yes, milady. Just finishing up. I'll meet you there."

I frowned back at her. "Do you know the way?"

"A servant will show me, milady. I'll find it."

Ah. She wanted an excuse to network. Hadriel had
had the same idea. He was downstairs somewhere,
waiting for me.

Calia fell in step with me as I walked down the hall.
Dessia wasn't with her this time. Arleth and Delaney fell
in behind us, my overly large collection of guards
organizing themselves after that, no one jostling, no one
needing to utter a word. This crew showed very well.
Nyfain had been smart to choose them for this journey.

"You guys are just…a lot more intimate," Calia said
as we reached another hallway and she pointed right.
"You're a lot more beautiful in your feelings for each
other. I've never really cared about marriage and
children, but after seeing you two together…it might be
nice. If I had someone like him—" She swung her hand

to brace against my arm. "Someone *like* him. Not him. I'm not encroaching on your territory."

I laughed. "I knew that."

"You see? I've learned something about dragons. Which leads me to an uncomfortable topic." She cleared her throat, pointing right again at the next hallway. She was taking me out a different way than we'd come in. "I saw you notice Nyfain noticing Eris."

"His ex." Swirls of anger filtered through me, but only because of the past claim she'd had. I felt zero jealousy toward her. She and Nyfain would have been a true mismatch. Fate had done that woman a favor. I was actually surprised he'd kept his temper long enough to secure a promise.

"Yes. She'll be there today. She works the gardens for the healers."

"That's fine. If she doesn't bother me, I won't bother her."

"Yes, well, that's just it." Calia grimaced as we took a wide stairwell. Crystal chandeliers draped from the ceilings above us. "She had a few things to say about you yesterday and last night. My reports said they were not kind."

"Your reports?"

"Yes. I told you I'd be monitoring the environment around you."

"You spy even in your own kingdom?" I asked quiet-ly.

I felt Arleth's hand on my shoulder. That had been too blunt.

Calia smiled at me appreciatively, her eyes flicking

back to Arleth trying to rein me in.

"I enjoy you for being so forthcoming, Finley," she said. "It's refreshing. And rare. Please don't subdue that around me—"

"When you are with your own people or in a mostly private setting," Arleth added.

Calia's cheeks turned red. "Yes, sorry. I forget that you are still learning everything, Finley. And…"

She looked away as we finally neared a set of wide double doors leading to a large patio surrounded by lush green plants. All manner of flowers dotted the bushes and grew along the ground, spreading their fragrance within the warm sunshine. Staff in the same uniforms as yesterday, with their white gloves and long, flowing hair, held the doors for us as we passed.

"Yes," she murmured, now looking straight ahead to a cultivated path through a large expanse of gardens. "I do. The king likes to know what is going on, both abroad and in his backyard."

"So everything you tell me, you'll be telling him?"

Arleth cleared her throat. I was not behaving in line with her strictures. But dammit, I wanted to know. I liked Calia. I needed to understand how all this worked. I needed to know if we could ever be friends. How I could ever trust her if we were.

Calia studied me for a moment as we walked. Her gaze flicked to Arleth behind us and then back, turning intense. She didn't want to answer with an audience.

"He's a busy man," Arleth said, sounding bored and relaxed at the same time. "All royals are. They need only the pertinent information with which to do their jobs."

"Very true, Arleth," Calia said, clasping her hands behind her back.

"Has Eris been warned that she is not dealing with a faerie?" Arleth asked. "Has anyone mentioned that alpha dragons, even the females, do not shy away from unpleasantness? I understand that my son was on his best behavior when he was here. As Finley will be, of course, but I worry Eris thinks she knows more about dragons than she really does."

That was the most gracious, seemingly innocuous threat I'd ever heard. And it was akin to giving me the go-ahead to handle Eris however I saw fit. Hopefully I wouldn't need to bother. After seeing Nyfain again, all scarred up and proud of it, the woman must know that he would be way more than she could ever handle, comfortably or otherwise. I bet they hadn't rage-fucked once. How boring.

"She has not been warned, no." Calia squinted a little. "I thought I might broach the subject with Finley first to gauge her reaction. I can certainly pass that on."

"I don't think there is a need, do you, Finley?" Arleth said. "I'm sure it was a shock to see a past acquaintance again, especially since he has moved on. She may lament her misfortune at losing the status he might've brought, and rage at another woman for gaining it. But soon enough she will realize that a dragon was never a good mate for her, and she will remember her place. Don't you think?"

"Yes, of course," Calia said. "I don't doubt it."

In other words: *Don't interfere. Let Finley handle it.* Except I was crazy and violent and tended to make a scene. That wasn't how things were supposed to go in courts, Arleth had been very clear on that when she was training me.

I turned to look back at her, an obvious question in my eyes.

"Oh, Finley, look at this." Arleth grabbed my arm and moved me to the side, pointing at nothing.

Calia continued walking for a spell before slowing, waiting patiently for us. She didn't ask what Arleth had seen. She was clearly giving my mate's mother a chance to coach me.

"The way you taught me to handle jealous squabbles in court doesn't seem to apply here," I whispered as Arleth pointed at something else.

Delaney pushed in close, pretending to look too.

"It's a risk, letting Finley handle this her way," Delaney murmured. "Not just because of how taken aback everyone will probably be, but because of the baby."

"The baby is not a concern in this situation," Arleth replied. "Eris is…a gardener."

"*I'm* a gardener," I said.

Delaney scoffed. "You're good at gardening; you're not a gardener. You're an alpha dragon."

"Yes, exactly," Arleth said. "Finley, this is not like handling someone from our court. Most of the faeries, unless specifically trained to be fierce, are a softer sort of people. This isn't a regular court issue, either. This woman didn't have a dowry when Nyfain knew her. She obviously still doesn't, which is why she is unmarried and will never rise in the ranks. She has a legacy of status from her father, and that is all. It will die with her. It was a terrible match for him, way below his level, but he was desperate. She took advantage of that."

I nodded because I remembered Arleth teaching me that unmarried people were looked upon unfavorably in this court. It meant they would either have children out of wedlock, something their society frowned upon, or they would never have children at all, which was not good for the court. A good bloodline was expected to be continued.

Eris had to be bumping up against the end of her childbearing years at this point. She wouldn't be kicked out of the court for not producing, but her position might be encroached upon by someone more powerful rising in the ranks.

"I mean...did anyone mention to her that dragons have a hard time impregnating?" I asked. "Or is it easier with—"

I gritted my teeth, not able to finish that thought.

"I doubt he did," Arleth said. "He was desperate, as I said. I was pushing him to get out, and not a lot of people would be willing to take on a refugee dragon prince of a mad king. He had the Syflora magic, though, and they wanted that bloodline."

Delaney clucked her tongue and shook her head. "He would've been continually pressured to reproduce, but without a heat or even love, it would've been for naught. He would've been miserable."

"Less miserable than with the king," Arleth said softly.

"Can we please talk about something else?" I said as

my rage throbbed in my temple. I felt my dragon trying to appease Nyfain's dragon, who was getting worried something was happening to us.

"Sorry," Arleth said. "Anyway, this is a squabble about a man. If Eris acts out, it will be irrational—"

"In regards to court politics," Delaney told me.

"Right, yes." Arleth nodded. "Additionally, she has middling status, and your status is equal to that of a king. No woman in this kingdom is so powerful. They probably doubt your position. At this point in time, at any rate. So you must make an example of Eris. She should not speak out of turn to a queen, number one, and if she speaks out of turn to *you*, then you must handle it…however you do."

"Colorfully," Delaney said.

"When someone disrespects the king or his title," Arleth said, "he reacts brutally. Harshly. Traditionally, his queen would not. She'd have the offender punished much more subtly. You're like a king, though, remember? You need to act the part. Get the message across."

"Okay…" I tilted my head, staring at a waxy green leaf on the bush. "I'm hearing two different things, here. You're telling me to deal with it how I normally might…and also telling me to handle it brutally, like a king would."

Delaney and Arleth shared a look, smiles pulling at their lips.

"Is there a joke I am missing?" I asked.

"Yes. You," Delaney said.

I scrunched up my brow.

"Handle it like you normally would, Finley," Arleth

said. "Whatever happens, just handle it. What we're saying is that you shouldn't try to be someone you're not in the healing tents or in the gardens. Be you."

I took a deep breath and let it out slowly. "Well, that's awesome. That's a little treat I wasn't expecting. Not that it'll really matter. The idea of Eris triggers me more than the actual person. I doubt anything will come of her disgruntlement."

We returned to Calia, and I apologized for the delay.

"Very interesting bush just there," I told her. "We naturally had to examine it from every angle."

"Yes," she said. "Here we go."

She took a right at the fork in the lane, turning onto another beautifully cultivated path wide enough for two. As we continued walking, the tall bushes to either side reduced down and the path opened up into a huge garden.

"Oh...wow."

They'd said tents, but I hadn't imagined these tented monstrosities—four in all, each as large as a small building. The flaps were partially open, revealing that two of them were greenhouses, open to the elements, and the other two held several workstations.

A sprawling garden existed around them, straight and orderly rows of plants and herbs and a couple of tiny trees bearing strange-looking fruit. Each area was marked with little signs saying what it was.

Workers bent within the various rows, pruning or collecting or planting or maintaining. White sunhats protected their skin from the warm rays and aprons were draped across their fronts.

"It's really something, isn't it?" Arleth said, pushing up close. She had a fond smile. "You will love working here. It is unlike anything you've likely ever experienced." She turned to Calia. "May I?"

"Of course." Calia motioned her on. "I'm sure you know one or two people from the times you've visited in the past."

Arleth and Delaney walked ahead, separating at the start of the garden and starting to wind their way through it.

I turned toward the guard and held up a finger. "You can only follow me if you mind the plants. Do not crush or even brush any of them. They are delicate. I will toss your ass out if I see that you are disrespecting them in any way, got it? These plants can make the difference between life and death. They deserve respect."

"Yes, alpha," Weston said, lowering his gaze to my feet. He was being official, not using my name. He didn't use royal titles for Nyfain and me either, instead treating us like we were pack. Many dragon royals would probably hate that, but neither of us cared in the least.

"Tamara," I said, turning, "I assume you know the drill."

"Yes, milady. I'm well versed in the protocol of the operations of other kingdoms."

"Operations, right," I murmured as Calia led us toward one of the work tent monstrosities. I'd almost forgotten that they used the goods from this production for the monetary benefit of the castle and kingdom.

"I've organized the whole day for you to work as you please," Calia said. "It was a special favor to me from the king. If you prove your worth, I can almost guarantee you'll be invited back. Arleth and her ladies-in-waiting were always welcome here, I've been told."

"And there is no magic in this production?" I asked, stopping at the edge of the vast gardens and bracing my hands on my hips. I didn't want to go to the workstation yet. I wanted to peruse the natural offerings.

Calia gave me a sly smile and then laughed. "Since there are none of my people within earshot, and your handler isn't here…" Her eyes glinted at me. "I will be blunt, shall I?"

"Please."

"I know that you were told our guests are prohibited from examining the castle's more robust magical operations. I also know you were told that yes, there is some magic employed in these particular operations, and it won't be explained. So then, what was the real point in asking? I don't understand plants like you do."

I turned my face away to hide my smile. "I don't know how to be clever with my words. Hopefully that won't bite me in the ass. Want me to be honest?"

Her smile had slipped, but she nodded. "Yes, I'd like that."

"I want to study some of these potions, the ones that use magic, to see if I can devise something like them."

"Ah. Yes, I thought it might be something like that." She looked behind us at my people waiting. "Let's take a walk, shall we?"

Unease niggling at me, I followed her into the rows of plants, aiming away from anyone who might over-hear.

"Listen, Finley," she said, slowing way down, her voice a low murmur. "I have a duty to my people. As do you. In time you'll learn to navigate that. Until then, please know that I am rooting for you. My desire to be with you and yours isn't just about repaying the service you rendered my people and family. It isn't just about monitoring your kingdom to see if we might want to align with you. I do, genuinely, enjoy your company. Dessia has latched on to Hadriel. She feels comfortable with him in a way she hasn't felt comfortable with anyone in a long time. One day I hope we can be friendly, if not friends. I have so few friends. I know all that might take a while, though."

"Not as long as you might think if you're just up-front with me until I learn all Arleth's annoying lessons about subtlety."

She laughed. "Yes, of course. Well, then. I will tell you this, and you will see how much I am willing to bend my duty to support a friend." She bent and plucked a little yellow flower from a plant I didn't recognize. "I have set you up with a workstation at the back of the tent. Some might think it a slight, but there are benefits to the situation. Mainly that no one will be working in either of the stations between you and a snarl-toothed woman with a surly disposition two tables away in the corner. You might notice her...work habits and *special skills*. You might also find that if someone has information she wants, she will grudgingly trade for it. Often she will reveal things she really oughtn't."

"I don't think you're quite clear on what I meant by up-front, but I think I catch your drift."

She laughed as we continued on our way. "She's the magical one."

"Yes, I got that."

"I would get in grave trouble if it came out that I'd told you that."

My heart felt a little squishy. Nyfain had said that in order to even partially trust, it was often necessary to hold one another's secrets. She was offering me an olive branch. She was trying to find a way to be friends, and trusting I'd do right by her.

"Thanks," I said softly. "Hopefully one day I'll get the hang of all this, and I'll be much less awkward. In the meantime, you're safe in knowing I'm shit at politics without my handler."

"I like awkward, and I hate politics. I much prefer your court, where everything is about hard work and unity. It feels more...genuine. But..." She shrugged and looked around. "I'm a faerie with a prized role in a prestigious court. Things could be worse."

I chuckled. "I'm a commoner queen with zero idea how to function in a court and even less inclination to try. I know things could be worse."

She huffed. "Now you're just feeling sorry for yourself." She rolled her eyes. "Anyway, good luck. Oh, and please, where is Hadriel? My sister went off to stalk him around the castle. I thought he was going to end up here by now or I wouldn't have let her."

"Why?"

A shadow crossed her expression but cleared in a moment. "She has a habit of getting into mischief."

"And you think Hadriel is going to save her from

that?" I asked.

"No. It's only that Vemar was with Hadriel, and he won't let anything happen to either of them. There are worse things than a dragon bodyguard."

"Ah gotcha." I shook my head and looked back the way we'd come. "I'm not sure, honestly. He was supposed to be here by now, but he doesn't usually go in a straight line when more interesting things could be seen in a zigzag. He also might've gotten lost in your enormous castle."

Her eyes took on a keen edge. "Yes, that is true. Well, I'll go hurry them along."

I wasn't sure if she was actually worried about her sister, or a known shit disturber wandering around the castle. If not for the look in her eyes, I would've guessed the latter. I'd have to ask Hadriel about it.

Until then, though, I was going to dig into these plants, and I absolutely intended to spy on that faerie who could do actual magic. If I could somehow make potions, Wyvern would really be rolling.

CHAPTER 37

ARLETH

T HE SECOND CALIA left, Dee and I met Finley and shadowed her through the gardens. We'd worked with many of these plants on past visits, learning about them from the locals. But they'd kept more secrets than they shared, especially about the plants used to make the most lucrative poultices and salves. Those were the money plants.

Back in the day, we hadn't pressed. But back in the day, we hadn't had Finley.

I had a sneaking suspicion she'd charm information out from under our hosts, giving little in return. After all, her knowledge mostly centered around the everlass plant, which was a tricky plant for non-dragons to work with. The faeries had been mystified by it for years. Generations. They couldn't get the knack, calling it an obtuse weed, perfect for dragons.

Finley would give them knowledge they couldn't use, all while robbing them blind. She was the perfect thief.

"Oh wow!" She crouched beside a flowering plant

with bright blue blooms and spindly leaves. "I've read all about this one!" She rattled off a name I'd never heard of. "This is great for the skin. It clears up acne and reduces redness—Oh goddess, you devious little thing." She stepped over the row she was currently in and squatted down to a leafy, light green shrub. "Look at *this*! This one is rare because it is so finicky to work with. There are only three of them here." She narrowed her eyes. "I thought I read that they like a lot of space. This wouldn't be nearly enough. But that book was old, so who knows. Maybe the information is outdated."

She worked her way through the garden, moving along the outskirts at first and then weaving farther in, recognizing the pattern. The faeries were incredibly organized, putting like plants with like. If this one helped the skin, that one likely did too. Similar but not the same. In the large middle area were the all-purpose plants, used for a variety of things.

Within each grouping, Finley recognized most of the offerings. She'd either worked with the plant or read about it. When she didn't recognize a plant, she'd analyze its leaves and gently touch its flowers. She even noticed which kinds of insects landed on them and how they likely pollinated. The woman was a walking directory for plants. I knew a lot, but her range of knowledge was incredible. She'd spent a lot of time with her nose in a book, both in her youth and preparing for this trip, and it showed.

Well on our way toward the work tent, Finley gasped and stalled, holding out her hand to stop my forward progress.

"What is it?" I asked.

A woman down the way glanced over, her eyebrows raised.

It was then I saw it, and my heart surged. I was careful not to let the sentiment show on my face.

"What have they done?" Finley asked, aghast.

"Oh yes." Someone, a pretty woman in her thirties with dirt smeared across her apron and her hat pushed a little off her forehead, wandered over. She smiled as she looked down at a plot of land hosting five everlass plants in horrible condition. "We've kept those going since Nyfain—excuse me." Her expression turned bashful. "Since the king of Wyvern was here last. They grew because of him, of course. Because he's a dragon. Well, you know that. We've been able to keep them going." She preened.

Dee gave me a sly look with a small smirk. She was thinking the same thing I was. They still couldn't figure out how to keep everlass healthy. They'd need to rely on Wyvern for the good leaves.

"You call this keeping them going?" Finley stared down in obvious horror. "They're... You're..."

"Is there a problem?"

I glanced behind me and very nearly let my joy show.

Plain face, loud clothes, not nearly good enough for my son. Eris.

He'd thought she was nice. Easy-mannered. A good companion.

It had all been an act. She'd been trying to seal the deal. To everybody but him, including her own people,

she was nearly unbearable. I would've terminated the
alliance several ways over if it hadn't meant Nyfain's and
my freedom.

I'd heard the things she'd said about Finley last
night. About how fragile she clearly was, having to be
carried. How common her roots. How disgusting her
scarred back, very unladylike, and how ugly her scales.
About how she'd stolen Nyfain away, using her pretty
face and spread legs to do so.

She'd said all this to anyone who would listen.

What an absolute fool.

Of course, Finley wouldn't have cared about any of
that. She likely would've laughed it all off. It was only the
idea of someone claiming Nyfain that riled her up, not
this particular woman. Finley clearly saw little value in
Nyfain's old intended, same as me. Same as Dee. Same as
her people, for goddess's sake. There were many in a
faerie court who would marry for the bloodline, even
without a dowry. The woman had to be tolerable,
though.

But mess with the everlass, and suddenly Finley did
have a problem. A big one.

Thank the goddess. Finley needed to prove she was
Nyfain's equal by making a dragon-scale show of
violence.

Finley turned just her head, a glimmer of recognition
sparking in her eyes before concern for the plants
washed it away.

"Are you joking?" she asked Eris.

Eris's eyebrows lowered. "I asked if there was a problem."

Finley turned her body this time, very slowly, very purposefully. The air crackled with barely contained rage. With power. Her gaze burned into Eris.

"What do you do here? You're a gardener, is that right?" Finley asked in a tone laced with menace.

Eris lifted her chin and crossed her arms over her chest defensively. "The *head* gardener, yes. A job *I* got through skill and hard work."

Unsaid: *not through my appearance and spread legs.*

Dee's brow pinched in anger.

"Skill?" Finley leaned in a little closer, and Eris's whole body went taut. "Let me ask again. Are you joking? Here's another question: who the fuck are you kidding? Do the people around here who make the elixirs check your work, or do they just assume these particular plants aren't as useful as they thought?"

Eris's jaw clenched. "What would you know about it? You're common. You didn't get any sort of royal education before you traipsed around in front of *my* fiancé—"

Finley moved so fast that I couldn't have stopped her if I'd tried. She grabbed the other woman and, in a show of power that made my eyes widen, spun and threw her way up and out. As Eris flew, Finley launched into the air, and suddenly her dragon burst forth, taking to the sky with mighty pumps of her wings. Her clothes dropped in tatters to the ground behind her. Her burgundy scales glittered with gold, so incredibly beautiful. She dipped her head and snatched Eris out of the air.

The other faerie near us exclaimed something in her

language, probably a swear.

"Maybe we shouldn't have told her to handle it like normal," Dee said in a wispy voice.

"It wouldn't have mattered. I didn't think she'd react to a claim on Nyfain made by that woman. Clearly, I was wrong. Let's hope Finley's bite doesn't kill her."

Dee clucked her tongue. "She hasn't learned the kind of control Nyfain has mastered. Not many have. You better start thinking of how you're going to do damage control."

I shrugged. "It's a pressurized situation. May-be…that'll make a difference…"

Eris screamed and struggled, her arms and legs flailing. When they were high in the air, Finley's dragon opened her mouth.

"Welp, that's one way to solve the problem," Dee murmured.

"Holy fuck, what did I miss?" Hadriel came running from the path. A pink loafer went flying from his foot. Hannon and his brother and sister jogged after them, all of them looking up at the falling faerie.

Vemar sauntered out last, his hands tucked into the small pockets in his blazer, a crazy grin twisting his lips. He didn't look up but veered a little to the left when he could, well out of the path of the falling faerie.

Eris, windmilling her arms and kicking her legs, screamed so loudly her voice turned hoarse. Finley swooped down in a beautiful, easy glide and snatched the faerie woman into her mouth again.

"Do you see blood?" Dee asked as Hadriel made it to us, one foot bare.

He was breathing heavily. "Hannon and I are away for one fucking hour, and suddenly Finley's dragon is playing catch with one of the faeries? Arleth, my darling, this was absolutely *not* in our plan!"

"What's going on?" Hannon asked, watching as Finley took Eris up high again.

"Eris made a comment about Nyfain being her fiancé," I told them, looking behind me at all the faeries in the field, who were watching the scene unfold in shock.

Finley again dropped Eris, who continued to scream.

"Well, she obviously won't be invited back here." Hadriel threw up his hands, looking at me in bewilderment. "What the hell is she going to do with herself if she can't work the plants?"

"Read?" Hannon suggested as Vemar finally made it to us. "There's a really nice library here."

"What happened to the everlass?" Dash asked as he looked down at the withering plants.

"They haven't taken very good care of them, it would seem." Hannon resumed looking at the sky.

Finley swooped down again, plucking Eris from the sky one more time. Instead of heading back up this time, she dipped at breakneck speed.

"She better not fucking crash," Hadriel hollered. "Finley, don't you fucking crash! The master will go absolutely crazy if you put the baby in that sort of danger. Do you know who will get a foot up his fucking hole? I will!"

"You're probably focusing on the wrong aspect of that scenario," Hannon told him. "You might want to worry more about the baby, no?"

"Oh, give me a break, she'd never do anything to hurt the baby." Hadriel waved his hand in the air. "She's crazy only to a certain point. But the master—Fuck, I'm calling him master again. The fucking king is not rational where she and his child are concerned. Finley! Do you hear me—"

Finley angled quickly, her wings out, catching the wind to nearly stop her. She dropped her head and let go of Eris. The woman tumbled out in a mess of limbs, rolling across the ground. Finley shifted back before running at her, yanking her up off the ground and hoisting her into the air at face level.

"That is a warning," Finley said, and fire crackled to life across her bare skin. "If you ever make any sort of claim on him again, past or present, I will kill you. Gruesomely. Now get the fuck out of this garden so that I can fix that patch of everlass in peace."

She tossed Eris away before turning around. The flame flickered again before diminishing and going out.

I wondered if Eris would get to her feet and demand justice. Demand someone do something. Instead, she just lay there shaking. The rest of the people in the garden let her.

"Hadriel, go find Leala and tell her I need some new clothes," Finley said. "Have someone send a note to Nyfain that I'm fine." She braced her hands on her hips and looked down at the everlass. "Hannon, in the meantime, go find someone with an apron, would you?"

"Sure." He pointed at the kids. "Stay here with Finley and the others. No wandering off."

"Hannon," Sable whined. "It's not dangerous here.

Everyone says so."

He didn't respond, just headed toward the work tent as though he'd been there countless times. No one stopped him from walking in.

Hadriel held out his hands, staring at Finley with wide eyes. She didn't notice. Instead she pointed at the nearly crowded plant between the others and gave me a look.

That plant was dangerous, but to explain why would reveal our secrets about the crowded plant. It wasn't something I wanted the faeries knowing.

"Pull it," I told her.

She reached down and yanked it out by the root.

"Sorry," she told it quietly, and from her tone, it was clear she meant it.

"Excuse me," a woman with a snaggletooth said as she walked forward, her face a little pale. In fact, all of their faces were pale. They clearly weren't used to seeing this sort of violence. "Just what do you think you are doing?"

Finley tossed the everlass plant to the side and faced the woman, utterly naked and not bashful about it. Those days had long since passed.

"Eris tried to claim my mate, and—"

"Not about that. I heard what she was saying. She deserved what she got. No, what are you doing, pulling that plant out?"

She came to a stop a few steps away from the everlass plot, giving Finley a wide berth.

Finley held up a hand to her, shaking anew with rage. "Here's how this is going to go. I'm going to fix up this piece-of-shit everlass patch. You people have mangled it. *Look* at them!" She took a deep breath. "More will spring up in the days and weeks before we leave. You have my word on that. I'll have Nyfain help with the process. Dragons will be visiting them around the clock. In fact, you'll need to clear more space." She pointed to the neighboring plants. "Those can be rehoused without a problem. Those can be killed. They're useless compared to the half-dozen other plants in this huge garden that do the same thing. Give me some space, both in the ground and personally, and I'll make these plants flourish. Then I'll show you how to harvest them and dry them so that you get the most out of them."

Dee grimaced, but the promise was out. We couldn't take it back now. We'd just have to hope they couldn't manage to care for the plants on their own. It would be hard to lose such a valuable trading commodity.

"If I make the plants flourish," Finley went on, "they'll work for you like a motherfucker. In return, I'll want to use a nice, big workstation so I can work with a lot of the different plants in this garden that I've only ever read about. Yes? A trade. A fair trade." She didn't wait for the approval. "Now fuck off. I'm pissed off at what you've done to these plants, and at that fucking cow for trying to claim my golden dragon. I'm not in the mood for fuckstains who want to waste my time and goddess-given talent. Dash, since you're here, you can help. Sable, start singing the song Nyfain taught you. These poor things are starved for a little love and attention."

And with that, her family quickly bent to the plants, working as a team in a way that spoke of the long years they'd toiled together. They pruned quickly, petting and stroking the plants, as Sable filled the space with a tune that would melt your heart and then steal your soul.

Faeries drifted over from all over the gardens, their eyes lighting up at Sable's voice. At what she would almost certainly flourish into when she came of age. Finley didn't think Sable had the Syflora gift, since her singing hadn't helped the plants prosper in the past, but she'd learned what she knew from books, and maybe those books hadn't mentioned that the gift sometimes didn't manifest until a shifter's first change. It was something I hadn't mentioned, either, not wanting to get anyone's hopes up. Seeing the faeries reacting like this, though...

Well, maybe it would be true after all.

ANOTHER HANDFUL OF hours passed in a flash. Eris had finally gotten up and moved on, taking herself back to the castle to recuperate from her fright. No one seemed to notice. All eyes were trained on Finley. She'd gotten their attention with her brutality, confused them with her tender care of the everlass, shocked them with how she spoke to their matriarch, and then wowed them with her knowledge of plants, those she knew and those she'd just read about.

Finley had come out of the demon occupation a diamond, and I'd cut her into a shape that sparkled and entranced. Still, she'd kept the qualities that made her such a fighter, including her stubborn ability to shove

K . F .   B R E E N E

her way into the space she wanted and take up residence.

She'd been allocated one work area. She'd taken up three without apology.

Everyone was too afraid to tell her to move.

Then she did what Dee and I had known she would: she blew their operations wide open.

She methodically worked her way through the garden, picking from plants she'd read about and wanted to try. If she didn't know the plant, she listened to a faerie's brief rundown before nodding without comment and tucking a sample into her collection satchel. Just like in my time, there were some plants no one would explain. Properties they kept to themselves.

She meandered through the tents, all of them, checking out their stores of dried plants and herbs and looking into their pots. Her gaze was so sharp and intelligent, her presence so authoritative, that people talked. They didn't seem like they could help themselves. She'd bark a question, and they would answer bluntly and honestly, something they had *never* done in my past visits.

Only one person refused to answer her questions. Only one seemed impervious to her presence. It was the snaggletoothed woman. She'd fucked off and left Finley to it, but she was a closed book when it came to her work.

That didn't seem to bother Finley. When she didn't get what she wanted, she got to work. She did what she did best—experimented.

It took her no time at all to figure out what the mystery plants did. Like was planted with like, after all. She folded them into her everlass creations, the leaves having been brought from her stores in the castle. Soon she had the whole tent looking over. She created by sight, by smell, and, most of all, by feeling.

Making her rounds in the work tent again, she'd stop at the various stations and ask, "Have you tried using this instead of using that?" Then she'd launch into an explanation of why she thought it might help. She'd wait for the rebuttal, ready to discuss other options, always leaving the faerie ready to try something new. Couldn't hurt, right? What was the loss? "That plant negates the effect of this one. You're fucking yourself. I'd use—"

She was a whirlwind, entirely in her element. Her beauty was even more radiant because she was steepled in what she loved—working the plants. Nyfain and Sable might be able to sing plants into health, but Finley could care for them better than anyone I had ever seen. She could understand them in a way that could only be described as divine. It was incredible to watch, even more so because she was in a place that should be foreign to her, meeting several of these plants for the first time.

Dee and I joined in, helping, offering suggestions, and taking over more of the faerie workstations. It wasn't that we'd been welcomed, it was that they'd acclimated to our presence. We just *were*, like they were. We worked there now, simple as that. Finley had forced a place for us, and they didn't think to be affronted.

I'd never heard of such a thing. I'd never heard of faeries being this open with outsiders. Not ever.

By the time we left, our stations had been declared ours for the duration of our stay, and we were told they'd be left open for us on future visits.

"If I hadn't lived it, I wouldn't believe it," Dee whispered as we made our way back to the castle, tired but enthused. It was time to get ready for dinner. We hung back from Finley a little so we could talk. "I would not believe it."

"I know. I knew Finley would weasel her way in, but that…"

"She loves it. She loves all that. It's her calling. They saw it in her just like we did."

"Yes, true."

"She's going to make Wyvern a *lot* of money." Dee sucked her teeth. "We just have to figure out how to get some of those faerie plants on the shadow market."

"Only a few kingdoms allow the shadow markets, and they are all less prestigious. I doubt my son will want to visit them for the purpose of his mother's questionable dealings. We'll need to be clever about how we make the request."

I watched with a smile as Sable and Dash ran in and out of the bushes, playing tag. Hannon walked next to Finley, listening to her chatter away about the new plants she was excited about.

Hannon had stayed the whole time, of course, wanting to be with his family. He'd stood idly and watched over the kids, or wandered the tents with Finley, giving her a sounding board that didn't actually sound. He'd had zero purpose, since we weren't sharing about his special ability with the everlass. He couldn't help with the plants like Dash, running to and fro to collect, and he couldn't sing like Sable. He didn't tell hilarious stories and jokes like Hadriel, giving people something to do when they took a break, or offer charismatic anecdotes like Vemar, who played off Hadriel in a way that had most people bending over laughing, wiping tears from their eyes. And maybe if he hadn't been such a calm, sure presence, or maybe if he'd been less broad and hand-some, or less...whatever it was that seemed to draw a person in and make them want to stay forever, he would've stood out. As it was, he blended in. He was part of the beautiful tableau Finley had painted within the faerie garden, and I knew in my bones that she'd go back home and immediately create the same sort of work area and inject her sense of family into it.

Under her steady leadership, we'd have the best plant-working operation in the world.

And after I got home, we'd also return to having the best library. The faeries had really upped their game in that department. They'd had sixteen years to expand and collect more volumes.

I hated to be outdone when it came to my library.

Plants and books, that was where our kingdom would shine above all else.

The first day had gotten off to an amazing start. It was better than anything I could've expected.

Dinner started off well too. King Starvos wanted to hear from the various people who'd been kept in the dungeons.

I understood what he was after—he wanted to see what kind of a case we had against the demon king. While Calia had a lot of power in his court, she was essentially a spy. Her grievance against Dolion would be easy for the demon king to swat away. She'd been trespassing, after all, in and out of dungeons all through the world. She couldn't be trusted.

Then there was Nyfain. His father had bartered with the demon king. Sure, Dolion had treated the kingdom abominably and taken far more than a creature of worth and merit ever would, but...they were demons. That was what they did. That was why no respectable party would deal with them. Finley, though certainly a gem, had found her way into the dungeon to save Nyfain. It could be claimed she didn't have a legitimate grievance either. That she'd put herself into the situation.

Hence Starvos's dilemma, but it was a dilemma that was soon laid to rest.

Micah was strong and powerful, well mannered, educated, and attractive. He was a shining example of a capable dragon. He spoke eloquently, sharing his story, and Weston addressed the king next. The epitome of an alpha wolf, he nonetheless spoke to the king with respect and even subservience, his manners impeccable. He shared his story about why he'd left the Red Lupine court, focusing on the family angle, and spoke of his time in the dungeons.

Tamara and her guard, whose imprisonment had not been part of my husband's deal, knew exactly how to speak to the king and the other members of the court. They'd had a lot of practice, after all. Weston's wolves followed their example, respectful when answering questions and not speaking to those of higher status unless spoken to.

Hadriel and Vemar spoke hardly at all, on their best behavior, something that probably killed Hadriel, and

Leala hadn't been invited after all. There were limits to Starvos's curiosity, it seemed, and a lady's maid was beyond it.

Everything was going so well. I got lucky enough to sit close to Starvos, who liked nothing better than to have his ego stroked. This was the arena in which I excelled, and I danced to his tune seamlessly. I thought we were going to pull it off flawlessly, as a group. As Nyfain and Finley's group.

And then, halfway through dinner, everything changed.

CHAPTER 38
FINLEY

"**U**GH." CALIA LOOKED around her with her hand on her empty crystal goblet. A ring of red had settled in the bottom. Staff walked behind the diners, checking on plates and glasses and seeing if anyone needed seconds or refills. We were on the main course of a fucking amazing meal. I'd already mentioned three times that we need a faerie cook. Our current cook was fine, but...I mean...some things transcended "fine," and this meal was one of them.

"Really, though?" Calia said under her breath, a line between her eyebrows. She looked at me in exasperation. "They are always so slow on my refills. The king doesn't think I can do my job blind drunk. And sure, he is right, but sometimes I just need to let loose."

Nyfain smiled from his position at my side, the place where I was supposed to be sitting. The one beside the place of honor at the head of the table.

We'd walked in the room at the head of the crowd, directly behind King Starvos and Queen Ayre. The king and queen had been escorted to the other end of the large table, where the queen waited beside her seat for the king to sit first. Once he did, she was helped into her seat.

The same scenario was supposed to play out with Nyfain and me. Except when we reached the other end of the table, Nyfain tugged me toward the head seat. The staff member, ready to push the chair in for him, hesitated at the sudden change in the seating arrangement. Until Nyfain stared him down, that was. With a little jump, the staff member was suddenly all action, tucking me in and delicately placing my napkin in my lap for me.

Nyfain then took the seat meant for me, leaning to the side like a playboy bored of this whole affair. He reached his hand across the corner of the table and took mine while waiting for everyone else to sit around us.

He'd done that in our kingdom, offering me the place of honor. I hadn't expected him to flout custom in a foreign land, though. It seemed a little risky for him to not only proclaim his queen equal in power, a first for our kingdom, but to make a show of giving her the place of most importance.

I knew better than to protest, though. It would ruin our image of a united front.

Starvos had taken notice, of course, his gaze pinging between Nyfain and me. The queen had paid attention too, a smile slowly soaking up her expression. But neither of them had commented, and then everyone else filed in. The food was placed on the table, and the moment was seemingly forgotten.

"I know exactly what you're talking about," Nyfain told Calia, using two forks to delicately pry the white meat of the fish from the rib bones. "My fath—the king of Wyvern allowed me two glasses of wine or mead at any given dinner, no matter how long the dinner lasted. He didn't trust me to have any more. I have no idea why because I'd never embarrassed him or myself with too much alcohol, but…" He shrugged. "I'd advise you to play nice while you're in his company and then take a bottle from the kitchens, head out into the gardens or your rooms with a few close friends, and drink to your heart's content."

"That would be great…if I had any friends." She pulled her lips to the side as she speared some of her fish with her fork.

"Am I not your friend?" Dessia asked.

"No. You're my sister, and you get nervous when I drink too much."

"That's because, unlike King Nyfain and his…the last king, I have seen when you drink too much. It's hard to keep you from drowning yourself in the toilet."

Calia rolled her eyes. "You exaggerate." She leaned toward me, her violet eyes shrouded in the low mood lighting of the dining hall. "She doesn't drink. She thinks overindulgence is cause for alarm."

I laughed as I daintily worked at my fish like Arleth had taught me. "Well, you're welcome to mine if you'd like." I gestured at the goblet of wine left untried in front of me. "I'm not going to drink it, for obvious reasons."

"It's not so obvious here." Calia looked back again, spying a staff member with a carafe of wine. She stared him down, but he didn't budge. "Our culture doesn't forbid a pregnant woman wine, just limits it. I'm sure they gave it to you assuming you'd have a glass with dinner."

Nyfain didn't tense or so much as glance in my direction, but unease rolled through the bond, from him and both of our dragons.

I laughed. "The dragons and man are much too overbearing for something like that. You know what they say about choosing your battles. Wine in small quantities isn't worth the headache of their overprotectiveness."

"Just in large quantities," Calia said, laughing. "Yes, I understand. Not to mention your mother-in-law—or mate...parent you call it, I think. She would probably run down here and slap the goblet out of your hand, not caring about possible offense to the resident king and queen."

"Very likely," I agreed.

"And you, King Nyfain?" Dessia asked, her fish half-eaten and her silverware laid down. "Why don't you drink your wine?"

Nyfain glanced at his full glass, then at me. He shrugged. "It doesn't seem fair for me to indulge when she can't." He grinned at me, his eyes soft. "It's our baby, together. I want to share in all the delights of her experience, and it seems unfair if I don't also share in the...drawbacks. Those that I can, of course."

"Careful, King Nyfain," Calia said dryly, tapping the base of her glass absently. "If you're too perfect, you'll ruin other men for my sister and me, and then one day we'll lust after you and be treated to flight training via

Finley's dragon."

They all laughed, and I felt a spark of unease. Truthfully, I'd gone a little overboard this morning, and I knew it. I was pretty sure Arleth hadn't meant I should handle the situation *that* way. But in the moment…I hadn't been thinking about anything at all. The drive to end the threat had consumed me, and then…well, I'd let my dragon go a little crazy.

"I'm far from perfect, I assure you." Nyfain laughed before taking another bite. "I won't mention this to Finley…" He leaned toward Calia and her sister in faux intimacy. "I am very glad I don't have to actually birth the infant. I've witnessed it once. It made me glad females handle that part of things."

"Please don't remind me," I muttered. I hadn't thought about that bit yet. It was too far in the future for me to worry about, especially given there were so many worries in the present.

He put down his fork and reached out for my hand. I pushed out my elbow at him, playfully denying his touch.

Calia laughed and swapped goblets with me. "Fine. You've convinced me. King Nyfain, hang on to yours. I'll get to that when I'm done with this one. We'll pretend I am now drinking with friends, even though absolutely none of you are drinking with me."

"I am one hundred percent sure Hadriel would be glad to drink with you," I told her before laying down my utensils. Delicious or not, the fish was just too annoying to eat the "proper" way. Hopefully there would be a few more courses to ease my hunger. Courses that I could just saw into and stick in my mouth like normal people. "Vemar would, too. Leala certainly would. A few of the wolves and dragons would give their left arm to drink with the pretty, violet-eyed faerie, and none of them would tattle on you, not after the initiation into real partying we've all had."

Calia took a sip and leaned back. Her eyes were serious when they beheld me. "My word alone is not enough to make my king act against the demons," she said in a low voice. "That's why he didn't allow me to take warriors with me to help you reclaim your kingdom. He didn't want it to seem like an act of war. I'm often alone in other kingdoms, so he allowed me to bring a tiny team."

"I know," Nyfain said, lowering his knife and fork and glancing down the table. "Your king danced around that issue pretty thoroughly. Dolion has a lot of power and influence, and many of the prisoners he trapped can be ignored. Weston was no longer a member of the court, your position requires some level of anonymity, and we essentially put ourselves into Dolion's care, directly or indirectly." He shook his head. "I hadn't realized how it would be perceived. I'm glad I decided to visit this kingdom before we address the council. With the information our very well-informed demon allies have, I can drag Dolion through the fire. I might not be able to declare war at first, but I can back him into a corner and wait for him to do something foolish. *Then* I can declare war."

"Given the king allowed the demons to be moved into the guest wing with you earlier today, I'd say he agrees with you," Calia murmured.

Nyfain dabbed his mouth, speaking from behind the napkin. "I enlightened him on some of the things Govam has shared with me. About the location of certain funds and resources that can be reappropriated if Dolion is taken down with the council's approval. They'd be the spoils of war."

I frowned at Nyfain as he lowered the napkin again and finished his fish. I knew Dolion had been pilfering from others like he'd taken from Wyvern, but I hadn't realized Nyfain was maneuvering to get the stolen riches back. It was wise, though. It was a good incentive for Starvos to help.

Calia took another sip of her wine and gently pushed her plate a little farther away. "Yes, there is hope. This dinner gives me hope. Your visit will prove fruitful, I think. You've shown that you are just as aggressive and volatile as dragons are reputed to be. You're vicious, but you're also a caring mate with good breeding. You're domesticated, so to speak. That's what I think the king will decide. Word of Finley's actions in the garden has spread far and wide. The ruthlessness with which she handled the...threat, we'll call it"—she smiled—"and then her delicate dealings with the plants and potions...well, it got people talking. And then there is the big, scary dragon with all the scars and the golden predator's eyes...doting on his pregnant mate, carrying her, and treating her with reverence and delicacy. Your emotional range has startled our people. The former king and Arleth were predictable—him for being mean and vicious, her for being graceful and easy. Everyone around them always acted with the utmost decorum. Then there's you two and your retinue, with Hadriel and Vemar's crazy outfits and the whip-toting lady's maid who just wanders around the castle talking to people…"

Calia laughed, holding her belly.

"I knew it would go like this," Dessia said, also smiling. "I knew it would. I knew the uniqueness of King Nyfain's court would be…" Dessia frowned, looking at her sister's face. "What is it?"

Calia's smile had slipped. She coughed politely into her napkin before taking another sip of wine. "I'm fine." She shook her head, patting her neck now. Then coughed again, her brow pinching together.

"Too much wine?" Dessia asked, sitting forward and turning, bracing her hand on the back of her sister's chair.

"That's only my second glass. That's…" Her face flushed, one hand on her stomach and the other now gripping her throat. Fear sparked in her eyes. "My throat feels like it's…getting tight. Like it's starting to close up."

She coughed again, bending forward.

A cold sweat broke out over my body. I knew these signs. They were classic, and she'd just drunk my wine.

"Fuck." I pushed up to standing, my heart suddenly galloping. "Hadriel, Hannon—someone! Run for the green chest. The antidote chest. *Hurry!*"

"I got this. I'm faster—" Vemar sprinted from the room in his bare feet, leaving his green loafers behind.

"Calia, listen to me." I picked up the goblet and handed it to Nyfain as I told him, "Do not drink this or the one in front of you. Save them. I want to analyze it."

He took it as Hannon and Hadriel appeared next to us, everyone else still confused, looking around and trying to see what was happening. Only a few people in this room knew the precautions I'd taken to learn about and ward off poison. This was why.

"Calia," I said, yanking her chair to face me. I met her scared eyes, panic setting in. She gripped her throat with two clawed hands, struggling to take a breath. "Listen to me," I barked, infusing the command with my will. "You will not die. I will not let you die. I know how to fix this. I have about five minutes after you stop breathing to do so—Hannon, get hot water, dammit." My brother took off running to the kitchens. It had been his job to know where they were in case of a situation like this. "You have to stay calm. If you stay calm and slow your heart, it'll give me more time. Okay?"

She nodded, wheezing.

"What are your symptoms? Stomach pain and closing throat?"

She nodded.

"Anything else? Headache? Blurry vision? Uh…heart racing? Racing before you realized what was happening?"

I got a nod to the mention of her heart, head shakes in response to everything else.

My mind raced, poring over all the possible poisons that might have caused her symptoms, narrowing down the possibilities. The problem was, I'd learned all of this when I was calm and collected. When someone I liked wasn't succumbing to poison right in front of me.

I felt her head. Fever, though that was expected.

"How about saliva? More than normal?" I asked.

She nodded.

"Dessia," I said, turning. "Get water and dab her forehead. Put a cold, wet cloth on the back of her neck." My attention back on Calia, I said, "Just stay calm. Trust in me, okay? I'll see you through this. You need to give Vemar more time. Your castle is fucking huge. He's got a long way to run."

Her smile was pained, but it was there. She closed her eyes, and I motioned for Nyfain to lift her up.

He did so as I ran my arms across the place in front of her, knocking glasses and plates and utensils to the ground.

People were yelling now. Screaming. The king was demanding to know what was happening.

I shut it all out. Arleth would handle their questions.

"This will be more comfortable." I motioned for him to set her down on the table where it would be easiest for me to attend to her. "Go ahead and curl up into the fetal position. That's what the body will want to do."

No seizure—that was good. She was conscious still, and probably would be until her throat completely closed and she ran out of air.

I checked her body. No rash. No shivering.

I nodded, rolling through the options, not finding anything that the crowded everlass couldn't take care of. Whoever was trying to kill Nyfain or me didn't know what a crowded everlass elixir could do against poison. That was why it would remain a secret, hopefully, passed down through the generations with care, only discovered by those who would use it well and keep their mouths shut.

"You're doing really great, Calia," I said, leaning over her and rubbing her back.

She swallowed once, then again, jerking on the table.

Shouts and screams accompanied people asking, "What's happening? What does this mean?"

"It means her throat has closed up," I said as Hannon jogged back in with two mugs and a small pot filled with steaming water. "It means we're on the clock. There should be plenty of time, don't worry. As soon as Vemar gets back here, we can get this sorted."

A sudden panic gripped me that Vemar would be accosted while trying to get that trunk. A panic that partially cleared when I remembered Leala was in our rooms with Urien, putting things away and organizing post-dinner clothing for us. While I wasn't sure Urien would be of much help, no one would get to Vemar with Leala playing defense. She was an expert with that whip. All he needed to do was get to her.

"You're going to lose consciousness soon, Calia," I murmured as someone fought to get to us. My people kept them at bay. "It's okay. It'll be scary, I'm not saying it won't, but it does not mean you're going to die. It means you'll have a good story to tell your new friends after you wake up, okay? I won't let you die. I have this firmly in control—"

"Here!" Vemar sprinted into the room, the trunk in his hands, sweat dripping down the sides of his face. "Got it."

"Thanks," I said, moving quickly but not hurrying.

I took a deep breath. Then another. Oxygen helped

the brain think clearly. It steadied the nerves.

"Dessia, take my place," I said calmly, trying to ease the panic I could see written across Dessia's face. "Rub her back. Murmur encouraging words to her." I put the trunk at Calia's head. I didn't want her to spasm or thrash and hit it, spilling the contents.

Hannon stepped in beside me, mug in hand. "How are you going to administer the antidote with her throat closed?" he asked.

"*I* am not. *You* are going to give her a shot with the serum. Fuck, I hope I don't kill her."

"It wouldn't matter if you did. She will die without you. She might live if you try to help."

Deep breaths.

Watch closely as Finley tries injecting crowded ever-lass plant into a person for the very first time, I thought, sweat sliding down my temple. *Let's see if she fucks up, kills the prized faerie, and then gets blamed for poisoning her. A real nail-biter, folks.*

My dragon didn't comment. Thank fuck.

I mixed the ingredients, adding a few things to speed up the effect of the crowded plant but nothing that would make it more potent. After a quick and dirty grind, I motioned for Hannon to fill the mug with water.

"Time," I barked. "I need a timer for thirty seconds."

"On it," Hadriel said. He retrieved a syringe and handed it to me.

"Right. Okay. Let's all just take a deep breath. Everyone take a breath." I pushed Dessia out of the way and traced my fingers down Calia's limp arm before poking her chest. Chest would be faster. I didn't need to get it into a vein, just into her body. The chest had more circulation. It also had a lot of bones. I felt down by her ribs.

"Go, Finley," Hadriel shouted.

"Here we go." I took the syringe from Hannon before bending to the mug and smelling. I closed my eyes, inhaling deeply. A little more acidic because of the rough grind. That meant it was a little more potent than a normal dose I might administer.

Nodding to myself, I didn't fill the syringe as much as I might normally. It was better to err on the side of caution. I could always give her more. I could not give her less. This should be enough to allow her to breathe, and I could chase the rest of the poison away before it did further damage.

"Here we go," I said again, and handed the syringe to Hannon. I picked a spot between the muscles in her upper arm. "Here."

I stepped away, letting Hannon take my place.

With the calm, deliberate movements that made him excellent at nursing, he emptied the contents into Calia.

My heart raced, but my dragon fed me power to keep me going. To clear my panic.

Nyfain's hand closed around my forearm before his solid warmth slid behind me, lending support.

Hannon pulled out the syringe and stepped back. "How long?" he asked.

"Not long. A minute. Two. Is her heart still going?"

He pushed her onto her back. Another glass fell off and crashed to the ground. He felt her pulse.

"Slow and weak," he said before placing the heel of

his palm on her chest, his other hand pressed over it, and beginning to pump. He kept the rhythm steady and normal, helping her heart keep going as the crowded everlass *hopefully* did its job.

"After thirty seconds, try to help her breathe," I told him, turning away. I didn't do this part. I wasn't good at it. "That will probably be too soon, but it's better to start too soon than too late."

"What's happening?" the king barked. "Why is she leaving?"

Nyfain shadowed me. "This is how the siblings work. She makes the draught, and he administers it. They've been doing this since they were old enough to know how. They've had a lot of experience. Give it a moment."

"How long is a moment—"

"That's thirty seconds," Hadriel called out.

I squeezed Nyfain's hand. Faced the wall. Thought about leaving the room.

People kept crying, yelling out. It sounded like there was some sort of scuffle. I didn't let any of it seep into my thoughts. I just stared at the wall and let Nyfain hold me.

"One minute," Hadriel said.

"I can get air in," Hannon said, out of breath. "Her throat is not fully open, though."

"Fuck," I said under my breath. "Keep trying!"

If she were a shifter, we'd have more time, but faeries weren't as hardy. They didn't heal as fast. If she didn't get enough oxygen in her brain—if she didn't start breathing on her own—in four or five minutes, six tops, she probably wouldn't come back from this.

"Breathe, Calia," I said, resting a hand against the wall.

"C'mon, Calia," Hadriel said. "Breathe, love. Let's breathe together, okay? I've been in your position. I wasn't poisoned—it was the curse being a cunt—but I still nearly died. Did I ever tell you that? Finley and the master saved me. Come back, and we'll have a toast to celebrate being saved by pretty people with unbearable rage issues. Maybe not wine. You've probably gone off wine now, but something else. Maybe something stronger? Preferably not poisoned, am I right?"

The room fell into shocked silence. Hadriel could confuse anyone.

"Here we go, my love," he coaxed. "I know you hear me." I looked back, seeing his hand holding hers. He was patting it with the other. "Here we go. Big breath, now. Don't take your sweet time because you like that Hannon is essentially kissing you. He's hot, love, but he's not worth dying over. Come on, big breaths now. I'm sure he'll let you cop a feel when you're better."

Calia coughed, her body jerking with the effort of it. She sucked in a breath and then started coughing again. Clawed at her throat and rolled to her side.

Hadriel looked up at me desperately.

"It's okay," I said, putting up my hands. I laughed in relief. "Oh fuck, it's okay. She's going to be okay."

I hurried to Calia's side again.

"It's okay, you're all right," I told her, stroking her back. "The remedy is working. We'll give it a little more time to work through you, and then I'll reassess, okay? We'll make sure all of the poison is gone. But you're going to live. Just take slow, deep breaths. It'll get easier. As for the stomach issues, you might throw up or shit yourself. I can give you something else for that. That's your body's reaction to the poison, not the poison itself anymore. Okay? So when you need it, I can make you something."

"Don't be embarrassed about shitting yourself, love," Hadriel told her, his hand now on her shoulder. "I've had experience with that, too. Goddess help me, I sure have. I'll tell you some *stories* one of these days. You'll be glad you did it because of poison. Cecil wouldn't tell the whole fucking castle that story, at least."

I felt the surge of power, belatedly realizing what it meant.

"That glass was intended for my mate," Nyfain growled, across the room and grabbing the king before anyone could even open their mouths in surprise. "Are you trying to kill my mate and unborn child, Starvos? Is that why you invited me here?"

Nyfain rammed the king against the wall by the throat. Hot and heady power slammed into Nyfain and washed over us all, the faeries' response to the threat to their king. I felt the slap of bone-crunching agony through the bond.

It didn't show in Nyfain's posture. I doubt it showed on his face. He was no stranger to magic trying to force him to submit. He was well used to pushing past pain or ignoring it.

My dragon fed him a huge swell of power. Nyfain's dragon added to it. Fire rolled over Nyfain's body, then mine as I pumped out more power.

Faerie guards rushed to help. My people didn't know what to do, if they should interfere.

So I did.

I ran toward him, flinging out my will and locking the two kings in a cage, impenetrable to interference by anyone else. I would not disrespect Nyfain by pulling him off. Just as he hadn't called me down for how I handled the situation with Eris. We were a team, and we'd fight and die by each other's side, whatever the reason.

"What do you get out of it?" Nyfain asked the king, slamming him against the wall once, twice, banging his head off the wood. "Are you working with Dolion?"

"It wasn't me!" Starvos yelled. "It wasn't me, I swear. You are here because I am interested in an alliance. I just needed more information. I don't know what this is about. I had nothing to do with it!"

Nyfain leaned into him as Starvos's hands slapped at his shoulders uselessly. The guards tried to pry into my cage of will, and I sucked in more power to keep it in place.

"You have a breach," Nyfain said in a rough voice. "You better clean house. If my mate is harmed in this kingdom, I will burn it to the fucking ground. Do I make myself clear?"

"Y-yes," Starvos stammered. "Yes!"

Nyfain released him and stepped back, bumping up against my will.

"Call off your guards, or I will authorize mine," Nyfain said, watching the other king closely.

Shaking, Starvos looked around, seeing his guards

struggling to get to him and not getting very far.

"How... How are you doing that?" he asked, his voice trembling.

"Call them down!" Nyfain commanded with a rush of power.

"Y-yes, of course. Stand down." Starvos put out his hand and tilted it a couple of times. "Back. Get back."

Slowly, the guards relaxed. They adjusted themselves and stepped back, weapons still out.

"It wasn't me doing that," Nyfain said as I dropped my will and took a deep breath. "It was Queen Finley. You must've underestimated her. Not surprising, since you clearly underestimated me. Your magic scared the late king of Wyvern. It does not scare me."

He rolled his shoulders, adjusted his livery collar, and turned his back on the king.

"I'm okay," I heard, drawing my attention to Calia.

Hannon and Hadriel helped her sit up. Her sister held her hand.

"I'm okay." She kept her hand on her throat, her voice scratchy. Her beautiful violet eyes blinked open, finding me and then filling with tears. "Thank you. Oh, Finley, how can I ever thank you? You've saved my life twice."

"Well, I mean..." I wiped the sweat from my brow. "That glass was intended for me, so I guess thank *you*!"

Nyfain picked up the full glass that had been in front of him. "How can we figure out if this one was also poisoned? That might help us determine who did it."

"Well, we all know who did it, don't we?" Hadriel said. "I mean, who has access to a bunch of plants and also hates Finley? I can think of one..."

CHAPTER 39
FINLEY

URIEN AND LEALA met us in our rooms, the pandemonium from dinner still raging through the castle.

"Of course it wasn't Eris," I said as Leala took my livery collar and crossed the room to secure it. I didn't even remember taking it off. I must have done it sometime in between realizing what was happening to Calia and figuring out she would be okay. "She isn't a cook or a server. How did anyone expect her to deliver the plants into our drinks?"

Nyfain walked over to his dressing area so Urien could strip him of his finery. I followed suit to mine to make things easier on Leala. Usually I helped her, but today I just stood there, exhausted and strung out, and let her handle it.

"I know. And I knew it wasn't the king trying to poison us," he said, looking over at me. "I just didn't want him to think we were behind Calia's poisoning."

I frowned at him. "Why would he think we'd poison

her if we were the ones who saved her?"

He huffed. "You're very green, sweetheart. Very pure of heart. Someone would do that to gain favor with the king. He might've seen it as me showing your worth. The facts were stacked against us."

"How so?"

"You sat in a seat intended for me. Neither of us touched our wine. Your actions can be explained away, but mine can't. He wouldn't understand my decision to abstain because *you* are pregnant. It's not a normal custom. You offered Calia your wine. She was affected, and you then saved the day with a remedy that just happened to be pre-made and worked quickly. A couple of those things—okay. But to an outside observer, it would appear too convenient. I didn't want us implicated in any way, so I made a show of it. I showed him my genuine fear turned aggression, something he'd understand." He rubbed his face as Urien stripped his pants. "It *was* genuine, make no mistake. My fear that you could've been poisoned was real, just directed at the wrong person. I went overboard."

"Will you be needing clothes tonight, sire?" Urien asked Nyfain when all his clothes had been removed.

"Just a night slip, Urien. Thank you." Nyfain donned the slip and crossed the room to sit in a large, overstuffed chair by the darkened window. "I didn't temper my rage. I scared him."

I let my own slip fall over my head and down my body before I joined him. He held out his hands, and I sat on his lap, tucking myself into his embrace and leaning my head against his shoulder.

"I can't really say boo, can I? I played catch with your..." I gritted my teeth. I still couldn't go there. I wondered if I'd ever be able to.

"About that." He chuckled softly. "I'm surprised you didn't kill her."

"It wasn't a killable offense. She was just pissed and hurt and insecure. If she'd touched you, however..."

"No, I mean, most dragons don't have soft mouths. They can't control their bite reflex well enough to hold a creature between their teeth without killing them."

I leaned back and looked into his beautiful golden eyes. "You can."

"I'm rare."

"And what? You think I'm average?'

He laughed and hugged me closer again. "No, but you are new to flight and your dragon and training. I didn't think you had that kind of control yet."

"My dragon probably doesn't, normally—"

Oh ye of little faith, my dragon scoffed.

"But we couldn't kill her, and my dragon was hell-bent on...going crazy."

"Good training exercise, then." He shook his head. "In fairness, it must be strange for Eris. One day she had a certain life, and the next day she had a bunch of stuff that didn't belong to her and no memory of why it was there. She gets her memory back after all this time has passed, then I show up again with someone new. A mate. A pregnant, beautiful mate, whom I made my queen."

"Yeah, that does suck. Except she had sixteen years to find someone else. It's not like she was mourning you or missing anything. It was basically the same as her life right before she met you. She had all that time, but she didn't do anything else with it."

"And that is why I don't feel sorry for her." He rubbed my back, and Leala and Urien tidied up. "Knowing what my life was about to be..." He let his head thunk back onto the chair cushion. "What a huge mistake I was about to make. It was a mistake of convenience, but... Goddess help me, imagine never feeling this kind of love ever in our lives, Finley. Imagine never knowing someone you cared about more than yourself. Someone who got you in a way you didn't think anyone could."

"I know," I whispered, snuggling closer.

"The question is, if it wasn't Eris who put the poison in our drinks, who was it? Who in this kingdom has motive to kill us? The king seemed truly baffled."

"You know the answer, right?"

"It seems likely that Dolion has someone in this kingdom working for him, yes. Without any proof, though, we need to watch ourselves." He slowly tensed, and unease bled through the bond. "What if you had been drinking? What if the poison had been in your soup? Or your fish, or if it had appeared later in one of the other courses?"

"Then Hannon and Arleth would've had to handle the situation."

"Hannon needed direction. He administered the antidote, he didn't prepare it."

"Your mother could have."

"Mom didn't spend months studying poisons. She wouldn't have known what to make up and how much to administer."

"Which is why I would've walked her through it."

"Damn it, Finley." His arm tensed around me, crushing me to him. "You handled that whole situation from beginning to end. You were still barking orders after Calia had gone out. You figured out what to do and had to make adjustments when things didn't work out perfectly with the crowded everlass. There was precious little time to get it right. Without you, Calia would've died. If it had been you poisoned—"

He gritted his teeth, and a blast of explosive power rocked into me.

"We can't have you getting poisoned," he said. "I'll be changing the way we do things. Your poison trunk will need to be fully stocked at all times, and it will be with you whenever there is food or drink consumption. Someone will taste everything meant for you, and we'll wait to make sure it is safe before it gets to you."

"You can't have someone do that! What if it is a slow-acting poison? What if it is an *immediate* poison?"

"If it is slow acting, then by the time it affects them, you will know how to administer it yourself. If immediate…well, maybe we need to have one of the locals be your food taster. *They* will need to make sure it isn't poisoned before it touches your lips."

"Random germs from strangers, goodie. That's not gross or anything."

"Better to be grossed out and alive than dead."

I shook my head and looked away from him. "This is ridiculous."

"The reason you're not fighting me harder is because

you know it is necessary."

"I'm not fighting you harder because I am trying to pick my battles."

"And this is a battle you would not win."

I narrowed my eyes, fuming. He was right...about everything. I absolutely would've died. I hadn't even been sure Calia would make it. Dealing with crowded everlass required a lot of guts and a lot of knowledge. There was no "perfect situation" when it came to using crowded everlass. Arleth wouldn't have been able to smell the difference in its potency. She wouldn't have changed the dosage, and that alone likely would've killed me. No one else had grown up using all their senses to familiarize themselves with plants. They hadn't needed to, since they'd had actual training. My expertise was unique, and it had shown in the way I handled the situation with Calia.

"I'll need to train someone in poisons," I murmured, pushing away from him a little. I hated losing arguments, no matter how mild. "We need to have someone specific on staff that is an expert on how to diagnose and then cure them."

"Agreed." He tried to pull me closer, but I didn't feel like budging just yet. "Many kings have one. I was shortsighted in letting you take full responsibility."

He leaned forward, since I wouldn't lean back, pulling my slip at my neck and exposing my shoulder. He ran his lips against my suddenly heated flesh, getting to his mark and sucking. I groaned. I couldn't help it.

"Starvos asked me how we'd managed to get two marks each," he murmured. "He mentioned he hadn't

531

seen that before."

I tilted my head to give him more access. If he wanted to ease the sting of winning the argument by giving me pleasure, I was inclined to let him.

"I told him it was rare. Only true mates may mark each other twice." He ran his tongue along the shell of my ear before sucking in my earlobe. "He complimented me on finding such a great beauty. You would've hated it." He laughed as one of his hands touched down on my bare knee. He moved his palm along the inside of my thigh. "I doubt that's all he sees now. Not after you showed your power this evening. Your power and your exceptional ability to handle dire situations."

His hungry mouth was back on my neck, sucking and licking to my throat. His hand kept traveling up my inner thigh, faster now, heading for his target.

"Urien, Leala," Nyfain barked, his power blistering across me, his lips still against my skin. "That will be all. Take the rest of the night off. We'll see you in the morning."

"Yes, sire," they said in unison, bowing and curtsying. They dropped what they were doing and showed themselves out.

"I've wanted to taste you all day," he growled, his hand still climbing. The other hand gripped the back of my neck and pulled me back a little so he could suck along the vulnerable spot in the middle of my throat. He ran his teeth across it, making me shiver. "To lick up your slick folds and suck down your sweet nectar."

I moaned as his hand reached my upper thigh and stalled. My legs spread of their own volition, needing his touch. His mouth trailed fire down to the top of my chest, where he met fabric.

"Or maybe you'd rather have me tease my cock against your needy cunt until you beg me to fuck you?"

His thumb trailed a light touch along the very edge of my pussy. My breathing sped up as all my focus narrowed on that light, teasing touch.

"Take off that slip, Finley," he said in a low, rough voice.

I hurried to pull it up from under my butt and over my head. He dipped his head immediately, licking across the hard peak of my breast before sucking my nipple in, hard. His thumb traced another line, just barely nudging my clit.

"Hmm, more," I breathed, my arm looped around his shoulders. I pulled him to my breast and pushed my legs even wider, trying to invite him in. "Yes, Nyfain, *more.*"

He continued to suck, the sensation spearing down through me as his fingers trailed along the outside of my folds, almost tickling. He turned his hand, fingers pointing down, and applied a little more pressure, still too far from where I needed him. He followed the curve of my body until he almost reached my asshole, finding a trickle of my wetness dribbling down.

"Hmm, you're so wet," he growled.

He released my nipple with a pop before repositioning me over his hard cock. He leaned me back farther, his hand playing with me again, dragging wetness up and over my clit, getting everything slick.

I slowly gyrated my hips, clenching and unclenching

the muscles in my cunt.

"What do you need?" he murmured, running his knuckles to either side of my clit, teasing me. "Tell me what you need."

"I need your hard cock." I panted. I couldn't get enough air. My body boiled under his touch. "I need you to fuck me with your big cock."

He slid his scorching mouth back up my neck as his hand roamed down my slit yet again, pausing on the very inside of my thigh. His thumb lightly wiggled over my clit this time, his touch still light and teasing.

I gyrated harder against him, spread wide, focused on every point of contact.

"Please," I said, gripping his shoulders hard.

He pushed his fingers to my entrance. His hand rested against me, the heel of his palm against my clit, and I pushed my hips forward to press harder against it. Then back and forward again, fucking his hand.

I moaned, dragging his lips up to mine. He lifted his butt, my weight nothing to him, before yanking the slip out from under him. I leaned back long enough for him to pull it over his head and toss it aside. I didn't go right back to his lips, though. Not right away. Instead, I feasted on all that scarred and inked muscle, hard and cut. I traced my fingers down it, giving him a light kiss before scratching my nail across one of his nipples.

He groaned softly, applying a little more pressure to my clit. I pushed into his fingers, frustrated when he backed off. I was still on the verge. My body wound tighter. Frustrated but enjoying it.

I yanked on his hair, dragging his head back, and

then kissed him hard. I could feel his lips curve upward under mine before he plunged his fingers into me. His thumb pressed against my clit, and then he started rubbing just right.

"Oh fu—"

The orgasm made me shudder against him. His growl of approval preceded him turning me to face him, guiding my knees to either side of his. He cupped my cheek, his eyes hooded, his face so fucking beautiful I couldn't stand it. He pulled me down to him, sucking in my bottom lip and running his teeth across it. His other hand kneaded my ass cheek while he brought me into position.

"Slide that wet pussy over the tip of my cock," he ordered me. "Get my shaft all nice and wet."

I reached down and grabbed his base, keeping him steady while I angled my body forward. His tip slid between my folds. I paused at my clit, rubbing him across it, and shivered in delight. I angled my body a little more, sliding down the underside of him.

He pulled his hands away from me, settling back against the chair. He spread his arms to either side, watching me push forward again, running along his cock until it was again pressed on my clit. Forward, grinding against him, trapping his cock between my wet cunt and his lap. Wetness ran down over his balls, and I reached back to massage it against his skin.

"That's right," he murmured, his eyes on fire now, drinking me in. "Work me however you want me. Take what is yours."

I stroked up his shaft, trapping it between my body

and my hand, and then paused with his tip right at my opening. He watched where his cock touched me, glistening now, so hard. I kept it there and leaned forward, running my hands down his neck and then tickling over the marks branding his skin.

His groan was soft, and his eyes drifted shut.

"Watch me, Nyfain," I said, infusing my words with power. My dragon scraped it through his body. "Watch your pretty mate fuck you."

His smile was whiskey smooth as his heavy eyelids drifted open again.

"As you command, my queen," he said.

I felt down over his delicious pecs before slowly lowering. His cock disappeared into my wet flesh. It was so large and thick, filling me in the most amazing way possible. I watched my fingertips trace over his cut abs.

He left his arms wide on the armrests, letting me do all the work. Taking his pleasure as I took mine.

I smiled as I bumped down, flush, his cock buried deep.

"I want you to fill me up with your cum," I told him, rising slowly and swiveling my hips. I moaned softly and let my head fall back. My long hair dusted his thighs. "I want you to fuck me, over and over, in every way imaginable, with no help from the heat. I want you to keep going until I am sated and dripping with you. And then I want you to fuck me once more to put me to sleep."

I rolled as I sat back down, a little quicker. Back up, I dragged that hard length against the spot inside me that made me melt. Glorious shivers danced across my skin. I pushed my palms up over my breasts and pinched my nipples.

"Hmm," I said, sitting down harder, driving that cock in deep again.

He grunted, and through a small slit in my eyes, I watched the muscles tense in his mouth-watering torso.

With a wicked smile, I rose again, running my hands up and over me, pulling up my hair. I rolled my body, hitting all the right areas.

"Tomorrow I want to be sore when I get to the work tent." This time I sat down *hard*.

His grunt accompanied a jerk this time. His shoulders tensed, then his arms, and he gripped the edges of the armrests. His eyes burned. Lava pooled through the bond.

I laughed, riding the fire.

"That's right, baby. Try to resist touching me," I taunted him, rolling my hips as I lifted. When he was nearly falling out of me, I lowered a fraction. Just a fraction. Then back up. Down and up, working my hips, just moving him over that one spot in my pussy. "Let your queen play with your cock."

I kept at it, feeling his thighs tense under me now. His jaw was clenched.

Still I worked, keeping the penetration shallow, pleasing myself and leaving most of him untouched.

"I want to work the plants with your cum dripping down my thighs," I said boldly, jerking now. I let my hair tumble down and grabbed one of my nipples with one hand and rubbed my clit with the other. "I want part of you inside me and your smell all over me. I want those women to know the golden dragon king, as handsome as he is powerful, as ruthless as he is caring, is *mine*."

I slammed down onto him as my fingers worked. A hot spike of pleasure sent me over, rocking through my body. I cried out, torn apart by the climax.

"Be careful what you ask for, my queen," he gritted out. "You just might get it."

And then he was standing, still impaling me on that hard cock. He held me with one hand and used the other to throw my arms around his shoulders. He cupped the back of my neck and pulled me closer, claiming my lips.

He walked me into the other room, leaving me to hold myself against him while he clutched my hips and worked me up and down his cock.

"I don't need the fucking heat to keep going," he said. "I'm going to fuck that pussy raw. And then I'm going to lay into your ass. I'll have you dripping a trail of my cum to the garden if you aren't careful."

He laid me on the edge of the bed carefully, worked up but obviously not forgetting about the pregnancy. That didn't stop him from slamming his cock into me, groaning with the wet slap.

"Fuck yes," he said under his breath, starting a fast pace before ripping himself out and flipping me over. "Brace yourself on the bed with your arms. Don't lie on your stomach."

At this early stage, lying on my stomach wouldn't affect anything, but I did as he said anyway. I liked his protective urges.

He gripped my hips and pulled me back as he thrust forward, slapping against me again. And again. The sounds of sex filled the room, my two orgasms adding to the wetness.

"This one is for me," he told me, pounding into me. "You'll take your pleasure, but you won't come. You'll be ridden for my benefit only. Do you understand?"

I whimpered as he kept going, hammering home, my body so wound up I didn't see how I could possibly hold back.

"Do you understand?" His power tore through me.

"Ugh, yes," I said, letting my head drop forward, my elbows bending from the pleasurable onslaught. "*Yes!*"

He reached over and grabbed a fistful of my hair, yanking back. "Good girl."

His cock beat a fast rhythm. My clit throbbed with the need to be touched, but if I did, I'd go over the edge. I gritted my teeth, the pleasure coursing through me, the need to come pulsing.

"Nyfain, please," I said, shoving back against him. "*Please.*"

"No. I'm going to leave you on the edge while I empty inside of you."

True to his word, he let out a vicious growl and then shuddered. He took two thrusts to finish and then pulled out slowly, breathing heavily.

"Are you desperate for more cock?" he asked in a dark tone.

My pussy ached with need. I clenched and released, clenched and released, needing him to fill me again. To suck me. To touch me.

"Yes," I breathed.

"Yes, what?" He rubbed his palm flat against my

pussy, careful to avoid my clit. He rubbed the wetness all over me.

"Yes, alpha."

"Not alpha..." He pushed two fingers into me, just barely grazing my front walls. A spark of pleasure added to my delicious misery.

"Yes, my king."

"That's right." He dropped to his knees and tasted me. "Hmm," he said, running his tongue through my folds. "We're even better together. Do you want my tongue, cock, or fingers?"

Between my spread thighs, I could see him working his dick while he licked and tasted my sex. All I'd need was a flick of his tongue to my clit. A plunge of his fingers in the right place.

But I wanted that cock. I told him so.

"Say please," he said, standing again.

"Yes, my king, fuck me again with your cock. *Please.*"

He slammed into me, reaching around and applying pressure to my clit. With a loud cry of pleasure, I tore apart at the seams. My arms lost their strength, and I pitched forward, face first into the bed.

He wrapped his arms around me immediately and hauled me back up, keeping me off my front.

"Careful now," he said, his voice so soft. It was such a fast change from a moment before. "Let's not put too much pressure on our baby's home, hmm?"

He pulled up my leg by the knee, bracing my foot against the wooden frame of the bed. He threaded himself back into me, wet and sloppy. So fucking hot.

"Let's get you another one right like this." He held me with one hand and worked my clit with the other, thrusting again, hard and fast. Half delirious, wondering why the fuck I'd incensed him earlier when I no longer had the heat to buffer me, I fell into the sensations. I fell into the magnificent friction. His arm held me tight. His fingers worked me just right. My heart was full, and my body was burning, and I did what he said. I kept going and hit another high. Then again in another position, keyed up as he shook and shuddered behind me, following my command and filling me up. Over and over.

Toward the end, he pushed me forward and helped me crawl across the bed, taking me to my side before using our releases as a lubricant to push up into my ass. His fingers on my clit and his mouth on my scales turned the painful slide into an erotic ache. He took his pleasure as I groaned against him. The world dropped away until it was just the two of us, our bodies tangled together and our pleasure spiraling.

He could've gone all night if I'd let him. The heat was well and truly over, having done its job, but I'd challenged him. There was one thing you didn't do to an alpha dragon unless you planned to see it through.

Just after midnight, after hours of orgasms coming hard and fast, I had to call it. I had to give in. I didn't even mind that he'd won that round. Eyes droopy, I drifted into sleep wrapped in his arms, ignoring the smugness coming through the bond.

If I'd known what the night would bring, I never would have challenged him.

CHAPTER 40
FINLEY

THE SCREAM TORE me out of sleep. I sat up with a gasp, ripping myself out of Nyfain's grip. The sound had been so faint that Nyfain hadn't stirred. But it wasn't just the sound that had awoken me. Some things couldn't be explained, and the feeling of a family member in danger was one of those things.

I knew without a doubt it had been Sable's scream.

In a moment I had my dagger from the nightstand and was running toward the door. That was when more sounds filtered in. A yell. A bang. Something was happening.

"What is—"

Nyfain cut off, probably hearing it too.

I grabbed the door handle and yanked it open as Nyfain's footsteps pounded after me.

"Finley, wait," he said, but the door was already swinging open.

The hall was filled with movement.

"Oh shit," I said, pausing for one moment.

I didn't take time to make sense of it.

Instead, I launched forward, everything slowing down in my mind's eye as adrenaline dumped into me.

Down the way, Hadriel turned slowly, too slowly, as though someone controlled him. His hands were at his sides. He tilted his head back to watch a demon raise a large, curved sword over his head.

Sex demons. Fuck! We'd been expecting a faerie attacker working for the demons, not the kind of demons that could control minds.

"No!" I yelled, running faster, trying to get there in time.

The sword hit its zenith and then sliced through the air.

I tried to use will, but they were too far away.

The demon burst forward, his back arching and head snapping back as two large, dark-skinned arms wrapped around his chest. The fingers on the sword hilt didn't release, but Vemar barreled the demon past Hadriel and to the floor in a vicious tackle. And then Vemar's movements slowed. Turned gooey and jerky, as though he was no longer in charge of his limbs.

Vemar rolled off, as placid as a lamb. The demon pushed up, dragging his sword off the ground.

He should've glanced up.

I reached him and kicked his hand off the sword. Bending quickly, I slammed my blade into the back of his neck and wrenched.

Nyfain reached me and then jumped in front.

"Wait for your guard," he yelled as he kept running, roaring as he reached a demon grabbing Govam by the back of his shirt. He launched the demon into the air, hard enough to crack his head on the arched ceiling above. The demon fell to the ground, limp.

I yanked my blade out and followed. He shoved his way past a fighting demon, knocking it against the wall. Denski was there a moment later, stabbing it through.

Govam caught up with me and yelled over the din as Nyfain reached more fighting.

"Incubi and succubi tried to sneak in," he said. "Their goal was to get to you and the golden dragon, I have zero doubt. They didn't mess with anyone else until Sonassa felt them and sounded the alarm. They must not have known we were with you."

"That's good news. Dolion might have informants, but they can't be too high up. The king wanted to be discreet about you guys. Where are the rest of the demons?"

"I told them to get into the room and lock the door so that they wouldn't be mistaken as the enemy. I was confident Denski and I were known enough not to be in danger."

I stalled when I saw Hannon in the doorway of the suite he shared with Father and our siblings. He nodded when he saw me.

"They're okay," he said. "Sable was headed to the restroom when she heard the commotion. She poked her head out and screamed before slamming the door and locking it behind her. No one has tried to come in, but I've been waiting out here just in case."

"Stay with them," I said as I kept going.

A demon's body lay on the ground with its arm bent

at an unnatural angle. More followed, the halls littered with bodies. Not only the demons had fallen. A wolf and a dragon were among the dead.

"Damn it," I said under my breath as Tamara ran around the corner up ahead.

"Your highness!" Blood had spattered her neck and cheek. She held a dripping sword. "Thank the goddess you're okay."

Lucille and Jade ran closely behind her, in a similar state.

Tamara's gaze zipped back and forth between Denski and Govam, then she looked behind us. Hadriel and Vemar were jogging our way, their eyes cleared of the daze.

"They closed us off from getting to you," she said, trying to catch her breath. "Even with the extra guards the king stationed with us. The faerie guard showed up, though, and helped us push through."

"How many are there?" I jogged around the corner, seeing a flurry of activity.

Our people fought in nightclothes, in the buff, or as wolves. Demons tried to cut through them, but it seemed their objective had changed. They weren't trying to get to our rooms anymore—they were trying to get away. Nyfain descended on them with a sword he'd clearly gotten from one of the bodies we stepped over. He cleaved his way through the mass with Weston in wolf form at his side. More battling dragons were ahead of him, and down the way, I could make out guards in white, cutting and slashing their shining swords, taking down anyone they could.

"There's more than just succubi and incubi," Govam said in a low tone. "Dolion really wants you two dead. He must think the threat to him will die with you."

"He wouldn't be far wrong," I said, reminded of what Calia had said.

A few demons broke through the line and ran like hell for the stairs. The faerie guards were after them immediately, trying to catch up.

"Shit! Calia! We need to make sure they haven't gone after her." I increased the pace of my jog, but Tamara shoved her arm in front of me.

"We need to wait for this to clear. The last thing you need is a surprise knife to the gut. You might live through it, but we don't want to risk the baby."

I gritted my teeth, knowing she was right but feeling like dead weight anyway.

We followed the crowd, the demons racing from our people, only to crash up against the faeries. More and more of them broke through, though, running madly. Wolves went after them, faster on four legs than anyone's two.

"Finley, you're okay," Hadriel said, breathing hard as he pushed his way to our side. "Fucking demons. Don't they take a break? First the poison, now this?"

Nyfain slowed as the last of the demons broke and ran for the stairs, quickly followed by the wolves. He turned back for me, quickly checking me over.

"Calia," I said as I caught up to him.

"Let's go check it out. Stay with me," he said, grabbing my arm. "Be careful."

I held out my free hand. "I haven't joined the fight,

have I?"

His lips twisted into a smile at my irritation. He nodded and hurried us the rest of the way down the hall, pausing at the wide stairway to make sure the danger had moved off.

"What do you make of this, Govam?" Nyfain said as we made our way down.

Govam told him what he'd told me earlier.

"He will try again," he finished. "If he is putting this much effort into killing you, he'll keep trying."

"How?"

"I can't say for certain. My guess would be more of the same—sneaking. Using the succubi to slip in, or some of his stealthier spies."

"I'm surprised he's being so open about trespassing on King Starvos's territory," I said as we hurried across a large foyer.

"It seems King Starvos has been diligent about staying neutral," Nyfain replied as Leala ran out of a large arched entranceway in a nightdress, whip in hand. A line of guards emerged a moment later, slowing when they saw Govam and Denski.

Nyfain held up his hand. "They're with us. I'm monitoring them personally."

"Oh good, you're safe," Leala said on a release of breath as the guards passed us, not picking up the pace quite yet.

"Where the fuck were you?" Hadriel asked.

"I was being spanked by a couple of the servants when I heard what was going on," she replied.

"Well, you nearly missed me getting my head

chopped off. Vemar had to save me, and now I'll sound like a real asshole if I tell him not to call me little buddy."

"I don't get your logic, but I like the outcome," Vemar said with a chuckle. "I had to get saved too, though. It's all good."

I shook my head, ignoring the others. "What do you mean, he likes to stay neutral? Surely this warrants a reaction?"

"If Dolion hadn't already imprisoned and then tried to poison his favorite court member, he'd likely have been appeased by a grand gesture, like an apology and compensation," Nyfain said. "He wouldn't think about going to war. Dolion came after us, not his people. When they realized the faerie guards were getting involved, the demons tried to take off. They were likely under orders to do just that."

"That would be my guess, though they could just as easily be cowards," Govam said.

"Fortunately for us, Dolion *did* imprison Starvos's favorite court member, and he also—indirectly—almost killed her. Hopefully that works in our favor."

"Dolion is usually good about knowing which lines he shouldn't cross," Govam said as we reached another set of stairs and jogged up. Servants ran around in chaos the closer we got to Calia's area. Nyfain sped up, wariness rolling through the bond. When we made it to Calia's suite, though, we found a line of guards waiting in front.

"King Nyfain!"

Starvos's voice cracked through the air.

We turned to see him striding down the hall wearing

pants and an untucked shirt.

"Leala, find us clothes," Nyfain murmured.

"Here, take mine for now, milady." Leala shed her nightdress. "Vemar, give his highness your clothes. You're the only one close to his size."

Calia's door opened and she peered out, her expression screwed up in worry.

"What is the meaning of this?" Starvos asked as he got closer. "I have reports of fighting and bloodshed in the guest wing."

"Demons attacked us while we were sleeping," Nyfain answered. "It looked like they meant to finish the job they'd attempted at dinner."

"Demons? Here? Preposterous. King Dolion wouldn't send demons here."

"You're welcome to go see for yourself." Nyfain gestured back the way we'd come. "We killed plenty of them. We've come to make sure Calia is safe." Vemar handed over his pants, and Nyfain stepped into them.

"Goddess comfort me, what has happened to you, man?" Starvos asked Nyfain.

"Protecting my kingdom came at a price. Every night, I fought off demon creatures intent on killing my people. And as you've seen…" He turned me around before I could get Leala's nightdress on. His fingers trailed across my back. "This was done by Dolion's minions. I'm sure you've also seen Calia's back. You've yet to hear all the stories, but I warned you what sort they would be. Dolion wants me dead because he knows how dangerous I am to him. He knows that I can give an accurate picture of his dealings. I am living proof of his misdeeds. You'll either need to send us on our way or get serious about protecting the castle. He's tried to kill us twice without being successful. He'll keep trying."

Starvos blustered as I pulled on my nightdress. "I've never heard of such a thing. He's a known menace, but no one's ever spoken of him going this far."

"Hard to tattle when you're dead." Nyfain glanced at Calia. "You good? Did anyone try to come this way?"

"No, sire," said one of the guards in front of her.

"I set them to watch her after dinner," Starvos said.

"If they see the demons coming, they'll do great." I finally pulled the dressing gown over my head. "But if sex demons get too close, the guards won't be much good. Calia knows all about that."

"Yes, sire, she's right," Calia said.

"I can mix an elixir tomorrow to protect them against the sex demons," I went on. "I don't have enough everlass to make it for the whole castle, though. Not yet. You'll need to pick and choose which of them you'd like to oversee the rest."

Starvos shook his head. "This is preposterous. You act like we're under attack."

Nyfain pointed at the guards protecting Calia. He didn't comment, though. We could both see that Starvos was in denial.

Nyfain put his hand on my back and guided me toward the stairs.

"Thanks for checking on me," Calia called, stepping out of the door.

I put up my hand to her as she turned to face her king.

"The demon king might switch his efforts from them to me," I heard her say. "He might act like he follows the rules of the magical world, but it's just that: an act. I tried to tell you that. Now you see."

"We'll talk about this in the morning," Starvos said right before we were out of earshot.

"We stay together from now on," Nyfain told me as we descended the stairs. More servants were running around, frightened looks on their faces. "We have another three weeks here before we all go to the council. We'll need to be vigilant."

THE NEXT DAY, Nyfain came with me to the gardens, our guard and my family fanning out behind us. This time a few of the demons came, too. Sonassa trailed behind us, guarding our rear, and Govam and Denski flanked us. The rest stayed back at the castle.

We had faerie guards, Starvos not trusting the demons, or maybe us. He was not having an easy time reconciling the fact that demons had barged into his castle to attack his guests.

"Son, Queen Finley," Arleth said by way of greeting, her gaze lingering on my belly. "That could've been a close call last night if those demons had reached you."

"Their magic doesn't work on me," I told her, pointing at Vemar and then at the patch of everlass. "Vemar, grab some other strong dragons and sit here, will ya? I need to get more plants growing as quickly as possible."

"It doesn't work on me, either," Nyfain said, stepping in amongst the plants. "I would've woken up before they reached us."

"Still." Arleth shook her head. "The council meeting can't come soon enough."

"Nyfain, I need you and my sister to sing to the plants, okay?" I said. "Make them grow big and strong. I'll get busy making that elixir, and then I'd better find something more challenging to focus on."

"Hey." Nyfain pulled me closer, his golden eyes trapping mine. "We're going to be okay. I won't let anything happen to you two."

I gave him a small smile before leaning into his warmth and security. "I know. But I'm high-strung. I need to keep busy."

He kissed me softly. "Just as long as you aren't worrying. It's not good—"

"Do not tell me that it's not good for the baby. Our kid will need to be tough to deal with us. They might as well start now."

"It's not good for *you*."

"Or the baby," Arleth called.

I sighed in annoyance and headed toward the tent. Hannon followed me, carrying a couple of items I needed that didn't grow in this garden.

"Sable, sing with Nyfain," I instructed as I made my way.

"Okay, *bossy*, sheesh," Sable muttered.

NOTHING OF SIGNIFICANCE happened for the rest of the week. We worked the plants and took meetings with Starvos, telling him more about life in the demon castle. It pained him to learn what had happened to his people, and I wondered why Calia hadn't shared more about her experiences previously. Then again, she hadn't hung around long enough to really get into it. And maybe she simply hadn't wanted to.

When nothing happened, and nothing continued to happen, I started wondering if Dolion had realized he'd crossed a line. Maybe he was planning on taking this up politically instead of attempting to murder us again.

I should've known better.

This time, though, when he came for us, he made it personal.

CHAPTER 41
FINLEY

A LOUD RAP sounded at the outer door of our suite. Leala paused in what she was doing by my dressing table, looking over at me with a lifted eyebrow. She was asking if I was expecting anyone.

I lay curled up between Nyfain's legs on a settee pushed back from the window, leaning on his chest with a book in my hands. He held a book as well, his arms draped around me and his chin pressed to my temple. It was a quiet reprieve after a long day of politics, working on my elixirs, and a raucous dinner to which only the very high court members had been invited. Everyone had really let down their hair. If only Hadriel had been allowed to go—he would've delighted in the dirty jokes. Turned out these faeries weren't so prim and proper behind closed doors, especially not when plied with wine.

I tilted my head back to Nyfain as the knocking sounded again, fast raps that would've sounded urgent if they weren't so light.

"Not me," he murmured.

Leala looked to the right, where Urien was probably standing, out of sight from our position. She nodded, adjusted her holster on her hip, and walked away, presumably to answer the door.

"Finley!" Sable came rushing into the room with tight eyes and an air of panic.

I sat up, dropping my book slowly. "What's up? Are you okay?"

"No. I don't know." She twisted her fingers together, and a thrill of unease pushed through the bond. "Dash left one of his little figurines at the garden tent earlier today. He insisted he needed it for his bath. You know how he gets. We just *knew* he'd sneak out to look for it."

I snapped the book closed and stood. "Where is he?"

"He's with Dad. He didn't go out. Hannon said he'd get it after dinner. So we ate our dinner with all the other unimportant people"—she gave me a *look*—"and listened to a little music, then went back to our room. Hannon went out to find the toy."

"Okay…so what's the problem? Is Hannon not back yet?"

"No! That's just it." Her expression crumpled. "We thought maybe he just couldn't find it. And maybe he can't. Dash seemed positive about the location, but you know him. He says it's in one room and it's really in another and—"

"Sable, how long has he been gone?" I grabbed a sweater off a chair back.

"Maybe he's still looking! Hannon wouldn't leave until he found it, you know? He—"

555

"Sable!" I barked. "How long?"

She glanced at the darkened windows. "A couple of hours."

"*A couple of hours?* And you didn't think to come before now?" I snatched my dagger off the nightstand.

Your dagger, really? my dragon thought, power starting to pump through my veins. *You're planning to take a knife to a teeth-and-claws fight?*

I let out an exasperated sound before putting it back and starting to strip.

"What should I do, milady?" Leala asked.

"I'll go." Nyfain jogged into the other room. "I'll go look. You stay here."

"You think I am going to sit here while my brother is out there somewhere? You're out of your fucking mind, Nyfain." I pushed down my loose pajama pants and said to Leala, "Go tell Hadriel. Tell him to put everyone on alert. It might be nothing. But if it isn't…"

She nodded and ran out of the door. She knew better than to use decorum in a possible emergency.

"The guards haven't sounded any alarms," Nyfain said, walking back in in his robe. "Starvos has them positioned all around the castle and in the grounds. If there was something out there, they would've blown the trumpet."

I was about to mention that demons could've just slit Hannon's throat in the darkness or whisked him away, but Sable was hanging on to our every word.

"True." I pointed past her. "Sable, go back to Father. Lock your doors, just in case. Wait for us, okay? It's probably fine. Hannon is probably still looking, like you said, or is chatting with a pretty faerie and the time got away from him."

Her brow furrowed, but she didn't give me the *ew* response she'd usually roll out for a comment like that. Instead, she swallowed and nodded.

"Okay," she said. "Make sure he is okay, Finley. We lost Mom. We can't lose him too."

"I know. I will. I promise."

She sprinted out of the room, and I looked at Nyfain, worry starting to curl through my gut.

"He's fine," Nyfain said, grabbing my robe and coming toward me. "I meant what I said about the guards. Starvos won't let a breach of his territory happen again."

I laughed. "Starvos isn't used to dealing with the demon king. Or anyone attacking him, really. What is that for?"

Nyfain paused with the robe held out. "To get us through the castle."

I shook my head and turned toward the window. I opened it, getting a blast of frigid air.

Ready? I asked my dragon as Nyfain said, "Finley, wait—"

Go, my dragon replied.

I stepped up into the window frame and then launched out, spreading my arms wide for reasons unknown. My dragon surged and took over, pumping her wings immediately after coming into her body. We soared up into the sky, slowing so that Nyfain could catch up. It only took him a moment. He wasn't about to go through the castle when I was already in the air.

Go the direction Hannon would've walked, I said,

pushing up close to the surface of my dragon's consciousness, watching the ground.

Guards dressed in white looked up as we passed. There were thick clusters around the actual castle, but their ranks thinned out the farther away we got. Only one walked the path we usually took to the gardens, and a sole guard idled in the gardens themselves, staring out at nothing. He or she glanced up as my dragon sailed over, swooping low and searching the ground for Hannon. In a moment, though, it became clear he wasn't there.

My dragon landed near the guard who'd turned to face us. I took over, resuming my human form and walking toward him as Nyfain continued to circle above.

"Have you seen my brother?" I asked the guard as I got closer. "He's the tall and kinda robust ginger? A couple years older than me? Real calm. Always very pleasant. Have you seen—"

The smell hit me first. The funk. And then the guard's skin changed, turning a little darker and then greenish. The creature smiled.

"Yes, I saw him. If you hurry, maybe you can save him. You'll need to offer yourself in his—"

I was on him in a moment, wrapping my arm around his neck and leaning back so that his suddenly flailing arms couldn't reach me behind him.

"Where is he?" I demanded as Nyfain sent up a mighty roar before landing not far from us. He was in his human form quickly and running our way. "*Where is he?*"

"Back in the forest, toward the water," the demon

wheezed, scratching at my arm now, trying to free his neck. "Go alone if you want him to live."

Rage washed through me as another dragon sailed overhead. Vemar. Then more, Tamara and the rest of my guard. Micah followed them.

"Oops. Too late," the demon said before starting to cackle.

I released him, but only so I could grab his face in my hands and twist. His neck snapped, and he slid to the ground at my feet as I turned around. Rage and power still pumped through me…but also terror. Fire curled across my skin.

"You heard him. I'm supposed to go alone," I told Nyfain, pushing back so that I could shift.

"You're going to believe a demon?" Nyfain shook his head. "Their goal will be to kill him regardless. The best we can do is try to pry him from their hands."

Wolves ran out of the bushes all around us, Weston in the lead. He'd been moving into position to surround a possible enemy. He jogged closer and then slowed, waiting. He'd heard the situation and stood ready.

"Fuck!" I said, the terror making me wobble. It felt like I couldn't get enough air. "Goddess help me, don't let them hurt Hannon," I said as I pulled my dragon to the surface.

They couldn't hurt him. They *couldn't*. Not kind and gentle Hannon. Not the backbone that had held our family together after Father got sick. All he'd ever tried to do was help others. He didn't deserve this. He didn't deserve to be in danger.

My dragon rose into the air as Nyfain's did, cutting

across the sky in the direction the demon had indicated. That could've been a lie too, for all we knew, but what other choice did we have?

Our heart thumped against our ribs as we flew, leaving the castle grounds behind. The trees condensed the further away we got, but nothing moved within them. We flew slowly so the wolves could keep up, silent shadows running below and behind us. We didn't see anything, and neither did they. All was silent.

Fuck, what if that demon was trying to draw us away? I thought, my dragon scanning the ground. *What if their goal is to storm the castle?*

They are definitely trying to draw us away, but not to storm the castle. We're the ones they want. They want to get us away from the king's guards, and they found the pressure point with which to do it. They found Hannon.

All this time they'd probably been waiting patiently for an opportunity, and Hannon had provided it to them. Dolion was no fool—he'd know I would sacrifice everything for someone I loved. I'd done it for Nyfain, after all.

A plethora of emotion pushed through the bond, and then I saw what Nyfain had.

Oh goddess please, no!

Adrenaline roared through me. Then came power. My mind went blank, and my dragon's vision tinged red.

Up ahead was a large clearing at the top of a little hill. Horrible creatures like the ones that used to grace the Royal Wood were tied to the surrounding trees. Their horrible, twisted jaws dribbled saliva as they pulled at their tethers, intent on the human offering in the middle.

Hannon.

He stood straight, his arms pulled behind him and secured around a thick wood post. Blood leaked from a gash down the side of his face and wet his white shirt near the breast. Another wound had soaked the pant leg on the right. The monsters growled and chomped at the air, desperate to get at him.

Despite all that, he stood perfectly still, his shoulders relaxed and his demeanor easy. Even now, in the middle of bloodthirsty monsters secured with simple rope, he was calm in the face of the storm. He didn't seem overly troubled. Resigned, more like. Sad, maybe, that it had come to this.

My heart broke.

They'd been waiting for us. They'd wanted us to watch him die.

Nyfain was right: they weren't looking to make a trade. How stupid that notion had been. They were offering up my brother as a lure, knowing we would try to save him, giving them a chance to kill us in the process. If he died, it would be solely because of me.

Get to him. Quickly.

One of the ropes snapped. The monster lurched forward with a snarl. Then another rope whipped in the air. And another.

No, they weren't snapping. They were being cut.

Demons must be lurking in the trees, out of sight. They'd seen us coming and were springing the trap to get us down there faster.

No, please! I begged the goddess, or maybe my dragon, or maybe the old gods from the legends. *No!*

The creatures rushed forward, all of them loose now, running toward Hannon in the middle of the circle.

Hurry, help him! I thought-yelled.

Heat rose from down deep. It rushed through our middle and up, scorching out through our mouth and nose. My dragon dove, shoving past Nyfain, who was trying to cut us off from the fray. Fire erupted from my dragon's mouth, blasting the ground. I would've been shocked as shit if the situation wasn't so dire.

Kill them all, I thought as she directed the thick stream around him. Two creatures screamed and wailed, humanlike sounds, before curling up within the flame. The rest were untroubled, though. They were not susceptible to fire.

Damn it! I thought, my terror as elevated as my rage. *Get down there.*

She let the heat consume her middle once again and spouted fire onto the ground on the other side of Hannon, taking out what creatures she could before diving fast to the ground. Once there, she banked quickly, plucking a creature off the ground and crunching its middle.

Hurry! I shouted within her head, seeing two creatures get in front of the pack, each nearly at Hannon. *Hurry!*

She swung her tail as Nyfain's dragon landed on the other side. He darted forward to grab one of the creatures in the lead, but another got in the way. He crunched through that one, ripping its head to the side before trying for its friend.

My dragon grabbed another as a scrape ripped down our side. She roared, fury riding her, and turned to clear a wide area with her tail.

Don't worry about that—we'll heal, I told her, anxious because she'd turned, and I couldn't see Hannon anymore. I couldn't see how much time he had.

The wolves rushed into the scene, but they were smaller than the demons' creatures and unused to fighting them. They teamed up against those on the periphery. They wouldn't be able to get to my brother in time.

My dragon turned toward the apex of the hill, and our heart jumped up into our throat. Her roar was desperate, chorused by Nyfain. One of the creatures had reached Hannon, its massive claws coming up to strike.

Hannon was looking at me with a sad smile on his face. His expression held no fear.

The creature's claws came down and raked across his throat.

No! I screamed, my ears suddenly ringing even though they weren't actually my ears. My dragon's roar of anguish drowned out the rest of the fighting. It slowed everyone, making the enemy freeze and the others flinch, wondering what had happened.

Nyfain snatched the creature he'd been after, crushing it between his teeth and dropping it to the side, and then jolted forward to get at Hannon.

Hannon's neck had been opened in a huge gash, blood gushing down his front. He jerked on the post, still held tight, unable to protect himself or do anything to retaliate. The creature's second strike landed as my dragon shoved her way forward. It sliced across his middle, making his insides bubble out.

Oh goddess, no. Oh please no, I thought, suddenly numb, not willing to believe what my eyes were telling me.

Nyfain reached the creature and pounced, ripping off lumps of flesh and scoring its body with his claws as the wolves fought the other creatures around us. More demons charged in with swords and knives, slashing and ripping.

Fire rained down around us from the dragons in the air, but when it didn't affect the creatures, the dragons landed amongst the wolves and fought on the ground.

I didn't care about any of it. I couldn't.

Pain welled up through me as my dragon reached Hannon, and I surged up to take over. Nyfain roared in frustration when I changed into my human shape, but I didn't care. I went to Hannon with shaking hands, untying him as quickly as possible.

"Goddess help us," I heard, and then Hadriel was there, nude and freshly shifted. "No, please, no," he said, and in his voice I heard his heart breaking just like mine.

"I can fix this," I said, cutting the ropes and catching Hannon as he fell. "I can fix this."

Hannon gargled, trying to speak.

"No, Hannon, don't talk. Save your strength. I can fix this!" Tears poured down my face. "Please, goddess, help me fix this!"

"I'll hold him, Finley," Hadriel said, his hand pushed to Hannon's middle to keep his insides put. "I'll hold him. Carry us to the tent."

"No. I can't. What if—"

"Carry us both, damn it," he shouted, taking a bloody Hannon into his arms. "You can do it. You *have* to do it. He won't survive if you don't."

"Okay," I said, stepping back to make room. "Okay."

A creature charged me, but I didn't even flinch. I kept backing up as Nyfain burst forward, crashing into the enemy and killing it in no time. He'd said he would protect me. I'd taken him at his word.

My dragon pushed to the surface and took over, filling the space and then delicately reaching down with her mouth open. Hadriel tucked himself and Hannon in, one hand on Hannon's middle, the other on his neck. There was blood everywhere, all down Hannon's clothes, dripping onto the ground, dripping into our mouth.

I can fix this, I thought, willing it to be true. *He's a shifter even if he's never shifted. He's strong. He might not heal quickly, but he's strong. He'll hang on. He knows he has to hang on, for our sakes if not his own.*

My dragon didn't comment, focused on keeping her mouth soft. She wouldn't have really cared if she'd accidentally killed that woman, but this was different. This was Hannon and Hadriel. She couldn't mess up. She couldn't afford to have an oops.

Even still, she flew faster than she ever had in her life. She pushed hard, cutting through the sky, keeping low so it wouldn't take as long to land. Once in the garden, she touched down next to the body of the demon dressed as a guard, which appeared undisturbed, and gently lowered Hadriel to the ground.

"Hurry, Finley," Hadriel said, cradling Hannon.

"He's not moving. His pulse is so faint…"

I shifted back. "It's okay." I sprinted to the tent. "Fuck, the fucking water isn't hot. It's fine. This is fine. I've been nearly dead a million times. I always came back. He can come back."

I heard wings as I made room on the worktable right near the fire pit.

"Finley."

It was Vemar. The guy could always be counted on to show up in a bind and save the day.

He had to save the day if I couldn't.

"Vemar, hurry!" I put kindling onto the mostly cold coals before stirring things around to spark it up a bit.

"What do you need, Strange Lady?" he said, jogging into the tent.

"Build up this fire. Quick as you can. I need hot water."

He took one look at the coals and said, "Fuck that. I'll fly back to the castle. I'll be back in two shakes."

"Don't get killed by a demon," I yelled after him. "Some of them are dressed as guards."

"Do I look that stupid?" And he shifted and took to the sky.

Moving my hands fast but not enough so to make mistakes, taking deep breaths as often as I could think of it, I moved around the table I'd come to know.

"How're we doing?" I yelled out, putting the ingredients I needed into a mortar and grabbing the pestle.

When I didn't hear a response, I yelled again.

"Hadriel? How is he doing? Tell him to hold on!"

Still no answer. My heart was beating too quickly.

Sweat coated my forehead.

"Good enough," I muttered, stepping out to look for Vemar. I noticed wings in the sky immediately, coming this way. I turned toward Hannon, and then my whole world drained of color.

A weight filled my chest as I jogged over, finding Hadriel curled up around him, rocking back and forth. Hannon's head hung back awkwardly. His hands were splayed out to the sides, limp.

"He just needs a heartbeat," I said as I fell down next to them, grabbing his wrist. No pulse. "Damn it, Hadriel, get out of the way!"

I tore Hadriel off him, ignoring his racking sobs and the wide tracks of tears down his cheeks. Trying to remember to breathe, trying to be as good at this as Hannon, I quickly laid him out. His neck was gaping, no longer bleeding. I could see his insides through the gashes in his stomach.

"Oh goddess, Hannon, oh..." I shook my head as wind from Vemar's wings washed over me. He dropped a shining metal canister to the ground before landing and shifting. "Come on, Hannon. Don't give up yet. Don't give—"

I pushed on his chest in the correct rhythm, then breathed into his mouth. Back to his chest.

"Vemar," I yelled, before breathing for Hannon again. "Vemar!"

"I'm here." He ran and slid to the ground on the other side of Hannon. "I'm here. Oh fu—What do you need?"

"Do you know how to—"

"Yes, yes. Go make the potion. The magical worker is coming. She can probably help, right? She can help."

"Yes, thank you. He needs a pulse. Just keep him alive, Vemar. Keep him alive."

Hadriel had curled up into himself, covered in blood. Leala sprinted down the path and toward us. Behind her ran some of the gardeners. The magical worker wasn't as spry. She'd take a little longer.

"It's fine," I said, running back into the tent, scooping up the canister as I did so. "This is fine. He'll be okay. We have time."

Remember to breathe, my dragon thought softly. Sadness welled within her.

"He'll be fine," I yelled at her, knowing what her feelings meant. Knowing what I'd seen.

I couldn't believe it. Not yet. I had to try to save him. I had to do something!

I opened the canister with shaking hands. Steam issued from within it. I poured the water into the mortar and then swore at myself. I needed it in a fucking mug.

Mug in hand, I poured the contents of the mortar into it and rushed out as the gardeners and other faeries reached us.

"Can we help?" the first asked, and I was surprised to see it was Eris.

"I need the magical worker. I'm not sure what she can do, but…" I hurried just as fast as I could without spilling the contents. "If you have any lifesaving remedies, I'm happy to try them."

"She's on her way. We'll get what we have."

Vemar kept up a steady pace, the sweat on his brow

catching the light. He breathed into Hannon's mouth and then went back to his chest, eyeing me for directions. Leala sat at his head, watching, likely ready to jump in if she needed to.

I felt for a pulse. Nothing.

"Fuck, Hannon, come on." I pushed in close. "Lift him up, Leala. He needs to drink this. We just need to get it down his throat."

"He's not bleeding anymore, love," Hadriel said so quietly I almost couldn't hear him.

I wished I hadn't heard him.

"It's okay. The everlass will help him." I tried not to look at the deep red bloodstains down his front. His gaping neck. "Oh, Hannon," I said through a tight throat, putting the lip of the mug to his mouth. "Oh, Hannon, please."

The liquid, too hot, dribbled in and then down. Some flowed over. He didn't gag. He didn't fight for breath.

He's not unconscious, my dragon thought delicately.

He was not unconscious. He was dead. That was what she was saying.

Tears blurred my vision. I couldn't stand to think that. I couldn't allow myself to think it.

"Where's that magical worker?" I hollered, feeding him more, then pausing for Vemar to breathe into his mouth. Then more.

I stared at Hannon's white face. I waited for a sign that the elixir would help him cling to life. That was all I needed. I just needed him to cling to life. If he did that, I could save him, I knew I could.

Guards ran into the space, forming a large circle around the garden.

"You're too fucking late, assholes," I ground out, still staring at Hannon, looking for some sign of life. "Hadriel, get up and make sure none of those guards are demons. Do it in wolf form."

Hadriel didn't say a word, moving slowly.

"Go!" I barked, power infusing my words, tears dripping from my chin.

"Here." One of the faeries knelt beside me. I recognized her from the other tent. She held out a syringe. "This is the strongest medicine we have. It is designed to magically kick-start the heart. If you get the heart working, we have a chance."

I took it immediately, my hand shaking. I wasn't good at this. Hannon was always in charge of this part.

Sobs racked my body.

"In his vein?" I asked with a trembling voice.

"Yes."

I nodded and attempted to see through watery eyes. After a deep breath, I found the vein and injected the potion or whatever it was. Then waited.

"How long should it take?" I asked as more wings beat at the sky.

"If nothing happens after two minutes, it hasn't worked," she said quietly.

"Do you want me to jump in?" Leala asked Vemar as he started pumping Hannon's chest again.

"No, it's okay. I've got it."

The wait was agonizing. I kept my fingers on his wrist, feeling for a pulse, hoping it worked. *Needing* it to work.

Dragons landed all around us, shifting back into human form. Wolves raced into the area. I didn't look at any of them, so intent was I on watching Hannon, feeling for signs of life.

The hand on my shoulder undid me.

"Time's up," the woman said softly, so softly I didn't think I heard her properly.

"A few more minutes," I said, clutching Hannon harder. "Just a few more minutes."

Leala lowered his head and sat back, softly crying. She folded her hands into her lap.

Vemar looked up at me. "I can keep going, Finley, if you want. I can go as long as you want. Tell me what you need."

He wasn't asking what Hannon needed—he was asking what *I* needed. He was asking how he could ease the blow of my brother dying.

CHAPTER 42
NYFAIN

"CAN I DO anything, alpha?" Weston asked as I watched Finley huddle with her family.

The faerie guard circled our small encampment, moved from the garden area to a place where they prepared the dead for their transition to the afterlife. Hannon was inside a small wooden house-like structure, lying on a wooden slat covered in white satin and flowers. The faeries were washing away the blood and stitching him up before they dressed him in such a way that his family could see him without being pummeled with the evidence of his gruesome death.

I wanted to turn away. I wanted to rage and take to the sky and bluster and blow. I wanted to declare war against Dolion right then and there, or at least have a do-over of that battle so we could kill them all a second time.

I didn't want to lose another dragon and three wolves, though. Hannon hadn't been the only casualty.

"See to your wolves. Make sure they are looked after," I told Weston, glancing at the other little houses. I'd already visited the others' lifeless forms and given condolences to the men and women who'd bravely fought beside them.

Fucking Dolion.

Fucking Starvos for not taking this threat seriously. Though I supposed he wasn't to blame. He had the castle locked down tight. People knew not to wander far at night with the current threat looming. Hannon had just been in the wrong place at the wrong time without any protection.

I turned away, drowning within the grief and sorrow coming through the bond.

"I'm sorry about this," Calia said as she walked closer. Her sister followed behind her with a wary expression, probably awkward around strangers and emotion. "I am so, so sorry. Hannon was well loved."

"He was, and for good reason." I watched Mom approach Finley and her family with a special tea that would help them relax.

"The king is taking this hard." She braced her hands on her hips, looking at the little houses, then shifted her attention to Finley and her family. "I know that doesn't mean much to you now. He is not a man who takes well to failure. There wasn't just one guard out here. There were five, and all were killed. He knows it could've been far worse for him if the demons hadn't drawn you away."

Starvos hadn't expressed any of that. He'd come to offer his condolences and apologize, but then he'd left us to our grief. I told her that.

"He hasn't been transparent. He wasn't a great fan of

your father and wasn't entirely sure about you. He definitely didn't want to take on the demons if he could help it. But this... The demon king underestimated how far he can push the king."

"Or else he was taking necessary risks."

"Or maybe that."

Although Finley got her family to take the tea, she refused it for herself. Sable objected, but her father pulled her in for a tight hug to squash her outrage. My mother pushed the tea on Finley again, trying to get her to take it.

"Are you going to help Arleth?" Calia asked, watching the scene.

I shook my head. "Finley won't listen to me any more than she'll listen to my mother or anyone else. She was incredibly close to Hannon. They helped each other through hard times. She won't want to wash away the pain. She'll think she needs to feel it—"

I cut off my words and looked away, getting choked up.

"Why?" she asked softly as Finley finally took the mug, held eye contact with my mom, and then poured the contents out. She handed it back with a stony gaze.

"Because she feels guilty. She thinks she's to blame for what happened to her brother."

"That's ridiculous."

"Grief doesn't follow logic."

My mother finally relented, proving which of them was the most stubborn. She ushered the others back toward the castle. I knew she'd get them situated, offer them more tea if they needed it, and stay to comfort the little ones. It was what she did best. She'd had a lot of practice with me when I was a child.

"What should we do?" Dessia asked, the first time she'd ever spoken directly to me.

"You don't need to do anything. What's done is done."

I blinked quickly to wipe away the moisture in my eyes. Finley wasn't the only one who felt incredible guilt. I'd pushed Hannon to be a part of our government, hoping he'd protect his kingdom—*my* kingdom—the way he seemed hard-wired to protect his family. I'd insisted that he come on this journey, wanting him to see what other commodities were out there to buy and sell. I'd let him bring his family, knowing he'd want to look after them. It wasn't Finley who had instigated all of this—it was me. And then I'd left him vulnerable. I'd let him get taken and used against us. What kind of king did that make me? What kind of man?

"What *can* we do?" Dessia said more firmly, edging around her sister so that she could meet my eyes.

Finley watched her family go before staring at the little house that held Hannon. Guilt roiled through the bond in intense waves, meeting my own.

She'd told Sable that she'd make sure Hannon was okay. She'd promised.

She hadn't been able to save him, first physically, and then with her plants. She'd lost him as she'd lost her grandma and then her mom. The pain I felt from her was indescribable. I wondered if she was reliving the pain of losing all of them all over again.

"Just be there for her," I whispered, a tear slipping

out of my eye. I turned away again. "Be there for the grieving. Help them cope. Let them cry. It's all we can do."

In another moment, Finley was walking again, checking on the wounded and speaking to the faeries who worked with plants or potions. She nodded frequently but brushed aside what were probably condolences. She hugged the others who'd lost their friends and pack mates, and the dragons who'd lost a childhood friend.

Finally, when I could feel the weariness dragging on her, she made her way back to me, her eyes shining in the moonlight. Without a word, she folded herself into my arms and then let go, sobbing so hard she had to turn away to throw up. I didn't bother taking her back to the castle. She wouldn't want to go, anyway. I just found a soft tuft of grass and sat with her, holding her in my arms and rocking her. It was all I could do.

FINLEY

I'D LOST TRACK of how many hours I'd been crying. All night, I supposed. At some point I might have fallen asleep, because I saw Hannon's kind face, happy and healthy. He'd just finished his first ever woodworking project, a misshapen table that could barely hold a mug. He'd been so proud. As young as I was at the time, I'd recognized that. Now, grown and somewhat experienced, I understood he'd also felt a sense of accomplishment. Of achievement. He'd always loved pushing himself to learn something new and master it. In fact, he mastered so many tasks, big and large, that by the time the curse ended, I had taken all his amazing abilities for granted. It felt like I had, anyway. It felt like I'd stopped giving him the praise he so often deserved. That I'd forced him into my shadow and left him there, forgotten and alone. Ripe for the picking. All the demons had needed to do was wait and snatch him up.

"Hey, hey," Nyfain said, kissing my brow and rocking me softly. "What's happening?"

I started crying again. I wasn't sure when I'd stopped. Or maybe I'd just started crying harder.

"He could've been so much more," I said, my voice hoarse. "He could've had so much more. I held him back."

"You lifted your whole family up. Your father will tell you so."

"My father is bamboozled by the idea of royalty and the court. Hannon didn't care about all that stuff. He stayed around because of me. They all stick around because of me."

"Finley, they'd have to stick around regardless. They live in the kingdom you rule. Even so, we both know Hannon wouldn't have come if he didn't want to. He didn't do anything he didn't want to do. I witnessed him pushing you around. He wasn't all flowers and rainbows when he needed something done."

"He didn't want to die."

He rocked me harder as I buried my face in his shoulder.

"I let him die," I wailed, clutching his shirt and pulling so hard I ripped the seams. "Oh goddess help me, Nyfain, I *let him die*."

"There was nothing you could do," Nyfain said, his voice breaking, his own guilt coming through the bond. "*Shh, shh,* there was nothing you could do, sweetheart. Nothing any of us could do."

"He was innocent. He was the money man, for goddess's sake. He only fought to protect people. He shouldn't have been mixed up in this. He shouldn't have been the sacrificial lamb."

In my dreams, Hannon's face had changed in a blink to the man who'd grown up. The man who'd helped me through the darkest times of my life. All our lives. The man who'd been the bedrock of our family after our mother died, even before Father got sick. The man who had always, without fail and without needing thanks, put his family before himself. Always.

The pain was so incredible that I couldn't think through it. I couldn't get around it. I felt like I was suffocating within it, dragged down to a black place without a name. A place where only revenge mattered. A place that threatened to consume my very soul.

"Hey, hey, I'm here," Nyfain said, squeezing me tightly, still rocking me. "I'm right here."

I felt a comforting hand lower onto my shoulder, and then another. Calia and Dessia. They'd been here all night, not leaving my side. When I cried so hard I threw up, one of them wiped my face while Nyfain continued to hold me. The other held my hair. They'd watched the little wooden house with me in silence, lending support, certainly not because they harbored a slender hope, like I did, that Hannon might walk back out of it at any moment. As though this had all been a horrible prank and he wasn't gone forever.

Not far away, Hadriel and Leala sat holding each other, their grief just as raw. They'd gotten very close to Hannon in the demon dungeon. Vemar was sitting with them, offering his quiet support. Weston and Micah and my guard were also keeping vigil with us. A lot of the other dragons had stayed close, too, and many of the wolves, those that didn't need to sleep to resume their guard.

Several faeries had joined us, many I didn't know and had never seen before. It wasn't their custom, sitting out all night rather than viewing the lost before burial, but they did it anyway. The garden staff had stayed, and even the queen had come to sit with us for a time. Everyone shared in my devastating grief, in the grief of everyone who'd lost someone this night.

When the first rays of the sun painted the sky, I blinked up in confusion. It didn't feel right, the sunrise. Light didn't belong here. It felt unnatural.

"We should send for something to eat," Nyfain said, stroking my face.

"I'm not hungry—"

"I'll take care of it." Leala jumped up, turning to go, but her step slowed. She looked around. "Do you hear something?"

"Is that…" someone else said, and everyone's faces started to slowly turn toward the houses all lined up in a solemn row. "Is that smoke?"

I looked over in confusion.

As though it were waiting for me to notice, the little house that contained Hannon burst into flames.

Nyfain jumped up, hauling me up against him, and then rushed forward and barked commands. The scene quickly turned to chaos, shifters bursting into wolves and rushing to secure the area, trying to find whoever might've set the fire. The faeries were quick to follow them, not trusting foreigners to secure the castle grounds. Dragons shifted and took to the sky to get an aerial view as those left on the ground rushed to the woodshed, issuing commands to get water and put out the flames.

I stared in horror. I couldn't fathom who would try to kill my brother again. There was a personal grievance, and then there was this.

The fire burned hot and bright in the new morning. Black smoke rose into the sky, disrupting the beautiful colors of the sunrise. The little house was quickly consumed and just as quickly burned down to the ground. The fire must have been magically charged, because matches and fire starter never could've created that effect. No dragon could've burned it that fast.

As the wood fell to a blackened crisp and the flames died, a great, fiery beast rose into the sky. As large as a dragon but with slender, more efficient wings, it was a beautiful sight to behold. Flame shivered out from its feathered yellow-orange chest and blasted through its deep red wingtips. Its clawed feet flexed and curled, as if it was testing them out, and it gnashed its pointed beak. The feathers on its head, long and wild like a tornado, caught the light and threw it in a beautiful kaleidoscope of color.

Its head swirled until it saw me. The flame minimized until it was just a whisper, curling along its wings, and then a soft glow of power that reminded me of those illuminated everlass leaves.

"Hannon?" I whispered softly, knowing what this beast was. I'd read about its kind in books, although they were always described as mythical. No one believed they had ever been anything but a great, magical, fantastical story.

The story of the phoenix.

The story of a creature who would never die from violence. Only old age could kill the mythical being, and its age was clocked in hundreds, sometimes thousands of years. Or so the stories went.

The creature beat its wings and rose a little more before flying forward, toward me. The house behind it was a pile of blackened wood. Nyfain's hand tightened on my shoulder.

I expected people to scatter, to give the creature more space, afraid of a beast whose firepower was greater than any dragon, even Nyfain. Instead they rushed toward me, standing in front of me. Dragons crowded overhead, dipping low, ready to battle.

"Hannon?" I asked again, tears again filling my eyes. Hopeful tears this time. Tears of desperation.

The phoenix dropped low, hovered so that those in front of me would give it a little more space, and then landed gracefully.

He's even better at landing than us, and it's his first

time trying it, my dragon grumbled. *That's some bullshit.*

I moved to step forward, but Nyfain held me fast. Those in front of me didn't budge. Not until the phoenix shifted.

A swirl of color and light reduced the great fiery bird into a man again. Into my brother.

"Oh my—" I threw Nyfain's hand off and then shoved my way through the people still standing in front of me. I threw my arms around Hannon, hugging him so tightly I wondered how he could still breathe. "You're alive. Thank you, goddess. Thank you! You're alive."

He pulled back before wiping away my tears with his thumb. "I'm so sorry to have caused you pain. It was the thing I worried about most when they took me."

"You were being taken to your death, and your biggest concern was the pain it would cause me?" I asked, touching his shoulders and then his hair, just to make sure he was really here. Just to make sure it was really him, healed and whole.

"Yes," he said, as though that were natural.

"But you didn't know you'd come back. Or did you?"

He shook his head. "No, I didn't know. I just knew I wasn't worried about dying. I haven't been for…I don't know how long, actually. I never thought about it until I went to the demon castle. That's when it occurred to me. I've always been worried about everyone else, not myself. I guess maybe I instinctively knew that I…"

He looked down at himself and then lifted his hands, shedding power easily now.

"Am I really a phoenix, Finley?" he whispered, his eyes widening. "Is this real?"

I laughed through new tears. "It better fucking be real, Hannon, because I don't want to go back to a few moments ago when I thought I'd lost you."

Nyfain stepped up then, supreme joy on his face and pulsing through the bond. He put out his hand for Hannon and then pulled him into a tight hug instead, pounding his back with a fist.

"You gave us a big fucking scare there, buddy," Nyfain said, pulling back and clutching his shoulders. "A big fucking scare. I'm sorry I couldn't get to you in time. I thought I'd let you down. That I'd let your sister and your family down."

Nyfain blew out a breath, and I noticed that he was choked up.

"Glad to have you back," he finished, stepping behind me a little, apparently using me as a shield against showing his emotions. "Please don't challenge me, though. I don't think I can back down, and you can't die. So..."

"Oh, I can die," Hannon said, running his hand through his wild red hair. Hair that looked like the flaming feathers of his mythical beast. "Dying is not at all pleasant." He chuckled. "I was still alive for the stomach strike and then riding in the mouth of a dragon. I really don't wish to do either again."

"Hello?" Hadriel had his hands on his hips and was tapping his bare foot. We'd all put on slips to make the faeries less uncomfortable, but no one had bothered with slippers or shoes. "Hell-fucking-o?"

I stepped to the side with Nyfain, clearing space for Hadriel.

"You bastard," Hadriel said, launching himself at Hannon. He hugged him as tightly as I had. "I thought you'd fucking died, you asshole."

Leala piled on. "I'm so glad you're back, Hannon. I'm so, so glad."

Calia stepped up next, her expression grim. "I'm going to just go ahead and be the bearer of bad news here." She swallowed and lifted her chin before turning to look at Nyfain. "He is going to be the focus of the entire magical world. They'll want to coax him to their kingdoms for his status and power and bloodline. If he won't take their very generous bribes, they'll try to take him by force. He has the gift of healing. He has the gift of agelessness. The gift of long life. He can bestow these blessings at will, and a certain magic exists that can force him to do so. That magic, thankfully, is just as rare, but it exists. He has the power to destroy the world—"

"Okay, okay, whoa, whoa." Hadriel waved his hands. "Let's just pull our hysteria back a little, shall we? The guy barely even knows what he is. We have no idea what's true and what's not. I mean, fuck, he *literally* just came back from the dead. Let's give the poor fucker a glass of wine or something before we start tearing into him about destroying the world."

"Hadriel is right," Nyfain said, but unease filtered through the bond. "Hannon needs to see his family. They'll want to know he is okay. As for the other…" Nyfain paused before meeting Hannon's eyes. "You know I'll do everything in my power to protect you. If you are taken, I will make sure you are recovered, no matter what it costs."

Hannon gave him a knowing smile. "You won't have the chance. Finley will already be tearing apart the world to get me back. Don't worry about me leaving your kingdom, by force or otherwise. My animal—my phoenix, I guess—is confident we won't be taken. And I am confident nothing would be worth leaving my family."

With that, Calia uncomfortably got out of the way as someone gave him a slip and then made room for everyone else to hug him or shake his hand, all of us happy we'd at least gotten one person back. If they were enthralled by his animal, they didn't show it. Maybe they were just too tired and emotionally drained.

The faeries, on the other hand, stared at him with wide eyes before bowing like he was royalty. A few kept bowing, treating him like a deity.

He ignored all of this as though it wasn't happening, which made me laugh.

On the way back to the castle, I kept my arm wrapped around his, so desperately happy and relieved and thankful. And I got right down to business.

"I am absolutely going to be using you," I told him. "I'll make sure no one else will—or they can if you want them to—but me? I'm using you. Although...how is it you heal people? Wait—"

I pulled back from him, my eyes narrowing.

"No," I said, shaking my head in mock anger. "No, this is bullshit. You're the nurturer. *I'm* the healer. Are you trying to one-up me? When I said to get out of my shadow, I didn't mean *replace me.*"

"Doesn't a phoenix need an agent to transfer its healing powers?" Hannon said with a laugh. "I transferred my power to the everlass, but you still had to make the elixir to actually use it. You make the agent. I just help it work."

After a moment, I narrowed my eyes and grumbled, "Good answer. We almost had a problem there." I chewed on my lip. "There has to be a more effective method, though."

"And I'm sure you'll figure it out."

I took a deep breath, watching the sky change colors as the morning aged. "Last night was the worst night of my life, Hannon, and I've had plenty of bad nights. Please don't ever do that again. I know you can't die, but watch yourself. Don't get taken. Don't do anything risky."

"I won't. And you have one thing I haven't one-upped you on. You have a true mate."

I remembered that he'd always wanted one. I was the one who hadn't ever worried about it.

I just squeezed his arm. He'd have a damn long time to look around for her, and he wouldn't have to lose his boyish good looks to do it.

CHAPTER 43
HADRIEL

I INHALED THE sweet air and exhaled slowly, my nerves fucking fried.

"I can't believe he's a phoenix," Leala said, fatigue showing on her face as she walked beside me.

"Yeah, right? Thank fuck. That ol' cunt of a demon king actually did this whole kingdom a favor in the absolute shittiest way possible."

"They have to die to shift for the first time," Leala said as though reciting from memory. "They die, and then the first rays of the new day bring them back to life. Right?"

"Well, obviously. Were you not there?"

"Crap, I need to go set out something for Finley. She won't think about her clothes, and that slip she has on is practically see-through."

She ran ahead, dodging around people in an attempt to make it to the castle first.

I slowed so that Vemar could pull up to my side. He looked down at me gravely.

"Quite a night," he said softly, grabbing my forearm and slowing me further. "I know about your secret."

I tensed, running through all the things in my head that could possibly constitute secrets. I wasn't coming up with anything. I'd never been good at keeping my embarrassing things to myself.

"Drawing a blank," I told him.

He pulled me aside a little, letting others pass, and lowered his voice. "About Dessia."

Cold dripped down my center. "How do you know about Dessia?"

"I have a long ear. You need to tell the royals. That can't be kept a secret."

"She's not any more dangerous than anyone else. A basilisk can't kill a dragon, in dragon form, with just a glance. It just hurts really badly, apparently."

"That's bullshit and you know it."

I licked my lips, really wishing he'd believed that. "Well, maybe it would kill most dragons, but not the king's dragon. Probably not Finley's, either. With their bond, they are powerful enough to withstand it. Anyway, it doesn't matter. We have Hannon. He'd stop her from doing anything crazy. Which she won't. You know she won't. She's a sweet girl who's had a hard life. We have no reason to fear her. Just drop it, okay? The poor fucking thing accidentally killed her parents when she shifted for the first time. If you overheard her, then you know she was taken and used as a death device before her sister could recover her. She has a troubled past. She hates what she is."

"She might hate what she is, but she can be used,

same as anyone else."

"And the dragons can help Hannon stand against her, same as anyone else."

"I'm not talking about the dragons, you thickheaded cuntmonger."

I was stunned speechless for a moment. Then I put out a finger. "Credit where credit is due. That was a good word. I'm going to use that one. Anyway, if you're not talking about them, who are you talking about?"

Vemar stared at me like his will alone would infuse me with knowledge.

"Turn that long ear into a moving mouth, will ya?" I said.

"The *certain type of magic* Calia mentioned, the kind that can control phoenixes, belongs to a basilisk. The phoenix's one true enemy is a fucking basilisk, Hadriel. They can trap creatures in time, which is death to a phoenix. Real death, the permanent kind. And their blood can be mixed into a special blend to will a phoenix to use its magic. No one is immune from everything, not even mythical creatures."

"How do you know all this? Are you sure?"

"What do you mean, *how do I know all this?* How do you *not* know all this? Didn't you get an education?"

"What sort of education involves mythical creatures and their mortal enemies?" I looked back at the two women, walking slowly behind everyone else, their heads tilted together. "What are the fucking odds, you know? What are the motherfucking odds?"

"This is how it works, though, isn't it?"

"How *what* works?"

Vemar gave me a flat stare. "Read a fucking book, bud."

I lifted my eyebrows. "They don't cover phoenixes in gardening books. Tell me what you know, quick. I need to figure this shit out."

He huffed as he shook his head. "Power needs to be balanced. In the mythical stories about phoenixes, the phoenix always has a mortal enemy and a savior. We just found out who the enemy is."

"She's not the fucking enemy. She's no one's enemy. She hides her magic for a reason, damn it. The king doesn't even know. She's on record as a null. As a faerie whose power is locked inside of her. At the *latest*, a faerie's power will manifest by the time they're twelve years old. The very latest. She was eighteen when she first shifted. By then, no one cared about her. She's able to stay with Calia because Calia says her unique magic can tap into Dessia's power. Which is true, but not in the way they think. The girls want to keep this hushed up because they know the king will use her. He'll officially enter her into the court and into his army. That's the last thing Dessia wants. She's safe if everyone thinks she's useless. Trust me, Vemar, she's not a threat to Hannon. He's a threat to her."

"How is that the case?"

"Now who is being dense?" I noticed someone glancing over and pulled Vemar a little farther away while lowering my voice. "Look, she ran away soon after she killed her parents. The people who came after her obviously realized what she was. They covered it up and sold the information to...I forget who. That party tracked her down and sold her again. Her captives used her as the bringer of death, basically. She doesn't just kill people with her eyeballs, she also has poison fangs that apparently work great for torture. Anyway, her sister, the spy, heard about the situation in her travels. Calia had already been looking for her, so she knew which questions to ask. She broke Dessia out, and they killed everyone who'd held her captive. Dessia did. She can apparently be quite destructive. Calia brought her here, where she forced Dessia to spill about the real deaths of their parents, they had a reckoning, and now Calia protects her. So if people find out about her, then they might want to use her to get to Hannon. Hannon being a phoenix is trouble for her, don't you see? She wants to keep what she is a secret."

"Why in the fucking world did she tell you all this? You of all people?"

"Oh, you didn't hear all that with your long ear, did you?" I rubbed my face. "Because Calia went to that late dinner with the castle people, and Dessia was lonely. She has no friends. She's scared to get close to anyone. But there is safety in a mediocre butler who dresses like a clown. Well, there *was* until a certain handsome dragon *also* started dressing like a clown and then hanging around."

"We'll get back to you calling me handsome in a while. I love my ego being stroked. But for now, we have a serious problem."

"I take it back—fuck you, and no we don't. Not if we don't tell anyone. Look, if Hannon was anyone else in the entire world, he would have for-real died when someone killed him. Instead of a whole world filled with people who could kill him, he has one. Big fucking whoop. And if we don't tell anyone who that is, it won't be an issue."

"Listen, I've known about Dessia for months now and didn't bring it up. Why? Because I believe you're right and she just wants to stay in the shadows. She doesn't mean anyone harm. But the thing about phoenixes is, there always has to be *someone* who can kill them. It balances the power. The same is true of a basilisk. The two are mortal enemies. The savior? It's Finley, of course. She has two wolf parents but turned into a dragon, the true mate of the most powerful, fearsome fucking bastard in the whole magical world. In history, I'd wager. Together, they're his protection. Against Dessia."

"First of all, you don't even know if any of this is true. You're getting this information from stories written by men and women who have a flair for the dramatic. You aren't reading the ledgers of a taxman; you're reading the fantastical versions of cowards who should've been there, weren't, and decided to write about it instead. Mortal enemy? Give me a break. That's preposterous."

"No one being can have too much power. Nature makes sure of it."

"Oh good, a dragon who thinks he knows it all is talking out of his ass." I gnashed my teeth. Finley was going to *freak*. She was already hypersensitive about harm coming to her brother, and after his death-turned-rebirth, she'd be a headcase about it. She wouldn't take this information lightly.

"We have to say something," Vemar pushed as Calia and Dessia drew closer.

It occurred to me that they were walking even slower now. Calia was playing it very cool, but Dessia had always been shit at hiding her nervousness.

"Ah fuck. Well, fine, I guess this is happening."

I strutted out to the middle of the path, braced my hands on my hips, and prepared for a chat. Before they even reached me, I laid it all on the line...in a way no one else would be able to decipher.

"This eavesdropping fuckstain knows all about the *things*, and he thinks we need to blab to Finley and Nyfain."

"Let's go back to when you called me handsome," Vemar murmured.

Calia and Dessia pulled up short, and then Calia strutted forward, pulling Dessia behind her. She pulled out a little vial from some hidden pocket and held it up threateningly.

I stuck out my finger. "Do not fucking magic me, faerie."

Calia rolled her eyes before throwing it onto the ground between us. Purple fizz bubbled up before it hissed. Smoke wafted around us and then turned into a sort of bubble, closing us in.

"That is a soundproof bubble," Calia said. "It lasts for fifteen minutes. You can leave at any time."

I crossed my arms over my chest, trying not to feel foolish. "Fine. Well? What are we going to do about this?"

"How much does he know?" Calia looked pointedly at Vemar.

"He knew the worst bit, and then I tried to fill him in on the background to soften him up, and then he started on about phoenixes and mortal enemies and—"

Calia sighed. "Just our luck, we found an educated dragon who obviously knows his folklore."

"I do not like this continued misinterpretation that I am uneducated—"

Calia interrupted me. "We've known that a phoenix would emerge. Basilisks and phoenixes tend to come in pairs. They balance each other."

"See?" Vemar nudged me.

I narrowed my eyes but tried to ignore him as Calia went on.

"When Dessia first felt Hannon, she wondered. Her...animal felt a strange sort of energy from him. Not long afterward, he crossed the bridge in the demon castle without feeling its affects. The Bridge of Doom, you all called it. She was highly suspicious then. She didn't feel anything from the bridge either, even though it made the rest of us feel like jumping into the lava. She didn't need me to make the crossing, she just pretended she did. After that, we stayed close. We watched. We waited. We hoped we were mistaken."

"You suspected the truth this whole time?" I asked. "And you didn't say anything?"

She ignored me. "When he died last night, we held our breath, wondering if the coming of the dawn would bring the phoenix. For Finley's sake, of course we hoped he would live. But for Dessia's sake..."

"Never finish that sentence," I murmured.

"You obviously know that if you try to kill him, I will kill you first," Vemar said without even a hint of rage or aggression. He was just stating the facts. He wouldn't even kill in a dragon's rage—he'd kill in cold blood.

I shivered.

"Yes, dragon, I know that," Calia spat. "What would be the point in her trying to kill him? How would that keep her hidden? Don't you see that she can be used just as readily as him? He can be used for healing and health. For ageless—"

"Yes, yes, we know," Vemar interrupted, though I didn't really know. I needed to read up on this stuff.

"Well, she is the opposite. She is the harbinger of death. Of pain. Of destruction. He can't cure the armies she can fell. No one can. The few who knew what she was as a girl, who sold her information, are dead. I killed them myself—"

"Goddess tickle my pecker, and here I thought you were sweet and innocent," I said in surprise with my hand pressed to my chest. "Fuck me, but you are good at deceiving."

"Those who knew of her…animal are also dead," she continued, mostly talking to Vemar now. "She had that privilege. Right now, she is a ghost. Better yet, she is a useless faerie to all but me. There are only four people in this world who know for certain what she is and that she is still alive, and they are standing within this bubble."

"Whoa, whoa." I held up my hand as Vemar shifted his stance, ready to strike or shift. He'd apparently taken that as a threat. "First, let me get something straight." I pointed right at her face. "You weren't actually spying for your king in Wyvern, you were spying for yourself?"

She blinked at me in utter confusion, just long enough for Vemar to snatch Calia by the throat, reel her in, and spin her around. He wrapped his arm around her neck in a chokehold and yanked her off the ground.

"You have to meet my eyes, basilisk," he said with his eyes closed, not at all troubled about Calia whipping her legs and scratching at him, trying to escape. "Before you shift or bite, she'll be dead. Let's talk about this."

Dessia stared at him for a very long moment before sliding her gaze my way. Her eyes had turned a nerve-racking shade of red.

I lifted my eyebrows and my hands.

"Can you really blame the guy, though?" I asked in my most disarming voice. "She threatened him. That was a threat. You've been inappropriately spying for long enough to know how dragons react to threats."

"It did sound like that, yes." Dessia nodded, then turned to the dragon. "Vemar, easy. She won't kill you. *I* won't kill you. Let Calia down so she can explain. She handles the maneuvering."

Vemar looked between Dessia and me before lowering Calia until her feet touched the ground. He loosened his hold, and she sucked in a deep breath, holding on to his corded forearm. But he didn't let her go.

"I think that's good enough." I winked at Dessia. "That's good, right? Let's go with that. He's touchy about the threat thing. Dragon, remember? He'll loosen up when she tells him the plan. You do have a plan, right? Because I'm also a little nervous about the threat."

"It wasn't a threat," Calia said with a red face, sucking in breath. "She shouldn't have told you, Hadriel. We fought about it after the fact. But she did, and Vemar overheard. Fine. There are four of us *right now* who know what she is. I ask that we keep this quiet until after the summit. *Please.* Once they hear that the legendary phoenix again walks the magical world, they'll know a basilisk must also exist. And then the search will be on. Rumors will start. Various little threads of knowledge we've left behind without realizing it will surface. Eventually, they will find her."

"Well, then who is her savior?" I asked. "Hannon has one, so who is hers? The king, right? You're in good with him. Tell him."

Vemar released Calia, giving her a small shove to force her to step away.

"Basilisks don't have a savior," he said, dropping his hands. "Basilisks, in all the stories, are the villains. They are the ones to defeat."

Now it all made sense. She'd be used, or she'd be killed. Her story was never meant to have a happy ending.

"Fuck," I said on a release of breath.

"Now you see," Calia said. "*Finally.*"

"Let's not get hurtful." I ran my fingers through my hair. "So what are you asking of us? Obviously you know that Vemar won't be keeping this a secret forever."

"I'll tell you what you should propose," Vemar said, crossing his arms over his chest. "You should propose that we all go straight to the king and queen of Wyvern and come clean. Dessia can't help what she is, and we all know what it's like to be used. They'll protect Hannon, and to keep him safe, they'll have to protect Dessia, too. And they will, because they won't fear you. The golden dragon king would rather die than bow down to the pain you could inflict on him. If you're looking for safety, you should be looking his way. And if no one here knows you're important, then they won't stop you from leaving this kingdom."

"They'll care if I leave," Calia said.

Vemar slowly swung his dark eyes her way. "I wasn't inviting you. Finley's going to be mad as hell that you lied about what you were doing in the kingdom not once, but twice. She's the forgiving sort...kinda, but everyone has their limits."

Calia deflated. She nodded. "Anything else?"

"Yeah, I could use a hot meal and a fucking bath. My balls itch for some fucking reason, and I want to stroke the lizard."

That didn't sound like a half-bad idea, and it wasn't because I wanted to be anywhere else but in the room when Finley found out about all this. Especially the part where I'd kept it all from her.

CHAPTER 44
FINLEY

"WHAT A CRAZY fucking life we are living," I murmured as I watched the shore approach. It felt like we were sailing to our doom.

Starvos had barely been able to wait a week before leaving. Dolion had unintentionally lit a fire under the faerie king's ass. Starvos might've been on the fence about aligning with us and going after Dolion, but his tune had changed since the attack on his lands, especially since we now had a phoenix on board. He didn't plan on asking for permission, either. It sounded like he intended to show up for the meeting, state his claim, and go for Dolion's throat.

This was a good thing, obviously. This was what we wanted. The problem was that Starvos planned to take the battle to Dolion. He wanted to rip into the castle of the demon king and kill anyone who got in the way, just like Dolion had done to him. He wouldn't hear me when I told him Dolion had built a fortress, and going there might be a suicide mission.

The other issue was that Nyfain had no idea how the council would react. Starvos thought his boldness would scare anyone away from standing against him, but Nyfain wasn't so sure. He worried some of Dolion's existing allies might stand with him.

"How do you mean?" Nyfain asked as we watched the shore. He was dressed in finery that befitted a king, his posture perfect and his expression unyielding, but I could feel his anxiousness curling through the bond.

We stood on our private deck in a very well-appointed faerie ship that routinely transported King Starvos across the seas. He had *insisted* we accompany him to the council meeting as his special guests. Translation: he wanted everyone to know we were allies.

"Well, I'm a queen, first," I replied. "And my brother is a fabled mythical being that people didn't actually believe in. Oh, and the whole bit about every phoenix having a mortal enemy is apparently true, and she just so happens to be the cute, very shy, and incredibly dangerous girl we met in a demon dungeon. Then there's the part about us heading into a very old and established magical council to start what might turn into the next magical world war. Something that hasn't happened in hundreds of years. I mean…need I go on?"

"Speaking of…Dessia," Nyfain started, and then rubbed his stubble with his free hand.

He'd purposefully refrained from shaving. He wanted to embody a quintessential dragon—ruthless, volatile, and scary as hell.

"Calia asked that we protect Dessia. Monitor her, of course, but protect her," he said.

"I know. I was standing right there."

"Yes, but you'd just finished piecing together Calia's double cross, and I wasn't sure you were really listening. You did punch Calia in the face right after that."

"She deserved it."

"I'm not saying she didn't. Not even her sister blamed you for it."

"I asked Hannon what he thought about the whole thing."

"Did you mention that our options were basically to keep her close or kill her?"

I frowned at Nyfain. "Obviously not. He'd never agree to letting me kill her just because she was born as the one creature in the entire magical world that could kill him. I just told him the facts. That she has a history of being captured and manipulated, and if the wrong person gets a hold of her, she could be forced to act against him."

"And what did he say?"

I sighed. "Can't you guess? Hadriel could. He mimicked Hannon's voice and everything."

"He thinks we should bring her into the fold."

"No. Well, yes, but he has volunteered to be her protector. He wants to help hide her so that she can finally live in peace."

"He wants to protect his mortal enemy." Nyfain laughed. "Sudden fame hasn't changed him much."

"I pointed out that he was the last person who should be protecting her. I mean…" I leaned my elbows against the wooden railing, and Nyfain slid a hand around my back. "Look, I know this isn't really such a big deal. So he's got *one* person who can kill him. Big whoop. I have thousands. Hell, I could slip, fall off a step, and crack my head. Dead. One shy woman with a troubled past and thick emotional scars isn't a very big deal, even if she's captured by some villain. So he is forced to use his magic. So what? It's for healing and good things. Whatever. She is not a huge concern to him. That is unless the two are together. That's just asking for trouble. It is literally asking for someone to try to take them both. They should be split up."

"They probably should be, but Calia worries someone will follow the breadcrumbs they might have unintentionally left behind and track Dessia down. She wants to stay with Dessia, but that is impossible given Calia's role with Starvos."

"Seriously, I was *right there*. I heard her. I can still hear when I'm mad, you know," I said. "If she joined us, and Starvos ever figured out what she is…"

I let the thought trail away. Nyfain turned and looked at the closed door behind us, making sure no one could hear. The salty sea wind whipped past me, tossing my hair.

"We tell him we didn't know. He doesn't know, so how could we? It would be easy to pass it off as her being drawn to her natural enemy, Hannon, and using us to keep him close. Keep our enemies close…"

I shook my head and looked away. "She freaks me out. Not her, but…what she is."

"I'm sure she would freak a lot of people out. That's why it's best to hide her. One of the reasons, at any rate."

I let out a breath. I wasn't really worried about Dessia. She didn't want to do us harm. Dolion was ten times more dangerous, maybe more so, and he was hellbent on our destruction. As long as he didn't know about her abilities, and the fact that he'd hidden her in a dungeon suggested he didn't, all was probably well.

"What if the council says we can't go to war?" I said softly. "What if they side with Dolion, and it is all of them against us?"

"We have Starvos. He's a very powerful and respected king. He, alone, will provide all the support we need. It'll be fine."

"Until we get to the demon lands and wash up against Dolion's fortress. Trust me, Nyfain, he and his predecessors built that place to withstand a serious attack."

"We have Govam." Nyfain glanced toward the stern of the boat. Govam and his demons traveled in the ship behind ours. Despite recognizing their usefulness, Starvos hadn't wanted them on this vessel. "He said he knows several ways in. We have Hannon. He is supposed to be able to cut through stone with his fire."

"Hannon doesn't have one clue how to use his magic. He can't cut through anything but wood at the moment, and that's because the fire is hot. It burns more than cuts."

Nyfain kept rubbing my back. "This has to happen. There is no other way. We're prepared. Or we will be."

I shook my head, the worry rising. He was right in that this had to happen. Dead right. But still...

"I guess I should make peace with the fact that Calia is a damn good liar," I said, my thoughts jumping all over the place. "I can't believe she fooled me twice with—" I cut myself off as my temper rose.

I told you something was off with her, my dragon thought.

No, you fucking didn't. You literally never brought it up. Ever.

You just don't listen.

"I wish I could rip my dragon out of my center and throw her overboard," I grumbled, straightening again. "I better go and see Leala. We're nearly there, and not all of us can pull off the tousled, grumpy, gorgeous *look* you're giving off right now. I have to be silky and slinky and sexy. I should get ready for battle."

"Civilized battle."

"Yes, I know. Your mother has been lecturing me for days. How I'm supposed to keep my temper in check after Dolion sort of killed my brother, I don't know, but she seems to think I have it in me."

"Hannon will be with you. He's always a calming influence."

"Except as a reminder of the whole 'Dolion killed him' issue, sure."

Annoyed, frustrated, hating Dolion more than I could express with words or fire or screaming or sulking, I made my way back in to Leala.

The last week in the faerie castle hadn't been much different than the three previous ones except for the enormous bargaining chip that was my brother. Nyfain had worked it hard, negotiating for future fighting aid should we need it, discounted trading deals, a united front against Dolion, and a plethora of other favors.

Meanwhile, the faeries who worked the tents had raided the library, trying to find ways to harness Hannon's magic into cures. I stepped in to buffer him, as I'd promised, but he just gave me a small smile and offered to help them in any way he could.

He'd been involved, if peripherally, in my attempts at healing most of our lives. Even after the curse was broken, he'd still hung around the plants and me. At last he'd found an official purpose. He was no longer in my shadow. Now he was the one who created the shadows, and he did it just as humbly and calmly as he did everything else.

That irritated my dragon to no end.

In the end, they'd found a few things that satisfied them. None of them, however, worked so well as the illuminated everlass, a secret we'd chosen to keep. I would've been happy to share, but Arleth and Delaney got right up in my face and threatened me with a lifetime of lectures on how to protect a kingdom's best trade interests if I dared to open my mouth. They said it was bad enough that I'd taught the faeries how to tend the everlass they had.

It had been a very compelling threat.

While the faeries were working with Hannon, I was busy learning everything I could from their magical worker. While I manipulated her, she thought she was manipulating me. She sang like a canary to keep me distracted so her fellow gardeners could monopolize Hannon's time. Any question I had, she answered. It was amazing. She even offered me a tour of the faeries' more robust magical operations, but I declined. They did real magic, like spells. Plants couldn't mimic that. I didn't want to waste my time on something we couldn't master.

When we said our farewells, the gardeners had presented us with an assortment of seeds and starter plants for our royal gardens. And Eris had offered me an apology. The former was likely because of the now large, robust plot of everlass we'd helped them cultivate, but the latter was heartfelt, and I accepted it.

Now the real work would begin. We couldn't afford any mistakes or mess-ups. We had to present a united front with Starvos, and we had to show our strength at all times. This was what we'd been working toward all this time. Ready or not, it was time to decide our future.

CHAPTER 45
FINLEY

W E ARRIVED AT the sprawling castle behind King Starvos and Queen Ayre's procession, allowing us to watch their grand entrance from our carriage as we awaited our turn. Their guard formed two columns, and they walked through with their entourage following behind. They glittered with jewels and sauntered like they were the most important people in this whole place.

"I'm not sure I can pull off that level of overbearing self-importance," I murmured as the last of them passed through the large arched doorway and their guard followed them inside.

"That's their style, not ours," Nyfain said, taking my hand. "We're the rough and ready dragons. We're too dangerous to be thought self-important."

I smiled as one of the castle staff opened our carriage door and stepped aside so we could exit the coach.

"Who owns this castle?" I asked, sweeping my gaze across the flat land and artfully crafted landscape.

"No one and everyone. Each kingdom pays a sort of

tithe for it, and a steward is in charge of keeping it up. We are all its master and none of us are. It doesn't rule any land until we meet, and then it rules all the lands."

"That's confusing."

He laughed as he stepped down beside me and curled his arm around my body. He hooked his hand on my hip possessively before leading me forward.

"There are many things that are going to seem confusing at first," he said, looking straight ahead and letting his people fall in around us. "I remember learning all this for the first time. It made my head spin. I hated the lessons. My mother told me that she did, too, when she had to learn."

"Fantastic. Now I'm really looking forward to it."

I felt his humor, but his smile quickly dropped away. Weston's wolves in human form lined up on one side, and Micah and his dragons lined up on the other. My guard would take up the rear, following behind us in rows.

Hannon met us at the beginning of the column, as planned. His new place would be directly behind us. Arleth would walk behind him, followed by Hadriel and Vemar, then the guard. It was decided that the rest of my family would enter with the staff, staying out of the public eye. My father didn't want my brother and sister directly associated with Nyfain and me, worried they'd be used against us somehow. I'd tried to convince him that powerful people had enough spies to know exactly who they were—might as well take the place of honor that was their due—but he wouldn't hear of it. I'd dropped the matter. Hannon's whole ordeal was still so fresh, and I didn't want to push Father so soon.

Nyfain didn't step in front of me and lead the way as King Starvos had done. He stayed by my side as we crossed the threshold and entered a large, well-appointed foyer. Columns rose around us to a very high ceiling decorated with lines of gold. A huge crystal chandelier hung down, glittering in the afternoon light. It reminded me a little of Starvos's castle. At the back of the expansive space, two sets of wide stairs curved toward an exposed balcony that curved around the foyer, allowing people to watch those entering.

Power flooded me, pumped up by my dragon, and small flames licked at my skin as we slowly made our way. They ran from me to Nyfain and back, traveling over our bodies as though dancing between us. Behind us, colorful light swirled and shed from Hannon, who had a much easier time accessing it now that his animal had made the final transition.

As expected, people stopped and stared, looking down at us with wide eyes. The hustle and bustle ceased entirely because everyone was staring at us.

A bald man with deeply bronzed skin and a pristine white suit walked forward to greet us in the middle of the space. His smile was slight and didn't meet his eyes, and a waiting team of staff, also dressed in white, waited behind him.

"King Nyfain." He bowed. "So good to see you again. I was sorry to hear about the late king of Wyvern."

"Porfino, hello. Yes, thank you. Let me introduce you to Queen Finley."

He offered me a bow. "Hello, Queen Finley. Your

reputation precedes you, of course, but descriptions of your beauty are but a pale representation of your lovely bloom."

I tried really hard to make my grimace into a smile. Really hard.

"Nice to meet you," I lied, inclining my head.

"And Hannon, whom we've lately learned is the mythical phoenix," Nyfain said, separating from me for a moment to allow Porfino a glimpse between us.

Porfino's eyes glittered, and his bow was just that bit lower. "Yes, the news reached me. Honored, of course. I hope you'll grace us with your flight."

Hannon didn't respond, and I guess it didn't really matter. He was a fucking myth come to light. If others were insulted by his actions, that was their problem.

I'm annoyed that I'm jealous of him, my dragon grumbled.

This time I tried not to snicker. I really did.

"And you remember my mother, the former queen of Wyvern." Nyfain waited for Hannon to step to the side a bit, allowing Porfino to welcome Arleth, before stepping closer to me again.

"Well, fantastic." Porfino clasped his hands behind his back. "Our people will take you to your wing. You'll find the itinerary in your rooms. We'll have the formal meet-and-greet tonight. If there are any problems, please let one of our servants know immediately, and I'll handle it personally." He bent at the waist a little but didn't step to the side just yet. "I would like the opportunity to mention that I heard about the trouble you had while staying at King Starvos's castle. I assure you that nothing of the sort will be tolerated here by *any* party. This is a neutral zone, as I'm sure you remember, and we'll be very careful to watch all food and monitor all areas for any hostile activity."

Nyfain's stare could've cut stone.

He didn't comment, just inclined his head and waited impatiently for Porfino to bow once again and step out of the way. Once we were walking, I asked him quietly what was wrong.

"He was warning us against retaliation," he replied, not looking around as we walked the halls and took the stairs up to the third floor.

"And why should that make you angry? You knew they wouldn't want us retaliating here."

"Because of the way it was handled," Arleth said, pushing up next to Hannon. "He made it sound like we were upstarts here to cause trouble." I could hear her anger. "He must assume the other kingdoms intend to ignore the attacks on us and back the demon king if we try to retaliate."

Her mouth firmed into a straight line, and she kept silent until the castle staff showed us to our rooms and then receded. Weston, Micah, Vemar, and Hadriel ducked in with us, obviously eager to take part in whatever conversation went down about the council.

Arleth went and stood by the windows, looking out over the grounds. "*This* is why Dolion has been able to get away with his shady dealings for so long. He is operating under the correct assumption that no one will want to upset the status quo. They're all afraid to push back."

"They are afraid of war," Nyfain growled, stripping his livery collar as Leala stripped mine. "Which is understandable. War is disruptive and expensive, and everyone knows the demons are ruthless and cunning. Dolion has been bullying them into silence and acquiescence by being the biggest threat in the room."

"Dolion is no longer the biggest threat in the room," Weston said, standing in front of the door with Micah. The others had made themselves at home, Vemar loitering in the corner while Hadriel wandered through the room, looking in drawers and opening cupboards. "Even without Starvos, soon everyone would see that there is a new game in town. Us. And we will have our vengeance."

"Fuck yes, we will," Micah growled, flexing.

"Well, I'm sure Leala and I can corrupt Dolion's minions," Hadriel said, exiting the washroom. "He really hated when his demons got involved in kinky fuckery. That'll at least piss him off."

"I could use a little debauchery anyway," Leala murmured.

Nyfain picked up the itinerary. "Go for it, Hadriel and Leala—just keep it quiet. We're allowed to bring one guard to the meet-and-greet tonight. Weston, that'll be you. I want the royals of the Red Lupine Kingdom to see you. I don't want it to look like I am hiding you. Hannon, you've been invited to attend as well. Get used to that. I assume you'll be invited to everything and likely treated as a sovereign nation. Beware what you say and what you agree to. Dolion isn't the only royal who relies on cunning to get what he wants."

He dropped the piece of paper onto the desk before scanning the room.

"Everyone break. Get some food and rest. Be on your guard, though. Regardless of what Porfino said, there is danger here. Dolion doesn't follow rules."

With murmurs of assent, the others left us alone, although Leala and Urien continued to unpack and see to our things. Nyfain slipped his hands around my waist, running his fingers lightly across my belly.

"All I want is our happily ever after," he whispered before running his lips down my neck. "I'm sick of all this worry and danger. I'm sick of being plagued by that demon king."

"We'll get it. Soon, we'll get it. Starvos is about to fast-track this thing with Dolion. We just have to get through tonight, and tomorrow everything will turn into chaos."

He huffed out a laugh and shook his head. "The calm before the storm."

"The cocktail hour before the storm, yeah. So annoying. Can't we just cancel?"

"It would be nice. But no." His sigh washed against my skin. "I need to lose myself in you for a moment."

He sucked in the flesh holding his mark.

"Just a moment?" I whispered, fluttering my eyes closed as he trailed his hands down my hips and then fisted the material of my gown before pulling it up.

"Maybe longer than a moment." He tugged it up over my head before dropping it to the floor. My undergarments followed shortly thereafter, and I heard Leala and Urien heading for the door. They knew the drill.

"I want it soft and sweet," I murmured as he slid his fingers over my breasts before stopping and lightly pinching the nipples.

"As you command," he replied, hardly more than a wash of his breath against my fevered flesh.

He turned me slowly before bending, sucking a budded nipple into his scorching mouth. I groaned as pleasure washed through me. Straightening so I could work at his buttons, he claimed my mouth, his kiss hard and consuming. He devoured me, his passion unfurling like a live thing and lighting me on fire.

"Hmm," I said, hurrying to push his jacket and shirt off his large shoulders before ripping at his pants.

He helped me, quickly stepping out before falling to his knees in front of me. He reached up to steady me as he pushed one of my knees over his shoulder. He parted my folds, licking up my center and making my whole body tighten. He sucked in my clit as he pushed his fingers into my pussy.

"Yes," I hissed, rocking into his mouth. The pleasure increased, building higher, his suction hard and his fingers just right. "Yes," I repeated, louder, grabbing two fistfuls of his hair.

He fucked my cunt with his fingers, not quite as soft and sweet as I'd originally asked. Thank the goddess for her wisdom in giving me what I needed, not what I'd asked for. I rode his face with fervor, right on the edge, chasing my orgasm.

"Faster," I said, head thrown back. "Harder."

His tongue swirled my clit before he sucked it in

pulses. His fingers kept going, pushing me higher, making me squirm against him.

I hit the peak with an explosion, crying out my delight, shuddering against him.

He didn't wait for me to come down. While I was still trembling from the aftershocks, he swung me up into his arms and walked me to the bed. Once there, he laid me down and pressed himself between my spread legs.

And he did listen to me then. He dragged the tip of his cock through my drenched folds before entering me slowly. I could feel his reverence through the bond, and also from the way he moved against my body. He thrust firmly and deeply, slowly pushing in until he ground his hips against me and then sliding back out as I clenched my pussy around him. He groaned softly, wanting more, needing it, but continuing with the slow, methodical fucking. So sweet. So sensual. So frustrating.

My body tightened up around him. I swirled my hips for more friction then changed the angle, making his cock drag against my inner walls, but it was still too slow, torturously slow.

"I take it back," I said, panting. "Fuck me hard."

"Now, now, my queen. You gave a command, and I intend on following it."

He slid his lips along my chin as he thrust in, grinding for longer now as I clenched and unclenched my pussy. Pulling out, slowly, so slowly, he left only the tip inside me, driving me wild.

"No, Nyfain." I rolled my head from side to side, squeezing my eyes shut. "Don't stop."

"Look at me."

I snapped my eyes open, falling into his golden gaze. He held eye contact as he pushed back in. More sparks lit my body. I wound a little tighter. I craved more of his hard length. I needed it harder. Faster.

I reached down for my clit, but he caught my hand and pulled it over my head. I tried with the other hand as he started moving again, but he caught that one too, pinning my wrists with one of his hands. He leaned his weight on it as his other hand found a breast. His thumb traced circles against my nipple.

I arched into his touch and tightened my legs around him. When he stalled again, I lifted myself and pulled with my legs to get him back into me.

This time he complied, ramming hard.

"Oh!" My shout of surprise turned into a moan as he pulled out a little faster this time, still taking too long. Still driving me crazy.

The anticipation mounted. I was hypersensitive to his every touch, hyperaware of his large cock slowly working in and out.

I couldn't decide if I loved this or hated it. If I wanted him to keep going like this for hours to increase the exquisite torture or if I just wanted him to bang the shit out of me already and make me come.

His mouth swallowed my moan as he increased the tempo. Then he slowly increased it more until I was writhing and whimpering under him, my mind blank of everything but the feel of him. One hand roughly held my wrists, but the other was gentle as he teased my nipple. His thrusts in were hard and forceful, but he'd drag his cock back out slowly. I couldn't get a handle on it. It was unraveling me little by little until I was a mindless, wanton creature begging him to make me come.

Finally he pushed up a bit so that he could slide his free hand down my body and run his knuckles along the sides of my swollen clit. I bucked, shaking my head from side to side.

"Do you want me to fuck you properly now, my queen?" he asked in a rough voice.

His touch teased me. His cock pounded in before grinding. I rocked against him, feeling the fullness of him inside me. He'd taken me right to the edge and was holding me there. Endlessly holding me there. He was firmly in control, and I had utterly lost it.

"Yes, please, Nyfain, please, fuck me properly. *Please.*"

"Please what?"

Back out and hold.

I mewed as I tried to push up. I slid him into me just a tiny bit more, only enough to continue the endless teasing. I fucking loved it and hated it at the same time. I was so deliciously on edge that I couldn't imagine giving this up even to reach a climax while needing to at the same time.

"Fuck me, alpha. Fuck me properly, alpha."

"That's a good girl."

And he pinched my clit while driving forward.

"Oh shit!" I yelled as the orgasm crashed into me.

He kept going, hard now, fast, working my clit and driving harder.

"Oh shit oh shit oh shit—" I gritted my teeth as the orgasm kept rolling.

He shouted an unintelligible word, and then he was climaxing into me, shuddering. With a last couple of thrusts, he collapsed onto his elbows over me, dropping his head until his cheek was pushed against mine.

"That was intense," I told him, the waves of pleasure finally starting to subside.

He sucked in air as he rolled onto his back and pulled me up against his body. "Yes, it was. I should listen to your commands more often."

I narrowed my eyes at him. "You should always listen to my commands, even when I change them halfway through a thing."

"Right, yes, that's what I meant."

I laughed and closed my eyes. Might as well get a little nap in before we went to the meetup and instigated a fight.

CHAPTER 46
FINLEY

"**I**'LL BE TRYING all of your food before you do," Hannon whispered to me as we made our way to the drawing room that would hold the royal meet-and-greet. This was apparently a cordial engagement designed to reacquaint everyone with each other. It would also introduce Nyfain and me as the new royals of Wyvern.

"How about I don't drink anything?" I replied. "I'll just hold my glass."

"What if you forget about it and take a sip and it's poisoned?"

"Just let him taste it," Nyfain said. "After the issue in Starvos's castle, I doubt anyone will comment."

"I don't like that suddenly he's the one protecting me," I grumbled. "I'm supposed to be the family protector. First there's you, and now there's him. I don't like this big-brother role-reversal bullshit."

Shit. I was starting to sound like my dragon, something she underscored by thinking, *Neither do I. It's unnatural.*

Neither of the guys said anything. Apparently I'd have to just sulk rather than argue. How annoying.

Two staff members waited on either side of the grand doors. When we stopped in front of them, Hannon directly behind us and Weston behind him, the men pulled the doors wide for us to step forward. Another staff member waited just inside the dimly lit room, his arm folded up across his chest. He waited for us to stop beside him before calling out our names to the large room. He announced Hannon as well, making note of his animal, and said nothing about Weston.

Weston was noticed, though.

The king and queen of the Red Lupine Kingdom, King Xeno and Queen Annise, zeroed in on him immediately, tracking him as he moved to the side and found a position there. He didn't glance their way, and if he was uncomfortable, he didn't let it show.

King Xeno stood up and plastered a slick smile on his face. Anger simmered in his eyes.

"King Nyfain," he said as he approached.

It was rude not to give an approaching royal one's attention, which kept me from scanning the rest of the room to see if that slime Dolion was lurking somewhere. It didn't matter. He wouldn't be going anywhere.

A staff member in the customary white approached us and asked for our drink order. Xeno waited until the staff member had left before speaking.

"It's a pleasure to see you again." He stopped beside Nyfain, but his body was angled toward Weston against the wall. "I'd forgotten you existed for a minute." He laughed like it was a grand joke.

I angled away, what Arleth had taught me was a polite slight. It was too early in the evening to be blatantly rude. Or so I had been told over and over again. She clearly knew me well.

"King Xeno, hello," Nyfain said with a very obvious tone of boredom. "Please meet my mate, Queen Finley. And her brother the phoenix, Hannon."

"Charmed." Xeno showed his teeth when he smiled at me, a not-so-slight show of displeasure, or perhaps a warning. I wasn't sure how he meant it. Wolf nuances were still tricky for me. He barely glanced at Hannon. "Aren't you going to introduce me to your new…commander, I think you call it? Or is a dragon *stooping* to use the term beta for his second-in-command?"

Nyfain didn't glance Weston's way. "Weston is the commander of our wolf shifters. A beta is a fine term, as well. I really couldn't care less what his role is called, as long as he does his job. He seems to agree."

"Does he now?" Xeno turned just a bit, his teeth gritted and his eyes on fire. Every line in his body screamed frustration and anger. "Is that what you're doing now, dragon? Poaching from other kingdoms?"

Nyfain glanced at him and then started laughing. When he spoke again, he reduced his tone to a low growl.

"That's rich, Xeno, coming from you. I don't have the magic to poach wolves, as you well know. And my guess is, you haven't found anyone as strong as Weston to continue illegally doing that for you either."

621

Xeno's face blanched.

Nyfain nodded. "I know all about it. We both know all your efforts to reclaim Weston were in vain. He walked away and never looked back."

"How'd you get him, though? I heard he'd died. His pack confirmed it."

"He didn't die. He was taken by the demons. He was kept in their dungeons and tortured. That is, he was tortured when he wasn't being sold to wealthy demons to be their plaything. It was my mate who saved his life—who rescued all of the prisoners from the dungeons—and Weston repaid her by helping us rid the kingdom of our demon invaders. His desire to stay was all his own. *He* approached *me*. It seemed he thought he had nowhere else to go. If he wanted freedom, at any rate."

Xeno's lip curled. "Bullshit. The demons wouldn't poach from my land."

A flurry of emotions rolled through the bond, but Nyfain kept his composure.

"There's that word again, Xeno. Poach. I think the word you're actually looking for is *kidnap*, don't you? That's what you were doing, right? It is certainly what Dolion does. You kept people in a prison of magic. He keeps them in a dungeon."

Nyfain turned to him, over a head taller, much more robust and wickedly scarred. He couldn't have hidden the danger radiating from his person, or the vicious intent sparkling in his eyes. He didn't try.

"Isn't it interesting," he continued in a low, rough tone, "that you both seem fine with the practice. And while you may *think* you are knowledgeable in his operations, I can assure you that you are not. He absolutely *poaches* from your lands. Weston is proof. Too bad Dolion isn't in the habit of telling others about the prizes he acquired from their shores, or you might've gotten your prized wolf back. Too late. But let me mention this to you: if you plan on siding with Dolion when I raise my grievances against him, I'll be happy to see you on the battlefield. We both know Weston will be there, and if he is, your wolves won't be *your* wolves for very long."

Xeno's eyes narrowed. "Is that a threat, dragon?"

"Yes. And here's another. If I hear of your continued...*poaching*, I will end you. However, if you play nice, I won't feel so inclined to mention your past wrongdoings in the council meetings. Stay out of my way, and I'll stay out of yours. Otherwise, you're *mine*."

"You'll end me?" Xeno snarled, and out of the corner of my eye, I could see faces turning our way. The tension between Nyfain and Xeno tightened and twisted, seeming to fill up the air. "The amount of dirty deeds your father—"

"The former king is dead. My slate is clean; the demons made sure of it. You have nothing on me. Nothing. But I have all sorts of colorful information about you. Don't get in my way, Xeno. I'll only tell you this once."

"Everything okay here?" Porfino had his hands behind his back as he led the server our way.

Weston had stepped forward, on the offensive. Another guy on the other side of the room had done the same, his muscles rippling and his hard eyes trained on Weston. He had to be Xeno's beta.

"That remains to be seen." Nyfain stepped forward

623

to take two drinks off the tray and hand them both to Hannon. They were waters, and clearly Hannon was meant to try mine before I did. Nyfain grabbed the last and held it.

Xeno didn't comment, his hard gaze beating into the side of Nyfain's head. Without a word, he spun and walked toward the door. It seemed he'd lost his taste for cocktails. A few moments later, the queen followed him out.

Porfino studied Nyfain for a moment until Nyfain looked his way. There was something wild and primitive in his stare. An obvious challenge.

Porfino dropped his gaze immediately and turned, heading away.

"He seems to think he has some kind of power in this place," Nyfain murmured, waiting for Hannon to give me back my tasted glass before walking me toward a collection of couches in the middle of the room. "He seems to think he's a peacekeeper."

"And he isn't?"

"No. That is beyond his duties as steward."

He didn't elaborate as he scanned the room. I felt his tension and followed his gaze to the back of the room.

Dolion. That rat bastard.

He lounged in the corner, shadows draping across his stupid black suit and the ugly horns curling away from his blue hair. He had a little smirk on his face, but that didn't fool me. At this point I was intimate with the ass basket. I'd seen the way he acted in his own kingdom, with no one of importance watching him. He lost his temper constantly, punishing his people at the drop of a

hat. He was the kind of shitbird who'd cruelly kick a
sleeping dog—or person—just because they happened to
be in his way.

I'd watched from my cage as he walked through a
demon party gone wild, pretending to smirk or smile
when people talked to him, and I'd seen that carefree
facade drip away the moment they couldn't see his face.

I'd watched his eyes burn with fear and rage as Nyfain stared him down, or when he smelled Nyfain's scent
on me.

No, he didn't fool me for a moment. He waited in
that corner, with tense shoulders and a full glass, because
he was worried. He hadn't been able to kill us, and he
knew he couldn't shut us up. Worse, we would seek to
destroy him in any way possible.

I met his shadow-shrouded gaze and couldn't help
myself.

I paused on the way to the couch, tilted back my
head, and laughed.

When I was done, I lifted my glass to him and said
loudly, "You made my life a nightmare. Cheers!" Still
smiling, I took a sip.

Fuck that guy. Fuck this pretending. I'd do what was
expected of me up to a point, but I wouldn't play nice
with that asshole. I'd earned my right to push back. And
goddess slap me, I would fucking take it, and I'd do it in
front of every powerful person I could find.

This room was a great start.

"King Nyfain, hello."

A man I recognized from the drawings I'd studied
rose from one of the couches with a lazy smile. He had

dark eyes and darker skin, with a powerful build and
nearly as much height as Nyfain.

King Caron, co-ruler with Queen Yuna, both wolves.
They ruled the Flamma Kingdom that housed the
dragons in their mountain villages.

"King Caron." Nyfain unfurled his arm from me so
he could shake King Caron's hand.

"Do you remember my lovely Queen Yuna?" Caron
put out his hand, prompting Yuna to stand. She had
long, flowing golden hair and small features, except for
large brown eyes heavily coated in thick black lashes.

Her smile was wide and eyes sharp as she met Nyfain's gaze and took his proffered hand.

"Hello, King Nyfain," she said. "So nice to properly
meet you. I remember hearing of you throughout the
years. Your mother, the former queen, was from our
kingdom, correct?"

"Yes. Until recently, she had moved back there. I've
still never visited."

"Well you should," she replied, all emotion hidden
behind her polite exterior. She was good at this. As good
as Arleth, I'd bet. "And how is former Queen Arleth? I
hear she didn't succumb to the heinous fate of your
kingdom. I am so sorry to hear about that."

"Yes, I couldn't believe when suddenly I remembered your kingdom again," Caron said, looking
troubled. "I felt half-mad for a moment."

"First, let me introduce my queen and co-ruler,
Queen Finley." Nyfain slipped his arm back around my
waist.

"Hello." I stepped forward with my hand outstretched, shaking first Yuna's hand, then Caron's. I had no idea whether the order was right. I'd forgotten that bit. "Nice to meet you."

"Queen Finley, I've heard so much about you." Caron's eyes crinkled at the corners. "You gave the faeries a run for their money with their healing ointments."

Clearly he had someone *in the know* in Starvos's court.

I laughed delicately, just like I'd been taught. "It was the first time I'd gotten to see someone else's operations. I may have pushed my way in and taken over a small area."

"Quite right." He laughed.

"And may I introduce my brother, Hannon." I turned and held out my hand. Hannon came forward slowly, clearly not wanting to be here at all. A part of me took grim satisfaction from the fact that he now had to endure all of this posturing with me. We'd always been a team, enduring the worst together, and now nature had forced him to travel the same path I was on. For now, anyway. "He recently learned he shifts into a phoenix. Hannon, this is King Caron and Queen Yuna."

Yuna's eyes sparkled. "Hello, Hannon. So great to meet you. A phoenix—wow! Did you have any idea?"

"Please, everyone, let's take a seat." Caron gestured to the couches around us.

"I didn't, no." Hannon sat in an armchair to my right, leaving the loveseat next to Caron free for Nyfain and me. He put his glass of water on an end table. "Our animals were suppressed for most of our lives, Finley's and mine." At their blank stares, he said, "Because of the curse placed on our kingdom by the demon king. I'm sure you've heard?"

"Now, now." Porfino walked quickly to Hannon's side, making it clear he'd been eavesdropping. "Let's not engage in slander. We're aiming for a routine, amicable meeting between the kingdoms."

Hannon blinked a couple of times before turning his face up to Porfino. "What part of what I said was slander? I'm sure everyone knows that the former king of Wyvern entered into a deal with the demon king, cursing Wyvern and trapping us within the borders? Along with the curse, the demon king suppressed all our animals, which inhibited our ability to heal, and then plagued the villages with a sickness that slowly killed us. I lost half of my family to that sickness. Do I suddenly not understand the meaning of slander, or are you an idiot? But please…" Hannon's eyes turned intense, and he adjusted in his seat, his chest now facing Dolion at the back of the room. His eyes dropped that way, too, and light started floating into the air all around him. "Let's bring the king of the demons over here to discuss this. He visited our kingdom often enough to know what was going on."

His body was relaxed, his demeanor calm, but his stare was hard and aggressive. If he'd had his chef's knife or axe, I would've worried he'd jump up and settle this matter once and for all. As it was, the rest of the room wondered if he'd give them a taste of his magic.

Too bad he didn't know how to work his damn magic. We could've done with another couple of months to figure it out. I should've let Nyfain kill Hannon that one time he low-key challenged him.

"Why are you chuckling?" Nyfain whispered.

"A few reasons. Never mind."

"Yes, of course, it's just that, were you royal," Porfino began, "you'd understand that we don't disparage the other rulers within our looser-styled meetups. Any grievances we might have should be addressed in a formal capacity."

"Correct me if I'm wrong, but if you think there is a problem, it is *you* who is passing judgment," Hannon said with an air of confusion. "I'm merely stating facts, as I said. I'm sure everyone knows about the curse."

"We didn't know your animals were suppressed, actually," Caron murmured. "Or about the plague."

"How about King Dolion stealing everything of value from our kingdom?" Hannon asked with his calm indifference that was working so well right now. "Or sending his demons to the castle and villages to twist the minds of the people and turn their behavior deviant? That was eye-opening, I can assure you."

That magnificent genius, my dragon thought. *He's playing them all.*

Yes. He was. I hadn't known he had it in him. Beneath the calm exterior, Hannon was clearly mad as hell, and this was his chance to say something about it. No one could fault him, either, because he was so mild about the whole thing. Except for his hard stare, he didn't seem angry in the least.

"That is something we could well imagine," Yuna mumbled, suddenly very interested in the part of her dress that draped over her lap.

"That's quite enough," Porfino said. "Let's steer the

conversation elsewhere."

"Yes, let's," Nyfain said, studying Porfino. "There is plenty of time for the *royals* to discuss the deeds of King Dolion. Anyone who would like a firsthand account may set it up with me directly. That'll be all, Porfino. You've inserted your presence into your benefactors' business long enough."

"And what do you mean by that?" Porfino pulled himself up indignantly. "I am in no one's pocket."

Nyfain's eyebrows lifted slowly. A little smile played across his lips.

"Are *we* not your benefactors, Porfino?" he asked before leaning back and crossing an ankle over his knee like he owned the place. He tilted his head a little, a look of bemusement on his face belied by the white-hot rage burning through the bond. "Why should you assume I was singling out one person?"

Porfino stared but didn't comment. Sniffing, he straightened his back and walked away. I caught his glance toward Dolion's corner, though.

In no one's pocket, indeed.

"King Caron, Queen Yuna, I had wanted a word," Nyfain began, running his fingers down the middle of my back.

When I leaned into his touch, he pulled his hand back a little, coaxing me to sit back against him like I didn't feel the tension pulling at the air around us.

Dolion was in his corner seething, I could see it. He was watching Nyfain and Hannon dance around with their words, making him look bad. It wouldn't be long before he snapped. He was sizing Nyfain up, and soon he'd try to reassert control.

"Of course," Caron and Yuna said in unison, and then smiled at each other like they were sharing an inside joke. They probably answered together all the time.

"I did not intend to pull so many dragons from your kingdom without speaking to you first," Nyfain said. "Unfortunately, my kingdom was, until recently, incredibly fragile. We'd been cut off from the world for sixteen years and had seen a lot of sickness and mass murder. We didn't have a leg to stand on. Finley and I couldn't leave to make an official visit. I hope you understand."

"We don't," Caron said somberly. "About what your kingdom endured, I mean. Not the whole of it. I think I'd like to understand a little better, come tomorrow."

He meant in the formal meetings.

Nyfain shook his head. "I do not plan to raise that as a grievance. The late king helped create that nightmare. My people weathered it as best they could. But afterward we had a lot to rebuild, and that is why I couldn't approach you directly before now."

"And…" Yuna leaned forward just a little.

Dolion, in the corner, had gone utterly still. He still hadn't taken a sip of the drink he held. He clearly wondered if I'd poisoned it, knowing I was a lot more effective at the practice than whomever he'd sent after me. I wished I had.

"How did the dragons come to know you had a place for them?" Yuna put a hand to her chest. "Please under-stand, we are mostly ignorant to…well, all of this, really. Suddenly we remembered who you were, and then trade opened back up, and dragons started to leave our kingdom in droves. It seemed to happen all at once. We're still a little in shock, I think."

Caron nodded, watching Nyfain closely, probably looking for a lie.

Here you go, Dolion, you fucker. Here's a little more to choke on.

I held out my hand. "I'll keep the first part of the story brief so we don't have Porfino running over here with more accusations of slander."

I smiled despite knowing it didn't reach my eyes. Given Yuna and Caron didn't even pretend to take up the joke, they could read me easily. More power to them.

"I traded myself into Dolion's…care to help Nyfain's kingdom. I wasn't queen at the time. I was a commoner."

"And his true mate," Caron said.

"Correct."

"But you could've broken the curse as soon as you knew about your true mate status, right?" Caron narrowed his eyes. "Or do I have that wrong?"

"Yes, but we were a kingdom on our knees," I said. "Many of us were gravely sick and dying. Our animals were suppressed. All we had as protection from the demons was Nyfain. He kept the kingdom from utter ruin. Under the terms of the curse, Dolion could not kill Nyfain. Without the curse, though, we had no such protection. If we'd broken the curse then, he would've attacked with all his demons and killed us. I know that because that's exactly what he did after the curse was broken. Except by then we'd formed enough of a defense to chase him away. Anyway, my deal with Dolion essentially meant his dungeons were my new home. Thankfully, Nyfain's stench scared the demons, or I would've been forced to be a sexual slave for his people, like everyone else—"

"I keep hearing my name."

The voice rang out across the room, holding all the power and authority he'd always used in his court. It really put into perspective what he thought of the sanctity of these meetings.

I didn't bother acknowledging Dolion as he pushed off from the wall. I was never going to do Arleth proud, I knew that now. I was never going to be the perfect queen playing nice with a bunch of assholes. It just wasn't in my nature.

I continued speaking.

"Dolion had imprisoned several dragons from our kingdom, and as Nyfain will address that tomorrow, I won't bore you with the details. But he'd also taken dragons from yours. And wolves from various places. And faeries. They decided they owed me a debt for helping them escape. They helped us free Wyvern from Dolion's grip, and then they stayed and helped us rebuild. They'd grown attached by then. They'd found their kind, and Arleth wanted to stay with her son... I'm sure you can understand. The wolves stayed, too, most of them. It has turned into a great place. You should visit sometime."

"As I said..." Dolion wandered closer, his drink held as a prop. A slick smile twisted his lips. "I keep hearing my name."

"That's because I'm talking shit about you." I crossed

my legs, and now I did lean back. I gave him a genuine smile. "So nice to see you again, Dolion." I held up my hands. "I don't have any guards surrounding me this time, though. That must make you nervous, huh? No guards, no bars, no weird-looking creatures with whips. It's not at all like old times, is it?"

He glanced at Hannon. "There is a large representation of Wyvern in this room. I wonder who greased the wheels, so to speak, to make that happen?"

Nyfain started laughing.

"I can leave, if you'd like?" Hannon asked, bending forward.

"Don't be absurd, Hannon," Nyfain waved his offer away. "You are a phoenix. Everyone is curious about you."

"I must admit, I am." Caron laughed, but his heart didn't seem to be in it. Was he trying to defuse the tension?

"Have no fear, everyone," Nyfain said. "Hannon's animal is new to this world. He's still learning his way. He is no great threat."

Keep your damn face neutral, my dragon thought. *Don't let them know he's full of shit.*

I'm trying! Though it's mostly true.

It's not even remotely true. The second someone he loves is threatened, his phoenix is going to go fucking crazy. I can't wait to see the sparks.

"King Dolion actually assisted in Hannon's first shift, did you know that?" Nyfain asked pleasantly.

A muscle twitched in Dolion's jaw. "Careful, dragon. There is a law against hearsay. The penalty is steep."

Nyfain's brow notched upward. "A law against hear-say? Is that right? I can only imagine who would benefit from such a law. I'll look at the verbiage later, and we can discuss it in more detail this week. Until then, I will simply state what I know, how's that? Hannon was...*poached*, I think is the word you and King Xeno use, from King Starvos's inner gardens and held against his will until we came to claim him. Demon creatures attacked him before we could, however. That was what initiated his first shift: being murdered. The others who died weren't so lucky, however. I lost some of my people, and so did King Starvos. He won't be here tonight, sadly. It was a long journey. He's tired."

The way he said *tired* gave it a double meaning. Tired from travel, and tired of Dolion's leash.

"I think that is probably about enough for the night." Porfino hustled back over, his mouth set in a grim line. He stopped next to me and bent down to take me by the upper arm. "This sounds like it is getting away from us."

A flash of rage tore through the bond.

But I'd already reacted to Porfino's reaching hands.

My will slammed into him. He flew back, landing on the edge of the coffee table. It crashed to the ground, and he rolled beyond it, bowling into two chairs and toppling them.

"If you attempt to muzzle me again, Porfino, or grab my mate," Nyfain growled, and my small hairs stood on end, "I will do much worse than the shove my mate just gave you. Do you understand me? I'll be discussing how much power you *think* you have this week. If we make it that long. No, no, where are you going, King Dolion? I was just singing your praises for unveiling the phoenix."

Dolion stopped on the other side of the furniture as though he were a naughty child caught trying to escape his punishment. He turned slowly, the set of his shoulders telegraphing his terror of Nyfain's dragon. A dragon that now lacked the curse's magical leash. I couldn't contain my glee.

"After Hannon died in Finley's arms, and her brother, sister, and father, who'd already lost so much at the hands of the legendary demon king, grieved the loss of the family's eldest son, we sat in mourning all night. At the coming of the new day, the phoenix was born. So you see, Dolion, it was thanks to...your demons, we'll say, that Hannon discovered the truth. It was a gruesome death, but it worked out for everyone, don't you think?"

What we all heard but he didn't say was: "Except for you."

"Hear this, dragon," Dolion said. He was on the verge of losing control. "Whatever you are trying to do won't work. The magical world has been running peacefully without dragons for sixteen years. We—"

"There were dragons," Nyfain said with an edge to his voice. "They were just locked in my kingdom, killed one at a time, locked in your dungeons, also killed one at a time, or stashed away in the Flamma Kingdom, where they were mostly ignored. And what did we get from the lack of dragons? A disgusting, conniving group of demons known for their honeyed words and dark deeds. Goddess help me, why would I want to barge back in and strive for a little equilibrium?"

"Equilibrium?" Dolion sneered. "Is that what you

think we had when your dear old dad was running amok through here, buying favors and intimidating people? Do you plan to follow in his footsteps, *King* Nyfain? Or is all this just so that you can win a few allies, attempting to make me nervous enough to give you your kingdom's gold back?"

Nyfain stood slowly, and fire licked across his skin. He turned so his shoulders were squared with Dolion's, and even though there was a couch in the way, he looked like he suddenly had Dolion by the lapels.

"Give my kingdom's gold back? *Give* it, Dolion?" His smile set my heart to racing. "No, I don't want you to *give* me a damn thing. I want to take it, by force. And I will. I will take all that is mine, including my vengeance, and I will take your head with it. I don't know why everyone has allowed you this much control and freedom, but your tenure is at an end. Sleep tight, demon king. Your kingdom is about to burn."

CHAPTER 47
NYFAIN

M Y RAGE COULDN'T be contained. It was alive, burning through me just as the flame had danced across my skin. Every muscle in my body rippled with tension as I watched Dolion leave the room. None of that had been part of the plan. I hadn't played the role as I was supposed to, subtle and cunning, but had instead walked into the room waving a conversational mallet.

I did not give a fuck.

I could not bear what this mockery of a council had turned into.

"What does he have on you?" I asked, turning toward Caron and then Yuna. "Why are you turning a blind eye to him? I know you've heard what was going on in his dungeons. The dragons who came to my kingdom lately said you were approached by their elders. You must've heard rumors of people disappearing throughout the world. Then this…" I gestured at Porfino, shaking in the spot Finley had thrown him. "What the fuck is this? Since when don't you talk business in closed-door meetings? Since when do you let a non-royal decide what you can and cannot say?"

"We think it best to keep the peace at these things," Yuna said with a raised chin.

I stared at her for a solid beat, not sure what to say to that utter bullshit. The flames dancing across my body licked higher. Caron sat forward, and I saw movement in my peripheral vision, their beta edging closer. A soft shuffle behind me warned that Weston was moving closer as well.

"Hey, hey. Whoa, whoa." Finley's light touch ran up my arm and over my shoulder. I hadn't heard her get up. "Don't mind him." She snuggled into my side. I hooked my arm around her waist without thinking about it. "He's prone to fits of manic rage. He's not challenging you. Not physically, anyway. The betas can be called off. They won't be fighting here today. Well...Weston might. I have a feeling Dolion is going to try to kill us in our sleep again, and things will probably get hairy."

Caron and Yuna didn't so much as blink. They must've heard about that already. They'd heard what Dolion was up to and were still attempting to go along with this farce.

"It's fine." Finley rubbed my chest. "It's okay. Let's just have a chat."

"I don't think I'm calm enough to sit down and have a chat," I growled.

"Look, here is the situation," she said to the royals, maneuvering me so I would return to my seat on the couch. She sat beside me. "As he said, you have to know Dolion is doing some shady fucking things that should never be allowed in the magical world. Some *shady* fucking things. Human trafficking? With your own people? Come on." She leaned forward, almost across me, bracing her hand on my thigh. "You're not okay with that. Maybe you don't have proof, and maybe you don't want to talk about things that are *hearsay* because something bad will happen to you, like him attempting to kill you in your sleep, but it can't be allowed to continue. You must know that."

Caron licked his lips, and his eyes darted to the side. Behind him, two royals from smaller kingdoms had stood up and edged closer. They'd left plenty of distance, though—they wanted to hear, not talk.

Finley took notice of it as Hannon moved near her. She glanced at other royals, all of them focused on us, none of them wanting to actually take part in the conversation.

"Ah," she said, nodding. "Hmm."

"I think it is time for you to leave now, Finley," Hannon murmured, standing next to her with his hands at his sides. His eyes were wary. He had the ability to feel emotions in the room. Clearly whatever was happening wasn't good.

"Oh yeah? Was it something I said?" She huffed out a laugh, but I wasn't going to stick around to see what happened next. Not with her here.

"Let's go." I pushed to standing and dragged her up.

"You have no idea what you're talking about," Yuna said, her voice almost too low for me to hear. "King Dolion has money, power, and a seemingly endless army—"

"Not to mention powerful allies," Caron murmured.

"He has ways to sneak into bedchambers and turn people to his will. He has people always watching, reporting." She shook her head. "Look what he's already done to you. He has too much power for us to stand against him. It's better for everyone to…just…"

She couldn't finish the sentence.

Finley stared at her. Then she put her hands to either side of her temples and exploded them outward.

"That just blew my mind, right there. Look what he's done to me?" She swiveled around to look at the others. "Do you know how many people successfully escaped his dungeons? As many as came with me. How about the number of people he can turn to his will after I've given them my elixir?" She held up a fist. "None. Zero. Ask the faeries. You're worried about his armies? What fucking demon in this world has a chance against a band of dragons working with a team of wolves? No, no, don't look so scared. I'm not talking about you cowards. I'm talking about the best fucking alpha wolf this world has ever known"—she hooked a thumb at Weston—"teamed with mean, powerful fucking dragons who cut their teeth in Dolion's dungeons. Dolion has come after us multiple times since we freed our kingdom. Multiple. The only demons left alive were the ones that escaped with him. It wasn't us scurrying out of here earlier, either. So yes, I know what *I* am talking about. You're the one who doesn't have a clue." She held her arms wide, and fire spread across her skin dramatically. She could sure make a statement. "The dragons are back, and this time they are united under the golden king and flanked by wolves.

Be very careful which side you pick, fuckers. Very careful. I hold a grudge."

Hannon stepped forward and pushed her to get moving. I was by her side in an instant, daring anyone to so much as move in her direction. I would rip their arms off if they touched her.

My mother was going to be so pissed. *So* pissed. We'd messed up in so many ways, I didn't even know what to say. But fuck it. Starvos had decided to go in hot anyway. I now saw why. The magical world was afraid of the demon king. He'd pushed and beaten and manipulated them until they were afraid to act.

Hopefully we'd just given them some confidence.

If we didn't, Starvos would tomorrow.

"Hannon, what'd you feel?" I asked as we entered the halls at a fast pace. I wanted to get back, get our nightly protections in place, and then fuck my mate. Her speech had me on fire for her. Desperate to feel her tight cunt wrapped around my cock.

"There was mistrust in droves," he said. Weston walked beside him. "Along with suspicion and nervousness. I'd bet at least half have some sort of deal with the demon king or whoever else he is working with, and the other half are afraid of the repercussions of standing against him."

"Caron and Yuna?" I asked, turning a corner and finding some staff lingering, chatting with one another.

They went to bow, but fear widened their eyes when they looked at me, and they hunched instead.

"Fear," Hannon replied. "Caron and Yuna, I mean. Not those staff right there. Though…they are also afraid."

"They clearly haven't seen an alpha dragon in a while," Weston murmured.

"I wonder if there was more to Caron and Yuna ignoring the dragons in their kingdom than simply a creature divide," I said to myself, seeing more staff scurry away instead of bow to us.

"You think Dolion was encouraging them to turn a blind eye?" Finley asked.

"I don't know. It doesn't matter, though. The dragons can come to us. I don't much care if the royals give a shit. They had their chance to include dragons in their affairs. They let it pass."

"You seemed genuine when you apologized to them," Hannon said.

"Royals in that situation rarely are, but we have to go through the motions. And directly after my apology, I called them out on their inadequate response to the dragons, and now we all know where we stand. My mother will be displeased I couldn't control myself better."

"The Flamma beta lacked in power compared to the Red Lupine beta," Weston said. "I would bet the Red Lupine pack is still strong and well organized. The pack with the most power will pull alpha."

"The Red Lupine Kingdom has aligned with the demon king," I said, turning down another hall and finding it bare. "I obviously have no proof, but you heard our conversation. That would make the Flamma royals even more hesitant to deal with us."

"What about you?" Hannon asked Weston. "When it

comes to pack power, how do you stack up?"

"We have more powerful wolves but a much smaller pack. I'm a stronger alpha, without question, but with our tiny pack, they'd pull alpha."

Finley looked back, incredulous.

"What?" Weston asked.

"You have a large and still-growing pack of *dragons*. Ain't no bunch of wolves pulling alpha on us. Fuck that."

Weston laughed. "And here I thought you didn't have the typical arrogance of a dragon."

"Come on, give me a break," she replied, slipping her hand into mine as we walked. "We're mighty because we work together, dragons and wolves. Don't discount the dragons when you wolves get ready to measure your cock sizes."

"Dragons specialize in enormous cocks," I said with a grin. "We'd win that contest any day."

"Goddess help me, their arrogance is insufferable," Weston said to Hannon, but I could hear the humor in his voice. Also the excitement. For a moment, he really had forgotten that his pack was so much larger than the wolves in its ranks. He had literal firepower at his disposal. It mattered.

I also wondered if he sensed the danger coming. Dolion felt the walls closing in on him. There was a reason he'd been trying to kill us to keep us from getting to this meeting. He'd wanted to shut us up. Now he knew he couldn't. He'd take drastic measures to get rid of us and hope he could cow the rest of them into overlooking his crimes.

Starvos had gotten it right: politics didn't matter.

Tiptoeing around the issue wasn't the right way to play it. The magical rulers had descended into chaos. Dolion had dragged them into it, and there he reigned.

Or, I should say, he *had* reigned.

He'd dragged me in too, and now he'd discover it was a place where dragons thrived. Finley as well as myself. He'd made a deal with the wrong sort of creature. Now we got to prove it.

"Weston, does everyone have their demon-be-gone elixir?" I asked as we neared our wing. There were more staff here, standing by in case anyone needed anything.

"We're set," he replied, his tone back to professional. "Our guests are separated between the various rooms on cots." He meant Govam and his demons. "We've arranged for them to be guarded by equal parts wolves and dragons at all times."

"And the castle staff?"

"I kicked them out of the area, as you asked me to."

"Good. Be ready for anything. War starts now. Hannon…"

"Yes, sire?" Hannon responded. When he went formal, he knew he was on duty. I'd finally found a way to incorporate him in our kingdom—one that fulfilled him. He was no longer just the money man. He needed to use his animal to help protect his home.

"Don't feel like you need to keep watch. Get sleep. We have someone watching your family. I want you fully rested if something happens."

"Yes, sire."

As Weston had said, the hallways were bare of any staff except ours.

"Finley," I said, my mind churning out all the ways Dolion might come for us tonight. "Hadriel knows to consistently check in with our people and make sure no one has turned informant, correct?"

"Definitely. He's also learning the details of every single letter that goes out and comes in. If he can't beguile the information out of people, he makes Vemar shake it out of them. Literally, I think. Hadriel and Leala are also on a mission to make friends with the staff."

"Good. We're set." I turned back and nodded to Weston, leaving him at the mouth of our wing.

Hannon continued on with us, even after we passed his suite. At our rooms, Finley frowned at him, and then sighed dramatically and let him enter our suite first.

"This has already gotten old," she said as Hannon had a look around. "I'm the knife-wielding one, Hannon, not you. I don't like this change in dynamic."

"In times of peace and when you aren't pregnant, I won't be so overbearing, I promise." He checked in the washroom and opened the closet.

I'd told Leala and Urien to take the night off. I wanted them well rested in case we had to flee in a hurry.

"Isn't this annoying you?" she asked me. "You're an alpha dragon—surely you don't need my brother mollycoddling you."

I laughed. "I'm protecting you while he checks out our rooms. His animal is driving him, just like mine is driving me. Suck it up."

She rolled her eyes, watching Hannon work. "You're not even really checking!" She walked into the room but stopped when I put a hand on her shoulder.

I pushed my body up against hers, sighing softly at her warmth and her soft, feminine scent. I ran my hand down her back, fluttering my thumb over her scales. She shivered.

"I don't need to see," Hannon called from beside the bed. "I can feel if someone is there by their emotions."

"What if they don't have emotions?"

"Everyone has emotions. Some people just choose not to express them. Soon people will figure that out, and I'll have to use my eyes."

"Or a wolf's nose," she replied.

"Yeah, or that. They can die, though."

"Hannon…" She threw up her hands in exasperation. "You can't be a bodyguard for everyone for the rest of your life just because you can't die. That's unreasonable."

He met us back at the door and nodded at her. "When you're not starting a war with a demon king, we'll talk about it, okay? Until then, I can keep you safe, so I *will* keep you safe."

He nodded to me as he slipped by. She watched him go down the hall, her eyes narrowed.

I laughed and gently pushed her into the room. "Let him baby you. His animal must be riding him hard to do it, and it also attaches him to the kingdom."

She held up her finger as I locked the door behind us. "Don't talk about the best ways to trap my brother. I won't let you use him. *I'm* the only one who can use him. If you try, I'll just get mad, but since you won't let me properly fight you, I'll have no way to expend my rage."

"Sure you will." I ran my hands up the sides of her

hips and dragged my teeth along one of her marks. The tension quickly left her body. I pulled the straps from over her shoulders and let her dress slide to the ground. I growled when I saw her lack of underwear. "You'll just have to ride me hard until you come all over my cock."

"Not the same," she whispered as I ran my lips down her flesh before turning her around and licking across a budded nipple.

I sucked it in as I undid the buttons on my shirt before pushing that and my jacket off. I worked my way down, kissing and licking while running my fingers down her scales and then over the swell of her ass. I undid the buttons on my pants with one hand as I licked her clit and ran my fingers through her slick folds. She spread her thighs, allowing me more access. Her hands curled into my hair.

"Lick my pussy, Nyfain," she said in a breathy moan.

I stood instead, leaving my pants and shoes on the floor. I took her lips with mine, the kiss starting soft and deepening quickly. Her taste drove me wild, fresh and sweet and *her*. Walking her backward, I waited until she bumped off the wall before lowering again, wanting to give her something to stabilize herself against. A hard surface to fuck her against.

I paused at her belly, running my hands across the flatness and yearning for the days and months to pass so that I could watch her grow. So that I could be there for her, laughing at her annoyance as I did everything I could to assure her comfort and provide for her. I couldn't wait to feel the baby move, and I could barely contain my excitement at the thought of meeting him or her for the first time. I hated that Dolion was standing in the way of our peaceful happiness. I hated that, even now, he was trying to ruin my family.

Anger sparked, hot and raw. Soon this threat would be over. I would see that demon and all his minions with their heads on spits.

"Hmm," Finley said, responding to the power pulsing within me. "Say night-night to baby and then move on to other things." I felt pressure on the top of my head.

I laughed. "Mommy is pushy," I whispered, kissing her stomach, taking a moment to hold her waist and gently brace my forehead against her. "I love you so much, Finley. I love the family we're making. I've wanted this for so long. I never knew how much I wanted this until now."

She ran her hands through my hair, and then I needed her with a passion that was hard to describe.

I bent to her center, putting my hand under her knee and lifting it to the side. I licked through her slit, and her taste exploded across my senses. We moaned together as I threaded two fingers into her cunt and rubbed in that spot I knew she loved. I sucked her clit in pulses, working her fast and hard. Her pussy gripped my fingers.

I stopped and straightened, running my hands up her smooth skin and turning her. Her palms hit the wall. My hands on her hips, I pulled until she backed up toward me, ass out. With my foot I tapped each instep, getting her to spread further before returning my fingers to her sopping cunt. I moved her juices to her clit, rubbing in lazy circles until she started to squirm again. Once again, I pulled back from letting her climax.

She whimpered in protest before pushing out a little more. I gripped the base of my cock and ran the tip through her glistening folds. One hand on her shoulder, I kept the other on my dick as I let it catch at her opening. Slowly I watched it sink into her wet depths. Her heady moan gave me a jolt of pleasure and almost shook the hold I had on my control. I struggled to keep it for a little longer, though. She liked a little teasing. She liked to stay on the verge of orgasm until she was delirious.

I bottomed out, grinding against her. Her heat gripped my cock as she tried to work a little more friction out of me. I didn't make her wait. I pulled out and thrust back into her, starting up a hard and fast rhythm. Her grunts of pleasure started to unravel me, slowly at first and then faster. I worked into her, reaching around her with one hand now to work her clit, and nearly grabbing her hair in a fist. Instead, I grabbed her shoulder and raked my thumb across the top of her scales.

"Holy...*fuck*!" She shuddered violently. Her pussy contracted around my cock with her orgasm.

And then I was lost.

I gripped her hair then. I held her tightly as I thrust into her, animalistic, chasing my orgasm. Her climax dripped down my cock. The slick slide of her frazzled my brain. It was as though she'd found the thread of an old sweater and yanked it apart. I rubbed my chest across her back, her scales scraping me, and continued to work her clit. She whimpered again, squirming.

Pleasure mounted. My balls tightened up. Almost there. I yanked her head to the side and bit down on her neck. She cried out, shuddering again as I sucked, and then I hit the edge and blasted out over it. The orgasm consumed me, ripping me apart and scattering me around. I filled her with my release, pumping it into her with three more hard thrusts as I shook against her.

Breathing heavily, I draped over her, holding myself within her for a moment longer. She angled her head so her cheek would be against my face. I smoothed her hair away and planted a soft kiss to the side of her neck.

"Let's get some sleep. I'm worried we're going to need it."

CHAPTER 48
FINLEY

L OUD POUNDING SOUNDED from the door. A shout rang through the room, a woman's voice, but I couldn't make out whose.

Nyfain threw the sheets away from him, swinging his legs over the mattress. The frantic pounding stopped only to be replaced by a loud crash. Wood groaned. Again, like someone was trying to bust down the door with their shoulder.

"I'm coming, I'm coming!" Nyfain yelled, jogging.

I pulled the sheets away, shaking off my dreams and pushing up from the bed. Light flickered outside the windows along the far wall. I hurried over, and my breath caught for a long moment.

Bodies washed over the grass toward the castle. Demons. Moonlight shone down on them carrying swords or torches or larger weapons. Demonic creatures ran within them, their hideous faces screwed up in rage or their snouts or maws open, exposing glistening teeth and stringy drool.

More shouts rang out from behind me.

"Finley, hurry," Nyfain yelled from near the door. "The castle is under attack. You need to get to safety with your family."

"Fat fucking chance," I said as I spun toward him. "I can blow fire now. I can help."

Amazingly, he didn't argue.

"We need to get to Starvos." He waited for me with an outstretched hand.

I didn't bother with a cover-up and ran past him and to the hall. Weston waited for us with shining eyes and a composed face.

"There are wolves running through the castle," he said as we jogged past him. He kept pace. "Red Lupine. From what I gather, they're trying to keep the kingdoms opposing them separated."

That confirmed it. They truly were working with the demons. Well, they'd regret it.

"Sire," Micah said, waiting for us on the right with all the army dragons lined up behind him. Tamara stood on the other side, my guard stretched out along the wall behind her. Beyond them, crowded around the entrance of the wing, waited Weston's wolves.

Every door in the hall was open, the rooms housing those who couldn't fit in the hallway, the demons, and other staff members.

"Put my family and the staff in the dragon rooms," I said as we slowed to get organized. "I doubt anyone will go looking for dragons."

"What about the demons?" Tamara asked.

Govam stepped out of the room two doors down on

my left, turning sideways to get between the dragons. He watched us without expression, awaiting orders.

"Keep them to the rooms," Nyfain answered. "Let them guard the family and staff for now. Their value is in the knowledge they have, not on the battlefield. I don't want them to get confused with the enemy and accidentally killed." Nyfain stared at Govam for an intense beat. "We have no reason to confuse you with the enemy, correct?"

"For us, there is no fate imaginable worse than being captured by him. Our survival is in your hands."

Nyfain nodded. "Then guard the innocent." He turned back to Weston. "What of the enemy wolves? How big of a threat are they?"

Weston's smile was wicked. "They should've known better than to shift. I need the dragon portion of the pack to create a big distraction. Once the enemy wolves are fully in battle mode, they'll be mine."

Nyfain looked at Micah as Leala came running down the hall in a leather bustier, a leather thong, and shiny black-heeled boots. She had her whip in hand and speckles and dots of something all over her chest and neck.

"My love, don't you ever take a break from information gathering?" Hadriel asked her quietly as she slowed in the center of the dragon column, everyone suddenly falling silent in her presence.

"Why take a break when I can get orgasms at the same time as information?" she murmured, catching my eye. It wasn't hard, given I was staring. "Milady, we've got trouble."

"We know, dove," Hadriel said. "We're literally getting ready to confront it, or didn't you notice all the naked people?"

"Is that…candle wax all over her?" someone asked.

Leala licked her lips. "No, I mean, they are targeting you, milady. I tied up and pleasure-tortured one of the staff members who services the demon quarters. It took a minute, but I finally got good information out of him. He overheard the demon king telling one of the others to take you out. He thinks you're the key to the golden dragon's destruction. If you hide, they will search you out."

Rage ballooned within the bond as Nyfain turned to me. Down the way, Arleth and Delaney stepped out of their suite, having clearly heard Leala's warning. They wanted to know what we'd do, and to me it was a no-brainer.

"If he wants to target me, he might as well go after my dragon," I said, feeling the fire of battle. "In the air would be the safest."

Frustration and regret washed through the bond but didn't show on Nyfain's face. "You stay near me. Understand?"

"I'm not going to be dead weight, Nyfain," I said. "I can handle myself. I know how much I can do and still be safe. I won't endanger our child, nor will I endanger our people by hiding. Lay off."

"I love domestic arguing as much as the next person," Hadriel said, "but we don't have time for it, Finley. Just agree with him now and do as you please later, like normal."

Hannon jogged out of a room down the way. "Demons are surrounding the castle. We need to move if we don't want to be overrun. It looks like the demon king had a large force on hand. He was ready for this."

Nyfain swore under his breath. "We need to get to Starvos. After that, we'll meet the demons."

"When the battle turns in your favor, watch for a change in their organization," Govam called out over the sudden din. "At some point, the higher-powered demons will take over. When that happens, it means Dolion has left. They'll try to scatter. Let them. Chase him. Try to get him before he gets back to his castle."

"His fortress, you mean," Vemar said.

"Yes," Govam replied. "I can get you in without being detected, but if you fight him there, it'll be close quarters, and you won't be able to use your dragons. The odds will be in his favor."

Nyfain grabbed my hand and urged me forward, running by Govam. It wouldn't take Dolion long to take off, I knew that much. He'd nearly gotten eaten by a dragon, so I imagined he'd be a bit scale-shy.

"As soon as you have the space, shift," Nyfain called out behind him. "Barrel through the enemy wolves. Scatter them. If they don't get out of the way, that's their—"

Nyfain cut off as a demon ran around the corner in a staff member's outfit. He skidded to a stop upon seeing us, shifting his appearance to look human. Almost lazily, Nyfain grabbed him by the neck as we passed by. He ripped him sideways and slammed him into the wall. His head thunked hard before he slid bonelessly to the ground.

"—that's their problem," Nyfain finished, reaching the stairs and stuttering in his step. Three wolves waited at the base, looking up. Beyond them were more, the first line of offense.

"They're small and likely have very little power," Weston growled. "They have been left to die. I'll shift now. I don't need dragons to take these wolves in hand."

"I am *so* glad he's on our side," Hadriel said from somewhere behind us.

"Okay, little buddy, this is goodbye for a while," Vemar told him as Nyfain walked us down the hall to give Weston room to shift. "Make sure to watch that asshole."

"Vemar, love, you really need to learn when and where that actually applies," Hadriel muttered.

Weston jogged between Nyfain and me as we headed toward the stairs. The enemy wolves growled, their ears flattening against their heads...and then suddenly they weren't growling anymore. One and all started to back away, their tails tucked firmly between their legs. A moment later, they started whimpering. Each lowered slowly, flattening to their bellies.

"My turn." Another of our wolves, powerful in his own right, on the next tier of Weston's hierarchy, shifted. He jogged down as Weston prepared to move on, his hackles raised and tail high.

Nyfain and I jogged past them, the rest of our team following. Weston returned to his position between us, and a glance back said the enemy wolves were now allies. We could turn them all loose when this day was done, but for now they would help rather than hurt.

Down the next flight of the stairs, we found the same situation, which Weston quickly handled, plus a few wolves loitering in the hallways.

"They are alerting the others of our progress," one of the wolf shifters behind us said as we continued on.

"Lot of good it'll do them," I said, finally reaching the wide, curved staircase that would land us on the bottom level at the front of the castle. More wolves waited there, larger than the others and much better organized.

"These are the power players," the wolf shifter behind us said as everyone started making room to shift. "Time for the dragons to help us make this easy."

Power built within the link. Nyfain's and my dragons shoved it back and forth, building quickly. They knew it was time to go to war.

"Watch that asshole," Nyfain told me with a smirk and a wink, and I couldn't help but laugh as our power pumped higher. He glanced behind him. "Okay, dragons, cause havoc."

Nyfain walked down a few steps. Weston and another wolf quickly fell in beside him, their hackles raised and their lips pulled back from their teeth in twin snarls. The wolves at the bottom backed off a few paces, ready to battle. One of them jerked, though, and then another, their ears twitching. More followed, hunching a little, their growls growing louder. Another shook itself, probably feeling Weston's call to join our pack and trying to shake it off.

Nyfain started to shift, and the wolves fell back as the

dragon grew and grew. On the landing behind me, Vemar did the same, not waiting for his turn. Then Tamara and Jade followed, crowding the area.

Nyfain's dragon ran forward, and Vemar's dragon jumped out over the balcony, flapping his wings once to slow his descent before landing with a thud. He'd learned the tight jump-fly technique to get across the lava near the Bridge of Doom. He lifted his head and roared as wolves ran in to bite or scratch him. They were wasting their time.

Vemar barreled into them as Nyfain ran through the wolves at the bottom of the stairs. Tamara hopped over next, and I rushed forward, shifting as I went.

"Finley, wait," I heard. Hannon. He didn't know how to fight on the ground. He had two bird feet instead of four sturdy dragon legs.

At least we have that working for us, my dragon thought as we followed Nyfain through the scattering wolves, who were not sure how to organize or hold their ground in such a small space with such large predators in their midst. They weren't used to dragons fighting on the ground.

You really need to let that competition between you and the phoenix go. It's not a good look, I told her as she swung her tail to the side and took out an entire sitting area under the second-floor landing. *Don't wreck the castle, either.*

First, I'll let the competition go if you admit that it's good that Hannon is going to look after you while you are in a delicate *condition—*

You are clearly out of your mind—

—and second, she continued, veering to the side of the space to scare a wolf and run over a couch. She crushed it under her feet. *The demons and wolves started it, and if the people who run this place have allowed a war to break out within their walls after all the warnings we gave them, they deserve what they get.*

But we'll have to chip in the money to pay for it, idiot, I told her as Vemar crashed through a door, taking the walls around it with him. Thank the goddess the ceiling was at least high. *This place is run by the collection of kingdoms.*

It needs updating anyway.

Nyfain roared out his battle cry, the sound shaking the walls and vibrating the ground beneath us. Wolves ahead of us visibly quailed, sinking down a little on their haunches. He dodged right and ran through a well-organized cluster while we went left, swiping the sides with our tail and taking out more furniture.

You're just doing that to be destructive, I accused her.

Yes.

Moving through the next room, my dragon scattered more wolves, slashing with claws and swinging with tail. My dragon swiped her head to the side, bashing her thick skull into two wolves and knocking them aside. They rolled across the floor and then shook, Weston coming up behind us. Any sort of vulnerability empowered him to shift their allegiance.

A look back saw the dragons lumbering along behind us. My guard was trying to catch up, but there was simply not enough room. The first level had grand rooms and entrances, but that was only for human-sized creatures. Our dragons barely fit.

Across the castle we went, more and more wolves joining our host. It was the one factor I was sure Dolion hadn't accounted for. If he had, he would've forced them to stay in human form. Since the Red Lupine monarchs *had* known, it would seem Dolion wasn't the only one keeping secrets from his allies.

Nyfain crashed through a smallish doorway, headed first to Starvos before we confronted Dolion's troops. Wood and paint fell like rain as he thrashed, forcing the hole wider, clearly forgetting he was the largest of the dragons. Of any of the creatures, actually. We ran along behind him, finding the set of stairs we needed and breaking the banister as we lumbered up.

At the landing, though, Nyfain shifted back to human before stepping to the side and waiting for me to do the same.

"Wait for a moment," he said, catching his breath from the shift.

The hallway in front of us looked empty, but that didn't mean it was. The other dragons had slowed to a stop below us, looking around to make sure there were no other enemies to knock around or confuse.

"Weston, I need some of your kind up here," Nyfain said. "Dragons, stay here until I come for you."

He waited for the wolves, Weston among them, to run up the stairs and flank us before we jogged down the corridor. Weston growled, a sound echoed by the wolf to our left, slightly ahead of us.

Two faeries popped out with large, shining swords held high, dressed in tight red outfits and with eyes promising violence.

Nyfain raised his hands. "I need to see Starvos. Our wolf alpha has thoroughly reined in the Red Lupine wolves. We need to meet the host of demons outside so that our dragons can be of more use. Time is of the essence."

One of the faeries rattled off something to the other in their language. There was a brief pause before they nodded, turned, and started jogging in front of us. We followed. All the doors were closed, but we found more faeries along the sides of the hall, tucked into nooks or hidden behind tapestries or curtains. Finally we reached the last door.

The faerie on my right knocked in a pattern, two fast, three slow, one more. A woman with fearful eyes and her hair in a bun opened the door. One of their staff. She saw us, and relief crossed her expression before she glanced behind us like she was searching for something.

She's looking for that damn phoenix, I'll betcha, my dragon grumbled. *He doesn't even know how to work all the things.*

What things?

He doesn't even know what things! He doesn't know what he's capable of!

"Janine, who is it?" Starvos called from within.

She stepped to the side, allowing us admittance.

Starvos stood at the windows dressed in red battle regalia with a stylized metal breastplate and cuffs around his forearms and shins. His warriors waited in the other rooms, standing tall and ready. Calia and Dessia sat in the far corner. Their eyes were tight, and they breathed a sigh of relief when they saw us.

I didn't have time to notice anyone else as Starvos glanced back. "Cocktails got out of hand, it seems," he said by way of greeting.

"Were you waiting for us?" Nyfain asked, taking stock of Starvos's fighters.

"Yes. I didn't know what else to do. There were wolves blocking us in. We could've gotten through them, but we would've taken damage. And then what? Have you seen what surrounds us?" He turned back as his lip curled. "That demon knew it would come to this. He knew all along that you had—that *we* had—enough incriminating evidence to knock him from his throne. I didn't expect him to accept it gracefully. I expected him to force us to take action, but *this*?" He gestured to the window. "There hasn't been a battle here for…hundreds of years. This is sacred land—"

"All due respect, Starvos," I said, "but we don't have time for outrage. That can come later. We need your people, and we have to cut through those demons. Our wolf alpha has the Red Lupine wolves under his control—"

"What?" Starvos blinked at me as though slapped out of a daze. "How?"

"He's more powerful than them, basically," I replied. "The royals used to use him to bring wolves into their pack and hold them there. It's a long story. Regardless, he's doing it now to add to our host and shrink theirs. We need your faeries, though. We've come to ask you to join us. United we are stronger. I just ask that your faeries fight *with* the wolves and dragons, not independently of them."

"*With* the…dragons?" Starvos looked at Nyfain, then back to me. "You can have warriors on your backs? You see…they've killed the stabled horses. The disgusting creatures brought them out there to kill them where we'd see the remains. It has crippled our army. Without horses, we'll be overrun immediately."

I glanced at Nyfain. Starvos was smart and usually sharp, but he was also up there in years, and while we'd expressed a lot of these concepts to him in our various meetings, they clearly hadn't sunk in. This was new territory for him. We needed to get over the informational hump. Time was wasting.

"Starvos," Nyfain barked, infusing power into the word. "We have wolves and dragons. Work around us. We are worth a thousand horses, because we have teeth and claws and fire. Would you let them beat you? Rise up!"

His last words were a growl, his voice like a whip crack. Starvos flinched, and then his back straightened. He braced his hands against the sides of the windows. "Yes. Okay. Wolves and dragons." He tightened his hand into a fist. "Dragons! Yes!"

Calia furrowed her brow at him before she slid her gaze to me. She'd clearly never seen him this scattered. I wondered if he'd ever had to go to war. It didn't seem like it, which explained why he'd put it off for so long. Fear could turn a person blind, even a king. Maybe especially a king.

Nyfain turned away from them and started meeting the eyes of the waiting faerie warriors. With a grin I couldn't help and eyes that were probably manic, I did the same.

"I've always said there's no stronger force than one that includes all the creatures fighting together," I told one, giving him a shoulder pat that was hopefully inspiring. "Well..." I moved on to another and touched her on the arm. Still another, holding up my fist in front of him and shaking it in anticipation. "Not exactly always. But since I started fighting demons. That counts."

"Work within the pack," Nyfain said as he headed for the door. "Don't fear the dragons. We won't burn you with our fire, and we won't trample you if we're on the ground. We've trained to fight alongside ground-bound troops. Trust in our ability. We'll scatter their troops and kill anyone we can. You and the wolves take down anyone we miss. Are you ready?"

As one, they answered with a crisp word I didn't quite catch.

"Be careful, Finley," Calia called after us, and I gave her a thumbs-up as I jogged out of the door.

Nyfain and I ran back down the hall, gathering up the wolves to flank us again as we went.

"What of the warriors in the hall, sire?" one of the faeries asked as we went.

"Leave them to protect those staying behind. We have what we need."

"They use magic when they fight, right?" I whispered as we reached the stairs and quickly descended. All the wolves were organized in neat lines, some shaking or lying on their bellies, probably struggling to get out of the magical pack lock. They'd have to endure it a while longer. Their current situation was better than being dead.

I did wonder where their king had gone, however. Maybe he was trapped just like the rest of them. That would serve him right.

Nyfain stopped at the top of the stairs, looking down on those waiting below. Various squeals and roars lifted into the night from outside. A slow thump, like a sword hitting a shield, kept up a steady rhythm. And then a demon ran into the castle from the way we'd come, screaming. Another followed.

"Attack!" Nyfain shouted.

CHAPTER 49
FINLEY

IT WAS VEMAR'S dragon who responded first. He turned with a roar, swiping his tail across the fast-approaching demons. It took out three before he raced for the widened doorway, trampling any demons foolish enough to charge toward him.

"Remember what I said," Nyfain told me before giving me a quick kiss. "I'm trusting you."

"I'm not sure anyone is really going to be after my asshole, but I'll take it under advisement."

I just caught him shaking his head before he started running. I was right behind him.

Another dragon didn't wait to go through the door. He crashed right through the window and wall, breathing fire as he did so. More followed, knocking holes through the structure that could hopefully be mended. Wolves raced out after them.

The faeries followed us down the stairs and then surged out, running through the new doorways, as first Nyfain and then I shifted. My guard was on the other side, none of them having bothered to take to the sky. They stomped their way forward, taking out demons with their claws, teeth, and tails, nearly as comfortable on the ground now as Nyfain.

A bright flash of fire caught my dragon's attention to the left. Hannon rose into the sky. Flame swirled up from his head, flowed over his feathers, and dripped down from his body. Sparks and embers and waves of light drifted out into the sky behind him as he moved, rising higher before letting out a great *caw*.

I could feel my dragon internally snicker. The phoenix was cool, but he definitely didn't sound it.

My dragon rose to meet him before turning and diving low, feeling the fire rise through her. We'd practiced this a lot over that last week with the faeries, and she'd learned to use her fire with great accuracy.

She let out the fire in a thick gush to start, rolling it over the enemy to see if they would be affected. Almost at once they started screaming or screeching, dropping to the ground and writhing. Another stream and down they went. Dolion clearly hadn't wasted anti-fire magic on these troops.

Hannon did the same, flitting and swirling and doing loop-de-loops as he sprayed and dripped and...possibly shat fire on the demons below him. This fire didn't burn them to death, though. It killed on impact, instantly.

Loop-de-loops? my dragon thought as she did another dive, spraying fire. *What sort of boob does that in a battle? I thought he was frolicking when he was doing that in the faerie kingdom. You know, showing off for them or something. I figured he'd know better than to do it in battle. This is embarrassing.*

He's shitting fire. Just let him be. He's got bigger problems than loop-de-loops. For example, Hadriel mercilessly making fun of him after this.

This is true, my dragon replied.

The other dragons rose into the sky, raining down fire. Nyfain's dragon flew by our side like this was a fun outing rather than a battle. It seemed a little too...easy. And in no time at all, the demons were scattering all over the place, running away.

These demons don't seem very powerful, do they? my dragon asked as we sprayed a group running for the distant trees. They didn't get far.

I let that thought sink in for a moment as she continued to burn them down and the demon swarm started to break up and scatter.

Fuck. I would grit my teeth if I had access to them. *Fuck! He's playing us. He's stalling us. Call everyone in. Let these demons scatter or leave some of the dragons to chase them and burn them. We have to get ready to go.*

You think the demon king is already heading to his fortress to lock himself in? my dragon asked before roaring her command with will.

Yes. He knows we'll follow. Of course we will; we've been gearing up for this for months. Dolion knows he doesn't stand a chance on our soil, so he's going to give himself the best odds. He's way ahead of us.

She landed at the hole in the wall closest to our staircase. Nyfain joined me there a moment later, shifting after us and walking closer.

"He's already headed home," Nyfain said, and waited for my affirmation. "Fuck." He shook his head. "I thought he'd play the game a little bit first. But Starvos is clearly in over his head, and the Flamma wolves are obviously hiding. We're the only ones Dolion actually fears. We're the only ones he hasn't manipulated into a corner. My father—the mad king, I mean—was always beyond his control, I think, and then they made their deal. It allowed Dolion to get the dragons out of the way, and the former king was just mad enough, and desperate enough, to fall for it. Dolion probably thought he'd kill me during the curse. I was a useless playboy back then. Flippant. It was an act, mostly, but he didn't seem to know that. He was trying to shut us down."

Arleth landed, followed by Delaney and Micah. Nyfain repeated his musings for their ears.

"It stands to reason," Arleth said. "Dolion did effectively get rid of the dragons, and he then bullied his way into a sly sort of power over everyone else. He needs you dead."

"And we need him dead." I spread my hands. "Govam is about to earn his keep. We'll need to get into the demon fortress.

"Who is going to tell Hadriel we're headed back to sea?" Delaney asked with a slight grin.

"Not it!" the group chorused.

That chore ultimately went to Vemar, who didn't mind in the least. He broke the news and then laughed at Hadriel's tirade about puking and shitting over the bow of the boat.

Starvos had regained his composure by the time we

returned to his rooms, and though he didn't say anything, I could tell he was embarrassed by sending his
warriors with Nyfain and not even following or standing
in a place where he could watch the battle. He'd let
himself and his people down, and he knew it.

To make up for it, he had his fastest ship send word
to Wyvern to get everyone moving. The battle was on. It
was time to meet Dolion where he felt the safest and
prove to him that nowhere was safe on the run from a
very determined dragon.

"THIS PLACE IS a shithole," Nyfain said as we drifted
toward the dark shores of the demon kingdom. It barely
qualified as such. It was more like an insufferable island
with constant wind, rain, and darkness, with only one
useable beach and crashing waves along the cliffs.

The castle, which looked more like a multilevel fortress built by a drunk designer and finished in different
eras, sat on top of the highest part of the island. The
long, dark building plunged down into the roots of the
land.

"The ground levels have arrow slits," I said. "I'm sure
they'll use them. They are covered over in glass, but
that's easy to get through."

I held a large sack containing Arleth's sword. Well,
technically it was my sword now, since she'd given it to
me, but it felt like a gray area. Hers or mine, it suited my
purpose. Many places inside that castle weren't big
enough for my dragon. I'd need something to fight with,
and since this sword and I had history here, it was
perfect. Hopefully I'd get the chance to kill Dolion with

it.

"They'll use arrows, yes," Govam said, standing to Nyfain's other side with the rest of the demons gathered close. It was time to see if he'd been playing the long game on Dolion's behalf, or if he genuinely did want change.

Nyfain studied the castle. "That is stone, right?"

"Right," Govam replied. "It isn't going to burn."

"Not with dragon fire," Hannon murmured, rubbing his chin. "I don't have dragon fire. I have brimfire, apparently. I borrowed a few books from the faeries, and I've been reading up on phoenixes. Brimfire can slice through almost anything if used right."

A loud, slightly worrying burp announced Hadriel's arrival. "But do you know how to use it right?"

"I tried on the council lands, and it killed people on impact."

"Is that when you shit yourself and hoped no one would notice?" Hadriel asked.

"You're projecting your situation onto me, Hadriel," Hannon said as he studied the castle in the distance. "I don't think anyone has ever shit themselves accidentally as often or as flamboyantly as you have."

Tamara, standing nearby with Vemar, started laughing despite the severity of the situation.

"But to your point, no, I am not positive I can do it," Hannon said. "I have not tried on actual stone, and I don't want to try in the ship in case I sink us all."

"What about the ground, though?" Tamara asked. "Did you leave divots or holes or anything?"

"Brimfire does not react to the ground as it does to

other objects. It will burn it, but it will not eat through it. I'll learn why that is when I have more time."

I blew out a breath. "Okay, in summary, our options are essentially to"—I held up one finger—"sneak in a few of the staff entrances that Dolion either doesn't know about or hasn't thought about"—I held up a second finger—"try to break in heavily barricaded doors that are armed with magical or poisoned traps"—a third finger—"or see if Hannon can cut a hole in the side of the building. If he succeeds, though, we'd have the whole interior of the castle on the other side, waiting to attack." I put my hand down. "That about the gist of it?"

"What a slew of very promising options," Hadriel said dryly. "Tell me again why the demon king wouldn't know about those entrances?"

"Servants are below him," Govam replied. "And those doors belong to the lowliest servants. He would be disgusted to know too much about them, and it wouldn't occur to him that someone of my caliber might concern himself with them. Usually, he would be right."

"And in this case?" I asked.

"When you are trying to document all possible ways of escaping without dying, you stop worrying about social tiers."

"Fair enough," Tamara murmured.

"We have no choice," Nyfain said, his arm coming around my back. "We'll follow Govam's plan. We'll divide up and go through the staff doors. Once inside, we'll try to sneak our way to the staff mess hall to meet up. Then we'll attack. That's the only way. The faeries and wolves are good in close combat. The court dragons know the sword, and some from the villages do as well. The dragons who don't will stay with Hannon. Hannon, you'll need to distract them and figure out how to shit fire through that stone"—Hadriel spat out laughter—"or whatever you have to do. Don't get killed, though. We can't wait for another dawn for you to come back to life. We don't have that kind of time. Finley, you stay with Hannon and direct the—"

"Don't even say it." I pulled away from him. "That is absolutely not going to happen. We talked about this on the way here. If you go down, who do you think Dolion is going to go after next? Me. Except I don't have even a quarter of the knowledge you do, and your mom doesn't know anything about warfare. If he takes you down, it'll only be a matter of time before he gets to us. We work best together, Nyfain. You know we do. We have to stay together. Dragons are tough, you said so yourself. Our child must be tough as well. We will all be fine, so long as we *stick together.*"

He stared at me for a long moment, anguish plain in his eyes. "Fuck," he said under his breath, turning to stare straight ahead at nothing. "How do you always get your way?"

"By speaking sense. Okay, let's stop fucking around. We need to go see Starvos, give him the plan, and then get underway."

WET FROM THE rain and cold but not feeling it because of adrenaline, part of our host gathered on the weather-battered side of the island in a cave mostly cut off from the elements. We'd taken a precarious rock path to get here, up from a tiny inlet that had been impossible to see from farther out. There were only four entrances that might work for us, all of them too small for our party to go in together. Govam had volunteered to lead our crew, clearly knowing that Nyfain would want to keep his eye on him. Denski led another, and Sonassa and another demon led the third and fourth groups.

A gently used firepit sat in the middle of the floor with a stack of wood sitting on top of wet straw. Little droplets of what looked like rust dotted the side of the cave in a line, leading from deep within the cave to the opening.

"Blood," Govam said without being asked, leading us deeper into the cave. "The dying or freshly dead are given to the officers to be made into creatures. Sometimes the body is too old and has to be disposed of in a different way, though, and other times someone doesn't want to see a friend made into one of those things. They use this exit to dispose of the bodies."

"Where do they put them?" I asked, glancing behind me at the wide expanse of sea on the horizon.

"They pitch them over the side to the rocks below."

"Dismal," Vemar said, a curved dagger in his hand.

"Becoming one of the creatures would be more so," Nyfain murmured, following Govam with me behind them.

Deep into the cave, the light dimmed to nearly nothing. I glanced back to make sure faeries could hold on to dragons or wolves, leading them through. The cave walls pushed in and the ceiling pressed down on us, making Nyfain stoop.

Govam reached the end and turned back, placing a finger to his lips. "*Shh.*"

He felt down along the crack, hit a groove, and then moved his hand over to the right. He pressed.

Click.

He didn't push the door open right away. Instead, he moved his hand to his hip and freed the blade in the holster. With his free hand, he opened the rock doorway very slowly, flattening to the side before peering in. Halfway open and he reached in oh so slowly, and then he sprang into action.

He pushed forward and then flung his whole body back, dragging a demon with him. He spun, his back to the door, his knife coming up.

Nyfain lazily jabbed forward with his short sword, piercing the demon in the chest. Govam flinched and dropped his sword. Then he clapped his hand over the puke-green demon's mouth. The wail was muffled but prolonged, so Nyfain jabbed forward again, this time with perfect precision through the enemy demon's eye. In a moment, it was all over.

Nyfain grabbed the body by the putrid rags it was wearing and handed it past me. Vemar grabbed hold, turned, and passed it on. At the back, a light scrape was the only sound I caught as someone clearly went to dispose of the body.

Govam took a long moment, staring at Nyfain.

"Sorry, did you want him alive?" Nyfain whispered.

"No. I just…didn't give you credit for the cool efficiency with which you can spontaneously kill. If you'd been in the dungeons, I wouldn't have survived you."

"And now we know where we stand."

"We've always known. I just have a new appreciation for it." Govam picked up his knife and turned back, pulling the door open a bit wider. "Keep your voices down. I'll tell you when we need to be quiet again."

The area beyond the door was swathed in darkness. A rusty metal stool, leaning left, sat beside it. Govam—or Nyfain, I guessed—had just killed the guard. Or maybe the door monitor. It was hard to say, since the creature hadn't had a weapon and there were no weapons here, either.

Shelves lined the walls, heaped with piles of things I couldn't make out, and baskets dotted the floor. Dirt and straw were strewn about, although I had no notion why. The room was long and narrow, no light whatsoever.

Govam slowed to a stop, then turned back again. He again put his finger to his lips. "*Shh.*"

He pulled a rope attached to a door, the soft click making him pause as a sliver of light cut across his face. He watched for a moment, his eyes darting around.

Nyfain waited right behind him, most of his body in front of mine. Not a sound drifted through from the space beyond.

Govam glanced back at Nyfain before slowly opening the door, freezing when it issued a soft *creak*. When it was all the way open, he stepped to the side, gesturing for Nyfain to go through. Nyfain paused for a moment, studying Govam, before he did as the demon indicated, reaching back to grab me to keep me close.

I slapped his hand away. It stressed me out when I didn't have room to move.

A larger room, just as messy, waited on the other side of this door. A rotten stench, like dead things covered in mold, assaulted my senses. The air almost felt gritty against my tongue.

I pressed my palm to the middle of Nyfain's back when he started to slow, letting him know where I was so he wouldn't divide his focus and glance back in an overprotective search for me. The door clicked behind us, and then Govam made his way to the front again.

There were two doors to choose from this time. Without a second thought, Govam angled right. He tried the handle, liked what he found, and then turned back with his finger to his lips. He didn't make the sound this time.

He went through the same motions as with the other doors, and we walked through three more messy, disgusting rooms. They seemed almost like storerooms for missing people parts, or maybe some gross kind of food. I didn't know for sure, but the good news was that there'd only been that one demon in our way.

That was, until we reached a dimly lit area up ahead.

CHAPTER 50
FINLEY

GOVAM STOOD WITH his hand on the back of the door and his head bowed. I couldn't tell if he was listening or willing himself courage. Finally he turned to Nyfain, paused, and inched closer to my huddle with Nyfain. His knife hand was near me, the weapon held low. It was an easy position to uppercut into my middle.

Nyfain saw it, and in a flash he reached across and grabbed Govam's wrist.

Govam didn't flinch. He inclined his head, like that was fine, and continued moving a bit closer to us until he was pressed against Nyfain's arm, his face close to the space between ours.

"This is one of two precarious rooms," he whispered, so softly I had to strain to hear. "This is a guard break-room. They stop in after a shift to grab some snacks and a drink, maybe a change of clothes, and go on their way. Someone might be around the corner at any time, ready to come through. We'll need to clear it as quickly and quietly as possible. We must kill anyone we see and throw them in here, out of the way. If we can make it through without being detected, we'll have some time to continue through the castle. If someone is allowed to sound the alarm, though, we're fucked."

"How big is the room?" Nyfain asked.

"Not very. We have room for a few people, no more. When the demons are cleared, we'll have to hurry through."

Nyfain jerked his head at the door. Clearly he just wanted to get on with it. Very confident, my mate.

Govam nodded and backed up slowly, making no sudden movements. Nyfain let him go, and he returned to the door. Nyfain held up his finger, though, and then took the lead. He turned to me, gave me a long look, and then leaned against the wall by the door. Caution came through the bond.

He's trusting you to be careful, my dragon thought, as though I didn't understand my mate's silent cues, *but also letting you know he needs you because you're good in a tight spot.*

I didn't bother commenting. Adrenaline coursed through me. This was it. This was one of what was sure to be many points where everything could go horribly wrong.

I felt a hand on my shoulder and turned to see Vemar with his eyebrows up. He was asking if he should go with us.

The wolves edged forward as well, and I could just make out Hadriel in their ranks. Leala, who'd insisted on coming, stood to the side with her whip coiled in her hand.

Nyfain waited a moment as I nodded to Vemar and then Tamara before shaking my head at the rest. It sounded like there wouldn't be enough room for any more people.

My stomach somersaulting, I pushed up close to Nyfain, sword clutched tightly in my hand. I felt the power thrumming through us, the anticipation. My breath came a little faster, matching my pounding heart.

A wave of urgency rolled through the bond and then Nyfain ripped the door open and surged into the moderately lit room beyond. I was after him in a flash, going left as he went right. A guard was headed for the door, his back to me. I grabbed him around the face with one hand and stuck my sword into his kidney with the other. I wrenched his head one way and stuck him again until he died.

I should've brought my dagger. It was easier for slitting throats.

I ripped him away, spun, and stabbed a surprised guard in the corner through the sternum. A quick step, and my hand was covering his cry as I stabbed him again and then let him slump to the ground. Tamara stuck another guard, and Vemar grabbed the downed bodies and threw them like sacks of flour. They sailed through the open door and landed with a thud in the dim interior of the room we'd just left. Nyfain grabbed a guard coming into the space, making quick work of him.

"Hurry, hurry," Govam said, glancing at the spilled blood but not stopping to do anything about it. He got around me and was about to lead us out when a foot scraped against stone. We all froze. A guard stood halfway through the door, staring with wide, disbelieving eyes.

Before Nyfain could move, the guard turned to sprint out of there, but a long brown cord flew forward and wrapped around his neck. It pulled taut, yanking the guard back into the room.

No, not a cord. A leather whip.

Leala stepped into the doorway and yanked, forcing the choking guard to take another step, delivering him directly into Nyfain's hands. Nyfain wrapped his hands around the guard's head and jerked. The loud *crack* announced the guard's snapping neck. He picked the guard up and tossed him through the doorway; our people in the other room hurried to get out of the way.

"Go, go, *go!*" Govam whispered, motioning me on.

Nyfain caught up with us quickly, his hand landing on my arm as he hustled me through the remainder of the room. With the others following, we ran down a narrow stone corridor covered in grime and took the open doorway to the left. There Govam stopped, tapping our shoulders to keep us moving.

I saw now why he had been adamant about smaller groups. This one was almost too large for our frantic plight.

Nyfain pushed into the corner of a small, dank room as the rest of our people filed in. In a moment, Govam threaded himself through everyone to get to us, shoved past Nyfain, and pulled a latch that opened a door I hadn't even seen.

This would've been impossible without him. Absolutely impossible.

On the other side, he motioned us through, trying to hurry everyone behind us. As the last of our group filed out, he shut the door quickly, making sure the click was as quiet as possible, and then fell back against it, sweat shining on his brow.

The sound of hard breathing filled the space, followed by Govam's long, deep breaths.

"Some maid," he whispered. He was obviously talking about Leala's save back there.

I put up my hands. "Right?" I said, nodding. "She needs a raise."

"You good?" Nyfain asked me, his lips to my ear as Govam made his way through everyone and started to lead again.

I gave him a thumbs-up as we wound through a small tunnel resembling a secret passageway more than a hallway. At the end, Govam stopped again and turned to face us, finger at his lips. Having learned from his previous misstep, he handed Nyfain his knife before leaning in to talk to us. It was probably more comfortable than an alpha dragon's grip on his wrist.

"This is the hardest part, right here," he whispered. "We need to get the key to the mess hall. The others will be waiting for us at their doors. It's on us to let them in. To do that, *we* have to get in. To do *that*—"

"We need the key, yes, yes," I murmured.

Does he think we're stupid or something? my dragon asked.

"Shh," I told her. Then, when everyone looked at me, I realized I'd said it out loud. "Dragon," I whispered.

"The guard of the watch is in the chamber beyond

this door," Govam said. "He will very likely be at the window looking out at the beach, watching our boats drifting slowly nearer. Or maybe they are anchored by now. Worst case, he is at his desk. We can't kill him, though. The key is right behind that, hanging on a hook."

"Why aren't we killing the guard?" I asked.

"Because he checks in often. They will know very quickly if he is gone. Killing him is our last resort. Our worst-case scenario is if he sounds the alarm." He paused to make sure we had that. "We need someone who is stealthy. Someone who is small, preferably, and easy to miss. Someone with opposable thumbs."

I looked back at the faeries, because no way could a dragon do it. Our feet might be quiet, but our menace was very loud. Before I could choose, though, I caught Leala edging forward, her eyebrows up.

Then I remembered her animal.

She shifted into a slow loris. It was a little monkey-like being with a poisonous bite. Most importantly, though, her animal had thumblike appendages. She could grip.

I motioned her forward.

"Yes, milady?" she said quietly.

I explained what we needed, and a determined expression covered her face.

"Okay, milady. What happens if he notices me?"

"Can you kill him?"

"Not quickly."

"Then we'll rush out if something goes wrong."

She nodded, stripping quickly and shifting down

into the big-eyed, small-bodied monkey thing. Govam stepped back with wide eyes, then lifted the flats of his feet, as though what he really wanted to do was dance away.

She scurried toward the door, and this time he flinched and staggered backward, like it was a mouse he was afraid of.

"Where's the latch for the door?" I whispered.

He watched her like he might a deadly viper, closing in on her slowly. He reached way over her head, stuck his fingers into a little groove, and very slowly peeled the door open. She looked out, those huge, luminous eyes blinking as the light sparkled against them. She held up her hand, and he flinched again, dancing backward as she darted out.

I shoved Nyfain to take his place. I did not know what Govam's deal was, but if he kept acting like that, he was going to get us caught. Not to mention it was ridiculous. Her little form was super cute.

Nyfain leaned against the wall, sword in hand, watching Leala and preparing to intercede if necessary.

Scratching sounded against the wall. Govam shuddered and rolled his shoulders. In a moment, Leala's animal darted back through on three legs, holding something to her chest.

Nyfain slowly closed the door, which latched with a soft click. Leala set down the precious cargo and then looked up, probably to make sure it was the right thing. Govam waited for her to back off and shift before bending to pick up the few keys on their scarred golden key ring.

"That image will haunt me forever," he murmured, and I nearly had to slap my hand over my mouth to keep from laughing.

He led us through another tunnel, turning a few times, until we came to a dead end. As before, he felt for a groove and opened the way, gesturing us through.

"How did you find all of this, man?" Vemar asked as we gathered in a darkened room with two doors. Both had locks. "And why couldn't we have used a lockpick?"

"I spent a lot longer trying to escape from this life than you did trying to escape from that dungeon," Govam said, looking at the keys. "This lock is impossible to pick. It has a specialized key integrating a very old magnetic component. It's from before Dolion built the top level. The mess is a safe room of sorts. The royals and court members would gather in here when the castle was under siege. It is built with stone—Well, you'll see."

He fitted the key into the lock and opened it.

"Why is it no longer used?" Nyfain asked as we walked into what looked like a cemetery for ugly furniture. The room had oddly angled walls, six in total of various lengths, and a dais for two thrones, one of which lay on its side.

"Dolion has a better one." Govam hurried across the room to let in the others, who would hopefully be waiting behind those other doors.

"Wait." Nyfain's voice rang out, and Govam stopped in his tracks. Nyfain caught up with him and shadowed him, clearly not wanting to be double-crossed and locked in this room without the special key.

Govam opened the door without complaint. "Dolion

was not as clever as the kings of old, however. There was a reason they put the room in the middle of the floor, fitting it in so awkwardly."

Sonassa strutted in with Micah on her heels. I'd made sure to give that group the elixir to stop her magic from affecting them. Micah nodded to Nyfain and me before turning to make sure his group had made it in okay.

Govam went to the next door. "They wanted it to be far enough away from the walls of the castle so that the room would stand if someone used a battering ram, for example."

"What floor is this?" someone asked.

"The third floor," Govam responded, letting the last group in. "Demons in this world have always been cunning, greedy, tricksters, so it should come as no surprise that this castle has seen plenty of sieges. But the royals of old weren't so selfish. Dolion built his safe room into his chambers. The idea was that he'd tuck himself into the safe room if the fifth floor was breached."

"And there is no way into the safe room?" Nyfain asked.

"Well...there wasn't." Govam lifted his brow, looking at me.

"Hannon," I said. "If Dolion makes it into his safe room, Hannon will have to cut through the building with his fart fire or whatever to get him out."

One of the wolves snuffled, and I realized it was Hadriel's. Clearly they found humor in that.

"Yes. But also..." Govam walked to one of the old

cupboards, the only one not covered in a thick layer of dust, and dragged out a few rolls of paper. He spread them across a huge table on the far side. "Dolion wasn't thinking about protecting himself from dragons who can throw themselves in and out of windows to shift. He has protections against fire, but he does not have protection against a dragon who crash-lands through a window."

"No," Nyfain said immediately.

"Hell, I'll try it," Vemar said. "What's the worst that can happen?"

"You miss and fall to your death," Nyfain answered. "Is there another way into his rooms?"

Govam leaned over the papers, which I realized were floor plans of the castle. "Yes. Two. One that is probably impossible. We'd need to fight our way to the other. If we do that, though, there is a strong chance he'll make it to his safe room, and his fate will be in an inexperienced phoenix's hands, all while the rest of the castle bears down on us."

We all exchanged looks.

"Sounds like the shits," Vemar said. "Let's do it. I still volunteer to try that window thing. Strange Lady can catch me if I fall."

"Let's get to it." Sonassa joined Govam at the table, followed by Denski. "We need to get to the top floor. That's where all the power is. Take out that top floor of power players, change the future of this kingdom."

"Get ready to battle," Govam said ominously. "Dolion isn't going to make this easy on us."

CHAPTER 51
HANNON

I STOOD ON the bow of the ship in the rain, looking out across waters that I had hoped to never see again. The castle I also had hoped to never see again loomed large on top of the island, silent and forbidding. No movement gave away what was happening inside.

"What are you waiting for again?" Calia asked, standing at the railing with me, constantly looking over and trying to read my facial expressions.

I soaked in her fear and worry, internalizing it so my animal could morph it into power. "Finley's sign that she's ready."

"Ready for you to help her?"

"Yes."

"What's the sign?"

The wind mussed my hair. My animal was content to bide his time. He refused to worry about Finley. Worrying would waste our resources. She needed us to crack that castle open like an egg, and that would probably take an exorbitant amount of power.

"I'll know it when I see it," I responded. "Finley isn't subtle when she's doing things like storming a castle."

"Huh."

She licked her lips and looked at the beach, where the rowboats were unloading those who couldn't fly. Most of the fliers were already down there in dragon form. They hated that they'd been left behind. They wanted to be helping right now, not standing around while the most important people in the magical world were locked in a castle, dependent on rogue demons.

"If they fail, the magical world will fall into dark times," Dessia said softly, her eyes rooted to the castle.

I couldn't feel her emotions. I had never been able to, although I'd never known why.

I guess now I did.

"They are the only ones who can take on the demons," she said. "The demon king knows it, and he lured them here to deal the deathblow. If he does, we're all fucked."

"Yes, thank you for the summing up," I said through a tight jaw. A trickle of fear wormed through me. "They won't fail."

They couldn't. Not just because of the fate of the magical world, but because my family had already lost so much. We couldn't lose Finley and her child. It would destroy us all.

I told you not to think about that. Just wait for the sign, my animal said.

It's difficult not to worry about my family and the future of my kingdom when someone reminds me of what's at stake.

Try harder.

My animal had always been very easy to get along with. Until now. Clearly stress didn't agree with him.

Calia stamped her foot in impatience. She looked back for a long moment before strutting away, probably to go see what was taking King Starvos so long.

"Did you know, Hannon," Dessia said calmly, "that some of the demons were actually crafted from our kind?"

I didn't want a history lesson, especially not one that started with demons.

I tried to squint through the driving rain, looking at the windows for signs of movement. Had they made it far? Were they fighting yet? If I didn't leave now, would I be too late?

"Should you really be talking about that out in the open?" I asked her.

"Have you not wondered at the similarity of demons ingesting certain emotions and turning them into power?" she asked. "Or why we were unaffected by the Bridge of Doom?"

"I feared I was one of them," I admitted.

"No. They come from us, not the other way around. If the blood of our dying bodies is mixed together just right, with a little bit of vampire magic, they can create a whole spawn of super demon. That's what the books say, at any rate. You cannot imagine the fear I felt of being discovered within their dungeons."

"Their super demons don't stack up very well next to dragons," I responded, my insides starting to squeeze together. This was taking too long. Finley should've been fighting by now. She wasn't the patient sort, not when it came to that.

"All they have now are remnants of power from that time. Our kind, yours and mine, weren't the only big powers in the magical world. There were other creatures, made creatures, that could destroy everything. Our kind came into existence to combat them. We are a relic, really. One of a few."

"Fascinating," I said, unable to help my dry tone.

"Do you think so? *I* think it's terrifying. Thanks to you, the demon king knows there is a phoenix. He'll know that a basilisk must exist somewhere, and that the two of us would be incredibly useful to his arsenal of demons. Our dying breaths would spawn a whole new era of hell. If your royals don't take him down, then the entire world will be in grave danger. Even the human world will be in peril. They have stories of demons and phoenixes and basilisks as well. Because it's happened before. The magical world is stealthy in their world at present, but bring forth a superpower bent on ruling, and they won't be safe anymore. If we don't win here, everyone will lose."

My heart sped up, and adrenaline started to dump into my middle.

"We are the protectors, Hannon. I am the killer. You are the healer. We were born for a purpose. For a duty."

"I know that. I am getting ready to do my duty."

Calm down, my phoenix urged me. *It's not time yet.*

"You are getting ready to protect your family and your kingdom," Dessia said. "That's noble, but it's not enough. You need to think bigger."

Anger flared within me and I rolled my shoulders, trying to shrug off her words. Ever since I met her, something about her had always rankled. Usually I didn't mind women looking at me for prolonged periods of time, but she wasn't like most women. She wasn't just looking at my shoulders, arms, chest—whatever. She wasn't admiring my surface attributes. That piercing gaze cut right through me. It seemed like she was stripping away my outer layers, one at a time, and looking deeper. Much deeper, uncovering all the things I preferred to hide.

I'd tried to stay away from her, and she hadn't ever sought me out, but her presence always seemed to overshadow everyone else's until it felt like I couldn't breathe. And not in that good way. No, it made me feel suffocated, cornered, or like I was being buried alive. It felt like she was constantly challenging me, even with her glances, and the only way I could thwart the effect was to answer the challenge.

Except I wasn't a fucking dragon, and challenges and rage weren't something I reveled in. At least until I met her. She drove me fucking nuts. It would just be so good to punch her right in the mouth. Or…pitch her overboard. Something like that, without a threat to my family, would've horrified me before my phoenix, before her.

It was even more annoying that she was absolutely gorgeous, and my body seemed to respond to her in ways that were mostly uncomfortable. My dreams had turned downright filthy. It wasn't natural.

Silence stretched in the wake of her words. I felt the

weight of her expectation pressing heavily on my shoulders. My chest tightened, and suddenly I couldn't stand still. I couldn't pretend to feel composed.

I turned to her in a rush. "*I* need to think bigger than that? What are you doing besides standing on the deck of a boat, watching a battle you have no desire to take part in, while hiding the magic that could potentially save the most important people in the kingdom? Instead you stayed hidden to protect yourself. Your lectures aren't going to stave off the demons, Dessia. Your selfishness and the cowardice of your king are fooling no one. You have the ability to help me, and yet you stand there and run your mouth, wasting my valuable resources on fear, worry, annoyance, and anger."

She tore her eyes away from the castle for a moment to lift her eyebrows at me. A little smile tugged at her perfectly sculpted lips, as though a master carver had etched them out of marble.

"Hmm," she said. "I wondered if you had any fire under that calm exterior."

"My beast is literally known for its fire. Of course I do."

"Having it and giving in to it are two different things, Hannon." She wrapped her fingers around the railing. "Well, since you asked so politely, I will tell you what I am doing. I am bringing a naïve boy, who has lived in the shadow of his fierce dragon sister, up to speed on what is actually expected of him. I am trying to help the world by incensing the phoenix. You don't need to hoard stolen resources. Those are for healing, not battle. That light you shed around you? That's essentially the magical fumes of the deep well of power within you. I shed various shades of shadow, some so dark they swallow the light. You need to tap into that well to reach your full potential. It's there, waiting for you. You need to grab your fire, soak in it, become it, and then expel it."

"Is that what you do?"

"No, Hannon. It is not. We have different beasts. I'd dearly love to switch. As it is, I grab something much viler than fire, and I learned how to do it from the worst sort of people."

I tilted my head, willing Finley to give me something. Needing a reason to go help and also to get out of this troubling conversation with someone who was supposed to be my arch-nemesis.

The itch that was her presence flared. It wouldn't be ignored.

"You had everyone fooled," I blurted. "We all thought you were sweet and troubled and broken."

She laughed as her eyes swung back to the castle. "I am definitely troubled and broken. But sweet? In my youth, maybe. Sweet won't help someone like me, Hannon. Of the pair of us, my job isn't to be sweet. Far from it. And neither is yours, really. Not when it matters."

She flinched and then pointed at a body crashing through the distant window of the castle, turning end over end as it flew toward the ground.

"Is that the sign you were waiting for?" she asked.

I stepped back in a hurry, shedding my clothes, something I still wasn't quite used to doing in front of others. Something downright embarrassing in front of her.

"Yes, that is the sign. I must go help them."

I stepped up onto a platform at the very edge of the bow. Right before I shifted, though, my irritation got the better of me.

I said, "I hope you enjoy the show from your lofty perch of safety."

And then fire consumed me.

CALIA

I BARELY CAUGHT the flash of color, followed by the swirl of fire eating through it, as I jogged toward Dessia's position at the railing. The driving rain beat at my face, making it hard to see. I didn't have the right magical ability to dispel the cold from soaking into my skin and making me shiver.

"What happened?" I demanded, watching the beauty that was Hannon flutter through the sky before streaking fire toward the castle.

"Hannon got the sign," Dessia said softly, her gaze still rooted to the castle.

The dragons on the shore rose immediately, following him with vigor. The wolves peeled away, racing forward.

The faerie warriors looked back at the ship.

"Damn it!" I turned back to look up at the captain's deck, where the king stood surveying the barren, dead landscape. "He does not have the resolve for this. He's been threatened by the demon king one too many times. It has taken root. He's afraid he'll lose everything."

I laughed without humor. "Does he not realize that to do nothing will mean that he *does* lose everything?"

"He cannot overcome his fear. He's useless in this." I turned back to the warriors who were waiting for orders. "Go!" I shouted, waving them away. I pointed at the others heading to the castle. "Fight for your kingdom! Fight for the golden dragon! Fight for the dragon healer!"

That was all they needed. Those who'd brought horses mounted and tore off across the grounds. The others started running. I somehow doubted they'd be late to the battle. This was the end game of the demon king. It would all be decided here.

This victory would not come without a cost.

I glanced back again and then jogged along the railing, looking for a small rowboat I could operate. The one that was supposed to take the king would be impossible for me and Dessia to get across the water.

"Here! Here's one!" I untied one of the ropes holding it to the side of the anchored ship. Dessia didn't run back to help me. "Dessia?"

She stayed by the railing, still as a statue, looking at the castle.

"Fuck," I murmured, leaving one rope still tied and jogging back to her. "Hey," I said gently, running my fingers through her long white-blond hair. "I thought you said you wanted to be on hand in case the battle turned against us?"

"Why do you think, after all this time, our father still

insists we hide our relation to him?" Dessia asked in a flat tone.

I stared at the side of her face for a long moment. She hadn't brought this up for a while. I wondered why she was doing so now, and how I could put the subject to rest and get us to the castle. Everything hung on this battle. *Everything.*

"You know the answer to that, Dessia." I continued to comb my fingers through her hair, trying to keep the urgency from my movements. She'd always found that comforting. "He's the king. He needs his heirs to have a clear line of ascension to the throne. We had to be sent away so as not to muddy the waters, so to speak."

"Two of us born to the same woman. He couldn't stop after the first unwanted child? He had to go for two?"

"He must've liked her very much."

"She was a *servant*. He used her for her beauty. And when she grew with child, he hid her. Then he tossed the child away to perfect strangers to protect his image and the future of his *legitimate* children. He liked her?" She huffed. "Not enough to let her keep her children. Not enough to keep her in the castle after he grew tired of her."

I sighed, glancing back to make sure we weren't overheard. "We were raised by loving people. That's more than most people can say. And it is a good thing we are related to Starvos. He treats me as a favorite—"

"That is because of your magic, not your affiliation with him. If it were the latter, he'd give a shit about me as well."

"Whatever the reason, you get the comfort and privilege of the castle because of your ties to both him and me. You get to stay hidden because he wants your affiliation to him hidden. It is the perfect setup for you."

"Yes. As long as I keep it a secret."

"Yes. Which is what you want."

"The golden dragon's parentage was a secret."

I frowned at her before movement near the castle caught my eye—another person flying out of the fifth-story window. Hannon was nearly at the castle now. The backup dragons were close behind. I could see shapes in the lower windows. Probably archers. They were getting ready to defend their castle.

Adrenaline pumped through me. I was not a good warrior in battle. No, I excelled at being a stealthy fighter. The woman who slipped a knife into your ribs. The poisoner. I got information, and I got out of there in any way possible. My weapons would be of no help in that castle, but the faerie warriors needed someone to lead them. Starvos wouldn't be doing it, so it would have to be me. I was the most senior member here.

"The golden dragon...has his own problems," I said, unsure where this was heading but knowing it needed to get to its destination soon so we could get moving. "He triumphed over them."

"His secrets set him free."

I shook my head. "I don't know what you mean. What are you talking about?"

Hannon reached the castle and blasted fire against the side of the building. Windows burst open, glass raining down the side of the building. He twirled in the air and tried another blast. More windows, but the stone wasn't affected. He wasn't producing brimfire.

"Phoenixes are tricky to maneuver," she said, as though in her own world. Her animal must be riding her hard right now. She always got in these moods when her animal was anxious. "They are steeped in all that is pure and good, in light and love, in healing and sunshine. But he farts fucking fire, for goddess's sake. Underneath that calm, protective nature is a beast waiting to emerge. I tried prodding him. I got somewhere, but it wasn't enough. He needs more incentive to unleash his full power."

"Seeing Finley in danger should do it."

"Finley *is* in danger. Grave danger. You know how many demons Dolion has at his disposal. You know how much power he has accrued. And he's very well aware that Nyfain and Finley have demon spies. He assumes they'll get in, I bet you anything, and he correctly assumes the phoenix is too inexperienced to help her get back out. The demon king has sprung his trap. He has accounted for everything they can throw at him." She paused, her eyes turning haunted. "Except one."

My stomach clenched. "No. They can do it. They are smart and savage, and Hannon is courageous. He'll figure it out. They'll kill Dolion and his upper tier, and the rest will scatter."

"The ones that would have scattered were set on us at the council. Don't be daft, Calia. It was our studies of the demon king that landed us in the dungeons, after all. We know what he's about. He has the upper hand. He will win."

"Hannon will figure brimfire out, Dessia, you don't need to—"

"It is not the human that needs to figure it out. It is the beast, and the beast has much to learn about himself. I know this because I had to learn the hard way. It took time. And pain. Lots of pain. The basilisk finally emerged because she needed to protect me. The phoenix needs that same lesson, and there is only one who can give it to him."

"You can't do this. If you emerge, Starvos will see. He'll try to control you. To use you. I won't be able to protect you."

She turned to me and smiled. "He didn't claim me as his daughter. He didn't claim me for his court. I am a visitor. A guest. An embarrassment because he thinks I have no magic. And now, I will be beyond his ability to control. Just like the golden dragon, my secret will set me free." She turned toward the boat I had partially readied. "I am not a naïve and scared girl anymore, Calia. I do not need a kingdom. I do not need protection. I am death walking. I am a literal nightmare. Only the phoenix can kill me, and he would never do it."

"But Dessia, people can use you."

"They can try."

CHAPTER 52
FINLEY

I DODGED A swipe and then stabbed forward, taking the demon in the middle and then ripping my sword free. Claws swiped through the air, right for my head. I bent back, heard my back crack, and brought my sword up in an arc before turning away. An arm, severed at the elbow, went flying.

Wolves rushed around me, slamming into the cluster of demons and scattering them. They made short work of them and ran forward, trying to catch up with Govam.

"Finley!" Nyfain called out, on the other side of the large room.

He grabbed a demon in his way, stuck it through with his sword, and then flung it wide. It hit a window and kept going, bursting the glass out and down.

"We need to be in the next room," he shouted.

I fucking knew that. Govam had quietly gotten us up to the fifth floor, killing everyone in our way without tripping any alarms. But he hadn't expected the clusterfuck of demons awaiting us as soon as we made it to a grand hallway leading back to Dolion's rooms. He'd expected them to be nearer the ground floor, ready to meet the troops from the ships. The place was fucking swarmed, demons packed in to the point where they were sometimes stabbing each other when trying to get to us.

I'd been the first to throw someone out the window to make room. Now that was our aim.

A line of fire erupted across my back, and I turned and thrust without thinking, catching a shorter demon in the throat. That would do it. Another came at me from the side, though, using claws, and a third charged from the other side.

There are too many of them, my dragon thought. *Shift. Let's crush them.*

The ceiling is too low. It's like Dolion built this whole fucking floor with dragons in mind.

He might've.

Yeah, he really might've. It was not ideal.

I cut and slashed my way through, making headway. Worry ate at my gut, though. There were so many of them. He hadn't been worried about us barging in. He'd been ready.

"Come on, Hannon," I said, converging with Nyfain and fighting my way forward.

A wave of heat rolled into the room from the left. We reached the doorway and then ducked out again as a blast of fire seared the air.

"Great timing," I murmured, stabbing a demon in the gut and chopping at another.

Nyfain picked one up with his free hand and slammed it into another, knocking the whole lot of them back. Vemar dodged forward, stabbing them as they fell then kicking one that was flailing on the ground.

He grinned and winked at me like the whole thing was hilarious.

When the heat winked out, we turned into the room. It had been so crowded that I hadn't really noticed the layout, but the demons and wolves had rolled for cover behind the dozen or so small walls placed throughout the room, each a little more than head height and about three people wide. On the sides facing the windows sat chairs or couches or tables with decorations. The other sides, away from the windows, were empty.

Dolion had absolutely thought of dragons when he designed this floor. These walls were meant to protect people from fire coming through the windows.

"We can't be in here," I said in sudden panic, seeing Govam and Denski fighting back to back down the way. Wolves snarled and lunged, ripping at demons. Faerie warriors slashed and thrust, spearing or blasting their enemies with magic. "If Hannon does brimfire, we'll be fried."

Nyfain nodded, catching sight of something outside the window.

Fire shed from the great bird, dripping like it had at the council battle. Fire washed across his feathers and swirled through the air around him. He twirled like some sort of dancer and then swooped toward the windows. His great beak opened, and I felt my eyes widening.

"Get out of the way!"

Nyfain grabbed me before I could dive, spinning me and stepping at the same time. Fire washed through the room as we hit one of the walls. A demon ducked in with us, and I grabbed him and tossed him into the flames. He died instantly, but the wall behind him held up.

"Or maybe Dolion specifically erected these to combat brimfire?" I asked, out of breath.

"There is no way Dolion could've thought of that. Hannon is using his magic, but he isn't using enough of it to create brimfire. He probably doesn't know how."

"Fuck," I said, taking another long look at that window. I could get to safety. Nyfain, too, and a few of the other dragons. But the wolves and faeries would be fucked if we left. Leala, too. There were no exits up here for those who couldn't fly.

Dolion had trapped us in.

HANNON

DIG DOWN DEEP, I told my phoenix as he did another pass and blasted the building with fire. *You heard what Dessia said.*

I am. I'm killing the demons outright like last time.

But you aren't getting through those barriers.

Do we want to? my phoenix asked. *Our people are in there. They can't withstand the fire any more than the enemy can.*

That was true. What had we been thinking?

Go to the other rooms. Find Dolion, and start ham-

705

mering him.

A dragon roared below us, the sound full of pure rage. The great orange beast punched fire through the third-floor windows. Screams floated back out. Another dragon, flying lower, was braving the arrows to do the same thing. A third crashed into the side of the building, scrabbling for purchase, grabbing a demon through a newly busted window and wrenching it out. I knew more dragons were around the other side, doing the same thing. But it would only force the demons to retreat deeper into the castle. We weren't killing enough to help. We had to get Dolion.

Fire swirled around us. Heat and light throbbed within us. It wasn't enough, though. That blasted woman had been right about that. It was frustrating that someone so delicate-looking and pretty could be so dark and annoying. It would be easier on my logic if her personality matched her image.

She's only annoying you because she seems to know you better than you know yourself, my phoenix said as he blew fire into the next room over. Demons jumped out of the way, but many of them didn't move in time. We thinned the herd, killing the bastards on impact.

She doesn't know me; she knows you. It's different.

Fine. She knows me better than you do. Better than I do.

Her animal and you are cut from the same cloth, that's why, I said as he looped through the air and went back for another round. They were ready for us, though. They jumped out of the way faster and stayed there longer, knowing they couldn't withstand my fire. *I am the light. She is the dark. Together we are the whole. Enemies. Allies. Apparently it changes constantly.*

We flew by a section of castle without windows utterly closed off from the outside. Beyond that, we saw him, standing in the middle of his room with only three other demons. He faced the windows with his hands behind his back, grinning.

Fire curled up from deep within me, summoned by the memory of what he'd done to my family. To me and my kingdom. I felt the heat before passing it off to my phoenix, and he let it explode outward, blasting through the windows and into the room.

As though he was waiting for it, the demon king and his minions gracefully stepped behind the white half-walls erected throughout the space. Our fire washed over and around them, hitting the back walls and furniture and setting them ablaze but doing no further damage.

The demons stepped out when it had passed, one and all with simpering little smiles on their faces.

They knew we couldn't do brimfire. They knew we were utterly useless.

What do we do? I asked, willing him to go back and check on Finley. *Get some weapons and go in there on foot? We're useless in the sky if we can't figure this out.*

It was then the phoenix saw the shape traveling across the barren land below. Her thick purple cloak fell from her shoulders as she moved, her back straight and her head bent forward in determination. The rain pelted the silky dress that draped her small frame, plastering it to her slight curves. Her hands moved down her front, at the buttons it seemed like, then pulled the gown from her shoulders.

She's going to help. My thoughts were wispy. My heart surged of its own volition. *She's going to sacrifice her safety to help Finley.*

She's helping us all. She must assume the situation is hopeless without her. She's probably right. You heard her; she is concerned about what will happen if Finley and Nyfain fall.

I didn't care that her reasons were probably selfish. I cared that she had great power and knew how to use it. We needed that right now.

She dropped her gown, stepping on it as she continued on toward the castle. Her undergarments were discarded a moment later, and I had a strong urge to turn away and allow her some privacy. But she wouldn't be concerned about such things, and I shouldn't be noticing her full, perky breasts or the gentle sway of her hips as she walked toward her unveiling, something that would change the course of her future forever.

Why are you so bashful? my phoenix asked, watching her flick off her shoes and pull something from her wrist before tossing it away. *You are a shifter. Shifters aren't bashful.*

It doesn't matter. Never mind.

Her chest swelled as she took a deep breath, and then she looked behind her. My phoenix followed her gaze, seeing a lone figure way back at the crest of the hill leading down to the beach. Calia, watching her sister.

Then Dessia looked up at us, and I could almost feel the darkness swell around her. I could feel it reach into me, way down deep, deeper than I thought I went. It traveled to my very center, where a strange spark glowed at the base of my person.

No, not my person. At the connection between my phoenix and me.

I felt that darkness pressing on us, as if a great weight.

Fear curled around us, a strange sort of panic. My phoenix's breath came faster and his chest tightened.

The weight increased as she walked toward us, looking up, always looking up. Murder was in her gaze, I could see it, even from the distance. I could feel it pressing hard inside of us.

My phoenix's wings flapped quickly, and we dropped low in the sky, almost hitting a dragon. Still the horrible feeling persisted, and then it occurred to me: this was how she killed us. She found that part of us only she could reach, and squashed it. She crunched it within her magic, like the press of time.

This was the way to really die. To forever die.

Images flickered through my mind, of Finley's tear-streaked face when I emerged from the burning shed in the faerie kingdom. Of Dad's hollow eyes and Sable and Dash's desperation, their hopelessness. I thought of all the people who'd sat with Finley in the faerie kingdom, mourning what they thought was my loss. Hadriel had hugged me so tightly. Everyone's faces had lit up when they realized that death hadn't ended me, not because of what I was, but because they cared about me.

Dessia's words had a way of crawling under my skin and taking root, and so my thoughts grew bigger. I thought of all the children in the world wanting nothing more than to play and act silly. Who should get a chance to grow up and grow old amongst their family and friends. I thought of the parents who should see their children grow without the horror of a curse.

I had a duty. Not only to Finley, not only to my kingdom, but to the magical world. I'd been born with a responsibility, and it was time to accept it.

It was petty, but I hated that Dessia was right.

I let the fear consume me so it would show me the way. Those thoughts beating in my head, my ears, my phoenix flew beside the building, looking in. Dolion still stood in the room in the corner, his furniture no longer on fire and his three people lounging on their chairs. They weren't worried about Finley coming through. They thought they were covered.

My heart sank when I realized they were right.

A host of demons waited in the room Finley was fighting toward. More than a few of her party were limping or bleeding. She pushed forward with Nyfain, and I could see the fatigue dragging at her. Her sword strikes were a little slower. They didn't land as fiercely. Nyfain, too, was flagging. He kept glancing at her and then the window. He was thinking of throwing her out. He must know she'd catch herself.

She wouldn't stay out, though. She'd rush back in to his aid. There was no saving her when her loved ones were in danger.

Focus! I yelled at my phoenix. *Find that well. Find that magic!*

I'm trying!

Just then, Dessia shifted. Her form grew and grew,

bigger than my phoenix. Bigger than Nyfain's dragon. A great serpent's head with four spikes reared up on a long, snakelike neck connected to a lean body with four feet ending in claws and a serpentine tail. Its mouth opened wider than that of a dragon or normal animal, revealing long, sharp teeth. It was like someone had crossed an enormous snake with a skinny dragon and forgotten to paste on the scales.

She darted forward. Her body bent back and forth as she moved like a lizard. She slammed into the front of the castle with such force that the whole thing shook. The door burst in, and the walls crumbled, her size and strength like nothing I had ever seen.

That's probably why we got brimfire, my phoenix said, in awe. *We need something strong to combat a creature like that.*

And then the weight of her darkness inside of us bore down with such force that my phoenix's vision grew spots. The choice was clear.

Fight or die.

CHAPTER 53
FINLEY

T HE GROUND TREMBLED, and the sound of a huge crash rumbled through the windows. I held out my hands for balance as everyone looked toward the window.

"Don't stop," Nyfain said, hacking and cleaving at the startled demons around him.

I did as he said, stabbing forward before a claw dipped low and raked across my thigh. I grunted and turned to stab as screaming sounded from below. Govam fought just ahead of us, slowed from the effort. We'd made headway. There should be just a couple rooms left before we reached Dolion.

Hannon flapped just outside the window, lowering dramatically for a moment and then coming back up.

A shock of fear froze me until I remembered he couldn't die. Whatever was happening to him, he'd have to work through it himself. I had my own problems.

Govam slashed through a demon and turned for the door, five feet away. As he brought up his sword, a demon on the ground thrust up with his bloody dagger, sticking Govam in the ribs.

"Oh shit," I said, trying to hurry.

He pulled away, his free hand going to the wound. Denski rushed over to him immediately, and then Sonassa was there as well, fighting the enemy demons back so Govam could get clear. He limped two paces before he staggered, looking at the blood coating his palm.

"Oh no," I said, trying to hack through our enemies to get to him. There were just too many fucking demons! They weren't as powerful as us, or as good with swords, but it didn't matter. There were more. Too many more. This was the worry we'd had from the beginning.

"Damn it, Hannon, please," I said, holding on to my power and willing it to give me more energy.

"You need to get out of here," Nyfain told me. He must've come to the same conclusion about the size of the horde. "Hannon clearly can't make it happen. There is no other way out. Jump free and get clear. You'll need to be the hope of the kingdom. You'll have to fight Dolion another way."

"There is no fucking way I am saving myself and leaving all of you behind."

Nyfain grabbed my upper arm and muscled me over to the window. Vemar crowded in, blocking us off from the fighting.

"There are going to be more demons in the next room," Nyfain told me, his eyes on fire. "We might get through them all, but we might not. And even if we do, Dolion can lock himself into his safe room. Then it

K.F. BREENE

would just be a matter of time before the demons in this place overpower us. Someone needs to get clear to keep the kingdom running, and that is you. Join my mother. You're a natural alpha, Finley. You can lead on your own. Protect our heir. *You need to get clear.*"

"No!" I said savagely. "I need to fight and help you win—"

Nyfain's eyes widened as something caught his attention outside the window. I looked just in time to see a long tail, like a big snake, disappear into the castle below.

"Is that…" I swallowed, my eyes widening.

"Dessia is joining the fight," Nyfain said softly, his eyes coming back to me. "But that doesn't mean we can get—"

Bright white light flickered through the windows. I squinted, putting up my hand to protect my eyes from the glare. When it subsided, I saw Hannon glide by. Fire so bright it looked like pure light dripped from his feathers, some of them his tail feathers, and no, he would never live farting fire down. His wingbeats were hard and purposeful, like he knew exactly where he was going.

To the end of this floor.

To Dolion.

"He's got it." Joy burst through me. "Dessia is helping, and Hannon's got it! Thank fuck!"

The floor trembled again, and another loud crash sounded outside. Screams echoed, and then a great many of them cut off suddenly, like someone had snuffed a candle. Fear curled within me, but I didn't have time to ponder on it. The bright light flared again, this time not flickering. A loud rumble shook the floor and walls. Earsplitting cracking and booms preceded the shaking and jolting of the floor.

Demons staggered and looked around wildly. Faeries had wide eyes, looking to us for direction. The dragons and wolves used the lull to their advantage. They doubled their efforts, slamming into the confused enemy, ripping out necks, tearing off heads, and poking demons full of holes.

"Nyfain, Finley!" Govam called, jerking his head toward the door.

Nyfain yanked me with him. Vemar followed closely behind. Demons had cleared the way or been cleared, some panicked and still confused, and the demons on our side had taken advantage of their state of mind just like the wolves and dragons had.

Our people flocked to us, forming a group. Some demons continued the fight, but many of them rushed to the windows, probably knowing we had a phoenix and guessing that phoenix had learned to properly attack. Dolion's people were only courageous when they thought they were winning.

Denski ripped open the door as Sonassa helped Govam stand. Blood trickled down his side, and I couldn't remember if demons healed quickly or not. Not that it mattered right now. There was nothing I could do for him in the middle of this mess.

A swarm of demons waited in the other room, most of them with their gazes directed out the window. Holy shit, this would've been hell to get through. It almost seemed like Dolion had concentrated his entire force in just these few rooms. Maybe he had. Maybe that was why it had been so easy to get up here.

"Look out!" someone shouted, and then white light seared through the room. I barely saw the stream of what must've been brimfire, no more than an arm's thickness, through the glare. It cut through stone like his fire had cut through glass, slicing through the back wall and cutting demons in half.

Denski dove back out and Sonassa shut the door, as though that would do anything. Nyfain grabbed me and turned, shielding me with his body as though *that* would do anything. The building rumbled and something huge crashed in the next room, one closer to Dolion. The light disappeared from under the door, and then there was banging and pounding. The door flew open and a stream of demons fought each other to run for the door on the far side.

They would run right into something arguably worse than a phoenix.

"Go, go, go!" Denski motioned us forward. "We have to get to Dolion before he escapes."

Part of the ceiling had fallen down. Debris lay everywhere. The fireproof walls had been sliced in half and lay in rubble. A gaping hole had been carved into the side of the building, letting in the driving rain.

The phoenix fluttered just outside before curling up his wings and diving in a little. He stumbled, awkward on the ground, before shifting into Hannon, breathing heavily.

"Did he come this way?" Hannon asked, looking around as though Dolion might pop up at any moment. "He ran this way to get away from me. He was in the room at the end. I got two of his people, but he had one more with him."

"No." Govam struggled forward, limping and hunched. "He'll be in the safe room. It's the one without windows. Can you use brimfire to punch through the walls?"

Hannon followed Govam, helped along by Sonassa.

A demon popped up from behind one of the half-walls, eyes wide. Before he could move, a whip crack rang out. The demon grabbed its throat as two wolves launched at it, tearing into it.

"Leala is still here, at least," I said.

The next room over held a narrow corridor with a torn-off door at the end. Through that was the same sort of havoc as the room we'd just come from.

Screams drifted from behind us, but they sounded like they were coming from outside and drifting in from open windows. Dessia was still making her way through the castle. She was cleaning house.

"There might not be much left of your kingdom after this," I told Govam.

"Maybe that's not a bad thing," Govam murmured, slouched against the stone wall.

"Are you going to make it? Do you heal well?"

Govam huffed out a laugh and then winced. "You were always such a peculiar dragon. You're always thinking of healing, even if it's your enemy."

"Not if it's my enemy, no. Them I kill."

He nodded. "I do heal, though not as fast as a dragon. This won't heal in enough time to keep me out of death's door, though. I don't care. I'll stay until Dolion is dead. If that means I die too, so be it."

"Punch through the wall here, Hannon," Nyfain said, indicating the door. "Basically, aim for the middle if you can. Flush him out this way. Hurry. Finley is going to want to save Govam."

Govam looked at the place Nyfain was pointing at for a long moment.

"This is where it counts," he said, grunting with each word. He struggled for breath. "When he teleports, it's essentially his body traveling through space at an incredibly fast rate. He is only invisible because he's moving too fast for your eyes to see. But his body is there. Stab at the air. Position yourselves at every exit and stab all around. A wound will slow him down and make it easier to catch him."

More than a few of us took deep breaths. Adrenaline coursed through me. Rage and vengeance rushed through the bond.

Hannon gave me a pointed look, which didn't communicate anything to me, and then he jogged back the way he'd come. The sound of fluttering suggested he'd taken to the sky again, and we all backed away from the spot Hannon would be aiming for. If he missed, it would mean bad things for all of us, especially if he could punch through both walls in a single go—and depending on how thick the walls were, there was a good chance of that.

The firelight is cool, my dragon admitted as we waited. *Too bad it also drips out of his ass, though. That's gotta be embarrassing.*

The light in the next room flickered through the

darkness. A loud crack and then a boom sounded before a stream of pure white fire tore a hole right next to the door. It swept a little to the side and down before cutting off, leaving a door next to the door.

Nyfain stuck his blade into the hole, pointy side facing the outer wall. A body screamed, appearing on the blade, and then it was forced through the opening as though someone was pushing from behind. I stepped forward, but Vemar got there first, blocking the way. He shoved back as though struck by an unseen blow, grunting. Dolion appeared in front of him, a dagger in his hand, the end embedded in Vemar's stomach.

"Fuck you," Vemar said, not pulling himself off the blade, but instead grabbing hold of Dolion and holding on tight. "Let's see you get away now, you shitbird."

"Throw him," Govam shouted. "Throw him now—"

Dolion disappeared, and Vemar was ripped forward. He didn't let go, though. He was pulled along, digging in his heels despite his wound. Nyfain was there in a moment, grabbing the air and ripping Dolion to the side. The demon king flew, his body becoming visible, right for Govam.

Govam didn't get out of the way fast enough. Dolion's body struck him, and his sword clattered to the side.

"Govam, here!" I slid my sword across the ground. The hilt hit off a little debris, making it spin but not altering its path.

Govam winced, lurching. He scooped the sword up, and as Dolion hit the ground, he twisted and stabbed. The blade sank a little way into Dolion's back, and might've stopped there, not deep enough to do mortal damage, but Nyfain reached them and bore down, adding his weight to the hilt. Then he stabbed the demon king again, issuing a fierce roar. Releasing the sword, he grabbed the demon king's neck and crotch and lifted him into the air. With a fast twist of his body, Nyfain slammed Dolion's middle down on his knee. Dolion's back cracked in half. I winced with the sound of it.

The demon king wailed, and Nyfain flung him onto the ground before yanking out Arleth's sword and stabbing down into Dolion's heart.

The scream cut off abruptly.

Nyfain stared down at the creature who'd been tormentor for a long time, and I could feel a cocktail of emotions rolling through the bond. The most prominent, though, was relief.

"We did it," I said, sagging for a moment as my pulse pounded in my ears. I walked to Nyfain on shaking legs. "We did it."

He cupped my face and gave me a fierce kiss. The bond glowed with our victory.

"We did it," he said when he pulled back, his eyes roaming my face. "Thank fuck, we did it. Now maybe we can go back home and raise some kids in peace."

I smiled up at him, tears in my eyes, the moment not seeming real.

"Yes," I said, then kissed him again.

"I concur." Vemar staggered to the wall to lean heavily against it, knocking me out of my reverie. "What do you say we add some of the luxuries they had in that faerie kingdom? That place was nice."

"We need to clean everyone up." I hurried to Vemar. "How bad?"

He waved me away. "It hurts like a motherfucker, but I'll be okay. He didn't stick it in deep. I don't have anything coming out of the hole, unlike Hannon's creature." He wheezed out a laugh.

"Are you sure?" I pushed his hand away and inspected the wound. Blood oozed out, but he was right: it wasn't deep enough for a mortal wound.

"Don't look at my dick while you are there, Strange Lady," Vemar murmured. "It might just react, and then your very sparkly mate will make the hole a lot bigger."

I gave him a flat look. "Yes, clearly you are fine."

Govam was half sitting, half lying.

"We need to get you out of here, bud," I said, motioning for Nyfain to lift him. "I have supplies on the ship. I can fix you up, no problem, okay? Just hang on."

"If you die, you won't get to be king of this shithole," Nyfain told him as we headed for the nearest hole in the wall.

The room groaned menacingly.

"You'll want to get everyone out of this place," I told Nyfain. "Send Hannon after Dessia before you do, but then get them out. This floor might go. I'd hate to see a victory turn into a catastrophe."

"As you command," he said, his golden eyes twinkling.

Grinning like an idiot, so fucking relieved I could barely comprehend it, I jumped out and shifted. My dragon roared long and loud, and we heard a cheer go up from the fifth floor. We swooped around, got close, and let Nyfain gently secure Govam into our mouth.

"Thank you," Govam said as we flew him back to the ship. "Thank you for saving us. None of this would've been possible if you hadn't traded yourself to Dolion. You didn't just save your own people, you saved the entire magical world. I will make sure no one ever forgets it."

CHAPTER 54
FINLEY

"THERE IS ABSOLUTELY no way I am going with you, Strange Queen," Vemar told me as we stood within the partially ruined demon castle, at the door that would take us down to the dungeons. "I swore I would never go back in that place, and I do not intend to change my mind, no matter how much I like you, respect your mate, and want to watch over my little buddy."

"Coward," Hadriel told him, dressed in a pair of lime-green sweats that matched Vemar's. "And stop asking Cecil to make you my stuff in your size. We look fucking ridiculous wearing the same loud sweats. For the last time, I wear the loud shit and you should try to look a little more normal so your craziness isn't as alarming."

Vemar laughed and slapped Hadriel on the back. "Don't be silly."

"I swear to the goddess and beg for a hand job, I honestly cannot take that man," Hadriel murmured, staring at the door.

"Does anyone ever actually believe you?" Vemar

asked him, still smiling.

"No, they don't," Leala said, standing beside me. To Nyfain she said, "Are you sure you want to see this, sire?"

Nyfain held my hand. His sword was strapped to his back. "Want to? No. I do not want to see the conditions in which my mate was tortured for those many months. Do I need to? Yes. I've heard her story, all your stories, but I have a feeling I didn't really grasp the magnitude of the situation. I want to have better context. I want to share in the horror so that I can better offer her—and you—support and compassion."

"If you didn't break a demon over your knee or routinely succumb to fits of rage, I'd say you were getting soft, your highness," Hadriel said. "As it is, I assume you'll make a great dad and mate, but I will continue being wary of your moods."

"Wise, Hadriel."

"Yes, sire. Thank you, sire. That didn't improve my mood. If we're going to do this, let's do it."

I looked behind us to the host of people who'd decided to go with us. Only some of them were past residents, like Micah, Tamara, Weston, and a few of the others. Most wanted to see what the people they knew had been through. Other people, like Hannon and Dessia, wanted to personally make sure the demons down there were dead. They'd volunteered to go first, since the only person who could kill each of them was the other.

Then there were the demons. Govam had fully healed in the two days since the battle, having consumed my usual elixir mixed with one of the illuminated everlass leaves. He'd been helping us go through the castle and find demons that were still alive, identifying those that needed to be killed on the spot and those that could adjust to a new, less loathsome, order. More were saved than killed, especially in the lower power scales.

He'd wanted to come down to the dungeons to make sure we didn't get lost, and in case there were any problems. Denski, Sonassa, and a few of the others had the same thought. They'd already been through here, though. They'd made it their job to kill all the new officers that had been created. The two factions had never liked each other anyway, and it saved us from having to do it.

"Let's go." Nyfain squeezed my hand.

The smell hit me, and memories immediately came flooding back. The pain. The pleasure through the bond. The parties. The torture. Nyfain looked up at the ceiling in the main room, tracing the large stone columns with his eyes.

"This is the whipping post." Micah stopped next to it, loathing in his expression. "The dragons spent a lot of time here. A lot of my blood was spilled on that ground. The knives were the worst, I think."

"I wasn't partial to the whips, myself," Tamara said, her hands in her pockets. "They were unpredictable."

"We didn't get whipped as much," Weston said as the newcomers toured the area and the rest of us replayed our horror. "I was probably whipped the most, because I had the most power to offer, but I was also worth more at the parties."

Nyfain stiffened, bowing a little and looking at the

ground as we walked. He didn't comment.

"This is where Finley poisoned all the officers." Hadriel stopped beside the large copper container that had once held the officers' drink. It lay on its side on the ground, empty. "Those fucking creatures were so weird. They all looked nearly identical."

"They were all fashioned after the first officer," Micah said. "He made the others in his image."

"And how was he made?" someone asked.

Tamara and Micah and Weston all shrugged.

"We didn't have a lot of quality conversations with those creatures," Tamara said. She looked at Govam.

He shook his head. "I was never privy to that side of things, and I was fine with that. They weren't creatures I liked dealing with."

Uneasiness crawled through the bond as Nyfain and I separated down the stairs. Govam stopped on the first landing and looked down the middle of the cells.

"This was the non-dragon grouping," he said, waiting as some of the others moved through it. "They were used a lot in parties because they were easier to manage. It means they were tortured less."

"We were tortured plenty," Weston said. "Just in a different way."

"True," Tamara murmured.

"Why not use the dragons more in parties?" someone asked. "Goddess alive, look at these cells. A bit of straw, a bucket…"

"The dragons made a sport out of killing guards," Denski said. "They were too volatile. They only attended the larger parties that had more security."

Down the next set of stairs and Nyfain blew out a breath.

"The one at the end?" he asked, starting forward slowly. "That's what you said, right?"

Hannon walked with us, and I noticed the everlass had withered and died. It hadn't been able to survive without the dragons.

"Yes." I stopped in front of it as the others stopped in front of their former cells.

"I thought I would die in this place," Micah mumbled.

"Me too," Tamara said. "I just wanted it to end, but something in me couldn't give in."

"Me too," Weston said, to murmurs of agreement from the others.

"I thought I would die in this place too," Govam said, looking around. "And a whole lot sooner than any of you."

"You were the only captain that didn't." Tamara grinned.

"I'm only alive because of Govam," Denski said. "I can't tell you how many times he saved my ass from the dragons."

"I nearly got you," Micah said.

"Me too," Tamara replied. "Vemar nearly got you three times."

"He had it out for me specifically for some reason." Denski's expression was grim.

"He hates to fail," Tamara replied.

"And then the new dragon walked in here like she'd chosen to," Tamara said, looking at me. "She shuffled in wearing the queen's sword, trying to pretend she was as weak as that muskrat that came with her. I wanted to kill her—you—for wearing that sword, highness."

"What'd you want, Micah?" someone asked with a chuckle.

"Don't continue along that train of thought," Nyfain growled.

"Yeah, she wasn't fooling anyone with the weak routine," Micah said, wisely ignoring the other comment.

"I knew she was different the second I saw her," Weston said. "It was the first time I had felt any real hope for a very long time. Especially when the faeries took notice of her."

"And then in came the weirdest fucking scene I'd ever witnessed in my life." Tamara bent over laughing.

"You better not be talking about me," Hadriel grumbled. "I was your fucking savior, damn it."

"You were wearing a maid's outfit." Tamara laughed harder.

"And then Leala called one of the officers daddy." Micah started chuckling, leaning out to grip the bars before flinching away.

"It got weird in the parties after that," Weston said.

"Very weird," Denski mumbled. "Very, very weird. I wasn't ready for it. Half the time I didn't know where to look."

"It saved the day, though, didn't it?" Hadriel demanded.

"It definitely saved the day, little buddy," Tamara said with a grin.

Hadriel put his finger up with a warning in his eyes.

"Don't you start."

Tamara broke into laughter again.

"That's what you slept on?" Nyfain asked softly, and I could see his eyes flicking from one bloodstain to the next. "This is where you stayed?"

"Yes," I replied. "I kept your letters in the back there."

"And she orgasmed on the floor in there, as well," Tamara said. "Sometimes because of pain, apparently, and sometimes just because she needed a holiday or something. I need to get me one of those bonds."

There were murmurs of assent at that.

Nyfain wrapped me into his arms and put his chin on top of my head. He breathed me in, hugging me tight.

"It's over now," he said. "We're done here. Let's get everything wrapped up and go home. We need to sort out the council, but the worst is over. The biggest threat has been extinguished. Now it should be business as usual."

"Why doesn't that sound comforting?"

He laughed. "Because you'll have more lessons with my mother, no doubt. She isn't very impressed with how we lost our cool."

He pulled back before tilting my face up. "Your battle is over for the time being. Now you'll rest and be pampered and endure my possessiveness as you swell with our child."

"Please don't mention the swelling bit," I murmured with a smile.

"As you command." He kissed me before turning me toward the exit.

EPILOGUE
HADRIEL

Five months later

I KNOCKED ON the door, paused, and knocked again.

"Hello, little buddy." Vemar walked up behind me and leaned against the wall. "I got here too early. I was hoping you'd have already drawn the king's wrath by now for interrupting them."

"I tried to wait as long as I could. I'm really hoping he's left by now. He has to meet with the advisors."

"Hey, guys." Hannon joined us, his hands in his jeans pockets. He had on a T-shirt that stretched across his broad shoulders.

"Oh good, yeah. Hannon." I stepped aside and motioned him forward. "You go in first. The king never yells at you."

"He does, but not in front of Finley."

"Yes, exactly." I motioned him forward.

Hannon glanced at my jacket and nodded. "That's good of you."

"What?" I looked down, smoothing the fabric across

my chest. Vemar wore the same one, of course, just much larger to fit his frame.

Hannon pointed. "The vaginas."

"*What?*" I leaned in a little closer to my jacket, but it was hard to get a perspective of the print from up close, so I shifted my attention to Vemar's. "Where?"

"There. Well, all over." Hannon pointed a little closer. "Is this because of that penis jacket you wear sometimes? Are you trying to equal things out?"

Vemar started laughing. "I love that dick jacket. Remember when we wore it when Calia came to visit, and she stared and stared before pulling you aside and asking if you knew the design looked incredibly phallic?"

Calia visited every few months, checking in with us and spying for her king. She didn't try to hide it, and she made a point of leaving the room when she thought we were talking about things that should be kept private. She was trying to make her job work around her friendship with Finley, and also keep an eye on Hannon for her sister's sake.

The only thing was, she didn't know where her sister was. That was what she said, anyway. No one did. After we left the demon kingdom, Starvos started making grand plans for the basilisk who would grace his court. Only she disappeared. Starvos had blamed us, of course, accusing us of taking her. He'd come here searching. When he didn't find her, he thoroughly questioned Calia. Dessia hadn't turned up, though. She didn't want to be used. She'd always told me that. She didn't want to be a pawn.

She also didn't want to scare people with her mere

presence.

I felt for her. I wished she could've come here with us, since having her around would have put people at ease, but she must not have thought it would work.

I hoped she was okay, and I hoped she stayed hidden. The worst thing in the world would be if someone found her, captured her mind, and used her as they had in the past.

"They aren't vaginas!" I looked a little closer. "They're flowers! It's a floral print."

"Really?" Vemar squinted as he looked again. "I'd thought they were vaginas, too. They look like it."

"They have fucking stems…" My words trailed off.

The flowers themselves *did* look like vaginas. How had I missed that?

"Fucking Cecil!" I yelled. "I asked for floral, and he gave me fucking vagina flowers! That bastard. He knew it wouldn't occur to me."

Vemar threw his head back and laughed. "Good one."

"Good one? You're wearing a vagina coat too."

Vemar shrugged. "I can ask girls to count the vaginas, and they'll think it'll be the real number, and I'll say there is one more and ask if I can see it. They'll get confused, and I'll—"

"No." I held up my hand as Hannon laughed and turned back to the door. "Don't continue. That didn't work with the dicks, remember?"

"Well…" Vemar toggled his hand. "It did and it didn't."

Hannon rapped softly before opening the door and

crossing the threshold. We followed him, my mood suddenly blackened. I'd thought the seamster and I were getting along okay. He hadn't pulled any practical jokes in a while. Clearly he'd just been biding his time until I wouldn't suspect him anymore, and then *wham.* Vagina coat.

Finley lay against Nyfain on the oversized couch that had been placed near the window overlooking the garden. The weather had turned chilly, and the flowers and plants sparkled with the light rain outside.

They each had a book, but while Finley was reading hers, Nyfain had his cheek resting against her head and his hand on her large belly. His eyes were distant, and a soft smile warmed his handsome face.

Hannon stopped a ways away from them, and light flowed around him in colorful waves. Vemar and I stopped, using Hannon as a shield. Clearly it was not a good time to approach them. The human was bad enough, but the dragon could go from calm to fucking insane at the drop of a hat. He apparently just forced his way to the surface and took over, and the human didn't fight nearly hard enough to keep it from happening. His level of protectiveness was ball-shriveling. It was best to always approach with extreme caution.

Nyfain rubbed her belly in large circles and kissed the top of her head. "He or she has strong kicks this morning."

"Hmm," Finley said, leaning her head back against him for a moment.

"Is this a bad time to ask to feel the baby?" I whispered to Hannon, my heart surging. I couldn't contain my excitement. Just a few months now! We'd have a little baby to play with and hold in just a few months. I'd need to alter my jacket choices so spit-up would blend in.

Nyfain glanced over, his hand stilling. Then, miracle of miracles, he took his hand away.

"You can since Nyfain took his hand away," Hannon replied.

I stepped out from behind him and slowly approached the couch. Nyfain tracked my progress with the dragon lurking behind his eyes. I could see it. I could see the crazy barely kept at bay.

Finley lowered her book and smiled at me, and she'd never been lovelier in all her life. Which was certainly something I'd thought yesterday, and the day before, but it was true every day.

"I love you," I told her, then wanted to punch myself in the face, cut off my dick, and just throw it to the side as I ran the other way so the dragon would get confused and not know what to chase.

I held out my hands and backtracked.

"Strictly platonically, obviously. Friend love. Family love. I-would-fucking-die-for-you-and-your-infant kind of love. Not the kind that wants a challenge from the fucking dragon, okay? My love is not romantic. I'm not into the mighty vagina."

"Stop talking," Leala called out from some-fucking-where. She was a rock of sense.

"Are you sure you're not?" Nyfain asked me, arching an eyebrow, his gaze slipping to my jacket.

"Fucking Cecil," I said between my teeth. At least the

king was in a good mood and the dragon wasn't muscling his way up to take over.

Finley laughed and reached for my hand. "Come here. You can feel. And I love you too. Most of the time, anyway."

"Oh yes, I get it. I'm insufferable to even myself some of the time."

Giddy, smiling like a fool, I felt her rounded belly, hard to the touch. Almost immediately, I felt a little push against my hand.

"Oh my gracious, hello!" I knelt down beside them, getting my mouth closer to her tummy. "Hello, little one. My, aren't you so strong. You're giving Mommy some good kicks." I felt another, and another, beating against my palm. "Definitely a dragon." I laughed.

Finley was still looking at me with a smile, and Nyfain was stroking her hair. Hannon stood behind us, watching the scene, his light show going full force. It was at moments like these that my heart glowed. I felt like we were all family. They were pack, an extension of Weston's pack, and I'd never felt a greater sense of belonging in my entire life.

THE BIRTH

"FUCK, OH FUCK, oh fuck!" I ran through the castle, tripped on a stair, nearly fell on my head, and put out my hands to gain composure. "It's fine. We have time. It's okay. She just started. This is okay."

I took a deep breath, because that was supposed to cure panic, and hurried to the back door.

"Hey, bub, watch where you're goin', will ya?" a ruddy-faced woman yelled at me as I ran past.

"I didn't even touch you, you dick-fuck." I screwed up my face and shook my head as I went. "I can't even come up with a good put-down. Damn it! Breathe, Hadriel, breathe!"

Instead, I sprinted.

I ran out the door, across the patio, and through the plush green grass to the everlass house. The king was in the fields with Sable, singing to the plants. Arleth, Delaney, and five other people were out there too, gardeners all. The large expanse of gardens stretched out on the other side with all manner of vegetation, some of the plants extremely rare. Arleth had some sort of plant hookup that she didn't share much information about. I got the feeling it wasn't strictly aboveboard. Regardless, Finley and Arleth had outdone the faeries, without question.

But I didn't care about that now.

"Sire, Arleth. Sire!" I stopped just outside of the plants. I was forbidden to enter. The dragons were a little touched in the head to think so, but they said the everlass held grudges. "Sire!"

The king stopped singing and turned toward me, waiting for news.

I swallowed roughly and caught my breath enough to speak. "She's labor gone, sire. Gone into labor, I meant. She's in labor!" I held out my hands as he started forward immediately. "I was supposed to tell you that she has just started, her water has just broken, and it will likely take a long time to—"

He brushed past me, heading for the castle.

"Right, yes. You don't care. I thought you wouldn't." I hurried behind him as Hannon poked his head out of the everlass house.

I didn't want to yell the news to him just in case the king got weird about it, so I made a circle over my belly, made a face, and pretended to be in pain.

Hannon started jogging after us.

"Oh good, at least there's a good healer on board," I said, jogging after the king like a little puppy. My heart raced and sweat dribbled down my back. I was so fucking nervous! I shouldn't be. I was supposed to stay strong, Arleth had said so, but it was hard because I knew childbirth was painful and potentially dangerous, and also because I wanted to meet that little baby so bad. I wanted to play peekaboo and "what is this thing, oh it's my hand" and roll through the grass. I'd never been an uncle. I really wanted to be one.

"This is exciting, huh?" Sable said as she caught up, dancing and running at the same time somehow. Her curls bounced. "I'm going to be an auntie."

FINLEY HAD BEEN put in the birthing room, which was usually a place only women went until the baby was born. Thankfully the room was on the ground floor, because the person who had told the king that had been thrown out the window in a fit of rage.

The king stopped in front of the open door and shook himself out before crossing the threshold. The tension in his shoulders and bearing melted away until he was loose and confident and ready to take on the world.

"Hi, sweetheart," he said as he approached her bed.

Finley was in a loose, flowing white gown, nestled into the pillows and with a blanket pulled up around her large belly.

He bent to kiss her forehead. "How are you? I hear we're getting started."

Her eyes held panic, and she reached out for him, clutching his hand and taking a deep breath.

"I'm okay. A little worried," she said. "I just don't want anything to go wrong."

He flicked off his shoes, took off his pants so he was only in boxer briefs, and stripped off his shirt. Then he crawled in behind her with his legs on either side of her and his hands on her shoulders.

"I'm right here, okay?" he said softly. "I'm going to be right here the entire time. I won't let anything happen to you."

She nodded as she sighed, closing her eyes and soaking in his touch.

And he did just that. He helped her through her breathing, walked with her when she needed it, distracted her when she wanted it, and then stayed right by her side when the contractions came hard and fast. He never faltered. He never showed fatigue. He never got worked up. He was a strong, calming presence for her the whole time.

Hannon checked in now and again until things got rolling, and then he was there constantly, monitoring her progress and the emotions of those around her. When necessary, I told jokes to distract people, or shut up when I was too distracting. Meanwhile, Arleth helped the midwife, giving Finley support and coaching her when to push and when to try to rest.

The labor was long, but finally the newest member of the family worked her way into the world. A girl.

Arleth wrapped her up with tears in her eyes and handed the squalling infant to Daddy. He cradled her with the utmost delicacy, looking down on her little angelic face like it was the most beautiful and miraculous thing he'd ever seen in his life.

Almost immediately she stopped crying, content to be held by the most fearsome alpha dragon in the world. And why wouldn't she be? She wasn't five minutes old, and already she had him wrapped around her little finger.

The king handed the infant to an exhausted Finley, and when Finley started crying, holding her baby against her breast, I wailed.

"Behold, the first female to inherit the title of Queen of Wyvern," Arleth said, laughing happy tears. "Welcome into the world, little princess."

And so it was. We were watching history in the making.

Finally, it was my turn.

I sat in the rocking chair by the window as the dawn light filtered through. Finley slept soundly in the other room, exhausted from her efforts. The king held little Tabitha against his chest as he bounce-walked to me, such a little tiny thing against a large, muscled, and scarred man. He held her with such reverence. Such tenderness. My heart broke into a million pieces, and I was crying again, so fortunate to be able to witness it.

"Are you ready to hold her?" the king asked in a hush.

"Y-yes," I said, swallowing down the emotion.

He gently handed her to me, and I cradled her close, my heart glowing.

"Hello, little Tabitha," I said with a smile, feeling her silky-soft skin with my finger. "Aren't you a cute little thing? And look at this. Look at this, hmm? You have all your little fingers, and I bet under this blanket, you have all your little toes. And two eyes, there they are, and a little button nose. I hope you look just like your mama, but I hope you act like your uncle Hannon, yes I do! Yes I do! Uncle Haddie can't handle another rage-monger in the castle, no he can't."

I rocked her gently and held her close and couldn't imagine wanting to be anywhere else in the entire world than in this spot, in this moment, with this little princess. My life had been rocky at times, but for this moment, it had all been worth it. I was truly blessed.

FINLEY

A WEEK AFTER Tabitha's birth, I sat in an overly cush-ioned loveseat in the garden as the sun crawled up from the horizon. The first rays of the morning sparkled against the beautiful illuminated everlass plant, a gift from my brother the phoenix. That guy was super famous at this point. We had people writing in from all over, asking for an audience with him, asking for youth, asking for cures to various ailments, big and small. Some promised him gold; some gave him a sad story.

He ignored them all.

I didn't ask him why. I assumed he was completely overwhelmed. I would be.

Little Tabitha lay at my breast, her soft cheek against my skin, drowsy from having just fed. I ran my fingers gently over her fuzzy, soft head. Her little body curled up against me and I just lay back, content in a way that I'd never experienced before. The tranquility of these mornings, and the soft glow of my heart, infused every fiber of my being. I'd thought I was happy before, but it was a pale representation of what she had brought into our lives.

"Good morning, sweetheart," Nyfain said softly as he stepped out of the glass sliding door.

I lifted my gaze to him with a small smile, drinking him in. My mate was so fucking handsome it was distracting. These months of virtual peace had been great for him, and my pregnancy and now Tabitha's birth had been even better. He'd relaxed some, but more importantly, he was happy. Deliriously happy. I could feel it through the bond, matching my own feelings. So was his dragon, and mine. We had each other, more in love every day, we had family and friends around us all the time, and we had song and love and laughter to brighten our days. The people of the kingdom respected us, trusted us, and the court was down to earth and helpful to the kingdom at large. The kingdom was absolutely thriving.

Arleth and I had created a garden and a library that should outshine any other in the world. And if it didn't, we'd damn sure start improvements. Both of us were a little overbearing about those points, and I was glad we agreed on it. With her help, and Hannon looking over the books, not to mention the incredible operations team we had in place, and of course Hannon's magic, we were making money hand over fist. Money that we liberally put back into the kingdom to ensure the people as a whole could thrive, safe and healthy.

Weston and Micah still headed up the armies, working together even though they didn't necessarily like each other, and Tamara kept a tight rein on my guard, training with the others for the eventuality of my battling. Not that that would happen anytime soon.

After the clusterfuck of a council meeting where we fought Dolion's demons, the other kingdoms had learned firsthand what sort of might we possessed. They learned how incredibly strong of a shifter Weston was, and how vicious and effective our dragons were. We also had a phoenix, and we'd taken down Dolion. If there was a kingdom on the "not to be fucked with" list, it was ours.

My mate's achievements and his happiness had softened all his hard edges and blurred all his scars. His golden eyes with the little flecks of burgundy sparkled as brightly as his glittering scales did in the sunshine.

"Do you need a break?" Nyfain crouched down beside the loveseat. "I'm sorry, I didn't hear her crying or I would've gotten up and brought her to you."

I smiled and pulled an arm away from Tabitha so that I could lay my palm on his forearm.

"You don't have to wake up with me every time she needs to be fed. I get to rest all day, with people to attend me. You have to play king *and* queen until I return to my duties."

I said the words because I needed to, but I knew they didn't have any effect. One might say he was working hard to ensure he didn't turn out to be a father like the mad king, absent or abusive, but that wasn't it. He was the father he should've had, patient and loving and absolutely devoted. Arleth got misty-eyed when she watched him with Tabitha and admitted that he reminded her so much of his biological father, her lost love. Nyfain would do anything for his daughter. For me. He would make no end of sacrifices and endure no end of hardship. He was hard-wired to thoroughly protect and provide, and that included his time and his love. He woke up with me at night because he wanted to be a part of every moment of her life. He did it because he wanted to ease my burden of constant feedings and chapped nipples any way he could. He did it because it comforted him to help soothe his crying baby and tired mate.

He did it out of love. The love of a proud papa dragon.

His smile was soft as he stood and then crawled in beside me. He gently gathered me up into his arms, careful not to wake the baby, and put his large hand over mine, his thumb still able to stroke her velvety-soft back.

"I love you," I told him, leaning my head against his

shoulder.

He kissed the top of my head. "You are my everything. You've brought me such happiness, given me the whole world. You're my true love and you've helped me find my true destiny. My life couldn't be any more sublime, Finley. Thank you."

My heart swelled, full to bursting. Tears stung my eyes.

"You're my dream come true and you always will be."

You're still absolute shit at making speeches, my dragon thought, though it didn't interrupt her purr. I chuckled softly and closed my eyes. After an upbringing of nightmares, I was finally living my dreams.

THE END.

About the Author

K.F. Breene is a Wall Street Journal, USA Today, Washington Post, Amazon Most Sold Charts and #1 Kindle Store bestselling author of paranormal romance, urban fantasy and fantasy novels. With millions of books sold, when she's not penning stories about magic and what goes bump in the night, she's sipping wine and planning shenanigans. She lives in Northern California with her husband, two children, and out of work treadmill.

Sign up for her newsletter to hear about the latest news and receive free bonus content.

www.kfbreene.com